2019
PUSHCART PRIZE XLIII
BEST OF THE SMALL PRESSES

EDITED BY BILL HENDERSON
WITH THE PUSHCART PRIZE EDITORS

Note: nominations for this series are invited from any small, independent, literary book press or magazine in the world, print or online. Up to six nominations—tear sheets or copies, selected from work published, or about to be published, in the calendar year—are accepted by our December 1 deadline each year. Write to Pushcart Fellowships, P.O. Box 380, Wainscott, N.Y. 11975 for more information or consult our website www.pushcartprize.com.

Acknowledgments
Selections for The Pushcart Prize are reprinted with the permission of authors and presses cited. Copyright reverts to authors and presses immediately after publication.

Distributed by W. W. Norton & Co.
500 Fifth Ave., New York, N.Y. 10110

Library of Congress Card Number: 76-58675
ISBN (hardcover): 978-1-888889-88-8
ISBN (paperback): 978-1-888889-89-5
ISSN: 0149-7863

for
William and Hunter

INTRODUCTION

"All children smile in the same language."
—Dorothy Galloway

Last year we dedicated this annual celebration to Barack Obama, the writer.

This year we honor William and Hunter, newborn identical twin boys.

As of this writing, William and Hunter are almost three months old, and yesterday they smiled for the first time at Lily, our daughter, their mom. And she smiled back. And they smiled and laughed with her.

For Lily and for her husband, Ed, this was a huge day. The boys had come out of their infant dreaming. They were strangers in a strange land and they had made their first contact with an alien world, a smiling and laughing mom and dad. Welcome! So much to figure out in the years ahead.

For many of us, we too live now in an alien world dedicated to power and lies. It is hard to laugh and smile. This is not the world we cherish. It is tempting to just retreat into tribal clusters, or surrender it all to a drugged wasteland.

But of course we cannot and will not retreat.

It might be helpful to remember where small press writers have come from. Way back in 1973 when Pushcart published its first book, *The Publish-It-Yourself Handbook*, from a Yonkers, New York studio apartment, commercial publishers, both legit and vanity scams, had almost total power of what could be issued. They told us who could seek readers and who was forbidden.

The contributors to that *Handbook*—Anaïs Nin, Leonard and Virginia Woolf, Stewart Brand, and others—showed us another way, the underground, if you will. Well today that underground is definitely not subterranean any longer. Thousands of small journals and book presses flourish, and formerly powerful bottom-line businesses are fading along with huge bookstore chains. The local independent bookstore is back. And most wondrous of all, twelve thousand writers and presses assemble each year at the annual AWP convention, a literary gathering that was unimaginable fifty years ago.

So do not despair about our contemporary blasts of power and lies. Stay calm and carry on writing. Eventually the power-obsessed will destroy themselves.

✻   ✻   ✻

Through the decades many writers have offered encouragement in difficult times to other writers in these pages.

Jayne Anne Phillips, in her Introduction to PPIX noted: "Writers form a continuum. That continuum forms what is, to the country at large, almost an underground knowledge, the knowledge is needed now . . . writers have collectively edited this Pushcart Prize. These are the voices that are speaking now."

In PPXI, Cynthia Ozick stated: "The American writing sound gives us our nationality. And this, while it hasn't much to do with keeping talents warm for the big trade publishers . . . is precisely the nature of The Pushcart Prize."

Tess Gallagher, in her Introduction to PPXIV, considered small press writing and reading "an effort which, while it asks for our generous involvement without promising fame or even a large readership, insists at the same time, in the words of William Carlos Williams, that 'you got to try hard!' and operates outside the trade publishing world of wins and gains, buying and selling."

Russell Banks in PPXV wrote: "I don't care what they say, those large commercial presses and the so-called slicks, about their love of literature and the life of the mind. I know what they love . . . profit, dividends, increase."

Banks continued with a warning about the danger to small presses and writers from too much self-congratulation: "I know about the *drek*, the merely competent and the self-indulgently incompetent, the reams of narcissistic self-expression that thrive in the pages of many small press magazines and books."

And so over the years, with the help of these writers and thousands of others, literary publishing has changed for the better. The point: do not despair about the present situation where truth is denigrated, facts depend on whatever power brokers say they are, and hype and celebrity seem to rule the national mind. Our struggle is worth it. We are not back in the era when non-commercial writers wrote for their desk drawers only. This is a true, quiet revolution. Let's keep it.

❈   ❈   ❈

In the past forty-three years our Pushcart Prize multi-voiced collective has been recognized, awarded and celebrated. As Charles Baxter put it last year, "The Pushcart Prize has changed the face of American literary publishing and has given untold numbers of young writers a boost."

But I find it impossible to pretend that all of the "best" (however you define what "best" can mean) is only to be found in our few hundred pages. Over the decades, the quality of independent writing has surpassed any attempt by a mere anthology to capture all, or even most, of that "best."

So I think it is fair to consider the following pages to be a sample of the excellence out there in the worldwide universe of literary endeavor. Please pay particular attention to the Special Mention section. All these writers have won a Pushcart Prize to my mind.

❈   ❈   ❈

Since I began this Introduction with a tribute to the innocence and joy of William and Hunter, I end it with a farewell to Sedgwick, our eleven-year-old Portuguese Water Dog. I found Sedgie as a puppy advertised in the pages of a local Long Island newspaper. He was a ribbon-wrapped Christmas present for my wife, Genie. All kisses and wiggle and bounce, he was unacquainted with depression. Every day over his many years was an adventure for Sedgie. He was a handsome critter, mostly black with a big white bow tie on his chest. His only threat was that he might destroy a stranger with kisses. He died after a furious round of play at the dog park with dogs half his age.

We word slingers could learn a bit from Sedgwick about wonder and love. Quitting for him was not an option. Think on these things in the current age.

"Dog is God spelled backward" is for me not just a funny cliché. Non-literate beings have much to teach us.

※　※　※

In the pages that follow you will discover stories, essays and poems from sixty-two presses (a record number). Thirteen presses are new to the series.

I won't even attempt to describe the immense variety in theme and style of what follows. All of these selections touched me and came our way thanks to the nominations of hundreds of presses and our two-hundred plus Contributing Editors for this edition. Special thanks to our guest prose and poetry editors: Rebecca Hazelton, Christopher Kempf, Keith Ratzlaff, Allegra Hyde, Mark Jude Poirier and Sujata Shekar.

We wouldn't be here without the support of our diligent distributor, W. W. Norton & Co., and our generous contributors to the Pushcart Prize Fellowships Foundation listed later. Perhaps you would like to join them? We seek no institutional or government grants and rely on the support of our enthusiastic readers.

As always, thanks to you dear reader. Without you we would have been long gone years ago.

Keep the faith. We all need you in the uncertain days ahead.

Love and wonder. Good-bye Sedgwick.
Hello William and Hunter.

B.H.

THE PEOPLE WHO HELPED

FOUNDING EDITORS—Anaïs Nin (1903–1977), Buckminster Fuller (1895–1983), Charles Newman (1938–2006), Daniel Halpern, Gordon Lish, Harry Smith (1936–2012), Hugh Fox (1932–2011), Ishmael Reed, Joyce Carol Oates, Len Fulton (1934–2011), Leonard Randolph, Leslie Fiedler (1917–2003), Nona Balakian (1918–1991), Paul Bowles (1910–1999), Paul Engle (1908–1991), Ralph Ellison (1913–1994), Reynolds Price (1933–2011), Rhoda Schwartz, Richard Morris, Ted Wilentz (1915–2001), Tom Montag, William Phillips (1907–2002). Poetry editor: H. L. Van Brunt

CONTRIBUTING EDITORS FOR THIS EDITION—Steve Adams, Dan Albergotti, Carolyn Alessio, John Allman, Idris Anderson, Antler, Tony Ardizzone, David Baker, Kim Barnes, Ellen Bass, Claire Bateman, Charles Baxter, Bruce Beasley, Marvin Bell, Molly Bendall, Karen Bender, Pinckney Benedict, Bruce Bennett, Linda Bierds, Marianne Boruch, Michael Bowden, Krista Bremer, Fleda Brown, Rosellen Brown, Michael Dennis Browne, Ayşe Papatya Bucak, Christopher Buckley, E. Shaskan Bumas, Richard Burgin, Kathy Callaway, Francisco Cantú, Richard Cecil, Ethan Chatagnier, Kim Chinquee, Ye Chun, Jane Ciabattari, Suzanne Cleary, Michael Collier, Martha Collins, Lydia Conklin, Philip Connors, Stephen Corey, Lisa Couturier, Paul Crenshaw, Claire Davis, Chard deNiord, Jaquira Diaz, Stuart Dischell, Stephen Dixon, Daniel L. Dolgin, Chris Drangle, Jack Driscoll, John Drury, Karl Elder, Elizabeth Ellen, Ed Falco, Beth Ann Fennelly, Gary Fincke, Maribeth Fischer, April L. Ford, Robert Long Foreman, Ben Fountain, H. E. Francis, Alice Friman, John Fulton, Richard Garcia, Frank X. Gaspar, Christine Gelineau, David Gessner, Nancy K. Geyer, Gary Gildner, Elton Glaser, Mark Halliday, Jeffrey Hammond, James Harms, Jeffrey Harrison, Timothy Hedges, Daniel Lee Henry, DeWitt Henry,

David Hernandez, Bob Hicok, Edward Hirsch, Jane Hirshfield, Jen Hirt, Charles Holdefer, Andrea Hollander, Chloe Honum, Maria Hummel, Karla Huston, Allegra Hyde, Colette Inez, Mark Irwin, Catherine Jagoe, David Jauss, Leslie Johnson, Jeff P. Jones, Laura Kasischke, George Keithley, Christopher Kempf, Thomas E. Kennedy, James Kimbrell, David Kirby, John Kistner, Ron Koertge, Richard Kostelanetz, Lisa Lee, Fred Leebron, Sandra Leong, Daniel S. Libman, Ada Limón, Gerald Locklin, Jennifer Lunden, Margaret Luongo, Matt Mason, Dan Masterson, Alice Mattison, Tracy Mayor, Robert McBrearty, Rebecca McClanahan, Davis McCombs, Erin McGraw, Elizabeth McKenzie, David Meischen, Douglas W. Milliken, Nancy Mitchell, Jim Moore, Joan Murray, Michael Newirth, Aimee Nezhukumatathil, Celeste Ng, Nick Norwood, Meghan O'Gieblyn, Dzvinia Orlowsky, Alicia Ostriker, Thomas Paine, Alan Michael Parker, Dominica Phetteplace, Andrew Porter, C. E. Poverman, D. A. Powell, Melissa Pritchard, Kevin Prufer, Lia Purpura, Keith Ratzlaff, Donald Revell, Nancy Richard, Laura Rodley, Jessica Roeder, Jay Rogoff, Rachel Rose, Mary Ruefle, Valerie Sayers, Maxine Scates, Alice Schell, Grace Schulman, Philip Schultz, Lloyd Schwartz, Maureen Seaton, Asako Serizawa, Diane Seuss, Sujata Shekar, Floyd Skloot, Arthur Smith, David St. John, Maura Stanton, Maureen Stanton, Patricia Staton, Pamela Stewart, Patricia Strachan, Ben Stroud, Terese Svoboda, Barrett Swanson, Ron Tanner, Katherine Taylor, Richard Tayson, Lysley Tenorio, Elaine Terranova, Susan Terris, Joni Tevis, Jean Thompson, Melanie Rae Thon, William Trowbridge, David J. Unger, Lee Upton, Nance Van Winckel, G. C. Waldrep, Anthony Wallace, BJ Ward, Don Waters, Michael Waters, LaToya Watkins, Charles Harper Webb, Roger Weingarten, William Wenthe, Allison Benis White, Philip White, Jessica Wilbanks, Joe Wilkins, George Williams, Kirby Williams, Eleanor Wilner, Eric Wilson, S. L. Wisenberg, Mark Wisniewski, David Wojahn, Pui Ying Wong, Shelley Wong, Angela Woodward, Carolyne Wright, Robert Wrigley, Christina Zawadiwsky, Elizabeth Ziemska

PAST POETRY EDITORS—H.L. Van Brunt, Naomi Lazard, Lynne Spaulding, Herb Leibowitz, Jon Galassi, Grace Schulman, Carolyn Forché, Gerald Stern, Stanley Plumly, William Stafford, Philip Levine, David Wojahn, Jorie Graham, Robert Hass, Philip Booth, Jay Meek, Sandra McPherson, Laura Jensen, William Heyen, Elizabeth Spires, Marvin Bell, Carolyn Kizer, Christopher Buckley, Chase Twichell, Richard Jackson, Susan Mitchell, Lynn Emanuel, David St. John, Carol Muske, Dennis Schmitz, William Matthews, Patricia Strachan, Heather McHugh,

CONTENTS

WHAT HAS IRONY
DONE FOR US LATELY

by PAM HOUSTON

from ABOUT PLACE JOURNAL

1

In 2014 I lost Fenton Johnson the Wolfhound—Mother's Day weekend was his last—which, I know from experience, will make all the Mays from now on a little sadder.

Eleven years is a big number for an Irish Wolfhound, and Fenton had made excellent use of every one. I named him after my dear friend, the writer Fenton Johnson, and as Fenton the dog grew up, he revealed more and more ways the name was apt. Like Fenton the human, he was wise and reticent, the best kind of grandfather even when he was only middle-aged. He wasn't big on asking for affection, wouldn't wiggle up to you like a Black Lab or a Bernese Mountain Dog, wouldn't even very often bump his head up under your resting arm for a pet. He preferred to sit nearby, keeping a loving and watchful and ever so slightly skeptical eye, as if the humans were always potentially on the verge of making a really bad decision, and he would be ready, in that case, to quietly intervene.

When Fenton was a young dog, he would bound through deep snow with an expression of such pure joy on his face it could make even a non-dog person laugh out loud. He would only drink water out of the very edge of a bowl, and only then with his top teeth pressing firmly against the metal rim. When he wanted something he would come over and scratch on the chair or the couch I was sitting on, as if it were the wrong side of a door.

When he was happy—for instance, if I rose from a chair with a leash in my hand—he would wag his tail heartily, but when he was ecstatic,

19

like when I came home after a week of working on the road, his tail would make huge happy circles, the scope of his happiness too big to be contained in a movement that only went from side to side.

To say Fenton was intelligent, to say he had a wider range of emotions than anyone I dated in my twenties and thirties is really to only scratch the surface of what a magnificent creature he was. He was the ranch manager, hyper vigilant but not neurotic, keeping his eye on everything—animals, people—making sure no one was out of sorts or out of place. Because of his watchfulness, he had perfected the art of anticipating what would happen next better than any person could have. He knew all of my tastes and my tendencies, and he was always ready to be of service in any undertaking—moving the sheep from one pasture to another, walking the fence line to look for breaks, riding into town to drop off the recycling, cheering me up on a sleepless night by resting his heavy head across one of my ankles, reminding me to get up from the computer after too many hours of writing and go take a walk outside.

This last year, though, the arthritis that first made itself known when he was about eight years old was getting severe. He'd been on Rimadyl—the canine version of Advil—for years. We had had good results from acupuncture, massage, and glucosamine chondroitin. Doc Howard had shelved his country vet skepticism to give a laser gun a try and had been surprisingly impressed with the results, using it on many patients for pain relief, as well as on his wife and himself. Once a week I loaded Fenton in the 4- Runner and we drove to Doc's, donned our Keith Richards goggles (Fenton got some too) and Doc's granddaughter gave Fenton six shots of laser light in his back end. Lately, even the laser gun treatments were reaching the point of diminishing returns.

I'd been away for a few days, in Boston, when I got the call from Kelly, my house-sitter, that Fenton was down and didn't seem to want to get up anymore. A wolfhound isn't meant not to be able to stand and walk around, however comfortable we might be willing to make him.

Months before, I had written on my calendar the following words, "This weekend keep free in case Fenton . . . ," and there was the old boy, as obliging as ever, doing everything, even dying, right on time. I flew to Denver immediately, and invited some of Fenton's closest friends to the ranch for the weekend, knowing that in order to come, they would have to brave the predicted Mother's Day blizzard during the five hour drive from the Front Range to the ranch.

In Boulder, at the Whole Foods, I bought dry-aged organic beefsteaks for everyone I thought might make it, plus a mountain of other groceries. I figured if we were going to be sad—and we were going to be sad—at least we were going to have good food to eat. When I selected the steaks, the Whole Foods butcher, whose name is Jerry (and whose dog's name, I would learn later, is Gristle) took a lot of time and great pleasure describing the dry-aging process, and when I asked for six T-Bones, one for each of the potential guests and another for the old boy himself, Jerry said, "you must be having quite a party." And since he had been so kind and thorough in *his* explanation, I said, "Well, what I am actually doing is having a kind of living wake for one of the best dogs who has ever lived, and I want to buy the very best for him, and for his friends who are making the drive up to my ranch in Creede to be with him." Jerry lifted one of the massive T-bones off the top of the pile sitting on the scale.

"You should have said so to begin with," he said, "In that case Fenton's is on me."

My friend Tami Anderson had a wonderful dog named Taylor who she was as deeply connected to, I believe, as I was to Fenton. I have loved all my dogs, of course, but there is the rare dog—I have had two so far in my life—that asked me to transcend my human limitations and be, at least occasionally, a little more evolved, like them. Fenton was such a dog, and so was Taylor. Taylor and Fenton were puppies together, and they loved each other truly all their lives. When Taylor was coming close to the end, she and Tami would often lie on the bed together and look into one another's eyes. One day, Tami told me, almost in a whisper, they were in such a position, and Tami said, "Maybe next time, I'll be the dog."

But Tami couldn't be there for Fenton's weekend, and neither could my partner, Greg, so it turned out to be me and Kelly, and Linda, who had cared for Fenton so often over the last five years of his life he belonged to her nearly as much as he belonged to me. She had flown in from Reno and met me at the Denver airport and we had driven together. The storm had kept everyone else away.

The weekend was everything all at once. It rained and snowed and blew and eventually howled, and I slept out on the dog porch with Fenton anyway, nose to nose with him for his last three nights. The storm seemed to have been ordered especially for the old boy, who loved the cold and snow most of all, who hated the wood stove and preferred it when we kept the house in the 55–60 degree range, who all his life would literally raise a disapproving eyebrow at me the moment he suspected I was going out to chop kindling.

Linda and I gave him sponge baths and rubbed his face and ears until he didn't want us to rub his face and ears anymore, and then we sat quietly beside him. I will admit to even loving cleaning him up, changing his dog beds, washing and drying him, fine tuning my attention to meet his every need.

When I could stand to tear myself away from him, I cooked—giant pots of soup and pesto and grilled vegetables and salad. I had no appetite but the kitchen was warm and smelled good whenever I walked into it. Fenton ate Jerry's giant dry-aged t-bone in three sittings over two days and enjoyed the bone as much as I've ever seen him enjoy anything in his life, even though he'd mostly lost interest in other food by then. There were times I was sure we were doing exactly the right thing by Fenton, times I thought that if *my* last weekend could be like his, it would be better than pretty much anybody's last weekend I had heard about in the history of the world. Other times, I was in a flat panic. How could I be trusted to make this decision? What on earth gave me the authority or the wisdom to decide when his quality of life had crossed over some determinate line? And all that aside, how would I live in a world without him, without his tender presence beside me, without his increasingly stiff rear end galumphing down the driveway to meet me, without his quiet vigilance as I sat in a chair and did my work?

Fenton was my seventh Irish Wolfhound and my tenth dog overall. I was not new to being the decision maker, but no amount of times down this difficult road made it any easier. At one point I got myself so freaked out I thought maybe we would get in the car together—just him and me—and drive and drive and see if we could outrun death.

On Monday morning I saw he was getting the very beginning of tiny sores from sitting still for so long, and I knew Tuesday morning would have to be his last. My friend Kae called from Denver and said she had tried to make it on Sunday, but they had closed highway 285 because of black ice and so far it had not reopened. She asked me if I was okay, and I told her I was. I have always called Kae the moral center of my large and wonderful group of women friends, in part because she was raised by preachers, in part because she has so much backbone, but mostly because she has a remarkable way of orienting toward true north.

Kae and I have the same exact Prius—year and model—and when she pulled in the driveway ten hours later Fenton got more excited than I had seen him all weekend, even though I was sitting right there beside him. Like there might be two of me, and I might come home all over again and start caring for him as I already was. This was another

22

unexpected gift of the weekend. How many hundreds of times had I seen Fenton at the bottom of the driveway, his tail going in giant crazy circles? But because I was always the one *in* the Prius I had never before witnessed that moment of recognition, the moment he became sure *that* car was my car. Who in your life has ever been that ecstatic over your arrival? Someone, I hope. Some living being.

But of course, it wasn't a second me who got out of the Prius. It was Kae, and when he recognized her, he danced and danced, on his front legs only, because he loves her too, and he knew she had come to see him. As a culture, whenever we want to treat someone or something inhumanely, we declare they don't have emotions, but anyone who thinks dogs don't have emotions should have been on the porch that night in the snow.

Kae had driven ten hours in whiteout conditions, doubling the length of the drive. When I asked her if it was awful, she shrugged and said, "You never *ever* ask for help, so after we talked, I figured I needed to get here."

I said, "I don't think I asked for help this time."

"Maybe not," she said, "But you were close."

We bedded down on the dog porch in sleeping bags under the swirling snow. She said, "You are doing the right thing, Pam. He's not going to get better."

I said, "It feels like a betrayal no matter what I do."

And she said, "I don't think betrayal is a word that belongs on this porch."

I teach sometimes with the Colorado writer Laura Hendrie, and she gives a craft lecture on something she calls the Jaws-Of-Life character, the person who sweeps in and pulls your protagonist from the burning car just when it seems all hope is lost. Kae Penner-Howell was my Jaws-Of-Life character that weekend. She came just when all my intrinsic strength and broad-minded philosophy about the cycle of life was about to fail me. She drove ten hours in a Prius on black ice to sleep on a hard wooden porch in a poorly rated sleeping bag with Fenton and me on his last night on earth.

I didn't want to go to sleep because the hours were short now and I didn't want to miss a minute. After we had been quiet a while, a coyote barked and another howled back from a greater distance. Before long and for the last time, Fenton joined their song.

A few hours later, when it was barely getting light, I lay nose to nose with him and petted his perfect ears and said, outloud, "You did such a good job, Fenton. You did such a good job taking care of me." He looked right at me, right into me. He wanted me to know he knew what I was saying. "And I think you already know this," I said, "but you don't have to be afraid." I didn't know where those words came from—if it were me getting the shot in the morning, I sure as hell would be afraid—but I knew when I said them they were the most important ones. In the gathering light he looked in my eyes not with fear exactly, but urgency. He said, *now it's my turn to trust you* and I said, *you can.*

An owl hooted, some geese honked, and Kae stirred in her sleeping bag. One of the lambs started baa-ing, Queeny, probably, the one with the higher voice. I heard Roany nicker softly, heard him walk around on the crunching snow. Somewhere in the distance, the sound of a woodpecker. All the sounds the ranch makes every morning.

Doc Howard came at ten am, through the snow, to give Fenton the shot. Doc is getting older and had told me he would be sending his granddaughter in his place, and I didn't protest, though I know he heard the disappointment and fear in my silence, so I was unsurprised and very grateful to see his small grey head behind the wheel. When I saw he did not have the sedative most vets give initially, before they give the drug that stops the heart, he again heard my unasked question. Doc said, "What's in this syringe is the world's biggest sedative. I don't like to mess around with lots of reactive drugs." Fenton was calm—almost smiling—for the very few minutes it took to put him to sleep forever. I believe he knew what was happening. I believe he was ready to put his head down on my lap one last time.

Everybody cried, even sweet Jay, Doc's brand new vet tech who had only met Fenton a couple of times. When I found my voice again, I told Doc the story about Jerry and the steaks, and he said, "Pam, it turns out there are a lot of really good people in the world."

After we loaded Fenton's body into Doc's truck to be taken to the morgue for cremation, Kae and Linda and I took a pasture walk in his honor. A couple of inches of snow covered the ground, and the Rocky Mountain bluebirds who had returned recently hoping for better weather were almost too beautiful against the freshly whitened pasture to bear. The sun came out, and we fed all the equines apples and carrots from our hands.

Eight hours later I found myself back in the Denver airport which was full of opportunities to do the things I hadn't found the time or the wherewithal to do all weekend: drink water, go to the bathroom, eat food. My plane was delayed two hours, and the corn chowder at Elway's

Bar tasted miraculous. I was riding on something I recognized as "having lived through the thing you thought you might not live through" adrenaline. I marveled at all the people around me who weren't grieving, who had had a normal weekend with their families at home. I wasn't sleepy exactly. It was more like the insides of my eyes had been scoured with a Brillo pad.

Fenton the human sent me a text saying Fenton the canine loved and was loved all his life, and there is no condition in all our living and dying that could be more satisfying. Months later he would write Fenton a eulogy that quoted both Thomas Merton (*What we have to be is what we are*) and Whitman (*Life is the little left over from the dying*), and saying, "Fenton the canine, was a teacher . . . he taught through the simple fact of being who he is, who he was. . . . In the losses lie the lessons. . . . if we would only embrace death as another aspect of life—if we would let the animals teach us how to live and how to die—we might just treat each other and our animals better than we do."

As I waited for my plane I found myself thinking back, as I had many times that weekend, to Jerry at the Whole Foods pulling that steak off the top of the pile. He might have thought what he did was a small thing—though the price of those dry-aged steaks make it at least a medium thing, even by the most objective measure—but the relative magnitude of his kindness to me, at that moment, was frankly immeasurable—and I held onto it all weekend, and for the weeks of grief to come.

2

Back in 2000, to help pay for the ranch, I took a teaching job at UC Davis, requiring me to be there for two ten-week quarters each year. I chose spring and fall, because summers are glorious in the high country and miserable in Davis, and because farm animals die most often in winter. I hired a series of house-sitters to tend the ranch while I was gone, often former students who needed a place to finish a book. Twice yearly I'd trade my down, fleece and Xtra Tuffs for corduroy and linen. Twice yearly, I became a teacher who rode her bright yellow bike to school, who formulated sentences containing phrases like "contemporary fabulism" and "Paul Celoyn-esque," who had regular meetings with the Dean and the Provost, and who usually brushed her hair for them. I read my colleagues' books on *Noir Cinema in a Post Colonial Age* and *Situatedness* and spent a fair amount of time apologizing for my 4-Runner and the percentage of my clothes bearing sports logos.

In Creede, there is no movie theater and no drug store and no one who would ever use a phase like "Paul Ceylon-esque." In Creede I talk to my neighbors about shrinking water tables and bingo at the Elks on Saturday night. When I go to the Monte Vista Co-Op to buy sealant to shoot into the water trough, and mineral licks, and big tubes of Ivermectin horse wormer and Carhartt overalls, I notice how different it is from the Davis Co-Op where I buy organic turmeric and homeopathic allergy medicine, and where people take their groceries home in environmentally friendly macramé nets. To the people in Creede I am intelligent, suspiciously sophisticated, and elitist to the point of being absurd. To the people at UC Davis I am quaint, a little slow on the uptake, and far too earnest to even believe.

In Creede, people believe in hard work, the restorative power of nature, and, in many cases, God. What stands in place of belief within UC Davis English is something you might identify as extreme verbal agility and analytics. God has been replaced by literary theory, of course, which has rolled all the way over, in the seventeen years I have taught there, from Deconstruction to Marxism with brief side trips into Feminism and the Post Colonial. In Creede there is no need for literary theory of any kind because there is such an overabundance of things that are actual. Cold, for instance, sometimes minus fifty degrees of it, and wind and drought, and wildfires that can chew up ten thousand acres in a day.

When I began teaching at UC Davis, it was still the home of the poet Gary Snyder. It was then, and still is, one of the finest environmental literature departments around. But times change, and over the years the talk has changed from riprap and plate tectonics to cyberspace as environment, Prius commercials as representations of nature, the suburban lawn as (and here I quote) "a poetic figure for a space, or spacing, around or under figurality—The lawn therefore a figure for what is excluded in the idea of figure itself—the very substance and/as dimension in which figurality can emerge in itself."[1]

My colleagues are brilliant, and so is their research, which proves to us, mostly, our own absurdity—tending our lawns, saving the earth with our Prii—the hollow chuckle aimed at ourselves. Departmental lectures focus on global systems and global currencies—the yen and the yuan hot topics in recent years. Last winter, a colleague taught a class in some-

---

1. Morton, Timothy, "Wordsworth Digs The Lawn", *European Romantic Review*, Vol.15, No. 2, June 2004, p.318.

thing called "distant reading." Because I have spent half my life teaching *close* reading, when the grad students first told me about it, I thought it was a joke. But distant reading, according to the New York Times is "understanding literature not by studying particular texts but by aggregating and analyzing massive amounts of data."

"It's not actually done by people," my student Becca told me. "You take a body of literature, say, all the books set in Paris from 1490 to 1940, plug them into a computer, and the computer can tell you how many mentions of the Pont Neuf there were." It was, I understood, an attempt to repurpose literature. As if all beings are best understood only in terms of their aggregate, as if by making things less particular, one made them more powerful or clear.

I thought about the books that had shaped my sensibility as a young writer: *A Pilgrim At Tinker Creek, Silent Spring, Sand County Almanac, Refuge, A River Runs Through It, In Patagonia* and *Desert Solitaire.* When I asked my classes, as I did each quarter, how many people had ever spend a night sleeping in the wilderness there were diminishing numbers of hands these days, usually only one, or zero. For the first time in my teaching life I was finding myself standing in front of a room full of students for whom the words *elk, granite* and *bristlecone pine* conjured exactly nothing. Was it feasible, or even sane, anymore, to write unironic, non-dystopian books about the natural world?

One answer, of course, was no. My colleagues are realists. They understand as far as the earth is concerned, we are way past game over. In recent years, our government has launched what Robert Redford and others have called the most sweeping legislative attack on our environment ever. The earth is lost, and all that's left is to study the simulacrums, the Man Versus Wild Video Games and Survivor. To write a poem about the loveliness of a newly leafed out aspen grove or a hot August wind sweeping across prairie grass or the smell of the air after a three-day rain in the maple forest might be, at best so unconscionably naive, and at worst so much part of the problem, we might as well drive a Hummer and start voting Republican. If we stand back for just a moment and think about what effort it has actually taken to destroy a whole planet that hadn't even been correctly mapped a couple of hundred years ago, it really staggers the imagination. And now, as we head for the cliff, foot heavy on the throttle, doesn't it seem pointless to write a poem about the essence of a tree? Maybe. But then again, maybe not. Maybe this is the best time there has ever been to write unironic poems about nature.

I have spent most of my life walking in nature, but for the last twelve months, I have been walking five miles a day, minimum, wherever I am, urban or rural, and can attest to the magnitude of the natural beauty that is left. Beauty worth seeing, worth singing, worth saving, whatever that word can mean now. There is beauty in a desert, even one that is expanding. There is beauty in the ocean, even one that is on the rise.

And even if the jig is up, even if it is really game over, what better time to sing about the earth than when it is critically, even fatally wounded at our hands. Aren't we more complex, more interesting, more multifaceted people if we do? What good has the hollow chuckle ever done anyone? Do we really keep ourselves from being hurt when we sneer instead of sob?

If we pretend not to see the tenuous beauty that is still all around us, will it keep our hearts from breaking as we watch another mountain be clear cut, as we watch North Dakota, as beautiful a state as there ever was, be poisoned for all time by fracturing? If we abandon all hope right now, does that in some way protect us from some bigger pain later? If we never go for a walk in the beetle-killed forest, if we don't take a swim the algae-choked ocean, if we lock grandmother in a room for the last ten years of her life so we can practice and somehow accomplish the survival of her loss in advance, in what ways does it make our lives easier? In what ways does it impoverish us?

We are all dying, and because of us, so is the Earth. That's the most terrible, the most painful in my entire repertoire of self-torturing thoughts. But it isn't dead yet and neither are we. Are we going to drop the earth off at the vet, say goodbye at the door, and leave her to die in the hands of strangers? We can decide, even now, not to turn our backs on her in her illness, we can still decide not to let her die alone.

3

I have always believed that if I pay strict attention while I am out in the physical world—and for me that often means the natural world—the physical world will give me everything I need to tell my stories. As I move through the world, I wait to feel something I call a glimmer, a vibration, a little charge of resonance that says, "Hey writer, look over here." I feel it deep in my chest, this buzzing that lets me know this thing I am seeing/hearing/smelling/tasting on the outside is going to help me unlock some part of a story I have on the inside. I keep an ongoing record of these glimmers, writing down not my interpretation of them, not my imagined connection to them, not an emotional contextualization of them, but just the thing itself. Get in, get it down, get out and move on to the next glimmer. Then, when I have some time to write, I read through the glimmer files in my computer and try to find a handful that seem like they will stick together, that when placed in proximity with each other will create a kind of electricity.

I try to keep my big analytical brain out of this process as much as possible, because I believe my analytical brain at best only knows part of the story and at worst is a big fat liar. I believe—like religion—that the glimmer, the metaphor, if you will, knows a great deal more than I do. And if I stay out of its way, it will reveal itself to me. I will become not so much its keeper as its conduit, and I will pass its wisdom on to the reader, without actually getting in its way.

In addition to being my method, the way I have written every single thing I have written, it is also the primary way I worship, the way I kneel down and kiss the earth.

4

On Memorial Day weekend, 2015, I drove the dogs back to the ranch after ten weeks in California. They were good sports about our time in Davis but there was no mistaking the smile on their dog faces when we crested the top of Donner Pass and got back over to the leash-less side of the Sierras. We stopped every four hours for walks along forest service roads or multi-use trails all the way across Nevada and Utah, but nothing is better than the first pasture walk back at the ranch.

On Sunday morning, we did what we call the large pasture loop, out to the back of my hundred and twenty acres and then over the style into the national forest, up Red Mountain Creek and across one edge of my neighbor's twelve thousand acres, and then back down alongside the wetland and back over my fence again. It was me, William, Olivia, the pup, and the writer Josh Weil who would be watching the ranch for the next several weeks while I went off teaching in Vermont, Marin County and France.

We were nearly back to my fence line when we heard a high pitched cry, which I first thought was a red tail hawk, until it cried a few more times and I realized William had found himself a baby elk. We ran up the hill, called off William, and watched as the calf took a few sturdy steps and then settled back into the underbrush where she had been hiding. Satisfied she was unhurt, we went another 100 yards down the hill only to find a dead cow elk, the blood in the cavity still wet where the coyotes had pulled the guts out.

I tried to make the hole in the neck look like something other than an entry wound—the tooth of a coyote perhaps or the peck of the little known round-beaked vulture. I did not want to believe one of my neighbors would shoot a cow, illegally, at the peak of calving season, right here at the edge of my property where my horses spend summer nights grazing the edges of the wetland. I didn't want to think anyone would shoot an animal for practice, for pleasure, and then leave the meat to spoil.

"That baby doesn't have a chance," Josh said, as we stared down into the cow's pecked out eye, as we kicked at the wet grass that had been pulled out of her stomach. "It's probably starving already."

We both knew the rule of thumb was to leave abandoned calves alone; we also knew we might be in the presence of an exception. Those unspeakably long legs, those airbrushed spots, the deep brown eyes, and slightly pugged-up nose.

"I wish we hadn't seen the cow," I said, stupidly.

"I do too," Josh said, "but we did."

We were both thinking of the two rejected domestic lambs my previous house-sitter had been feeding, and the mudroom full of milk replacer. We were both looking at the sky, which had begun serving up one of Colorado's famous May blizzards: the temperature was dropping, the snow was sticking, and the wind was starting to howl.

"Let's take the dogs home," I said, "and heat up some milk and bring her a bottle. If she is still here when we get back, if she lets us approach her, maybe you carry her back to the barn."

We took our time getting the bottle. If her mother was still alive we wanted to give her plenty of space to react to the distress cries once we were out of there. We drove the 4-Runner around to the closest road access, so Josh would have to carry her 300 yards instead of 3000. We found her easily, and she blinked up at us sweetly, apparently unafraid. Maybe she was already too weak from hunger to save, I thought, and yet she had jumped right up to get away from William.

I sat down beside her and offered the bottle. She wasn't too keen at first, but when I gave up and drew it back across my chest she stretched herself across my lap to give it another sniff and chew a little on the nipple. She'd only take a little at a time but before long we'd gotten about a cup down her. She put her head in my lap and started to go to sleep. Josh said it might be a good time to try to transport her.

She did not love being carried. She wiggled and squeaked like she had when William had found her, and I prayed a giant elk cow would come crashing through the trees to fight us for her, but the woods were quiet and Josh held on tight and once we got to the 4-Runner she curled up in the dog bed in the back like she had been doing it all her life. Back home, Josh carried her the short distance to the barn, where we made a bed of straw for her, which she rejected in favor of the dirt floor, and I went inside to heat some more milk. That time she drank almost two cups. She shivered in the cold, and I rubbed her warm with my jacket. It was at that point Josh named her Willa.

The Internet said it wasn't uncommon for cow elk to leave their babies for several hours, because the babies could not keep up with the herd at the pace of their daily grazing. It said the calves were scentless, and would not attract predators, and the herd would come back and pick them up around dusk.

"If the dead cow isn't her mother," I said to Josh, "we may have just done a really bad thing." But it was snowing in earnest now, the wind screaming, and mistake or not, Willa was warm and dry in the barn.

I did what I always do in Creede when I don't know what to do and that's call Doc Howard. He said there was a sanctuary near Del Norte that would take her and raise her. He told me to call Brent, the wildlife officer, and that Brent would come get her, take her to the sanctuary, and while he was at it investigate the shooting. He said, "There are several other things you could do Pam, but not without being in violation of all kinds of laws."

I knew everybody had gotten freaked out about elk since chronic wasting disease became a thing in Colorado, but I also knew we had never had a case of it in Mineral County and they checked every elk the hunters took out. Still, I didn't really want to raise an elk baby with a bottle. What I wanted was for some yahoo not to have shot her mother. The website said to feed your orphaned elk four cups every four hours, so I left Brent a message and went out with more warm milk. This time she was interested and drank with less coaxing. She followed me around the stall, and when I would sit down in the straw with her, she would touch her nose to my face and hair.

Josh and I spent another hour with her, watching her walk around on her long long legs, greeting her when she wanted to make contact, feeling what it was like to be in her presence—which had a mystical quality to it, a visitation from some other-worldly being. So calm, she was, so delicate and full of light.

"Now, Pam, I'm going to need you to trust me a little bit," Brent said on the phone, and because of the tone in his voice when he said it, I did. "The sanctuary in Del Norte won't take elk anymore because of chronic wasting. There's a place in Westcliffe I might get to take her, but her best chance at the life she is meant to have is if you put her back out there, exactly where you found her. There's a good chance the herd will come pick her back up."

"Even if the dead one is her mother?"

"Even if," he said. "If the herd has another cow nursing, she'll probably be okay. I'll come up at seven in the morning and if she's still there I'll put her in a kennel and take her to Westcliffe."

It's hard to put a week-old elk calf back in the woods at sunset within a hundred yards of a ripped-open elk carcass the coyotes already know about, but by the time we talked ourselves into it, I had gotten two more cups of milk down her, it had stopped snowing, and the last sun of the day was warming things up a bit. Josh carried her back to the 4-Runner, we drove her around to the back fence and Josh carried her, kicking squeaking, back to the exact tree where William had found her. We didn't know what we were going to do if she followed us, but she didn't. She curled back in right where her mother had put her, and waited, we hoped, for the herd to come at dusk.

"What a story she'll have to tell her friends," I tried, as we turned our backs on her.

"Oh, she just thinks this is what happens to everybody," Josh said, "On the seventh day of being an elk you get to ride in the back of a car."

The next morning, I had to leave for the airport at four-thirty, and the air was clear and full of stars and twenty-nine degrees on my car thermometer. I said another prayer the herd had come back for Willa, that her mother had not been the shot one, and nobody minded she smelled a little like humans and the back of a 4-Runner usually occupied by Irish Wolfhounds. "We might have messed up," I said, to whoever I thought might be listening at that hour—some genderless Druidic earth power, I supposed, perhaps the mountain itself—"but we talked it out every step and tried to make the best decision."

I watched seven come and go as I drove father away from Creede and closer to the Denver airport. I knew news wouldn't likely come until nine, but every minute after seven was torture. Finding her dead would have been the fastest outcome; loading her into the kennel and sending her off with Brent the next fastest after that. Searching the woods for her would take the longest. It was hard to even know what to hope for.

Finally, when I was sitting at gate B23, Josh called. The cow had been shot; that was certain. They had looked long and hard for Willa and found no sign of her. They had also looked up and down the road for a shell casing to help identify the poacher and had also not found one of those. Brent would go up to Spar City and ask around, but he wasn't hopeful he would find out anything more.

I have decent intuitive skills, which have improved with the onset of menopause, so I tried to quiet my mind to get a sense of Willa. For whatever it is worth, she did not feel dead to me. I know how potentially self-deceiving that sounds. But she was, among other things, a magical being. Josh and I gave her up to the mountain, and I believe the mountain took care of her.

5

It is hard to be ironic about a dying dog. It is hard to be ironic about an elk calf when her nose is touching your face. It is hard to be ironic when the young writer who tends your house and cuddles your dogs and who you know loves the earth with the same passion you do is walking behind you down a dirt trail with thirty-three pounds of baby elk in his arms. It is hard to be ironic when your pasture erupts after an unexpected May blizzard into a blanket of wild iris. It is hard to be ironic when the osprey who returns to your ranch every summer makes his first lazy circle around the peak of your barn.

Last January, I was speaking with an environmental scientist who said he was extremely pessimistic about the future of the earth in the hundred-year frame, but optimistic about it in the five-hundred-year frame. There will be very few people here, he said, earnestly, but the ones who are here will have learned a lot. He also said the carbon driven period will be looked at as the most barbaric, most irresponsible period in the history of the world.

There are times when I understand all too well what my colleagues in Davis are trying to protect themselves from. Times when seeing the world's bright beauty is almost more than I can bear, when my mind is running the grim numbers the scientists have given us right alongside. And it is also true, had I never laid eyes on Willa, I would not have spent five sleep-deprived hours weeping—often sobbing—in the car that morning on the way to DIA. If I hadn't slept those three nights on the porch with Fenton, it would have been three fewer nights of my life spent with an actively breaking heart. But a broken heart—God knows,

I have found—doesn't actually kill you. And irony and disinterest are false protections, ones that won't serve us, or the earth, in the end.

For now, I want to sit vigil with the Earth the same way I did with Fenton. I want to write unironic odes to her beauty, which is still potent, if not completely intact. The language of the wilderness is the most beautiful language we have and it is our job to sing it, until and even after it is gone, no matter how much it hurts. If we don't, we are left with only a hollow chuckle, and our big brains who made this mess, our big brains that stopped believing a long time ago in beauty, in everything, in anything.

What I want to say to my colleagues is that the Earth doesn't know how not to be beautiful. Yes, the destruction, yes, the inevitability, but honestly, Doctor Distant Reader, when was the last time you actually slept on the ground?

How will we sing when Miami goes underwater, when the raft of garbage in the ocean gets as big as Texas, when the only remaining Polar Bear draws his last breath, when fracking, when Keystone, when Inhofe . . . ? I don't know. And I imagine sometimes, often, we will get it wrong. But I'm not celebrating the Earth because I am an optimist—though I am an optimist. I am celebrating because this magnificent rock we live on demands celebration. I am celebrating because how in the face of this earth could I not?

Nominated by About Place Journal

34

THE TORNADO AUCTION

fiction by KAREN RUSSELL

from ZOETROPE: ALL-STORY

I. AT THE SALE BARN

You know, there was never any money in it, even back then. If you were a breakeven, you were a success.

I'd been fully retired for nearly fifteen years when I decided, on a whim, to return to the sale barn. Driving home from the pharmacy, passing the shoals of purple corn, I watched the wheel turning in my hands. The barn's howling interior, with its warrens of wind hoses, was as familiar to me as my home, but I recognized almost no one. How young the faces had become! Just about everybody I've ever wanted to impress, I've now outlived.

Baby southerlies whinnied around, shrieking their inhuman sounds. Violet funnels chased one another beneath the shivering ducts. Crocus blue mists, soft as exhalations, fogged their incubator walls. I felt a growl under my navel as I passed chute seven—the doorway out of which my own twisters had flown, once upon a time. New lunacies greeted me on either side. What a catalogue of weathers my peers were now breeding, dreaming up on their ranchlands. Clouds branded Pink Cauliflower and Lucifer's Bridal Veil. Clouds almost too bloated with rain to move. I found plenty to admire, despite the grim forecasts I'd been reading all year.

Moisture began to clot on my glasses, so I removed them. Some things, I swear, I see better without correction. Tornadoes, for one. My eyes often snag on irrelevancies, when I'm wearing my glasses; without them, I can take in more. The panorama, you know, the whole sublime blur. Estelle,

I think, hated the sight of my naked face. (*Jesus, Robert! Do you know how scary you look, wandering around out there like Mr. Magoo?*)

The national anthem cranked up, and everyone stood. By the old custom, one of the local families had donated a runty funnel, set to manifest at the crowd's off-key crescendo. So while we sang, hands on hearts—"And the rockets' red *glaaaare* . . ."—a howler blew out of chute one.

"Oh my God," I breathed. And I felt the way I always hope to feel in church. As the twister kicked and spun around the arena floor, the howl rose from its center, throbbing without discrimination into and through each of us, and row by row we fell helplessly to our knees.

The auction is a quarterly event, and until my retirement I attended every one. You'll read in the papers that ours is a "graying community," a defunct way of life. But on auction day, it never feels so. Scattered around the parking lot, over a hundred twitching, immature storms dimple the roofs of their trailers, like pipping chicks testing their shells. Their wailing surrounds and fills the barn, harmonizing with the hum of machinery. The viper pit of hoses, the blue convection modules stuck to every wall like big, square dewdrops—the various modern wet nurses that keep a developing storm alive. "Back in the Dark Ages, all we had to work with was liquid propane and the real wind," my old man liked to remind me.

On my way in, I'd passed a quintet of freshly weaned storms, all sired by the same cumuliform supercell out of Dalhart. Beautiful orphans, thriving independently. I'd known this line of clouds my whole life; that Dalhart stud cell was famous when I was a kid. Its signature thunder went rolling through many a turbulent generation, and I smiled to hear it once more. In the refracted glow of such a shimmering lineage, you get the child-joy, the child-fever. I'll turn seventy-four this March, and it doesn't matter: that joy regresses you.

It's been a bad season for seasons. Not just here in Gosper County but all across the country. After the anthem we sat, while the flag was attacked by the last of the purebred gusts and the cloud danced itself out. Then I saw the one face I'd been counting on seeing, as surely as flipping over a penny to find mournful Lincoln: the Rev.

"I don't care what your politics are," the Rev crooned. "I think it's time we all admit that the weather is changing . . ."

36

A few boos, though most were nodding, hat bills stabbing at the air like a bunch of dour woodpeckers. Everybody here has been hit by the warming. This year, if you wanted cold, moist air, you had to pipe it in. The dry-line days on which we breeders rely did not come.

Guilt rose from the bleachers like a rippling stink. Relative to the West Texas cloud-seeding corporations, our approach here in southern Nebraska remains pretty Amish. Still, when you're raising weather by artificial means, it's hard to pretend you don't have a hand in the Change.

I feel less culpable than some because I always stayed small—I didn't mess with the supercells or the silver iodide, I didn't go for broke with the ten-thousand-dollar anemometers, the quarter-million-dollar accelerators. One twister at a time, I raised almost by hand.

And I raised them for demolition. This was the seventies, on the ranchlands of Tornado Alley. You can bring down a city block with a rental tornado, and I had contracts. My twisters have felled fire-damaged silos and bankrupt casinos, foundering Chick-N-Shacks and neglected libraries. Pry bars, reciprocating and circular saws, jackhammers, trenchers, wrecking balls, human crews with their human needs and fleshy vulnerabilities—all unnecessary. So long as you properly configured the chute and programmed the expulsion vents, a tornado would roll toward a condemned building as inexorably as a pregnant lady toward rocky road ice cream, as Estelle used to joke in her joking days, when the girls were still small. Elsewhere, I hear, they rent out beehives to pollinate fruit trees. Nowadays, of course, armies of American litigators have made weather-assisted demolition illegal. I suppose that's progress.

Prices for violent storms have bottomed out, and farmers are downsizing, doing dirt devils, doing siroccos. Walls of dust raise themselves, some reaching eight thousand feet under the blazing sun, swallowing the gas flares over the oil wells. The jet stream is not cooperating. Neither, for that matter, is the economy. To survive you have to sell out to the rodeos, the monster-truck rallies. We don't suffer alone. Offshore rigs report that water spouts have all but dried up, and voltages in the high-desert lightning fields are down forty percent. Here on the Plains, an early frost snuffed every budding funnel cloud. These days anybody with sense farms winds. Winds are the growth industry. Clean energy. You want to get out ahead of the apocalypse, get into winds.

Supercells, those alpha storms that bulge with precipitation like muscle, cost too much in upkeep and insurance for all but the corporate outfits. From their Piper Cubs, mercenary armies of pilots pulse infrared beams into the wild cumulonimbus, watch rainbows go flickering under their fuselages. The accountants work their profit-and-loss models to determine whether a cloud should live or die. Culls deemed unfit for sale are left to spin out in the green canyons, thousands of acres of privately held weather graveyards. A few family farms are still hoping to develop prestige twisters; I'd seen two in utero while driving into town. Sister funnels, housed in adjacent incubators. They looked lonely out there, spinning on their single toes. Purple monsters, twice the height of the cork-colored barn, yawing up and down, consuming bitter air. What it must be costing to irrigate them all through July, to keep those updrafts tight, I shudder to imagine.

Any storm you see at auction was artificially bred, artificially maintained. Coriolis Farms, our family's outfit, was no exception. The tornadoes we reared were a miniature sort, typically rotating around sixty or seventy miles per hour, rarely more than fifty meters across. EF0, EF1. Compact enough to rage in a corral and strong enough to flip a car.

But even corporate-raised stock is far less powerful than the Act of God twisters that destroy whole towns. I've seen mobile homes conscripted into a cosmic game of kick-the-can, and that evil is beyond humanity; it's assigned randomly, by forces unknown. Weather damage is the inverse of a victimless crime: victims lose everything, and there is no culprit to lock in a cage.

And still, so many of my fellow farmers are bewildered whenever one of our ground-traveling clouds gets loose and vigilante mobs show up at the breeder's ranch. Give people a name to blame for their suffering, and you, too, can expect a flood of furious attention. On the night my storm escaped me, the entire county read the damage swath as my autograph.

Just when I'd reconciled myself to anonymity, Lemon Guyron slid onto my bench with his oldest son beside him. I've known Lemon for decades—his skin like grainy brown mustard and his fortressed smile.

"Can that be Wurman? I almost didn't recognize you!"

"We've got some age on us, I guess. How've you been, Lemon?"

"Never better, never better. Bad year for weather, but that'll pass, of course." A grin spread like a moat around his face. "I got no complaints."

Lemon's son, what was his name?

"Actually, Mr. Wurman," said this forty-year-old boy, who'd inherited his father's speckly skin but not his relentless affability, "we've had a helluva time finding a buyer this spring. A lot of the state fairs are moving away from tornado riding. Too much liability, and the kids aren't interested." He smiled with his gums, lifting his moustache into a gloomy rainbow. "Like jai alai and unprotected group sex, it has seen its day." We chuckled our stage-chuckles, staring ahead. You have to force a chuckle sometimes, just to get your tires out of the mud; otherwise years might pass without another word spoken.

"You in the market this year, Wurman?"

"I'm not buying," I said. "Just fantasizing."

"Looks like something's coming down . . ."

Knee to knee, we all craned in, stubby number twos poised above scratch pads. The clouds were loaded in the pens now, coerced into a temporary calm, like genies in their bottles. Bodiless, they could not paw the earth. But we heard them readying for expulsion, whining for release, behind every steel door.

Chute two opened first, and out whirled a dirt devil, shrubby and meek, gyring in place like a music-box ballerina, already dissipating into the golden afternoon air.

"It would exhaust itself right here," I murmured to Lemon, "if it weren't for those hoses stringing it up like a corset."

"That's what the Ahmad brothers are putting up?"

"I heard they had some trouble with their incubator."

"Looks like bad breath."

The Rev chanted over the gusts: "One thousand, now two, now two, who'll give me two? Two, now three, now three, who'll give me three?"

Last year, the nation's top recorded price for a storm was a quarter-million dollars for an EF4 tornado named Jericho, raised by Gomez & Daughters, one of the last matriarchal weather ranches in Texas, and sold to Franklin Fair & Rodeo. That may sound like a lot of money, but consider what it takes to run an aeolian generator, and redo the math; like I said, if you're a breakeven in this strange industry, you're doing better than ninety percent of breeders.

Two rows down, a kid with bad razor burn and a bony white Stetson is saying, "I don't think the market will fall out of bed, but I'm saying the highs are in place."

These dumb-ass young men, in for the day from Dallas or Denver, wearing yellow slickers with the sales tags still dangling down their necks, constantly chatting to distant bosses on silver devices. The conglomerates buried us. Wiped out our last hope of any profits. Now they send their agents to outbid us in our own towns. Puffy-faced flunkies with their indoor sunglasses and their show dimples, their fake-friendly hellos and BA degrees in subjects that sound phony: environmental business management, sky-ag biochem.

The Rev called speeds into the clown-nosed mic, singing the praises of the yet-to-be. This one, full grown, was sure to be another "storm of the century." That one, the "future terror of the Great Plains." I can tell you what was happening inside the buyer's mind, as the Rev seeded us with his enthusiasm: a second tornado was building. Bigger, faster, stronger, and immensely profitable, the sort of sublime weather that reduces grown men to bed wetters.

Four plummy funnels were rotating around the corral; mush-roomy and odd as she was, I couldn't take my eyes off the white one.

"What's got you pinked up? Not that ugly loaf?"

"Maybe so. Who sired it?"

"Supercell Four. Molly's outfit."

"You don't like it?"

"I don't like the looks of it, no. Everybody knows they ionize with junk from China."

"Molly does?"

"Oh, heck yes, Robert. That downdraft look natural to you?"

"I'm not buying, anyhow—"

Molly's cull rolled over the sandy soil like a drunken marble, wobbly and slow, a beautiful foggy light streaking its center. My pencil never touched the scratch pad.

"Three thousand, who'll give me four?"

I lifted my paddle.

"The *hell* are you thinking?"

Lemon turned his stare on me. His wintry eye, assessing.

"You're a fool," he offered. "You want to burn up all your kids' money?"

"The girls are grown. They don't need my money."

He laughed angrily. Scared for me, or maybe of me.

"Find a new hobby. Golf, Wurman. Have you thought about golf?"

Another paddle went up, jumping the price a thousand dollars. The man's powder blue Head in the Clouds vest revealed him as a stooge for one of the big Texas weather factories.

I lifted my paddle.

"You're mad at the girls, I can see that."

"This has nothing to do with the girls."

"Be angry. You have every right. But this is a mistake."

"*Twelve* thousand, do I have thirteen?"

I lifted my paddle.

Outrageously, the hired goon raised, as well. It wasn't his money, was it? Possibly he'd decided his duckling pride would be injured, losing a cloud to the likes of me.

I lifted my paddle.

"Fifteen, do I have sixteen?"

"Yep!"

"Jesus, Wurman. You don't have that kind of money."

"Who are you to tell me what I've got?"

"You really want to ruin yourself, go jump in the river—it's quicker."

I lifted my paddle.

"Going, going . . ."

Gone. She was mine.

"It's a bad bet."

"My worst," I happily agreed.

II. ALL SALES FINAL

"It may die before you get home. You're aware of that possibility?"

The ranching of storms has come a long way since wranglers drove those silent clouds, black and distended, up the Goodnight Trail, or captured Colorado River mists on horseback. But the sale of a tornado is still very much a handshake business.

"I am aware," I said to the seller's fat-lipped manager, wondering what I had just done. Never in a long career had I bid so highly on a maybe.

(*Bobby, what did you expect would happen?* One of my wife's favorite questions, whenever things went sideways for us.)

At the loading chute, I clutched the hauling papers, watching the young storm flatten, straighten. Lemon, bless him, had loaned me his trailer to get the bucking cloud home. Moisture found my tongue, settled there. *This is what she tastes like, then. My storm. Mine to keep spinning, mine to make strong.* And moisture dribbled onto my cheeks, amazingly of my own manufacture. Never when I'm called upon to cry can I wince out a tear. At Estelle's funeral, to my girls' disgust, I was a dry teat. Couldn't plug my eyeballs into what I felt deep below. Something is wrong with my wiring, I have always known.

The pale funnel pulsed out and contracted, like a star exploring its cosmos. In the sunlight, against the dark walls of the chute, it became a ghostly gramophone needle, leaping and falling, lightly and blindly, searching for the groove.

These days such mishaps are rare, but every rancher has heard or told that anecdote about the fledgling twister that burst its trailer, escaped onto the highway. In the rearview I saw only the solid metal cylinder. But in my mind's eye I beheld her, a cone of swiftly moving air. Traffic hung four car lengths behind me.

I drove south through successively finer meshes of rainfall, until by the end there was no water to speak of and only hot grit steaming up from the underbelly of the truck. Nobody emerged from the house to scream, "Robert, what have you done?"

III. CONSISTENT INSTABILITY

My first thought on waking was, *Did she live through the night?*

From the bedroom window, I have a clear view across the parched grass to the tornado shelter. Cottony mist enveloped the gray and yellow silo. Let's admit it was a dumb-ass move, to buy a twister on credit, at an age when I cannot realistically expect to raise it to tornadic speed and stature, much less sell it for a profit. To buy a twister at this most vulnerable stage in its development without having set foot in my own shelter in half a decade. An impulse purchase is cinnamon gum, not an unvetted cloud.

I pulled up to the shelter to unload and found everything still functional. Incredibly, the great air bladders that had been idle for years were swelling and falling. Every one of the fans had clicked on. I got the hoses fretworked to maintain the updraft, tubed in some ice crystals. Checked the vertical vorticity levels: all excellent. Warm winds and cold winds charged into the system—the collision of temperatures that keeps a baby spinning, breathing. The goal is to get that rotation sufficiently strong to be self-sustaining. It's an art, no doubt, to calibrate all your inputs and to fight off homeostasis in pursuit of a paradox: consistent instability. As Estelle and our girls would tell you, if I have one talent it's for this: divining what a developing storm needs to stay angry, to live on.

The highest terrestrial wind speed ever measured was 301 miles per hour, when the Bridge Creek-Moore Tornado touched down in the

Oklahoma City area during the early evening of May 3, 1999. An EF5. The twisters we raised at Coriolis Farms were modest, relative to their wild counterparts; our shelter can harness clouds that rotate at no more than a hundred miles per hour. The last one I bred that escaped my control clocked at eighty-nine. A solid EFl. Fortunately, she unraveled within a mile, knocking out only a power line. I have it on video, all that potential snuffing itself in our western pasture, along with the fourteen thousand dollars I'd poured into her. We watched the funnel slow until it went slack as a rope, dissipating into the whitish horizon.

Raising a tornado, you're always dreaming of its dying day. That's the breeder's ultimate vision—to build a storm until it can unwind spectacularly, releasing all of its cultivated fury, evanescing before your eyes. Whereas with my daughters, I have to pretend they'll live forever. The alternative is too terrible to contemplate. If there is a life after this one, I'll be dead myself and still pretending.

My oldest daughter was four pounds at birth, and her appearance flooded the earth with an infinite number of horrors and perils, a demonic surge of catastrophic possibilities out of all proportion to the tiny mass in my arms. Love unlids Pandora's box. Is that obvious? Before her, I honestly did not know it. What I felt for her was of a wholly different order than what I felt for Estelle. Never before had that heat collided with the icy possibilities of accident, of death. Not at these speeds, not with this intensity, and constantly. They were born at the same moment, twins: our baby daughter and the dangers.

"She's alive!"

I couldn't recall the last time I'd been so happy about anything. In my tone I heard the man whose girls were still young and whose farm was operational. Stretching between the shelter's frame and the house's porch beams, a quarter mile to the east, was tensioned cable with a set of wind chimes at either end, the line my dad had strung up in 1957 to maintain contact with our storms, like those tin-can walkie-talkies. They'd been dormant so long, I'd neglected to check them at the house, but on this end they were singing hysterically, bouncing over their thin shadows.

Tornado shelters, if you've never seen one, look a little like grounded rocket ships, made of oxidized glass and reinforced steel and buried in the sod. Incubators or caskets, pending how your young storm fares. Ideally, I'd never sleep, monitoring my baby's rotation through the night. I circled the shelter, peering through the viewing windows.

43

The funnel was suspended between the floor and ceiling vents, look-ing more irritable than powerful. The anemometer reported no gain in speed, and the wind girdles showed a fairly consistent circumference. But that sound spiraling out, I'd forgotten how a roar like that can fill you up entirely. Hearing loss is part of aging, I suppose, yet I hadn't guessed you could go deaf even to a sound's howling absence. To the absence of all pleasure in your life. Now it seemed absurd, impossible, that I'd endured so many years without a storm to nurse. How had I survived the peace and quiet? My ears were deluged, until there was no longer any room for thought. I moved, and it was the sound moving me. I knew what she needed.

Two transparent tunnels run from the shelter to the shining fence line between the birches. Cost a fortune to put them in, and then I got only a decade's use out of them before Estelle delivered her ultimatum. I hit the lever that releases the doors, and the antsy cloud burst into view, flying the length of the tunnels, blown up and back by the fans.

There's another tornado shelter that we never finished, on the other side of the house. There it sits, accusing me still, with the bald eloquence of our skeletal cars, a zoo of rusting metals in the bunchgrass. (*Robert, would you fix those things or sell them? Please?* Estelle would plead. And I'd tell her, which I thought was a pretty good joke, *I'm forming an artificial reef.*) I initially insisted the second shelter was at "an early stage of completion," then it gradually became a "stalled construction"; it was years before I used the word *abandoned.* Now, thanks to my recent pur-chase, I would die penniless, all good intentions still waiting in the rain.

For some reason, the sight of grass poking through and smothering the ruined planks of the foundation filled me with relief. Wind plucked at my shirt, tugging at the collar like fingers. In a cooperative spirit, I undid the buttons and shrugged it into the breeze.

Nobody would find me out here on my knees and hands, crawling around the periphery of the shelter to check its ventilation. Nobody would comment on my slack, hairy belly. Nobody would say a word for or against me, because nobody was paying any attention at all. I watched my shirt fly a great distance, sail-white, and snag on a birch branch. There it hung, waving its empty sleeves. I grinned and waved back.

Around noon, the good feeling broke into articulation, and I could voice precisely what had been making me so happy. Because I'd finally done it, hadn't I? I'd outlasted my life. The girls were grown, Estelle was gone. There was nobody left for me to hurt.

Live long enough, and your life becomes your own to gamble with again.

IV. ALONE TOGETHER

Two weeks rolled by in a silvery blur. Not a soul had been out to the property; it was just me and the prairie grouses with their lurid orange goiters—the only suns I'd seen in days. Rain had returned to southern Nebraska! A terrific downpour had battered the county back to misting green life, and I'd gotten drenched by it myself, lying outside the shelter to hear my funnel crooning to the outer air. The sky was overcast again, spongy-gray and thick. Inside the shelter, the white pendant had swollen to fill the entire chamber, and I swore the machines were just accessories to her rising fury. It's a beautiful thing to watch an infant becoming independent. Centrifugal forces were pushing air faster and faster around the partial vacuum of her heart.

By Friday of our third week, we were broaching a level of instability that would allow the funnel to double in strength. I was spending twelve, fourteen hours a day by her side, monitoring her growth and cooking the hot wind into her, holding my ear to the throbbing hull of the shelter as a kind of hypnosis. Her rising and descending wailing followed me home at night, and into my dreams. Something wonderful had happened to me, and my sleeping and waking lives were now identical, filled with singing storms.

It was so thrilling to be back on the job that I kept forgetting to take my medicine; one afternoon I woke up on my back, watching the real sky darkening above me. Flat, white clouds glided serenely overhead, so that for a moment I felt like I was at the bottom of a lake, staring up at a hundred floating docks.

My old man returned from Germany at twenty-seven already scoliotic with his freight of nightmares and medals. When I was a kid, I hated him for spending so much time away from us; I'm not angry about this today. The same need burns in me, and I wonder at the mechanisms by which such things are inherited. Memories went darkly leafing through my dad, growths he couldn't control. Of course he had to leave us to be with his storms. He had my ma, three midget sons wearing his face and always chanting his name, glomming onto his knees—there was no respite in the house. I imagine a tornado must have been the only ax that could level the entire Hürtgen Forest inside him—again and again, as often as necessary. When you're thickly sown with ghosts, it makes no sense to plug your ears against them. Those cries come from within.

I was always late for dinner. *Eat without me*, I'd beg my family. Outside every window, they could see our black storms feeding. Some nights we had to scream over their howling: *How was school, girls?* I'd grip the table with knuckles popping to avoid running right back into it. The howling was a magnet, pulling at my spine. The house was a cardboard box, and nowhere I could be for very long. *Our house*, I had to remind myself, because it was Estelle's domain; I did my living outside. At night we left the windows open, so that I could pretend I was amphibian, straddling the inner and the outer worlds. Dawn released me back into the lake of the sky. Springtime meant air filled to brimming with secret moisture, begging to be captured and spun into the yawning wombs of my twisters. My daughters' gnat-like little voices, I'm sorry to say, were no match for the howling.

When I was a younger man, I liked naming the storms. Shiva, Smash-N-Grab, Jack B. Limber, Calypso the Queen. My daughters got quiet names, each one as sweet and forgettable as a sugar cube dropped into a teacup. Anna, Megan, Laurel. You see how it goes for the Chantelles and the Rainbows in this world; unlike my tornadoes, I wanted the girls to travel anywhere they chose without causing a stir.

Six weeks after the auction, kneeling at the midpoint of the tunnels, I clocked my twister barreling overland at fifty-one miles per hour. My throat was on fire before I realized that I was screaming along with her.

Then the bad moment came, when she blasted through the boundary and into the open air, swelling marvelously in diameter, uprooting the centenarian elm, and rooster-tailing a wall of red dust. The force of her exit knocked me into a quivering heap in the dirt; I shook my head clear and stood to find the funnel moving straight for me, swallowing the distance between us like brush-fed fire.

I regained consciousness on the far perimeter of the field, resting my head on a pillowy lump that seemed to be made of my own skin, bulging out of the back of my skull. The cloud was sucking topsoil from every direction, turning a muddled brown as she spun off to the east and kicked my truck onto its side. I neither saw nor heard the windows shatter—without my glasses, the whole scene before me was one streaming tear.

Had she picked a different day to escape she'd have been dead already; but as it happened, atmospheric conditions at that moment were ideally suited to support her life. All morning, a thunderstorm had been brewing on the western horizon, moving over the dowdy spires of the grain silos. Major precipitation, cherry-sized hailstones, sporadic lightning. Warm surface winds had been pushing up from the Gulf, and the sky overhead was deep blue for miles; she was glutting on that warmth, pulling it into her whirling body. I found myself thinking, insanely, that my cloud must have realized this, planned her break accordingly.

She was angling for the house. My hands muffed my ears, came away sticky and red. The sight didn't bother me; it was only my blood, after all, and I knew the next sight would be my house splintering apart. In instances of similar stress, people report their entire lives flashing before their eyes; I saw sticks, a stack of bills. Why didn't I stand then and run to save myself? But this part of me has always been the broken one. In boyhood, I remember feeling very generously toward my fevers.

Good luck is luck I don't deserve, and yet this is simply what happened: the wind changed. At the precise instant when all seemed lost, my funnel spun 180 degrees, pivoting with an arbitrary mercy that I had to fight not to take personally as grace from on high. A rear-flank downdraft from the massing weather system might have turned her; I can offer no worthier explanation for what I saw. With the same howling serenity that she had targeted my house, she flew back the way she had come, blowing in a clean line. She seemed almost human in her retreat, retracing her steps through the gouged pasture; and disappearing inside the shelter once more, she sucked the doors shut behind her.

"Good girl," I breathed, as a spear tip hiccuped inside me, lodged in my left side; I spit up muddy-pink phlegm and felt proud of my cloud, wondering if she'd broken my ribs.

"I thought I was finished today, Estelle," I spoke into the cave of the house. Sandy air settled on my gumline; I'd taken to leaving the windows and the doors open for the company of my storm's chiming at all hours. "I thought I was finished, but look at how quickly a man can be resuscitated."

"Unscathed, I wouldn't say that," the doctor said, frowning down at me with his expression of Ivy League constipation. "A cracked rib can easily lead to pneumonia, if you're not careful about your breathing."

"Doc, if you'd seen how fast she was going, believe me, you'd know how lucky I am to be breathing at all."

The doctor removed his glasses, and his blue eyes were unshaded lamps. He was a new doctor, a young doctor. Very telegenic. Definitely looked the part of concerned physician. Color me fooled. Because when I told him I needed some relief, his whole face crumpled like a kite in a tree.

"I'm going to suggest an excellent physical therapist. In the meantime, I'd make sure to keep taking all your current medications."

"I was sort of hoping for some painkillers, to be honest with you." I coughed and winced, splinting my ribs with my palm. "Just a vial or two of tide-me-overs."

I've never been a man for theater, and it feels lousy to perform real pain for a stranger. His mouth puckered further, the lips tugging into a little heart, and I wondered why his pen wasn't moving.

"Tide-me-overs. I see." He placed the pen on the desk. "What exactly did you have in mind?"

His shining eyes didn't fool me now.

"Do I look like a drug dealer, doctor?"

The doctor smiled at that. "Do I?"

It got so quiet I could almost hear the gavel rapping inside him.

"Can I be honest with you, too, Mr. Wurman? You look like a man who's falling on hard times. And I promise you, this is not the cushion you want to land on."

V. UNDER THE RAINBOW

She was sucked into the heart of the storm, spun above the shelter, dropped almost a quarter mile away. She did not break a single bone. The newspapers nicknamed her "Dorothy" and TV cameras swarmed our farm. We felt misused by them. They made her eyeball fodder, filler between commercials. Flowers and cards poured in for about a week, and then months of sidelong glances. To this day, on Laurel's rare visits, folks will wink and whistle as if she were up on a parade float—"Hey, Dorothy!"— blind or indifferent to her wincing. It's a notoriety that never relents.

Afterward, Laurel was skittish around me. Whenever I tried to touch her, she gasped as if scalded. She couldn't even get to anger, and I worried about that at night. Some natural progression had stalled out inside my daughter, and I knew what that felt like, one forlorn note repeating itself, your song in a rut.

The deal we struck was this: Estelle wouldn't leave me, and she wouldn't send the girls away to board in Omaha, where her sister was a teacher at the Academy of the Sacred Heart—I pleaded with her on that count—but I had to agree to something, too. No more howlers in the shelter. I conceded, thinking I wouldn't last a month. How could I live without that roaring? The simple fact was that I didn't know how to do anything else.

"So learn," my smart wife suggested.

I got a job at a friend's wind farm, cash-cropping zephyrs. It was hack work, the semi-luminous. I hated the minutes of my life. I wanted to do what I always had, better than it had ever been done. I wanted to put my head in an oven. But I did what I'd promised, and collected my checks, and raised the tame weather. And eventually, I retired.

Laurel is twenty-seven now, a paralegal, and she says her day-to-day is very full. But our daughter, "miraculously unscathed," never really recovered. It's as if her body was simply incapable of restoring its default settings. The skittishness became a permanent trait, sunk deep—though ultimately she did get to anger, a static rage that ignites only in my presence.

She was unconscious when I found her, so she couldn't know that as I set my palm to her cheek, she spasmed, her whole body jerking in the coppery dust. She couldn't know that I cried out, shuddering with her, as I was seized by a childhood memory: a Swainson hawk circling overhead with a baby prairie hare in its talons, which it dropped, the hare falling and clapping itself against the rocks. When people ask her, "Who found you out there?" she knows to answer, "My father," but she couldn't know that I gathered her into my arms and held her.

Nothing shattered for me in those moments while I cradled Laurel and rushed for the house; quite the contrary, all the pieces of my life fused into a mirror, spun at last by this event into a glassy coherence, and I saw, I understood, that in fact I had always been the greatest danger to my family. I was the apex predator. Duly noted. I made the revision. Guiltily, I dreamed of the day when I'd be alone, my shadow roving over my land, unhindered by the fear of hurting anybody, especially those I'd loved so recklessly.

One by one they blew off—first Estelle, then each of the girls in turn. Today they are far away, safe from me.

After the injury, I more or less gave up driving into town. I couldn't move fast enough to sidestep the staring people. Their cold glances turned me into Bambi on the ice, slipping and sliding all over. Who can price-shop for soup amid that kind of judgment? I bought about a month's supply of milk and cereal, eggs and canned chili, hamburger meat, buy-one-get-one frozen pizzas. A head of lettuce and some freckly bananas as an after-thought, because the doctor had begged me to eat foods with minerals, rich in whatever.

Wes Jeter netted me on my way out the door. His struggle to smile was almost comical—how upset he looked as he grabbed my free hand, pumped!

"I assume you made out better than the cloud."

I beamed at him. "We both survived. I got her back into the shelter. Tell you what, Wes, it was a goddamn miracle. She's there now, fattening up on the hoses. Wind speeds of fifty-five this morning."

"Well, you need to put it down, Robert."

"Excuse me?"

"Robert, you look . . . unwell."

"Unwell?" I laughed. People were mincing words for me now, as if I didn't have the teeth to bite into the apple.

"I ran into Lemon Guyron a few weeks back. He told me what you bid—"

To my surprise, his eyes began to water. Who knows what Wes really felt in that fluorescent aisle, thinking about my cloud. Very possibly Wes was jealous. His wife was still pink with health, their place seasonally mobbed by a hundred grandkids; and he himself had been retired for years, without any obvious pressure-relief valve. So maybe Wes was crying for himself.

"Wes," I hissed, "I haven't felt so alive in years. Try to be happy for me. Or, if that's too much to ask, try never to think of me at all. It shouldn't be difficult."

VI. DEVELOPING A STORM

Here's how the fury forms:

Towering supercells can reach seventy thousand feet into the atmosphere. These are the storms that breed tornadoes in nature. Countervailing winds roll air into a moving tube. (The "corpus" of the storm, some call this. Though a storm, of course, is bodiless.) From ground level, sun-warmed air begins to rise, updrafts that push into the center of the horizontal vector, causing it to bulge. A spectral mountain develops in the sky, energy sheeting down either side. Condensation releases heat, driving the updrafts higher. Two vortices are born, the weak twin dies, the survivor becomes the heart of a new system, the mesocyclone. A funnel descends, tightens, inhales more of that warm surface air, and accelerates its rotation. When that swirling horn makes contact with the ground, it's officially a tornado.

What kills a tornado? Theories vary. Here's what I've observed first-hand: Eventually, the cold outflow of the downdrafts knuckles around the warm inflow, resolving and unwinding the tension that fuels its rotation, that keeps the chaos bounded and mobile. As the rotation slows, the funnel disintegrates. Out like a lamb. A white wisp, swallowed back into the thunderclouds.

Black heaven spiraling down into a phantom drill bit—this is what you likely know of tornadoes from the movies. What you may not know is that there have been several reported cases in which a breeder's twister has gotten loose, jumped a fence, and ascended toward a passing supercell. Spiraling *up*, not down, and fusing to the placental, moisture-rich belly of the feral storm. Turn your gaze skyward in the aftermath of such a coupling, and you'll behold a jaw-dropping wall of cloud.

To attempt to engineer that kind of celestial monster by, say, failing to bar the doors of your shelter would be an unspeakably dangerous and selfish act; and whenever rumors circulated the sale barn of a rogue breeder who'd done just that, I sputtered my reproof along with Lemon and the rest. But even as I did, I was lit by wonder: Suppose you could do it once and be guaranteed no casualties, no catastrophes. Imagine the cloud you'd raised embraced by the cumulonimbus, forging the bridge between earth and sky. What could be more gratifying to a tornado farmer than standing witness to such an assumption? Can you see it? I can, but I've had a lifetime to practice.

VII. DRIVING HOME

I can tolerate cities, the crowds and the sounds of cities, but city people often get deeply spooked when they visit our sandy prairie. They call it empty, which isn't true at all, but an error of perception that must result from the absence of tall buildings, groaning subways, or any clustered trees to wall off sight lines. A vast presence comes swarming at you overland, waving and yellow, airy and blue. A radial horizon. I did fine in New York, where I spent three days when my middle girl got married. I didn't spook. I didn't complain about wading shin-deep through trash bags in Times Square, or the festival of elbows. You add stuff in, and I can manage; you take stuff out, and a city person is undone.

On their less and less frequent stopovers, the girls all refer to it now—"the emptiness." Anna spent two days here in November and complained the whole while. She could no longer hear the land exhaling all around her. That saddened me; I didn't know someone I'd raised could turn so numb. Ask the crowded stars if they find this country empty. Ask the howling guest behind our house.

I'm an inland man, but I've always loved the dial tone, the salty wash of sound that floods into your ear, like the ocean, I imagine, so round and full that it rinses your memory clean, too, until eventually you forget that you're listening to anything at all. Midnight is the best time to apply this treatment to your ear. You lift the phone, call no one. It works on me the way the TV did back when the house was full. In the fallow years, after giving up the storms, I needed noise piped into my skull.

The phone is a yellow rotary, a perfectly functional piece of equipment that slyly became an antique on our wall. I hate the newer models, which look like plastic antlers. I don't have that little window that tells you the name of the intruder, the caller ID—which was never a problem when no one called. But since I'd quit town the phone had started ringing daily, then hourly, sometimes every ten minutes, the sound fireworking through the kitchen until the tape would roll and transmit one of three shrilly familiar voices.

"I just called Amy at the pharmacy, she says you're not picking up your medicine . . ."

"So you're at it again. I cannot fucking believe this . . ."

"I am not bluffing, Dad, I will board a plane tonight if you don't answer . . ."

"Dad, Daddy, pick up, we're all worried . . ."

I considered picking up and telling them they should have been worried a lot earlier, because as it turned out I'd been depressed for years, and only now was I coming out of it. But I knew that I could, and should, conserve my energy. Save my breath, save my strength. Everything I had on reserve was for my cloud; nobody would suffer for want of my presence except for her.

"We were tornado farmers in Nebraska," I've heard my daughters say, "we had no childhood." They seem to hold me accountable for some miserable early life that is entirely their fiction, as adult women. I'm not sure what the motivation is there. Maybe they're ashamed at how little they actually did suffer, relative to Estelle and me and folks of our generation. Whatever their reasons, our girls have recast their carefree youth into some campfire tale to entertain their city friends, or to chastise me for events long past. I feel outside of every story that they tell about me. "But you were always outside," the middle one, Megan, likes to snap. "Always up, up, and away. We had to scream to get your attention."

Against that last accusation, I won't defend myself. But they forget that I had to scream, too, at the top of my lungs. And still, they never understood me, did they?

Anna and Megan left five messages apiece. Laurel called only once, on a Tuesday, or a Wednesday or a Thursday or a Sunday—I admit I've lost track—at dusk, but it was Laurel who finally baited me into answering. I won't let her voice languish inside the machine. So I picked up, thinking of the hare on the rocks, and before I could get the receiver to my ear she was already laying into me.

"Are you insane, Dad?"

"I taught you better manners than that. Want to start with 'hello'?"

"Mr. Jeter called. He says you're driving without a windshield. And he tells us you bought a tornado, with what money I don't know."

After a moment, I was almost relieved. Old Wes. What a meddlesome prick. He must have really done some detective work, to hunt up Laurel's New York number. Farewell, Wes. One less person to worry about.

"Mr. Jeter loves you, Dad. He was concerned about you."

Her shallow breaths reminded me that it had been forty minutes since I'd checked my cloud's precipitation levels.

"I appreciate your calling, girl, I really do. But now I gotta go."

"Wes loves you. Do you not understand that?"

For a swimmy second, I forgot which one I was talking to.

"Megan says you haven't been making your insurance payments."

Right, Laurel, the resentful one. Though these days, that's hardly a unique distinction.

"How the hell would Megan know that?"

A great pain fanned out behind my eyeballs, and I felt suddenly so very tired.

"Nobody can get hurt this time. Nobody lives out this way. And not that it's any of your business, but the windshield isn't gone, it's just a little broken."

"Can you see through it?"

"I know the roads."

"What you're doing is *selfish*, Dad."

"I don't see how my storm affects anybody but me. But if you want to be upset, that's your choice. This is America. You're free to be whatever you want to be."

"Yes! America, home of the free! Why didn't I think of that? OK, I choose not to care whether you live or die."

In the quiet interval that followed, I listened to our breaths collide over the line, my daughter's and mine, cold air and warm.

"Goodbye, honey."

"Your friend loves you, OK? That's why he called."

My mind bloated on a single note for a full minute, a pure, consoling sound, before I realized that I'd hung up on her.

I considered calling Wes, to chew his ass out, but the simpler solution, in the end, was to unplug the phone.

VIII. BREAKING FREE

Most of the guys I came up with are gone. Who knew that an exit to that hall of mirrors existed? Once when I was boy, I ran away from my family. Down the boardwalk, under the pop-eyed red and yellow lights of the carnival, toward the quiet rectangle of blue that waited at the edge. I reached that place, and instantly regretted it. The great, turning cyclops of the Ferris wheel loomed behind me, a blind and indifferent monster, and I could hear only the wind sharpening itself against my scalp. I ran too far, didn't I? Out of sight, out of mind.

One by one they died, my mother, my father, my brothers, my bosses, my rivals, my storms, my wife, and turned my world into an afterlife. You might discover yourself here one night, and you can tell me then if you find invisibility to be a blessing or a curse.

You know, I've always hated that expression, "a blessing or a curse." As if anything in life were so neatly divisible. Let's try this: a freedom, or something worse.

IX. DAMAGE SWATH

The morning sky was clear and the mercury low, but I knew on waking that rain was coming; and within fifteen minutes the thunderheads rolled in. I switched on the portable to the sirens screaming—a tornado watch, the first of spring: "At 10:28 a.m., National Weather Service Doppler radar detected a severe thunderstorm capable of producing a tornado near Gosper County, Nebraska—" And then the patter of a hundred fingers against the kitchen window, when I'd expected the hiss of rainfall. I slid up the sash and looked down to what remained of the wind chimes, scattered about the porch like spent shells, and then over to the shelter, which seemed to convulse before my eyes, the locking bars spinning in their cylinders and the domed roof vibrating; *It will hold*, I thought, just as the steel walls buckled and my twister smashed out. Sucking surface air, she tore a black furrow through the pasture, and within seconds of hitting the atmosphere her pearly color began to mutate, as she absorbed the stain of whatever tumbled through her—now she was woodsmoke, now pollen, now gravel, now red dirt.

Crossing into the far meadow, the funnel bloomed and vaulted skyward, reaching into that vast electric field that rolls without boundaries over the West; and as she made contact she started to lift off the ground, howling up and up like a flying top, bumping at the base of the storm. The anvil was already a mile in diameter, easy. The whole purplish wound pushed northeast, self-cauterizing with lightning.

I did a limping sprint to the truck, dropped my keys twice before getting them into the ignition, and then watched the needle jump by ten-mile increments as I raced to catch her. A half mile from the shelter, she purled the barbed fencing that separated my farm from Yuri Henao's and began to drill across his flowering gardens. Yuri is a middle-aged man who breeds gentle sunshowers in horseshoe-shaped convection pods, and the guilt I feel today about the devastation to his land was not audible to me then, nor was any real concern for his safety—all swallowed by the high whine of my joy.

As forked light raked the eastern prairie, I tracked the spinning cloud—bouncing down the highway, defining her trajectory, she seemed predatory now, certain of her quarry. She reeled in the galvanic atmosphere, doubling in size while the portable prattled on: "The National Weather Service has issued a tornado watch for Gosper County. A thunderstorm capable of producing a tornado was located over the town of Elwood, moving south at fifty miles per hour. Residents are advised to take caution and begin necessary preparations—"

Next came the infinite moment. Never in my lifetime had I witnessed anything like it.

Two hundred yards ahead of me, the funnel shot across the road, picking up speed and color, turning darker and darker, and then simply levitating. I braked hard, and the truck fishtailed, settling sideways in the empty lane. My hands cramped on the wheel, and every muscle in my body went taut as my eyes lifted with her: *The gust front could snuff the connection. The downdraft—*

All at once, my mind was serene. Beyond the dusky whirl of my twister, the black mass of the supercell rose, forty thousand feet at least, erasing the horizon, and she went spiraling into its heart. Within seconds, they were one. Wherever this behemoth system touched down next, nobody would guess that a part of it had been reared on Coriolis Farms; they'd mistake it for an Act of God.

The anvil took on the aspect of a rotting orange, the bruised clouds pierced everywhere by citrus reds and golds. I wasn't thinking then that what I had just done was the equivalent of loading a bullet into a gun. I wasn't thinking at all. My thoughts had merged with the sirens on the radio, as the reports escalated in urgency: The storm now spanned two miles. Winds 140, 150, climbing still. And then the watch was over; the tornado had materialized.

"Flying debris will be life-threatening to those caught out. Mobile homes could be lifted from their foundations, damaged or destroyed. Residents are strongly advised to seek secure shelter immediately—"

I felt no fear, no remorse, my senses attuned wholly to the rattle of wind through the truck cab. My body was folded into the driver's seat, but my mind was nowhere at all, floating out through the spider-webbed windshield and up the ladder of my cloud. It had become a tornado, a real tornado. At this distance, perhaps three hundred yards off, it looked like a landlocked tsunami, a gray wave rearing up and back, dancing foamily around the empty highway. Belatedly, I felt the prickle of conscience, yet a spiral check showed only the bucking prairie and miles of hard rain. Thank God. It would die out, I thought, before it could break even one window. Or it would kill only me.

To my right and left were tractor access roads, quickly turning to mud. If I wanted to run, I'd have to make a U-turn. I cut the engine, pulled the keys from the ignition, settled in. Rodeo of two. I'd only ever wanted to know what my cloud could become.

The vortex loomed before me—a colossal door careening on screaming hinges. Between blinks it seemed to redouble in power, rocketing overland, stiffening its rotation. I saw, quite clearly, my truck smashed against the maw of a concrete culvert, my body lying in the field beyond, pale as an armadillo. Waiting like a shed skin to be discovered, photographed by the coroner. Which was perfectly fine by me; I was nothing, or I was breath absorbed into the spinning wind. I would follow my cloud into the storm's vacuous core. I would want nothing. I would be spun apart. This mind of mine, already guttering, clocked its last memory: my old man pumping air into a dark chamber beneath the moon.

But then the image changed, and it was Laurel—curled in the red dirt, mouthing my name with bleeding lips, assuring me that she was happy, that she didn't blame me, that my love had been enough, although we both know this isn't true. I blew on deeper, up and over my still body, into a future where I am past, where my daughters stand beside a gurney, drawing back the white sheet. I wouldn't disappear entirely, would I? Someone would have to identify me. That sight would live inside my girls, twisting, howling.

And then I was back in the truck, and the truck was back on the road—the key turning, the engine rumbling to life. I kept my eyes level with the dry horizon, turning away from the only thing I'd ever wanted to see. I imagined my storm disintegrating, pulling apart into brown, scudding clouds, but I dared not look back. I couldn't bear to watch her die out, and if she lived, I couldn't risk becoming spellbound again. What a backward way of discovering you are loved—in the damage swath of your death. The moment I plugged back in, the phone would start ringing, and I owed my girls some answers. Rain sheeted over the cracked glass as I sped homeward.

To be clear, this is not my happy ending. Nothing destroyed me and nothing is over—and here I am, breathing sky with you on earth.

Nominated by Zoetrope: All Story

INTO THE MYSTERY

by TONY HOAGLAND

from THE SUN

Of course there is a time of afternoon, out there in the yard,
an hour that has never been described.

There is the way the warm air feels
among the flagstones and the tropical plants
                          with their dark, leathery green leaves.

There is a gap you never noticed,
dug out between the gravel and the rock, where something lives.

There is a bird that can only be heard by someone
who has come to be alone.

Now you are getting used to things that will not be happening
    again.

Never to be pushed down onto the bed again, laughing,
and have your clothes unbuttoned.

Never to stand up in the rear
of the pickup truck and scream, as you blast out of town.

This life that rushes over everything,
like water or like wind, and wears it down until it shines.

Now you sit on the brick wall in the cloudy afternoon and swing
    your legs,
happy because there never has been a word for this,
as you continue moving through these days and years

where more and more the message is
                              not to measure anything.

Nominated by Krista Bremer,
Rebecca McClanahan, BJ Ward,
Charles Harper Webb,
Eleanor Wilner

THE TELL-TALE HEART

fiction by ANTHONY MARRA

from MCSWEENEY'S

after "The Tell-Tale Heart" by Edgar Allan Poe

Your Honor, I stand accused not only of first degree murder by the prosecution, but of mental unfitness by my *own* defense lawyer—the charlatan in the polyester suit over there—and in light of this treachery, I have no choice but to confess to the former charge to defend myself from the latter. Please listen, Your Honor, to how reasonably, how rationally I describe the gruesome business—and then try to tell me that I am not mentally fit.

To begin with, I had nothing against Richard. No, just the opposite. He was my roommate and friend, the cultural and civic leader of our two-bedroom apartment at 2359 Green Pine Ave, #3A. He was a kind, soft-spoken young man. He liked to think of himself as a rebel and had several piercings, which his mother made him remove when they went to brunch—I knew it was Sunday by the studs and hoops soaking in a teacup of his grandmother's Polident denture cleaner.

His only shortcoming, if you can call it that, was his iPhone. Every experience he dutifully engraved via tweet, post, or status in the marble memory of the cloud. Reality was only visible to Richard at 326 ppi. He had thousands of friends on Facebook, most of whom he'd never met, and when I saw the whole of his sturdy frame hunched over that glossy four-inch screen, tapping furiously, there seemed something pitiable about such a tall man submitting to something so small. It was clear he yearned for connection—he was no different than you or I, Your Honor.

The night he signed up for Tinder, I spied him through a crack in the bathroom door. I pressed my eye to the gap and watched as shirtless, stern-mouthed Richard nearly herniated himself trying to dredge a weak wedge of muscle from his padded abdomen. Again and again, Richard pointed his phone at the mirror, snapped a picture, and studied it. I studied him. I expected pride, self-satisfaction, but no, his face reddened in a flush of self-loathing. Not even he would sleep with himself.

I should've backed away and slipped into my bedroom, I know. That would've been the end of it. And I would have, but just when I'd made up my mind to leave Richard to his private discomfort, his eyes flashed to the mirror and I saw—or imagined—that his found mine in the reflection. His eyes were the deep blue of a vulture, and you can call me *unfit*, but if you stood at the cracked door, with those pale blue points pounding into your soul, your spine, too, would have wilted. But he hadn't even seen me, Your Honor. It was only a trick of the light.

When Richard went back to the bathroom the second night, I tried to concentrate on the book I was reading, told myself to focus, but was drawn—propelled, even—back to the gap in the door. This isn't me, I told myself. I'm no voyeur. But the previous evening, I had witnessed Richard's unvarnished self-doubt, had trespassed into an intimate space, and you may call me strange—mad, even—but I felt a greater connection to Richard in those moments than I'd ever felt to another person.

And so, that second night I stood in the narrow slab of light that sloped through the cracked door, and I again watched Richard watch himself. Floss-launched saliva asterisked the mirror. Richard stared into it with carefree composure that lasted as briefly as the camera flash. I pushed the door gently, oh so gently, until the two-inch crack widened to three. Still—still!—he didn't see me. He pressed the red delete button and the phone emitted a crumpled crush as the image disappeared. He sighed, drained of everything but relief. Over the next hour, he took dozens of self-portraits, and every time he deleted them, he sighed. Destroying the Richard of two seconds earlier seemed to fortify him. He wasn't taking pictures for his Tinder profile anymore. He was taking pictures to delete them—and my lawyer says *I'm* mad. It was terrible, seeing him there, at the sink, taking and destroying picture after picture, as if each one brought him closer to erasing his own face. His shoulders loosened as mine hunched. His tendons relaxed as mine stiffened. That was the moment when the idea came to me. Your Honor, my only madness was mercy. I was no more than a forefinger on the red delete button, finishing what he had himself begun.

Each night for eight nights, I stood at the bathroom threshold, and each night for eight nights, I cracked the door a few careful inches wider.

61

Each night I watched with a kitchen knife hidden behind my back. Not that I was planning anything—no, of course not—only because the presence of the knife pressurized each moment with thrilling possibility. Then, finally, the eighth night. I cracked the door inch by inch until my own face was visible in the corner of the mirror and still—still!—he refused to see me. He stood shirtless at the mirror and as one photo became ten became twenty, each of which he erased, Your Honor, I swear I nearly turned away. But in that moment I noticed that Richard was holding the iPhone at too wide an angle to capture his own reflection in the mirror. The dark-pupiled camera lens stared directly at me. He took my photo, examined it, and went to press the red delete button, but before he could, a roiling terror uncorked inside my chest; tuning pegs tautened my nerves; what happened next was no more premeditated than your next heartbeat. I stepped forward and raised the knife. When I brought it down, his eyes finally met mine.

We needn't go into the gory details. You've all seen the crime scene photographs. I stoppered the puncture wounds with cotton balls. I checked his pulse, but anyone could see he was gone. I slid his favorite oxfords onto his feet, washed the blood from his face, and clothed him. What does one do with a corpse? I had it worked out so plainly, so perfectly: I pried open the living room floorboards and entombed him within the dusty cavity. For the rest of the night, I scrubbed the bathroom, washing blood from the walls, Cloroxing the tiles. When I finished erasing the evidence of Richard's death, I began erasing the evidence of his life. I trashed his toothbrush and wiped the mirror. I zipped the contents of his closet into two suitcases and cleared them into the dumpster out back. I worked all night and fell asleep in the purple dawn light.

Three sharp knocks flung me into the somber afternoon. I sat up, my face and chest damp, and tiptoed to the door, half-believing I'd dissolve into a puddle of perspiration before reaching it. Could the authorities have been summoned? Had I been too loud? Had Richard shrieked as he died, or had I as I dreamed?

But the woman behind the door wore an expression of cautious optimism. She fidgeted with her hair. I stood back from the peephole, having already spent too much of my life watching the inner dramas of others.

"Yes?" I asked, opening the door.

Her smile was a cheerful breath intruding into the apartment's gloom. "I'm here to see Richard."

"How do you know him?"

The corners of her lips tightened as she tried to parse an answer. "We met, well, we haven't met yet, but we're supposed to hang out."

"I'm sorry?"

"We have a date," she said.

I couldn't believe it. He'd actually met someone on Tinder.

"He isn't here yet?" She checked her watch. "I guess I'm a couple minutes early. You mind if I wait inside?"

She must've been from some idyllic Midwestern province where people leave their doors unlocked and instruct their children to say thank you when accepting candy from strangers. But I had nothing to fear; I'd been too careful, too crafty. Your Honor, you should have seen how sanely I smiled as I invited her in.

A faint buzzing came from somewhere, but I ignored it. I was too busy being convincingly stable, the kind of roommate Richard always wanted me to be. She tapped on her phone while we talked.

There! Again! A murmur beneath the floorboards. Dear God—was he still alive? No, he couldn't be, impossible. I had held him in my arms and felt the soul sigh from him. And yet I crossed the room to stand on the floorboard but my weight wasn't enough to silence the throbbing beneath.

She frowned. Had she heard it too? She must have.

"Is something wrong?" I asked.

"He isn't responding," she said, sending another message on Tinder. "I'll try again."

"No, no, no," I said. One *no* too many.

But I barely heard her because the hum beneath the floorboards had grown to an audible shudder. The vibration pulsed from the wood grain through my shoe soles so that I was not standing on a floor but on the very frequency of Richard's heart. His heart, preserved in that cursed phone, shaking with each message she sent! I'd recognize it anywhere, the two-part clamor so imprinted in my consciousness while I'd lived with Richard that I heard it in foot shuffle, in cricket legs, in my own beating chest. I must have slipped the phone into his pocket as I dressed him—the carelessness! I wanted to shout, to pull my hair, but the woman now looked at me curiously—oh God!—she pretended not to hear, just as Richard had pretended not to see. I had no choice but to maintain the charade.

"Maybe you could call him?" she asked again, checking her watch. "Or maybe better not. He seemed like an alright guy when we were messaging, but man, standing someone up from a hookup app? That's just demoralizing."

"No, it's not that." My voice slipped, my hands trembled. The gears of my dark imaginings spun by the pedal power of my pacing. "He'd never do that. There must be an emergency holding him up."

"Really? Now I'm worried," she said, setting her hand on my forearm. "Please call him."

I reached for the landline and dialed his number. My breaths quickened to gasps. Richard's heart had stopped on the floor in the bathroom—it had!—I had felt the pulse silence beneath my finger tips. Now the short, shimmying pulses grew louder, louder, louder still beneath the floorboards. The clamor resounded and—God, oh God—I was resurrecting him! I was putting the drumbeat back into his muted heart! He would rise from beneath the floor, I was sure of it, and then— I was sobbing—ranting—weeping—he spoke to me from across the chasm of death: *Hi, you've reached Richard. Not here, obviously. Leave your name and number and I'll call back.*

The floorboards beneath me had silenced, but I still heard Richard in the static-laced stillness of his afterlife.

The woman now tormented me with an expression of grave concern. She asked if I was okay, if I was sick, if I needed a doctor. Could she not hear the vibrations of the phone? The beat still thundered in my ears— booming! banging! blaring! How could she just stand there asking if I needed help? Mad—she must be! She knew! She heard! She had! Yet there she stood, torturing me with kindness! It was too much. I couldn't bear it. Anything was better than this anguish. I dropped to my knees, pried up the floorboard, and reached into the dusty cavity to extract Richard's phone. "There!" I howled. "There he is! Take it!"

I thrust it into the woman's hands, and she stared at me, first dumbfounded, then horrified, and before she accepted the phone, before she snatched it and charged outside to call the police, she looked from Richard to me, from Richard's empty eyes to my own, and the three of us shared a moment of genuine connection.

Nominated by McSweeney's

THE ARMED LETTER WRITERS

fiction by OLUFUNKE OGUNDIMU

from NEW ORLEANS REVIEW

It all started with a letter, slapped smack in the middle of our street sign. It was Uncle Ermu who saw it, and he was livid.

"Ermu . . . an affront on the ermu . . . hard working residents of Abati Close ermu," he stuttered.

It wasn't a formal letter; it was a letter, from one dear neighbor to another. It was a spidery cursive scrawled on A4 paper, in black ink.

Hello Everybody,

We are coming for a visit soon. We will convey to you the days we will be visiting Abati Close by and by. We will appreciate your maximum cooperation. Do not aid the police in anyway. Please be warned that all trouble makers shall be dealt with, severely.

Mr. God-Servant kindly appended his signature on behalf of our local chapter of the Armed Robbers Association (ARA).

The letter was perused by the Abati Close Landlords and Land-ladies' Association. The Head of the association Mr. Kole, passed on the letter to the District Police Officer, Inspector Sulu. It went through another round of perusing and investigating at the Police Area Office Z which culminated in the dispatch of two police officers, Sergeant Wale and Corporal Juba. When the two officers arrived in Abati with the letter, Uncle Ermu couldn't recognize it anymore. The letter was in a very sorry state. Uncle Ermu visited and mumbled in all the nine houses that made up Abati Close, about the current state of the letter, he said it was smudged with fingerprints and spots of palm oil. It had a torn corner, probably chewed off by a rat.

His mumblings eventually got to Inspector Sulu, who invited Uncle Ermu over to Area Office Z for a talk. It was a short talk between Uncle Ermu and two police bullies. At the end of this conversation he got booked for defaming the good name and work of the police. He was thrown into the Police Area Office Z, Cell 5, which was filled with cranky "under-police-investigation detainees" for two nights. When he returned to Abati, he had knuckle marks all over his body, two black eyes and a missing tooth. He explained to us that he'd sleepwalked into Cell 5's walls at night. When asked about the letter, he clamped swollen lips together and walked away from us.

The two police officers, Wale and Juba, prowled and sniffed around Abati for a few days. Their well worn police boots stomped up a storm of dust as they swung their batons at our doors.

"By the authority vested in us as officers of the Nigeria Police, we command you to open in the name of the federal government."

People opened their doors and peeped from behind their curtains, and they answered them out of the corners of their mouths. No one wanted to be seen cooperating with the police; the Armed Robbers Association had warned against that. Sergeant Wale asked the questions while Corporal Juba nodded jotting in his tattered note pad.

"Did you see who posted the letter?"

"When was it posted?"

"Do you know the members of the Armed Robbers Association?"

"Are they men, women, or children?"

"No"

"No"

"No."

"Spirits?"

"We don't know."

We all responded. A yes would have resulted in a night or two in Cell 5. After they finished questioning Abati, they turned to Uncle Ermu.

"Where did you find the letter?"

"How was it posted?"

"Was it in an envelope?"

"Did the envelope have a stamp?"

"How did you remove it from the signboard?"

"Did you read the letter alone?"

"Where did you read it?"

Uncle Ermu, looked at the two scraggly enforcers of the law and told them, he had looked up at the street sign one morning and saw the paper stuck perpendicular to the "A" in Abati. It was about five centimeters from the pole. He knocked it off with a stick. It wasn't in an envelope nor did it have a stamp, and he read it by the pole, alone. When the officers asked for more information, Uncle Ermu told them to go read his signed statement, which should be in the case file in Police Area Office Z. He knew his rights.

Only one road led in and out of Abati Close. The other end was blocked by a steep sewage canal that runs on the other side of the road and curves behind the nine houses before it straightens again and carrying away the waste from the neighborhood. One morning during their investigations, the officers stood beside house nine, outside my window. They walked to the edge of the steep slope of the canal and looked into it.

"Shouldn't we look into the canal?" Corporal Juba said.

"Why should we?" Sergeant Wale said.

"It may be a possible way of escape for the robbers."

"Why do you think so? Are you one of them Juba?"

"No, sir."

"Should we go into the canal?"

"Can you tell me why your head isn't working well today?"

"I have no idea, sir."

"Does the government pay you to poke your nose in what does not concern you?"

"No, sir."

"Does the canal in Abati Close concern you?"

"No, sir."

"As your superior officer, I command you to about-turn. We have wasted too much time looking into people's waste," Sergeant Wale said.

The police officers turned to the other witness they had: the street pole. It became the center of their investigation—only God knows how many times they went round the grey pole, staring at the green sign board attached to it.

"If it wasn't made and installed by the state government we would have asked how much it cost," Sergeant Wale said.

"With proof of receipts of its fabrication, of course," Corporal Juba said, and noted this in his notebook.

"Or of the name of the welder that made it? Where he bought the metal from or the paint he used?" said Sergeant Wale.

"But of course," said Corporal Juba.

They fondled it, hit it with their scarred batons, talked to it, whispered to it, growled at it, and finally left it alone when it couldn't tell them who pasted the letter.

We, the residents of Abati, were left with no choice but to respond in terror, and we did. We made our windows and doors burglar-proof by reinforcing them with steel rods. We drenched them with floods of holy water and rosaries blessed by pastors, reverends, fathers, and bishops, attached Imam blessed tirahs to them or smeared on jujus procured from Babalawos. Tall fences grew taller and became topped with layers of broken bottles, metal spikes and barbed wires. Flood lights were added to fences; they lit up Abati so brightly, that shadows ceased to exist in Abati at night.

One month passed and nothing happened, Abati Close chose to forget the letter with determination; we stopped thinking about it. We stopped talking about it. The police stopped coming by. It must have been a prank they told us. We stopped locking ourselves indoors by 6 p.m. Windows were no longer closed before 7 p.m. Music blared out of speakers at our dusk-to-dawn, open-air parties. We forgot to switch on the security lights at dusk. Our hearts stopped flying out of our chests when we heard roofing sheets contract at night or when wind rustled through the patch of bamboo in the canal behind Abati Close.

We forgot our fear until we woke up to the promised rejoinder; it was pasted on the street sign again. This letter was typed in Times New Roman, double-spaced, and on letterhead paper. The letter had a unique emblem on its letterhead—two crossed, long nosed pistols with two captions "carpe diem" in Latin and "seize the day" in English, joined by an "equals to" sign in red italics beneath the pistols.

Dear Neighbors,

The local chapter of the Armed Robbers Association will visit Abati Close on August 1, from 12 a.m. to 5 a.m. We plead your indulgence that you cooperate with us and our list, and kindly hand over the things on our list. If you don't, you will face the consequences of your actions.

Please do not bother to inform the police. We have dropped a copy of this letter with them at the Zonal Office A.

Thank you for your anticipated cooperation.

Your Neighbor,
God-Servant for the Armed Robbers' Association (ARA)

The Landlords and Landladies' Association passed another letter to the DPO. He showed them his copy. Our very slim, very cold, very closed, dusty, forgotten case file was reopened. The DPO dispatched policemen again to sniff, shuffle, and prowl. We, the residents, went through another round of questioning.

"Did you see who pasted this letter?"

"Can you speak Latin?"

"Do you know anyone who can speak Latin?"

"Have you ever seen the emblem on the paper before?"

We answered:

"No."

"No."

"No."

"No."

Abati Close stopped sleeping again. Jujus, holy water, and tirahs returned to our doors, windows, and gates. People stopped staying out late. The security lights came back on in Abati Close—brighter. We held all night prayer vigils and slept with both eyes open. Uncle Ermu was put in charge of the committee set up to proffer solutions. Mr. Kole and Mama Londoner, a landlady, were members. The meeting was held on the last Saturday of July. It was open to all the residents of Abati.

Mr. Kole's compound was filled with residents sitting, standing, squatting, or leaning on walls. Uncle Ermu started the proceedings at 10:12 a.m.

"Ermu . . ." he began. "My people, this ermu ad hoc meeting was called to find a solution to the menace that is about to strangulate, annihilate, exterminate. . . ."

Mr. Kole cleared his throat interrupting him. "Ermu . . . us!"

Uncle Ermu glared at Mr. Kole and continued. "All sensible suggestions are welcome. We must rise, ermu . . . against . . . this ermu. . . ."

Mr. Kole grunted louder. "This very grave threat!" Uncle Ermu shouted before he sat down.

Mr. Kole opened the floor by asking for suggestions. Mama Londoner said, "Why was Abati chosen out of all the Closes in our local government area by the thieves?" She peered at us through her thick glasses. When none of us could answer the question, she answered, "The insect that eats a vegetable lives on the vegetable plant. If a wall does not open its mouth, a lizard cannot come in. It is the house-thief that invites the outside thief into a house."

We fell silent, necks turned and craned around, looking for the insects, thieves, and lizards living in Abati. Our brains whirred as we picked out suspects, our eyes locked on them. And we sat in judgment over them. We handed down immediate sentences. We didn't bother to hand them over to the police, where they would have had two clear options: a) Walk out of the police station on a carpet made of naira notes and come back to rob us; or, b) Be handed over to our underfunded judicial system, which was filled with spineless wigs with overflowing case-in trays that would pass our suspects on to the pot-bellied wardens of the Nigerian Prisons Service where they would be detained in crumbling prisons, built during the colonial era, and held for years without trial. There they would emaciate on the generosity of the government in bedbug-infested cells, eating beans swimming with weevils.

Still in our heads, we opted for our own option and dispensed justice. We imagined piling all the thieves together at Abati Close junction, throwing rings of old tires over them, pouring petrol over them, and setting them ablaze. This option was carried out by nameless hands and faces, of course. We lawful citizens watched the scene from behind the haze of smoke and the nauseating smell of burning human flesh and hair. We shook our heads at the actions of these nameless hands, but we watched until the robbers stopped writhing in the fire and the tires stopped glowing red.

It was Mr. Kole who finally moved us past this very bumpy silence by requesting suggestions. He stopped our whirring brains and brought us back to the meeting.

We threw suggestions all over the floor.

Twenty-four hour surveillance of Abati Close by the police.

Twenty-four hour surveillance of Abati Close by the army.

Twenty-four hour surveillance of Abati Close by the air force.

Twenty-four hour surveillance of the canal that surrounded our local government by the navy.

Employ the services of private security operatives.

Fortify our Close with juju from a strong babalawo who has not seen or felt the sun in twenty years.

Cries of "God forbid" by Christians and "Awusubilahi" by Muslims tore the air. The man who had made the last suggestion shouted louder— he had a Sango shrine in a corner of his compound.

It took the combined efforts of Mr. Kole, Mama Londoner, and Uncle Ermu to stop the shouting war. Mr. Kole stood with both hands raised; Uncle Ermu and Mama Londoner begged us all to settle down. We did after a while, but the mistrust didn't leave our eyes. We now looked at each other through the dust of the religious fervor we had whipped up.

Mr. Kole reasoned with us, "I think arguing will not solve the problem at hand, nor will looking at each other with evil eyes. I suggest that we start a roster for a neighborhood watch group. Each house should provide two men to the cause every night. That's eighteen men per night."

We roared our approval, and shouted and clapped.

"Can women participate?" Mama Londoner piped up. In her excitement, her wig slipped down her forehead. Uncle Ermu helped put it back on right. She thanked him.

"Those interested in making up the first group of eighteen, please raise your hands," Mr. Kole said.

We went quiet again. Hands were carefully arranged by sides or politely placed in pockets. Uncle Ermu stepped into the silence. He said he would solve the problem with a series of integrals and differentials. After some minutes of calculations, accompanied by a lot of mumblings, Uncle Ermu eventually showed us the roster he had drawn, but it was not adopted—the living breathing variables kept protesting at the top of their voices, and no one could agree to their slots. The conclusion of the meeting? The landlords and landladies were empowered by the residents to choose the people who would come out every night. They agreed to increase house rents by 400% if we failed to comply. Madam Londoner and Uncle Ermu seconded the motion. Uncle Ermu gave out all the available emergency numbers and moved to adjourn the meeting. We were told to be our neighbors' keepers to be vigilant and report any strange activity to the police. They reminded us of the police force's new public announcement: "police is your friend" jingle.

Landlords and Landladies chose the volunteers for the visit on the first of August. Residents of each house saw them off at their respective gates, wished them well, and locked the gates after them. The volunteers gathered at the head of the Close. Car owners had to contribute a used tire pile which provided fodder for two bonfires blazing at the bottom and the top of the Close. We, the residents of Abati Close, contributed to the world's pollution with a good excuse. The two bonfires lit up the neighborhood watch group, whose members sat on stones and used tires in the midst of empty bottles of manpower and kai kai—they were all male.

At precisely 12 a.m., our visitors announced their arrival with a procession of cars and with volleys of *ka ka ka kau ka kau kaus* into the still night. It wasn't the local guns of the hunters or the reluctant rusty police Kalashnikovs. These guns were happy to boom, and did so loudly, with pride in the quiet night. The neighborhood watch group on-call evaporated into the night, condensing into human form behind bushes and inside gutters.

Indoors, residents dived under mattresses and tried to muffle the sound of wildly thumping hearts. We had saved on our phones all the emergency numbers on speed dial. One for Inspector Sulu, two for the Police Rapid Response Squad, three and four for the State Commissioner of Police hotlines, five, six, and seven for the Inspector General of Police hotlines, eight for the ambulance service, and nine for the fire brigade just in case a fire started. We tried to call the numbers, but the untiring electronic voice at the other end kept saying "all lines to these routes are busy." All the residents of Abati were dialing at the same time—if only we had taken turns calling, or had assigned somebody during the committee meeting as the caller we could have gotten in touch with the police. God was an afterthought, but we remembered Him, happy that all lines to His route would not be busy. We prayed until our throats dried up and our tongues stuck to the roofs of our mouths. But the guns kept booming.

Our visitors from the Armed Robbers Association didn't break down doors or locks. They simply knocked and asked politely that we open our doors and give them everything they had on their checklist. The 60-inch curved Sony smart LED TV that glowed through the French windows in house number two's balcony at night. The seldom-driven Buggati parked under a tent in house three. (The owner of the car, Alhaji Sadiq, couldn't find roads without potholes to drive it on.) Uche, the business man, had a bag filled with dollars in house four. Laptops, tablets, and phones weren't on the list; our visitors considered it a grave insult to be offered them.

The first house they visited was Mr. Kole's, the second Mama Londoner's. They both cooperated fully. They opened their gates and ushered the armed robbers into their houses. God-Servant led in three guys, he introduced them as Smally, the Black One and Long Man. Smally flipped through a sheaf of papers and pulled out the one with the correct house number on it. Mr. Kole and Mama Londoner handed over everything on the checklist. It was Uncle Ermu who was a little bit difficult. He did not open his gate to let them in. He waited for them in his sitting room, in his armchair. Sweat poured off his body and soaked the armchair; a small puddle formed underneath his feet. His wife and children whimpered behind him, telling him to go open the door. But he refused, stubbornly sweating into the armchair.

Our visitors broke through his concrete fence and sawed off the burglar-proof rods on his windows. Thirty minutes after they came to his gate, they stood before him and asked for the things on the checklist. He told them he was a retired university lecturer who had served the nation with pride, honesty, and hard work in its foremost ivory tower. Smally told him to clean his fat ass with his pride or honesty—he could choose whichever—but begged him not forget to make use of his talent for working hard and to keep his mouth shut hard except when he was spoken to. He waved the checklist before Uncle Ermu again. God-Servant told Uncle Ermu what Mr. Kole and Mama Londoner had given them. Uncle Ermu reminded them that he didn't have that much. He was a retired professor of mathematics specializing in coordinate algorithms in multiple sequences. God-Servant sighed and told him to stop talking. This wasn't a lecture and they weren't his students.

Uncle Ermu sputtered a couple of ermus, and then declared from his armchair that all fingers are not equal. The Black One asked him to place his right hand on the table so he could see for himself. Uncle Ermu complied—it was after all a scientific experiment. The Black One brought down his double edged machete on Uncle Ermu's fingers. "They are equal now," he said, and wiped his machete on Uncle Ermu's shirt. Uncle Ermu wet his pants, defecated, and fainted. The sequence of those events are still hotly debated by the residents of Abati. Unfortunately, Uncle Ermu can't recall which event happened before the other. His wife and children can't either since they were busy, over his prone body, complying with the contents of the checklist.

The armed letter writers went through the nine houses, collecting items on their checklist. At house six, our visitors ate ofada rice and spicy locust beans sauce, but not before they had emptied a very famous jewelry box, the contents of which were well known in Abati and its environs. These pieces are splashed in the glossy pages of society magazines, peeping through the thick rolls of fat draping their owner's necks. The local chapter of the Armed Robbers Association left Abati Close just as they came, in a convoy of cars and volleys of *ka ka kaus*.

No sooner had they left than several police trucks skidded into Abati. The noise of blaring sirens and screeching tires filled the morning. Black uniforms spilled out of battered trucks—special anti-robbery rapid response trucks—and reluctant Kalashnikovs coughed into the air.

"Where are they?" the police asked themselves.

"Have they run away?"

"They should come out now."

"Where are they hiding?"

"They couldn't wait for us," they answered themselves.

We allowed them to empty the chambers of their reluctant guns into the air and into our fences. We knew well of cases of accidental discharges by unknown policemen, guns shooting bullets into human bodies by mistake—faceless police officers cannot be prosecuted. After the smoke from their guns had cleared, it revealed a confused, malnourished, ill-dressed police force. Residents of Abati trooped out of their houses throwing accusations and allegations into the night.

We blamed the police for our woes and the police blamed us for not calling on them.

We blamed the non-performing telecomm networks.

"The police don't regulate them," they replied. "Send a petition to the regulatory commission."

"How could you not have heard the gunshots?" we said. "After all, Zone Z is just a few kilometers away. Even the deaf could hear the sound of those booming guns."

"But you didn't call us," they replied. "We didn't know the exact community that was under attack. We didn't want to encroach into Zone Y's jurisdiction. We have to clearly log complaints into our logbooks before officers are dispatched to crime scenes."

This brought us back to the beginning, and we repeated the accusation-allegation cycle again and again until day broke and the armed letter writers got farther away with our valuables.

❄   ❄   ❄

It took some weeks to gather truths about the night of the visit from our local chapter of armed robbers because the next day we retold the story laced with lots of untruths. We had to sift through dense layers of lies to patch together a story of the events that happened. Some truths came out in our statements at Police Area Office Z. Sulemon had gone there to report that his laptop was stolen on the day of the visit.

"Lie," the police officers on duty told him.

From a file, they pulled out the letter the Armed Robbers Association had sent the police, informing the police of their visit. They pointed to a line at the bottom and read out aloud; "Laptops, tablets, and phones will not be stolen."

The policemen shook their heads at Sulemon, "He who tells lies will one day steal."

They gave Sulemon paper to write his statement.

"Describe the men who had stolen your laptop," they told him. His description fit the brother-in-law of the sister of the uncle of the DPO.

They filed his statement and threw him in Cell 5. Sulemon returned to Abati Close after two weeks. He was released after he wrote another statement saying that he had been temporarily insane when he filed the earlier complaint. The police officers also added this page to the file.

Some of us made fun of ourselves, laughing out loud with tears in our eyes. Gbenga had run out of the house and hid in the canal behind Abati, leaving behind his very pregnant wife and seven children. His wife never fails to tell everyone about his abandonment. Pius had joked at a neighborhood party that he had heard a neighbor, whom he would not mention by name, beg the armed letter robbers to let him join the association so that he could rat out the residents of Abati who had gone to the police with the letters. The robbers had told him to shut up: a snitch was always a snitch; we don't like snitches. We all laughed until Oke, his roommate, told him to shut up. Pius was the one who had begged. Pius denied this vehemently.

Some of us whispered to God in prayers. Abeni was overheard in a church toilet cursing the robbers about her stash of gold jewelry which had been stolen. She had kept them in an air-tight container at the bottom of her chest freezer. The robbers didn't know she had the stash. In her fear, she had given it to them even though nobody in Abati knew she had jewelry. She never wore any.

Some of us mumbled or cried in our sleep, and our partners comforted us back to sleep. Some of us dribbled out stories after a beer or two, or more—those stories always livening up beer palors in the evenings. And we laughed at ourselves all over again.

Uncle Ermu learned to write with his left hand. He started an NGO, which has the sole mission to identify and catch the members of the Armed Robbers Association. Nobody in Abati wants to be a part of it. Uncle Ermu is the chairman, secretary, treasurer, and only member of the NGO.

Our story takes on several layers of untruths—depending on who is telling the story and where the telling is taking place—but the essence is the same. There were two letters and a visit; on that we, the residents of Abati, all agree.

Nominated by New Orleans Review

CAROLYN

by STEVE STERN

from BAT CITY REVIEW

I don't want to write this. I'd always counted on C.D. Wright—she was always Carolyn to me—outliving me long enough to say inappropriate things at my funeral. It gives me vertigo to find myself hanging about on earth in her absence. Forgive me if I tend to view her as somewhat larger than life—problem is, she was. I knew her best back in our scruffy Arkansas days. A friend of somebody's friend, she turned up one afternoon on the Ozark commune where I was living in a tepee, sweltering in summer and sleeping in winter under five blankets and two dogs. This was 1973. Somewhere beyond the hills that surrounded our parched parcel of land, a war was ending too late, generations of insulted and injured were finding and losing their voices, and this saucy uninvited visitor had the audacity to intrude on our mountain fastness with news of the outside world. "You folks never heard of Watergate?" Our attitude was: shoot the messenger. Even so, her caustic alertness to history unfolding gave her, in the face of our lotus-eating society, a peculiar gravitas. More even than her coltish figure and abundant chestnut hair, I was struck from the first by her sardonic smile: I was taken with the nasal jew's harp twang of her voice as she made tongue-and-cheek observations about the squalor of our flyblown, snake-infested dirt farm. "Tobacco Road!" I remember her exclaiming. Everything about the Aquarian Age depravity we lived in—the VW bus raised on cinderblocks, the never-completed geodesic dome, the feral children—seemed to tickle her, and I was somehow grateful to be an object of her amusement. I followed her around like a puppydog all that afternoon, fascinated by her wit and self-possession, qualities that made you want from the instant you met her to win her approval. Later on, with the bad conscience I still harbor for having abandoned my fellow communards, I re-entered history in order to write stories. It was all I'd ever really wanted to do. I arrived at the university in Fayetteville with my jeans still caked in pig shit, hair like a burnt shrub, where I'd been told there was something called a Master of Fine Arts degree. It was there I sought out Carolyn Wright again and reminded her that she knew me, sort of.

At that time I believe she was still flirting with the idea of a career in law. She had a clever, cherubic lawyer boyfriend with whom she had a teasing relationship ("Come over here, boy, before I switch you") that inspired a jealousy in me I could hardly suppress. A judge's daughter, she was possessed of a passion (now famous) for social justice and championing the underdog, an abiding theme that informs every aspect of her life and work: Outrage, though always leavened with a wry humor, was her birthright. "Your conscience makes cowards of us all," was my constant complaint to her. Ultimately the poetry jones got the better of the legal incentive—it wasn't that much of a contest—and she transferred into the university's graduate program in creative writing. It was directed then by the poet Miller Williams, Lucinda's father—though, knowing Miller, I can guess how it galled him to become known chiefly as Lucinda's daddy. (Back then she was a whip-thin little girl with a big guitar, playing in the dives along Dickson Street before she was old enough to drink.)

I took every opportunity to visit Carolyn in the small clapboard bungalow she rented with the law professor Bessie Osenbaugh. It was a kind of running salon for artists and activists, that house, which Carolyn presided over like a back-country Gertrude Stein. Northwest Arkansas was an unlikely place for the extraordinary confluence of talents—some of whom would become legendary—that had fetched up there in the mid-70s; there were giants in Fayetteville in those days. A remote hill town, it had little in the way of culture or beauty to recommend it; such fervor as the place laid claim to was largely generated by the university's football team, during whose games the population wore plastic hogs on their heads and drank themselves into an orgy of regurgitation. Nevertheless, Fayetteville was a magnet for renegades, misfits, and fugitives of every stripe, many of whom found their way to Carolyn's door. There was Ralph Adamo, the soulful gadfly whose poems extracted pure grace from an unfathomable sadness, and his outsize sidekick John Stoss, who some thought of as a yet-to-be-documented species, some as a holy innocent. John exuded poems, novels, and plays like a hemorrhage he was helpless to staunch, leaving a paper trail of manuscripts behind him as he moved from a fleabag apartment to a gutted sofa in a friend's drafty basement to the backseat of his antiquated Dodge sedan. Often homeless and penniless, he was one of a number of charity cases that Carolyn was frequently canvassing for, strong-arming us all for funds to make sure he had sufficient socks and underwear to see him through the winter. They were the rogues' gallery, Ralph and John and the scary outlaw poet Fred McQuiston, and a parade of combustible women espousing militant feminist causes, all of whom Carolyn suffered gladly: redoubtable women warriors like the Amazonian ceramic sculptor Tracye Wear, the gentle revolutionary Shelby Morgan, the photographer Deborah Luster, with whom Carolyn would collaborate on *One Big Self,* their gorgeous and harrowing album of Louisiana prisoners. A feminist rabble-rouser herself, Carolyn conspired with these women in their floating venues, one of which was the apartment I lived in with my then girlfriend Dorothy. When they met there in the evening, I was banished to walk the streets until their cabal disbanded.

Carolyn's very hospitable housemate, the big-hearted Bessie, had her own circle of intimates, who appropriated Carolyn as well. These included Bessie's closest friend, another lawyer named Hillary Rodham and her new husband Bill Clinton, both marking time teaching in the law school until opportunity knocked. The two of them were often in evidence in Carolyn's parlor, sharing sacks of chicken nuggets and fries—Bill with his bushy hair and the baby face that masked a ferocious intelligence, Hillary with her slightly nerdy affect, the helmet hairdo and goggly eyeglasses that were always smudged. I admit to having been charmed by them both; I was a sucker for Bill's earnest glad-handing and Hillary's combination of brass and vulnerability, which she later came to camouflage with her iron-clad pants suits. Their conversation back then, casual but relentlessly engaged, seemed to take for granted that the arc of the moral universe really did bend toward justice, and that you could shape its course with your will. How young they were, as was I, and Carolyn, who nonetheless kept that faith all her days. Is it any wonder that I recollect the personalities that frequented my friend's house, my friend included, as waiting in the wings before stepping on to the world stage?

I can't remember a time when her poems didn't take my breath and leave me half swooning from their erotic charge. In my memory her early efforts were, by her own admission, tentative: it surprised me that this quick, fearless, razor-sharp woman could lack confidence in any endeavor. Tentative maybe: there was certainly a persistent inclination toward ventriloquism in the poems, a facility for inhabiting fictive characters; perhaps that might be viewed in some quarters as an avoidance of assuming one's own voice. But Carolyn ran the scales of those hardscrabble voices with a stunning vernacular ear; she conceived a haunting cast of characters, each of them bearing the trademark stamp of her fierce desire and stoic resolve.

> When he quit on me
> I thought I was dying.
> July come; I forgot the butterflies.
> Didn't water nothing.
> Didn't feed nothing.
> Didn't take a walk
> Until my rocker give it up.
>
> He must have found someone
> With more hair, a lower ass;
> Wearing pants with stripes
> Running both ways.

from *Alla Breve Loving*, 1976

(He'd liked her striped pants when they met.)

She might invoke a voice "trapped by bailing wire and broken glass," but I never knew that to be the case with hers. The edge was always there, and the music, sweet and sour in its bluesy cadence, its lyric pathos and identification with those of slender means. From the outset the words she chose seemed yanked from the earth with the wildflowers intact, the dirt and stinkbugs still clinging to their roots. Everything in her purview—"a hood slammed like meat hitting wood," a dark belly falling "like bread no one has kneaded," "a girl who shook her slip off her shoulders like a sapling getting rid of the snow," "a woman waiting for the wind to turn down her sheets"—all of it seemed sanctified:

> The perennials by the shed identifying
> Themselves by vibration alone
> The light discolored as a candelabrum . . .

Of course Carolyn would be the first to concede the profound influence her relationship with the poet Frank Stanford had on her work.

Of that I suspect books are currently being written. For a time, her poems were rife with the echoes of his idiom—the dream logic and the dark violence of his rustic conceits—and sometimes those echoes could be louder than her own original noise. I think this was especially so after the seismic trauma of his death, when she seemed almost to be channeling his voice. But in the end, rather than try in vain to wrench herself from his authority, she was able to assimilate his sensibility comfortably into her own. After that her work was free to contain multitudes. "Because no poet's death/can be the sole author/of another poet's life."

Like Frank Stanford, she occupied the medium of poetry as naturally as a cat inhabits its skin. But Frank was so much a creature of his own invention that you felt, without exaggeration, that the poems had engendered the man rather than the reverse. It's why he appeared so vulnerable when he materialized out of the rumor of himself to take up residence in town: then you feared the toll reality might take on active fancy, because Frank always seemed about nine-tenths make-believe. Carolyn on the other hand was so manifestly present. Whatever the extremity of her mood—and her moods could be very extreme—an unabashed joy would eventually prevail. Then she might take down the alto sax she was just learning to play, a little like Jack Benny with his fiddle though with her own antic flair, and blow:

I put the horn between my legs;
When I reached for that Godalmighty E
I felt the bell open.

The largeness of her character, the impishness that only thinly disguised her moral strength, made everyone who knew her want desperately to please her; you'd do most anything to elicit that pickerel grin or the full-throated cackle of her laughter. Just as you'd also take care not to cross her, because she was notorious for a temper disinclined to show patience to fools. In a culture whose response to iniquity was often *far out* and an academic environment that was mostly defined by old boys, Carolyn held firm in her certitude to the distinction between right and wrong. I remember seeing her, a wisp in the looming shadow of big Jim Whitehead, poet and former fullback, wagging a finger at him like a schoolmarm as she took him to task for some impolitic judgment. I can hear her threatening the poet Carl Launius, who was confined to a wheelchair and notably hard on his peers: "Mind your tongue, Carl, or I swear I'll push you down the hill." More than once I recall shuddering in my desert boots at the words: "Stern, I've got a bone to pick with you." Then there was the night she came running to console me when my dog was struck by a car. And the morning she struggled helplessly to control her hysterical giggling when we went to fetch a recently married poet to read on the radio show we hosted together. When no one answered our knock, we charged into his unlocked apartment to find him engaged in an acrobatic sex act with his new wife. Whereas Carolyn's moods were high drama, fluctuating between sunlight and storm, mine tended toward a neurotic sulking for which she mercilessly mocked me. "Stern, what is it you want?" I recall her needling me one night while driving me home from a party at Buddy Nordan's. This was Lewis "Buddy" Nordan, whose stories had been so derided by the lords of the workshop that he was virtually hounded out of the writing program. Then Buddy with his gin-blossoming complexion and salt-and-pepper beard, eyes perpetually moist from mirth, doggedly set about getting even. He stopped drinking and began to write stories that orchestrated the shot-gun marriage of hilarity and heartbreak in what resulted as a perfect equipoise. An irrepressibly lovable man, he went on to produce a spate of celebrated books such as *Wolf Whistle*, one of the single most moving and compassionate (not to say funny) pleas for civil and moral rectitude this side of *To Kill A Mockingbird*. After he left the university, Buddy's house became a kind of writing workshop in exile, and there were always parties. So Carolyn's nudging me on the ride home, "What is it you want, Stern?" And I lacked the courage to confess that the thing I wanted most at that moment was her. I'd nurtured a silent and unrequited crush on Carolyn Wright for who knew how long. Once I stayed awake an entire night trying to muster the chutzpah to tell her I wanted to be more than her friend. When I stumbled bleary-eyed and muddy-brained into her office at the college the next morning and made the appeal I'd been rehearsing ad nauseum, she replied in that classic reedy drawl, "Well, Stern, I hadn't ruled out the possibility." A few days later she introduced me to Frank Stanford.

Frank. People are often frustrated by the difficulty of reducing him to human scale. By now so much has already been written about the tall tale of his life that it's hard for even those of us that knew him to separate hagiography from fact. The facts are preposterous enough: he was an orphan adopted by a single woman and educated in a monastery; his mother married a civil engineer who built levees along the Mississippi, and Frank spent his summers in the river camps running with the children of black laborers in the days of Jim Crow; he wrote poetry

81

from the time he learned to write, eked out a living as a land surveyor, lived in the woods with an artist wife who painted portraits of him with panthers couchant and full orange moons. And so on. That it's all true doesn't diminish the quality of myth. His first book, *The Singing Knives*, had been passed around among our circle like a sacrament, and it remains one of the most savagely beautiful books I know. All this advance press had preceded his return to Fayetteville after having dropped out of the university years before. Then there he was with his lumberjack torso, a face with the kind of masculine prettiness you associate with an Elvis or Muhammed Ali; and I thought: Gimme a break! So naturally hero and heroine were drawn to each other; their alliance, notwithstanding its transgression (or perhaps enhanced by it), seemed to us to have been prefigured in some celestial storybook. It had the aura of inevitability. And like the storybook romance it was—"Only the brave deserve the fair"—it was bound to end tragically. But in the meantime Frank and Carolyn set up a household like no other, where the Word mattered unequivocally and imagination was free-range and every conversation over dinner had a rapturous dimension. I remember sitting in "the damnable dingy light" of their living room one evening, drinking and listening to John Coltrane, while Carolyn extolled the praises of her friend V. This was the inimitable Miss Vittitow, genius, martyr, and mentor of sorts, who was run out of Arkansas for her early embrace of the Civil Rights struggle and later became the subject of Carolyn's magisterial *One With Others*:

> A girl who knew all of Dante once
> Live[d] to bear children to a dunce.
> [Yeats she knew well enough to wield as a weapon.]

> **She had a brain like the Reading Room in the old British Museum. She could have donned fingerless gloves and written** Das Kapital *while hexagons of snowflakes tumbled by the windowpanes.*

At some point Frank had interrupted her narrative to propose, "Let's put on a pot of coffee and write all night." Carolyn laughed and concurred in that attitude of mutually assured gladness with which they approached their visionary enterprise; I never knew artists more intoxicated by their own gifts. But I was fainter of heart, and thought Frank's proposal like an invitation to travel beyond any known map. I had a sinking feeling then that my friends were departing—had already departed—for places I could never reach on my own steam.

I didn't think then that Frank's imminent destination was so close to home. He took his life not long thereafter, pulling the trigger a stupefying three times, and following a lost year or so Carolyn left Fayetteville for good. Others scattered as well, Ralph and John and Buddy retreating into their respective legends, the Clintons merrily absconding to lead the free world. Me to the dank cellar of a squatted house in London. In San Francisco Carolyn reconstituted her life in phoenix-like fashion and mounted the trajectory of her poetic project with a rodeo panache. Years would sometimes pass between our encounters. She did come to New Orleans in that limbo season after Frank's suicide, when I was in the city nursing my own broken heart over some failed relationship. Together, the walking wounded, we shuffled into Tipitina's where the Neville Brothers were playing, got soused, and danced all night; danced feverishly in that sultry barn as if we thought that, at least for a while, we could sweat out the toxins of grief. (And we did.) Once, on the way to Providence to take the job at Brown that became her headquarters for the next three decades, she stopped in Memphis where I was living with my recent and soon-to-be-ex wife. It was then she introduced me to her new man and my old jealousy flared all over again. Forrest Gander was insupportably handsome, and if that wasn't enough, he was warm and funny and obviously ass over elbows in love with his betrothed; even worse, he was talented to an absurd degree. Oy. It was clear that Carolyn had finally found herself a worthy complement: I could hardly forgive her for being so happy. Nor did she and my spouse, to put it mildly, hit it off. My wife probably also resented the humility she was forced to feel in the face of such an ideal match, because later that night in a bar, a nasty drunk, she actually threatened Carolyn with physical violence. And Carolyn, never one to shy from a fight, responded a touch gleefully, "I'll stomp you so hard you'll wish you'd died as a child." I think I slid discreetly under the table.

I attended her wedding in Eureka, a gala ingathering of motley admirers attracted to her light, but after that I saw her only sporadically over the decades. "Because the unconnected life is not worth living," we maintained an irregular correspondence, throughout which she chastised me for this sadsack pronouncement or that failure of nerve. "Dylan says, Nobody breathes like me. I say, Nobody moans and groans like you. Face it, Stern, you're a flop of a careerist—own it—you can live on less than anyone else in the developed world—join Sam's club and stock up on TP and peanut butter—sell your house and quit teaching." Regarding my anxiety about a current project set in medieval times: "I think the Middle Ages is perfect for you. In fact, if this isn't redux, I'll piss on my own gravestone." In response to my complaints about a series of surgeries: "I'm beginning to rally from whatever crawled up my bottom on a foreign mattress. But you, why are you on the table so much? What did you do to yourself? Is it all from the typing?" And a final verdict: "It's alright to be depressed just as long/as you don't let it get you down." Such esteem as I have for myself is due in good part to having known a woman of such spirit and heart. Though I've also moved around a bit, I always felt I was watching the Roman candle trail of her career (for lack of a better word) from the vantage of our shared past. I always seemed to be viewing her progress from the perspective of that charmed moment back in the Fayetteville of our youth. How better to gauge the distance of her journey, and marvel at the constellation of books that—by virtue of a perception upon which nothing was lost (nothing human in any case)—altered forever the firmament of American poetry. I mean, who has such a glorious life? Carolyn married a strong and devoted man, became the mother of a remarkable son, won all the prizes, traveled the globe, and left behind an indelible body of work. She also left behind a legion of friends for whom the memory of her very rich hours and sometimes even the work itself can only compensate so much for the absence of her infectious laughter.

> *Bless the fields*
> *of rocks, the brown recluse*
> *behind the wallpaper,*
> *chink in the plaster,*
> *bless cowchips, bless brambles*
> *and the copperheads, the honey locusts*
> *shedding their frilly flower*
> *on waxed cars, bless them*
> *the loudmouths and goiters*
> *and dogs with mange,*
> *bless each and every one*
> *for doing their utmost.*
> *Yea, for they have done*
> *their naturally suspicious part.*

from "Table Grace," 2002

Love whatever flows. Cooking smoke, woman's blood,
tears. Do you hear what I'm telling you?
                                        from "Clockmaker with Bad Eyes," 2002

Brothers and Sisters, Señors y Señoras, I tell you how it is that
    we live, and what it is that
we do, we get ourselves up off our much abused sofas,
Hermanos, Hermanas, to the old intolerable sound of hollow
    spoons in hollow bowls,
to insure that our love has not left the world or else
                                        from "The Obscure Lives of Poets," 2016

A version of this remembrance was first delivered by Steve Stern at
Brown University on November 9, 2016 as a part of Come Shining: A
Tribute to C.D. Wright.

Poems cited in this remembrance can be found in following collections
and publications:

Translations of the Gospel Back into Tongues (SUNY Press,
    1981)

Further Adventures with You (Carnegie Mellon, 1986)

String Light (University of Georgia Press, 1991)

Tremble (Ecco, 1996)

One Big Self (Copper Canyon Press, 2002)

Steal Away (Copper Canyon Press, 2002)

One with Others (Copper Canyon Press, 2010)

Poetry Magazine (February, 2016)

Nominated by Bat City Review,
Jay Rogoff

DANCING

by ROBERT HASS

from AMERICAN POETRY REVIEW

The radio clicks on—it's poor swollen America,
Up already and busy selling the exhausting obligation
Of happiness while intermittently debating whether or not
A man who kills fifty people in five minutes
With an automatic weapon he has bought for the purpose
Is mentally ill. Or a terrorist. Or if terrorists
Are mentally ill. Because if killing large numbers of people
With sophisticated weapons is a sign of sickness—
You might want to begin with fire, our early ancestors
Drawn to the warmth of it—from lightning,
Must have been, the great booming flashes of it
From the sky, the tree shriveled and sizzling,
Must have been, an awful power, the odor
Of ozone a god's breath; or grass fires,
The wind whipping them, the animals stampeding,
Furious, driving hard on their haunches from the terror
Of it, so that to fashion some campfire of burning wood,
Old logs, must have felt like feeding on the crumbs
Of the god's power and they would tell the story
Of Prometheus the thief, and the eagle that feasted
On his liver, told it around a campfire, must have been,
And then—centuries, millennia—some tribe
Of meticulous gatherers, some medicine woman,
Or craftsman of metal discovered some sands that,
Tossed into the fire, burned blue or flared green,

So simple the children could do it, must have been,
Or some soft stone rubbed to a powder that tossed
Into the fire gave off a white phosphorescent glow.
The word for *chemistry* from a Greek—some say Arabic—
Stem associated with metal work. But it was in China
Two thousand years ago that fireworks were invented—
Fire and mineral in a confined space to produce power—
They knew already about the power of fire and water
And the power of steam: 100 BC, Julius Caesar's day.
In Alexandria, a Greek mathematician produced
A steam-powered turbine engine. Contain, explode.
"The earliest depiction of a gunpowder weapon
Is the illustration of a fire-lance on a mid-12th-century
Silk banner from Dunhuang." Silk and the silk road.
First Arab guns in the early fourteenth century. The English
Used cannons and a siege gun at Calais in 1346.
Cerigna, 1503: the first battle won by the power of rifles
When Spanish "arquebusiers" cut down Swiss pikemen
And French cavalry in a battle in southern Italy.
(Explosions of blood and smoke, lead balls tearing open
The flesh of horses and young men, peasants mostly,
Farm boys recruited to the armies of their feudal overlords.)
How did guns come to North America? 2014,
A headline: DIVERS DISCOVER THE SANTA MARIA
One of the ship's Lombard cannons may have been stolen
By salvage pirates off the Haitian reef where it had sunk.
And Cortes took Mexico with 600 men, 17 horses, 12 cannons.
And La Salle, 1679, constructed a seven-cannon barque,
Le Griffon, and fired his cannons upon first entering the
    continent's
Interior. The sky darkened by the terror of the birds.
In the dream time, they are still rising, swarming,
Darkening the sky, the chorus of their cries sharpening
As the echo of that first astounding explosion shimmers
On the waters, the crew blinking at the wind of their wings.
Springfield Arsenal, 1777. Rock Island Arsenal, 1862.
The original Henry rifle: a sixteen-shot .44 caliber rimfire
Lever-action, breech-loading rifle patented—it was an age
Of tinkerers—by one Benjamin Tyler Henry in 1860,
Just in time for the Civil War. Confederate casualties

In battle: about 95,000. Union casualties in battle:
About 110,000. Contain, explode. They were throwing
Sand into the fire, a blue flare, an incandescent green.
The Maxim machine gun, 1914, 400–600 small-caliber rounds
Per minute. The deaths in combat, all sides, 1914–1918
Were 8,042,189. Someone was counting. Must have been.
They could send things whistling into the air by boiling water.
The children around the fire must have shrieked with delight
1920: Iraq, the peoples of that place were "restive,"
Under British rule and the young Winston Churchill
Invented the new policy of "aerial policing," which amounted,
Sources say, to bombing civilians and then pacifying them
With ground troops. Which led to the tactic of terrorizing civilian
Populations in World War II. Total casualties in that war,
Worldwide: soldiers, 21 million; civilians, 27 million.
They were throwing sand into the fire. The ancestor who stole
Lightning from the sky had his guts eaten by an eagle.
Spread-eagled on a rock, the great bird feasting.
They are wondering if he is a terrorist or mentally ill.
London, Dresden. Berlin. Hiroshima, Nagasaki.
The casualties difficult to estimate. Hiroshima:
66,000 dead, 70,000 injured. In a minute. Nagasaki:
39,000 dead, 25,000 injured. There were more people killed,
100,000, in more terrifying fashion in the firebombing
Of Tokyo. Two arms races after the ashes settled.
The other industrial countries couldn't get there
Fast enough. Contain, burn. One scramble was
For the rocket that delivers the explosion that burns humans
By the tens of thousands and poisons the earth in the process.
They were wondering if the terrorist was crazy. If he was
A terrorist, maybe he was just unhappy. The other
Challenge afterwards was how to construct machine guns
A man or a boy could carry: lightweight, compact, easy to assemble.
First a Russian sergeant, a Kalashnikov, clever with guns
Built one on a German model. Now the heavy machine gun,
The weapon of European imperialism through which
A few men trained in gunnery could slaughter native armies
In Africa and India and the mountains of Afghanistan,
Became "a portable weapon a child can operate."
The equalizer. So the undergunned Vietnamese insurgents

Fought off the greatest army in the world. So the Afghans
Fought off the Soviet army using Kalashnikovs the CIA
Provided to them. They were throwing powders in the fire
And dancing. Children's armies in Africa toting AK-47s
That fire thirty rounds a minute. A round is a bullet.
An estimated 500 million firearms on the earth.
100 million of them are Kalashnikov-style semi-automatics.
They were dancing in Orlando, in a club. Spring night.
Gay Pride. The relation of the total casualties to the history
Of the weapon that sent exploded metal into their bodies—
30 rounds a minute, or 40, is a beautifully made instrument,
And in America you can buy it anywhere—and into the history
Of the shaming culture that produced the idea of Gay Pride—
They were mostly young men, they were dancing in a club,
A spring night. The radio clicks on. Green fire. Blue fire.
The immense flocks of terrified birds still rising
In wave after wave above the waters in the dream time.
Crying out sharply. As the French ship breasted the vast interior
Of the new land. America. A radio clicks on. The Arabs,
A commentator is saying, require a heavy hand. Dancing.

Nominated by American Poetry Review

SINGULAR DREAM

by MARY RUEFLE

from POETRY

I was born in Speckled Eggs Garden.
I will die on Broken Egg Farm.
I'm hopping between them now,
I consider everything
to be friendly
and nothing dubbed.
I am a chick with legs
and yellow hair.
Oh Lord Almighty, creator of
all things beautiful and sick,
who prefers another life on top of this,
who are you to judge?
When Adam and Eve vanished
solemnly into the dark,
shrouding themselves in the forest,
I was timid and nibbling and
stayed behind, betrayed only
by the plucking of my beak
upon the ground you so graciously
provided (thanks).
I did noth with the best,
I am nothing now, do ye
noth with me or not?
Hear me now before I break

O Lord of the Margent,
Lord of noth and straw and all things
sent far, cheerio, sincerely,
I sleep on one leg too!

Nominated by David Baker,
Mark Irwin

WHAT'S WRONG WITH YOU? WHAT'S WRONG WITH ME?

fiction by J. M. HOLMES

from THE PARIS REVIEW

"How many white women you been with?"

The room was filled with good smoke and we drifted off behind it.

"What's your number?" Dub looked at Rye real serious like he was asking about his mom's health.

I leaned forward from the couch and took the burning nub of joint from his outstretched hand. We called him Dub because his name was Lazarus Livingston—Double L. His parents named him to be a football star. He could play once upon a time, but not like Rye.

Rolls, who was too high, chimed in: "Stop it, bruh, that shit's not important."

"Of course it is. I'm finna touch every continent," Dub said.

"White's not a continent," Rolls said.

"You know what I mean."

"I know you never won a geography bee," Rolls said.

The room was streaked with haze like we dropped cream in a coffee, but Rolls never cracked windows. He smoked like a pro even still, burned blunts and let it box out the room. He had the leather furniture from his dad's old office and we sank into it. These days, he got lit every morning before work, after his bowl of Smacks. His latest was shooting an ad for the ambulance chaser Anthony Izzo. I was about to ask him if he still painted.

"Why won't you answer the question?" Dub continued. "Gio would answer." He looked at me: "Wouldn't you, G?"

"Don't play this game," I said.

"How many?"

"Man, G don't count, he's mixed, that's a performance-enhancing drug." Rye tagged me light on the chest.

"He speaks!" Dub said.

"Shut the fuck up," Rye said.

"Whoa, peace," Rolls said. "My place is a sanctuary."

"Stop with the Buddhist bullshit," Dub said.

I put the joint out. Rye started rolling another.

Rolls stood, but put his hand on the armrest to steady himself. He straightened up. "It's Brahman," he said.

"Brah-shut-the-fuck-up," Rye said.

Rolls smacked his lips and looked at Rye. "You two belong together," he said. "I'm getting a drink."

"Get me one," I said.

Rolls wiped his eyes and left to the kitchen.

"Really though, why you being shy?" Dub nudged Rye. Their huge frames looked goofy sitting on the couch together, boulders sinking into the leather, jostling each other like idiots.

"Nigga, stop, I'm rolling. You'll ruin the J."

"My Gawd! You've never fucked a white chick."

"Don't be stupid."

"You haven't."

Rye began licking the edges and shaking the cone down.

"Don't pack it too tight," I said.

"Madie teach you that?" Rye said.

Rye knew I didn't roll well, but my girl rolled jays better than him and Rolls. She kept the jay loose enough to pull well but tight enough not to burn sloppy or canoe. I loved watching her manicured fingers at work. During one of our college breaks, I brought her back to the city and showed her around. She rolled our weed and talked above us, underneath us, and around us. My boys cracked jokes and looked out for her. They treated her like a long-lost, porcelain-colored cousin. She said our outdoor weed was garbage. We called it middies. She called it schwag. Both equated to trash. Rye said that Madie was the first woman he ever bought a drink for, but I'd seen his lying ass spend money on chicks in highschool.

"That's one hell of a white girl," Rye said.

"Don't change the subject. We're talking about you," I said.

"How is the old lady?" Dub said.

"You're gonna let him off the hook?" I said.

Dub pulled on his nose the way he did when he was thinking of some heinous shit.

"I just wanna know how the treads are," he said.

"Yeah, how's it hittin'?" Rye said.

I leveled my eyes at him. "That's wifey."

"Stop being soft," Dub said.

"He's team lightskinned. Let him be," Rye said.

"You're a fucking macadamia nut."

They both were silent a second, then started laughing.

"Y'all are stupid," I said.

"Sing me a love song, Urkel," Dub said.

Rye looked away. Rolls returned and handed me my drink. It tasted like straight coke and I told him.

"Strength is life, weakness is death," he said.

"Man, I don't even know why we come here," Rye said.

"Cause you're scared of your landlord." Rolls took the joint from him.

"Gandhi's got jokes," Rye said.

Rye's landlord was a fat Irishman with an absurdly thick neck. He didn't mind Rye moving in because he remembered watching him play football when Rye took the team to a state title. Rye kept his music turned down and entered the house without switching on the stair light when he came home real late. We could never smoke at his spots, now or growing up. At his mother's house, we couldn't smoke because she'd wake up and press us for some. Rye would pretend it didn't bother him, but she'd start wringing her hands and looking off because she wanted more than trees, and I would stick my head in the fridge and pretend there was something there to look at.

"My boy's not scared of that fat mick," Dub said. "But he's clearly scared of white pussy."

"Let it rest," I said.

"Fear is at the center of all hate," Rolls said.

"You're smoked out," Dub said.

Rolls passed me the joint and got up to throw on a record. In middle school, Rye and I used to bump Dipset, wasting our freshman highs on gangster rap with no dimension—sped-up drums, pitch-altered samples chopped up and arranged to bang like gunshots. We would smoke weed in my aunt Mary's basement because she worked a lot and was hardly home. We sprayed air freshener and enjoyed the cool mist on our skin as we walked through and back in a daze. She never came down, but we sprayed it anyway.

One day, he left upstairs to go to the bathroom and didn't come back. I waited a while, longer than that or shorter, letting the minutes bend around me and grow fat as I climbed into the high. I thought I heard a door shut. I sprayed more, thinking it was my aunt, home early for some reason. I tripped up the stairs, boots heavier than usual. No one was in the kitchen–living room. There were some orange peels. Rye always ate my food. He said football players needed the calories. I wondered if he'd gone to 7-Eleven for more snacks, but his coat was still on the counter. I went by the bathroom—door open, fan still on. Computer room— empty, but the computer was loading. I sat down to see what recruiting videos he was watching, but after a minute, he hadn't returned. I went into the hall. My aunt's door was open. I went to bust in and cuss him out, but came up quiet inside my high. In the room, he moved around slow, came to her dresser and studied her pictures. He picked the one of her standing next to her flavor of the year, Luca, on a beach in Rio. She looked tan in her purple bikini. Rye stared for a while. Then he reached his hand to open the top drawer of the dresser.

"What the fuck!" I said.

Rye was so shook he banged his knee on the shelf.

"Shit!" Then: "Why are you sneaking up on me?"

"What the fuck you doing?"

"I got lost," he said.

"You're not that high."

He sat on the bed rubbing his knee.

I gestured at the drawer. "That shit is weird," I said.

He stood and set the photograph upright again. Paused. "She's sexy, man."

I slapped him on the back of the head.

He made like he was going to tag me in the chest. I flinched. I made like I was going to tag him. He flinched too.

"She got those green eyes," he said.

"Fuck's wrong with you?"

He paused like the question was philosophical. "I been conditioned," he said.

Rolls cranked up the Impressions: So people get ready, for the train to Jordan. I loved that song, but I was surprised Rye and Dub let it ride. Years ago, Dub would've cut it off and tried to convince us to hit the clubs on Westminster, but we'd wind up at a house party with jungle juice and dancehall playing instead. Now we got higher and thought ahead to Thanksgiving, about chopping it up with whatever family we had left. Rolls had his attempts at abstract art hung on the walls. Maybe it was the smoke, or the way the red, green, and white paint seemed to pop

95

over the black roofing material, but the work was actually beautiful, balanced.

"He won't tell us because he hasn't been with any," Dub said.

"How many have *you* been with?" Rye said.

"Too many to count." Dub smiled.

"Stop lyin'."

"I like to take 'em in the shower. Let 'em bathe me," Dub said.

"You watch too much porn," I said.

"I even had this one, Cecile, after she finished washing me, she hit me with the Eddie Murphy line," Dub said.

"Bullshit," Rye said.

"Real talk. She said, 'The royal penis is clean, your Highness.'"

"You're lyin'," Rye said.

"Why would I lie?"

Rolls said, "You add to the mischief of the world."

I liked to wash Madie's hair when we were in the shower together. The way it trapped water and became heavy satin in my hands. She thought mine was waterproof. Her shampoo smelled of sweet citrus and vanilla. She let it air-dry in the kitchen while she made steel-cut oats with flax for breakfast. I drenched the hippie shit in syrup and told her how good it was.

"Ya, aight," Rye said.

"I just treat 'em how they wanna be treated, choke the daddy issues out of 'em. If they want me to play Dominican, I let 'em call me papi. Anything but gentle. Long as you know that, you're straight."

"Lyin' ass—" Rye started.

"Don't be mad at me. You should really do better for yourself. You played ball," Dub said.

"I've fucked white women," Rye said.

"Then tell us how many."

"I'm leaving if you don't stop," I said.

Rye took a deep pull from his drink. It wasn't his pace.

"You ain't gotta be mad. We ain't talkin' about Madie," Dub said.

When Dub and I used to slap-box in highschool, Rye would always break it up before we closefisted one another. Dub said I was too pretty to throw hands anyway. I told him his bulky ass was too slow to fade me. He'd say, Lightskin bruise like fruit.

"You think she been keeping herself pure for you?" Dub said.

"Easy, Dub," Rolls said.

"You think some big motherfucker ain't coming around to hit it right while you're away?"

I stood up. He leaned forward.

"You got something else to say?" I said.

He brushed some ash off his long leg.

"You heard me."

"Dub, fall back," Rolls said.

I kept my eyes locked on Dub.

"You fucking hear me?" I said.

The music changed tracks and went on. Old Cole.

"Now you're shook cause—"

I slapped the joint out of his mouth before he could finish. He was halfway up when Rye grabbed him in a bear hug, there on the couch. Dub threw his elbows a few times trying to break free.

"Calm down," Rye said. "Calm down."

"Nah, this nigga thinks that his girl isn't community property. It's a revolving door when you ain't here. Captain Save a Ho. You're the only nigga that kiss that bitch on the mouth."

I tried to get close enough to swing, but Rolls had gotten up and was standing in the way.

"Calm the fuck down," Rye said. "Go wait outside," he said to me.

"Fuck that—"

"I know niggas that piped!"

I lunged and swung at Dub's face, but at the last moment Rolls tried to step back in front and tripped on the table. My knuckles landed on the side of his jaw. I felt the connection like when the baseball hits the sweet spot of the bat—it caves with a softness.

Rolls fell against Rye then into the couch. Blood already outlined his teeth. Rye and Dub still struggled. I didn't know whether to apologize or keep swinging. I felt like I was in a pool of water and my limbs were weak and slow. Then Rolls kicked me in the shin with his heel.

"Get out!" he said. "Get the fuck out."

It was cold out and leaves scratched down the block. Rye said that Rolls was fine. We were faded. The night was dark. We headed toward East Ave., back toward Rye's. He stumbled a little bit, leaving the glow of the orange streetlight and falling into the shadow for a moment.

"I haven't had an empanada in a while," I said.

"Yeah," he said, "you've been gone a minute." His voice sounded far off. A car wheeled by with windows rattling.

"So were you."

Rye stopped, burped, and let it out into the night like dragon fire.

He took a quick right into the backstreets. I tripped a little trying to follow him.

"Forget the shortcuts?"

Stefano's yellow awning came up on the right, a high man's beacon to buñuelos and ramen hot enough to peel the weed film off our tongues—that was highschool.

The inside smelled the same as always—grease and incense. The baked goods in the case had gone cold, but if you told them you were going to eat it then, they fired it up hot for you. I got two chicken empanadas and a potato one for Rye. He thought they filled you up more. The man behind the counter was too tall for his job. He threw the goods in the toaster and turned the knob, then went back to his magazine.

"Drew still work here?" I asked.

He looked up. "Who?"

We stared at each other for a moment. "Forget it," I said, but he was back in the pages.

I thought about getting a strawberry soda. My tongue felt thick.

"Put the potato one in a separate bag," I said.

He separated them for me.

Rye didn't want his. He looked at the bag a long time before saying no.

"C'mon, we're lit. You're starving," I said.

"I'm not hungry."

"I don't even fuck with the potato ones," I said.

He stopped. "I'm not fuckin' hungry."

"Stop acting shady," I said.

"Shady?" he laughed. "What are we, in middle school?"

"Strange, weird, suspect, indignant. What do you want me to say?"

"Say my name, say my name," he belted into the night.

I was about to clown him for singing, but started eating instead. The chicken ones were too good and I was too hungry to wait for his bullshit to cease. They were hot all the way through. I missed cutting class to come grab a bagful with Rye, talking about which Coaches were after him. The day he got a letter from Morehead State, his mom broke down and started thanking God, even though she wasn't religious like that. He was going to school for free. I bought bottles and we found a nice

98

spot on the river, mixed Hpnotiq with Henny, and drank until we couldn't feel summer's absence.

"You know he woulda laid you out, right?" he said.

"What?"

"Dub. He woulda beat your ass."

I put my empanada back in the bag and stared at him.

"Fuck him, I—"

"Nah, he woulda fucked you up," Rye cut me off.

"You got something you want to say?"

"Why you mad?" he said.

"Why'd you stop him then?"

He looked off.

"Cause I didn't know you were gonna knock Rolls out."

I flexed my fist and thought about Rolls, bloody mouthed on the floor. I wished my car wasn't parked at Rye's. Madie would be waiting. She hated when I came home lit, but she liked getting lit with me. I visited her so many weekends, we were trying to figure out how to move in together. Our time was like repeated honeymoons, languid and blissful: takeout—perfect sex before and after, falling asleep in ways that only we knew, having worked them out together night after night until we fitted like matryoshkas.

He stopped smiling and watched the stoplight at the top of the hill change colors. The city was built on hills, with roads that curved and ended abruptly and led deeper and deeper into a labyrinth split with a snaking river that changed color with the season because of the dye left over from the textiles back in the day.

"I did sleep with one white girl," he said.

I crumpled the bag from the market and tossed it, wiped my mouth with the back of my hand.

"Why didn't you just say?"

He sped up a little and I lengthened my stride to follow.

"None of that shit would've happened," I said.

"Fuck you, you should've fought him forever ago."

"He roasted you just as much," I said.

He eased up on the pace.

"I'm just playin'. I didn't sleep with no white bitch."

"What the fuck is wrong with you?" I said. "What happened?"

"Nothing."

"Bro, remember when I caught you looking through my aunt's underwear?"

He shot me a look, then smiled.

"What-had-happened-was—"

"Man, shut up." The wind picked up to bring winter faster. "Whatever it is can't be that bad."

"Aight," he said. He glanced over at me. "Well, in the middle of it . . ." he started.

We were at the stoplight. There were no cars. He started to cross. I followed.

"When I was hittin'."

"Yeah?" I tried to catch up.

"She called me a nigger."

I fell behind a step, then two.

"That's fucked up." It was all I could say.

I thought about if Madie pulled some shit like that. I thought about the type of white women that went out in search of that, the ones who kept the word in the back of their throats—an ugly secret, a black appetite. Madie wasn't like that; guilt maybe, that was this country, but nothing dank and malignant. I wasn't on an auction block in front of her. I thought back to when we'd looked at each other in the mirror together, floor-length at her parents' in Manhattan, her hand around my dick, smiling. I tried for a minute to see what she saw. I told myself I wasn't on an auction block in front of her.

"Rye," I said.

He woke up.

"And?"

I reached the left onto his street before he did. Still he was silent, trying to lock something inside, back where it belonged. I saw him grow fidgety even in the shadow of the streetlight.

"Yo," I said.

He turned.

"I liked it," he said.

"Liked what?"

"When she said it." He paused. "I fuckin' liked it."

"How?"

"It made me harder."

We neared his steps.

"Like—hardened your resolve to find a strong black woman?" I raised my fist.

He left the joke in space.

I stopped as we reached his stairs.

"You're not staying?" he said.

"Nah, man."

He toed a spot where the stair was chipped and splintered.

"You're no better," he said.

I handed him his empanada.

"I just want to see Madie," I said.

He put his hand on the rail before he turned to go up and stopped.

"I loved it," he said. "It made me an animal."

"Yeah."

"No, you don't understand, man. I grabbed her hair and turned her face away. I don't know." He took a breath. "I wouldn't even let her look at me."

"She said it again: Fuck me like a nigger."

He stared at the ground for awhile.

"I wanted her so bad," he said. "She tried to turn her face toward me and I just buried it deeper. I thought I was going to break her. It's like I couldn't stop. I shoved my fingers down her throat with the other hand and she closed her eyes. I wouldn't even let her do that. I raised her eyelid so she had to keep an eye open. I bit her jaw until I saw teeth marks." He brushed his hand over his waves like he'd always done. "I lost my mind."

He went up the first step. The automatic porch light came on. I imagined him walking up the stairs to the second floor in the pitch black. Going home to no one, eating his food alone.

"Then it worked," I said.

"What?"

I took a few steps back. "She got what she wanted."

He held the paper bag tighter. His eyes softened. "Say hi to Madie for me." As I turned the corner, I heard the apartment door close.

Nominated by The Paris Review

101

LUPINSKI

fiction by MYRON TAUBE

from NEW LETTERS

So here I am, outside my Miriam's room, putting on that yellow plastic-paper they make you put on when you go in the offensive care unit. They don't want people to bring in their germs, so I put my arms in the sleeves and pull it over my head—it can be difficult, because the two bendles are in the wrong place—they shouldn't be hanging in the back when you got to tie them in front.

I see in the room where my Miriam is laying with those tubes in her arm and that oxygen in her nose. They put these other tubes where she pees and in her tochus, because she was making all over herself. She says this is no way to live; she can't take it no more. She says I should stop coming; I should stop being nice to her; she says I'm only being selfish. I'll tell you the truth, it was like a knife in my kishkes. I never thought of myself as selfish. Let me go, she says. This is my wife talking, how do I let her go?

So I keep telling her she's getting better. Even the people in the exercise room say she's doing better. She uses her walker and almost made it back to her room; then she made. That was two weeks ago, but now she feels better. I hope she feels better. I tell her, she shouldn't worry if she dirties herself; they clean her up. She'll come home. She says it's over, this is no way to live. Let me go, she says, and I think, No, no. Not after sixty-four years. This is the mother of my children. I don't just let go.

So I wave at her. And while she tries to sit up, and she tries to pull the sheet she uses for a blanket to her shoulder, she also tries to take the plastic oxygen mask off her nose so she can smile at me. She only got two hands, so she falls back on the pillow.

While I'm putting on this plastic thing over my clothing so I can go talk with my wife, this doctor in a white jacket with his name stitched in blue over the pocket comes up to me, a long thin face with gold-rimmed glasses. I don't know him, but he got a stethoscope around his neck and a bunch of papers on a clip board doctors always carry when they see patients. So I finish tying up my yellow raincoat and this doctor says, "I'm sorry to hear about your wife." He sounds like he means it.

"We're getting used to it," I says, thinking he knows my Miriam from the other times she was in this ward. I know some of the nurses, but I don't know him.

"That's not what I meant," he says, and he looks at me seriously.

"What's the matter?" I say, because I ain't heard nothing bad. In fact, I was hoping Miriam could start the rehab again. "You know something?"

He looks at his papers. "She hasn't eaten in three days. We put her on liquid support."

What's he talking about? I know for a fact, my Miriam don't like hospital food. She never did; she likes my cooking. I was here yesterday—maybe the day before, it don't matter—they give her a little chicken noodle soup and a roast chicken breast, which she said was dry like cardboard, and rice and peas. So I get this idea, I cut off little pieces of chicken and put them in her soup, and then I put in a few spoonfuls of peas and rice, and I mix it up with the spoon. It looks like regular chicken soup. And I feed her almost the whole bowl. All right, so she didn't eat the whole chicken breast, maybe a half, maybe a third—but that's not stopped eating.

I look in the room at my Miriam and she looks at me, and her face looks different, and I start crying. "What are you talking about?" I ask the doctor.

"Your wife told the nurse she doesn't want any heroic measures."

Heroic Measures. I remember those words from when we first took Miriam to the hospital, some nurse give us papers to sign: If you're dying, do you want Heroic Measures? To tell the truth, I don't know what they mean when they say Heroic Measures. To me, Heroic Measures is when Superman jumps in front of the girl and the bullet bounces off his chest and he saves the girl's life. But I know what "if you're dying" means.

Tears roll down my face.

The doctor changes the subject. "Do you have any immediate family? We think they should be here."

103

I can't stop the tears from running down my neck and soaking the yellow rain coat. Can we be talking what I'm afraid to think we're talking?

"Do you have any immediate family?"

"I got three sons," I say. "They got wives and children."

His face looks serious. "I don't know if you want the children—it depends how old they are." Then he looks me right in the eyes. "Would you like me to send for the priest?"

"What did you say?"

He shuffles his papers. "The social worker wrote that your wife wants the last rites."

I can't stop the tears from running down my face. My breathing makes it hard for me to talk. "My wife wants a priest, like a Catholic?"

"Aren't you Mr. Lupinski?" he says.

"My name is Epstein," I says. "Solomon Epstein. That lady"—I point—"is my wife, Miriam. And we're Jewish."

"I am so sorry," he says. "There's a mistake. I saw you putting on the gown, and I thought you were going into her room." He points to the room next to my Miriam's. Then he puts out a hand for me to shake, like now we're friends. "I'm sorry."

What can I say? I shake his hand, but my kishkes are all turned upside down.

When I go inside the room, Miriam whispers, "Sol, what's the matter?" Her voice is very weak, her eyes look funny.

I sit down on a chair and my heart bangs like a drum. I shake my head and try to stop the tears. "You don't know, I almost punched that doctor in the nose."

"Why are you crying?" Miriam says, trying to sit up. "He told you I'm dying?"

"No, no," I says. "You're not dying. Don't even think it. You just relax. You want a little water?"

"I'm OK," she says, and I push up the pillow to make her more comfortable.

"Why did the doctor make you cry?" She sounds so tired.

"It's all right," I says. "I think we had a little misunderstanding."

After a while, her breathing sounds heavy, she falls asleep. So I let her sleep. She needs her rest. I start down the hall, and I stop. In the corner of my eye, I see where the curtain in Lupinski's room don't close all the way. I take a step back and I see his wife is laying on the bed with her eyes closed; she's holding a cross on her chest and this priest is sitting next to the bed. He's got a purple scarf on his shoulders and he's reading from a black book. Then I see, standing outside the door, this old guy, he got white hair; he's sort of bent over, wiping his eyes with a handkerchief. This could be Lupinski. I go over to him, but I don't want to be stupid like that doctor.

"Excuse me," I say. "You're Mr. Lupinski?"

"Yes," he says. "Do I know you?"

"I don't think so. My wife is next door"—I point at Miriam's room. I put my hand on his shoulder. "I hear your wife wanted the last rites, so I want to tell you I'm so sorry."

"Thank you," he says. "Now she's at peace."

"Yes," I say, thinking I never heard nobody say that before. "If you got family, maybe they can stay with you and help a little."

"They're in Teaneck," he says, like that should explain things.

"Well, good luck," I say. "I'm sorry for your loss." And I walk to the elevator.

I get home, I make a little sandwich from some leftover meatloaf. You'd think, with all the children the boys got, somebody would like a little meatloaf, just to make sandwiches for school. But nobody wanted. So I've been eating meatloaf sandwiches for three days. Maybe tomorrow I'll bring a meatloaf sandwich for Miriam. I know she likes it. I make a meatloaf, it's different from everybody's. I take a hard roll, maybe a couple slices stale bread or I crumble up a left-over matzoh from Pesach, and I soak it in a little red wine. I squash up two or three little garlics and put them in. A little salt, a little black pepper. A chopped-up onion. Sometimes I cut in two or three mushrooms. And I mix in an egg. But my big secret, I put in little bits of red pepper, the hot stuff; they give the meatloaf a zing. Then I chop up another onion and spread it on the bottom of this bread pan. I open a can of tomato sauce, and I put a little sauce on the bottom to cover the onions to keep them from burning. Then I spread the meat so it fills the bread pan, and I make sure I sprinkle a little tomato sauce throughout the meat; it should mix with the juices from the meat and the onion on the bottom and make a gravy.

And I put it in the oven for two hours at three fifty. You got to love it. You eat with a couple slices of bread to soak up the gravy. You should drink a little iced seltzer water with it. My Miriam says, Sol, when it comes to meatloaf, you are the king. I'll bring her some tomorrow.

That night, I get a call from David, my son the doctor. He tells me my Miriam ain't doing good. "What are you talking about, Dovid'll? I was just there. I gave her some chicken I cut into the soup. She wants me to bring her a meatloaf sandwich tomorrow. She's eating good."

"Dad," he says, "I think you're confused."

"No, no," I says. "I was there. This tall skinny doctor with gold glasses told me the story. It was Mrs. Lupinski who wasn't eating, she wanted a priest. He thought I was Lupinski. It was all a mix up."

"Dad," he says, "something happened. What was it?"

"I'm telling you, that doctor is calling me Lupinski. He's telling me my wife don't eat no more, she don't want no Heroic Measures, she wants a priest, she wants the last rites. That's not my Miriam. I'm no Lupinski. Your mother is OK."

"He made a mistake," David says. He's a doctor, so he knows about this mistake business. "He didn't mean Mom."

"He almost give me a heart attack."

"Dad, it was a mistake."

"Certainly it was a mistake. You see, it all starts from the not eating. I told your mother, she got to eat."

"Dad," my son the doctor says, "he made a mistake about who he was talking to. He made a mistake about who you were. And he wasn't Mom's doctor, so nothing he said about Mrs. Lupinski had anything to do with you."

"That's what I'm saying, Dovid'll. It wasn't your mother. It wasn't me. I'm not Lupinski."

"Dad," Dovid'll says. "Don't get excited."

"I'm not excited," I says. "I'm just trying to get a grip."

"Dad," my son says, "I spoke with Dr. Hendrix, the head of the ICU. He sees no hope. She's going."

"She's going home?"

"No, Dad. She's dying."

"No, no," I says. I couldn't say more. The tears come down my face like a rain storm. "It's a mistake."

"Dad, it's not a mistake. They think the family should be there."

"No, no. It's like Lupinski, the wrong people . . . everything . . ."

"Dad, get dressed, I'll pick you up in twenty minutes."

It's the middle of the night, and I feel a little confused, like I don't know what's going on, I don't want to know. I feel around in the dark for my pants on the chair and I get dressed. My son the doctor rings the buzzer so I know he's here. I go downstairs. It's snowing, and I should have taken a scarf. Miriam knitted me some beautiful scarfs. I should wear them more often. I sit beside him in the car.

"Listen, it's beginning to snow," I says.

"I know," he says, and turns on the wipers.

I didn't want him to think that maybe I didn't know he knew how to drive when it snows. The man's a doctor. He knows how you should take care. "I just think you should drive careful."

"Dad, I'll drive like I'm transporting a baby."

I wanted to laugh. That's what his mother used to say. My Miriam. Sometimes, in the summer, we drive up the Bronx River Parkway to this little restaurant in the country. We have an ice cream with apple pie and then the boys run around outside on the grass. One time, we park the car, and my Miriam sees a couple Ferraris and all the Cadillacs and New Yorkers, so she thinks they're rich people from Riverdale. Sol, she says, I don't know why you take us here. It's so expensive. We could buy a quart of ice cream at home, and I can make hot chocolate. I'm listening to the boys shouting as they chase themselves around a tree. You think they're rich? I says to her. Let them look on me and see what a real rich man looks like. Oy, Sol, she says and squeezes my hand. She's smiling.

When we go there, if I put my foot a little on the gas, she says, Sol, watch the speed limit. We got the babies. It don't matter, the boys could be ten, twelve, thirteen; they were always the babies. It's all right. I used to know where I was going, what I was doing.

"What about Samuel and Jacob?" I say to Dovid'll.

"They said they'll be there," David says.

I watch the wipers going back and forth. "You know," I says, getting a little worried. "I don't want we should have to take her home in the snow. She could catch cold."

"Dad," he says, "she's not going home again."

"You know this? How?"

"Dad, I told you, I spoke with the head of the ICU. A doctor doesn't lie to another doctor. Not about a patient."

Everything was a little confused in my head. Outside the car, it was snowing, and in the car I was warm like toast. Everywhere I turned, there was a mistake. What was I hoping for? Did I expect Elijah to come? I'll tell you the truth, I was still thinking about that doctor thinking so much I was Lupinski, he tells me everything about his wife. But why? Do I look like Lupinski? Do I act like Lupinski? The only thing I can think of, Lupinski's wife—I don't even know her name, only that she's at peace—and my Miriam is in the hospital in a room next to her. That makes me Lupinski? My head is spinning.

We go into her room, the boys are there, Samuel and Jacob. The wives are there. Rachel and Helen. They must of got a babysitter for the kids. They give me hugs. They're crying. I look at Miriam. She breathes a little heavy. Her hand moves up and down, like she's calling me. Her eyes are closed, but I think she hears my voice, so I go sit down in the chair next to the bed. I hold her hand. It feels cold, so I rub to make it warm. She turns her head to look at me. She's breathing. She smiles at me. It's a small smile, but she looks happy, even with that oxygen mask on her face.

Then a doctor walks in. A little thing, she must be about twenty, I don't know how she could be a doctor, but she's wearing that white jacket with the name sewed on the pocket, and she got a stethoscope around her neck. The way she walked in, I didn't like it. She was very stiff, like she meant business and didn't want nobody to say something about how young she looked. She says excuse me to the boys and pushes past them and goes to Miriam's bed and lifts up the blanket and looks at the tubings and plastic bags.

"I'm checking her evacuations," she says, like she wanted my permission.

"Did you find something?"

She shakes her head. "She's shutting down."

"What are you talking?" I say.

"It's systemic," she says. "The lungs and heart can't support the system, and the failing systems can't support the heart . . ."

This sounded serious. Miriam's hand was cold like stone. I had to know the truth. "You're a doctor?" I says. "Not a nurse?"

"Yes," she says.

"You tell me the truth," I say. "She's dying?"

I hear the boys moving around. I think . . . maybe they heard us talking.

This little doctor looks at me. I think, I got grandkids bigger and older than her. She nods slowly. She says, "Yes."

I look down at my Miriam. I keep stroking her hand. What can I say? What can I say after sixty-four years that she don't know?

"I love you, Bubbele," I says.

Her eyes make a little gleam, and her hand slips away from my hand and her breathing stops and her face just relaxes like she's going to sleep, and she looks peaceful. And then the machine stops beeping and makes a long sound. *Bzzzzzzz.* A nurse comes and stops the machine, and the doctor looks at her watch and writes something on her pad.

The girls come over and one gives me a glass of water. I drink. Then the boys are standing around me and I think they're talking to me. Dad, dad. Are you OK? Of course I'm OK. My heart feels like stone. I just lost my life, I got to remember how to live. If she knew what she had just done to me, she would come back. One of the boys says he'll take me home, and I'm moving toward the door, and this nurse is standing there with a clipboard, and she looks at me.

"I'm sorry," she says. "I don't know your name."

I look at the nurse. She's very pretty in her white uniform. What can she know about life? I don't know what she wants from me. What can I explain to her? I see where one of the boys just kissed that old lady on the bed. I can't stand it. I got to go home to tell Miriam.

"Lupinski," I says. "Just call me Lupinski." I almost trip as I shuffle toward the elevator and press the down button.

Nominated by New Letters

YILAN

by KRISTIN CHANG

from THE SHADE JOURNAL

In Taiwan the rain spits on my skin.
        I lose the way to my grandmother's
house, eat a papaya by the side of the road,

        papaya in Taiyu meaning wood
melon. My grandmother's house is wood
        & always wet, as if absence

holds water. As if drowning
        itself. My stomach oversweetens
on fruit, wears a belt of rot. Pre-

        typhoon heat coiling back
like a punch. I take a train from Yilan
        to Taipei, the same route

my mother fled when the Japanese came.
        By the side of the road, she saw a child eating
another child's face. What my mother

        ate during wartime: five flies
in oil. The open sores of fruit & so
        much rain. Once, a girl gunned

down with her mouth full
           of milk. Once, my mother
bent to drink from another

           girl's mouth. In Taipei, I watch bodies
syrup in my heat-slow sight. A blonde
           woman in an advertisement

for skin bleach, looking like
           my ex, looking like my first
-world face. I watched

           the typhoon from the 65th
floor of the Marriot, watched
           smaller buildings lean

like thirst to water. After, a salt scent
           inflecting the air. In my mouth, a sea's
accent. In Yilan, they will gather the dead

           parts of the trees & burn away
the rot. It was my grandmother
           who taught me to burn

only what you must, then water
           the rest. Who taught me
that a tree is a body

           through which water becomes fire.
In Yilan, my mother harvested sugar
           cane, dragon's eye, unidentified

limbs, small & sickling like fruit
           fallen before it is ripe. In another country,
my mother watches soap operas

           in her native dialect, about time
traveling women who fall in love
           with Japanese soldiers. I dream about

111

being loved in another time
        zone. About meeting a woman here,
speaking in a Chinese that bursts

        apart in our mouths like fruitpulp.
We will pretend it is love
        that lasts. I pretend not to know

what men do. What women
        remember. I understand the news
enough to know another typhoon

        is coming, another estimated body
count: infinite. According to the news,
        it is possible to predict violence

like a storm. I call my mother
        & she speaks to me in three languages
but names me in one: Kristin, meaning

        bearer of Christ. In my name, too many names
for god. Through the second typhoon,
        I sleep with my fist against my jaw,

wake with my teeth hitting ache
        like a surprise pit. I dream of telling
my mother I love her

        country. I dream of telling
my mother I identify sexually as
        alive. Instead, I sleep

until evening, dream of frying
        Yilan in an oily dark. When
my grandmother died, we were asleep

        in America, 15 hours ahead
in the night, waking up
        in her future. When she died, I imagine

all the trees did too. I imagine
        the trees I touch are new
generations of the same

        loss. I left Yilan while the sea still
boiled with stormbirth. In Chinese,
        typhoon is *tai feng*, sharing a word

with *tai wan*. A nation named
        after its greatest disaster. My body
named for what it bears, what

        it bares: this nation,
where nothing is still
        waiting to be saved

& the dead are still
                dying.

Nominated by The Shade Journal

MURDER TOURISM IN MIDDLE AMERICA

by JUSTIN ST. GERMAIN

from TIN HOUSE

Just west of Holcomb, Kansas, on the lonesome wheat plains Truman
Capote famously described, stands what was once the world's largest
slaughterhouse. It was the first thing we found in our search for the Clut-
ter farm, on a Saturday in June so hot it felt like being ironed. The Tyson
facility was squat, bland, and beige, designed to mask its purpose, the
killing of six thousand cattle a day, each shot once in the head. If this
place had existed in 1959, *In Cold Blood* would start with the abattoir
at the edge of town; subtlety was not Capote's strong point. As it is, the
book begins with grain elevators rising like Greek temples from the
plains, a simile as subtle as a neon sign.

We stopped at the gates of the slaughter-house. Even inside the car,
the air smelled like death. The vegan riding shotgun didn't react how I
would've expected, not a word about that documentary on the beef in-
dustry: she just said we must've missed the turn. She was right. We dou-
bled back and found Holcomb proper, still pretty much as Capote
describes it, "an aimless congregation of buildings" wedged between
Route 50 and the Arkansas River, split by the tracks of the Santa Fe Rail-
way. *In Cold Blood* opens with an objective and somewhat dry portrait
of the town, its climate, landscape, layout, and location—"almost the
exact middle" of America. A few things had changed in fifty years. A
modest park at the city limits, across the street from a new school, was
dedicated to the memory of the Clutter family. The former Hartman's
Café, the gathering place and gossip node Capote frequented while
writing the book, had become a Mexican restaurant called El Ran-
cho, a signal of the demographic shift brought on by the meat industry.

114

South of town, across a ditch that used to be the river, steam plumed from a palatial electric plant. Otherwise, Holcomb looked the same as the rest of Kansas, hot and brown and level, all silos and grain elevators, an architecture of attempts to break the flatness.

Locals might be used to it, might not feel our vague unease at having no geography to contain us. We were tourists, full of assumptions, seeing everything relative to our frame of reference. We'd come from Albuquerque, a city at the base of the Sandia range, in a part of America where the skyline looks like the screen of a heart monitor, and so the flat ring of this strange horizon seemed to us like time itself, a noose drawing tight.

A week earlier, Bonnie—my copilot and de facto girlfriend—had asked if I wanted to drive with her to Minnesota. Her brother had been picked up by a pro soccer team outside the Twin Cities and needed someone to deliver his car. It was a bad idea, objectively, a four-day road trip with someone I shouldn't even have been dating; but it was summer in Albuquerque, all glare and ennui, a good time for bad ideas. Google Maps suggested a route that ran fifty miles from Holcomb. I said yes, as long as we could make a detour. She agreed to accompany me to a murder scene much more readily than I'd expected. Bonnie was up for anything, a trait that had attracted me to her, and that now made me keep her at arm's length, unable to imagine a relationship.

Going to Holcomb was a pilgrimage of sorts. I'd been writing a book about my mother's murder for the last five years, and to write about murder is to live in the long shadow of *In Cold Blood*. Capote's seminal book had become an obsession of mine. I'd wanted to write a response, a counter-argument, a true murder story that made a gesture his didn't: to present the victim as a person, not a narrative prop, and to treat their death itself as tragic, not as an occasion for a larger tragedy. A printed copy of the manuscript sat on the passenger's floorboard of our car; the final edits were due in a week, and I'd been reading it out loud to Bonnie on the trip, listening for false notes. It was scheduled for release in a year—from Random House, Capote's publisher—and, save for my editor and agent and a few friends who'd read an early draft, Bonnie was its first audience.

Somehow the contents of Capote's book, and what I'd read about the writing of it, failed to warn me how drastically plans can change on trips to Kansas. We'd set out on an impromptu road trip to deliver a car, but, earlier that day, as the Rockies dropped us onto the plains, like eggs onto a griddle, it had happened to us. She was driving like shit, playing a Philip Glass song about Wichita that sounded like madmen fighting a piano duel. Other cars became an event, a mystery of source and destination, and we wondered who lived in those distant houses shielded by trees, whether and how anyone could. We talked about time and technology, how we were piloting a dinosaur-powered vehicle across the floor of an ancient sea, what future civilizations would find here—all the insipid shit you can only say earnestly in a moment like that. Beyond her face, fields rippled into the distance, where in that plane of wheat I saw the curvature of the earth. We engaged in risky sex acts as we drove. The past got lost in the apocalyptic flatness, along with the reasons we were there, and why we shouldn't do something doomed and stupid, like fall in love.

* * *

If you're reading this, you've probably read *In Cold Blood*, and know it's the most important work of American nonfiction, the genesis of the true crime genre, a staple of high school and university reading lists. It boasts millions of copies in print, and has inspired multiple feature films, as well as a play, an opera, a hard-to-find documentary, a bad graphic novel, a book-length critical treatment, dozens of dissertations and theses, thousands of articles. Even now, fifty years after its publication, *In Cold Blood* has been in the news twice recently, first because the killers were dug up for DNA tests attempting to link them to another murder, and then because one of the detectives died and left secret case files to his son, who is—of course—writing a book.

The origin myth of *In Cold Blood*, which Capote himself carefully crafted, goes something like this: In November of 1959, Capote read a minor article in the *New York Times* about the murder of a Kansas farmer and his family. He'd been looking for a subject befitting a new narrative form he called the "nonfiction novel"; the unsolved killing of the Clutters fit the bill. Capote went to Holcomb and followed the case for five years, from the funeral through the arrest of the accused killers, their trial and appeals, finally their hanging. The book was serialized in the *New Yorker* in 1965, released soon after by Random House to sensational acclaim, and instantly became a classic.

Some of that's true and some isn't. For starters—and despite what he would later claim—Capote didn't go to Kansas to write about a murder case. He didn't even go to write a book. His original pitch to the *New Yorker* was a piece about Holcomb's reaction to the killings, the fear and suspicion and collective sense of shock, a sleepy town rocked by a gruesome act of violence.

And he didn't go to Kansas alone; he had help in the form of his childhood friend Harper Lee. Capote understood that, as an acquaintance put it, "people wouldn't be happy to have this little gnome in his checkered vest running around asking questions about who'd murdered whom." Lee was awaiting the publication of *To Kill a Mockingbird*, and presumably needed a distraction, so she volunteered to go with him. She helped in various ways, taking notes, attending functions, sitting in on interviews; he would later refer to her as his "assistant researchist," but her most important contribution was to grease the skids for her old friend. Lee, a warm and charming Southern woman, fit in with the locals in a way Capote, the pintsize dandy, reedy-voiced and effeminate, decidedly did not. He would later dedicate *In Cold Blood* partly to Lee, but he didn't mention her contributions in the acknowledgments, and she is referred to only once in the book, as "a woman reporter."

Five weeks into the trip, Capote and Lee joined a crowd waiting outside the courthouse in Garden City for the accused killers, Dick Hickock and Perry Smith, who'd been arrested in Las Vegas and brought back to Kansas for trial. *In Cold Blood* observes the scene from the perspective of two stray cats, a peculiar choice for a work Capote would later call "immaculately factual." Silence falls over the crowd as police cruisers pull to the curb and the suspects perp walk up the stairs, blinking in the camera flash. The cats don't notice Capote's reaction when he first sees Smith, diminutive and doe-eyed and brooding, so much like himself—there but for the grace of God went Truman. The moment everything changed: Capote's plan for the book, his career, his life. Lee would later call it "the beginning of a great love affair."

* * *

My copilot shared a name with the Clutter matriarch; beyond that coincidence, Bonnie would object to any portrayal I give. Slim, white, pretty, brunette, not unlike Capote's description of Smith: dark, moist eyes, black hair, "a changeling's face." I'd known her for six months, give or take; the duration of our relationship, like its exact nature, was a matter of dispute. She'd been married when we met, to a man who'd abused her, knowledge that evoked my mother's abusers and far too much of the fervid rage I'd tried to bury; she was still married, in fact, although she preferred to say "separated." She was a graduate student at the university where I taught; I preferred to specify that she wasn't *my* student. Then there was her son, the only incontrovertible fact between us: having had my share of stepdads, the last of whom murdered

117

my mother, it was one of the things I'd sworn I'd never be. I'd already become most of the others.

Unsurprisingly, we disagreed about who was supposed to get directions to River Valley Farm, former home of the Clutter family, scene of their grisly murders. Our phones had long since lost service. So we crept the streets of Holcomb in our borrowed silver Saturn, looking for a treelined driveway matching Capote's description. I'll save you the trouble: from old Route 50, go south on Main, west on Oak, follow it to the end.

We stopped at the entrance, where a metal gate hung open next to a pink-lettered sign prohibiting trespassing, then parked across the street and stood in a searing wind, wiping dust from our eyes, staring out across a wheat field at the house half-hidden by a shelterbelt. The night of the murders, Capote writes, the killers stopped in the driveway and stared in awe at the farm, the elms lining the driveway, the barns and fields, the green lawn and handsome white house. In his confession, Smith recalls thinking, "It was sort of *too* impressive."

Not anymore. All that irrigated wheat slowly sucked the aquifer dry, and drought did a number on Capote's beloved elms, to which he devoted nearly as much attention as he gave the victims: they were all dying or dead or stumps. The house was just another sensible Kansas farmhouse with a brown and patchy lawn. The disappointment reminded me of my hometown in Arizona, which tourists visit to see the O.K. Corral, where three men were shot dead, and now throngs of mid-westerners and Germans mill among the effigies, wondering why they traveled so far to see an alley by the highway. Another thing I'd sworn I'd never be: a fucking tourist.

On Oak Street, as we left, three men we'd passed on the way to the Clutter house were still slouched against the bedsides of a Chevy truck, tilting bottles of Bud Light and watching us. As we approached, the biggest of them walked out into the road and raised a hand. I stopped and rolled down the window. His words came in with the dust.

"You got no brake lights."

"Stay here," I said to Bonnie. The Samaritan followed me to the back of the car. He was the size of a small bear and grimy in the way I imagined farmers were. The other two men—a shifty-eyed teenager and an old man who could have been whittled from a twig—stayed by the truck. I yelled to Bonnie to press the brake. I meant for her to slide over into the driver's seat, but she got out of the goddamned car, big sunglasses and a little black shirt and cutoffs that clung to her ass, the source of high school nicknames. As the men watched her, I thought fleetingly of the two ex-cons breaking into that house up the road, all those years ago, and failing to get what they wanted.

The lights didn't work. The big guy said it was probably a fuse, mentioned an AutoZone in Garden City. I thanked him. My hand was on the car door when he said he'd seen us taking pictures. He stood behind me, thumbs in his belt loops, legs spread, like a gunfighter.

"We're just passing through." It seemed like something I was supposed to say, a line remembered from a script, what the stranger in town says to the sheriff. In the ensuing pause I tried to shut myself up. "I'm a big fan of the book."

The teenager, swear to God, spat into the dust. The old man's squint clamped down a little more; I remembered from something I'd read that Nancy Clutter's boyfriend, Bobby, still lived in Holcomb. The Samaritan jerked a massive hand in the direction of the house. "You can go on up the driveway if you want."

"Don't want to bother nobody," I said. The grammar of the rural poor sounded condescending, even though it had once been mine.

"Nobody to bother," he said. "I'm right here."

"You live there?"

"Yep." He shook my hand and said his name was Brian. "This happens all the time."

In that moment, I wanted nothing more than to get the hell out of Kansas, but we turned the car around.

❊   ❊   ❊

The first time I read *In Cold Blood*, for a college class, I admired it: the luridness of the story, the elliptical grace of the prose, the coy withholding that wound the plot. But Capote's portrayal of the victims bothered me. He describes the Clutters clinically, superficially, by heights and weights and ages, hair and eye color, the kind of details you get in an autopsy report. The book's subtitle is *A True Account of a Multiple Murder and Its Consequences*, yet it devotes just 35 of 343 pages to the victims. So much for consequences.

Holcombites took exception to Capote's treatment of the Clutters, especially Bonnie. *In Cold Blood* paints her as timorous, frail, depressive, frequently institutionalized. Many who knew her claimed Capote had exaggerated her mental illness. If so, it worked: Bonnie comes off as more sympathetic than her husband or children, more human and complex. Capote plays the others to type: Herb the teetotaling Methodist, a successful rancher who "cut a man's-man figure" and was "always certain of what he wanted from the world"; Nancy the straight-A student, the class president, the "town darling" who wore her boyfriend's signet ring and helped protégés bake pies; Kenyon the gangly, rambunctious teenager, building and inventing, scared of girls. Not Bonnie. She was afflicted by an unspeakable sadness, full of doubt and anxiety possessing a rich and dark and unknowable inner life. She dreamed of being a nurse, suffered crippling postnatal depressions, once spent two months in Wichita away from her family, which she enjoyed so much the guilt drove her back. She refused to cook, slept in a separate room from her husband; was the only Clutter who drank coffee, and may have been the source of the mysterious cigarette smell in the house; she was prone to cryptic, ominous remarks. She's the best character in the book besides Smith.

Her family disagreed. Bonnie's younger brother was still outraged forty years later, when he granted his only interview on the subject. And on the fiftieth anniversary of the murders, Herb Clutter's niece wrote an essay for her tiny local newspaper in New Mexico, detailing her response to reading *In Cold Blood*: "The Clutters became cardboard figures, hardly more than a backdrop for Capote's sympathetic depiction of the killers." The surviving Clutter daughters, both of whom remain in Kansas, claimed Capote had told them he was writing a "tribute" to their family and accused him of "grossly misrepresent[ing]" their parents and siblings for profit.

Imagine how that feels, your murdered mother misportrayed. Millions of books, multiple movies, half a million Google hits for her name. All of it wrong. The surviving Clutters made a family scrapbook to preserve their version of her. But what good is a version nobody reads?

❋   ❋   ❋

We passed between the rows of withering elms, which no longer cast any shade, and into a clearing. To the left stood a silo, a barn, and a mobile home with the wheels on; to the right, the Clutter house. Close up, it still looked like Capote describes it, although his description is imprecise; he calls it a "handsome white house," but the first story was pale yellow brick. It had been updated over the years, with new white siding and a split-log fence, a satellite perched on the steep angle of a red-shingled roof. In 1959, it was the kind of house that signified wealth. But to us, and Capote—whose Gothic descriptions of the farm focus on the elms, the wind, the bloodstains on the walls—the house was remarkable only

120

because of the story it suggested: Two men parked where we were, in the middle of the night, arguing in whispers, building up the nerve to take a shotgun from the backseat and cross that lawn, to that side door, in search of a safe full of money that didn't exist. The victims inside, asleep and unaware. I thought of the place where my mother died, a trailer in the desert a thousand miles away. The last time I went there, when I was writing my book, all trace of her had been erased. Was that better?

Back on Oak, the men were where we'd left them, and what had seemed strange now seemed sinister, their watching, our repeated trips up and down the street, this absurd ritual of visiting the house. I slowed the car to a crawl, cracked the window, yelled a thanks. The big guy nodded and pointed to the beer in his hand. I declined the offer and kept going.

"I couldn't tell if they hated us," Bonnie said.

Later I would learn on the Internet that the big guy's name is spelled Bryan, that his parents bought the house for a dollar after the second owner killed himself, that they briefly offered five-dollar tours until neighbors objected, that they listed the house at auction in 2006 but didn't get a satisfactory bid, that he sometimes shoots guns in the air to warn off trespassers. I don't blame him.

*　*　*

Capote acted as if he'd invented the true crime genre with *In Cold Blood*. He didn't; it dates back at least as far as Lizzie Borden. He probably borrowed the "nonfiction novel" approach from Lillian Ross's *Picture*, and he wasn't the first person to focus on the murderer, either—Meyer Levin did that nine years earlier, with *Compulsion*, his historical novel based on the Leopold-Loeb case. But *In Cold Blood* was more successful than its predecessors, and far more influential. In a 1997 article on murder in America, Eric Schlosser traces a trend of murderer-protagonists back to Capote's portrayal of Smith. Schlosser attributes the trend to curiosity: "When the murderer is the protagonist of a story we can vicariously experience that power." We want to know how it feels to kill someone.

In Cold Blood tells us exactly that, in Smith's words, a little more than halfway through, textbook timing for a tragic climax. In the backseat of a police cruiser somewhere in Arizona, Smith finally narrates that dreadful night in Holcomb. He tries to explain why he did it. In his version, he and Hickock lock the Clutters in the bathroom and search the house

121

for the safe. Instead they find forty dollars, a radio, and a pair of binoculars. Smith takes these outside to the car and stands for a moment in the driveway, looking up at the moon, savoring the November chill. He thinks about leaving, walking out beneath the elms and to the highway, hitching a ride. "It was like I wasn't part of it," he says. "More as though I was reading a story. And I had to know what was going to happen. The end." So he goes inside and slits Herb Clutter's throat. He says he didn't mean to do it: "I didn't realize what I'd done till I heard the sound."

He never said that. Capote wrote the last line into Smith's confession, the only account of the murders the book contains, a passage that makes Smith seem reluctant, full of regret, almost humane: sparing Nancy from Hickock's plan to rape her, placing a pillow under Kenyon's head, putting Herb out of his misery with a shotgun blast. *Esquire* sent a reporter, Philip K. Tompkins, to Kansas after the book's release to investigate its accuracy. He compared Capote's version of Smith's confession to the transcribed testimony of both detectives in the car, as well as to the transcript of the confession itself. Only in the book does Smith express regret, or mention any emotional response at all. "To judge from his confession," Tompkins writes, "Perry Smith was an obscene, semi-literate, and cold-blooded killer." Smith's autobiographical narrative, written for a court psychiatrist and quoted at length by Capote, suggests the same: it's aggrieved, incoherent, brimming with rage; at one point, he brags about having thrown a policeman off a bridge. (Hickock's statement also belies his characterization as the less interesting of the killers: he seems remarkably candid and self-aware.) Later in the book, Smith tells a friend visiting him in jail that he's not sorry, that nothing about the murders bothers him a bit.

People who knew Smith—the detectives, fellow convicts, his sister—spoke of him with contempt or fear. Most who met both killers preferred Hickock. Not Capote. *In Cold Blood* portrays Hickock as a pedophile and a coward, a lifelong convict with a disfigured face, a small-time crook in over his head. Smith gets the sympathy, as well as the space: more than one hundred pages, far more than Capote gives anybody else. In his biography of Capote, Gerald Clarke remarks on the "many unsettling similarities" between the author and his subject: both raised in broken homes and orphanages, both small and boyish, both bookish and artistic. Because he saw himself in Smith, and found that irresistible—a KBI agent later claimed they had hallway trysts on death row—Capote took a thirty-one-year-old felon others described as a dwarfish sociopath and portrayed him as a frustrated and mistreated dreamer, a guitar-strumming poet prone to fantasies of Mexican treasure and a big yellow bird that protected him in his sleep, a murderous Peter Pan.

From the beginning, Capote conceived of the book as a tragedy: hence the silos rising like Greek temples from the plains, the minor Holcombites who act as chorus, its classical story arc and emphasis on fate. Hickock is the second actor, the cops and justice system the antagonists, the Clutters vehicles for the hero's hamartia. The hero is Perry Smith.

❊ ❊ ❊

We had to make Salina, still halfway across the state, that night, and the sun was setting and our brake lights didn't work, and I didn't like the sound of six more hours on an interstate when nobody could see us slowing down. We stopped outside the old Holcomb School, where the Clutter children went, and I kneeled on the hot asphalt, pulling fuses from the box beneath the dashboard. I didn't know which fuse did what and we didn't have the owner's manual and it wasn't my car. The fuses came out one by one, and everything turned on and off—the radio, the blinkers—but the brake lights refused to kindle, and as the pavement began to cook my knees, déjà vu set in. I had never been to Kansas with another man's wife in yet another man's car, and I thought it felt familiar because that's the kind of situation I get myself into—the kind that's hard to explain—until I remembered where I'd seen this street before: on the cover of my worn paperback copy of *In Cold Blood*, which I'd lent to Bonnie.

She hadn't read the book until the week before. I'd read it five or six times, growing angrier with each read, more outraged by its moral project—the glorification of a half-wit murderer—and its legacy, how it made focusing on killers the default mode of murder narratives, laid a cornerstone of murderer worship in American culture. Now here I was, on a trip to Holcomb, reading to her my portrayal of a dead woman she would never meet, and it seemed absurd that I had never felt the weight of that before: a whole world of potential readers out there who would know my mother only from my book. What a thing to do to the dead, what an act of hubris: to preserve your impression of them for posterity, knowing they can't defend themselves. The same thing Capote did to the Clutters.

I had justified it during the writing process by telling myself I was honoring my mother, that her story would serve a greater purpose, call attention to the epidemic of domestic violence in America. But that was a hollow and self-serving rationale. My name would be on the cover, my picture on the jacket, the royalty checks in my name. I knew my book would never be as successful or widely read as *In Cold Blood*, wouldn't do much to change the cultural conversation about murder. Nobody wants to read about a victim; it forces us to imagine sharing their fate. And what good is a response nobody reads?

Capote must have reassured himself that he had a higher purpose: to advance an argument against capital punishment. The last section of *In Cold Blood* pleas Smith's case to escape the noose. But Capote also needed him to hang, because he needed an ending. Friends later remembered Capote's frustration in the years Smith spent on death row, waiting for appeals and stays of execution. An acquaintance told George Plimpton about a dinner in New York a few years into the writing of *In Cold Blood* at which Capote talked about the killers—"he seemed clearly in love with" Smith—and said the book was done except for the ending. "But it can't be published until they're executed," Capote said. "So I can hardly wait." At a party two years later, just after Smith's last appeal had failed, another partygoer heard Capote say, "I'm beside myself with joy!"

*   *   *

At the AutoZone in Garden City I scraped a bird carcass out of the Saturn's grille, replaced the brake light fuse—which didn't fix the problem—and asked the clerk if he knew how to get to the graveyard. He sent us to the wrong one. Bonnie got a miraculous bar of service and searched on her phone for nearby cemeteries while I watched the setting sun toast the fields of wheat and texturize the land around us, shadow fingers reaching out from tombstones.

Bonnie announced triumphantly that she had found it. She'd grown invested in our tour through Holcomb; most people would have thought it was macabre, but she's a poet, prone to finding romance in unexpected places, like graveyards where two mismatched lovers searched for murdered strangers. A few highway ramps and there we were, at Valley View. At least Capote gets the cemetery right: an oasis of trees and grass, "a good refuge from a hot day." As far as I had seen it was the greenest place in Kansas. We parked and went looking for the Clutters.

*   *   *

In Cold Blood never says outright who did what. Smith's confession claims that he killed Herb and Kenyon, and Hickock killed the women. Smith later admits to committing all four murders, but Capote suggests he does it out of sympathy for Hickock's mother. Later still, Smith tells a friend visiting him in jail that he killed the entire family. The lead detective in the case, Alvin Dewey, believed the original confession, but said Capote thought Smith killed them all. The book itself leaves the question unanswered. It must not have seemed important.

Capote did attempt to answer the question of why. A doctor quoted in the book claims that Herb Clutter represented everyone who'd ever wronged Smith, that he saw his entire past of pain and alienation writ large in his victim. Capote theorizes that Smith suffered a "brain explosion" and never made a decision at all: *I didn't realize what I'd done till I heard the sound.* The book suggests it was Smith's destiny to kill: a child of abuse and divorce and neglect, cursed by poverty, forged into a violent criminal by a society that gave him no other choice. Smith himself says it was at least partly a rational decision—before the murders, he and Hickock discussed their options—but that he did it because he was mad at Hickock for being wrong about the safe, and disgusted by his partner's desire to rape a teenage girl.

But Capote actively conceals the most likely motive: Smith had fallen in love in Kansas. Ralph F. Voss devotes a chapter of his book on *In Cold Blood* to its homosexual subtext, which was noted by critics after publication, but overshadowed then and now by the brouhaha over the term "nonfiction novel." Hickock and Smith were former prison cellmates. Throughout the book, Perry is repeatedly referred to as a "punk" and described in feminine terms; he rarely shows interest in women and seems jealous about Hickock's liaisons; Hickock calls Smith "honey" "sugar," and "baby"; at one point, they "pick up" a German lawyer and his male companion in an Acapulco bar and spend a few days with them; when the German gives Smith his sketchbook as a parting gift, it includes "nude studies" of Hickock. The two killers share hotel rooms all over America and Mexico, and stay together long after they have no apparent reason to. Homosexuality remains a subtext only because Capote refuses to acknowledge it. He deflected attention from sexuality while promoting the book, too, insisting in interviews that there was no sexual relationship between Hickock and Smith. But Capote was, above all, a savvy self-marketer, and he'd seen his previous books criticized for gay content; he knew that, in the mainstream America of the midsixties, having a gay protagonist would cripple the book's commercial prospects. (The same audience had no qualms about murderer-protagonists: Robert Bloch's *Psycho*—and Hitchcock's film adaptation—had proven that a few years earlier.)

125

In Smith's account of the night of the murders, when Hickock says he wants to rape Nancy, Smith replies, "You'll have to kill me first." Voss suggests that Smith stopped him not out of moral outrage, as the book claims, but because he was jealous, which would explain "one of the great ironies within *In Cold Blood*": Smith spares Nancy from rape moments before one of them shoots her in the head. In Voss's reading, Smith's tale becomes a different kind of tragedy, more Shakespeare than Sophocles, a story less about fate than it is about love: betrayal, jealous rage, the consequences of one catastrophic choice.

* * *

The cemetery was windless and calm, dappled by sunlight slanting through the trees. Near a junction in the path, Bonnie spotted the grave of Alvin Dewey, flanked by his wife and father. A moment later, she called me over to another grave. Capote writes that the four victims share a single stone, "in a far corner of the cemetery—beyond the trees, out in the sun, almost at the wheat field's bright edge." If that had ever been true, it wasn't anymore. A cypress tree draped the grave in shade, and the dead stretched for fifty yards in every direction. Herb and Bonnie Clutter were buried together under one marker, their children beneath smaller satellites on either side, all three stones tinted mauve in the dusk. Pinwheels spun on the kids' graves, plastic flowers for the parents.

In Cold Blood ends at the Clutter grave. Dewey is weeding his father's plot when he sees a friend of Nancy's. They talk briefly about how much has changed since the murders, and afterward he walks out beneath the trees, "leaving behind him the big sky, the whisper of wind voices in the wind-bent wheat." That last line always rang false to me, the melodramatic personification and sloppy second "wind," Capote's love of alliteration left unchecked by an editor. Maybe that's because it was; the moment never happened.

Capote altered facts and fabricated so much of the book. A few pages earlier, he shows Smith on the gallows, apologizing for what he's done, an apology none of the other people there recorded; according to some witnesses, Capote had left by then, unable to watch. Still, somehow the ending seems most significant. Capote couldn't bring himself to end with the hangings, a passage supposedly so difficult to write that it paralyzed his hand. He said he wanted "to bring everything back full circle, to end with peace." After hundreds of pages about the killer, his hard-luck childhood and thwarted ambitions and plight on death row, Capote couldn't end with the book's last vision of Smith, his dead feet dangling from the

126

gallows. So instead he leaves us with a gesture to the victims, a sentimental scene that never happened, one final look at their resting place.

Walking through the graveyard, on the way back to the car, I said I felt like a tourist. "Maybe it's good to be remembered," Bonnie said, and I wondered how a person could be so unapologetically herself. We talked about what we'd want done with us when we were dead, funerals and gravestones, whether or not it mattered, and how we might need to decide soon, because we were about to drive three hundred miles through the night with no brake lights. A joke, but I thought about it: we could die on the road, wind up buried in a place like this, leave our story to somebody else's telling.

✿ ✿ ✿

In Cold Blood made Capote a millionaire, the toast of New York, famous in a way few writers have ever been. It also destroyed him. He spent the next two decades descending into addiction and self-caricature, reaching his nadir when he appeared on a live TV show, having not slept in days and high as wheat in June, and predicted his own suicide. "I'll kill myself," he said, "without meaning to." And he did, five years later, in a friend's guest room in LA. He never finished another real book. In 1966, days after the release of *In Cold Blood*, Capote was already saying that if he'd known what the future held, he would never have stopped in Holcomb: "I would have driven straight on. Like a bat out of hell."

He was probably exaggerating. But you wonder what would have happened if he'd never come to Kansas. Some rare moments feel significant even as they happen: you see the future stretch ahead, flat and forbidding, like a highway across the plains. Capote had one in Garden City, on the courthouse steps. Smith had one on the Clutters' lawn before he killed them. I had one leaving the cemetery, watching the wheat bend in the wind just like Capote writes and realizing that whatever was happening between Bonnie and me was beyond our control. That night, in the last hotel room left in Salina, we threw our bags down and fucked like we were about to die, and in the aftermath I told her nobody had ever wanted her as much as I did, and she took that to mean I always would, although I didn't mean that at all. We made it to Minnesota the next day. Two years later, we did that drive again, to start a new life there, and six months later Bonnie passed through Kansas while leaving me, and six months after that I drove through yet again, in a panic, with a ring in my pocket. Capote got one thing right: there are only two kinds of endings, death and the ones we invent.

127

Bonnie wrote notes for a poem on the trip. They end with a moment that happened a few days after Kansas, when we followed my vet-student cousin into a basement meat locker where a dead donkey dangled from the ceiling, eyes and mouth stuffed white with wax. I think Bonnie liked the idea of coming full circle, from the slaughterhouse to the meat locker—they even smelled the same—and the strangeness of the moment. I touched her shoulder and she felt a shock and swore she saw the donkey sway. I just liked the sense of peace. The donkey was blind, mute, story-less. Nobody knew who'd killed it.

Nominated by Tin House

THE GREAT MEAL

by JUNG HAE CHAE

from AGNI

When the bell rang at noon at Five Ocean Trading, it was time. The swishing of scissors, the clacking of dies, the cutting of a thousand berets and beanies and bowlers and fedoras, the up-down-across ankle-pedaling of a sea of sewing machines, even the chattering of the AM-radio man or woman in the background—time to rise to something holy.

Or to lunch. The manager—we'll call her Ms. Cho—was always the first to arrive at the head of the table, with good rice. Good rice was important to her and to everyone at the table, for it signified a good foundation. Time, too, was important to her. Someone in her family or church or apartment complex was dying, always dying. On time, off time, in and out of time, dying. Once, she had seen a young man set himself on fire in her hometown in Jeolla province, a college student resisting the militaristic regime that followed the separation of North and South. Another manager, too, had been dying, for as long as anyone could remember—dying—of cancer or something. He was the kind of man who by now had become used to all manners of dying, by fire or water, by taste or temper, be it a home fire or home invasion, a lightning strike or not enough light striking inside the brain—he'd seen it all. His final cause might soon have been his liver, his face colored and textured like a tangerine gone brown, pocked and not quite edible. He liked to share bright things, spicy rice cakes a vigorous orangey shade his skin might once have been, or fried fish cakes so red they looked almost alive.

Then there was my buddy Jane, a perky twenty-year-old who liked to smoke Marlboro Reds and binge drink beer and soju, who had worked there longer than I, this being her second season. She came back for

129

"the people," she said. Jane was a people person. As the bastard child of a beer tycoon, she knew how to drink better and more than most middle-aged men. A veteran of all things unfit and outlying, she was like an outgrown prom dress or a truck-stop motel on a stretch of an unmarked highway. Sometimes she was lovely and unseasonable like a December rain. Not unlike me. She and I were meant to be college dropouts, not factory line workers. We didn't even like hats.

"Unni, when I save enough to pay my back-tuition at NYU, I'm outta here," she said.

"When I save enough to get to India, I'm outta here," I might have said.

It was important for me to distinguish myself from the sad people at Five Ocean. I was acutely aware of being ashamed, not only of my association with a not-totally-legit operation like Five Ocean that relied on an all-cash, all-talk, all-loose-paper business model, but ashamed in general, in a more abstract way. And confused, too. Ashamed because confused. So much so that I had *become* these two abstractions. Ashamed of having to wear a dual identity of sorts: at once an aspiring human with a lofty, though as yet unknown, purpose, a comrade-in-arms with the *Wretched of the Earth*, as my coworkers seemed to me then; and a thud of a human spiraling out of control. Ashamed, too, of having to support myself at such a young age by working at a factory, of saying "Five Ocean Trading," a name that seemed to defy correct grammar.

So I made sure to bring something different to the table. Each day, I concocted dishes that my coworkers could neither recognize nor name: spinach linguini with spam and kimchi, mung-bean-and-raisin salad, turmeric-seasoned tofu and cabbage. These were not Korean. The ingredients brought together the cultures I was confusedly trying on. They did not taste good to the Korean palate, likely because they contained spices and persuasions that were incongruous with the Land of the Morning Calm.

Sometimes I'd forget to bring lunch. Sometimes I forgot things that reminded me of my mother, who had died a few years earlier from a growth that started in the middle of her and spread upward. I had seen death before, but *her* death marked the first real tragedy of my young person's life. Mr. Lee, our boss, always the last to arrive, often brought a lunch bag with a matching bowl adorned with a flying phoenix. "That's a beautiful bag," someone would say. He would look up, as though one of the birds had come to life, and with a puzzled look on his face, nod. He had a habit of nodding to all that was said, no matter the content or subject or how he actually felt about it. Alone with me, he spoke of his child and wife back home in Korea and how he had lost the One Real Thing. He had been a kind of double agent for a covert operation in the Korean government. He had betrayed his people, he said, and if they found him, they'd kill him. I didn't ask what all that meant. I didn't ask because Mr. Lee, too, wore the look of someone who, nearing the end of life, yearned to have Meaning. Somehow, all his life, he'd been stripped of that right. Or is it a privilege? He needed to talk without a period at the end of the sentence. I listened, my eyes keen with yearning, too, for meaning. I listened, just listened, and sometimes while listening I imagined his Chinese lover, who had worked on the second floor as manager of the production line. That they were lovers was an open secret. I imagined her wiry arms and legs intertwined with his, a dark sea of sewing machines filling in the negative space around their snake-taut bodies. They rarely spoke kindly to one another; they rarely spoke. Their language was not a language to be spoken, under- or over-stood, but approximated into the human, broken into the smalls of backs and knees, toughened into skin. Eaten. I listened, just listened.

The Koreans were a nosy-noisy kind of people. When they ate, they kicked their tongues into the roofs of their mouths, wild and uninhibited in their chewing, setting up an uncoordinated rhythmic teething, ticking, click-clacking, and sloshing that signaled harmony or distress, either satisfaction or dissatisfaction with their meal. They spoke sparingly, allowing only grunts and awkward pauses between bites, as if to witness seasons passing. When they did speak, it was usually about other people's business: who owed whom how much money this month, who had left his wife for yet another woman in their congregation, who had gambled away his family's life savings earned from seven-days-a-week backbreaking work, whose kid had gotten into Harvard or Juilliard on full scholarship, who had fallen ill with cancer or cirrhosis of the liver or some other disease on the list of the most tragic and incurable but who couldn't be treated because of their illegal status. God was their only hope.

* * *

My preoccupation with the eating and sharing of foods and the philosophy thereof no doubt stems from my childhood in South Korea, spent mostly without adult supervision. Before I started school, I lived with my grandmother, several unmarried aunts, and an uncle in a traditional, old-fashioned Korean home, complete with courtyard and outhouse and no refrigerator. No refrigerator meant not becoming westernized and not living in a tiny matchbox in an apartment complex like the one my mom had lived in while working in a bustling city in 1970s South Korea. Fresh from divorce, ashamed and confused, she needed to build a life for herself and prove that she could make it without a man. With the pittance she made working in a university office as a secretary, she saved and saved unreasonably for the chance to buy a one-room apartment on lottery, so that one day she could bring her three children to live with her. That was the plan, anyway.

Not having a refrigerator also meant that much of our food had to be fermented, pickled, or spiced heavily, even buried underground to keep through the winter months. By mid-autumn, in preparation for the long harsh winter, the neighborhood women would come together to make a communal kimchi, a staple in Korean cuisine. The primary ingredient: pickled cabbage spiced heavily enough to awaken all six senses, including the sense of sorrow instilled deeply in the Korean people. They made giant batches of it, transferred them into brown, pear-shaped, earthenware crocks, deep-set and lidded tight, and buried them in the earth. Gloveless, their red-pepper-stained fingers reeked of garlic and scallions and fish sauce. They sang and told each other stories as they scooped, stirred, spiced, scraped, swirled, spooned, shut, and shoveled—a ritual as sacred as burying their ancestors. I watched entranced as the lady priestesses blessed the food they had created.

Then there were the daily rituals. Evenings I enjoyed following my grandmother into the kitchen, that musty underground gathering place of smells. Inside that sweltering pit, a deep-pocketed cast-iron wok bellowed up giant smoke-clouds, preparing me well for the great meal. When dinner was served—finally—we would take our places around the knee-high table and kneel down holy-like to eat. Rice porridge and a single fish. My uncle, the only man in the house—king!—would be served first, then the rest of us—one girl without a father and four women without husbands. Grandmother always last. She would claim the head of the fish for herself and make it last the whole week. First the scales, carefully pulled loose and unsmocked by her skilled fingers, which gradually exposed the gelatinous filigree beneath. The tips of her fingers were precise instruments that pried off the gills, the bones, and the bulbous brain matter; then the taste of sea infused deep in the eyes, the best saved for last. Pulp to blood, filaments to bone, sea to body. She fed us the good flesh.

❅ ❅ ❅

The Mexicans were not welcome at the table. They were the workers in the filthy, fume-filled back rooms who worked the sewing machines, dies,

and assembly lines carrying the various hats—all the menial tasks involv-
ing mindless repetition but requiring some level of risk. In other words,
tasks that no Korean would do because they were deemed too lowly. The
Mexicans smiled like children and said, "Hola!"—the only word in their
tongue spoken to Koreans. Somewhere in the belly of the factory, the
Mexicans huddled and spoke in hushed voices, in their own rhyme and
rhythm, and when no one was watching they bit into their own spiced
foods, smoked their own joints, pissed into their own holes. When they
retreated into their homes, one imagined, they made babies of their
own kind. They were used. They were used to being used.

Then there were the women: Jane and I, Ms. Cho the unmarriageable
workhorse, the Chinese lover, and her young daughter. Ms. Cho became
the unofficial caretaker of everyone, especially the men, who seemed
always in need of caretaking—if not for cancer, then something else. She
knew the bottom-most needs of these men, the pittance of warmth and
grunt of dignity they relied on for survival. After our meals she would
round up the bowls, consolidate the foods, and stock them in the fridge
with labels on them. Later she would dole them out to us in uneven
portions depending on what she perceived we each needed. She was
precise in her giving, but imprecise in her taking. She gave and gave.

The Chinese manager, who was beautiful and mostly silent, was in
love with Mr. Lee, our handsome boss, and took good care of him. We
suspected that she packed his lunch for our daily meals, a ritual to which
she was not invited. I wondered where and what she ate. I wondered
about her life back in China when she was a young girl or woman. I won-
dered about her other lovers and the techniques of loving and how she
had learned them, whether she had used them with Mr. Lee or with her
daughter's father, her now-estranged lover. I wondered and wondered,
though I did not ask about them. She lent me money before I asked. She
gave to the Koreans. The Koreans took from her; they did not give back.

It was the women who gave. The men talked. They were the sales-
men, the dealers and wheelers. They made the money. Sometimes it
came in bundles, inside handkerchiefs. As the bookkeeper, I was in
charge of it all, the coming in and going out. I liked the ritual of count-
ing: after dividing the bills into little stacks, I would grip each one by
its "belt," fold it mercilessly into a U, spit on my index and middle fin-
gers to keep it lickity-taut, then like a back-alley boss spit on the floor,
too, for good measure. Then count. I would count again and again until
I had the bills perfectly stacked and organized: ones, fives, tens, twen-
ties, fifties, hundreds, and the lucky twos. I made sure people got paid.

Sometimes, when there wasn't enough, I decided who got paid and who didn't get paid from one week to the next. From the employees who worked overtime to suppliers who needed payment for their shipments, they were all nice to me. They brought me coffee and treats. There is much power vested in the one who keeps the books.

Which was an important life lesson, for one day Mr. Kim, one of the salesmen, smiled at me even after I threw a box at him across the room. Mr. Kim was a fat man, in both physique and demeanor. Quickest with his chopsticks, he wasn't afraid to take the last morsel on the plate that we all shared as comrades and would have done so if it were our last meal on earth. He liked to tell jokes that no one laughed at. He smiled gratuitously. So I threw a box at him. But only because he was a thrower himself. Moments earlier, he'd thrown one across the room at Jane. I couldn't imagine what she must have done to deserve a box being thrown at her like that. So I did what any drinking pal would do in good conscience: do one up.

There were other men at Five Ocean, all of them needy. Made only more so because I held the ledgers. One Korean hat salesman asked me out after work. Seeing that I had nothing in common with hats or Koreans, I said yes, and even suggested we go out on a double date with his buddy and my buddy, Jane. Drinking is how Korean people bond, and so we bonded over a concoction of beer, soju, and whiskey, or whatever was around, all in one shot. We washed down our pipe dreams, our messy, off-the-chart paths, and the sorrows of our mothers and fathers who'd dreamed big for us and risked big things to come to America for us. We drank and drank. And we ate and ate, because eating is about more than just food for the Koreans. We ate and threw up our arms and sang karaoke and laughed gratuitously. We threw up together. Fighting is how Korean people bond, so we fought over who was going to pick up the tab, lest we be shamed for being cheapskates. Jane, grateful that I had "stood up" for her with Mr. Kim, treated us to a night of binge drinking. She and I often observed and philosophized about the men and women at Five Ocean, who increasingly became the men-children and the women-mothers. After work we would perfect the art of drinking until we sat numb, the stillness interrupted by nodding and a mutual one-upsmanship.

❊　❊　❊

The upside of being given something of a notice of impending death is that one can prepare for it. Ostensibly, your life does "flash before your eyes" when the end is near. Time collapses. You stop caring about what other people fill their buckets with. You start using the good crystal bowl you've been saving for special guests and start wearing the gold watch. You settle old feuds and stop to talk to neighbors and pet their dogs. The mundane fills with meaning. You appreciate the simple ingredients of life: water, wind, colors, flowers, children. My mother did strange things like that. She talked about how she regretted leaving my "poor father," who needed her because he couldn't take care of himself. Not because he was an invalid but because he was often passed out drunk, sometimes in neighboring towns, next to a bus stop. She talked about how she wanted to wash his dirty clothes and cook fish for our family, and how simple things like that would have made us happy. She regretted not having visited him at his hospital bedside, where he'd died after falling on the side of a road. Drunk.

In time, she could no longer differentiate between the sounds of *h* and *f* (or *ph*) since her vocal cords were affected by the spreading cancer; "Mrs. Hwang" became "Mrs. Fong." She broke into tears on hearing certain words: *phosphorus*, for example—or to her ear, *hwa-su*-phorus, hwa-su meaning *fire* and *water* in Korean—this she associated with her illness, and, in turn, with her sins, her wayward soul, her debts to humankind. She cried and cried, saying "Hwa-su-phorus, hwa-su-phorus" over and over, as if in a trance. God was her only hope.

Only later did we learn that she had called her job's HR department to make certain the beneficiaries of her life insurance policy and pension plan were her three children. She'd also contacted the church to oversee the arrangements of her funeral and other domestic affairs. She'd stocked up on groceries and cleaned the house and tended to her houseplants shortly before checking into the Christ Memorial Hospital on the eve of Thanksgiving 1992. For the next three weeks my grandmother, with her lifelong habits of eating and speaking in tiny portions, remained silent and sat with me in close vigil by my mother, her firstborn, as the doctors tried to figure out the "systemic shock" that had shut down her major organs.

My mother was born in December, was taken in December. Sometimes she was lovely, like the alchemic blue-azure that rains down off-season. Sometimes she was available whole to me for a small infinity, as if poised for some greatness beyond us. Always she was singular and an outlier. She was a hapless human not poised to let go of her children, to let go of the debris from all the fires that had been raging in her life, the phosphorus-hot mess that had consumed her. *To let go.*

It was forgetting that was at the heart of drinking, forgiving at the heart of communal eating. We seem able to forgive anything or anyone—

135

even the nation's traitor, or the lover who had made her wait in the maid's wing, or the mother-daughter who passed on without bidding proper goodbye. We pass on—when we share our foods and eat earnestly, noisily, morsel by morsel, with our good tongues. That is when the food is good for the body: it washes us of our debris, tears us down, builds us up once again to face the insufferable. My mother, too, knew how to eat well and drink well, the trait I seem to have inherited without shame or fatigue. Some nights I walk past the once-filthy storefronts, past his studio apartment, the top floor of a six-floor walk-up, and imagine Mr. Lee with his good rice, scooping up spicy anchovies into his mouth, the light reflecting off the brightly colored fish as from a fire, palming the lovely contours of his face.

Nominated by Agni

THE STORM

by MICHAEL COLLIER

from KENYON REVIEW

Our landlord, a federal bureaucrat, would sit in his car
across the street at the end of the month to collect rent.
He had a scarlet birthmark covering his neck
and tinting the lobe of his left ear. That's what
you got for a $125 a month on Capitol Hill
in 1981, a landlord afraid to enter his own building
and a 300-square-foot "garden" apartment.

I did odd jobs for him: painting the long, dark
brick passageway that went past our door
into the concrete yard and unpaved eeriness of the alley;
and twice repaired locks on apartments upstairs
that had been burglarized. One victim, a newly divorced
woman in her midthirties who lived above us, broke her lease
and moved out. She had dark hair in a style more suitable
for someone much older, combed over on top to disguise a thin
    spot.
In my mother's parlance, she seemed "ill-equipped to deal with
    life."

When I called the landlord to say she had "vacated the premises,"
a phrase that came out of my mouth involuntarily, he was silent
for several seconds before calling her a "fuck."
I thought she'd done the right thing considering how
shaken she was and that, among other things, as I was installing

a dead bolt, she said it felt as if she'd been raped—actually,
she used the phrase "gang raped," which seemed hyperbole
to me until I told my wife who without pausing said of course
that's what you'd feel if you were a woman.

Night or day it was the kind of neighborhood
where if something happened you couldn't trust someone
to come to your aid, like the evening my wife and I
were fixing dinner and heard over the radio's drone,
or perhaps through it, what sounded like shouts and screams
or cries, all three, I guess. Beyond the window we could see
a woman flailing, on her side in the street. By the time I reached her
she was up and pointing down the block to a figure running away.
Instinct of a kind I'd never felt sent me after the man
but only the distance of a house or two until another more familiar
     instinct
sent me back to the woman who was now rubbing the side of her
     face,
and from instinct, too, I put my arm around her and then
I don't know how else to say it, she "buried" her face in my
     shoulder.
"I'm sorry" she said. "I'm so sorry"

•

When one of my sons turned 25, I calculated how old
I would be when he turned 50, if I were still alive, and then
it occurred to me that after I die his age will begin
to catch up to mine, until at some point in the future,
if he lives long enough, we will for one year
be the same age, the only time in our lives, so to speak,
when I am not keeping ahead of him moving toward death
and he has not yet surpassed me, and in order for me to experience
what he will experience that day, I will have to live until
I'm a month shy of 96, which is how long my father lived.

•

The afternoon the Air Florida jet crashed in the Potomac
I was working in the basement apartment on 10th Street.
The blizzard had been accompanied by lightning and thunder,
big booms and flashes, as if there were a storm within a storm.

By noon the schoolyard across the street had close to a foot.
One of the many times I got up from my work to look out
the small window, I saw a group of boys tramping slowly
in a jagged file across the playground, each carrying a large,

household item: a TV with its cord dragging, a turntable atop
an amplifier, speakers, an IBM typewriter. The last boy dragged
a red plastic sled with a bulky, olive-green duffel bag as freight.
"Looters in the Snow," I thought, like a Bruegel painting.

We lived close enough to National to hear planes land
and take off, intermittent muffled rumblings I'd learned
to ignore, although at first I tracked them tensely
like a passenger strapped in his seat silently urging the plane up.

Back then, I was afraid of so many things, I dealt with fear
by acting brave and impervious, cultivating as well
an ironic bonhomie that covered up the effort.
Everything was an effort, so I made effortlessness my goal.

At night, what I'd avoided during the day appeared
in the form of my child self: a pale, chubby, asthmatic boy
brought too easily to tears, who could not say no for cowardice
the time at the state fair he rode "The Hammer" with an older boy
    he admired.

Rising in the gondola above the midway with its tantalizing lights,
he felt alive in a peculiar but appealing way as it rocked gently.
For a moment courage was like gaining altitude incrementally
and yet, from having waited his turn in line, he knew what was
    coming.

If you want to know what fear looks like, look at the boy
when he finishes the ride. He's smiling because he thinks
everyone is watching him, and that's why, too, when his friend
    suggests
they ride again he keeps smiling and can't believe what he's agreed
    to do.

•

Along with the hospice nurse—who kept increasing his morphine,
reassuring me she had the orders for upping the dose,
which meant she was hastening his departure—I was with my
    father when he died.
And yet the nurse, whose name I can't remember, although
I promised myself never to forget, had been trying hard to keep
    him alive.
She brought out a nebulizer to help him breathe.
"Robert, cough. Cough, Robert," she urged.
He hadn't responded to either of us for several hours, yet we could
hear him struggling to comply or maybe he was trying to speak.
No matter, a few hours later the nurse told me quietly he was near
    the end
and if family wanted to see him before he passed I should let them
    know.
What took them so long getting there I didn't ask.
The nurse stayed with us, meaning my father and me, as I kept   .
    waiting
for my sisters and brothers-in-law to come through the door, or kept
    hoping
they wouldn't so I would have the moment to myself, not to myself
but for myself, with my father, whose ragged breathing, occasional
    gasps
and, yes, coughing, had become thin and shallow, although his
    fingers roved
over the sheet and even jumped now and then. His head at an angle
on the pillow made it seem as if he were concentrating
extremely hard on the ceiling, as if, I thought, he was listening
to someone talking to him from up there and all the effort
he had been expending hour after hour to catch his breath, to let
go of the great sighing his lungs and mouth produced, the heaves
and groans, the agitated restlessness of his body, the unappeasable
shiftings of his discomfort, had left him, washed up, alone
and isolated as the tide that had been ebbing all night and into
the morning was so far out and had taken with it so much
shore that my father was left on a pedestal of sand, around
which a shallow moat dissipated the farther the tide withdrew,
and just as I in my exhaustion believed he was the island
of Mont-Saint-Michel—his head the cathedral nestled in the tightly
clustered village, his nose the spire rising from the bell tower—

140

just then his utterly blue eyes opened. Shocked by their own
   awakening
they looked at whatever it was they saw, which is why when his eyes
closed and he died, his mouth remained open. The last thing the
   nurse did
was to brush, no, to flick his hair up off his forehead.

•

The plane's tail hit the 14th Street bridge, sheared open
   automobiles
stalled in the storm-clogged traffic, and then went nose first
into the frozen river. Twenty years later, the sister
of one of the crash victims said, "There's a tenacity

the dead have on the living that no living person has on you."
When the rescue helicopter got low enough over the Potomac
the pilot could see through the whiteout a few people standing
on one of the jet's wings. To say the river was frozen

isn't really accurate. It was chockablock with ice floes.
The plane had opened up a lead in the ice between it
and the shore that was covered quickly with jet fuel.

•

For part of the war my father was stationed in DC as a flight
   controller
at National. Late one night, he guided Charles Lindbergh to a
   landing
and then went on the field to meet him. Since Lindbergh
was there only to refuel, they walked among the planes, talking.

For many years, my father carried in his billfold a dollar
Lindbergh had signed and given to him. He called it a "short snorter."
This meant if he ever met Lindbergh again, and couldn't produce
   the bill,
he'd have to buy him a drink.

When he was first assigned to National, my father lived alone
in an apartment that would eventually house my mother and oldest
   sister

who were then with family in Indianapolis. One night, awakened
by a tapping at the window, he hauled up the blinds to find

a man's legs and feet dangling from above. On the few occasions
I heard him tell this story, he provided little more than
what I've written here. I never thought to ask him, as I'd like to now,
what effect discovering that man had on his life.

I'd like to know, too, if he ever thought about killing himself?
A day rarely passes without my college roommate,
Jimmy O'Laughlin, who asphyxiated himself in his father's car,
coming into my thoughts or appearing in his bell bottoms

and flowery shirts, hair teased and ratted like Rod Stewart's
and his side of the room littered with crushed packs of KOOLs
and discarded cups of Laura Scudder vanilla pudding,
which he used to snuff out the butts. What might it mean

that during the semester O'Laughlin began to contemplate his
    demise,
I was writing an art history paper on Dadaist suicide.
Dada was like throwing a full garbage can into someone's backyard
or swimming pool, something I did with friends in high school.

We called it "alley aping." And Dada suicide was an act of such
nonchalance and indifference that I mistook it for courage.
When Giacometti was asked, "Have you ever thought of suicide?"
he replied, "I think of it every day, but not because I find life
    intolerable,

not at all, rather because I think death must be a fascinating
experience." That's not how I think of suicide. I think of it
as one among many solutions to the problem of living,
different than the others all of which involve staying alive.

Freud said it is impossible to imagine our own deaths,
he who imagined his down to its exact dosage in morphine.
When O'Laughlin climbed inside his father's car
and started it up in the garage, he had moved home to finish

two incompletes so he could graduate with our class,
that was his particular problem of living.

•

Twenty years ago, when I first wrote about the crash,
I began, "So, you were in a cave of your own making."
Meaning the 300 square feet of apartment where,
after my wife left for work, I rolled up the foam mat

we slept on, brought a chair in from the other room,
and worked at a narrow, plywood desk, a desk lamp
the only light—warm and intimate, but intense
and clarifying for the way it invited concentration.

And then I wrote: "You got up from the desk
and walked to the window covered by security bars."
That's when I saw the boys crossing the playground.
My first thought was "Looters in the Snow" because

I'd been memorizing John Berryman's "Winter Landscape"
that is based on Bruegel's *The Hunters in the Snow*.
As I looked through the bars at the freezing world,
what should have been a quiet scene shook with thunder

and was lit up with clouds that pulsed with lightning.
I recited the poem silently, slowly, and imperfectly,
as if I were lip synching sounds I heard in my head.
Sometimes I repeated the previous line to get to the next.

Here's the middle of the poem:

> Are not aware that in the sandy time
> To come, the evil waste of history
> Outstretched, they will be seen upon the brow
> Of that same hill: when all their company
> Will have been irrecoverably lost,
>
> These three men, this particular three in brown
> Witnessed by birds will keep the scene. . . .

•

The woman who had been mugged had written her
phone number and name on a scrap of paper I had torn
from a yellow legal pad I used for writing, and for several months
I kept it folded in my wallet. If I called her I'd be setting

in motion events beyond my control which is what
I must have wanted, but not enough. Occasionally, I'd take it out.
It reminded me of how when I put my arm around her
I also had brushed away her hair from her face with my fingers

and curled it behind her ear to stay in place.

•

The mnemonic that recalls the address of the Capitol Hill
    apartment
behind the Marine barracks on 8th Street, S.E., that billeted
the drum and bugle corps and honor guards for State functions,
the year my wife and I lived in DC (747 10th Street), is *Jumbo
    Jet.*
Four stories of watery-green brick, tallest on a block that marked
the edge of a neighborhood's stalled gentrification. Fall into early
    spring
on Friday nights, we could hear the sounds of the bands fade in and
    out
as if on a tide. Cannons going off ricocheted inside the parade
    ground
announced the ceremony's end. Our windows hummed, and once
a small jade horse stationed on a shelf fell over and broke a hoof.
The bands were called the Commandant's Own and the President's
    Own.

•

O'Laughlin was in Yale Psychiatric Institute recovering from
an earlier suicide attempt when on Tuesday, October 13, 1970,
the day Bobby Seal was appearing in New Haven for a pretrial
hearing as the accused for the murder of a fellow Black Panther,
O'Laughlin phoned-in a bomb threat but didn't specify
why or where so the police evacuated three courthouses.

At our tenth college reunion I said to Betty, his
former girlfriend, that if Jimmy had only known
how much he was loved. . . . "Are you kidding," she said.
"Give me a fucking break. He knew he was loved."

•

One night, a few days after the crash, I was driving back
from a party, late, alone, on the George Washington Parkway,
which because of high-banked snow was like a shallow,
roofless tunnel. Headlights reflected off the opposite side

of the road as I'd come into a turn, a blue-white, arctic
shimmer and as such the dark, clear night above pressed down,
or so it seemed, as if it had physical weight, but when the road
made a wide, broad turn and with the shoulders plowed

on either side flush to the pavement, the river came into view
and across it the dome of the Jefferson. Up ahead, brighter
than day, towers of high-intensity floodlights lit up
the near-end of the bridge. Suspended in the illumination,

rising by cable up a crane and dripping with water, was the tail
of the plane, growing larger but stranger as I drew closer.
Stranger because it was exactly what it appeared to be, or I should say
what I expected it to be, but at the same time it was larger,

monumental, a warrior's shield inscribed with a rune-like logo,
a Celtic or Arabic intertwining riddle, an empire's seal,
so much shaped metal, trapezoidal, hanging, twisting
as it came to a stop. But it wasn't until I was heading

into the District on the undamaged span that it became fully
what it was, torn off its body, a wounded appendage, an explosion
of peeled-back skin, bone and tendon and arteries severed, distended,
and no mnemonic or involuntary phrase to repair or rename what it
     was—

not a link in the chain of modern disasters, not a harbinger of
     wrecks
and salvages—the unceasing drone of cranes and claws loading barges

with misshapen beams and miles of wire and glass that didn't
    melt—
but a scrap of paper with a name, a power cord dragging in snow,

O'Laughlin hanging up the phone, my father's short-snorter,
a bit boring through the door, the airplane picking up speed,
thunder inside of snow, "God, look at that thing,"
one of the pilots said, "That don't look right."

Nominated by Marianne Boruch,
C.E. Poverman

KYLIE WEARS BALMAIN

fiction by SARAH RESNICK

from n+1

The summer passes in an ordinary way. Maria applies sunscreen on vacation in Montenegro. Nikki collects trash on a beach in Santa Monica. Megan ditches Brian to go it alone, she's always been so independent. Sandra scores a superhot *and* supernormal boyfriend. Selena wears a vintage cotton scarf; Taylor wears a cotton crop top. Whitney uses an electronic kiosk at Best Buy. Kylie celebrates her birthday—she's 18!—in a $9,000 Nicolas Jebran minidress. Kevin stretches his quadriceps before taking off on a run. Hope marries Robert at Villa Cimbrone in Ravello, Italy, as their 8-month-old son floats by on a cloud (thanks, Cirque du Soleil). Miranda replies to Blake on Twitter! Minka and Vanessa don the same striped off-the-shoulder midi from Reformation (it looks better on Vanessa). Michelle and Jonathan begin dating; they met through mutual friends. Kim wears custom Alexander Wang for an "LA art discussion." Jenna and Henry welcome their new daughter, Poppy, her name the childhood diminutive of her great-grandfather George (yes, *that* George). Britney debuts her total body makeover (she still eats fast food!). Ben fucks the nanny, and Jen, "in shock," escapes to Atlanta for downtime with friends.

Elsewhere, a woman is asked to leave her apartment. The landlords are expecting a baby. She relocates.

The woman's new apartment is dark, dank: a basement with seven-and-three-quarter-foot ceilings. She decides she cannot stay for long. She unpacks only what she needs, leaves the rest in boxes, lives amid a maze of cardboard. She nurses a chronic cough. She reads the first thirty-seven pages of *My Brilliant Friend* and then she doesn't read anything at all. She does her laundry obsessively, determined to exploit the apartment's one redeeming feature, a washer-and-dryer set in her kitchen. (The building's two other tenants use the appliances when she is not home.) She subsists on yogurt and teff and prepared salads she buys from LifeThyme after 9 PM when the food bar is half price. She goes to bed late and wakes at 6 AM when an alarm clock sounds in the apartment upstairs, and then again every eight minutes until her neighbor stops hitting snooze. This goes on for weeks, then months. She already has two jobs; still, it is clear that she needs to make more money. She is tired of moving, and she is tired of being broke. She devises a plan. She applies to work at *The Magazine*.

For the initial interview she faces S., who is research chief of *The Magazine*. They sit in a glass-paneled conference room at a wood table built for thirty. The table is a dark reddish brown. It reminds the woman of the kitchen and bathroom cabinetry in the cheap renos she has visited throughout Brooklyn. CNN plays on mute on a large flatscreen television suspended from the ceiling. (BREAKING: TWENTY-TWO FIREFIGHTERS FREE AN UNNAMED STUDENT FROM A MARBLE VAGINA SCULPTURE IN GERMANY.) S. examines her CV, says, "The work here can be slow, and there is a lot of downtime. Are you sure this is for you?"

Downtime appeals to her. The woman also likes the job title she will have: *researcher.* She thinks it has an eminent quality.

The woman takes the job. As she is leaving, S. hands her a copy of the most recent issue of *The Magazine*.

At home, now, the woman takes *The Magazine* from her bag. She pages through it. There are many pictures. Words take up less space. The woman has seen many of the people in *The Magazine* before—that is, she has seen their images before. These people are real insofar as they exist in the "real world." The woman had vaguely understood that this world consisted of Los Angeles and New York and sometimes London or the finer beaches of continental Europe. But there are new cities she did not expect: Tontitown, Arkansas; West Monroe, Louisiana; and Anderson, Indiana.

The stories in *The Magazine* are about a certain set of people doing things. The stories are also about how these people look while doing these things. More precisely, they are about how these people look when photographed doing these things. There are more women than men, and they look really good, usually—their skin luminous, their hair lustrous, their shapewear flattening in all the right places. And if they don't look good then the fact that they don't look good is (at least part of) the story.

When the woman was young, her mother subscribed to a magazine that was like this magazine but not this one. Her mother kept it in her room, on her nightstand, to read before bed. The woman, then a girl, never went looking for the magazine, having resolved somewhere around the age of 11 or 12 to be the kind of person who would care only about "important" things. Probably she just wanted to be different from her parents. As she grew older, the feeling stayed the same.

But here, looking through *The Magazine*, she worries this may have been a mistake. Behold, inside, the whole of America: fashion knock-offs, "diets that work," stratified wealth, divorce, couture latex, infidelity, single moms, contouring, God, fame, infamy.

She thinks, *All I have to do is check the facts.*

It is her first day. The shift begins at 3 PM; the magazine will ship to the printer that night. She and the other researchers sit in an area called "the pit," where they are joined by the copy editors. The pit is in the middle of the office, a large rectangle surrounded by a pony wall. The computers are circa 2009. She finds a seat at an empty computer.

S. stops by to run through the basics. For each weekly issue, every word and image must be reviewed twice by someone in research—once in "first" and once in "final." Not only those words and images that form "news" or feature items, but those that make up thematic commodity roundups ("Standout Sneakers," "Brushes with Greatness"), fitness advice ("Workout Moves You'll Love"), reviews ("My Top '80s Tracks"), the cover, the table of contents. Everything must be checked. The work is assigned by page. The pages are printed out on 11″ × 17″ sheets of paper. She must mark her corrections in red, then discuss them with the editor or the writer or both. She is to bring her pages to the copy editor tasked with entering the changes into the layout.

S. warns, "Even though Mariah Carey's age is widely known, we must never print it in the magazine."

One of the first stories she is assigned tracks five women who have recently undergone multiple hair-color transformations. That is, they have dyed their hair more than once in the past several months. For each, a series of images chronologically evidences the metamorphoses, with captions noting the date of the dye job as well as the star's natural hue. The captions mention the celebrity's last appearance on an album or in a television show or film, and sometimes also the colorist or the salon responsible for the latest look.

She spends an afternoon scrolling through Instagram timelines, looking for sudden changes in color. Much of the job of checking facts will entail prowling the depths of various social-media accounts. Later she will come to curse the platform for not providing a search-by-date function. For now she is enthusiastic. She begins to familiarize herself with the personae. She makes connections between the various stars—who sleeps in whose bed, who hangs in whose squad. She skims interviews for clues about the celebs' natural shades. Sometimes this information has been entered into IMDb.com.

A fellow researcher leans in to introduce herself. "I'm a poet." The poet points to one of the copy editors and recounts how he wrote his first book during downtime at the office. The copy editor is an associate editor at a literary magazine called δ. He went to Harvard. The poet reveals that she is working on an essay about the adverb *there* as used in works of literature over the past 300 years. It is for a publication of some note. The poet has searched for *there* in Google's Ngram Viewer and is assessing a list of titles published between 1748 and 1772. The poet says, "This job is great because it leaves me plenty of time to work on what is important to me." In the corner, another researcher is editing the Wikipedia entry for Judy Chicago's *The Dinner Party*. Next to her a third researcher is taking a BuzzFeed quiz: "Swipe Through the Founding Fathers on Tinder and We'll Tell You if You're Destined to Die Alone." The woman watches long enough to see the researcher left-swipe George Washington. *The Magazine* provides dinner—on that particular night, pan-seared chicken with herb jus, crispy Brussels sprouts, farro and tangerine salad, braised kale, flourless chocolate cake for dessert—and if she stays past ten o'clock, she can take a car home on the company's dime.

"It's so flush," she tells a friend.

She struggles, at first, with the complexities of Los Angeles's geography. When Porsha is spotted "carbo loading" at Crustacean, she can be described as having eaten her spaghetti either "in Beverly Hills" or, if space is limited, "near LA." But never can she be said to have been "in LA," even though Beverly Hills is in LA County. When Sophia exits a popular grocery store "with Lifeway Kefir and a bouquet," she can be said to have been leaving a "Hollywood Bristol Farms" or an "LA Bristol Farms," Hollywood being in the City of LA.

She ranks the relative exclusivity of LA's various gated communities (in order: Beverly Park, Brentwood Country Estates, Beverly Ridge Estates, Mulholland Estates, and Bel Air Crest). She dedicates an afternoon to untangling the Kardashian empire. She checks a map of the family's collective real estate, roughly 85,000 square feet of interior space distributed throughout Westwood (City of LA), West Hollywood, Calabasas (LA County), and the gated community of Hidden Hills (LA County). She takes special note: Hidden Hills, itself a city, is also part of the City of Calabasas. This, it seems to her, is categorically impossible. Still, she resolves to accept what she cannot understand.

She feels a sense of satisfaction with the new subject mastery she has acquired. An editorial assistant stops in front of her desk: "Wanna vote?" The assistant holds up side-by-side images of Ryan Gosling, Matthew McConaughey, and Chris Hemsworth, with beards and without. The woman squints. She performs the act of scrutiny. "With, with, without," she replies. The assistant marks down the woman's responses on the back of the page.

When she tells people that she works as a fact-checker at *The Magazine*, they often seem perplexed. "What does *The Magazine* need fact-checkers for?" they say. Or, when they want to be clever, "But there aren't any facts!" Others are surprised that a research department at this particular genre of publication is so robust when at traditional news magazines, many such departments have been all but gutted.

"But there are facts," she will say. Fact: Kylie posted on Instagram, "I love being able to take care of myself and others at the same time." Chiwetel Ejiofor spells his name C-h-i-w-e-t-e-l E-j-i-o-f-o-r. Jessica Biel wore a Giambattista Valli Couture 5 embroidered silk dress with Giambattista Valli heels to the Tiffany & Co. Flagship Opening on the Champs-Élysées on June 10 in Paris. Mango's polyurethane Zip tote featuring twin top handles and a snap-button fastener costs $60 on mango.com.

This is for the most part what her job entails: checking the accuracy of personal names, brand names, dates, locations, ages, times, prices (always retail, never sale), descriptive nouns (is that a midi or a maxi?), quotes (word for word if published elsewhere), web addresses, times married, children born, months pregnant, film or TV show last starred in, charities founded, charities supported, town born in, properties owned, square footage occupied, brands loved, weight lost, clubs visited, bandmates undermined, restaurants dined in, husbands abandoned, boyfriends dumped, carats worn, weight gained, lawsuits pending, rivals avoiding, orphans adopted, islands visited, Oscars won, designers worn, products used, cleanses completed, weights lifted, Emmys won, nannies hired, nannies fired.

Before working at *The Magazine*, the woman worked at another, much smaller magazine. She took the job at *The Magazine* so she could afford to continue to work at the other magazine. Now she works at the other magazine in a lesser capacity than she once did. Maybe she'll find time to write. She is not the only one in the pit who works at another magazine. There are two other editors from the magazine the woman works at. There is also the book-writing copy editor from δ and four of his colleagues: they don't get paid for their work on δ, which is why they work at *The Magazine*. All the editors are also writers. One of the editors is a writer and a dancer.

Then there are the poets, four of them, give or take. Performance artists, three. Dancers, including the editor-writer, two. Novelists, two. There is one visual artist, one oral historian, and one comedian. And there is one politician, a Democrat. All of these pit workers take shifts at *The Magazine* to support whatever else they do and care about. Most of these pit workers are women. The others in the pit (also mostly women) are "career."

This makes *The Magazine*, unbeknownst to its publisher, editor in chief, editorial director, deputy editor, design director, entertainment director, senior editors, writers, reporters, and the rest of its staff, most of whom tend not to demonstrate much interest in the pit workers, a benevolent sponsor of the city's high-minded literary and arts communities.

A not insignificant number of the people in the pit went to Harvard or Princeton or Yale or Columbia, or leave because they will be going to Harvard or Princeton or Yale or Columbia.

The people who work in the pit come and go.

For every story she is assigned, her inbox fills with backup forwarded to her by the story's writer or editor. The backup consists mostly of a

152

compendium of emails sent and received over the past several days, or weeks, or months, compressed into a series of attachments that open into individual windows. Checking a two-hundred-word story can mean navigating between twelve open windows, each window an email thread of its own. The emails contain links to stories at other outlets and to Twitter and Instagram posts. They contain press releases from publicists: "Irena wears MeMee's Luxe Ready High-Rise Skinny Jeans in Vaunt while out shopping on Melrose Avenue on April 28." They feature publicists hawking client brands—"Hi love! Can you run something on the new Charcoal Pure$_2$Vitamine Elixir by EVETA? Celeb fans include Lillie, Alicia, and Christiana"—and publicists issuing official statements: "It is with heavy hearts that we move forward separately. This was a very difficult decision, but we have come to an amicable conclusion on all matters. Our primary concern remains the well-being of our children, and we ask with profound gratitude that you respect our family's privacy at this very sensitive time." Sometimes there are publicists acting as sources: "There really was no drama. They tried to make it work but found they were headed in separate directions. They are still friends, and it's all completely fine."

In other emails, eyewitnesses relay reports ("She had her hand on his chest and the biggest smile on her face"), as do friends of celebs offering inside information ("It's nothing serious. They're just having fun"). Reporters file transcribed interviews, which get mined repeatedly over the years for direct quotes, and conduct favors for sources: "Can we please plug Heather's new bridal line in an upcoming Hot & Stylin'? She's been so helpful with celeb weddings." From time to time, experts offer expert opinions: "Marianne Evans, Nutrition Health Consultant, ThinNow, tells *The Magazine*, 'The last ten pounds is the hardest to lose. This is because when there was famine we have stored the fat to make us survive. That's how the human race has survived all these years.'" The woman squeezes the fat on her abdomen and rolls it around in her hand.

The Democrat is sitting to her left. He is affixing mailing labels to a stack of what must be three hundred envelopes. An equal number of nondenominational holiday cards fan out toward her keyboard and mouse. "They're for my donors," he says. The Democrat is a Manhattan district leader. He knows a lot about rent stabilization and neighborhood bike lanes. She is excited to know someone who has his own Reddit AMA thread. He is running for state assembly. She thinks he might win.

Outside the conference room, people are congregating. The woman walks over. Dinner has arrived: Happy Valley Meatballs, Seasonal Upstate

Mac & Cheese, Braised Beef, Charred Chicken, Golden Beets with Quinoa and Orange, Grilled Organic Tofu, Kale with Dates and Granola. A line wraps around the conference room. The line begins to move. The woman is next in line. A certain editor who believes she is too important to stand in line walks in front of the woman. The editor grabs a plate and begins to fill it, taking the last scoop of Seasonal Upstate Mac & Cheese. The woman waits for her to finish.

After a shift one evening, she meets with two friends. The friends are older than she is. They own a limited-liability corporation together. Actually, no, they are married, but sometimes the woman thinks there may not be much difference. They have 2-year-old twins. The twins are home with a sitter. The wife relays how they may consider investing in a third child. The husband lifts his Negroni, and the ice cubes clatter against the glass.

A server stops by to drop off a trio of delicately plated fish tacos. The husband turns to his wife. "I want a picture. Move in closer together." The woman nudges closer to the wife. She smiles awkwardly. The flash goes off. "You two look great."

The couple finds her job humorous and possibly a little worrying. "Maybe you should aim a little higher?" the wife suggests with some concern. "Maybe," the woman says. The wife sips her white wine. The husband's ice cubes clank louder now.

In the photo department, the woman passes an enlarged pap shot of Suri Cruise in a pink princess dress and matching headband. Suri is standing inside FAO Schwarz, her face red and covered in tears. The photo is pinned to the wall.

The woman hears the photo editor in his office, where he speaks in tones that sound important. She lingers and pretends to consult a reference book called *Celebrity Pets*. The editor is complaining about the fact that more and more of the images in *The Magazine* first appeared on Instagram. The old agreement has been upended. The deal used to be: the magazines offered an audience, and the A-list celebrities provided access. Sometimes the magazines offered money—one paid $4.1 million for the first pictures of Shiloh Jolie-Pitt in 2006. Now the A-listers just post the pictures themselves. Conversely, the celebrities who first rose to stardom on Instagram or reality TV—the D-listers or Z-listers—are eager, desperate even, to be in *The Magazine* because it confers legitimacy on their

154

status as stars (hence the appearance of Tontitown, Arkansas, and other Middle American cities). All this affects readership, which affects ad sales, which is bad news for *The Magazine*'s business model.

The woman tries to look busy. She turns to the entry on "Hannah" (Britney Spears's teacup Yorkie) and then to "Mr. Butler" (Olivia Palermo's white Maltese terrier). Now the editor is complaining about celebrity bloggers. Some of the earliest bloggers have agreements with agency photographers from a time when no one thought the internet would matter. The bloggers pay next to nothing for agency images and post them online hours, sometimes minutes, after they were taken.

By the time *The Magazine* appears in the supermarket checkout aisle, everything inside is old news.

The office is decorated with a set of dry-mounted paparazzi shots of various celebrities circa 2003, a time capsule of a onetime A-list: Catherine, Beyoncé, Kate (pregnant with Ryder), Scarlett, Nicole, Carmen, Katie, Cameron, Drew, Jennifer, Demi. These most precious of artifacts have been enlarged to something approximating life size and hung throughout the office. On one wall, the photographs are arranged in tableau fashion, an opulent dreamscape where women in floor-length gowns and pinned updos hover above an expanse of plush red velvet. This wall is her favorite. In the background are ornamented iron railings and gilded plaster detailing. Men, if they appear at all, serve as accessories, second only to the women's handbags and shoes.

It strikes the woman as odd that *The Magazine* has not replaced these images with the newest, hottest, most popular, best-dressed stars. Not that she is complaining. On the contrary, she welcomes the opportunity to familiarize herself with an earlier era. She has always loved history. And the photos are office landmarks, useful for providing lost newcomers with directions. To get to the women's bathroom, make a left at Demi Moore, then hang a right at Carmen Electra.

The Magazine's compulsive quantification is most rigorous when accounting for the passage of time—how long a star has lived, how long a relationship has endured, how long a star takes to get back her pre-baby body. For example, a wedding: "The reality star's 7-year-old son, Bentley, served as 'mini best man,' says Taylor, 29. The boy escorted his sister, flower girl Jayde, 16 months, down the aisle while pulling 4-month-old

Maverick in a wagon. Then Maci, 25, strode to her love of four years." In three sentences, six different measures of time. The woman must verify the accuracy of these quantifications by ascertaining the past date in question, then calculating the difference in years or months or days between this past date and the day the issue goes to press.

This is one way *The Magazine* elicits self-comparison ("Sooo glad that's not my life") and judgment ("*What* is she doing?"), usually of the moral kind, without being explicit about it. Were the woman to know nothing else about Maci, she could glean from this paragraph alone that Maci and Taylor had two children before marriage, and that Maci's eldest child was born to a different father, possibly out of wedlock, when Maci was just 18.

She sits next to B., the comedian. B. relies on an online age calculator to determine the ages of celebrities. But the woman, having read elsewhere in *The Magazine* that "doing math in your head can help prevent memory loss" and having long been worried about the prospects for her own memory, decides she will begin a preventative regimen.

She spends a lot of time looking at faces—the subtle asymmetry of a pair of eyebrows, the curvature of a chin. *The Magazine's* address, its appeal to intimacy, pivots about the face. The face—it is corporeal, physical, but it is also something more. It is a kind of artifact, something assumed or worn. Reproduced as image in an infinite stream, the face slips easily into the realm of the idea. It comes to stand for a concept— a set of traits, a collection of credits and commodities.

So that when she looks at a picture of Kim, she reads: *Family-oriented businesswoman, hypersexualized (but not vulgar!), with a domestic streak and an agreeable air.* When she looks at a picture of Angelina, she sees: *Compassionate global citizen, a cosmopolitan humanitarian and philanthropreneur.* When she looks at a picture of Bethenny, she reads: *Brassy, joke-cracking, down-to-earth hustler who worked her way up from the bottom.* When she looks at a picture of Taylor, she sees: *Wholesome emblem of girl power projecting indie cool and mainstream cool.*

They are the faces of women who flaunt the legacies of feminism and at the same time pronounce its irrelevance. They are the faces of women whom America can understand.

The copy chief and her deputy ("the copy ladies") occupy two large cubicles adjacent to the pit. They have worked at *The Magazine* for a long

156

time. The deputy arrived after being laid off from a newsweekly around the time the phone stopped being just a phone. The Xerox machine is stationed immediately to their right, which means any number of persons pass their desks. The ladies, who are chatty and affable, also entertain themselves (and others) by talking to these passersby. They talk to each other, to the designer who sits on their left, to whomever is in earshot. Pronouncements of the latter kind tend to ridicule a celeb or to praise her. Jennifer Aniston is an abomination, as far as the chief is concerned; Ice-T's wife, Coco, can do no wrong. These allegiances are so passionately expressed that they dispense with any need for justification. That the copy ladies have seniority, maintain the highest of standards, and are unanimously beloved by staff lends these declarations a certain level of authority. Also, they are funny.

"What do you call those cutout holes in dresses?" says the copy chief. "Dress holes? Slut vents? 'J. Law stuns in slut vents at the *Hunger Games* premiere in LA'?"

When their voices shift from pointedly audible to a low murmur— and this happens a lot—it is impossible not to want to know what they're whispering. Gossip, its public performance, is tantalizing. Inevitably, the woman strains to hear.

The copy ladies both have curly hair that falls just below their chins. Hair management is another important topic of conversation. (This is of particular interest to the woman, who also has curly hair.) The chief feels her curls are too flat, while the deputy feels her curls are too stiff.

The woman goes to a party in a museum for the opening of a new exhibition. A friend has brought her along as a plus one. She takes three laps around the floor and retreats to the bathroom, to use the toilet but also to take a break. She lingers in the stall, reads email on her phone. Four distinct voices enter the room. She can see the intruders through the crack between the door and the doorframe. They are laughing, twentysomethings, three brunettes and one blonde. Their hair falls to the middle of their backs and lacks not for volume.

The blonde shimmers in silver sequin tulle mesh that matches her four-inch booties. The first brunette stuns in an embellished silk mini and Louboutins. The second brunette models a leather-belted crimson jersey frock and black combat-style boots. The third brunette channels old glamour in a black velvet midi with long sleeves and a plunging V back. They crowd before the mirror and plump their hair. They lean in close to inspect their eyeliner. They powder the shine on their foreheads, drag highlighter across their cheekbones, coat their lips in color. Then the photo shoot begins, phone by phone, their lithe limbs in various tangled arrangements of BFF. Minutes pass. "Did everyone get the shots they need?" one asks. They swipe through their camera rolls, each looking for the shot in which she looks better than the other three, even as the other three still look very good. It's a fine balance. "Yes," the others respond. "Let's go then." They leave. The woman flushes the toilet and heads toward the sink.

The researcher who swiped left on George Washington is yelling into her cell phone in a Slavic language while carrying on a Gchat conversation ("huh ? / aight / lmfao / you dirty / VBG"). The research chief walks by and drops off a spread for the woman to check: "That's *Amore*! George and Amal Say 'I Do.'" The woman sits down with her plate of food—Mediterranean vegetable medley, kebabs, mini spanakopitas, pita triangles—and a dribble of baba ghanoush falls from her fork and colors the left margin. She wipes it away. It leaves a translucent mark that glistens on the page. *E! News* is streaming from someone's desktop at a high volume and no one turns it off.

She dials the number to Consorzio Motoscafi Venezia. The time in Italy is 4:00 AM. A man answers:

"*Pronto!*"

There is static. It is hard to hear.

"Hi. Do you speak English? I'm trying to find out . . . How long does it take to travel from the Cipriani to the Àman Canal Grande Venice in one of your water taxis?"

"*Scusi?*"

"I'm, uh . . . I'm calling from, um, a magazine. In New York. To travel from the Cipriani to the Àman hotel—how long would that take? It's for . . . George and Amal are getting married."

"*Ah, si!* Twenty-five minutes. Maybe twenty-eight."

She thanks the man effusively and hangs up. She drafts an email:

> Hi! The water taxi "ferrying guests from Venice's Cipriani hotel up the Grand Canal to the luxury Àman Hotel" takes twenty-five minutes, approximately, and not "seven," as the story currently claims. Do you want me to change it?

158

Also the suites at the Àman, according to the hotel recep-
tionist I spoke with, begin at 1150 euro, or around $1500 US,
so I'll mark this change as well.

She presses send and signs off. She watches a researcher and a new copy
editor flirt in the nearby conference room, an enormous croquembouche
towering between, them. A few of the profiteroles are missing, and the
pyramid looks a little lopsided, or so it seems from her vantage. A man
walks in wearing dark jeans, a button-down, and what looks to be a minia-
ture desktop computer passing for a watch: a visitor from *TechRadar*, the
tech and gadget magazine that occupies the other end of the office. Oc-
casionally the woman will go out of her way to use the Xerox closer to
TechRadar when she needs a reminder of the ongoing masculinity crisis.
Also, they often have snacks. The man eyes the croquembouche, circles
it once, warily. From his back pocket he pulls out a bushcraft knife and
removes it from its sheath. He jabs the knife into one of the cream-filled
puffs of choux pastry and frees it from its glazed edifice. He deposits the
profiterole into his mouth.

*   *   *

One day, as the woman is verifying the contents of Aja's bag ("'I have
a lot of stuff,' the star says of her Madewell leather tote"), she is inter-
rupted by the sounds of laughter and squealing delight. A small crowd
gathers in the area where the editors and writers sit. The woman
wanders toward them. Justin Bieber has sent over a special gift: twelve(!)
bite-size cupcakes with white and pink frosting. *The Magazine* has
favorably reviewed his new album, and he has sent a thank-you gift.
The cupcakes are gone before the woman can push her way to the
front.

Kim Kardashian joins snapchat. Kendall joins soon after, and Kourtney
soon after that. But Kylie was first, a full year ahead of her sisters. Within
weeks, the woman, who was surprised to find that Snapchat hadn't al-
ready gone the way of Friendster, finds that it is now a place where news
unfolds. For instance: "Kylie Raids Mom Kris's Fridge and Pantry While
Kris Is Out of Town." She asks B. if B. can explain Snapchat to her. B.
shows the woman how to set up an account and to record and caption a
video. B. says, "Now send me a snap." The woman cannot think of any-
thing to send.

She looks over at the copy ladies, who are whispering. She decides to walk over and pretend to make a Xerox. She hears the chief say, "They're saying as many as fifteen people."

The backup for a story arrives in her inbox. The story is about an ongoing feud between Alexa and Alana, two women on a reality TV show that documents how difficult it is to have a husband with a lot of money.

A source close to Alexa says:

> Alexa and Alana had a big fight when they filmed on Tuesday night over politics. Alexa is a huge Hillary supporter (she tweets every day about how great Hillary is and how horrible Trump is) and Alana is supporting Trump. Alana turned her back to Alexa at one point and refused to acknowledge her. Alexa interjected and said, "Let's keep politics out of this." Alexa doesn't like talking about it on camera. But Alana wouldn't let it go. She kept picking a fight with Alexa, calling Hillary a two-faced liar and telling Alexa that she was voting for a sociopath, and that if Alexa were voting for Hillary then Alexa must also be a sociopath.

The woman looks up. Three men with long, scraggly beards and black T-shirts are being led through the office by the editor in charge of entertainment. The men wear bandanas. "And here is where our writers sit," he says. He moves his outstretched arm in a sweeping motion. The apples of his cheeks are plump and the skin so taut it is shiny. She is pretty sure he has just had Botox injections. "And here is our fashion department," the editor says as he leads them down a corridor to the easternmost end of the office. The editor does not stop to acknowledge the pit. The copy ladies are speaking so as to be heard: "Why is *Duck Dynasty* here?"

> At that point Alexa tried to leave the room but Alana was like, "What, are you too scared to fight it out like a real man?" And then Alana threw her glass of wine onto Alexa (rosé, luckily). At this point, Alexa was furious and was like, "No. You. Didn't" She was soaked in wine but she got up in Alana's face and

160

screamed, "Take it back!" Then Alana pushed Alexa into the marble countertop and pulled her hair with one hand while with the other she grabbed a California roll from a nearby platter and mashed it into Alexa's forehead. Alexa fought hard to keep her cool. She felt like she was going to explode. "You bitch!" she said. Then Alicia and Ariana got up from the couch and came over and dragged Alexa out of the room.

Alexa is really upset about all this. She doesn't understand why Alana is always so mean to her. Alexa thought that by now Alana would be over the fact that Alexa is engaged to Alana's ex-husband and also that Alexa sued Alana for sole ownership of the company they started together. Alana didn't even like her husband when they were married. She was always spending his money on fancy lingerie but then not even wearing it for him, instead going out to the club and drinking and coming home in the early hours of the morning. She is a raging alcoholic. Her life is so sad and pathetic. No one likes her. Also Alexa feels like Alicia and Ariana always take Alana's side. She thinks they are always protecting her. Alexa is hurt by this. She wants them to show support for her once in a while too because she really likes them and wants them all to be as close as they once were. But Alexa won't stand for Alana's drama. She's not a

The woman finds the quote she is looking for. Sometimes it is painfully obvious when the subject of a story is also the source. The giveaway: the details are too extensive, the interior monologue too rich. The words of one of the career copy editors, who tends to speak at decibels appropriate for an auditorium, carry over from across the pit: "Are they talking about his NARB?" The woman must google what this means.

The managing editor has made changes to the schedule to get more done in less time. The number of freelancers on each shift has decreased. Dinner, formerly provided two to three times a week, is now provided once. For the woman, this means fewer hours of work, more meals to pay for, and more time to spend in her shitty apartment.

One day, twelve staffers are laid off. The mood in the office is solemn. A younger editor cries softly as she packs her belongings into a box. A younger writer consoles her. The managing editor is one of the staffers who is let go. The woman has never heard of a magazine that does not have a managing editor.

She turns to B. "What's a 'Glam Squad'"? B., who is watching stand-up on YouTube, takes off her headphones. "Is it, like, an official thing? Should I capitalize it?" B. is relentlessly kind and patient. "No," she says. The woman is glad to know her.

Dinner arrives: rigatoni in cream sauce with shelled green peas (taste frozen), penne with red sauce, eggplant Parmesan, lentil salad with parsley and lemon, tossed green salad, i.e., iceberg lettuce topped with sliced carrots, cucumber chunks, and canned chickpeas. No dessert.

The woman makes a mistake. She gets an email:

> Hey, do you know why Evan Styles's age went to print as 43 when he is only 36? I really hope you did not confuse him with Evan Styles the drummer. Did you? Styles is pissed. I need you to explain how this happened.

The woman gleans from the tone of the email and the thread that precedes it—Styles's publicist expressing how furious her client is to have been aged seven years—that she may lose her job.

The woman has only a vague recollection of the item. Who is Evan Styles? She's always been bad with names. There is Michelle Williams (*Dawson's Creek*) and Michelle Williams (*Destiny's Child*). There is Vanessa Williams (*Ugly Betty*) and Vanessa Williams (*Melrose Place*). There is Jason Alexander (*Seinfeld*) and Jason Alexander (Britney Spears's fifty-five-hour marriage). There is Dylan McDermott, Dermot Mulroney, and Dean McDermott. There is Minka Kelly and Moira Kelly, Mira Sorvino and Mena Suvari. There is Benoît David and David Benoit, Brie Larson and Alison Brie, Olivia Munn and Olivia Wilde, Channing Tatum and Tatum O'Neal, Seth McFarland and Todd McFarlane, Emma Watson and Emily Watson, Bill Paxton and Bill Pullman, Simon Callow and Simon Cowell, Colin Firth and Colin Farrell. There is Taylor Lautner and there is Tyler Posey.

Apparently there is also Evan Styles, drummer number three in a '90s emo band, and Evan Styles, a four-time contestant on various competitive reality TV shows. The woman is able to show that the internet is also confused about Evan Styles: a reliable and oft-relied-on source—reliable because it is maintained by publicists—lists the known birth date of Styles the drummer in the entry for Styles the reality contestant. *The Magazine* blames the error on the reality TV contestant's publicist. The woman keeps her job.

It is late when the woman returns home. She was at the office working on a story about the Sister Wives clan ("Kody, 47, secretly divorced Meri, 44, last fall and legally wed fourth wife Robyn, 36, months later"). She opens the door to her apartment and the lights are on. "Oh. Hi. I thought you were out," says her upstairs neighbor, the one with the alarm clock. The neighbor is leaning against the kitchen counter, reading an issue of *The Magazine* from the woman's bathroom. The washing machine rumbles. There is a lump of dirty clothes on her kitchen table. "I've got eight minutes left on this load. Do you mind if I wait for it to run through so I can throw it in the dryer?"

"OK," the woman says.

The neighbor turns the page. "Ugh. I can't believe Rob is dating Kylie's boyfriend's baby mama. That's a little distasteful, don't you think?"

"I guess," the woman says. "But, you know—it must be hard to be Rob. I think, like, if he's found someone who makes him happy, he should pursue it."

"Nothing is objectively hard about that guy's life," the neighbor says. The spin cycle picks up speed.

Tonight she is assigned a timeline. It tells the story of the Hiddleswift Romance. Taylor and Calvin break up. Reveals a source: "Calvin never appreciated her." Two weeks later, Taylor and Tom appear on the cover of the *Sun*, lips locked on a beach in Cape Cod. They drink espresso late at night and share a cream puff shaped like a swan. They clasp hands. Tom is "so, so smart and talented." Taylor is "over the moon." Taylor's friend Ruby defends their romance in a lengthy post on Instagram. Tom meets Taylor's parents, Taylor meets Tom's. Tom and Taylor holiday in Rome and head to the Vatican in a helicopter (#blessed). They stay in the 861-square-foot Picasso Suite at the five-star Hotel de Russie. Tom makes sure there are fresh flowers every morning. They eat breakfast on the terrace. "It was insanely romantic!" says a friend. Back in LA they have the "fight that nearly split them." Then they split for real. Two and a half months, start to finish, and it's over.

The story is well documented, each scene verifiable with photographic evidence and various articles online. A flurry of emails arrives in her inbox, a trail of reports from "pals," "onlookers," "insiders," and random people who tweeted about seeing the Hiddleswift descend on their local café. They furnish the story with conjecture. They offer their opinions.

When dinner appears, she pauses briefly. Pizza again. No one waits in line. As she walks over to the conference room, she passes the copy ladies, who are whispering. The chief says, "I think it could happen any day now." The woman grabs a slice with mushrooms, adds red-pepper flakes and garlic salt, and brings it back to her desk.

Were Tom and Taylor truly in love or just performing love? It is not the woman's job to know, to confirm or deny one or the other. Whether their affair was organic or a story line dreamed up by their respective PR teams is of little consequence, as far as fact-checking is concerned.

What matters, for her purposes, is that even if Taylor and Tom were not truly in love, they had still performed love for the cameras. Love or no love, there remains the *fact* of the performance. And in the fact of the performance, there is something one can call "truth," i.e., the performance happened.

If there is a fiction in the story, it does not originate in *The Magazine*.

Today no one is working. They are too busy talking. An email is circulating with a link to a local tabloid. The woman finds the story online: "Apollo Is Poised to Sell *The Magazine*, Layoffs Imminent." Reliable industry sources say the parent company is in trouble. Attached to *The Magazine* is a hefty debt now more than a decade old. There is no way to pay off this debt, given recent financial troubles within the company— the result of a plagiarism scandal at Apollo's *Sports Today* for which the company is being sued—so Apollo has decided to unload its largest liability, the debt-laden *Magazine*. There are several prospective buyers, insiders say. The woman googles to see if there are any other reports. She finds a longer article in a national newspaper: "Celeb Rag *The Magazine* Is Said to Have Suitor, in Late Stage Conversations." She skims through the opening paragraphs, then begins to read more closely.

The Magazine was born as a monthly to Apollo Media, whose publisher and editorial director, Augustus Apollo, had seen previous success with *Sports Today*, the sports-focused weekly he still oversees along with *TechRadar, Epoch, Wine Now, Look,* and *Luxury*. Apollo began *The Magazine* to compete with the thriving *Women & Men*, whose editorial mandate was to provide profiles of "exceptional individuals."

While *The Magazine* began by publishing lengthy profiles accompanied by studio photographs, its house style transformed in 2002 when Apollo sold half of *The Magazine's* shares to media conglomerate Triumph for $40 million. Under its newly appointed editor in chief, Emily Stern, *The Magazine* inverted the ratio of words to images and upped the number of unsanctioned paparazzi photographs chronicling celebrity life "off camera." Stern introduced the wildly popular "Stars So Ordinary" and zealously covered the reality shows that aired on networks owned by Triumph.

The Magazine's circulation and single-copy sales vastly increased, and its success inspired copycat magazines *Wow, OMG!, Whispers,* and, finally, the former standard-bearer, *Women & Men,* which co-opted many of its features.

In 2003, Apollo spent $280 million to buy back Triumph's share in *The Magazine*—seven times the original investment Nearly fifteen years later, the company still makes significant debt payments on the loan it took out to finance the purchase.

According to the source, who spoke on the condition of anonymity because the deal talks are private, Apollo Media is negotiating a price of more than $100 million. The source also said that as part of the deal, more than one hundred of the 150 staffers could be laid off. The talks are in progress, and a deal could still fail. The spokeswoman for Apollo declined to comment.

Two years after being diagnosed with lupus, Selena enters a treatment facility for "anxiety, panic attacks, and depression." Three months into her liaison with NBA pro Tristan, Khloé tests the depths of their romance. Three years after they both graduated from college, one of the fact-checking dancers performs in Paris while the other begins a history PhD at Harvard. Ten months into her jail sentence, Teresa remains

165

zen thanks to yoga. Two and a half years after his first book was published, the book-writing copy editor is finishing a second. One year after landing a spot in the Victoria's Secret Fashion Show, Gigi wins Spike TV's Our New Girlfriend award. Five years after their first visit as a married couple, the royals return to Canada for an eight-day stay. Seven months after running for state assembly, the Democrat is still a fact-checker. A year and a half after #nannygate2015, Ben is "fantastic," having just come out of rehab. Eleven years into their love, Liev and Naomi announce they will live separate lives. Twelve months after the poet completes her essay on *there*, she publishes her third chapbook. Hours after Blac Chyna delivers daughter Dream, Rob posts, "Today was amazing :) I am so lucky!!" Fifty years into being a vegetarian, Christie shares a recipe for a kale salad. Eight months after taking an improv class at Upright Citizens Brigade, B. starts her own podcast; it is available on iTunes. Seventy-two hours after getting "sucker punched in the gut" by wife Angelina, Brad is still "extremely upset." Nineteen months into her job at *The Magazine*, the woman still works at the other magazine (and her third job, as a proofreader) and calculates she may have just enough money, finally, to move.

The woman passes the conference room on her way back from the water dispenser. B. is inside. "Dinner is here," she says. On the table are two boxes of SpiruMEGA Protein++ All-in-One Meal Bars in assorted flavors. The woman recognizes the boxes. Earlier in the day they were out on the giveaway table at the tech magazine, alongside galleys of discarded books. Next to the boxes is a stack of paper plates. On top of the plates are a few misshapen napkins. Some plastic forks and knives are strewn across the table.

A handful of writers enter the room. "I'm famished!" one says. The anticipation on their faces quickly turns. "Seriously?" The writers stare at the table. The woman takes a bar.

Arriving early from a dentist appointment, the woman enters the office and walks toward the pit. The cubicle area is empty. So is the pit. She sees a few staffers from *TechRadar* as well as *Sports Today* and *Look*, but no one from *The Magazine*. Strange, she thinks. I must be the first one here. She turns on a computer and waits for it to load.

She opens her email. There is one new message, dated the day before yesterday. It is from the publisher, sent brand-wide. The subject line is "Farewell."

Dear All,

By now you may have heard that today I sold *The Magazine* to a major competitor. As part of the deal, the competitor will not be taking any of the current staff. If you are reading this email, you no longer have a job.

   The Magazine was once (and still is) a highly lucrative brand for me, and I am sorry to have to say goodbye to such a profitable venture.

   I wish all of you the best of luck. I do understand how dire it is out there; that's why I had to sell.

Yours sincerely,
Augustus Apollo

On the desk to her left is a SpiruMEGA bar in Peanut ChocoCream. She reaches over and picks it up. Then she grabs a copy of *The Magazine* from the stack next to her computer and flops it open: "The Girls Turn on Caitlyn." She tears open the meal-bar wrapper and takes a bite. She leans back in her chair, puts one foot on the desk, and turns the page.

Nominated by n + 1
Dominica Phetteplace

SECRETS DEEP
IN TIGER FORESTS

fiction by POE BALLANTINE

from THE SUN

Next door, in a run-down daiquiri-pink house with bed-sheets instead of curtains on the windows, lived Whitey Carr, who loved to pound me every Sunday with his tiny fists. My mother said I had to feel sorry for Whitey because he'd lost his mom, and his brother, Raja, had come back crazy from the war. Whitey was thirteen, a year older than I was, and my mother said his younger sister, Queenie, was already a tart. A tart sounded good to me. They sold them from outdoor stands in Balboa Park at the Old Globe Theatre, where my mother and father took me to see Shakespeare plays. Lemon tarts were the best.

Whitey's mom, Mrs. Carr, had died the year before. She'd been a pasty, nervous person who rarely left the house. When she did, she was always clutching a stack of books to her chest—headed off, my father explained, to college. She was going to get her medical degree and become a doctor, an unheard-of achievement in my working-class neighborhood.

The last time I remembered seeing her alive was when Boyd Johnson, who lived across the street from us, shouted to the whole neighborhood that she'd gotten sick on the sidewalk. We all dashed over and examined the orange splash with yellow bits that made the voices in my head whirl up in a crescendo of singing astronauts. Mrs. Carr was rushing into her pink house, leaning over, clutching her books. I tried to read the puddle as a fortuneteller might read a palm. Everything to me translated into colors and words spelled out in typeface in my head, l-i-k-e t-h-i-s. There were letters to be deciphered in the mess, I was sure, though I could not quite make them out.

168

Mr. Carr, Whitey's father, worked in one of the defense and aeronautics factories that ran for miles along San Diego Bay and made rockets, bombs, and planes for the war against communism. He was tall with a large, square head like a giant robot, and as pale as if he'd eaten a heaping plate of bad oysters. Whitey told me his dad had leukemia. Neither Whitey nor I knew what leukemia was, so I asked my schoolteacher dad, who said it was a cellular disease and that Mr. Carr probably did not have long to live. It occurred to me then that his wife was studying to become a doctor to try to cure him.

I never learned how Mrs. Carr died. Not long after, her oldest daughter, Mavis, who was fifteen, got "PG." That was the word Queenie used. Though she was younger than I was, Queenie had to explain many unfamiliar terms to me, such as q-u-e-e-r and s-c-r-e-w. PG meant p-r-e-g-n-a-n-t, which meant two people had "done it." (Done what?) Mavis dropped out of high school, got big, and had a ginger-haired baby that all the kids on the block said belonged to Mr. Carr, who was not long for this world.

Raja had gone away to war a serious boy in a uniform, but when he came back, he was no longer Raja. He was more like a luminous bird who tipped his head this way and that and stared down at you with his inscrutable dark eyes while he crowed and clapped his hands and tried to communicate with noises that sounded very much like the jumbled chorus of alien voices in my head.

It was fun to talk to Raja. I could tell by his wide and sunny soul that he would never hurt me. He would insist that you take anything he might have in his hand, including money. And whatever you said—whether you made a joke or were completely in earnest—he would laugh as if it were the wittiest thing ever.

Raja was the only happy-all-the-time person I'd ever seen. Clowns were not to be trusted. Comedians often described pain. Newscasters and scientists smoked cigarettes and shook their heads gravely as they foretold the end. Raja made me feel so good I thought he had learned some secret deep in the tiger-haunted forests on the other side of the world. I was always disappointed when one of his brothers or sisters would come to coax him back into the house.

Jay down the street had also returned from the war a different person. Before he'd left, he'd been a cool teenager with rolled-up sleeves who said he was going to kill him some g-o-o-k-s, but now that he was back, the coolness was gone, and he no longer seemed to remember any gooks. He glared at his neighbors, wiped his neck with a soiled handkerchief, and flexed the muscles in his jaw. He wore green coveralls to work on old cars in his driveway, his black hair slicked back with what looked like the same grease he used on the engines. He scowled at the kids who played near his house, and if a ball went into his yard, he'd turn red and shout, "This shit has got to come to a *grinding* halt!" My father said to stay away from Jay; he was a hairsbreadth away from going b-e-r-s-e-r-k.

I figured I would be sent off to war in a few years, and I wondered if I would come back crazy like Raja, or angry with a squirming jaw like Jay, or legless like Mike Juarez on the next block over, or dead in a box like Larry Brentwood three blocks away. I pictured my house with dark windows like Larry's and a sad mother inside.

Queenie said they were looking for a place to put Raja, because he was too cuckoo for them to take care of. He walked in his sleep at night, and you'd wake to find him standing over your bed with a j-o-k-e-r f-a-c-e, or he would scream and scream, awake or asleep, and no one could stop him. They were filling out the paperwork, though it was a long wait, since there were so many others like him home from the war who needed help.

I tried to imagine what had happened to Raja and Jay in their jungle battles with the commies and the gooks. Though my father, who opposed the war, had shown Vietnam to me on a map, it remained in my mind not a country but a crack through which hippies and drugs and assassinations and taunting voices poured. Raja had turned the war into a song and trilled and warbled it and looked deep into me, as if waiting patiently for me to understand.

There were three pine trees between our house and the Carr house next door. The pines had once been Christmas trees and had grown so fast and tall after we'd planted them that we had stopped buying live trees. But they were easy to climb, with a canopy so thick people couldn't see you inside unless they looked closely. Raja liked to sit cross-legged in the shade between these trees. I found him there one day chuckling to himself. He seemed at peace, as if he had left everything bad behind in the war or on the helicopter ride home. I sat down with him, and he smiled and made a cooing sound that bubbled like a flowing mountain spring. I had learned that I didn't have to try to have a conversation with him. I could just say, "Hello, how are you today?" and Raja would take care of the rest.

He would speak again one day, I thought. Until then, I'd enjoy seeing fewer spelled words ticking across the top of my head. A stray cat I'd named Kiki came along and began to wind herself around Raja's legs. He was delighted and petted the cat, and Kiki nestled into him and closed her eyes, purring.

Whitey showed up a few minutes later, a lit cigarette hanging from the corner of his mouth, and he sat down with us. He was so gaunt and blue-lipped and stringy-haired, it was hard to believe he could beat up just about any kid on our street. Whitey usually beat me up on Sunday afternoons. It was quick work. He had asthma, though, and later that evening he might come over to borrow my inhaler. But no matter what day it was, he never beat me up in the presence of Raja.

I asked Whitey to tell a joke, and he did, and I laughed loudly to show how much I appreciated his sense of humor, in the hope that one day he would call off his campaign against me. Raja laughed, too. His eyes danced, and he looked perplexed, as if for a moment he'd caught a glimpse of his old self and all the bad things he'd left behind.

Whitey liked to make his older brother laugh, but often in ways that seemed cruel to me. For instance, that day he said the word s-h-o-e-h-o-r-n over and over, and Raja doubled over laughing until he was gasping for air. Whitey kept saying "shoehorn" until I feared that Raja would suffocate. Finally Whitey slapped his brother on the back and said, "Come on, Raj. We gotta go inside for dinner."

I watched them walk away together and smelled dinner cooking all up and down the block: sauerkraut and roasts and Cakes and frying onions and chickens. African-village chanting started up in my head like a holiday by the river. The villagers sounded happy today, and I could hear the water slapping the shore. The sun slanted over the rooftops and sifted through the pines, which gave up the scent of medicine and vanilla wafers, and that, plus the good feeling that Raja had brought, summoned the memory of many Christmases past, so warm and far away.

Coming back from the 7-Eleven one cool, gray autumn Saturday with two grape suckers in my pocket and a bottle of Bubble Up in my hand, I saw Raja ride by in the back of a white car. The car had a wire grate between the front seat and the back. Raja was smiling. I waved at him, and he waved back.

171

When I got home, Queenie told me Raja had been taken north to a place called Vacaville, a f-u-n-n-y f-a-r-m for crazy veterans. Queenie had only recently grown breasts, and they wiggled as she talked. She said he'd taken a h-o-r-s-e p-i-l-l of mescaline, and he'd flipped. "Mescaline" sounded Mexican to me. Queenie made it sound as if the Mexican horse pill had been the cause of all his troubles. I wondered if he'd taken it before, during, or after the war.

There had been a song on the radio a year or so earlier called "They're Coming to Take Me Away, Ha-Haaa!" I owned the 45. The tune started up in my head now, and honky-tonk voices sang along, and I tapped my knee to the beat as Queenie wiggled her breasts and I thought about the funny farm at Vacaville and Raja cheering up all the inmates with his bird laugh as the sun angled in through the big stained-glass windows. Ha-ha.

At dinner that night my father said he had seen Raja taken away. The men in suits had come. They had stayed awhile. Raja had bid his family a tender farewell. He'd been smiling when they put him in the car. "That was a good boy," my father said. "What a shame."

"What's a horse pill?" I asked.

"A big pill," my father said, "like you'd give to a horse."

"And mescaline?"

"A drug from a cactus. Stay away from it."

That wouldn't be hard, I thought. I had trouble swallowing even small pills, and there was nothing tempting about cactus.

Everything made sense now: a pill you'd give to a horse, full of a drug from a cactus, taken after coming home from a war against gooks, final destination Vacaville, which sounded like a vacation or a vacancy in a motel, and through the window of that motel I could see a host of distorted and hellish faces and old peasant women with mangled teeth who yacked and yelled at me without a sound.

Nominated by Krista Bremer

BARBIE CHANG WANTS TO BE SOMEONE

by VICTORIA CHANG

from BARBIE CHANG (COPPER CANYON PRESS)

Barbie Chang wants to be someone
    special to no longer

have wet hair to no longer be spectral
    to be a spectacle Barbie

Chang wants to befriend the Academy
    which is the Circle

wants to eat meat with the Academy
    wants to share with the

cads who think there is a door to the
    Academy wants the key to

the Academy door wants to give grants
    and awards for words

but she never knew that life was about
    unraveling not raveling

that a tear is only a tear after it has
    fallen her parents never

called in favors never knew there was an
    Academy never learned

alchemy Barbie Chang wants to forgive
    the Academy for its

cattiness wants to hate the Academy
    and its Circle and their

certainty each year she buys climbing
    shoes to go up the tree

she tries but can't climb then sells them
    on Craigslist she gets a

new pair each year on her wish list but
    can't get past the first five

feet she stays on the street rolls herself
    flat so she can become

the street feel the bare feet of people
    pressing her deeper into

the earth there are aspirations of worth
    everywhere a stipple of

ants around the cement crack frozen
    from bug spray as if

they had meant to take the shape
    of an iris

Nominated by Copper Canyon Press,
Shelley Wong

174

A FISH IN THE TREE

by JOHN LANDRETTI

from ORION

One morning I saw a stick in a tree. Curved and broken, it lay across a
forked bough about six feet out from the trunk. The buds had yet to
open so I could see the whole of the stick, black against a red sky. The
tree itself, a young ash, stood in a park near my home. Late that winter
I'd walked past it a dozen times. But I'd never noticed the stick. And this
was no slender twig. It was a hefty, light-blocking chunk cracked off from
the interior. No one around here would have called it a *log* exactly,
though there are places on Earth where it would have enjoyed that sta-
tus and, thus appreciated, perished long ago under a soup pot. In any
case, it looked so exposed and awkward among its more delicate neigh-
bors that I was surprised I'd ever missed it. How had it come to so un-
likely a perch? Had a child hurled it up from below, or had it fallen from
above, storm-dropped like a toad? Whatever the means, it looked so
utterly settled into place that I assumed it must have been there a long
time. Perhaps the child, if it were a child, was just now lighting a ciga-
rette and merging into traffic. Perhaps the wind, if it were a wind, was
just now buffeting the cliffs of El Capitan. I let the possibilities come.
I added the stick to my life. There is just no end of things to wake up to.

Earlier that winter, I'd begun walking again. Each morning at dawn I
went out for a turn through the neighborhood. It was welcome disrup-
tion to a life lived mainly under rooftops. And, as much, spiritual exer-
cise. Considered spiritually such walks are less an act of leisure or fitness
than they are a practice in seeing. They restore an elusive perspective,
the effect of which recalls a favorite cartoon: beneath a curbside view of
a tin can and discarded tire, one reads, "Milky Way, close up." I often

175

imagine my walks as two circles of concurrent experiences. One circle is external and sensuous—footfalls and birdsong, rain—the physical journey; the other circle is internal and imaginal—ponderings and conjectures, dreamscapes—the figurative journey. Now and then these two experiential circles overlap, forming a mandorla. In their slender overlay I occasionally encounter an interfusion of both worlds: the imaginal strikingly present in common things. In a state forest I once came upon a pallid balloon, which must have sunk from the sky, and was then standing on its string deep in a shaded ravine, or the indigo dragonfly near a marshy rail bed, who had floated in among the cattails to alight just so on the tipped equator of a bobber. Each such outward encounter enters my awareness as a private symbol in the public sphere, one whose revelations are insistently partial and whose emanations lift like vapors from the lowlands of my inner walk. As years pass, these interfusions abide in memory. Whenever I consider my place in the vastness of space and time, they appear. They are the iconography of my quiet hours.

So, of course, the next day at sunrise I was back in the park. Once again, approaching the ash, I looked up at the stick. Its shape seemed to suggest something, how it appeared snouted at one end while toward the rear it presented a pair of knots, lobed and ventral, and I realized it looked like a fish. A fish in a tree! Amused, I slowed my walking and regarded it some more. The illusion brought to mind a pretty word for these tricks of the eye, *pareidolia*. From the Greek, it means "beside the thing you're looking at." When we discover a face in cracked paint or in the froth of our cappuccino, we are having a moment of pareidolia. While the illusion was charming enough, its discovery brought some disappointment as well, for I figured that the verisimilitude probably exhausted everything the stick had to offer.

A memory of an early *Peanuts* strip challenged this presumption. From a grassy hilltop, Charlie Brown is pleased to find a ducky in the clouds while Linus observes the stoning of Saint Phillip. Schultz's humor celebrates the quality of imagination and the complex way that imagination can texture life's sensuous side. Clearly, for Linus, those clouds had drifted beyond verisimilitude and into a mandorla of his own. In my own case, it seemed there was more in the tree than I first thought. Indeed, I got the feeling that the stick—now a fish—was not about to be dispatched by my categorization of it. As I passed under the ash, the silence above seemed nearly reproachful. The opprobrium had an oddly compelling quality to it, as if a cold little planet were pulling at my breast. I continued my walk, watching the lobed fins turn behind me

176

and then disappear among the branches. Pareidolia, it seemed, would not serve to explain the fish. Indeed, as I left the park the term had acquired new meaning: no more a category of optical hustle, but rather the name for a distracted third daughter in a fairytale, as in, *Once upon a time, young Pareidolia went into the forest and was accosted by a fish in a tree.*

Next morning, back in the park. Stars overhead, orange horizon; all the eastern branches looked like the wreckage of cathedral windows. I stopped just west of the fish. It was, as ever, at fat rest on its perch. The opprobrium was gone, replaced by a vacancy that invited consideration. I pondered the fish. Its skin appeared black with white fleckings that I guessed were fungi. I decided this fish was male. His circumstances seemed to reveal his sex, this being stuck in a tree for so long. A female, I guessed, would have detected the whereabouts of her interior and soon disappeared into it. But this fish seemed to lack such recourse, or refused to engage it, and so kept to that branch, day after day, resolutely finning his predicament. But if a male, what kind? Mythical, surely—an Ouroborus spread flat, or perhaps a Leviathan, a small one, who'd made a very unfortunate turn in the deep. Yet his silhouette, so factually piscine, refuted that deduction. *My form*, he seemed to say, *swims in taxonomies.* I tried a flying fish, a rainbow trout. But neither endured. His settled contours, his shadowed skin, suggested a creature foreign to sunny waters. He had that brooding somnolence one associates with bottom-feeders. A bullhead, then. Or a dogfish. At last a carp came to mind. Perhaps a venerable koi well into its second century. That appealed, at least aesthetically, this locating him somewhere between a Basho haiku and an Escher print. At any rate, if I lacked precision in pinpointing his species, I assured myself I'd gotten close enough. My prima materia, after all, was just a stick.

A few evenings later we had a late-season snowfall. All night the snow quietly loosed itself in the street lights. Next morning I got up earlier than usual. The snow was still falling, aimless and unhurried. In the park it coated the trails like poured cream. I paused before the ash. Heavy flakes wobbled to the birth-wrinkled leaves where they lit and went clear. Some touched the fish, cooling him, and made a place for snow to pile. Standing in that misplaced Christmas air, I was whelmed by an insight that turned tumblers in the deepest part of me. Indeed, it changed everything between me and the fish. I saw now that my strange companion was no carp at all. His home was not some pond among raked pebbles, but rather an ocean whose edges had long ago wandered away to form other oceans. I stepped from the trail into the fresh snow and smote my gloves together.

"A coelacanth!" I said.

When I was five years old, I received a starter set of the evocatively titled, *The Golden Book Encyclopedia of Natural Science*. I adored those four colorful books. Since my parents never added to the collection, I focused all of my attention on the contents of that introductory quartet; as a result I entered elementary school with an impressive factual grasp of the natural world that ended abruptly at the letter D. In the C book, of course, was the coelacanth. I learned of its discovery off the coast of Africa—a fish believed to have gone to fossil 65 million years ago. Photographs show a beautiful fish in an otherworldly way; the coelacanth's fringed body is flecked with scores of tiny white galaxies, as if graced with a tattoo of the Local Supercluster. The fisherman who dumped the creature from his nets had no idea what he was looking at. The article reported that as he reached to touch it, the coelacanth snapped at his fingers. That detail, so insignificant among the primary scientific facts, retains a rightness that has stayed with me for years. Things from the deep, it seems to suggest, scorn presumption. I've long admired the coelacanth, its ken having lived on with such mild unconcern despite our dismal inferences and bleak pronouncements. One cannot help but recall Mark Twain's "Reports of my death have been greatly exaggerated." Since my boyhood, the coelacanth has existed in the back of my mind as a compelling but elusive symbol of the contrary impression, a shadowy familiar from weakly lit depths. In that capacity he has been both encouraging and disturbing. In the coelacanth I find a flaw-wizened teacher full of secrets, foil to the death that lies in complete understandings. As a teacher myself, and one bent on clarity, I have not always appreciated his methods.

The following week brought April Fools'. The snow turned crisp and slipped away. Each morning I went out to walk. As always, I had to hike a ways—up the long street and then back into the park—before reaching the fish. The ash bordered one of the quieter trails in a section called AC-U3, or *Acorn Park, Upper Woodland*. To get there, I first had to pass through two small wetlands (AC-W10 and W5). All this I'd gleaned from a municipal report that detailed plans to restore the native flora. To that end, the City had coded the park's ecosystems and then flagged the invasives for removal. Indeed, last fall the crews had started their work:

where once my entrance to AC-U3 presented an illusion of wilderness, it now was a sparse woodland. The dark arches of undergrowth were gone, replaced by a view of taillights exchanging themselves in front of the Flameburger diner. But the crews had yet to cross the marsh that split Section AC-U3 into two woodlands. The young ash was at the marsh's far side, amid hardwoods still tangled in buckthorn and honeysuckle.

As April went by, the coelacanth appeared as ever on his branch. He grew quite ordinary. Some mornings he looked just like a stick. Now and then I'd pause to regard him, but most often I just nodded and kept on my way. While I would have liked to deepen our acquaintance, I understood that whatever might come, if anything, would have to come from the coelacanth. My part was simply to show up each morning and allow myself to see more in the air than a piece of wood. Perhaps that sounds easier than it was. But I'd fallen from practice. As mentioned, it had been a while since I'd done this sort of walking. The peculiar effort, to look for fish in trees, put me in mind once more of Charles Schultz, of Linus, who waits all Halloween night in a pumpkin patch for a conjuring only he believes in. Pathos ends that story when grumpy Lucy finds him shivering at dawn and shepherds him home. It is the genius of Schultz to end Linus's night in disappointment, but to leave the larger story open; we receive no indication that Linus rejects what has inspired him. We cannot say how his ardor will evolve, or what future guises his inspiration may take. What captivates Linus in such an insistent way—a Great Pumpkin!—includes a trajectory that others may ridicule, but which nonetheless remains an enchantment born of his integrity. It is a kind of love poem written just for him. That, anyway, is what I read into Linus's story. I admire the courage of this scraggly headed character. Linus has allowed himself to reckon strangely. He suffers his own originality.

When I finally got into elementary school I discovered that I was, as they say, a slow learner. Concerning natural science—as well as math and all the rest—I could not keep pace with my classmates. In an effort to compensate, I disrupted discussions and lessons with much anxious hand-raising and panicky questions. This behavior invited an alternate set of lessons on the playground. Overall, those dispiriting memories proved formative; years later, as a young teacher working with adults in poverty, I decided that the kindest thing I could do for my students, especially those burdened with lousy learning experiences, was to make a practice of answering their questions with exceptional patience and clarity. During that phase of my career I saw little value in the parsimonious disclosure of sages. After all, if one understands what a learner wants, then why not provide a clear answer at the level the question is asked? For many years, such solicitude seemed to me an essential characteristic of any good teacher. But, as I eventually learned, deft explication only serves to a point. Such efforts do little to nurture the curiosity of that Linus who sits wondering in the heart of any student. That insight came back to me one morning on the trail when I paused to gaze up at the coelacanth. By then it was late April and the young leaves had greened in around him. I imagined those same leaves in October, spotted and yellow. In their falling, they would surpass everything he knew. Come January he'd still be there, a stick on a branch at thirty below. The best lessons, he seemed to say, occur without explanation.

As the days passed, the coelacanth came more frequently into my thoughts. In the shower, I soaked my hair and considered him. At stop signs, I peered up through the windshield as if from the underside of water. My contemplations brought to mind a poem by Rumi, "The Phrasing Must Change." The poem offers the example of a woman who is master of her own originality, her strange reckoning. Each day, Zuleika sees her divine Joseph, her beloved, in the common things around her, in trembling branches and early light, in coriander seeds and softened candle wax. If she comments on any of it, she sweetens her phrases with inner meanings known only to her: when she says *the clouds seem to be moving against the wind, the willow has new leaves, the furniture needs dusting,* "it's Joseph's touch she means." When she's thirsty, "his name is a sherbet." At my office, I hung the poem about Zuleika above my desk where I could look at it while I ate my lunch. On the art of engaging a fish in a tree, Zuleika offered what seemed an instructive approach. The lesson lay not only in her ability to locate God in things like saffron and onion skins but also in the daily practice she made of courting her own discretion. Zuleika walks in a lush mandorla.

One morning in early May I went out overdressed for the weather. When I got to the ash, I stopped to knot my jacket at my waist. Looking skyward, I said to myself, *It's another orange dawn.* I said, *The curved branch is black against the glow.* My words went up among the twigs, and then I shared a little silence with the coelacanth. As I was regarding the shape of him a robin came to perch near his head. For an instant, as I gazed at both, I could not say which was more real than the other: the creature so labeled and understood to be a robin, *Turdus migratorius,* or the chunk of wood hove up from the duff (or dropped from above) and now a coelacanth. Though the moment lasted just a second, I marveled to experience such a startling collapse of categories, and in the instant that followed scrambled to preserve the sensation much the way a person struggles to remember a dream. As the perspective dissolved, restoring the familiar divisions, I realized that the coelacanth had made his move.

Or not. Surely the fact of a robin forever trumps the metaphor of a fish. Straightaway I heard a man's voice from those educational films of the 1950s: "This is a tree. Sometimes a log or other debris may become snared in its branches. These can create *interesting* effects. The ash, meanwhile, is a hard wood with many useful commercial properties." As I considered the robin I was forced to acknowledge its irrefutably sensible features—the signature eye rings and striped throat, the famous breast—any of which could be verified across a thousand robins. But what evidence was there for the coelacanth? I suppose I could wrest his crude likeness from the tree. I suppose I could lay the stick in a tray and examine every deciduous cell beneath a lighted lens. But despite my diligence, I would not discover a single scale of the coelacanth's numinous flesh. Alternatively, I could probe the heartwood, looking for a fossilized fishbone, for proof positive of the historical coelacanth. I might do one or the other for several hundred years. Either way, I'd be left with a piece of wood and an ocean of anxiety should I mistake so literal a thing for a fish that swims elsewhere.

My brief shift in perspective got me to wondering once more: what lies behind the artful surface, the spiritual intimation, that so beguiles our effort to net it in words? Precisely what is it, this fish that swims elsewhere? At evening I loitered at my window and watched the clouds. Have you ever gone looking? Lots of people have. Our literature is rich with elegant responses, each in its own way ending with ellipses. Over the next week or so, I leafed through a few books of reputable searchers— Plato's *Republic* and King David's Psalms, the fairy tale about the girl who looks east of the sun and west of the moon, the lectures on metaphysics by the good-natured William James, and the wild verses of Emily Dickinson, written as she rowed the seas in Eden. The writer Jorge Luis Borges scented it on a late Argentine afternoon. In a poem called "The Other Tiger," he introduces a creature of his own invention, a big cat "made of symbols and of shadows . . . scraps remembered from encyclopedias." He goes on to set this particular tiger apart from the physical animal, "the tiger of the vertebrae" pacing in Bengal or Sumatra. Then, most interestingly, he identifies a third tiger, a creature comparable to the first or second, but neither one nor the other. He calls his search for it "unreasonable," yet he keeps looking for this third tiger, which, he concludes, "is not in this poem." I think Borges would equate the fish that swims elsewhere with this third tiger. If he were to offer anything more, I imagine he would continue along the lines of his *via negative*, his negative way, pointing at all the places where a third coelacanth is not up in the ash tree, for example, or anywhere in this essay. The nuance of Borges's subject—cleaved thin to a vexing translucence—reminds me of a passage in the Gospel of John, the verse in which Jesus confounds the literal-minded Nicodemus by saying that the breath of the spirit is wind but not actual wind. I sometimes wonder what kind of Christianity we would now have had Jesus added that there is a third wind as well, and it's nowhere in Scripture.

If you say to a black man in America, "Good to see you," a sizable number will reply, "Good to be seen." That the compliment is not reciprocated is a nod to *Invisible Man* as well as a compensatory blessing for one who has gone unnoticed by whites for three centuries. Good to be seen, indeed. I suspect that the private symbols that come to us of their own accord, so illumined in imagination, so marginalized by an insistent literal-mindedness, might say as much. As well, such marginalization may also be the result of a less adversarial disposition, let us say one born of a bookish preoccupation with traditional symbols—our circles and griffins, ankhs, winged gates, and stars—the sheer variety of which would demand years to canvas and appreciate. Consider a man so distracted, who one morning steps into the world and spots a fish in the tree. Amazed, he exclaims, "Good to see you!" and the fish, if it replies at all, says, "Good to be seen."

When I search my past for the fish that swims elsewhere, I do not see much of him at all. He is a mingy haunter. Beyond *The Golden Book Encyclopedia of Natural Science*, I locate him exactly twice, and neither appearance is as apparent as his visitation in the tree. In each memory, he appears wholly suffused in a feeling, one whose signature complexity— profoundly unsettling, darkly assuring—enabled me to recognize him decades later in that late-spring snowfall. The first of these recollections occurred during a visit to a natural history museum. I was about fourteen. What linger are neither the Neanderthals nor the dinosaurs, but rather an unremarkable case that displayed a pair of tusk-shaped shellfish washed up on a beach. The broad window offered little else to look at. Painted on the back wall was a featureless sea. It receded to a pink horizon that may have been dawn but could have been dusk and has since become for me Wallace Stevens's "evening all afternoon." The moment was the Early Devonian, the Age of Fishes. What haunted me then was the implication, so casually presented, of time's cool democracy. Two shellfish on a deserted beach forty million years ago: the quality of that archaic moment was no different than any recent Saturday when I lay in bed reading, say, *The Golden Book Encyclopedia of Natural Science,* my two legs flung out on the sheets. As I stared at those shellacked tusks, I was awakened to a formative thought: whatever I hoped to preserve of my identity—the whole shebang of this John Landretti—was going to have to make peace with a process far more committed to anonymity.

Years later, one January evening, I had my second acquaintance while sitting alone in a Catholic church. Catholicism was the faith of my child-hood. As I'd come into my thirties, I found myself increasingly drawn away from its communal rituals and creeds and toward the solitude of its mystical backwaters. I read the Catholic mystics, Saint Theresa of Ávila, Meister Eckhart, and others, each of them wonderfully complex, each of whom struggled to reconcile the originality of their visions with the or-thodoxy of their time. Eckhart was tried for heresy, as well as Saint The-resa's mentor, the famous visionary Saint John of the Cross. While they each proved constant to their vows, I lacked such fidelity and was slowly thinking my way out of a religion. On that winter night, I had in mind something a priest had recently told me, that all religions were valid but that Catholicism was God's most perfect expression of that validity. I'd heard as much from various Evangelicals, each referring to a trans-lation of the Word that in its alleged perfection subordinated or annulled all others. In the dark of that evening, as I weighed these competing per-spectives, I noticed how peacefully the stained glass windows had given up their stories. From the vantage of memory, I might say that those dark shards lay against the night like the scales of stygian fish. As I lingered in the candle flicker, the great Catholic symbols of my youth—the Crucifix and Virgin, the Byzantine angels—all seemed to abandon their parochial unity and become the many faces of God. They touched my body with a single silence whose depth seemed equal to eternity: anonymous guest, that silence, amid the pews or out on the quiet seas, in all the midnight rooms where people lay wondering; it required no name, and none was given.

Symbols, especially a dream symbol, frustrate the modern mind. We are confounded by what the religious historian Mircea Eliade calls their "multivalence," their "speculative audacity." One night we dream a snake made of light or a tree filled with edible roses and if we dwell on either our purpose is not to let the image infuse us with its veiled and kindly disruptions but rather to figure the thing out, to turn its evocative weirdness into a manageable idea. Meister Eckhart nicely captures the ruin in this tendency: "The least creaturely idea," he says, "is as big as God. Why? Because it will keep God out of you entirely . . . it is when the idea is gone that God gets in." The dream image, the symbol that inexplicably haunts your waking hours—a tiger in your study or the Great Pumpkin, the fish in a tree (both the one in the ash and the other on Golgotha)—all elude the closure of ideas. They fail as done deals. Yet each offers the psyche a "speculative audacity" big enough for God to get in.

In a Zeitgeist so increasingly hostile to complexity and irresolution, so inflected with political and religious fundamentalism, how best to court the complex symbols that inhabit our lives? Apt counsel steers me toward a religion for which I feel some affinity. Within that community I might find guidance through its images and prayers, locate, as it were, a synchronistic Buddha or Christ in my coelacanth, and so follow an established path into what is finally ineffable. Or I might risk a more secular route, read a lot of books and poetry, sit with a candle in the woods on rainy nights and feel the inexplicable affection that haunts the shadows of the earth. In *The Interior Castle,* her field guide to the soul, Theresa of Ávila writes, "The important thing is not to think much but to love much; and so do that which best stirs you to love." To gauge the authentic power of a creative work—and a personal symbol is, if anything, a creative work—Vladimir Nabokov insists that a person should not respond to the impressions of mind or heart alone, but rather to a combination of both which he says occurs in the spine. With characteristic acerbity, he advises, "Rely on the sudden erection of your small dorsal hairs. Do not drag in Freud at this point. All the rest depends on personal talent." While Nabokov's subject is the assessment of great literature, I find his exhortation applies equally well to assessing the self's native mysteries; it reminds me to trust what wisdom I have and offers a practical way to distinguish an authentic symbol, one whose source is the unknown, from those allegorical toadies that now and then pop up to serve the ego while leaving one's dorsal hairs flat.

In a song called "The Knuckleball Suite," Peter Mulvey describes a summer evening in a small town. It might be somewhere in Iowa. His images offer up rain not long after a ballgame and pink clouds tall on the horizon. Mulvey describes a few people in this town. Four verses in, we meet Sally:

Sally's barefoot in the backyard calling out to that star above
  the pines
Sally's barefoot in the backyard calling out to that star above
  the pines
And for once that star answers, it says, "Sal, you are the wine,
  you are the wine"

I find it appropriate that the first line of the verse repeats itself, for it's clear that Sally has been calling out to that star for some time. She's made a practice of it. She has a relationship with it. And, as it happens, that evening—who can say why?—she is requited. I am fond of Sally. In a way, I regard her as one of my teachers. She reminds me of a Zuleika nearer to my own time and place, her bare feet well planted in the clover of a midwestern evening.

Of the power of questions, and of the difficult art of teaching, the critic Northrop Frye once observed that the reason great educators present far fewer answers than questions—more than the students themselves ask— is that merely providing an answer shuts down a student's process of self-exploration and deeper inquiry. As Frye points out, "Unless something is kept in reserve suggesting the possibility of better and fuller questions, the student's mental advance is blocked." As a teacher, Frye's goal was always to split the atom of presumptuous thought. My initial zeal to preempt such questioning, to deploy clarity in order to spare students the anxiety of their ignorance, delayed my appreciation of this tact. As an older teacher now, I recognize the wisdom in Frye's approach. Indeed, I've come to fancy that this "keeping something in reserve" is the instructive method of the divine universe itself; though we may wish it otherwise, God doesn't much condescend to hand out answers at the level we ask them. To do so, one might say, would be to make a tautology of enlightenment. This is why mystical writing is so trenchantly allusive; it precedes and follows the wisdom of Emily Dickinson by telling it "slant." My own way to engage the obliquity is to make a practice of those morning walks, to show up and keen myself to the nearly imperceptible subtleties of divine requital.

❖   ❖   ❖

Early one evening in July I walked to the park. It had been a couple of weeks since my last visit, as I'd been out of town with my family—a summer trip to the ocean. Near my usual entrance, the municipal workers had laid fresh timber for a bridge through the muck. When I crossed into Section AC-U3, I saw that the crews had finally crossed the small marsh. In the far woods, they'd cleared the invasives. Here and there, back in the duff, lay heaps of dropped brush. While the ash looked the same as ever, the forked bough no longer held the coelacanth. His disappearance, so unexpected, took me aback. As I stood there looking at his old perch, my loneliness surprised me. I wandered over to one of the brush heaps and poked around. At a second pile I poked some more. I felt like a grubber, selecting logs and tossing them aside. At last I stopped. For a few minutes, I stood gazing at the second pile. By degrees, I felt myself overtaken by that serene breathing which so often settles on us when we stare into something inconclusive and beautiful—like a small radiance of midges seeking one another in evening light. Above me, among the canopies, a jet was speeding along at altitude. Its contrail was vivid, a puffery as straight and purposeful as a professor's chalk line. Back a ways, in the air, the line was already coming apart; curls and points, a foreign calligraphy.

Nominated by Orion

ALL POLITICS

fiction by JESSICA BURSTEIN

from RARITAN

for Professor James Franco

Bob Dylan paid off all my credit cards. Bob Dylan finished revising my book. Bob Dylan gave me a foot massage. Bob Dylan explained Max Horkheimer and Theodor Adorno's "The Culture Industry: Enlightenment as Mass Deception" to me, and then he taught my graduate seminar on it. Then Bob Dylan told the horrible professor in my department to go fuck himself. Bob Dylan remembers the birthdays of all my nieces. Bob Dylan is a prince. But this isn't about Bob Dylan.

I wouldn't be writing this down, but it's been the best year of my life. I'm not ordinarily autobiographical but I've got some time now that several of my more taxing obligations have been met, and what with the massages I feel pretty relaxed. Bob comes over about twice a week. We talk a little—not about the Nobel thing—we're totally past that. But now that I know all about England I explained Brexit and Philip Larkin, and last week I read him a little Barbara Pym, but mostly we just kind of groove, and then he asks me if I want to take off my shoes, and I do. I'm not stupid.

Near as I can figure it, J. M. Coetzee must have given him my number. I was at Oxford earlier this year, for a fellowship they award to professors from West Texas teaching in the Pacific Northwest, or as we call it now, the Upper Left Coast. I was really happy to get the fellowship and, I don't deny it, surprised. I had proposed a series of talks on quote installation art, mostly earthworks. I'm really very interested in dirt. It turns out that dirt is big, big like you wouldn't believe. Anyhoo,

I had written up a proposal on the frontier and the art that started popping up sort of close to El Paso, along with the little pueblo walls, sort of indigenous speed bumps—and apparently Johnny Depp was on the committee and is really into native stuff, as in Native American—he's part Cherokee—and they loved it. Given, shall we say, recent events, Johnny Depp is looking into indigenous cultures again. (He really does take them seriously: have you seen that Sauvage commercial? Total dirt. Check it out.) Anyway I was so happy. You can't plan this stuff. It's kismet, I swear.

It was getting grim on the home front. Don't get me wrong. Seattle is a pretty calm-inducing place, what with the rain and everyone staying in to watch movies, and even with this *Fifty Shades of Grey* cultural renaissance and the new new postfeminism, Washington state is cool again. Ever since they had that big new show on Kurt Cobain at the city's main museum, you could tell Kurt Cobain jokes—"What was the last thing going through Kurt Cobain's mind?" "I don't know; what?" "His *teeth*!"— and people would laugh again. Even so, the problems with the state legislature never went away, and in these days of budgetary brouhaha, the university was getting it in the neck. And taking it, since basically American professors are spineless. By basically I mean unequivocally. Humanities professors are the worst. Or as we like to term it, the best.

This all means that there were a lot of budget cuts here at my university, things like taking out the phone lines, restricting our access to the copy machines (professors still love to copy things), shutting down the library, merging the humanities with the new Diversity in Diversity Zion Protocols Center, and moving the department's coffee machine into the main office where you had to put a dollar in a tiny little plastic cup that's in front of it every time you poured yourself a cup of joe, so the timing could not have been better. My passport had been revoked, along with everyone else's, but they paid to reverse mine, so off I went to Oxford. It's in England. Long flight.

Oxford was neat. They put me up at an apartment, or, as they say there, a "flat," and I pretty much stayed there most of the time, when I wasn't in the huge office they'd also given me. It had a fireplace! I couldn't find the switch, but they put them in weird places over there. Or I went to the gym. I gave a couple of lectures on American art and dirt, and they seemed to like that, but the thing is I mostly went to the gym, when I wasn't drinking, because they gave me, and I quote, an entertainment budget too, but I'll get back to that because I really want to talk about the gym.

The Oxford gym was like the gyms I'd been to back home, because I always went to the gyms where the black guys worked out and the equipment was shit. Not the black guys who work at the university; the other black guys. The other black guys were usually handsome, and always built, or, as they say in England, "sporty." I'm not black. I'm five feet tall and not black, so the most I could hope for was a sort of Dorothy-Parker-meets-distant-cousin-of-Spike-Lee thing, but I am a bulldog when it comes to the gym, so I was there more than a lot and when I got my hair dyed red, one of the guys asked if I was part black and when I said, "No, just a Jew," he said, "You must be, a little," and I said, "I do not demur," so I got the name Red DeMur. Later I found out Red was short for Redbone, so there you go.

In the United States I did whatever was the latest brand of cardio that was going for a goodly while. Even the shit gyms had treadmills, and then they would have step machines, mostly the kind for pussies, excuse me, but really they are. The good ones are the ones with real stairs, but they draw a lot of electrical current and shit gyms mostly aren't set up for that, so you'd get the elliptical trainers, if you were really wasting time, the ones with paddles for your feet. If there were women at the gym, they'd be on those, frantically paddling up and down, gripping the spindly little handrails like they were drowning, and for all the good it was doing they might as well be chewing. Chewing tapioca. So I would either run or do a stationary bike, which I know is sad, but the point is to mix things up. You don't want to plateau. Plateauing is death. And if I was really in the mood I would do the rowing machines, because no matter how old a rowing machine is, my friend, it will kick your sad ass.

So when I went to Oxford the shit gym didn't faze me whatsoever. I ran every day on the treadmill, either after I was done with a lecture or after I was done drinking the night before and trying to get rid of a hangover. I always ran for the same amount of time: fifty-five minutes. An hour is just too depressing. The treadmills were circa 1990s, circa Kurt Cobain, really old and without any video, with the silly LED displays, and the red button with the thick black cord and plastic gripper you were supposed to snap onto your shirt, attached for when you have a heart attack, fall off the treadmill, and die, but not because you have a knee injury because thanks to the safety cord the machine would have already stopped and you couldn't sue. I never used the cord. I would come in with my iPhone, wearing crappy gym shorts and my "Study Naked (Vote Drunk)" T-shirt or the sleeveless tee from the North Side of

189

Chicago Matadors Boxing Club or the really tight black shirt a lawyer friend of mine had sent me showing a cartoon woman blowing her brains out with a hand gun, where the blood turns into butterflies. Like the college student said in my Taylor Swift colloquium—we were analyzing the "Out of the Woods" video—it's very symbolic. The blood-butterflies shirt, I mean.

At the gym I always listened to the same thing: Madonna through the ages to get me through the first twenty minutes; then Ariana Grande and a little A-WA; then I'd take it further back with Haim and "Town Called Malice" because Paul Weller snapping—I assume it's Paul Weller snapping—makes for excellent pacing; and then some Coldplay because I was in England and call me old-fashioned but no matter how good that Goop Exfoliant Instant Face Melting crème is, I remain steadfast in the belief that Gwyneth Paltrow deserves to die; and then I'd coast with the Bey and perk it up with The Clash, which I realize Joe Strummer would have hated, but "Complete Control" is excellent for the "I'd open up the back door but they'd get run out again" trochees to run to.

I always used the same machine, because it was England and no one touches the treadmills. There was a row of five at the back of the room with cardio equipment, two on the left, then a space so you could walk up the aisle to the front, and three on the right. I always ran on the machine on the very far left. After a few weeks I noticed that once I'd be running for about twenty minutes, someone would start in on the machine to my right, and go for a while, then pace down and go away. I never paid any attention, because running is running. Then I'd get off, in the noncolloquial sense, and go do some free weights. Oxford is nice and all, but the fact is when you're at a shit gym it's a waste of time to try to use what our flabby betters used to call "the Universal Machine" (that's humanism for you). Universal Machines are those machines with a lot of different stations, as in of the Cross; each has its own little muscular target—the theory is you can just circulate around this contraption and work your triceps and then your lats and then your biceps—but my point is if the treadmills were from the 1990s, the Universal Machines were from the 1890s, or more like medieval, which is way earlier, so you just suck it up and go to where the free weights are, sit down on a bench with a dumbbell (I so won't go there) and try to get some honest work done before you go home and think about dirt or poetry or whatever it is you're paid to contemplate in a scholarly fashion. I never bother with leg exercises; that's what running is for, even though Oxford seems to pride itself on these abduction/adduction thigh machines, the etymology of which is almost as obscene as what you look like when you're on them, scissoring your legs together or—better—heaving them apart, while you're being stared at by some chemist-don with a skin condition. One difference between shit American gyms and shit Oxford gyms is that Americans grunt; the Brits just endure, quietly. I will give them that.

Now, one night I was at a sherry hour with the Master of one of the colleges—yes, they call them that, or provost, or president, or warden, or rector, or sheriff, depending on the college. A Romanticist I knew there said, "They call them just about everything except King of Thieves." Romanticists can be what you call wry.

So I was at this sherry hour, right before the Harry Potter High Table, and this tall red-haired dude said to me, "Have we met before?" I said no, but he wouldn't let it go: "Are you *certain*? I'm *certain* we've met. Did you *attend* Yale?" So I said, "Just off the coast of Yale, in Texas," and he laughed this squeaky laugh and said, "I saw you *exercising* at the gym yesterday, next to my favorite South African novelist," and I said, "Oh, I thought Nadine Gordimer was dead."

The Master of the College had appeared—they're excellent at circulating—and was all too happy to hasten to elaborate, which was fine, because there was no mention of Yale after that and I heard all about African novelists, more power to them, but the red-haired guy kept chipping in and he was not what you call wry. Not wry at all, but he made sure to sit next to me at High Table and kept correcting the Latin of the poor student schmuck who said the prayer or blessing or hex or whatever it is they say before you actually get to eat. Said schmuck was clearly petrified, and I felt for her, but what can you do? I'd learned enough to know you don't clap. So she crawled back to the table of minions from which she'd issued, and we of High Table set about being pandered to. Once you got past the empathy with the willfully oppressed (no one could mistake an Oxford student for someone in actual need of empathy), it can be, I have to say, pretty great in terms of the alcohol and, if not the actual quality of the food, its quantity. On the other hand, as I've mentioned, my unrequested red-haired dinner date wasn't going anywhere and if you can't clap, you certainly can't ask to switch seats. So then I heard all about Coetzee. Australia. What is it with that place? Whatever. And now he was at Oxford for a little bit, and giving a lecture or something, and all anyone knew is he worked out like a demon at the gym, mostly on the recumbent bicycles, which in America would have meant all the people who cared about fiction or nonfiction or whatever it is the guy does flooded the gym but it was Oxford, and so they didn't. My red-haired informant was, he said, an exception by virtue of the fact (and I hope you haven't eaten) that he'd had a groin injury and was on the abduction/adduction machine, he said, *constantly.* I'll spare you the rest.

Fortunately one of the rules at Oxford High Table is you can't sit next to the same person when you're having your dessert alcohol as when you are having your dinner alcohol, or as it is nonrespectively known, dinner and dessert. Actual dessert they call pudding in England, but what they call dessert is the event. I don't get it either. After High Table you troop off into a different room, shedding vicars as you go, and then you sit down again, and have pudding at dessert, and more alcohol. For dessert I was next to a vicious biographer of a vicious classicist, and we talked about being vicious. Now this was time well spent. Turns out you have to pass the alcohol counterclockwise, even if the person who wants it is directly to your left. I still can't figure out if that's democratic or not.

The next week I was having my cigarette out back of the shit gym as per usual and this skinny old guy came up to me and said in a weird accent, "You shouldn't be smoking," and I said, "Exactly, chum." He didn't go away, and he didn't take the Silk Cut I offered him, but we kept talking. I told him the Kurt Cobain joke and he laughed. Then he asked me who Kurt Cobain was, so I told him. Well, it turns out this was Coetzee. Wouldn't you know. I had absorbed from the earlier High Table Learnathon that the guy doesn't talk about his work, not that I blame him, so we chatted about epilepsy and Sibelius, and the next week we had a few drinks at one of the local pubs, the Devastating Preamble, I think it was. Sweet guy, and I don't really get why they say he's so quiet, because I absolutely could not shut him up about Ford Madox Ford. To his credit he was completely uninterested in dirt, but he showed up at one of my talks anyway. Sweet.

Well, like I said, I had an entertainment budget, and for all his sweetness, Mr. Nobel Prize for Literature turned out to be pretty tightfisted when it came to lucre, so we ended up doing a fair amount of drinking chez my office. We'd sit in front of the aforementioned fireplace and talk about this and that—taxidermy, how to get a tattoo removed, the sexual anatomy of angels, that non-trans girl model with no legs who runs marathons—but banter aside all this meant that I was the one who was supplying the alcohol. Not that it bothered me, really, but it's the principle of the thing and finally I told him he had to pony up something or other. So then he'd bring along snacks. But it wasn't as easy as it sounds. First he said there wasn't a convenient place to shop, so I walked him over to a mom-and-pop, pointed him to the snacks aisle, and said I'd wait for him at the front by the cash register, which in Oxford is basically an abacus. Whilst doing so, I bought a lottery ticket (stay tuned on that), and after about thirty minutes—the guy is like *totally* indecisive—he ambled up with some Cheese Doodles and Twizzlers. "Two snacks?" I said; "your cup runneth the fuck over." He started to put back the Cheese Doodles but I stopped him. So he shelled out and we went back to my office and I hauled out a South African chardonnay to reward the guy. They're not bad, actually, those wines; you'd be surprised. Anyway, the neural pathway was laid, and for a month after that he'd show up with Cheese Doodles and Twizzlers.

My last major contribution to literature was getting Coetzee to switch to Red Vines—told him they were fat free and that sold him. Every calorie counts, buddy. My very words. Done and dusted; Red Vines forever and always. So in toto we got along just fine for the rest of the year, and then he went back to Australia or wherever, and finally I closed up shop and came back home to America.

But not before I won the lottery. The ticket I'd bought from the abacus-wielder turned out to be a winner, so not only was I fit as the veritable fiddle by the time I left England, I was rich as whoever that guy is—I don't care; I was as rich as me. The taxes threatened to prove something of a liability, but after spending time at Oxford, I knew the difference between barristers and solicitors, hired me one of each, and flew away a wealthy woman. Like I said, a good year.

So I set up a charity in East Tennessee with the money I'd won. I really like James Agee and had read that his childhood home was torn down a long time ago in Knoxville, and I had a real-estate agent look for a lot in the area and she found one, so I bought a house that we converted to a charity for pregnant battered women and called it The Boo Radley Home for the Recurrently Distracted, and later someone told me that that was Harper Lee and Alabama not James Agee and Tennessee, but Monroeville is a little busy nowadays with the Zaha Hadid Foundation doing the new Watchman Watchtower rippling over the Marina Abramović Moral Compass with Breakaway Guiltine.

(I ran into Marina at the NeoHum Consortium—we're getting with the federal program and rebranding the Arts and Sciences as The New Humilities. Now that she's president of the MLA Marina is post-post-post-sugar. Oh, and that whole Rice Counting Center—since you don't actually eat the rice, you're also post-carb. And entre nous, I have never seen softer looking skin. I swear, the woman glows. Oh, and she's working on a sunscreen. Big bucks.)

But Monroeville, Knoxville, whatever: my pregnant battered women didn't care, and what with these new tax breaks the federal government gives a minus-hoot. Or as the French say, sans.

At the BRHRD opening, Alan Cumming and Tim Roth showed up—don't ask me why—but it was great because as it happens the three of us really like vodka martinis—well, to be frank, Tim Roth will drink anything—and we'd ended up in the basement with a bunch of throw pillows and shit-faced. Tim Roth had given a spontaneous little talk about how it was wrong to batter women, especially pregnant women, and all the pregnant battered women really dug him, and I left him chatting with them to get the lights set up for Alan Cummings spontaneous number, since he said he really wanted to sing "They Call Me Naughty Lola" and "Whatever Lola Wants": actually he said in that cute Scottish accent, "I want to sing every last song with Lola in it," and he was fabulous. Fab-u-lous. He didn't know the Kinks song, can you believe it, but I helped him out there. Anyway Tim Roth came up behind me at one point and whispered into my ear, "Give me tequila or give me or death," and I went, "Tequila mockingbird," as my private homage to Ms. Lee (RIP) and we went downstairs to where I keep the wet bar, and Alan followed us there—he's got a little crush on Tim, I think—and thus the vodka martinis.

First we made the martinis, and then we drank the martinis and then Alan said it was not humanly possible to sing the theme song from *Bewitched* right after the theme song from *I Dream of Jeannie*—Du-*duh*, *duh*-duh-*duh*-duh-*duh*; versus Duh *duh*, Duh *duh*, Duh-*duh*-Duh-duh-duh *duh*—which turns out to be surprisingly true, especially after martinis. Tim Roth ended up sleeping over. Not what you think; he just passed out, pretty much in the middle of reading aloud from a new translation I was working on of André Breton's *L'Amour fou* that I keep down in the basement and had left on top of the Kingsley Amis. I'm calling it *Crazy Love* instead of *Mad Love* and it turns out Tim Roth is really into the French surrealists and Van Morrison, and got excited when I told him about my translation, which I was doing as part of an application to a Patsy Cline Foundation for the Applied Arts fellowship, even though he doesn't like country-western music. So like I said all the pregnant battered women really liked him, and he was sweet to all of them, too, both Alan and Tim were really sweet to them and it was a great success, the whole thing. Turns out the place is actually making money. There's a lot of money in pregnancy nowadays. I found this great South African accountant who'd relocated to Australia (got the name from you know who), and all I do is sit back and let the ducats roll in.

I wrote a book last week, and sent it off to a publisher, a real one. I am totally done with those university presses: "Oh, yes, colored post-it notes will do just fine; why bother to pay me?" So it turns out that the real publishers really liked my book. Well, more than really liked it. The editor called me on my iHole—I am so over the iPad—and said they wanted it pronto. Jean-Louis Trintignant, Grimes, and Michael Ignatieff are coming over tomorrow to suggest some revisions. I am a really big fan of Eric Rohmer, so this should all be very interesting.

Nominated by Raritan

MY HOBBY NEEDED
A HOBBY

by DANA ROESER

from SENECA REVIEW

My hobby needed a hobby you know how you get a dog and you
    have a dog
and then Kurt says we need to get the dog a puppy the dog needs
    somebody

to play with her to teach and then you have a baby bossy baby needs
    a little
baby and littler baby and then like you have a thing that you don't
    get paid

any money for it's like an art you do it for the love of it sooner or later
though it gets you know it starts to make you nervous you get
    caught up

in politics it doesn't matter that there's not any money it's prestige
rankings and who's up and who's down so that thing you were
    calling this

vocation the thing you did for art's sake you know you didn't want
to get paid for because you loved it so much it was like you loved

the work it felt like play I mean you looked up after several hours
you were so absorbed you didn't even know where the time went
    then it

gets onerous because this currency is being traded and you know it
    is starting
to get heavy it starts to be as heavy as coins people even use
    expressions

like coin of the realm my stock went up or my stock went down or
    somebody
or other didn't use their political capital all that kind of crap so
    now

your hobby your art needs a hobby that feels completely free and
    doesn't
have anything to do with the buying and selling attaching your
    worth to some

chips or tokens markers or whatever so you've got to get a new free
    thing
where you get completely absorbed and work feels like play well so
    I found

one my pet the pet little sister of my first pet is some horses well
    then I get
to the stable forget about time waste like five hours at a pop after a
    few years

start wearing a watch but am not going to worry yet so I am
    washing off
Berto the horse that I am helping to pay for but still it feels pretty
    free I don't

go to horse shows I'm like sixty-three years old people consider it a
    miracle
that I'm even staying on which I'm barely doing my trainer and I
    spend half

the time gossiping to the point where we decide we probably have
    to go
to lunch so I am washing Berto off and Berto is starting to squirm
    a little about

his pet out in the pasture he can just make out through the fence I
     can tell
he has a pet the horses all have buddies his pet is Vinny the donkey
     and when

I went to get him before my lesson he was chasing the red horses
     because
he thought they were bothering Vinny he does tolerate Love Bug
     the white pony

though because Love Bug is Vinny's little brother his inseparable
     companion
his familiar I go to get Berto he's in a herd of the black horses and
     one starts

to pin its ears and foment a little stampede but I yell my hateful yell
     and it stops
and Berto walks peacefully to the gate with me he acts sometimes
     like I'm his buddy

which makes me shine all over never mind the transactional aspect
     the treats and
carrots I'm loaded down with most of the time ban the word
     "transactional"

and also any consideration of the fantasy lovers mine and probably
     my husband's
not exactly pets or little brothers the priest tonight said we each
     have an angel

this is really the first I'd heard of it and I started picturing my crush
bathed in light oops no my angel I mean my real one though I don't
     think

it he she is my pet but more like I'm its I'm surrendered as
     somebody's distraction
from their day job their support poodle crossing buddy safe space
     spice cake

Nominated by Marianne Boruch

SPECTRAL EVIDENCE

fiction by VICTOR LAVALLE

from PLOUGHSHARES

"They think I'm a fraud."

"They think I'm a fraud."

I like to repeat this to myself in the mirror before I go out and do my job. It might seem weird to say something cruel right before I perform, but I thrive on the self-doubt. If I go out there feeling too confident, then I don't work as hard. It's easy to get lazy in this trade but I take the job seriously. For instance, the word *psychic* does not appear anywhere in the window of my storefront. I never say it to my visitors. I call what I do "communication."

The other value in staying behind the curtain for a minute is that it gives the guests a chance to sniff around the parlor. They want to peruse the decor. They yearn to leaf through the handful of books I keep on the low shelf by the chairs. They're here for a performance too. If I stepped out too soon they wouldn't have the chance to reconnoiter, and then while I'm talking they're casting their eyes around the room and I have to repeat myself. Or, even worse, we just never make a connection. I'm not here for the ten dollars I charge during the initial visit. That money doesn't even cover the cost of all the coffee I drink in a day. Of course I'm in this for the money, everyone's got to make a living, but even that isn't the real goal. As I said, I am a communicator, and when a session works right all of us in the room play a part in the transmission. And at the end I get paid, so what's wrong with that?

I like to start work in the morning. Not many others do. Most folks who do this kind of work don't even open their eyes until mid-afternoon. Their days start in the early evening and run through the dawn. But

199

that's not my way. For one, there's too much competition and I'm not part of a family or a crew. For instance, the Chinese work in small groups and cater only to their own. I tried to learn Cantonese for about fifteen minutes but one of them took a liking to me and explained that no Chinese person would ever go to an American woman for help, so what was the point? I didn't take offense to it. She communicated something important to me. The only thing I can still say in Cantonese is *Can I have your address?* At least I think that's what it means.

The other reason I like mornings is because it means I get mostly old people coming through the door. You know why they're here? Most of them just want to talk and it turns out I do too. The cards I turn over at my table are secondary. Their loneliness is what blew them into my store. Isolation is as powerful as a gale force wind. There are times when we've been going at it for an hour or three, and before they leave they actually force a little more money on me, as if I'm a niece who should buy herself a new dress or something.

Which is why, I admit, I'm baffled by the three folks who are in the parlor right now. Can't be more than nineteen or twenty. Girls. They might be drunk. People who are drunk at eleven in the morning are scary, no matter what. They're so far gone they can't even talk quietly. Even when they shush themselves they only come down to about a nine on the dial. Immediately, I figure they were passing by and decided to stumble in for a laugh. The best I can hope for is to get them in and out quickly, collect a few dollars, then greet my usual morning crowd. I'm already looking forward to hearing about someone's endless concerns for a grandchild compared with corralling three drunks for half an hour. But work is work. They came in and I called out that I'd be there in a minute. Then I gave them five minutes to poke around. I tend to wait until they get to the books. The shelf is low and right by the chairs, so if they're reading the titles, it means they're probably sitting down.

"*Wonders of the Invisible World*," one reads aloud. She moves on to the next. "*The Roots of Coincidence*."

"Just sit down, Abby."

"Where is this lady?"

"It's too dark in here."

They're getting impatient. I give myself one more look in the mirror. I've been trying out this new look, a scarf wrapped round my head, one that drapes down around my neck as well. It makes me look like I'm from the silent movie era; think of Theda Bara in *Cleopatra*. But last week when I came out wearing it the guy in the chair asked me if I was a Muslim, and things only got tense after that. But these are three women and I tell myself they'll appreciate the flourish. More than that, I like the look.

I give the scarf one last touch and whisper the five words to myself. "They think I'm a fraud."

Then it's time for the show.

* * *

Two of them want to leave after ten minutes, but it's the third who won't get out of her chair. Abby is her name. Her head is down for most of my reading, hair hanging over her eyes. Her friends find her exhausting, but I try not to be hard on them. After all, they haven't left her side. Abby is the only one who doesn't ask silly questions. I know how that might sound to some. Any serious question at a storefront psychic's must be, by definition, "silly." I get it. There's hardly room for all three of them on the other side of my table, it's a little wooden countertop that's really only made for two. But it doesn't really matter, only one of them wants to be sitting across from me.

Abby's mother died six years ago, that's what brought Abby here. As soon as she says this, I find a part of my heart warming to her. Suddenly she doesn't look all that different from my Sonia. What would she have been like if I'd died when she was twelve or thirteen? Would she have ended up in a place like this, with someone like me, or much worse than me? I find myself feeling even more grateful for her friends, no matter how impatient they're becoming. They will not abandon her, at least not today. I wish I could remember either of their names.

"I just want to know if . . ." Abby whispers. Even though she seems tortured I don't think she's going to cry. She sounds resigned. "Is there something . . . after all this?"

I have a few things I usually say when people skirt close to this subject, the whole point of being here. But I can't think of them, because I've never had someone ask the question so directly before.

"OK," one of the friends says, rising to her feet. She's the smallest of the three, but the most potent. This one is the sergeant-at-arms when they go out to the bar. She looks at me. "We're going to miss our train back if we don't leave now."

The other friend is in worse shape, she sort of oozes off her chair. For a moment it's not clear if she'll fall flat or stand up. She stands, puts a hand on Abby's shoulder but it doesn't look like comfort, only a way to keep her balance. It looks, for a moment, as if she's crushing the poor kid.

Abby nods and finally rises as well. Is it strange that I'm thinking less of Abby and more of her mother? Trying to guess what I'd want some stranger to have said to Sonia if she'd come to them pleading for answers, or at least comfort. I guess the obvious choice is to say something simple and uplifting, but I can't do that about something so serious. Anyway, I can tell that's not what she really wants to hear.

While I'm struggling Abby opens her bag and finds three ten-dollar bills. She hands them across the table to me and of course I do take them. We've been together for a half-hour, exactly as I'd expected. I hold Abby's wrist. What should I say? What should I say? All my talk about putting on a show and I've got no preplanned act that will work for this.

"Yes," I say and squeeze her hand. It's the best I can do. The friends are already at the door, opening it and letting in cold air and sunlight. "There is more."

Abby looks at me directly; chin up. It's the first time I get to see her eyes. They're red from lack of sleep. She cocks her head to the left, seems surprised to hear me being so definitive. Then she pulls her hand free and follows her friends out of my life.

My daughter died a year ago this July. Sonia went to the Turning Stone Casino in Verona and jumped from the 21st floor. We hadn't spoken to each other in almost four years by that point. I hadn't even known she was living upstate. The coroner's office sent me an envelope with her last effects. Inside I found loose change and receipts from the ATM in the casino lobby, a flip phone that had somehow survived the fall, and a broken watch. It had been the watch that tore me open. I'd given it to her when she graduated high school. I didn't know she'd kept it all that time. It's not as if it had stopped at the moment of impact or anything, the hands weren't even still attached. In a way, that seemed more accurate. For her and for me time didn't stop, it shattered.

It's nearly eight by the time I get home. I've been in this apartment for three decades, raised Sonia here. After Abby and her friends left, I welcomed my stream of regulars, but I thought about Abby the whole time. Most of my days are as long as this one. I leave early for work and don't come home until dinner. All I do is sleep in this place now. I avoid it. I should admit that to myself.

I come through the front door with my late night pickup of Thai food, and in the kitchen I make a plate. For a little while—all of last year—I would eat the food right out of the container. There were times when I didn't even take the container out of the bag. It got to be too sad. So now I pull down a plate and utensils. I find the white wine in the fridge and pour myself a glass. I even sit in the same spot I've been using since my daughter was old enough to sit up in a chair by herself. She made such a mess when she first learned how to eat on her own and I never acted too patiently about it. Even before she died I found myself fussing at details like that, trying to trace a line from how she fell apart to something I'd done when she was still a child. Somebody is always to blame and most of the world tends to agree it was the mother.

How do I know I'm a true New Yorker? I actually believe the city goes quiet at night. Sonia used to have trouble sleeping because we lived next to the BQE and all night she would hear the trucks and cars speeding by, but by the time I had her, I'd long learned to tune that stuff out. It was only if I got in bed with her, like if she'd woken up and couldn't get back to sleep, that she'd point out the noise and I'd finally hear it.

Dinner done, I wash the dishes and pop the cork back into the wine. I can't even claim I tasted the food. The apartment has one long hallway with rooms branching off from it. I pass Sonia's old room. The door is shut. I never open it anymore. In the bathroom I take a slow shower, putting in the time to wash my hair, a nice way to slow myself down. My bedroom is at the end of the hall. I get in bed and turn off the lamp by my bedside and I listen to the sounds of this city.

"It's too dark in here."

The words came from the hallway, but I don't even roll over. I know who it is.

It wasn't a week after Sonia died that I started hearing from her. She only ever says the one thing. When it began, once I decided to believe it was happening and not just something caused by my grief, I had her body exhumed. I thought that might be what her words meant. She didn't like being buried. But it didn't help. She kept on talking. I begged her to tell me what she meant, but I couldn't get her to say more. I kept longer hours at the storefront because I wanted to be around other people. When I'm alone I can't drown her out.

"It's too dark in here."

She's come down the hallway now and joined me in my room. She'll go on like this all night.

❊   ❊   ❊

A week later I get a walk-in first thing. It's a middle-aged white guy, which is pretty unusual for me. He's standing on the sidewalk when I show up at nine. He asks for me by name. I bring him in and ask him to wait. I slip in the back, but when he's looking at the bookshelf, I take a moment to part the curtains and snap a photo of him with my phone. At least if he kills me the cops will find his picture. This might seem paranoid to some, but I don't care. It strikes me as a completely rational thing to do. I've had more seeing-eye dogs in here than lone middle-aged men strolling in.

I look at myself in the mirror, but this time I don't chant, not trying to charge myself up for a fine performance. Maybe he's a cop; that's the kind of energy he's emitting. They still do undercover operations on storefronts. Two years ago, a guy gave away over $700,000 to a pair of psychics in Times Square. I won't put on a show for this one, that's what I decide. No scarf draped across my head and neck. He won't see Cleopatra, only me.

When I get to the table, he's already laid out the ten-dollar bill. There's something insulting about seeing the cash before I've done anything. It looks new. Maybe he went to the ATM right before he showed up. Immediately, I wonder how many more fresh notes are waiting in his wallet, then I feel angry at myself for being so easily enticed.

His hair is white and thinning and slicked back and his sharp nose slopes down until the tip hovers right above his top lip. He doesn't seem to blink, even as I sit there quietly watching him. There's something predatory about him. As if he's a bald eagle and I'm a fish. I'm used to people looking at me like I'm a fraud, but not like I'm a meal.

"You're an early riser," I say, trying to be chatty.

He holds my gaze. "Where's the cards? Don't you people use cards?"

"We can," I say. "We will. But I like to talk first. It puts my visitors at ease."

He hasn't moved. Still hasn't blinked. His hands are flat on the table, but that doesn't make me feel any safer.

"What kind of things do you say? To put visitors at ease."

I look up and count how many steps it would take me to reach the front door. Seven maybe and I can't say I'm in any shape to run. The backroom has a bathroom, but there's no emergency exit. I could lock

204

myself in the bathroom and call the police, but how long would it take for him to smash his way in? "What did you say to Abby, for instance?"

He says the name with emphasis, but I admit I don't know who the hell he's talking about. Do you know how exhausted I am? I hardly sleep at night. At this point, I just lie there with my eyes closed listening to Sonia. How am I supposed to think of anything else?

For the first time, he moves, crosses his arms, and leans forward in his chair. "You don't even remember her," he says. He almost sounds happy about it, like I've confirmed his worst intuition.

"Abby," I say. Then I repeat it. I'm trying to get the gears of my memory to catch. When they do I snap my fingers. Maybe I look like a child who's happy to have passed a quiz. "She came into my store a few weeks ago."

"One week ago." He breathes deeply and his crossed arms rise and fall.

His eyes lose focus and he stares down at the table and the posture is exactly the same as Abby's had been. That's when I recognize him. It's not their faces but the way they hold their bodies.

"Who is she to you?" I ask.

"One week ago," he repeats.

I calculate my path to the door again. Maybe I could make it in five steps. This old girl might have one more sprint in her.

"What did you say to my daughter?" he asks.

I don't understand where this is headed. Is he back to ask for her fee? All this over a few dollars? The story of an overprotective father scrolls before me, the kind who won't ever let his child become an adult. I'm insulted on her behalf.

"She's a grown woman," I tell him. "What I said to her is confidential."

He drops his arms and slips one hand below the tabletop so I can't see what he's doing. Reaching into his pocket maybe.

"You're not a lawyer," he says. "You're just some scam."

The words settle on me heavily, a lead apron instead of a slap. I find myself needing to breathe deeply, so I do but it hardly helps.

"Did she report me or something? Are you here with the cops?"

He pulls his hand out from under the table. He's holding a tiny flashlight, like a novelty item, a gag gift. There's a bit of fog on the inside of the protective glass, where the bulb is.

"I gave this to her years ago," he said. "It was still on her keychain when her body was recovered."

The blanket across my chest feels even heavier now. I think I might get pulled down, right off the chair.

"What did you say to my daughter!" he shouts and he throws the flashlight at me. It flies wild, goes over my shoulder and into the back. As soon as it leaves his hand he looks horrified and chases after it. He sends his chair flying sideways and it knocks into the shelf. A few of the books fall to the carpet. He hurtles through the curtain and he's in the back and suddenly I'm alone. I get up to run for the door. I'm sure I can flag down a cop car on the street. But then I hear her.

"It's too dark in here."

Now I plop right back down onto the chair, can't move my limbs. My mouth snaps shut and so do my eyes. What did I say to his daughter?

Yes. There is more.

He steps back through the curtain and he's got my scarf in one hand, Abby's flashlight in the other. I wonder if he's planning to strangle me with the scarf and, for a moment, consider that I'd deserve it. The death of my child was already my fault, so why not his as well?

"I thought you would've run," he says quietly. He stands over me, holding up the scarf and the flashlight as if he's weighing the two.

"There's nowhere for me to go," I say.

He sits on the ground right there beside me. It's strange to see a man my age cross-legged on a carpet.

"I won it for her at the Genesee County Fair," he says of the flashlight. "It's funny what kids hold on to."

Now I understand why he grabbed my scarf. He's patting at his face, his tears.

"Maybe I said something to her?" he asks. The words come out so quietly that my first instinct is to lean in closer, but he isn't talking to me. I need to get an ambulance for him. I rise from my chair and slip my cell phone out of my pocket.

"I'm going to call someone for you," I say and he nods softly. Now I'm surprised I thought he seemed angry, when he's only delirious with despair.

After I call I crouch down beside him and wait for the sirens. This makes my knees start hurting instantly, but I can endure it. I grasp one of his hands between two of mine and I remember the way I touched his daughter when we spoke. They have the same delicate wrists.

I'm afraid to tell him what I said to her but not because I fear for my safety. Instead, I wonder if Abby thought I meant something hopeful when I told her there was more to existence. If she lost her mother, if she missed her mother, maybe she thought I meant the woman waited for her across the veil, that they'd be reunited in a better place. Why wouldn't she think that? It's the story people prefer. What if I told her father the same thing now? Would he be tempted to try and join Abby? I couldn't be responsible for such a thing, so I say nothing and simply hold his hand.

The EMTs arrive and help Abby's father to the ambulance. After taking some information from me they drive off with him, then I go back inside the store. For the first time, I can see the place like so many others must: the silly dim lighting, the bookshelf of mystic texts. It's such a cliché. No wonder my visitors viewed me as a fraud.

I go to the back and make myself some tea. While the water boils, I lift the chair Abby's father knocked over. I gather the books that fell, but instead of putting them back on the shelf, I go in the back and drop them, one by one, into the trashcan. I find the scarf and leave it in the garbage with the books.

My work changed after Sonia died. There is an afterlife and it's worse than the world we live in. That's what I know. I don't understand why I kept the news to myself.

"It's too dark in here."

The kettle whistles in the other room but I can still hear my daughter. I suppose that will never stop. I make my tea, then I sit at the table and wait for visitors. From now on whoever comes to see me is going to hear truth.

Nominated by Ploughshares

I LOVE YOU BUT I'VE CHOSEN DARKNESS

by CLAIRE VAYE WATKINS

from GRANTA

I spent the morning on myspace looking at pictures of my dead ex-boyfriend. The phrase *my dead ex-boyfriend* is syntactically ambiguous you can't tell from it whether this boyfriend and I were together when he died. We were not. We'd been broken up for about two years. We were together for three then apart for two then he died. He died in a car crash that's how he died.

Myspace is still with us. You could dogear this page literally or figuratively bookmark it set aside the volume or magazine or swipe to a new screen new beginning and find my myspace page or yours assuming you were aged fourteen to say twenty-five in the early oughts. The reason myspace failed isn't because it was populist or ugly or bought by news corp but because it was hard to talk about: *my myspace* is harder to say than *my facebook*. The uncooperative cadence of the phrase *my myspace page* perfectly encapsulates the awkwardness of the early oughts when our story begins.

His name was Jesse but in the years between our breakup and his death he went by Jesse Ray meaning his new friends and his new girlfriend called him Jesse Ray. I never called him Jesse Ray. No one from our old group ever called him that. We all grew up together don't talk about him much now maybe because we don't know what to call him.

I remember his body best of all because it was covered in tattoos. Not covered that's lazy. His body could not have been covered in fact because his tattoos were a secret from a few important people—his parents

208

mainly and the people in their church. It's not that his parents didn't know him as I thought then but the him they knew was not the him I knew. There were at least three Jesses at the time of his death: Jesse, Jesse, and Jesse Ray. His parents knew one I knew another his new friends and new girlfriend knew a third. The only person who knew them all was probably his biological mom K she lived in Elko and knew everything. Jesse and I once fucked in the sacred vestibule of the Mormon Church in Ruth Nevada while his grandfather's ninetieth birthday was taking place in the multi-purpose room down the hall and she knew about that for example. K had been a waitress her whole working life she was basically omniscient.

Clothed Jesse was just a tall lean white guy. Long feminine fingers goofy mop of glossy brown curls he was vain about a stupid soul patch sometimes sometimes a mustache eyelashes of a fawn. I'm still attracted to men like him. But when he undressed he exposed torso biceps and thighs crowded with ink: a scarecrow and graffiti he photographed in the Reno railyard and his own let's say underaccomplished drawings. His collarbones read I LOVE YOU BUT I'VE CHOSEN DARKNESS. with a period as in end of discussion. We'd been friends of friends in high school where his stepmother was a biology teacher who didn't believe in evolution. I'm being unfair. She was a lot of other things too—my own sister—but the combination of her courses' difficulty and her stern piety made her stepson's secret rebellion first-rate gossip. And he'd had many of these tattoos done with an improvised apparatus built of a bic pen.

Jesse was on the football team wore eyeliner and sometimes other makeup with his jersey on home games suit on away-days. He dated evangelical girls who would only permit him anal sex another secret from his parents theirs too I assume. His father was a bearded giant a/c repairman taught karate led a Saturday night home church of his own strict eccentric doctrine. Their study was based on a code he had developed for unlocking the secret meanings of the Bible something about every seventh word or fourth word and each in their small congregation had their own three-ring binder with highlighted decryption glyphs in plastic sheaths. Jesse's father had had a shipping container buried somewhere on their property stocked with supplies to wait out the days between y2k and the rapture. All this I gathered from Jesse for though at that time I still possessed my anal virginity I was never recruited. This could be because my stepfather rocked prison tattoos on every region of his corpus including his neck and hands but was probably because my family didn't have a church. Work was our church my mother

209

said though for most of my childhood she attended her Friday night AA meetings religiously.

I paid little attention to Jesse in high school because he was a rollerblader and I preferred skateboarders suspected him gay. I was fifteen sixteen seventeen and didn't know how to spend time with a boy who didn't want to fuck me. Then all of a sudden it was August and all the swimming pools in town gone mouth-warm so you didn't even want to swim until after sundown and Jesse was back from college and I was headed off to the same one in a few weeks. He was working a/c wrung out from crawling under trailers in 120-degree weather in long sleeves so his dad wouldn't see the markings on his arms.

We were at our friend Sean's drinking budweiser with clamato Sean's dad made us—where I come from if you work you drink, no matter that we were eighteen nineteen years old. By dusk Jesse and I were alone in Sean's parents' semi-above-ground pool. I gave him a shoulder massage— his shoulders pallid his neck and face sun-leathered save for little white hyphens at his temples where the arms of his sunglasses rested. After the massage Jesse said, in the voice of an animated luchador from a web series we all watched then, 'Maybe you want to take your top off?'

I was somewhere between willing and compliant. *Down* we called it as in *she's down* short for *down to fuck* or *DTF* which is what it said beside my name on the wall in the football locker room Jesse said. CLAIRE WATKINS = DTF. Inked as an insult but I've never taken it as one. I was indeed down to fuck. I was curious liked exploring other bodies I also liked to be liked who doesn't.

'This is why I have no respect for rapists,' Jesse said, cupping the white triangles of my boobs and glancing into the house to see whether anyone was watching at the sliding glass door. We couldn't tell didn't care.

Jesse said, 'Girls are really nice. Most of them will do whatever.'

I told him that was because he looked like white trash Ryan Phillippe.

He blushed turned the color he would ask me to dust across his cheekbones some mornings in the bathroom in the one-bedroom guesthouse we rented behind a halfway house off I-80. 'You just have to ask. That's all they want. All consent is is asking. If you can't even ask, you're a pussy.'

'You're using that word wrong,' I said lifting myself topless to the edge of the swimming pool.

'What, "pussy"?'

I pulled him close worried about my stomach rolls. I had probably been reading my mother's copy of *Our Bodies Our Selves*. 'You're using it as an insult meaning weakness,' I murmured into his neck. 'The pussy—by which I assume you mean the vagina, vulva, clitoris, cervix, uterus, and ovaries—is the strongest muscle in any body. The clitoris has twice as many nerve endings as the penis.'

Jesse had freed his from his swim trunks. 'No for real pussies are tremendous,' he nodded.

'Also,' I said, 'it's a term that belongs to a community. Like the n-word. I can say it but you can't.' I pulled the crotch of my swimsuit to the side and we kissed.

I said, 'I can use it as an insult or in reference to my anatomy. I can say, "Fuck my pussy, Jesse." Or, "Let's fuck, you pussy."'

All this was mostly fun and erotic though we rarely came but it was also my survival strategy. You could question its efficacy since it made sweet boys afraid of me so that I always ended up with the crazies but in this manner I went from being raised by a pack of coyotes to an academic year on the faculty at Princeton where I sat next to John McPhee at a dinner and we talked about rocks and he wasn't at all afraid of me.

Anyway I didn't like sweet boys. I liked filthy weirdoes who scared me a little and I still do.

Someone eventually shooed us out of Sean's pool and Jesse and I drove out to BLM land and lit off fireworks and fucked a few times in the back of his little pickup where he said, 'How do you like it?' and 'No, I'm asking' then we were boyfriend and girlfriend and then we lived together up in Reno working retail and fast food and taking night classes and Jesse quit drinking and proposed on Christmas and I reneged on New Year's and Jesse started snowboarding and going to shows and doing hard drugs and I started writing and Jesse fucked a girl in a tent up at Stampede Reservoir and another girl at the Straight Edge house and I tried to fuck a kid whose dad had an amazing cabin at Tahoe but I chickened out and in this manner Jesse and I broke up about a dozen times and eventually tacked a curtain across our living room and that became my bedroom where I would occasionally find Jesse napping in my bed because he missed my smell or on my computer without my permission doing homework or jacking off.

Jesse lived like he was dying a saccharine nugget of pinspiration terrifying to actually behold. Take it from me you do not want to room with anyone who lives like he's dying. His body was coiled with eros, anarchy and other dark sparkling energy. He looked for fights at shows or by wearing eyeliner and little boys' superhero shirts he bought at walmart to strip clubs waited for someone to call him a faggot and then he beat their ass. He had been on the club boxing team before he dropped out and snow bros in town for bachelor parties did not expect his long arms nor his gigantic martial arts father. After he went to awful awful for an awful awful or a buffet for prime rib.

He got gnarly nosebleeds all the time and our best talks happened with him in the tub letting the blood slide down his face and red the warm water. He was in the mug club at the tavern around the corner an investment he called it not because a mug club member received his beers in a grand customized stein though that was appreciated but because members could purchase another pint for a friend for a dollar which Jesse did often and then sometimes he smashed the pints on the floor to emphasize a punchline or one time into the side of a guy's head because the guy called Jesse's favorite milf waitress a cunt.

He liked to sing classic rock karaoke and uproot street signs and use them to smash too-nice cars parked in our bad neighborhood. He once shit his pants while skateboarding to work then worked his whole shift like that. He owned three skateboards two snowboards and about a dozen books in a crate beside his sleeping bag until he read *Walden* and said I don't need this crate! We had taco night at our apartment every Tuesday for all the runts and strays in our friend group and Jesse cooked the meat. He cut all the lilacs from the bushes on campus with his leatherman and piled them on my unmade bed even though we were broken up because the previous spring we'd been walking together and I guess I'd stopped and smelled them. He was very good at keeping secrets. Needless to say he became a junkie junked out on all sorts of things near the end but he was also very much alive.

One day I came home from my new job forging signatures for my butch women's studies professor at the subprime mortgage company she owned with her partner and Jesse was at my computer a piece of shit dell I'd maxed out my credit card for. He must have gotten a nosebleed during because he was jacking off covered in blood. I let him finish kissed him during then told him it was time to get the fuck out and he agreed said he would after the World Cup because we'd gone halvsies on the cable.

There is no story—he was there then he was gone. I am a dumb lump scratching my head baffled by this basicmost constant the ultimate fact: he was there then he was not.

I found out he'd died from my sister who found out on myspace. His current-now-suddenly-former girlfriend was in mourning black hair black clothes black makeup long all caps passages of pure screaming grief. No syntactic ambiguity. You want to know whether I hated her I did.

People die on the internet now really die we can watch them die in real time every gruesome frame if we like and sometimes if we don't. Periscope into dorm rooms into cars off bridges black people executed by the state unarmed fleeing autistic hands up fathers mothers children sisters star in snuff films screened in airports.

Of Jesse I have only pictures—his body on myspace. I like the selfies best you can see his gaze in them see what he thought was hardcore what he thought was punk. The last he posted before he died are of some operation he had throwing metal horns beside staples in a savage line from his sternum to his navel then around the navel a few inflamed sutures beneath the navel disrupting the outline of a new tattoo on his abdomen one I don't recognize not a very good one never to be completed.

There was a car crash someone was fucked up probably everyone though I don't know that for sure. I heard Jesse was thrown through the windshield flung into the desert off the highway on the way out to BLM land the place we first made love. I'd like to put it that way.

He kept secrets hated condoms. I watch his then-current-now-ex-online for signs and symptoms. I check his myspace and I know she does too since she is me is my own sister. We have the same thing living in our blood now. I am not doing a good job of this.

Jesse always let me be the good guy. He did not pay much attention to what I was doing and this is the version of freedom I have grown most accustomed to most protective of. He saw I was a watcher and gave me something worth watching. He was not violent but he enjoyed violence he was a vandal and a fighter but he was never mean never tolerated meanness. He was the person I called when I was afraid. He walked me anywhere I asked him to though he admitted the only time he felt unsafe on the street was anytime he had a girl with him. He always let me be the better person even though I wasn't better than anyone. He wasn't cracked up but he let me be the steady hand made me make myself feel safe. When I was with him I was always in control and this was true somehow even the night we drove to Berkeley to see radiohead and after drove a little stoned across the bridge and slept at my sister's place

213

in the tenderloin on the living room floor because we were twenty twenty-one.

He was harmless there the street was noisy and the living room was lit orange from the soda streetlights and we collapsed into a mess of sleeping bags and yoga mats and pillows and somewhere in there my sister's cat making my eyes itch. I woke up with Jesse rolled atop me wanting sex. I was tired didn't want it he was not at all violent but also not relenting his body unyielding his long arms beefed up from snow-boarding all winter and from lifting boxes in the stockroom at work. He held me down.

I remember thinking in italics. *Is this when it happens?* And then I answered myself. *That's up to you.* I decided that it wasn't it was sim-pler. I was determined to make it out of college unraped an actual goal I had though before I even started college I met a kid in the shoe store where I worked who invited me to a party but the party was just play-ing cards and so I was playing poker a tourist's game with him and some other people and drinking a corona then I woke up and it was morning and I was on the bathroom floor sore with my pants around my ankles. I walked into the master bedroom looking for this kid the kid who'd invited me whose apartment it was the only person I knew at this party. He was in bed asleep with an erection no blankets and another girl I didn't recognize naked spread eagle on the bed her hands were tied to the bedposts I think but I could be wrong. I didn't want to wake him wrote my phone number on his bathroom mirror with what I am just realizing now must have been her lipstick. This was in Los Angeles.

What's your family church? Jesse's father asked me the one time in three years I had dinner at their house. We don't have one I said or maybe I said work. Work was our church and laughter too. Farts and laughter and work and words. Rocks and photographs and dogs and TV. Breaking into houses for sale viewing things at night building materials casino decor landscaping elements once some mature water lilies and some koi. My sister my mother and me around the kitchen table bullshit-ting. The earth the body the sisterhood.

My husband has a dead love too. We traded them on our first date by my count the night we were the last two left at the bar and we walked to the united dairy farmers on high street for ice cream and took those to a hipper bar open later where we sat on stools playing footsie and drinking beer and eating sundaes with the ghosts and thereafter went home and dry humped without kissing in my bed where eventually Dap slept with his jeans on. This was in Ohio.

It was the first real conversation we had as intimate with another person as I've ever been. I told Dap about Jesse which was my way of telling him about my mother. Dap would not know her name for months.

Dap's love had been in grad school. She went on a research trip to South America something with biomes spores got an infection but didn't know it. She came back to the States and died in her sleep. Her room-mate found her in the morning cold in her own bed. She'd had bulimia some thought and that compromised her immune system possibly.

Dap never got to see her body. I never saw Jesse never saw my mother. She was cremated while I finished my midterms. By the time I got home she was ash. We spread her in our garden at the Tecopa house the so-called Watkins Ranch on supposed Sunset Road. My sister and I put some of her ashes in the backyard at the Navajo house at the tree she planted where she'd buried her beloved hound Spike. I don't know where Jesse is now.

Jesse, I wish you were here. America is violent and queer as fuck. The snowbanks are rising and every morning I drive over a frozen river past a mosque an elementary school this week sent a letter threatening *a great time for patriotic Americans*. I pass a kid who looks like you walks like you did I pass a sculpture by Maya Lin called *Wave Field* which is like a bunch of waves made of grass covered in snow so like a bunch of bumpy snow. Pretty cool. I drive to a strip mall and smoke weed in my SUV and do rich bitch yoga with these fierce old dykes and Indian grandmas and public ivy sorority alumni and other basic traitorous cunts and for $20 each we all come out an hour later looking like we just got fucked all of them my sisters.

Maya Lin also designed the Vietnam Memorial. Ross Perot called her an eggroll remember? We were kids. Did you ever get to see the Vietnam Memorial? I don't think you did. I've seen most of the monuments in DC. I've been to New York and Paris and The Hague and Antwerp for a night and London and Toronto and the Amalfi coast in Italy and Wales twice. I've had coffee with Margaret Atwood lunch with Justice Stephen Breyer and a beer with the *Game of Thrones* bros while Anne Enright sang hymns. Once I was talking to Michael Chabon at a party and Ira Glass interrupted Chabon to talk to me and then—then!—someone cut in to talk to Ira it was Meryl Streep.

Sorry. I only have so many people I can talk to about these things.

My sister came to visit and she had this strange look on her face and I said what what and she said do you realize that our parents could not have afforded the dollhouse version of this house? I spent the morning looking for you on myspace and trying to untangle a sad mess of white cords made by slaves and this too is America.

We have electric cars sort of and any day now the tesla gigafactory outside Sparks will be the largest building in the world. We have virtual reality headsets and as you predicted people use them mostly for porn. We have HD porn. My sister knows a woman in Albuquerque who was raped repeatedly by her husband and he liked to watch porn on his VR headset during. I can't shake that.

I can't shake the pictures you posted of your body hundreds of them on myspace. In some you are Jesse Ray alive but dying actively dying looking dead choosing darkness. In none of them in an unnamed album you are finally truly dead. You are a torso beneath a sheet in the desert. There is a shattered windshield a cop car an ambulance a fire engine tilted on the soft shoulder of the highway lights blazing. The sun is rising and the mountains are indigo above you. Someone has tucked you up so none of you is showing so we don't have to see the parts of you we don't want to.

You were here then you were gone.

Jesse, Jesse, Jesse Ray, my dead ex-boyfriend, my son, my stepson, my own sister, mom, Martha Clair, I have a daughter now she knows your name.

Nominated by Granta,
Steve Adams,
Lydia Conklin

LIKE SOMEONE ASLEEP IN A CINEMA

by MARY JO BANG

from VALLUM

Like someone asleep in a cinema who wakes to lean over into your space and mock your open-eyed wonder. That's how it was then, the eye movements of others tracking my every reaction on the stage that ends by design *sans everything*. When everything is over the shape of the moon will still feign a bathtub boat in the underworld, at rest on its side. I'll be the flower I've always been, held by a woman wearing a hat, half-veil, half-opened lips, the whites of her eyes matching the moon as the sun reflects off its surface. The pockmark above my right eye will also match. I so wanted to be stone but never achieved it. Wanted to lie to get what I wanted, without wondering, *What will happen if I lie*? My face still stings from the hand that slapped it. My teeth taste of some *Naptha*-brand soap. Every act is literalized. The clock no longer flips one to two, time is a hissing *is*. Lying is now in fashion. Lie down with me, people say, when they hold someone back from the edge of that insane remembering. What floats out of the mouth is the suds of tomorrow since I will never be clean as long as I live. We watch unrealizable shadows and make something of them—an eye watching the lashes fall.

Nominated by Vallum

MIDWINTER

fiction by D. NURKSE

from PLOUGHSHARES

Could you love God in a world without death? Teacher asked.

And we children shouted, a bristling forest of raised yearning arms. *Yes! No! Depends!*

We didn't know the answer, or even the question, just wanted to be admired for alacrity, vehemence prompted by authority. Some of us took the opportunity to punch our neighbors, or, in our excitement, ourselves.

Yet we felt sorry for her. There were lines like a ledger stave ruled in her forehead, and the wan scuff mark a key might leave on the edge of a lock at the corner of her chapped lips. This morning one of the buttons on her gray blouse was open. How could that happen? No one had buttons like Teacher—huge sofa-buttons, the holes hidden by a scrim of fabric.

Come to think of it, one of her earrings was missing its Neiman-Marcus pearl: just a dangling wire clasp.

It was the winter after Inchon. Our uncles were fighting in a very distant country, frigid one day, tropical the next. We knew the names: Pusan, Red Beach. We imagined the campaign. How do you cross a name, from one side to the other? A little like wading, a bit like swimming. They bore burdens: a bazooka, canned peas, pictures of us.

But now Teacher had picked an older boy, called him to the board, and was considering his answer gravely, though he was spouting complete nonsense (it was Victor Lasarello)—*probably for half an hour*; now she called on a shrimpy adenoidal girl who never spoke, who stood cowering, somehow covering herself with chalk dust just by proximity, her pale lips fluttering.

Yet Teacher listened, leaning forward, with the attention of a patient when the doctor speaks. In the hush you could hear the constant ping of heat-pipes, teachers in higher classrooms, droning with a heart-stopping authority, and the squeak of the hamster's wheel.

Oil it! We said under our breath. Who knows why it never happened—who skipped a day on the task chart, who was distracted, why that small trapped creature is still advancing, there in the darkest month, in the cage of a circular journey.

Nominated by Alice Mattison,
Joan Murray

THE BAR BEACH SHOW

fiction by OLABAJO DADA

from THE SOUTHAMPTON REVIEW

Every other Sunday, the army hosted a sold-out show at the Bar Beach. They ran flashy advertisements in the *Daily Times* a couple of days prior to the event, promising "a show like never before" while occasionally announcing a hike in the gate fee because of the surge in gas prices, or to offset the cost of new swings and slides they installed on the beach for "energetic Nigerian tots." On the day of the show, while children played soccer and flew kites around lovers moseying along the shoreline, who patronized hawkers peddling snacks, and swimmers rose and fell with the waves, soldiers set up barrels right next to a bamboo stage where invited musical guests entertained the crowd just before the show's most popular attraction. Then, with much ceremony and to deafening cheers and jeers, the soldiers paraded newly condemned criminals and tied them up to the barrels. And while they wailed and pleaded and ceaselessly declared their innocence, the soldiers yanked out their assault rifles and mowed down the convicts like inanimate paper targets. Their bodies, which were thrown far out into the water according to a new decree, sometimes returned to the beach after a day or two, always naked and often missing several succulent appendages.

Every other Sunday, more often than on other days, these images flickered with little weight through Akanji's mind as he hauled planks of wood from the sawmill to his workshop, which doubled as his wife's kitchen. And even though Aina was now in a wheelchair, she wouldn't let him cook or even clean the dishes. She seldom complained as the loads of wood he brought in turned into wall high stacks of coffins, or when he let sombre strangers in to haul the coffins away; she dusted off wood

220

shavings from her pots and stove and endured the ear-splitting rap of his hammer well into many late nights.

She did complain that she didn't like cooking with the dead, though. And she would have complained even louder if she knew he kept the money from his sales in the house.

He tiptoed down the ramp he had set up for her at the kitchen entrance and gingerly opened the bedroom door.

"You dey go Bar Beach now?" she asked when he stepped in, patting his bald head as he bent over to slip in her flip flops. He didn't expect her to be awake yet.

He nodded.

"Careful o! You sure say time never reach to stop?"

He chuckled. It wasn't time to stop. Not for him. "E remain small, dear. No dey fear." He brushed her hair and tied it in a bun. "Make I dey go now."

☼   ☼   ☼

No half-eaten carcasses washed ashore that sparkly Sunday morning, however. The ocean rocked sprightly as if on a seesaw, lapping at the beach and occasionally flaunting its waves at the breeze. And even though the tides had retreated four hours prior, the narrow stingy road overlooking the Bar Beach was still wet and its potholes were still puddles. But one watching from above wouldn't have noticed this if not for the parting of the horde on the road whenever traffic came through. You could see a little space open up before each car or bus or motorcycle and then close up behind it. The show began at noon—not a minute later—and the entrance gate was shut once the clock struck 12. The soldiers weren't much for condoning bloody civilians' lackadaisical attitudes to punctuality. After 12, they would only allow anyone in who could pay double the gate fee and complete 700 frog jumps under the scorching sun. But until the gates were opened, everyone had to stand outside.

The beach was barricaded with a barbed wire fence that stretched farther than anyone would bother to walk or even drive to get around. Soldiers patrolled it anyway, so the labour wouldn't exactly be worth broken bones or busted joints or bullet perforated torsos. As the gates opened after they had sweltered under the sun for hours, the thousand-strong crowd thinned into two lines. Spectators with their gate fees shuffled in on the left, while traders who had stalls on the beach and hawkers with business permits entered on the right. "Exact change only," the soldiers warned as the spectators showed their naira notes and dropped them into an open barrel at the entrance. "We no dey carry change. We're not petty traders!"

Many of the people had skipped church early to get a good spot in front of the beachhead. Others who didn't go to church had been there since daybreak, chatting with the sentries about that day's performers. People trooped in and ran towards the ocean, stopping just shy of a huge arc cordoned off with a thin row of bamboo stakes. They chose their spots and settled in with their mats and soccer balls and coolers full of drinks and gongs and drums. There was a row of stalls not far from the entrance, where spectators bought more drinks and food. You could buy pepper soup with fresh catfish from Mama Ufot, but you had to go to Calistus next door for beer, schnapps or gin—the soldiers had a *Zero Tolerance Policy on Business Monopoly*.

Humming along to Ras Kimono's "Natty Get Jail," which came from a ghetto blaster in a record store five stalls away, Calistus arranged bottles of drinks on a rack in his stall and wiped down the benches— sleazy planks that were balanced on 50-litre kegs filled with wet sand. He poured two shots and handed them to his first customers.

"Money don add o!" He told them sternly.

"How much?" one of the men asked.

"Five naira."

They balked. "No, lailai!" the man retorted. "Na three naira."

A truck rolled onto the beach as Calistus regarded the men with a sneer. There were three barrels on its bed. He abandoned them and stepped out of the stall. Two hefty soldiers off loaded the truck while a stocky officer stood by supervising, arms akimbo. Calistus waved at him until he got the soldier's attention. When the soldier beckoned to him, he stepped back into the stall and stared at the two men, who still hadn't touched their drinks.

"First time for here?"

They nodded.

"Una come from where?"

"Ibadan."

"I see," he said. "Welcome. But let me tell you; drink for here is five naira. If you like, I can call Major Okoro to explain to you properly." He pointed in the direction of the soldier.

Their eyes widened, and the one who had been quiet broke into a grin. "Ah! No need, bros. We understand well well."

After serving more shots to more customers, Calistus walked up to Okoro.

"Akanji never come?" he asked.

Calistus shook his head "E remain small. He go soon reach."

They watched the delirious crowd that had collected in front of the record store. Not too far from them, a guy who brought his girlfriend on a date was getting kicked on the ground by another soldier.

"You no dey hear word?" the soldier howled. "We say no camera for beach!"

The guy tried kneeling up but the soldier's boot bashed his head back into the wet, gravelly sand. Then he seized the expensive-looking camera and smashed it against a rock several times until its lenses broke into multiple pieces and the film slithered onto the beach like a baby snake. Two 8-year-olds in Speedos laughed at the guy and raced each other along the shoreline, kicking up the seawater at an elderly man in a white robe who was on his knees and had his hands to the sky. He ignored them and kept praying, even though he had a glistening sabre in his right hand. His head jerked in all cardinal points and sometimes swivelled on his neck.

"Only three today?" Calistus pointed at the barrels.

"Yes o! Colonel Thompson suspended fast-tracking trials indefinitely."

"Why na?"

"Public defender salary don increase. More overtime for them, more cake for him."

Calistus clenched his teeth. "Bastard!"

"Why are you complaining? You never spend money na. At this rate I'll need three or four more shows to complete the second floor and paint the house. And we are not talking swimming pool yet." He hissed and pulled three photographs from his pocket, handing them to Calistus.

"Find them and send them to my office."

Calistus watched his brother stomp away, followed by his bodyguards. He walked back to his stall and served his customers more drinks, and then stepped outside again and gazed over the beach with the photos in his hands. The crowd danced on as one song followed the next. The sun rose further in the sky, and so did the excitement, as the beach continued to swell with people.

❊ ❊ ❊

At the other end of the city, under a billboard that advertised the Bar Beach Show on one side and featured the picture of a beaming General Buhari on the other, brandishing a whip and begging LET'S MAKE

NIGERIA A BETTER PLACE, Akanji fanned himself with the stack of papers where he drew his casket designs, cursing under his breath at the long line in front of him. There was a motorcycle park across the street, where two soldiers sat on the arched back of an elderly man who had ignored the overhead bridge and had run across the road. Tears and sweat trickled down his face onto the floor, and he absently mumbled pleas to them. But the soldiers laughed and gleefully cheered on two shirtless teenagers who were sparring bare-knuckled on the sidewalk, refereed by a pot-bellied man in a wifebeater. A sign on the canopy behind them welcomed you to JAWANDO FITNESS CENTER. The road teemed with hawkers manoeuvring their wares around army jeeps, overcrowded rickshaws, four-wheeled metal contraptions and their thick exhaust fumes.

Whoever came up with such a stupid idea as standing in a queue just to get on a bus? Didn't these moron soldiers understand this was a waste of people's time? Surely there were more profitable things to do on a Sunday morning than squander precious time replicating a Lagos traffic jam in the name of the *War Against Indiscipline*. Not too long ago, if your destination was important, you wrestled your way into whatever bus came along. But now soldiers force you to stand behind saucy teenagers and talkative market women just because they got there before you. He kept his left hand firmly in his pocket so he wouldn't be tempted to look at his watch. He couldn't be out too long because of his wife.

Truth be told, the money he needed was ready, but he couldn't tell her that. He could make some more so they could afford a truck for him to make cement deliveries from the factory and quit carpentry. Maybe even a little more than that so he could lay the foundation for a small house. All she had to do was endure several more weeks—well, maybe months—in the chair. They'd come far. He might as well stretch it out. So, there was no returning home empty-handed today.

A bus arrived and left, and the queue shortened. Akanji's gaze returned to the motorcycle park. Those machines were faster means of getting around within Lagos, but very few people ever dared to take them across the lagoon to the island end of the city. The daredevil riders always belted along the shaky Third Mainland Bridge as if they were in a James Bond movie. And it wasn't uncommon for fishermen who prowled the lagoon to pull out floating bodies and shoes from time to time.

"Bros," someone tapped his shoulder from behind. "Bros, what is the time, abeg?"

224

Akanji hissed at the albino and reluctantly pulled his hand out of his pocket, showing him the watch before inadvertently glancing at it himself. His head ached. He felt blood and money draining out of him as the crimson second hand spun slowly and menacingly on his wrist. He wiped his brow with the paper and waved timidly at a soldier monitoring the queue. The soldier caught his gaze and pointed at Akanji with his rifle.

"Na wetin?"

Akanji trembled at the sight of the nozzle. "Shon sir! Make I come?"

The soldier beckoned. Akanji walked up.

"Officer, abeg, people dey wait me for Bar Beach. I have to be there before 12 noon."

The soldier took off his sunglasses. "Look at all these people," he pointed at the queue. "Where you think say them dey go? Even me, do you think I won't rather be there than keeping you donkeys in line on the streets of Lagos?"

Akanji sighed. "I know sir, but I have customers waiting."

"And they will be there when you reach. You dey fear to do frog jump?"

Akanji wished he could tell the soldier that that wasn't the point. He could get there anytime he wished and still be allowed in without hassle. Heck, he wasn't even interested in seeing the show. But his customers weren't the throng who went to make merry at the show. They hardly wanted to be identified at all, and he often wondered how they were strong enough to even attend in the first place. He should have just told this idiot that Major Okoro was expecting him. But saying that now would prompt more questions. He turned and looked thoughtfully at the motorcycle park. Then he turned back at the soldier and smiled.

"How much, sir?"

"Ehn? How much for what?"

"For your trouble. If I fit sharply follow the next bus."

❊   ❊   ❊

The barrels had been set up inside the arc by the time Akanji got to the beach. Further up the sand, a band was setting up their instruments on a stage. He hadn't seen this group before. They were women; all five of them clad in leggings and spaghetti tops.

"Just three today?" he asked Calistus as he knocked back a shot and gestured at the barrels.

"Ehen now! Who am I to ask questions?"

Akanji nodded and stared at the dancing crowd. He missed dancing with Aina. He missed the way she locked her arms around his neck and bounced her breasts in his face; how she remained spirited even after two miscarriages. She made him swear not to give up trying for a child with her, so when she got sick, he initially thought she was pregnant again. Then they realized she wasn't.

He shook the thought out of his head. At least he still had her. All would be well after the operation. No one could say the same about his customers.

"What happened to your head?" Calistus asked.

"Leave story, abeg. Where is Major?"

"Office."

"You find their family?"

"Two of them."

"Where are they?"

"Office."

❊   ❊   ❊

Major Okoro's office was a small wooden shed built under a coconut tree a good distance from the entrance to the beach. There was one table and one chair—anyone who had business with him had to stand through it. His official designation under the new Buhari regime was ARTISTIC DIRECTOR OF THE BAR BEACH SHOW. And he never shied from the publicity. He made verbose speeches before the show began every Sunday, espousing the regime's commitment to "law and order and public comportment," and its equal commitment to the arts by making a "creative spectacle" of the punishment of public enemies.

Akanji stood beside him and watched as he negotiated with two sobbing women. The taller one had swollen eyes and didn't utter a word throughout. She just cried continuously and blew her nose into her headscarf. *These are wives*, he thought. *Mothers never come.* What would Aina would do if he were arrested for theft and executed at the beach? Executed convicts, after all, were considered property of the state. He doubted she would wheel herself into the ocean like she threatened when he'd first told her of his business plan with Okoro. But he'd promised her: once he made enough money to pay for her surgery, they were done.

"Look," Okoro told them. "I can't release your husbands to you at that price."

"Oga please!" the plump woman wailed. "That is all we have."

He hissed. "Save your money, then. We'll just toss those good-for-nothing scoundrels into the ocean for the fishes. I hear they pluck out the eyes first."

The women went on their knees. "Major, please! Their spirits won't rest if they don't get a proper burial."

"Really? Did they give us any rest when they went around robbing and killing innocent people?"

This was the part of the job that Akanji hated. Did Okoro ever care about how these people would be able to afford their loved ones' funerals after he'd milked them dry to release their bodies and forced them to buy a coffin? Okoro glanced his way and nodded, and Akanji handed him the papers.

"Look," he said to the women. "I can't change that price because I've factored in the price for the coffin. And that's even at a 20 percent discount. But I will throw in a favour."

The women dabbed their faces and looked up at him.

"I'll tell my soldiers not to shoot them in the head or face. That way you can have an open casket for the wake. Then they can have a proper burial and rest in peace, and nobody feels cheated, not so?" He handed the papers to them. "Pick out any design you like and Akanji will make it for you. Don't forget to give him your husbands' measurements. He knows his work very well, so recommend him to your friends."

❊ ❊ ❊

"Wetin do your head?" Okoro asked after the women left.

Akanji touched his swollen forehead. "I saw the butt of a rifle."

Okoro cackled. "Why, did you try to bribe your way ahead of the line?"

"Ehen now! Time was going. What was I supposed to do?"

"But they let you get on the next bus, abi?"

Akanji nodded.

"See! We're not inconsiderate like you bloody civilians."

"The idiot pulled me by ear and dragged me all the way up the line. And he still took my money. But I'd have been saved all that humiliation if you would let me use your name."

"Why?"

"Because everyone knows you."

"Exactly!" Okoro picked up his beret and straightened up. "Come on, let's go out. It's almost 12."

Ten soldiers with Uzis flanked them on either side as they treaded the sand towards the arc where the barrels were set up. Moments like this made Akanji wish he had joined the Army instead of learning the carpentry trade after he dropped out of school. He knew he would have made it far. Maybe not as far as becoming a major, but far. But it was at that time that he met Aina, and she made it clear she didn't want a soldier for a husband. He wished he could rub it in her face that a soldier was helping him make enough money to save her life now that she was ill and wheeling herself around. She probably knew he thought so. She often knew what he was thinking. Okoro took one last drag at his cigarette and threw it in the sand.

"Look," he said to Akanji. "You know you can't use my name whenever you have a small problem. You know you're not supposed to call attention to me. Or yourself."

Akanji kept quiet.

"If you flash my name around, people will get curious. When they get curious, they will ask questions. And if people ask questions, they will find out things they are not supposed to find out. And that's because those who shouldn't talk will open their mouths, which is what caused the problem in the first place. You dey hear me so?"

Akanji nodded.

"Akanji."

"Yes, sir."

"Akanji."

"Yes, sir."

"Akanji!" They stopped walking.

"Yes, Major."

Okoro looked up at him and held his gaze. "How many times did I call your name?"

"Three. Three times, sir."

"Do you love your wife?"

"Yes, sir."

"And you want to see her get well?"

"Yes, sir."

"And you want to live long with her?"

"Hmmm."

"Then please continue to keep your mouth shut. This," he pointed in the direction of his office, "is *serious* business. Do you understand?"

"Yes, sir."

"We're making good money, Akanji. Don't ruin it." He sighed. "How Aina body, sef?"

❊   ❊   ❊

The crowd that had gathered around the stage went berserk when the Black Maria holding the three convicts rolled through the gate, but they knew enough not to run towards it. The three men watched from Calistus' stall. People high-fived one another and jumped in excitement. One little boy ran around with his hands spread out and the Nigerian flag tagged to his back like a cape, with the words "Indiscipline na Cancer" stencilled in Kandahar ink across the middle. Major Okoro laughed. Akanji, who had been fidgeting in his seat, got up.

"Um . . . I think I'll be going now, Major."

"Why now? The show hasn't even begun."

"Em, yes. But . . . you know . . . Aina . . ."

"Okay, no problem." Okoro fumbled in his back pocket and handed Akanji a 10 naira note. "Take am use for transport. See you soon?"

"Soon, yes soon. Thank you, Major. They should be ready by Friday."

They watched him hustle away and out through the exit gate. Calistus poured them two more shots of schnapps before he spoke.

"How long before his wife dies?"

"Not very long."

"But he's still saving for the operation?"

"Because the doctor told him it's operable, as I suggested."

"It's not?"

"It's cancer. And e don reach far for her body. He's still working for us because he doesn't know."

"Which he won't be motivated to do anymore once she dies."

"And you think I haven't considered that?"

Calistus smirked and shrugged.

"You're right," Okoro said. "I don't think we should delay any further. Find us another carpenter and I'll take care of him after he finishes this job." He stood up and patted his brother's shoulder. "Now let's go and wipe that blemish off our society," he said, gesturing at the Black Maria.

❊   ❊   ❊

Akanji held on to the seat as the motorcycle barrelled down the Third Mainland Bridge at breakneck speed. He had given up begging the rider to slow down. He tried to blot out the images of those barrels, or the thought of getting tied to one of them with bullets pelting him like angry hornets. Aina was going to be well soon. She was right about him risking his life to save her, but all he needed was two more jobs. And then he was done. She would have her operation, he would buy the truck (forget the house—no need to be greedy) and they would go away. Far away. Farther than wherever it was in the middle of the ocean that the convicts were offered to the fishes before the waves returned their leftovers to the beach.

Nominated by The Southampton Review

PARACHUTE

by MAGGIE SMITH

from PLEIADES

Because a lie is not a lie if the teller
believes it, the way beautiful things

reassure us of the world's wholeness,
of our wholeness, is not quite a lie.

Beautiful things believe their own
narrative, the narrative that makes them

beautiful. I almost believed it
until the new mother strapped

her infant to her chest, opened
the eighth-floor window,

and jumped. My daughter tells me,
after her preschool field trip

to the Firefighter Museum,
about the elephant mask, its hose

like a trunk, and the video of a man
on fire being smothered in blankets.

She asks me if she knows anyone
who *got dead in a fire*, anyone who

got fired. When will I die? she asks.
When I was a child, I churched

my hands, I steepled my hands,
and all the people were inside,

each finger a man, a woman,
a child. *When I die, will you*

still love me? she asks. The mother
cracked on the pavement—

how did the baby live? Look,
he smiles and totters around

the apartment eight stories up.
Beautiful things reassure us

of the world's wholeness:
each child sliding down the pole

into the fire captain's arms.
But what's whole doesn't sell

itself as such: buy this whole apple,
this whole car. Live this whole life.

A lie is not a lie if the teller
believes it? Next time the man

in the video will not ignite.
The baby will open like a parachute.

Nominated by Dan Albergotti
Michael Waters

A COUNTRY SCENE

by RICK MOODY

from SALMAGUNDI

The meth heads, if that is the correct designation, had been watching the house for months. Agreed, this presumes the meth heads had their shit together enough to watch anything at all, beyond NASCAR or *Alaska State Troopers*. Their hard, rural lives mainly involved sleeping in, for days at a time, in the extremity of despond, because that was what it felt like when the pollutants evacuated the relevant neurotransmitters. If they were methamphetamine users, rather than users of, e.g., crack cocaine, there is greater likelihood of transitory psychosis, ischemic events, seizure, and paralysis. Any of these side effects would have prevented the perps from effectively watching the house. And yet there is no conclusion but that they were, because they tiptoed onto the premises, according to neighbors, double-checking to see if it could be done, before going in big with a pickup and hand tools.

Did they start watching the house after they were rebuffed in their attempt to snow-shovel the driveway, for cash, on one occasion? Nine months prior, the owner of the house was out in the driveway, and the meth heads slowed down on the way past—from their own hovel, a couple houses down, where most of a decaying fir tree rested on the roof and a partially disassembled television was snow-covered in the yard—and they asked if the owner needed help shoveling, which he declined, citing good exercise. The meth heads may have illegally procured a snow blower that they were hoping to use as a revenue generator throughout the neighborhood. We can imagine their contempt for the owner as he lifted each wet, intractable shovelful of precipitation, when more practical methods were, for a paltry sum, being offered to achieve a like result. Maybe they wanted a closer look at the premises, while shoveling, as they waited for a climatically advantageous period, a period in which the owner of the house would no longer be likely to visit so frequently as he did in summer. It was, after all, his second home.

And so: the meth heads decided upon October, right after the birthday of the owner. They did not break in during a birthday celebration, during the eating of gluten-free chocolate-chocolate made from a box. Among the questions pursuant to the crime, including wondering whether the perpetrators were beaten frequently as children, was the question of whether they were observing through the windows during the two-day birthday celebration. Was candle extinguishing observed? Conjugal activity? Excretory episodes? And did they try the patio door with their crowbar before the burglary? As to the further question, the one you are about to ask, it is likely they were high during the heist, because otherwise they would not have been quite as gleefully merciless as they turned out to be. They had already driven into the driveway, per the testimony by the closest-but-one neighbor, and then turned around and gone back down to their falling-down hovel. They knew it could be done, this breaking and entering. They fired up beforehand, to kindle in themselves the hardness required for felonious activity, and then they drove on up the driveway, and pulled the car in a bit, so that anyone passing by would not think about it much. They didn't stop to admire the view from the yard. They went around back, they leaned on the patio door, a French door of a certain kind, and they quickly overcame the French door, in order that they could be, in earnest, lawless, upcountry sons of liberty.

In short order, across the threshold, the meth heads came to feel that all that was in the house *belonged* to them. The door swung back, and to the meth heads it was like the first time they non-consensually abridged the freedoms of a teenage learning-disabled girl. The prevailing order of things, in which, by and large, you leave to other people their ideas about property and ownership, was overturned, and the appurtenances of that house were theirs.

However, achieving the threshold of the premises also leads us to an important metaphysical question, one that is implicit in breaking and entering in the majority of circumstances, and that metaphysical question is: having had their quiet enjoyment of the premises would they *shit on the bed*, whichever bed; for many lawless, upcountry sons of liberty, this was a traditional part of the breaking and entering game, it was part of the folk literature of breaking and entering, a culmination even, and though they had performed just the four or five burglaries in the eastern Dutchess County area, they were well aware that shitting on the bed was practically de rigeur. According to their natures, they knew. They were pondering shitting on the bed while they turned off the electricity at the fuse box, and, with flashlights, began emptying closets and drawers of wearable items, looking for the baubles that could be presented to any unscrupulous pawn broker. Throughout it all there was a certain fecal pressure upon the collective bowel of the team.

On the second floor, they were laughing and belittling the possessions of the former owners of the house, especially possessions that indicated the undeniable vulnerability of the owners, for example striped socks or women's undergarments. This stuff was ridiculous to them, the signs of vulnerability were ridiculous, and the more laughably vulnerable the more they felt powerfully the need to *shit on the bed* while looking at, for example, a drawer full of boxer shorts. *Shitting on the bed* is considered a reasonable activity in few theaters of human conduct, because this posture would require one burglar to allow another to see him crouch as the waste product swung free from him, and yet which criminal has not wanted to feel so utterly liberated, so American, on the king bed of some interloper from the city, whose crime is that he pays exorbitant property taxes into a school district that will never provide services to him. Why not shit on the bed of a person like that? Why not evacuate last night's microwaveable meat product and hot sauce through the alimentary passageway onto the lavender comforter of that dog and his wife? It would be so satisfying! Kind of like pissing on a younger brother while he sleeps, or, for example, killing feral cats!

As the minutes passed, and the adrenalin and amphetamine combination settled down into a steady state, so that the meth heads—they were three, one a convicted felon, and two younger guys he had impressed with promises of riches and prescription drugs in abundance— were no longer quite so nervous. With their flashlights wobbling, they considered in the master bedroom pieces of jewelry that were not self-evidently worthless in the light of the flashlamp. *Just take it. We'll figure it out later.* The dressers in the master bedroom were emptied entirely, spilled out on the floor, and in these drawers they found the heirlooms that were hidden in sock balls and among lacy undergarments. Who would put jewelry in the sock drawer when everybody knows to look in the sock drawer? Man, these people who owned this house were *fucking dumb*, and they deserved to be robbed, because if you're this naïve you deserve to be robbed; they thought they were so smart the rich city fuckers who owned this house, they actually put jewelry in the sock drawer, which is *fucking stupid*, and there's no fucking alarm wired into the house, which is *fucking stupid*, and people like the meth heads could just fucking waltz in here, and if they wanted to *shit on the bed*, the three of them chortling about it, they could just *shit on the bed*. And yet the charismatic felon, the one with the leadership qualities, had to consider whether he truly wanted to see the quivering hindquarters of the two younger as they tried to offer up the precious load of microwaveable meat products; he had done time in the county lockup, and in country lockup it is the rectal productions of others that is inevitably a daily concern. You want to think about anything else but the assholes of others. *Take all of it*, he was saying, in his baggy jeans, and his backward baseball cap, and then he left the two of them in the bedroom and went through the attached bathroom looking for prescription medication that would blunt the edge of a diminishing buzz. There were no drugs at all! What kind of rich people don't have any drugs at all? The least you could do would be to have some Halcion. No kind of rich people that he knew slept easily; they were all taking sleeping pills for all their rich people problems. In his incipient dysthymia, he clomped down to the basement in his work boots, to get away from the other two, because heavy hangs the head that wears the crown. He wanted to think, and to know felonious solitude. He wanted to commune meditatively with his spoils. If you're not going to know the little endocrine thrill that is itemizing the inventory, then what is the point? In due course, he came upon all the musical equipment, there in the basement, which was a rich vein to mine. He threw open the basement door, and carried out the guitars, and the amp, and all the pedals, and all the cables, an entire milk crate full of ancillary pieces and parts, a violin, a melodica, and during this spree of accumulation, the convicted felon forgot, for a time, about *shitting on the bed*, because he was calculating amounts of drugs that might be purchased with the revenue to come, when these items were deposited in a pawn shop across state lines.

Of the two younger fellows upstairs, it is worth inquiring, for the moment, if either had ever attempted to have sex with a farm animal. It is an unfair characterization of country folk, that just because they live in the vicinity of animal husbandry they have attempted to mount livestock. Just because, like ordinary decent criminals, they are liable from time to time to sell pills out of their bedrooms—some Ritalin, some oxys, some Wellbutrin, some Abilify, some Ketamine—that they have a powerful need to defile any domesticated species. It is unfair to suppose that just because they watch NASCAR and *Alaskan State Troopers*, and

236

play *Grand Theft Auto,* and have unregistered guns and buy metham-phetamine from a would-be Satanist in a trailer up the road they have debauched Elsie. And yet. Did those two younger guys, just impressed into service, ever have sex with an animal, or consider having sex with an animal, or at the very least touch an animal just wondering if there was an aperture on the farm animal that might be of the correct gauge? Did they wait until dusk and go around back of the pig farm up 22 and con-sider whether to take a pig by force? Did the crack cocaine or metham-phetamine lead them, on occasion, to dwell upon the sexually punctilious quality of the pig? What is the effect of methamphetamine on country folk, on their sexual impulses, when surrounded by newly birthed calves, still wobbly on their calf legs? Did Ketamine boost the sexual prowess of country folk when they were in the thrall of non-consensual sex with a calf? Did it increase the staying power of the young drug connoisseur?

Or put it this way: the country, the forest, the sparsely inhabited lati-tudes summoned up in the writings of the American Transcendental-ists, down through the decades of our national literature, the realm of the transcendental, the realm of solitude, of the mind of the divine, the forest, the farmlands, the wildness of the country, is, in this story, the land of heavily acned amphetamine addicts in their early twenties, who have on multiple occasions battered family members, and who mostly watch television in a state of morose self-hatred and regret, but who every now and then rouse themselves enough to think about scaling the heights of passion with calves and/or goats or sheep, or who are willing to destroy a house in order to get a little money with which they can bewilder themselves, and so that they might *shit on the bed.*

Downstairs, the convicted felon—heavy hangs the head, etc.—having believed that he'd satisfied himself to the tune of a few thousand dollars with the musical equipment, moved onto a foot locker that he was con-vinced secreted away items of value, and as he stood there considering what was the best blunt force-approach to opening the foot locker, one of the other two sauntered down the stairs, interrupting the felonious solitude with which the convicted felon beheld these further posses-sions of the homeowners, and in violating this solitude, this other in-sured that the convicted felon hated him a little more.

Can we do it now? We'll just do it, and you can stay down here. And here the *henchman,* if that's the right technical term, laughed a tight self-satisfied laugh that resembled something from the pertussis family of medical symptoms. He was big, dumb, and clad in muddy work boots and old jeans, wore a hooded sweatshirt of the kind manufactured exclusively with Chinese sweat shop labor, and his voice, a mild high-tenor sort of thing that was out of phase with his lumbering exterior, was locked into these pertussis-like convulsions of laughter. It was unclear if this *shitting on the bed* had ever been something he'd done before, or if he was just coming to it now, believing himself to be in a group of like-minded men.

"You guys are little lost ducklings," the convicted felon remarked at this point, as the second henchman now joined the first, "and if I could pluck out your livers and make some kind of pâté out of them, I'd do it. I'd grind up your livers in some kind of meat grinder, and then I'd get like one of those expensive stone-ground crackers at the gourmet store, and I'd put your liver on the stone-ground cracker, and I'd make you watch me eat it. I'd eat seven of these crackers in a row, and then I'd throw the rest of the pâté out, dump it on the lawn, just for the fuck of it. It's like you're following your mother hen into the crosswalk with your webbed feet and making it *unmushed* over to the ice cream stand to beg for the last waffle cone, which will fatten your little duck livers up good. If I could, I'd prise open your mouth with a stick, and pour in a large helping of bovine brain tissue until you were fattened up. By the way, I know a guy killed his own aunt for insurance money and got away with it, cut her up and fed her to the pigs, and now he owns a tanning salon."

He flung a sheaf of old love letters, the convicted felon did, a sheaf of fervent love letters bound with a red ribbon, onto the floor. He trod upon these love letters without looking down.

"We are not going to shit on the bed, because shitting on the bed is obvious, because everyone shits on the bed, like shitting on the bed is a coming-of-age thing, you know, where a teenage boy goes out into the world to become a man. His dad has a wicker pallet, or mat, because that's how they live in the Pacific Islands, and the son has to sneak into dad's yurt, where the pallet is, and while the father is out hunting and gathering the son has to shit on his dad's pallet. At that point, he's ready to take a wife. But we are not like this. We prove our manhood in other ways. I have been giving this some thought, and what I really want to do is make some supper, or maybe a late lunch, you know, in a leisurely way. We're going to go up there, and we're going to try to get all the tastiest grocery items, like some barely defrosted health food from the refrigerator, like maybe rhubarb, and we're going to put all this in a pan, a no-stick pan, and then we're going to eat some of it."

All three perps in the basement, in the disconsolate last glimmering of dusk, overshadowed by the low, insubstantial Berkshires; in the distance, somewhere, fawns of the neighborhood gaped at the flashlights darting around in the interior of the house. Did we note that the third perp was a slightly rotund man with a goatee? That overbite should have been corrected. His eyes said vulnerable while the rest of him said impulse control problems. Now all three hesitated, in the basement, until in some empathic way they knew that they'd agreed about the supper plan, at which they climbed the stairs to the kitchen in single file. The kitchen was centrally located, situated for easy escape. In the following way they organized their repast.

Chicken Nuggets, Home Style

One ten-pound bag basmati rice
Sixteen ounces canola Oil
Unfiltered Extra Virgin Olive Oil (Fairway Brand)
Skippy's Superchunky Peanut Butter Natural
Sea salt, La Baleine brand
Black peppercorns, six ounces
Red pepper flakes, Simply Organic
Ground cinnamon, McCormick, one jar
Dark brown sugar, Domino, ½ pound
Sun-Maid Raisins, one pound
Sunrise Brand Crispy Maple cereal, one box
Leapin' Lemurs brand cereal, one box
Bob's Red Mill Steel Cut Oatmeal, one pound
Bob's Red Mill Gluten-free pancake mix, one pound
One box spaghetti, De Cecco, one box
Spike all natural vegetable broth, 32 ounces
Enjoy Life Gluten-Free Cookies, one box
Annie's macaroni and cheddar cheese
Lay's Original potato chips, 10 0z, $2.50×2
One half gallon almond milk (365 brand)
One half gallon Tropicana Orange Juice
One half gallon Newman's Lemonade
4×Maple yogurt Ronnybrook brand, one cup
Two dozen organic large eggs
Butterscotch pudding (Swiss Miss)
Apples (local, one bag of 12–15)
Vermont brand whole wheat bread, one loaf

Morning Star Chicken Nuggets (x2)
Amy's Frozen burritos, miscellaneous (x10)
Morning Star Griller's Prime patties
Morning Star Chickpea patties,
Newman's Brand frozen pizza (margherita)
One bag frozen corn
One bag frozen rhubarb
One bag frozen broccoli

Scatter entire contents on floor
Jump up and down on contents methodically
Rescue chicken nuggets from floor, from a box partially flattened,
place unmolested nuggets in frying pan
Heat nuggets on gas range, eat with hands, get bored after a couple
and leave remainder in pan for when the police arrive.

When they had eaten their fill, such as it was, the perps found themselves unaccountably hushed, complete, and therefore in a period of uncertainty about what to do next. It was then that they realized they were, at least for the time being, *fulfilled*, regarding their day's labors. The next dialogue was thus: *Did you bring the hacksaw? No, I thought you brought the hacksaw. What are you fucking stupid? I told you to bring the hacksaw. I don't have a hacksaw. You're the one who said he had a hacksaw in the garage. We're missing out on the copper downstairs. Good money at the scrap yard, good money. We got all this jewelry, I want to lie down. You don't know what you're talking about, worthless pigfucker.* Acrimony and distemper. Strained, distracted silence. The inadvertent beginnings of sobriety. How could they have gone through the ritual of eating together, and then become so selfish, so sullen and resentful, so quickly? The three of them in a triangular configuration, each hating the other two, until one of the henchmen muttered what all had been thinking, *Well, maybe we'll just have a nice shit on the bed.*

Questions for Further Study

1) How is class a particular feature of the burglary at the heart of "A Country Scene?"

2) Is it possible to write a story in which there are no conventionally sympathetic characters? Is the narrator in this story sympathetic?

3) What is the symbolism of the act of *shitting on the bed*? Is it an example of the Gift Economy?

4) Have you or anyone you know been the subject of a violent crime?

5) Would you be able to be impartial if impaneled on a jury to consider the crimes of the protagonists of this work?

6) Does this work of fiction imperil due process should the perpetrators come to be apprehended in the matter of this crime?

7) Where farm animals are concerned is a lack of audible consent necessarily identical with non-consent?

8) Is the interior of a sheep, during the act, like a) a velvety passageway, b) stubbly and unwelcoming like a cratered lunar surface, c) fragile and dry like rice paper?

9) Why did I personally have to endure the burglary described above, which was actually two burglaries, interrupted briefly by a visit from the police some hours after the action described herein?

10) Is it possible for the perpetrators of these burglaries, who took, for example, the ring I proposed to my wife with, to commit these crimes without ever undertaking to feel the loss that the violated party feels (and here I use the word *violated*, despite its overuse in this context, because I now understand precisely what it means)?

11) How can I go on doing my work, when the place where I did my work was the setting of this "country scene"? That is, a place defiled by these guys, and made more their home than mine?

Nominated by Selmagundi,
Mark Irwin

FACE

by TOM SLEIGH

from LITERARY IMAGINATION

I. M. Mark Strand

Mark came into the room and said, *Tom, you have*
the face of a dog. Alan, you have the face
of a horse. And me, I have the face of—

but Mark couldn't decide what kind of face
he had, or else I couldn't in the dream
remember or maybe it was that the dream

couldn't remember. And in the second part
of the dream Mark came into the room smiling
and laughing, and after a while he left the room

and Alan said, *It's only natural he wants*
to have a good time. And when Mark didn't come
back for a while, I went looking for him,

and though I knew where he was, I couldn't find him.
And in the third part of the dream, Mark came
back into the room and said, *No, Alan, you*

have the face of a dog, Tom, you have
the face of a horse, and me, I have—
but he never did say what kind of face he had.

And in the fourth part of the dream, Mark came
back into the room and said, *No, no, it's me!*
I have the face of a horse! I have the face of a dog!

And in the fifth part of the dream—
but there was no fifth part of the dream—
only Alan, me, horse, dog, and Mark

coming and going, coming and going in the room.

Nominated by Literary Imagination,
David Jauss

THE IMAGINATION RESETTLEMENT PROGRAM

fiction by ELI BARRETT

from PLEIADES

The first one I saw was a tiger with golden stripes—shiny gold, like metal—breathing fire in my front yard, scorching the hell out of my Bermuda grass. I still don't know where that thing came from, maybe a folk tale or a kid's cartoon. All I know is it scared the bejeezus out of me. I hunkered down in my house for days afterward, watching the news. At first, no one could figure out where all these strange creations were coming from. Then they started finding famous ones, like Tarzan and Tom Thumb, until finally a government spokesman came on and told us that centuries of creating characters had caused a crisis. The world of imagination was overpopulated and overflowing.

The displaced characters had to live somewhere, and the government thought it would give the economy a boost to pay people to board them in their homes. For years I'd been scraping by on disability checks, so in spite of that bad brush with the tiger, I decided to apply to the program. Some people got lucky. Imagine having Winnie-the-Pooh living in your house! Or Cinderella! I got Mary. She was a simple advertising character, but she turned out to be better than any fairy tale princess around.

They dropped her off on a chilly morning. She must have been freezing, because with my bad leg it took me a long minute to walk to the door. There was an icy sort of rain falling, like frozen sand, and it glistened all over her coat and blonde hair. "I'm Mary," she said, "the bridal detective."

"I'm Carl," I said. Normally I have the manners to welcome someone to my home, even though I haven't had visitors for a while. With her, I couldn't get the words out at first. I kept thinking, *What the hell is a bridal detective?*

Maybe I motioned for her to come in, because she stepped inside and handed me her coat. Underneath, she was wearing a strapless silk dress with a brooch shaped like two church bells. She held out her hand, and when I touched it, it was warm despite the cold. When she smiled, it was the most perfect thing I'd seen in a long time.

❈   ❈   ❈

Like every other day for the last four months, Mary makes lunch while I watch TV. It's deviled eggs again. Most of her cooking is finger food and has gotten repetitive, but I don't mind. She lays a napkin on my lap and sets the tray beside me. I ask her to stay and talk. Nothing is on TV except boring documentaries anyway. "Do you want to see the gown you bought me?" she asks. She twirls around, her new dress swishing around her legs. "It's perfect for a semi-formal rehearsal dinner."

I chew an egg and watch her pose with her hands on her hips. "It's gorgeous," I tell her. Not long after she moved in, I went to a bookstore in town and sat down with a stack of bridal magazines, trying to find where she came from. They were all on the factual straight-and-narrow by then—real brides telling real stories, painfully dull ones at that. Then a few weeks later, I was in a thrift store that sold old magazines for a dime apiece. I dug through them until I found her. She was in a half-page ad for a traveling bridal show, wearing the clothes she'd come to me in. Under her outstretched hand was a list of cities and dates. "I'm Mary the bridal detective," the tagline read. "I search for the best deals in bridal fashions." I stared at that page until I noticed damp spots were pimpling the paper.

"Maybe soon we can go shopping for a wedding dress," she says. "The new collections are out now."

The house could've surely used a little feminine touch, but since she's arrived, it's been more than just a touch. The windows have silk curtains, the tables have vases and china figurines, and the cost of all that is nothing compared to her dresses and shoes. It's too late to learn to say no to her. To get another check, I've been thinking about taking in a second character. I discuss it with Mary. She says it has to be my decision. I'm the man of the house after all, and it's not like we're married. I watch her real close after she says this last thing. It could be she looks blue because we can't be married. It is against the law. Even taking her to bed, which would satisfy at least some of what I feel, would get me

245

kicked out of the program. She smiles and picks up the tray. I can't really tell if she's as sad as I am, because maybe it's just me telling myself what I want to hear.

Even though my house is barely big enough for two characters, the government approves my application and tells me to expect the new character to arrive soon. Mary helps me set up a cot in the basement next to the water heater. She scrubs stains from the cement floor and sweeps away spiderwebs. But there's only so much she can do. The basement walls are cracked, and a draft comes from a hole near the ceiling that also seems to be a nesting spot for squirrels. Getting hurt and living off disability checks doesn't make it easy to keep a house up, but the truth is I let most things slide around here until recently.

When Mary is finished cleaning, I thank her and use my hand to brush a few cobwebs from her hair. She moves her head, and I accidentally touch the side of her face. I don't move. Closing her eyes, she leans her head against my hand. I couldn't go back to a life without her. Then like always, I remember there's only one way for me to have everything I want. "Mary," I ask, testing her like I've done before, "if someone asked you about this, would you tell them what happened?"

"Yes," she says, lifting her head. "Why should we hide the things that make us happy?"

I brush my cobwebbed hand on my pants. She still smiles at me, while I'm surprised by the pain growing inside me. At least a dozen times a day, this same pain fills me like a balloon, and I never see it coming. Mary already makes me feel hugely lucky. I can't risk losing her. It's a bittersweet hurt anyway, a young man's hurt. It's better than the ache of broken joints any way I look at it, so how can I complain?

* * *

A few days later, Tommy Lee arrives at my doorstep. If he wasn't wearing a cowboy shirt and a Stetson hat, it would be hard to tell he came from the world of imagination. He looks like a regular young man. Firm handshake, quick smile. Calls me sir.

He cranes his neck toward the kitchen when he hears Mary cooking. I ask him to sit down on the couch and tell me about himself. I can't just ask what movie or book he's from, because everyone knows they don't think that way. He tells me he's lived on his family's ranch his whole life until now. I ask him what state his ranch is supposed to be in. He has no idea. I ask him if his state was called a territory. He stares at me. His papa and older brothers ran the ranch, he tells me, and he mostly

246

did chores and mended anything that was broken around the place. Am I lucky or what? The house needs a pair of strong hands as much as it needed Mary's feminine touch.

"My papa is the greatest rancher around," Tommy Lee tells me while we wait for Mary to finish cooking. "A preacher too. He used to be the sheriff, but now he just helps fight the outlaws and Injuns sometimes." Then he tells me about his six brothers, his God-fearing mama, and how every night at bedtime his papa came into his room to share some words of wisdom with him.

Mary enters with a shrimp cocktail tray. Tommy Lee jumps to his feet with his hat pressed to his chest. "I'm sure happy to see you, ma'am."

"I'm delighted to meet you too," she says, "but I'm a miss, not a ma'am."

"A miss? Are the boys around here blind?"

"I don't think so," she says. "I haven't met any who are."

"I just can't believe the prettiest flower in the prairie ain't been picked yet," he says, pinching a shrimp between his fingers.

Mary looks confused, but quickly pulls herself together. "I hope you like what I made. Shrimp cocktail never goes out of style." She gives him a delighted smile, but I'm not sharing the joy. He chews the shrimp with a doubtful look on his face.

"I don't think Tommy Lee likes your food," I say.

"No, I think it's the best grub in the world," he says. "A man would crawl over broken glass for it."

"Why would anyone want to do that?" Mary asks.

"He doesn't mean it, Mary," I say. "It's just a silly way of talking. Tommy Lee, you think you can handle fixing a leaky roof?"

"That would be nothing for me, Carl," he says. "I'll get it to as soon as I finish talking to this fine lady."

"No, you better start now."

"You're the boss man, I guess," he says, putting his hat on. "Don't go anywhere, miss. I'll be back soon." Not long after, I hear him hammering above my head. I tell myself to give him some time to settle down. He might just be a young man who's full of overblown country flattery, the sort of man who'd praise another man's new truck or his new boots as quick as he'd praise a young woman's beauty.

I glance over from my recliner to make sure Mary's lost in her dress catalog, because the evening news is on and they are interviewing some joker who's saying that characters are all dirty freeloaders who should be forced to work for their benefits. Lately, that's become a common opinion. The time when everyone worried about Winnie-the-Pooh finding a decent home feels long gone. There's also the feeling that the government is throwing money at a crisis that's over. New characters have been banned all over the world, except in a few rogue countries, and the government experts have discovered that if enough people imagine a character, it will go back. Now every night instead of educational TV, we have repatriation shows. After the news ends. I stay tuned for the start of tonight's show, a performance of *Hamlet*. I try to keep my eyeballs on it so he can go back to a world where people understand the way he talks.

When it's dark outside, Tommy Lee comes in and sits on the couch next to Mary. He cranes his neck to see her catalog and then slides closer until their shoulders almost touch. I tell him it's his bedtime and show him to the basement.

"How'd you get lame?" he asks, eyeing my bad leg. "Did a horse throw you?"

"That sounds better than falling from a third-story scaffold," I say.

"So that's what happened to you!" he says. "I bet it was hard to walk again. You must've learned a lot from your suffering."

"Not a damn thing except that hospital bills are expensive," I say, "and that being a slow walker in a fast world is no fun."

"Papa was shot by outlaws twice. And he was bit by a rattlesnake while on a cattle drive. It took him three days to crawl to help."

"Okay. And he got wise right after those things happened?"

"That's how he can give me lessons before I go to sleep. Suffering, like you did, and what he learned preaching."

"Good for him." I reach for the cord to turn off the light. "It's time for you to sleep."

"Wait. What did I learn today?"

"You patched a leaky roof, but I think you already knew how to do that."

He flips over on his stomach so he's not looking at me, burrows his face into the pillow, and groans a little.

"You getting sick?"

He lifts his head. "I just want to learn something."

"Well, that's a worthy goal I guess. I got an old set of encyclopedias packed in a box somewhere."

"That's not what I mean," he says. "Where's my goodnight lesson? Even if I caught the barn on fire or even if I sold Mr. Dobson's horse so I could go to the carnival, my papa would sit beside my bed and give me a lesson."

248

Hell, I think. *This one is turning into a handful.* "Not every day in the world will bring you a lesson," I tell him. "Most days you're just here and that's it."

He pulls the pillow around his ears and shakes his head back and forth.

I once watched an educational show about different kinds of characters. Some sort of special event has to repeat in the life of some types of characters. A mystery has to be solved or a misunderstanding has to be cleared up. Without that, they can't let go of one day and move on to the next. So he'll sleep, I'll give him a lesson. "You should leave Mary alone," I say. "That's my advice to you."

"Why?"

"Because I'm older, like your papa, and we know about life."

He starts drumming the cot with his feet, slowly at first and then faster. "But you're just telling me what I can't do. You're not teaching me anything."

He kicks harder and faster, and the cot begins to shake. The flimsy frame squeaks and rattles like it's about to be wrenched apart. "Hold on," I say. "What I'm trying to teach you is that too much flattery can make a woman hate you."

The kicking stops. "Is that what happened to you?"

It was always the opposite problem for me, keeping quiet and shying away when it was time to lay out my feelings. But I'm not going to tell him that. "Yes," I lie, "There was this woman I decided to sweet talk. I flattered her so much. I said a lot of silly things. Then when I was finally finished, she said she could never believe me again. And she never did."

"That must've broke your heart clean in two. I believe you're right. Being too sweet to a woman straightaway isn't smart," he says, placing his head on the pillow. "You suffered, but now you have a lot of wisdom. Good night—" He pauses, and I know he's thinking of his papa, wherever he may be. He smiles and says, "Sir." I reach down and pat his shoulder before I turn out the light.

Now that Tommy Lee and his check are finally here, I can take Mary shopping like I promised. As we make the long drive into town, Tommy Lee looks out at the poor farms and rundown strip malls like they're wonders of the world. When we arrive at a bridal store advertising a big sale, I make him wait outside in the parking lot to guard my car against the gangs of outlaws I tell him have been seen in the area.

249

I wait in a chair in the corner while Mary disappears into the dressing room again. "Do you really like it?" Mary asks when she comes out. She lifts the skirt of a lacey wedding dress and lets it sway in her hand.

"It's beautiful," I say, "like everything you've tried on."

Shoppers in the crowded store look at us and whisper. A few give Mary unfriendly stares. She looks no different than any of them, only more beautiful. I suspect I'm the giveaway that she's a character. If she wasn't, she wouldn't be here with me. After I buy her the cheapest dress she liked, I carry it out hanging over my shoulder. "I saw you through the window," Tommy Lee says when he opens the door for us. "You were powerful pretty, like a rainbow after a desert rain."

"I'm glad you like it," she says, beaming. "Although my dress is very white, not like a rainbow at all."

Not that he notices, but I glare at him, wondering how he forgot last night's lesson. While we're arranging the dress to lie flat in the trunk, a woman crosses the parking lot. "I wish I could afford a dress like that," she says over her shoulder. "I guess being real doesn't count for much anymore."

"No one wants to buy you a nice dress anyhow!" I yell as she walks off.

I decide I'm not going to let a bigot stop us from enjoying the day, so I treat us all to lunch at a sit-down restaurant. People occasionally sneak looks at Mary just like they would any good-looking woman. Their eyes glide past me to Tommy Lee, the men's eyes jealous, the women's pleased. No one seems to guess he and Mary are characters. It makes me sad as hell, but the difference must be him. The shirt he's wearing today only cost me a few dollars at the thrift store, but it looks good on him and not too old fashioned. Probably they think I'm his father, the living proof of how far he's come from his lowly beginnings to nab a beauty like Mary.

When it's his bedtime, I give him another talk about treating women with respect, which of course means not flirting with Mary. He smiles and thanks me again for my wise words. Then the next day he's wooing her as bold as brass. For the next month, it's the same routine. The only difference is Mary. Maybe it's my imagination, but she seems to care as much for him as me.

* * *

I feel good for about ten seconds after I wake up and then I remember the awful news I heard on TV last night. I usually join Mary and Tommy Lee for breakfast by this time, but I stay in bed, turn on the radio, and listen with the volume low. I'm hoping somehow the government changed its mind while I was sleeping.

A morning call-in show is on. "I hope they get worked sixteen hours a day," a caller is saying. "They owe it to us taxpayers."

The host asks, "Do you think the politicians decided to phase out the resettlement program because of the election later this year?"

"They sure did. They're running scared now. They finally heard how angry the real people are."

"And do you believe the labor camps will be humane like the government says? There are a lot of very, umm . . . interesting characters who'll be housed in these camps and working together—maybe not for sixteen hours a day like you suggested but for long hours regardless. Do you think they can have a decent life?"

"They already sent the best characters back." The caller cackles. "So now it should be about getting a good life for us. The real people. You can't tell me that free labor from all those thousands of characters won't get the economy moving again."

"Let's hope it makes a difference, because things have been rough out there. Thanks for your—" I turn the radio off. My leg hurts like hell this morning, so to climb out of bed I have to use a cane. When I hobble into the kitchen, Tommy Lee is at the table, eating the thin pancakes Mary always makes. Tipping his hat, he says, "Howdy, boss."

"You're awake!" Mary says. "I'm sorry I started breakfast without you. I wanted to wait, but it was getting late." Seeing her act so concerned, just for making pancakes before I woke up, makes me feel even worse. The labor camp they'll send her to is no place for a woman who can get worked up over making tiny slights.

Tommy Lee starts talking to Mary about breaking horses and this one filly in particular named Thunderclap who never let anyone ride her except him.

"You think you can clean the gutters today?" I ask him. He spends most of his days working outside, not by chance of course. Even though I hate him half the time, I still manage to give him a better life than the government will.

He slowly chews his pancake before answering. "I already took care of those gutters," he says. "Been up working since six. I'm just enjoying these flapjacks from this good ol' gal."

"I'm so glad you like the crepes," Mary says. "They're great as hors d'oeuvres or as a cozy breakfast before a wedding."

251

Tommy Lee stands up and carries his plate over to the stove. "All I know is I'm a lucky son of a gun to get a hot breakfast from a pretty woman. I'd like to have that for life."

"I want you to rehang the shutters," I say.

"But nothing's wrong with the shutters," he says. "They're hanging fine."

"They looked a little crooked to me."

"How's that? They're plumb straight."

"This isn't an argument. Get out there now," I say. Shaking his head, he turns on his heel and leaves. I sit down and rub my pounding head. Mary brings me a plate and a cup of coffee. "There's something I need to ask you," I say. "What if we moved somewhere else?"

"With Tommy Lee?"

"No, he can't come. We'd be starting over fresh. We'd even have new names."

She spoons some batter into a hot pan. "You wouldn't call me Mary?"

"Maybe at home, if you want," I say, "but not around other people."

"I'm Mary the bridal detective," she says, a woman literal-minded as can be, which makes leading a false life nearly impossible. It's pointless anyway. I have no money, and my cane doesn't say much for finding the kind of rough, anonymous work I'd need to support myself and Mary.

Something smashes in the living room. I tell Mary to wait while I check, Tommy Lee, a hammer in his hand, is standing on a ladder outside the window. A pane is gone except for a few wobbly shards still attached to the grid. "I wasn't paying attention to what I was doing," he says.

"That sounds like the definition of sloppy workmanship," I say.

"If I broke a window on the ranch while I was daydreaming, my papa might make me fix all the windows in the poor widow's house down the road."

"Oh, would he? That sounds pretty darn complicated," I say, noticing the draft blowing in from the missing pane. "You can make up for your mistake by just fixing my window. I don't want the cold getting in tonight."

He climbs down from the ladder. "Let me do something more," he shouts, "so I learn something."

"I have to go to the store. If you want to show me how sorry you are," I say, "throw some grass seeds on the scorch marks that tiger left on my lawn."

"And then what?"

"Find something to work on," I say. "Something on the outside of the house."

On my way to the hardware store, I have to pull over for a bit because my eyes are too misty to see straight. The cashier asks if I've been crying. The hell I'm gonna tell him. When I get back home and open my front door, the house sounds like it has been holding its breath. "Mary?" I call. No answer. I rattle my cane across the floor as I walk to Mary's bedroom. I count to ten before I open her door. On the bed, Mary is sitting in her wedding dress. Tommy Lee is beside her, their hands entwined in her lap.

I catch my breath and say, "What the hell are you doing?"

"I'm marrying this little lady," he says, turning to Mary. Her face doesn't change and she stares past me.

"Are you crazy?" I say. "You'll do no such thing." I move as fast as I can toward the bed. To my surprise, he doesn't resist when I tug his arm. In fact, he seems to scoot over to the edge of the bed.

"You ain't gonna take her away!" he screams. "I'll run away with her before you do."

"Boy, she don't even want you," I say. Looking at Mary, I can tell she had no idea how to say no to him. Tommy Lee turns to look at her too, but she's looking past the both of us.

"I messed her up," Tommy Lee says. "What should I do?"

I yank his sleeve, and he springs to his feet right away. "Get out of my house," I say. He looks at me with his mouth hanging open, so I repeat myself. Now he's crying as he walks to the door. Once he's on the porch, he dries his eyes with his sleeve. "It must be my turn to suffer," he says quietly. "Maybe I can help some people right their wrongs along the way."

"Your suffering won't help anyone, not even yourself," I say. After I close the door, I peek out the window. He's nowhere to be seen, like he never existed. I wonder how long it will take the authorities to notice Tommy Lee suffering heroically. Before I can worry about that, I have to see Mary. She's sitting on her bed in a white slip, her gown hanging on its wooden frame in the corner of the room. "Did you agree to marry him?" I say, my voice sounding angrier than I intended.

"No," she says. There are tears in her eyes, but at least she's looking at me.

"Mary," I say. "You've been living with me for half a year. I have to ask you—do you want me?"

"What do you mean?"

"To marry. Do you want to marry me?" In my ears, my voice sounds high-pitched and scared. I've told myself a million times that what I want isn't allowed, but it was just me being scared, like I was standing at a door and counting to an enormous number before I went inside.

"I don't know," Mary says. "I shouldn't always be preparing for something I never do, but I don't know what it is."

There's no point in waiting anymore. The door is wide open and I'm going through it. I kiss her. After a few times, I wonder if her lips will kiss me back. I haven't totally forgotten what it's like to be with a woman, but I feel like I'm going through the motions. I slide my hand down the front of her slip, squeezing and kneading with my thumb like I remember. I think her neck is arching with pleasure, but maybe I'm pushing her head back with my kisses. She leans back on her elbows to make it easier for me to touch her, or it could be because my weight is on top of her. I slide my hand underneath her slip. "Oh Mary," I say, moving my fingers. "What did they do to you?"

Or what didn't they do? I've always sworn the person who thought her up did it two minutes before a deadline. She was never meant to be a bride, just a bridal detective. I search with my fingers again just to be sure. When I sit up, Mary stays on her back, staring at the ceiling. Her tears wait for her to blink so they can spill over her lashes. "I'm sorry," I say. She sobs and nods her head. "Things can be like they were before," I tell her.

And they could have been, except they come for her the next day.

* * *

There's a man I telephone. "Bridal detective?" he says. "Are you kidding me? Now I've heard everything. How about I make her a cop? I won't even charge you extra."

"No," I say, "I want her to stay the way she is in the ad I sent you."

"Suit yourself," he says. "You know how to wire money overseas?"

Vanity repatriation, they call it. There is a black market for writers who want to return their characters to the world of imagination. In third-world countries that didn't sign the character ban, there are thousands of people who eke out a living by watching videos or listening to books. It took me a long time to find the right phone number and even longer to save up the money.

After the deal is made, I slide open my dresser and take out a magazine that's as stiff and bumpy as a washboard. The experts say that when these characters are in the world of imagination, they can't see our world

254

at all. But maybe when Mary goes home, she'll know it was me who freed her. She'll know it was me who loved her. The magazine falls open to Mary's page. Like she wants to share a joyful secret, she's smiling up at me. She holds her arm out like she's ushering me toward a prize only she knows.

Nominated by Pleiades

CHRISTIAN SOLDIERS

by HAL CROWTHER

from NARRATIVE

> Under a government which imprisons any unjustly, the true place for a just man is also a prison . . . the only house in a slave state in which a free man can abide with honor.
>
> —*Henry David Thoreau*, Civil Disobedience

The death of Daniel Berrigan, a personal hero and one of the few men alive who was old enough to be my father, called up disturbing memories of a critical period in American history. One memory in particular. I was a fledgling journalist at *Time* magazine in New York, newly wed, and freshly radicalized by the terrible events of 1968, when Robert Kennedy and Martin Luther King Jr. were assassinated, Richard Nixon was elected president, and a misbegotten war in Vietnam divided this country as it has not been divided since—until, perhaps, at this moment of Donald Trump's ascension. One of my colleagues was dating a tall, pretty young woman named Ann Berrigan. A few of us were drinking at her apartment one late-winter night in 1969. A guest looking for the bathroom started to open a door in the hall—and Ann jumped up almost screaming to warn him, "Don't open that door—don't!" Everyone was startled, and mystified when she made no effort to explain.

After her outburst, the evening ended on a note of embarrassment. Back in the street waiting for a cab, Ann's boyfriend entrusted me with the story. Behind the bedroom door that night was her uncle, the Reverend Daniel Berrigan, S.J., a federal fugitive, a radical priest on the FBI's most-wanted list for his part in the incineration (with homemade napalm) of Selective Service records in Catonsville, Maryland, the previous May. Ann was protecting not just her uncle, he explained, but her guests as well. Anyone who actually saw Father Berrigan or could confirm his presence was legally obligated to call the FBI or, like Ann, risk felony prosecution for harboring a fugitive.

I had covered the occupation of Columbia University buildings by the SDS, interviewed its militant war chief, Mark Rudd, and witnessed policemen with billy clubs assaulting tenured professors. In New York I'd undergone a rapid evolution from Rockefeller Republican to pacifist and Berrigan fellow traveler, all while the long black shadow of the draft board still lay across my future like a napalmed corpse. But Dan Berrigan hiding just down the hall, on the other side of a thin apartment wall—this was closer to the heart of civil disobedience and radical royalty than I had ever imagined I would be. Later I heard Ann talk about her Uncle Dan and Uncle Phil—Dan's younger brother, a Josephite priest and a war hero—with pride in their exploits but anxious comprehension of the dangers to which these fugitives of conscience had exposed their friends and family. Every good Catholic family is proud of its priests, but the Berrigans had produced a fearless pair of militants the conservative Catholic hierarchy could never endorse or restrain.

Father Dan was the poet, the intellectual of the brothers Berrigan. His first book of verse, *Time Without Number,* had won the prestigious Lamont Prize in 1957, establishing him at thirty-six as a leading figure among Catholic poets. English poetry was my focus as an undergraduate, and for a draft deferment I had been teaching literature at a New England boarding school. As a federal fugitive, Dan Berrigan represented the confluence of serious poetry and nonviolent resistance to the government of the United States—to me, at that time, an irresistible combination. I read most of Berrigan's work that was then in print. Impressed by his craftsmanship and passion, I was an unlikely candidate for his brotherhood of faith. His poem "The Face of Christ" begins "The tragic beauty of the face of Christ shines in our faces." A pilgrim like me, from a family of agnostics, Unitarians, and hardheaded, freethinking Scots, is not instantly engaged. But what fascinated and haunted me was the life where his intellect and faith had led him, a life that in a few months would place him in a prison with felons who had never read a poem.

The Berrigan brothers' crusade against the Vietnam War and imperial America was one of the first unqualified examples of "high seriousness" I encountered, outside of a book. What they were attempting opened a wider avenue of dissent for so many of us, still politically unformed, who were trying to refine and respond to our consciences. The

257

"higher power" inspiring Dan and Phil Berrigan was so transparently, mountainously higher than the power represented by Nixon and Agnew (and the amoral, Machiavellian Kissinger) that it shamed a whole generation out of the adolescent patriotism we were raised on. Atheists or evangelicals, boys who followed the Berrigans' example and burned their draft cards understood—in a way most of their fathers never had—that defying cynical politicians and bad laws was not the same as betraying your country. And that betraying your conscience was the worst crime of all.

Raised like the Berrigans in a rural, predominantly Catholic community in upstate New York, I grew up with a weakness for priests. Maybe it was their celibacy, freely giving up the one thing I desired most, that intrigued me. But I always knew one or two, and I used to play golf in the early morning, on the dew-drenched fairways most duffers avoid, with an Irish priest who cheerfully tried to convert me to some respectable form of Christianity. I called him Father though he asked me to call him Tom. He looked like Nick Nolte and died young, of cancer. From my secular viewpoint, priests carried an otherness about them that Protestant clergymen did not share. Most of them assigned to our rural parish came from exotic places like Manhattan, Buffalo, Albany. The nearest university, attracting the best Catholic students from my school, was St. Bonaventure, where Thomas Merton had once taught English literature among the brown-robed Franciscans I regarded with exaggerated curiosity and respect.

Dan Berrigan revered Merton, author of the religious classic *The Seven Storey Mountain*, and always claimed him as an intellectual and spiritual father. I met Father Dan only once, many years after his imprisonment and rehabilitation, at a funeral attended by luminaries of the Left. I told him about the night at his niece's apartment, which he found amusing as ancient history. I didn't get a fair chance to sample his famous dry wit. It was his brother Philip with whom I made significant acquaintance, and from whom I received a late education in pacifism, commitment, and Christian sacrifice—a brief but not superficial glimpse of the singular mind of an individual who could live as the Berrigans lived.

In the eternal struggle between the flesh and the spirit, it was the weakness that I always understood. Phil Berrigan, as much as anyone I ever met, showed me the strength. In May 1994 he and two of his pacifist commandos were locked in the county jail in Edenton, North Carolina, awaiting trial for applying their hammers of justice to the nose cones of F-15E fighter planes at Seymour Johnson Air Force Base.

Phil, then seventy, had already spent more years in prison than Mohandas Gandhi. A former semipro ballplayer and an infantry lieutenant at the Battle of the Bulge, he was still physically imposing—to carry out his symbolic assault on the F-15Es he climbed an eight-foot fence, forded a freezing knee-deep stream, and crossed three-quarters of a mile of pavement on his hands and knees.

A tough cookie, this warrior-priest, who talked about his eleven-plus years in prisons the way scholars talk about graduate school. Sympathetic to his cause, I hadn't known what to expect from him or his fellow prisoners of conscience. I'm profoundly claustrophobic, and people who would give up their physical freedom for their beliefs, for any beliefs, stood well outside my experience. Maybe I anticipated some kind of feverish, hollow-eyed fanatics. What Berrigan showed me instead was the supernatural self-control, the peace and apparently impregnable calm that must come with a firm belief in a benevolent personal God. If I try to describe myself at that time—as my forties ended—*disillusioned* and *skeptical* are words that come to mind. I had not found a God like Berrigan's, and doubted that I ever would—but only an idiot would have failed to recognize the power that it gave him. One of the things I remember best about this strange encounter in the Chowan County jail is that the deputies and jailers—none of them educated or Catholic, I would guess—seemed almost as impressed with their prisoners as I was. They were respectful, almost gentle with Phil Berrigan and big John Dear, a Duke-educated Jesuit, and their younger disciple Bruce Friedrich.

At least in my presence they were gentle, and it's not as if I was Mike Wallace and the crew from *60 Minutes*. A mild irony was that Philip Berrigan, for all his sacrifice and the transfiguring power of his faith, was not immune to the call of the flesh. He secretly married a former nun in 1970, when he was still a working priest, and later fathered three children. This was a weakness he shared with the great Thomas Merton. Merton (not unlike Saint Augustine) earned a reputation as a libertine in his student days at Cambridge and was forever susceptible to wine, women, and song—jazz, in the latter case. The Kentucky writer James Still, a friend of mine, used to sneak six-packs of beer into Gethsemani Abbey to share with this imperfect monk, whose (avowedly) platonic love affair with a student nurse in Louisville caused a scandal at the abbey when Merton was fifty and world famous.

Dan Berrigan seems to have been the true ascetic, the one best suited for the priesthood or the monastery. For most of his ninety-five years he owned virtually nothing, and according to the people who loved him he never noticed the absence of material things that most Americans take for granted. This was an ideal condition to which I always aspired—of all the monastic vows, poverty would have been the easiest for me—but never quite managed to achieve. (Chastity, silence, obedience—are you serious?) In a diseased consumer culture like America's, uncontaminated citizens like Daniel Berrigan have been viewed as exotic aliens. Of all the quotes I've collected from compatriots whose wisdom was inadequately celebrated, my favorite is a premature self-epitaph from Patrick Hemingway, retired big-game guide and son of the famous Papa: "Say what you will about me, call me an underachiever, but I was never a consumer, and I was never a fan."

I like to think the Berrigans read Hemingway's boast somewhere, and shared it with satisfaction. The strength their neighbors squandered getting and spending, these brothers devoted to emulating Jesus, as they understood him, and pleasing God. I thought a lot about their faith after witnessing it in practice in the Chowan County jail. The essential work of their lives was conscience building—deciding (or learning, the scholarly Jesuit might have said) exactly what God expects of your conscience and obeying, without question, as long as you live. The voice of your conscience becomes the same as the voice of your God. A God I approved of, in their case, even if I couldn't share him. Theirs was no soft, malleable, spongy sort of God who forgives us for everything or who can be molded to any desperate purpose—the worst examples of this all-too-human heresy would be the KKK using the cross of Dan Berrigan's Jesus as a symbol of racist terrorism, or jihadists murdering Muslims (and others) in the name of a homicidal god. The Berrigans' God was a harder God they followed down a hard road; the best consciences I ever witnessed under pressure weren't half as strict as theirs.

Their brand of radical pacifism was too demanding to attract a host of disciples—Jesus barely managed double figures, after all—but the quality of their converts was very high. John Dear, the Jesuit from North Carolina who was jailed in Edenton with Phil Berrigan, has been arrested seventy times for nonviolent protests and served several years in prison. He was dismissed by the Jesuits in 2013 because his passion for peace, in the eyes of his superiors, had compromised his vows of obedience to the order. "Obedience to God comes first," I remember Dear saying, in his jail cell in 1994. But many of us in North Carolina are extremely proud of him for sustaining the work of the Plowshares Movement, for keeping the faith as he inherited it from the Berrigans.

Phil Berrigan died in 2002. Now Dan is gone too, and John Dear, a vigorous young lion of a priest when I met him, is nearing sixty. The *New York Times* describes the peace movement as "withering"; the Pentagon and the Society of Jesus operate much as they did before the Plowshares priests took up their hammers. The secretary of state who once stage-managed America's involvement in the Middle East carnage was narrowly defeated in the 2016 presidential election by a saber-rattling right-wing maniac who raves about bombing Arab countries until the sand glows. After thirteen years, at a cost of more than two trillion dollars and 4,500 American deaths, the United States of America—which defeated Hitler, Tojo, and Mussolini in less than four years—has failed to "secure" the single city of Baghdad or the highway to its airport. All Vietnam's lessons remain stubbornly unlearned.

"This is the worst time of my life," an eighty-seven-year-old Dan Berrigan said in 2008, the last year of the Bush-Cheney-Rumsfeld war machine. "I have never had such meager expectations of the system." But he was in firm command of the irony involved in making great sacrifices for an apparently hopeless cause. He preached that believing in God and doing the right thing, regardless of consequences, were the imperatives that kept a decent person sane. "The day after I'm embalmed," he vowed, "that's when I'll give it up." His refusal to retreat or despair reminded me of the day I spent with his brother Phil in the Edenton jail.

"Is there a temptation to despair and quit, to fold up our tents and go back to normalcy, to our personal requirements?" Phil asked himself, and his comrades. "I suppose. But the consequences of withdrawal are reprehensible. Silence lends assent, doesn't it? Jesus didn't withdraw. I preserve a lot of hope."

"We're prey to discouragement," he admitted when we were alone, the last thing he said to me before the cell door clicked shut on him again. "The public resists the lessons of history—it scarcely acknowledges history. Americans seem tired of perplexing social issues. It comes from the way we live in this country, I guess."

Neither their country nor their church ever lived up to the Berrigans' expectations, and nothing about the way we live in this country offers much hope that there will be another generation of radical priests to hold America's feet to the spiritual fire. There are no schools that breed Christian soldiers of their unbending creed, to insist as they did that war, militarism, and gun violence are all one disease, and one linked inseparably to all the other diseases—oppression, poverty, starvation, racism, environmental degradation—that threaten to bring the human adventure to a premature conclusion. War is insane and disgusting, and it will be with us always, undermining most progress in the direction of civilization. Frustrated pacifists find consolation in the conviction that we're on the right side of history. That consolation is more powerful, apparently, for those convinced that they're on the right side of a righteous God.

Can traditional religion, burdened by its own history, disrespected by science, crowded almost into the shadows by conspicuous consumption and metastasizing technology, still inspire unusual individuals to live heroically, on a consistently higher moral plane? The answer, for anyone familiar with the Berrigan brothers, is a confident "Yes." But there's always my other question, which I'd never be rude enough to pose to a man of faith: If God made and loves us all, why did he make so many of us cruel and stupid?

I've never forgotten a prayer I learned in summer school from the Jesuits of Canisius College in Buffalo, where an Alsatian priest taught me more and better French in two months than several expensive schools had taught me in six years: "Mère de Dieu, priez pour nous, maintenant et à l'heure de notre mort."

Nominated by Narrative

BBHMM

by TIANA CLARK

from THE JOURNAL

After watching the music video

Vm
P

I, too, want to be naked,   zebra-striped
in the almost dried accountant's blood,   sticky
and sucking   a fat blunt inside a Louis Vuitton
suitcase brimming   with the newest money.

This   is another way to see myself, too,
in the way Rihanna   nooses   a white woman   up
by her smooth feet, a blue-blooded pendulum   swaying
as her beautiful tits   look more perfect than ever.

Why did that image excite me so? No,   not the tits,
but the simulated lynching.   It feels so damn
delicious   to say bitch.   Bitch better/bitch better have
my money inside my mouth.   I hate it when people

talk about black artists   being capitalists.
Why can't we thrive in something rich and green too? And let us
be loud about it? Let us be loud   without consequence.
Remember, when we were dating? I wanted you   to pay

for every meal, and yes, the movies taught me that love—
was someone reaching for the check   first.
But *there is no such thing as a free lunch.* Someone
has to pay   with the fruit from their body.   Yeah, I'm spreading

my legs   for someone else, because I'm hungry   and always
at end of some kind of altar. Even now, I'm paying for my doctor
to reach and scrape inside me   to say   I don't have cancer.
She tells me   I need to start thinking about babies

because of my age.   I think, *Bitch* . . .   I'm not ready.
There will always   be tithes and offerings. At my church,
they called it *first fruits*.   My mother gave me quarters
and as a kid   I waited for the clink at the bottom

of the bucket being passed. I believed God heard this too.
Somewhere someone is counting the cash behind a velvet curtain.
Once, a boy said, *suck it, bitch*   with his heavy, dense hand
at the back of my head   pushing. Pushing   is

another way to mean   *pay me what you owe me.* I didn't forget.
Yeah, I see the total   at the bottom of the receipt.
I have so much   debt.
                  I am forever   in the wettest red.

Nominated by The Journal,
Chloe Honum,
Allegra Hyde

NO TIME LIKE THE PRESENT

fiction by **GABRIEL BROWNSTEIN**

from HARVARD REVIEW

Katya was a yoga teacher and very pretty, with a round face and little black dreadlocks, a degree in cinema studies from Bard College, and a tattoo of an infinity sign on the back of her neck. Her father was a doctor from Boston, and her mother a painter from Port-au-Prince. She had been called Catherine when growing up in Old Lyme, Connecticut. Tomorrow was her lumpectomy. She took a pill and kissed her daughter Nomi goodnight.

Sebastian Fishberger, her husband, was forty-four years old. He retained the build of a high school varsity tennis player, though perhaps more stooped. He owned a company that sold web-based learning applications to colleges and universities. While his wife brushed her teeth, Sebastian lay on the couch, drinking his third whiskey of the night, and reading a book that had helped Katya with her anxieties, *Tomorrow and Tomorrow and Tomorrow*, by Jonathan Garment, M.D. Sebastian sipped his whiskey. The ice melted in his glass. The first time Sebastian came to a half-familiar Sanskrit word, he thought he understood it. The second time, he was less sure. The third, he realized that his eyes were running over the same lines again and again. His eyelids got heavy. The ship of meaning came unmoored from the words. He held the book in front of his face, but now he dreamed he was on a boat, reading. The sentences became a noise in the background of his dreaming, a sound like the lapping of the tide. His little skiff ran past a spiny reef, and toward open water. Under the surface, he saw the creamsicle fins of a big orange fish. He heard a tiny click—he imagined it was the click of

Katya's reading lamp. His eyes opened. He thought of the front door—the door had come with the house, the ugly green front door—its knob was old and cheap and spotty in parts where the brass finish had worn off. The knob was sticky. The knob didn't work.

Earlier in the evening, he had been trying to take out the garbage, and had been unable to open the door on account of the broken doorknob. The trash had had a broken chicken bone in it, and the bone had punctured the bag, and the bag had started to drip brownish greenish juice all over the front hall. Katya had come to Sebastian's rescue, wearing a blue canvas apron. She had opened the door with a twist of her mindful wrist, a trick that Sebastian had been unable to duplicate. And now that she had taken her pill and gone to sleep, he worried. What if there were a fire? Would they be able to open the door and escape? If there were a fire, would they all be trapped?

Sebastian wore the clothes he had worn to work: a candy-striped Oxford shirt and a pair of steel gray jeans. He got the screwdriver from the cabinet above the fridge. The knob was loose. Where the knob met the door there was a circular piece—some kind of guard or washer shaped like a donut. It rattled. Sebastian tried to tighten the little screw at the knob's side, but the problem was inside the mechanism. There might also be a problem on the side of the door. Maybe the problem was with the catch plate. Maybe the catch plate stuck out a little, and that made it hard for the latch to retract. Sebastian turned and twisted the knob. He kicked the door. He tried again. The door opened.

Mist rose from the asphalt, past the parked cars and up to the streetlights and windows. Their cat, Hanuman, crept toward the front door, sniffing. Sebastian nudged the cat with his foot toward the living room and the coffee table. He knelt down in the front hall, to get a look at the catch plate. He couldn't fix it any tighter to the door's side. His wallet pinched, so he took it out of his right front pants pocket and laid it on the Ikea organizer, where the family kept its shoes. There, he forgot it.

He had fallen in love with his wife in the early 1990s, when she was in a band called Cat Fight Cat Fight. She had been playing bass at a house party in Annandale, a little girl with glowing dark skin and a big bright smile and a giant instrument and her afro popping wildly from the top of a multi-colored scarf. For the lumpectomy, Katya was going to leave before six in the morning. That was her plan. She was going to take the subway to the hospital on 168th Street. Sebastian was going to pack Nomi's lunch and walk Nomi to daycare, and from there follow Katya's path into the city and uptown on the A train. When the procedure was over, and the doctors discharged her, they would take a taxi back to Brooklyn. Sebastian had wanted to drive Katya to the hospital and to drive her back home, but Katya had wanted him to be home in the morning for Nomi. Katya had been adamant. She didn't want to hire a sitter. She didn't want to explain the procedure to their little girl until it was done. She had banned the word cancer from the house. Also, she didn't want Sebastian to worry about parking near the hospital. He knew she was being crazy, but he figured that since Katya was the one who had to the tumor, he might as well do what she said.

He pictured little pervert flesh cells reproducing in his wife's breast. They never said the word tumor aloud. She had excised it from conversation, by decree. But now it sat there, next to even their most ordinary remarks, like some kind of emoticon they couldn't scrub from their emails. She'd text, "Nomi's got dance at four tomorrow? or "Can you pick up some laundry detergent?" and he'd see it like a shadow on the screen. Was it the dancing crab emoticon? No, it was the pile of shit emoticon, the one with the little flies. Past midnight, he disassembled and reassembled the doorknob. He extracted the long, oily, toothed spindle from the center of the door. There was a conference call at four tomorrow with Port Jefferson University, and if all went well and he was back from the hospital, he'd call in. Sebastian put the long bolts in his mouth and the short screws in a little white espresso cup. A figure in green appeared outside the gate. Sebastian rose, screwdriver in hand, as though he were ready to defend his house from an invader. But it was only his neighbor Foley in his bulky sweatshirt, and Foley's labradoodle, Ringo. Foley's glasses glinted in the dark. Ringo wagged his club-like tail. Sebastian threaded the spindle back through the gears. He tried to fix the catch plate more tightly to the side of the door. He tested the knob. Then he shut the door. He could not open it again.

He cursed. He turned the knob. He pulled it. He said, "Fuck shit." He rattled it. He had fucked it. He kicked the door. He had fucked it good. He had made it worse. They were trapped. Before six in the morning, Katya would have to go out the back door without coffee or breakfast, and from the little back yard she would have to climb six sets of fences, through the Goldenberg's yard and past the chicken coop, all the way to the Lombardo's alleyway, just to get to the fucking hospital. Sebastian kept twisting and tugging on the doorknob, and finally got it open. The wind was picking up, the fog vanishing. The gray cat made a dash for freedom. Sebastian caught the animal in his arms.

Now that the door was open, he was afraid to close it again. It seemed he had only two choices: 1) to stand in the open door all night; or 2) to go to Home Depot and get a new doorknob.

Katya the yogi believed in the dharma. Sebastian did the stretches, he joined the chanting, he said the ohms, but he was more skeptical. In *Tomorrow and Tomorrow and Tomorrow,* Jonathan Garment, M.D., argued that a mantra turned signal into noise. A phrase, like "present moment," or "beautiful moment," through repetition became nothing but a movement of the lips and tongue, or if repeated silently, just a firing in the blackness of the frontal lobes. Sebastian wasn't sure how that notion calmed Katya. He also wasn't sure that Garment was right. Surgery was scheduled for eight-thirty. They'd probably be home by four. Sebastian knew he shouldn't care about the Port Jefferson University call.

At Home Depot, the clerks in orange aprons stood asleep at their stations. Music piped through wires into their ears. A familiar jingle played through the hangar space of the store: "A rainy day or a sunny day could be any day is a funny day." Sale displays of gas grills and backyard furniture looked like the remains of civilizations in which no one had ever wanted to live. Sebastian took out his phone to check the time. There was a warning on his screen: less than ten percent of battery left. He wandered down an aisle of front doors, past deadbolts and combination locks. Sebastian selected neither the most nor the least expensive doorknob. It was called Tuff Stuff. Its knobs were round brassy balls, and they were packed in a hard clear plastic with a hole at the top so the package could hang from its rack. The brand advertised itself as a "vestibule lock" and the label said that the only tool necessary for installation was a screwdriver. Odds were, they'd be home by four, in time for the stupid call.

It was past one in the morning. Only two of the dozen checkout counters were staffed. The checkout girl had greasy hair and pimples on her forehead and a small-featured face with big eyes. He put the doorknob on the counter. He touched his pocket and felt his phone. That was when he realized that his wallet was gone.

"Just a moment," he said.

She didn't look at Sebastian.

"I had my fucking," Sebastian said. "I'm sorry."

Her big lips were painted red, her eyelids coated with a green-blue powder.

There she was on her stool, like a mushroom on rot. When had he taken his wallet out of his pants? Had he dropped it in the car? In his pockets he had only three dollar bills, a dime, a nickel, and four pennies. The doorknob cost $18.39.

Sebastian said, "Excuse me, please."

Her plump lips neither closed nor opened. Sebastian returned to the aisle of doors and locks and chains. He hung the knob back on its hook. The identical knobs behind it rocked and swayed in a line. If he went back home for his wallet and then drove back here for the doorknob, it would be two in the morning before he even got to work, putting the new doorknob in the door. Or he could leave the store empty handed, drive back home, and get in bed next to Katya and the tumor in her breast. He would lie there and watch the ceiling, and he would worry about the house burning down, the doorknob not working, the three of them trapped. He'd smash a window. He'd lower Katya out, and she'd be standing by the planter where in springtime irises bloomed, and he would hand Nomi through the broken glass. Then he'd leap. Jonathan Garment, M.D. had a description of anxiety: "the thought that thinks less than it thinks." Katya had quoted that to him, and he'd been so annoyed.

"Well, read his book," she'd said.

He'd said, "I don't need to read the fucking book." He'd just been trying to make a simple point about anxiety: that sometimes anxiety prevented one from seeing things, but sometimes it helped one work things through. Then Katya had substituted the word *panic* for *anxiety*, as if that were nothing, with her chocolate yogi eyes, as if *panic* were not implicitly insulting.

And then he had pointed out that she had her own craziness, too— like it was craziness to outlaw words like *tumor* or *cancer* or *death*. When he said those words, she'd said, "Enough." She'd raised her hands, showing her pink palms.

Now he was wishing he hadn't said that. She'd left the room. She took her pill and went to bed. And on the couch he'd picked it up, that book by Jonathan Garment, M.D. Sebastian had never stolen anything in his life, but now he was going to steal the doorknob. He was going to do it for his family.

Dangerous-looking contractors rolled a dolly laden with wood and joint compound and sheetrock, and they looked around themselves suspiciously, as if Home Depot were the recreation yard of a penitentiary. The sad-faced cashier moved boxes into the cart of a bearded shopper, an orthodox Jew. Two guards in black shirts bantered by the exit. The shorter of the pair, a wizened, bespectacled man, raised a finger and lectured his younger partner. "Some like they fruit firm," he said. "Some like it tender." Sebastian felt it coming, Jew vs. Black, the eternal conflict of the Brooklyn tribes.

"What?" The shopper in the skullcap piloted his heavy cart toward the door. The tassels in his shirt swung in opposite directions from his gut. "You going to count every piece?"

"Yo yo." The younger guard was squatting, fingering the purchases and examining the long receipt. He had arms thin and long as an arachnid's. "You only pay for one of these."

Sebastian put his phone to his ear. He walked as though distractedly, while the guards and the shopper argued. "We can go real time," he said, as he flashed the doorknob in the guards' direction, "Or we can go asynchronous." The doors slid opened. He stepped past them into the parking structure, which smelled of urine and mildew. Under the low concrete pilings, dark liquid dripped from the back of a dented van.

"Young sir!" came a voice behind him.

Sebastian slid into his car. He dropped the phone and doorknob on the passenger's seat. The phone chimed, showed its corporate logo, and powered down to black. The guard in the rearview mirror had his mouth open and his hands high. Sebastian gunned the engine. He dropped the emergency brake. His wheels squealing, he turned to avoid a parked truck, then he powered past a stop sign.

It took two honking drivers for him to realize that he had forgotten to turn on his headlights. The elevated highway loomed above. He'd had three whiskeys before Katya had gone to bed. His heart was thrilled and pounding. He crossed the Gowanus in the wrong direction. He made a left turn down a quiet street with shuttered gates and piles of trash.

"Present moment," he told himself. "Beautiful moment."

But where the fuck was his wallet? Had he left his wallet at home? He jabbed his fingers under his seat, fishing for the wallet. He made another left turn on Fourteenth Street, past a row of garbage trucks parked like giant beetles at the curb. They had a video of him, casing the aisle of doorknobs and locks, standing in line and fumbling through his pockets. They had a shot of his license plate speeding off into the night. He came to a stop sign on Second Avenue. The plate number got typed into a search engine. Somewhere in Mumbai, a mouse pushed a curser across a computer screen, and up came Sebastian Fishberger's name, his address, his credit scores, his company homepage—they'd catch him. The compactor trucks were double-parked to his left and right. A taxi came whistling through the intersection, honking as it went.

"Present moment," Sebastian mouthed the words. "Present moment."

He was driving without his license. He'd never pass a Breathalyzer test. Best to go back and explain, to return the doorknob. The wind lofted plastic bags in spirals from the street. Sebastian imagined his wife asleep in bed. He imagined a double mastectomy. Fuck it, he thought. He stepped on the gas. The bicyclist came out of nowhere. Sebastian braked. He felt the rubber grip the road. The seatbelt grabbed his chest. The car careened forward. The bicycle was there, right in front of him, would not move from his squealing fender. He felt the contact through the steering wheel. The metal made its awful sound. Sebastian winced, leg rigid on the brake pedal. The body vanished. Sebastian heard a thump overhead. Then the body dropped out of heaven and through his rear view mirror.

Sebastian opened the car door. The pavement moved underfoot. He grabbed the emergency brake. He put the car in park. The bike was under his front left tire. The bicyclist was on his hands and knees, a big ugly white man with a shaved head, dressed in shorts and a Hawaiian shirt. He stood. He was bent double, breathing heavily, his pale scalp faintly greenish in the dark. In his hand he had the heavy chain of his bicycle lock.

"Thank God you're okay," Sebastian said.

The bicyclist faced him, blood on his mouth. He was ghostly, with narrow porcine eyes and tattoos on his hairless white forearms.

"I didn't see you," Sebastian explained. "You were coming from the wrong direction."

The bicyclist swung his chain. Sebastian dodged. The rear window of the station wagon exploded.

"Hey!" Sebastian put his hands up.

The bicyclist drew the chain back, and swung again. Sebastian's forearms took to the blow, but the end of the chain whipped back and one hard link pinged his forehead. Sebastian lost his balance. He was down on the asphalt. The bicyclist advanced, whip cocked for the final blow—and then suddenly, like he'd been sapped on the head, the bicyclist froze. His eyes rolled upwards. He stiffened. The wind picked up. The bicyclist, stiff as a cardboard cutout of himself, fell over backward, landing

271

hard. His chain clattered. He lay still. Sebastian stood. There was blood on his hands.

Sebastian got back into his Subaru. His head hurt. He plowed right over the bicycle, running a red light. His open door beat against the sides of parked cars. He reached out, and slammed it shut. Streetlights exploded off the cracks in his windows. He said, "Oh shit oh shit oh shit oh shit." The blood was on his sleeves, on his fingers, and on the steering wheel. He said, "Fuck fuck fuck fuck."

He had trouble parallel parking, first bumping the car in front of him, and then running his wheels up the curb. He pounded his fists on the steering wheel. There was a bump like an egg on his forehead. He turned off the ignition, then turned it on, thinking to go back and check on the man he'd just murdered. He smashed his rear bumper into the car behind him. He pulled forward, then back, then drove his front wheel onto the curb again. He screamed. He gripped his head where it hurt. When he walked out of the car and toward his house, it was all he could do to keep his balance. He had the doorknob in his left hand and his phone in his pocket. He tried to call 911, but of course his phone was dead. He screamed. He covered his mouth. "Get a grip," he told himself. He worried his neighbors would hear him.

Inside the house, he took off his bloody shirt. He bundled it in a plastic bag and shoved it in the kitchen garbage. The cat mewed. The wound was ragged on his arm and tender and swollen and greenish blue. The stupid song from Home Depot kept chiming in his head, rainy day, sunny day, any day, funny day. "I didn't," he blurted. "I didn't mean." He punched the wall. He hurt his knuckles. Sebastian washed his injured arm in the kitchen sink and pressed the wound hard with a paper towel. "Please God." he murmured. Then he slipped into his rubber Crocs and his hooded sweatshirt and after some difficulty with the front doorknob scampered down the street to the car again.

It was an awful parking job. He needed to make it okay. He needed to do it for Katya. He shut his eyes and thought of his wife in bed, and he listened to his own heartbeat.

The crack to the front window wasn't as bad as he thought. The back window had been demolished. There were crystals of glass all over the child's safety car seat. Maybe, he thought, he could tell Katya it was an accident. Or he could say that some crazy vandal had done that to their car! She'd have no reason to doubt it. She kept baby wipes in the glove compartment. Sebastian cleaned off the steering wheel, and the bloodstained seat. He wiped down the front fender and the windshield. How long until they found the body?

Back home, he shoved his sweatshirt deep in the laundry, and also his bloodstained pants. He washed his arm again and saw the blood run down the drain, and he dried the wound with toilet paper and dropped the paper in the toilet bowl and flushed and then taped a piece of fresh gauze over his forearm. Quiet as he could, he went back to the bedroom. He thought, "Fuck fuck fuck," but did not scream it. Everything was going to be okay.

He put on a t-shirt and pajama pants. In the bathroom, he looked at himself in the mirror and ran water through his hair and touched the greenish lump where the chain had pinged his forehead. His wallet! Was it in the fucking car? On the way to Home Depot, had it fallen out of his pocket and under his seat? He imagined the wallet in the street beside the dead body, just sitting there for the cops. Sebastian patted down his dresser top. All his panic was now focused on the wallet. He fumbled through his sock drawer. The cops would find the body and there would be his driver's license and home address. He got down on his hands and knees and reached under the bed.

"Bastian?" Katya said.

"It's nothing."

"Fuck time is it?"

"Sleep."

He sat up and knocked his head on the bedside table, and Katya's reading lamp fell and so did her P.D. James novel. The nightlight in their daughter's room cast a glow across sleeping Nomi. On the coffee table, the stolen doorknob sat in its clear plastic packaging, next to his empty whiskey glass. *Tomorrow and Tomorrow and Tomorrow* was on the couch, doing a split, its front cover a picture of clouds, its back full of sky blue praise. We are all one, wrote Jonathan Garment, M.D. The oak breathes out, and we inhale it. We exhale and are absorbed by the tree. We share our genes with the earthworm. Sebastian pulled the cushions off the couch. He found pencils, quarters, playing cards, and hair elastics, but no wallet. He moved old newspapers off the kitchen table. On his desk were charts and binders and a printout of a Power Point presentation. There was the screwdriver on the Ikea organizer where the family kept its shoes, and there beside the screwdriver lay Sebastian's wallet. Idiot! He could have just covered the catch plate with a piece of duct tape. All he needed was a piece of tape! He could have thrown the bolt of the front door and covered the doorknob latch with a piece of tape, or put a piece of tape on the doorpost. He was on the witness stand. "I didn't mean . . ." Sebastian kicked the door. "My wife." He punched it.

"Daddy?" came a small voice at the top of the stairs.

Nomi's curls were matted to one side. Her skinny legs poked out of her nightdress, the one with the fading fairies and the marks from chocolate ice cream.

"What are you doing, dads?"

Sebastian went up the stairs to her, and took her damp and cool little hand, and took her up to bed, and lay there beside her, listening to the city. His arm throbbed where it was injured. His head ached. "Present moment," he tried to tell himself. He'd argued with his wife so stupidly about Jonathan Garment. Katya took on regal calm when she was most pissed.

"It's just a way of saying, Sebastian." She kept her chin high as she spoke. "Just a way to let go."

"But what if we don't want to let go," he'd said. "What if we prefer clinging? I prefer clinging. Don't you?"

"I don't," she'd said. "No." Or maybe she'd said, "I don't know." But she'd lectured him on anxiety and then he'd called her crazy, and then he had said all those words that she had told him not to say. *Cancer*, *tumor*, and *death*. He wished he hadn't said them, on this of all nights. And what had she said. Panic? He flinched, and in his mind he felt it: the contact of the bike against his front fender, the sound of the body scraping the top of his car.

"Daddy?" Nomi asked.

"We're fine," said Sebastian.

She shifted her hips. Her hair smelled of sweet shampoo.

Most nights when he put her to bed, Sebastian told stories about the Tooth Fairy and Hanukkah Harry. He'd forgotten to tell her one of those stories tonight, after all the bickering with Katya. Of course, they never let Nomi hear them bickering, and they never used the word *cancer* around her. Nomi didn't know exactly what was going on tomorrow, but the silence had its own effect. She felt the tension. Like a scent it got everywhere: in the sheets, in the walls, in her scrambled eggs.

In Sebastian's stories, the old couple lived together in a split-level house in Wyandanch, Long Island. The Tooth Fairy was named Chedeline, like Katya's mother, and Sebastian imitated the Tooth Fairy by using his mother-in-law's sing-song voice. As the Tooth Fairy, Chedeline trotted the world, changing currencies and breaking large bills.

Hanukkah Harry was paunchy and arrogant, like Sebastian's dad. He worked only eight days a year, but spent the rest of his time in his study, reading toy catalogues, which he referred to as "the literature of the field." Nomi wondered what the Tooth Fairy and Hanukkah Harry were doing for Thanksgiving. Sebastian said they weren't really doing anything, because this year Hanukkah fell in late November, and Harry was overwhelmed, busy, and tired.

"But what about Chedeline?" He could feel her anxiety in her fingers and legs. "She wants a party, doesn't she?"

"Oh." He kissed her beautiful forehead. "I think she's pretty tired, too. Go to sleep, Sweetie."

"Are you going to sleep?"

"Oh, yeah."

He got into bed next to Katya. The clock read 2:49. He brought the sheet up to his chin, and he put his head on the pillow. He closed his eyes and imagined the man's head under his wheel, the skull popping beneath the shaven scalp, the brains coming into the treads of his tires.

"I'm not," Sebastian whispered.

"What?" said Katya.

"Shh." He hadn't known his voice would be audible. "Nothing. Relax, Babe."

Katya settled back on her side of the bed. He turned over his pillow and put his face to the cooler side. Her bras after workouts left lines in the skin beneath her beautiful breasts. He imagined a scalpel tracing that curve, the layers of skin parting, the blood coming out.

"Oh, God," he whispered.

He tried to pray. He thought of a football team linking hands, urging God to mess with their opponents' last-minute field goal attempt. But God was no die-hard Sebastian Fishberger fan.

He imagined himself in a raincoat after serving his jail term, smoking a cigarette, tawdry love affairs in Alphabet City. His bald wife with her scarred chest vomited in the bathroom. He wanted her body to remain against time, sexy and warm and close. He reached out. Katya inched away. He felt her thigh through her thin pajamas, and he was possessed of it: the urge to take her, to snatch handfuls of Katya, to have her from behind—

"Sebastian!"

He apologized.

He lay on his back. He breathed and watched the ceiling swell. To calm his erection he thought of the least erotic vision he knew: Fox broadcaster Sean Hannity. He pictured Hannity's frightened eyes, his massive hair, his liar's smile. Sebastian put his hands on the cold plaster wall. A plane moved over Brooklyn. The cat moved heavily down the stairs.

She said, "What, honey?"

Had he spoken? He didn't think he'd said a thing. He said, "I'm sorry." He should call 911. If the man wasn't dead, the man needed help. Why hadn't he called 911?

He went downstairs. He picked up the phone. But to call now, and from the home phone, was to confess. He couldn't get arrested, not tonight. Who would take Nomi to school? On one end of their mantle was a small wooden sculpture of the elephant-headed Hindu god Ganesha. On the other end sat a thin white ceramic Thai Buddha with arms aflame. Above the fireplace hung photographs of their grandparents, Katya's grandfather in black and white in military uniform, and pictures of little Nomi. The television in the hearth was a black flat screen. He put down the house phone. He picked up the doorknob. He struggled with its clear plastic packaging. He tried to open it up with a ballpoint pen. He stuck the pen in the hole from which the package had hung from the display rack. He tried to lever apart the two sides, but the pen popped out and stabbed him. "Shit!" He danced around the coffee table, cursing. He jumped. He stood at the sink and ran cold water on his arm. He'd drawn a big blue line on himself and gouged a hole on the hairless side of his forearm. On the hairy side was the bruise and the bloody gauze pad. Sebastian blotted the fresh blood with a handful of Kleenex. On his left arm was a crazy exclamation mark with a purple point. Then he got the poultry sheers from the knife block in the kitchen and used those to snip apart the packaging. Sebastian got down on his knees and took the screwdriver in hand. The lumpectomy would be successful. He'd be on that conference call. If the cops had been called to the accident, they'd be at his door any minute now. He'd left tracks, all those doors he'd scratched while driving.

The tip of his screwdriver trembled. Sebastian found the x at the head of the screw. His mind felt liquid. His hands were a tired old man's. He checked the instructions that came with the doorknob: *Rotates outside rose make sleeve projecting be symmetrical around the door.* Garment had a spiel about the workings of the human eye, how the wavelengths of light fluctuated and were never constant, and yet the mind invented colors, constant hues, like yellow and blue, and there was some argument as to whether a person could see a color for which he didn't have a name. The example was blue. The Greeks didn't have a word for blue, Garment said. That's why Homer called it "the wine-dark sea." But Sebastian had never seen a *blue* sea, not really. Maybe Greek wine, like the sea, was black or slate-colored, and didn't Poseidon sometimes have blue eyebrows in some traditions? Sebastian could remember the seat of the Greyhound bus in which he had read a book called *On Being Blue*, and he could remember the cover of the book, and the landscape flashing by the window, but he could not remember where he was traveling or a word that he had read. Sebastian tightened screws. He looked at the instructions one more time. *Push the boton before install back to inside knob.* Maybe he had only imagined it. Maybe there was no body in the street. Or maybe the bicyclist had awakened and taken his broken bike and gone away. *Projecting be symmetrical around door.* Sebastian closed and opened the front door. The stoop was icy on his feet. The wind blew the leaves on the branches of the sidewalk maple, and they trembled, and fell and scattered and collected into a bank alongside the wood that edged and framed the little tree. He closed the door. He tried to open it. The doorknob wouldn't turn.

There was a keyhole in the doorknob. He checked his pajama pockets.

"Fuck," muttered Sebastian. "Fuck shit!" He hadn't taken the key.

He'd stolen the wrong kind of lock. He didn't want a doorknob that locked! He'd have to go back to Home Depot tomorrow. He'd have to pay for this knob, and then he'd have to buy another one, and he'd have to get down on his knees in the front hall after surgery, and instead of the conference call, he'd have to take out the screwdriver and remove the fucking locking doorknob he had stolen. From the other side of the door, the cat meowed.

Through a gap at the side of the curtain to the closest window, Sebastian could see his book and his empty whiskey glass. He could see the clock. It was nearly five. He sat down barefoot on the cold stone steps. He put his head in his hands. He wasn't going to wake Katya, not now, no matter what. Let her sleep that half hour. He'd just stay out here, patiently. The cold blew through his pajama pants.

"Breathe," he told himself, and then he heard a police siren, coming closer.

Sebastian tried to keep his eyes closed, his legs crossed, his thumbs and forefingers in circles on his knees. The siren got louder. He opened his eyes. He could see the lights crossing Seventh Avenue. He would stand and present his wrists, and let them cuff him. He was on his feet and pounding the front door.

277

"Katya! Katya!" He could feel the collision in his hands. He could see the bald head of the bicyclist rising toward his windshield. "Katya!" He called. "Help!"

The siren flickered away, the sound snapped and stretched and then the cop car was gone, down the hill, two blocks away,

Sebastian could see the lights turning on in his neighbors' windows. An old woman in a wool cap sucked on a cigarette, kept her head down, and walked to work. From the avenue, he heard the squeaking brakes of a delivery truck. People were up and showering. Subways moved under ground. In the distance, on the elevated BQE, traffic was thickening. Nurses changed shifts in hospitals, doctors in New Jersey were silencing their alarm clocks. In Manhattan, policemen poked nightsticks into homeless bundles on Fifth Avenue. Sebastian's father never slept. He was probably checking his blood pressure right now. And Chedeline in her bed in Connecticut was dreaming, maybe another nightmare. The drums were coming, the drums were coming. His wife was coming down the stairs.

Sebastian wanted to explain everything to Katya. He wanted to apologize for saying cancer, tumor, and death. He wanted to be forgiven— he could feel his anxiety rising, metastasizing, expanding. She opened the door. Katya was barefoot. She wore thin pajama pants, and a torn shirt for a top. He saw her face, tired and ashy and lined, heavy with the Ativan she'd taken to sleep, and heavy with early morning. He saw also the face he had first loved, Katya, his rock-and-roll girl. "Time to go to the hospital," she said.

Nominated by Harvard Review

SKULL

fiction by DAVID LONG

from GLIMMER TRAIN STORIES

You're four hits into a bowl of two-hit weed, you and a waif named Keiko. It's the now-distant summer you sublet that rathole on Grosvenor Avenue, a time when your life still could go many ways. Inside, the flat is close as hound's breath, so you've been living on the fire escape since the third night of the heat wave. You've padded the slats with sheets of industrial cardboard from a loading dock and five-dollar sleeping bags from the Army Navy. No one uses the north fire escape, so it's your private crow's nest. In the months before this, dawn meant coming down zingy from whatever kept you up all night, but now when you wake, five, five fifteen, the air is pearly cool, traffic on the Dugan so thin you hear pigeons taking flight across the way, all at once, the wingbeats sounding like a sheet being shaken out, fresh from the clothesline.

Keiko has the skin of a china doll. She could be twenty or seventeen or fifteen. Her hair would be glossy as a rocking horse mane if washed and not so raggedy—it looks like she cut it with a jackknife in some public restroom. As always, she has on the black Pretenders tee, skinny-leg black jeans, worn-to-shit black high-tops. She showed up first with Joey de Souza and Phil Frost and others you know from busking, so you figured she was attached to one of them, but a week later she came alone, asked if she could hang, sat round-backed, paging through your strew of books, rolling immaculate little smokes of Bugler, smoking them to the nubbity nub, not saying two dozen words to you before stealing off into the twilight while you were inside taking a leak. The other time, she was already here when you got home, and how she managed that, being way too short to grab the drop ladder, is a mystery.

That was the same night she asked to see your fiddle. You snapped open the case, drew it out, caught her tiny flinch before letting you place it in her hands, then her *Oh* at how weightless it felt. When the strings left white powder on her jeans, you explained about rosin. She asked if the violin was old. *Not too*, you said, began to say your good instrument was back in Maine for safekeeping . . . but instead of going into all that you played, a Bach cello prelude transcribed for violin, segued into "Rickett's Hornpipe," then a hazardous Stéphane Grappelli riff you'd been nailing roughly once in every five attempts, but panached your way through this time without a bobble . . . seeing her delight, her fingers fluttering up and scattering as if the notes were incandescent bubbles.

Later, you told her if she needed a place she was welcome to crash there, found her a thin blanket, a pillow, watched how she untied her sneakers and set them side by side, like ceremonial slippers. The fire escape ended at your floor—above was only a scabby iron ladder to the roof, which meant no mess of slats between you and the sky. When Keiko seemed dead to the world you lay back, uncovered, looking up—even with a new moon, only a few bright stars were visible through the canopy of city light. After a while, you found yourself replaying Keiko's response to the music, the tile-white fingers flittering up spontaneously. If you'd worried she might get to be a pest, showing up whenever, it was then you stopped. You had no idea where she went when she wasn't here, but you liked it when she was, you realized . . . and you realized you had no desire to put any moves on her, which was novel and worth contemplating, but then you, too, were asleep, and when you woke at first light she was already gone.

Anyway, tonight: once you set the pipe down, you see she's not zoning out peaceably; she's crimpy eyed, headed the opposite direction. You're already thinking you should ask is she doing okay, when she wriggles a thick-folded sheet of glossy art stock from her back pocket, opens it square by square, passes it to you. You flatten it back and forth over your jeans leg, then angle it into the beam of Tensor light. It proves to be a crisp, wide-angle shot of a humongous underground room somewhere in Czechoslovakia made entirely of human skulls. *Thousands* of skulls. Not white like bleached bone, but filthy yellow like very old, maltreated piano keys, the domes of the foreheads sheened wherever people could reach them.

You break your gaze away, say, *That's freaky*.

When you go to hand the picture back she won't take it. You don't blame her. *Thousands of skulls*, you think, *and every last one of them somebody*.

280

Some nights a breeze wanders down Grosvenor, almost enough to cool the sweat on your temples, but it's dead still now, that leaden quiet before a storm, except there *is* no storm. When you look up again, Keiko is palpating her scalp, her fingers spread like spider legs, both hands, really pressing down—it's like she's inspecting her armor for frail spots.

Keiko? you say.

You touch her bony elbow. *Keiko—*

She looks at you, blinking, shallow-breathing. *My brain's right under here*, she finally says. *My . . . me.*

Not exactly a revelation, but weed has this way of rubbing your nose in the obvious.

You say, *Why don't we— Here—* and only now does she let you guide her hands down to her lap.

You sit back on your haunches and the two of you look at each other. You say, *Pretty buzzed, huh*, hoping to break the spell.

Keiko says nothing. You see her trying to wet her lips, which are kind of sticking to each other, but her tongue's gummy, too.

I'll get you something, you say. Just be a second.

You yank yourself up by the railing, stabilize, then duck through the window, and now you remember there's not so much as an RC in the medieval fridge . . . and even before this heat, its weeping doorless freezer barely managed slush cubes. *Okay, fuck, water then*, you think. At least you're together enough to not poke on the overhead light, a monster bulb dangling from the twelve-foot ceiling that comes on like Judgment Day if you happen to be stoned.

You run the tap, locate the oversized Red Sox cup, check for roach carcasses, swish it out, test the water with your little finger. Still warm. Waiting, you start to picture how far it has to come, up through five stories of rust-constricted old pipe—it won't feel cold until you're getting water that was *underground*, you realize, and then you're visualizing the supply line, buried in the dirt, five or six feet down, and suddenly you regret going down this path, so you decide to try the fridge, after all . . . and, miraculously, there's an *orange*, still good. You find your sharp knife, slice the fruit into eighths, and lay them on a paper towel as if the sections had just fallen open like petals . . . but then it seems like you've left Keiko alone *way* too long. You scoop up the towel, secure it against your T-shirt, hustle back outside. *What if she—?*

But, no, she's right there against the bricks. Except she's rocking, her elbows dug into her hipbones, fists at her mouth, tapping, almost hitting herself. And now you can hear the sound coming from her, the *Ooh,*

ooh, ooh, ooh people make when the ground starts giving way under them. You know this sound, you've made it yourself.

You tuck the orange slices out of harm's way, kneel, slowly bring your hands up to hers, and stroke her knuckles with your thumbs, after a while easing the fists open.

Her cheeks are wet, her gaze perfectly abject. *I don't want my skull to have nothing in it*, she says.

I know, you say, *I know. Nobody does. Nobody on Earth.*

You hold her head against your chest as she sobs and sobs, gradually enclosing it with your arms, then as much of the rest of you as you can manage.

Nominated by Glimmer Train Stories,

Steve Adams

KERNELS

by DAVID J. ROTHMAN

from THE NEW CRITERION

Kernels

When you told me about his whistling belt
And your cruel stepmother, who placed each kernel
On the hard floor then made you kneel, I felt
Like I had wandered into some infernal
Fairy tale. But it was real. How strange:
To sit in your calm home, crisp autumn light,
Jazz, coffee, hearing that. Failure to grieve
Can freeze what frees us up. I'm sure you're right
To try to let it go. And I believe
You have. What strength it takes to be that story,
See it clear, then give it up, conceive
It now as a mere childhood allegory.
You did the brave thing, learning how to live.
But me? They hurt a child. I don't forgive.

Nominated by The New Criterion,
Rachel Rose

A FLOCK, A SIEGE, A MURMURATION

by SU-YEE LIN

from BENNINGTON REVIEW

When they said, two hundred cases of bird flu confirmed, we kept to our houses and apartments. We avoided the outdoors and all its creatures. We wore masks to avoid breathing the air that could be polluted with just about anything. We looked askance at the chickens tied with rope to the fronts of tool shops, to the songbirds kept in cages in the trees. We thought to ourselves: we will live as though we are dying.

I was applying for med school in the States then, although living in China as an expat. I had an excuse to never leave my apartment but when the government asked for volunteers to cull the poultry from the wet markets, I went into their offices. They looked at me, masks over their faces like my mask over mine. I said, I want to help. And they said, why? For science, I replied. And they stamped the form and said, tomorrow. Six a.m. It was April 2013 in Shanghai and the sky was gray from morning to night.

We took a tally of the number of bird corpses we hauled out to the truck. White plastic bags of chickens and ducks, pigeons and geese. The geese were the worst with their long necks tangling with one another, those heavy feathered bodies. The pigeons looked so small and harmless and there were fewer of them—I, after all, had never seen them offered on menus around China although I'd heard of carrier pigeons still being raised by enthusiasts in tall apartment buildings. I'd even seen a coop myself, last year, dark and full of the cooing of birds, like a soft lullaby.

There was no blood shed: what unnerved us was the smell of cooking poultry when we put them through the incinerator, a smell that made our mouths water. To be hungry in the face of death. I saw this as practice. The same sensation one has with a human corpse, this odd feeling of hunger while dissecting, due to the formaldehyde. After all, I was interested in the processes of the body, of that tenuous boundary between being alive and not. The way certain chemicals, certain smells, can influence your thoughts and actions. All so rational and clear.

The culling of poultry was happening in all parts of the country, first these southeastern cities of Shanghai, Hangzhou, Nanjing. Then spreading west and south. The cases kept climbing, three hundred then four hundred then seven hundred. People were afraid to eat chicken, even in restaurants, as though you could catch the disease from eating the flesh of these birds. It was no normal flu. It shut down the organs. It made the air feel like water so that your lungs collapsed. Your skin would sink into itself, your bones would ache, your heart would slowly stop beating.

After the sterilization of the first market, the largest in Shanghai, I went back to my apartment that I shared with two roommates, both Chinese and not expats like myself. The scent of the protection suits, the gloves, lingered on my body. I did not wash it away. The next day, I went to the Department of Health again. I said, Let me help. They stamped my form. Again and again.

No one called me from the States. My parents were long gone and any relatives I had didn't care where I was or what I was doing. My roommates kept to themselves. Instead of writing essays or teaching Chinese students the Latin roots of difficult vocabulary, I looked at photos on the internet of all the different varieties of birds. Mandarin ducks and nightingales. Chickadees and red-tailed hawks. I memorized their details, their Latin names and coloring, the insects and grains they ate. I printed out photographs and highlighted the names in yellow, hand-wrote their details in dark blue ink that stained my fingers. I went out and I placed birds into sacks and pumped in highly concentrated carbon dioxide until they died. They fought it, they beat their wings and tried to rip through the bags but I'd put my hands on their bodies until they were still.

The death rate was 40 percent and it hit the young and old alike. The virus had yet to mutate so it wasn't yet contagious between humans. It was found that the virus wasn't only carried by farmed poultry but also wild sparrows and pigeons. Bird catchers were sent to the parks with nets every day. Afterwards, I held their bodies in my hands and released them into the fire.

I canceled my SAT classes. I traveled to other cities nearby to cull birds, on the high-speed bullet train with a commendation from the Health Department. This person has experience. This person is willing to do what is necessary to help halt a pandemic. This person wants to be a doctor. But that wasn't why I did it. At night, I'd catalogue the birds and think: There are so many out there. How will we get them all.

Nine hundred cases in a month and climbing despite the killings. No chicken or duck or goose served in restaurants. Many of the larger restaurants were shut down. The songbird cages that used to hang in the trees were all empty, probably hidden away. The sky was perpetually gray with the smoke from incinerators and the city smelled like roasted chicken. There were few people on the streets. The virus had now mutated and could be spread person to person. In People's Park, the only people around were the bird catchers—not even the marriage brokers were out. Life was at a standstill. On the subway, if a person coughed, you'd get out of the car at the next stop and go into another one. There were no tourists on Nanjing Road. I'd walk down it and see the salesgirls, bored, at the counters, masks over their noses and mouths, looking down at their smartphones and unwilling to speak to one another.

Once, I saw myself on the television. It was earlier on. A reporter had asked me, her lipstick perfect, her hair a shiny wavy dyed brown, "Do you think this culling is necessary?" I'd said yes, but my eyes betrayed me.

The wet markets had all been shut down and there was no poultry to be found in the city. I ate vegetables and noodles that I'd cook in a wok, the gas flaming hot so that I'd often burn it. I'd open the window and watch my contribution of smoke waft out into the air. My roommates still ate fish and beef and pork. They only bought it from the large supermarkets. They never offered it to me and I would think: if only you knew what I'd done.

During the day, I would watch the bird catchers who stalked around People's Park. There were very few birds to catch, and some days, none at all. They'd smile at me and I'd smile back, but we never spoke, for fear of the virus. I'd watch the clear skies and the trees blooming with flowers, but their color was faded by soot. A layer of dust coated my windowsill every morning if I left my window open. I thought about medical school. I thought about the feel of a fluttering bird's heart, the way their tiny eyes looked at you, the sharpness of their beaks. I thought about the corpses I would feel under my scalpel, the skin falling away to reveal fat and muscle. I thought about what disease can do to a body, how blood can pool under the skin, how the cells can implode, how the things inside of you can be transferred to outside the body.

When my roommate complained of cold in the apartment, of how her muscles ached so she couldn't get comfortable, the other roommate packed her bags and left the city. I was the one to call the hospital. They took her away in their white protection suits, on a gurney as though she couldn't walk, as though she were already dead. There was fear in her eyes, but also resignation. As though she had known all along it was coming. But didn't we all? I was only surprised I wasn't the first.

I went to Hangzhou, to Xixi wetlands, a national wetland park. There, swans still swam gracefully by the Misty River Fishing Village. They'd been tested and spared, one of the few concessions the government had given. I was alone and, for hours, I watched them drift by, and my mind was blank and white as the feathers on their backs.

Back in Shanghai, my walls were covered with lists of the names and details of birds. Color-coded and sorted according to species and families. In this city, the birds had been mostly eradicated, but not so in other cities. There were people that were pushing back, saying that they should focus on a cure, especially now that it could be transferred between humans. These were cities that were proud of their birds, their herons and long-necked cranes. The summer was in full swing by then, the trees a shade of green that looked unnatural against the sky. We had almost forgotten what the air should look like, smell like. But few people left their apartments, still. The hospitals were full. We were told to stay put. Don't travel. There wasn't anyone around to witness the trees and the flowers, but only to notice how the mosquitoes bit us at night, flying through those too-large holes in the screens.

Over a thousand cases reached, and the epidemiologists all remarked on how strange it was for this flu to keep on spreading, through the spring and into the summer. There was a ban on international travel and businesses were hurting. The parents of the roommate who had gone to the hospital showed up one day and cleared all her belongings out, their eyes intent and their mouths and noses hidden by a mask. I was unsure what it meant, whether she had recovered and was going home or still in the hospital or had died. They did not speak to me and all her belongings could be put into one large suitcase and a bag made of that plastic material used for rice bags and decorated with the cartoon sheep Yang Yang being menaced by wolves. The apartment felt terribly empty after they left and I wondered what I'd do about rent. I needn't have worried—the landlord never asked.

There is a feeling that you get in an empty city that should be teeming with millions of lives, like the day after a blizzard. But you get that a lot in China, in those ghost cities that jut out of the landscape, beautifully manicured but lifeless. Shanghai, though, wasn't coming out of her coma. Instead of birds, there were insects everywhere so that many of us didn't even want to leave our buildings anyway. What would we see, after all, but the way the insects had eaten the greenery of the trees with the dead heads of flowers rotting on the sidewalks. Rare to see a street sweeper or pruner of trees. Everyone ate from stocks of food canned years ago and made to last. I ate ramen from a package, not even bothering to cook it, as I added to the bird collection on my walls. Three thousand cases, thirteen hundred dead. I stopped watching television or tracking the news. Did it matter what others were saying or what was happening in other cities? I thought about the connections with the body and how it resists disease, the functions of red and white blood cells. I looked at the photographs of birds I couldn't imagine but for their pictures upon my wall and thought, if not for me, would they exist? To name is to own.

Fewer people dying now, and the hospitals were emptier as people recovered. The climbing numbers of cases slowed to a crawl, but people were still afraid to go out. When I wandered down the streets, they were often empty, with only the occasional hole-in-the-wall restaurant open. What was there to lose, though? The worst was already here. On Nanjing Road East, I met a Uighur man grilling lamb on skewers. Only three skewers on the makeshift portable charcoal grill, but the smell wafting from it was irresistible. That was the intention. His dark eyes peered at me from below his thick hair, his white cap perched on top. He smiled under his mustache. I was the only one around. Who are you cooking those for? I asked. He didn't miss a beat. For you, he said. How much? He slid a couple more skewers from a bag onto the grill. The first one, free, he said, after that, five kuai. It was more expensive than it had been, but he was the first one to come back and sell them in months, out in the open. A natural entrepreneur. All right, I said, give me four. They were mostly fat and cumin, smoky in a way that burned just a little bit in the back of your throat. The man watched me as he grilled a few more, maybe for himself, and, as I ate them one by one, the sweat dripped down my forehead from the summer sun and the spice. The street empty but for the two of us. Aren't you afraid of the virus? I asked. Aren't you? he shot back. I shook my head. He shook his. It's over, he said. It doesn't matter anymore. I thought about that the entire walk back. The subway lines had long since shut down.

It was over, yet it wasn't. There was a fatigue to the city, to the residents who were more wary, more paranoid than they had been before. There were cicadas that chirped endlessly and mosquitoes that grew fat on our blood no matter how many we swatted. Shanghai had been a city under siege and the siege was mostly lifted, but the weight of it was not. We didn't know what to do with ourselves, what we'd done before the virus. There were countless drawers of ashes in the cemeteries. There were no birds. I wondered whether my students still wanted to study for the SATs, whether there'd always be waves of children to cram for academic tests that would be their key to leaving the country. I couldn't bear to take down my walls of birds: the white-throated needletail or *Hirundapus caudacutus*, subspecies *nudipes*, native to southwestern China; the great crested grebe or *Podiceps cristatus*; the Steller's sea eagle or *Haliaeetus pelagicus*, the heaviest eagle in the world. What would it have been like to feel the weight of these birds on my shoulders, on my arms? Or to have held them in my hands and feel the weak fluttering of their hearts.

The city emerged slowly from its invalid state. The airports opened up again and the odd tourist could be found on Nanjing Road, a new Rolex on one wrist and a Louis Vuitton bag on the other. Disease was not the status quo, although for five months, it had been. Who had been at a standstill during that time? Was it Shanghai or was it the world? There was a peace to the new equilibrium and things were shifting now to the old. Middle-aged ladies started dancing in the parks again, but the matchmakers took longer to return. I heard the sound of pipes in People's Park that I almost mistook for a bird before remembering. One roommate returned, the one who had abandoned the other, but she wouldn't look at me, wouldn't say a word. Perhaps she was ashamed of what she'd done during that time, but she needn't have been. People are who they are; her actions under times of stress cannot be fully blamed. I began tutoring a fourteen-year-old boy whose parents wanted him to get a head start, so that he could eventually leave for a country without China's problems, they'd said, and take them with him.

It was November when I saw the first bird. A common sparrow, streaks of black and brown on his head. I enticed him over to me with crumbs of the thousand-layer sesame-and-scallion bread you can find all over the city and he came to my bench in the park, completely trusting. He hopped into my gloved palm. I laid my other hand over his head. I felt the rapid beating of his heart but he did nothing but flutter his wings. How easy it is to crush a life. How hard it is to save one.

Nominated by Bennington Review

BLOODY MARY! BLOODY MARY! BLOODY MARY!

fiction by ANDREW MITCHELL

from SOUTHERN INDIANA REVIEW

For his son's twelfth birthday, Frank Rudman rented the Party Cave at Pizza Piazza and invited Ethan's seventh-grade class for a Sunday afternoon of endless cheese slices and cake and twenty dollars' worth of quarters for the old pinball machines chiming in the back of the room. It was now one o' clock—the party started at noon—and so far only two other kids had arrived: a tall, sharp-shouldered boy named Chester Taft ("Yes, I am related to President Howard Taft," he'd told Frank solemnly, as though it were his superhero identity) and little Lucy Hadler, a breathless fourth-grader—a neighbor—who insisted on reading aloud the fortunes she interpreted from the lines on Frank's palms: lotteries and new loves and even an impending reincarnation as a bottlenose dolphin.

The Birthday Boy sat alone at a table, rearranging red pepper flakes on the Formica top with his fingertips as if attempting to solve some tiny puzzle. He glanced up at Frank and smiled, the sweet, brave smile of a boy benumbed to the bite of disappointment, and Frank could do nothing but smile back.

The Party Cave had been setup for twelve Party Animals. Frank had invited the entire seventh grade class, after all, and didn't the Law of Averages dictate that at least a dozen of those cruel, hormone-addled bastards would have shown up? There were twelve cone hats positioned at three tables and, in the back of the Cave, a big banner—HAPPY BIRTHDAY ETHAN!—which was signed by Chester, Lucy, and Frank. Most pathetic of all, though, was that Frank had forgotten to update the number of pizzas he'd ordered to coincide with the Party Animals who had actually come to the party, so that now three huge HOT N'

291

READY boxes lay open and mostly untouched like strange, disc-shaped aliens awaiting autopsy.

"I'll go check on the cake," Frank announced. Lucy clapped. Taft was hunched over a *Jurassic Park* pinball machine. Ethan blinked and said nothing.

"Hold tight," Frank said.

In the main dining room, Frank slumped into a vacant booth. Earlier that morning it had rained, and the sky outside the window retained a greenish, post-storm glow, as if a scrim of algae had drifted over the sun. From unseen speakers the Rolling Stones preached that you can't always get what you want, and God, Frank thought, wasn't that the truth? He had wanted to give his son a birthday that would take his mind off things for a couple hours—Frank's mind too, he had to admit—but had succeeded only in tying one more emotional brick to the boy's ankle. Like a callous attorney presenting evidence to a jury of Ethan's insecurities, Frank had submitted Exhibit A—the empty Party Cave—which proved beyond a reasonable doubt that Ethan had no one who wanted to hang out with him, save for Odd Oracle Lucy and the 27th president's pimple-faced heir.

Frank slouched deeper into the booth. Jesus, a pizza party? The last thing an eleven—no, twelve!—year-old boy wanted was a quaint bash at a kitsch, rundown, haven-to-the-1970s pizzeria, especially when he was plopped at the bottom rung of Outlook Springs Middle School's Social Ladder. Had Frank even asked Ethan what he wanted to do on his big day? No! He'd envisioned pro-Ethan throngs gathered at the Piazza's front doors, high-fives and laughs and Ethan exalted up on a throne of his new friends' shoulders, pizza after pizza being whisked from the groaning ovens in order to accommodate these uproarious multitudes. The fact that only Mrs. Taft and Ms. Hadler had RSVP'd had not bothered Frank, so complete was his faith in the allure of free pizza.

And look how that had turned out.

As often happened when he found himself botching the delicate process of raising a son, Frank's thoughts turned to Bonnie.

This pitiful showing would never have happened under her watch. For one, she would not have dreamed of hosting Ethan's birthday at the goddamn Pizza Piazza, and two, even if she had been conned into it, she wouldn't have allowed it to go unattended. She'd have gone door to door throughout Outlook Springs, recruiting Party Animals by the dozens, piling boys and girls into her Buick and ferrying them down to this bash in droves, her camera popping bubbles of light as she maneuvered about the Cave, capturing pictures of Ethan grinning as some cute girl kissed him on the cheek, as he ducked behind a table to avoid the manic cannonade of a Nerf gun.

But Bonnie was dead, and now Frank had the impossible task of trying to be as good as she'd been. God. He even forgot to bring the camera.

He sidled out of the booth and rang the little NEED HELP? bell at the front counter. He'd paid good money for the Party Cave—money he couldn't afford, if he was being honest with himself—and he didn't think he should have to come up here and ask for his goddamn cake.

"Hello?" he called into the kitchen. His hands were trembling. "The cake, please," he said. The cook came to the counter. He was a hunched, mustachioed man with flour in his sparse black hair. He wiped his hands on his apron, looking confused. "The cake," Frank repeated.

"There's no cake, sir," the cook said.

"Excuse me?"

"The cake is included in the Ultimate Party Package, sir."

Frank's blood throbbed in his ears. "I don't understand. I ordered that package."

The cook shook his head. He opened a drawer beneath the cash register and removed a heap of pink order forms. He thumbed through the pages and slid one across the counter toward Frank. "See?" He pointed at Frank's signature at the bottom of the form. "This is the Standard Party Package: access to the Cave, party hats, fountain drinks—"

"This doesn't make sense," Frank said. "I mean, who wouldn't want cake for their kid's birthday?"

There was judgment in the cook's eyes. "Many parents prefer to make the cake themselves, sir," he said.

"Many parents?" Frank said. "Jesus!"

He thrust his MasterCard across the counter, but the cook simply shook his head, as though it were a rabid rat.

"I have no cake prepared, sir," he said.

From the Party Cave, Lucy came zooming into the main dining area like a balloon with a pinprick leak. "Mr. Rudman!" she squealed. "Guess what?"

"Hold on, please, Lucy."

"I read Ethan's palm," she said. She lowered her voice to a conspiratorial whisper and added, "We're gonna get married!"

"That's wonderful news," Frank said.

"I wanna get married right here," she said. She looked around the Pizza Piazza as though it were Machu Picchu at sunset, and blew into a party horn. The checkered paper tube unfurled from her lips like some cartoonish serpent's tongue.

"Listen," Frank said to the cook, clutching the countertop with both hands as if to keep himself from sinking into the quicksand of his own incompetence. "Please," he said, "isn't there anything I can do?"

Lucy led the "Happy Birthday" song with a stirring falsetto as Frank entered the Party Cave with a platter of coffee cakes. The cook's wife had purchased the cakes at Rubio's Bakery that morning, and either out of sympathy for Ethan or some munificence sparked by Lucy's Pizza Piazza wedding plans, the cook gave these cakes and a package of candles to Frank at no charge.

Chester Taft hit the lights. The candles flickered in the mirrors that ran along all four walls—reflected orbs converging on Ethan from the north, east, south, and west. In the back, the pinball machines pulsed with a blue-red-green light. Frank placed the platter of coffee cakes in front of Ethan.

"I screwed this up, bud," he said.

Ethan said, "It's okay, Dad." In the dark, the lenses of his glasses caught the candlelight like two holographic coins.

"I'll get you a real cake on the drive home," Frank said.

"Don't you dare tell us your birthday wish," Lucy said. "It can't come true if you do."

Ethan stared at the cakes. He drummed his fingers on the tabletop. Then he inhaled.

"Hold on," Frank said. "I've got an idea."

"For a wish?" Lucy said. "That's cheating."

"No, not a wish. For a game we could play. Something I used to do as a kid. Have any of you heard of Bloody Mary?"

Frank surprised himself with the question. Back when he was about Ethan's age, he'd often go over to his best friend Seth Malamoff's house and play Bloody Mary with Seth and Seth's older sister, Trisha. Frank had a small—huge, mega, colossal!—crush on Trisha. Together, the three of them would huddle in the bathroom, shut the door, light one of Mrs. Malamoff's candles, and turn off the overhead light. Eyes closed as they counted down from three, Frank, Seth, and Trisha would chant in unison, "Bloody Mary! Bloody Mary! Bloody Mary!" The legend as they knew it was this: hearing the incantation of her name, a blood-spattered ghost would appear in the mirror, and if you looked her in the eye you would free her from the glass—she'd haunt you for the rest of your life. Sometimes during these ceremonies, Trisha would press her face into Frank's shoulder and scream, her breath hot on his neck, and he'd carry these little moments with him for weeks, months. Years.

Why had he thought about this again now?

Frank sat next to Ethan. He explained the rules of the game. Because wide-eyed Lucy was right there, he left out the details about the potential lifelong haunting, Mary wielding a giant axe, etc.

"Who wants to play?" he asked.

"I don't believe in ghosts or spirits or any of that junk," Chester said. "I think they're just carbon monoxide-induced hallucinations."

Lucy said, "I saw my grandpa dancing in the clouds when we flew to Santa Fe for his funeral. Mom and Dad didn't see him, though."

Chester's diagnosis was prompt. "Altitude sickness," he said.

"I'm sure there's more to it than that, Chester," Frank said.

In the coffee cakes, the candles melted like slow-burning fuses.

"Let's do it," Ethan said.

Lucy clawed her static-charged blond hair from her face. She rested her head against Frank's forearm. "I don't want to open my eyes, Mr. Rudman," she said. "Tell me if she appears, okay?"

"I will," Frank said.

Ethan approached one of the mirrored walls with the platter of coffee cakes. The others followed.

"Ready?" Frank asked. Everyone nodded. They counted down— "Three, two, one!"—and shouted, "Bloody Mary! Bloody Mary! Bloody Mary!"

There was a pause. Silence.

"Told you," Chester said.

Ethan laughed. "Not even Bloody Mary wants to come to my party," he said.

And then he blew out the candles.

Frank pulled up to Chester Taft's house and found Ms. Taft sitting on the porch with a glass of some dark green liquid clutched in her hand. She waddled down the stairs. She was a huge, tanned woman, and she wore nothing but a pair of jean shorts and a much-too-small bubblegum-pink

295

bikini top that did little to conceal her vein-scribbled breasts. She came right up to the driver's-side window of Frank's truck, leaned inside, and thanked him for inviting Chester to the party.

Frank stared hard at the odometer. "He's a good kid. I'm glad he came along."

"Thanks for the lift, Mr. Rudman," Chester said.

Driving home now, Frank could only imagine what the sight of Ms. Taft's huge, drooping breasts had done to poor Lucy's delicate psyche. Lucy seemed to read his mind.

"That didn't bother me, you know," she said from the backseat. "That big boob lady. Chester's mom."

"Oh," Frank said.

"It bothered me," Ethan said.

Lucy leaned between the front seats. "I hope I never get boobs like that, though," she said.

Steering the conversation far off the topic of Lucy's future breasts, Frank turned on the radio. The Red Sox were getting pounded by the Orioles heading into the sixth inning. Frank switched the station. Zero A.P.R. over at Midtown Motors. Switch.

"Leave it here!" Lucy said, and she began singing along to "Downtown" with Petula Clark.

"How do you know this oldie?" Frank asked.

"Daddy loved this song," Lucy said. "He used to sing it to me all the time."

Frank glanced back at her in the rearview mirror. Right around the time Bonnie died, Lucy's father had run off to Chicago with a man he'd met playing online poker. Frank had been too busy dealing with his own grief to keep up with the grief of those around him—including Ethan's, he hated to admit. However, he'd heard bits and pieces of the story from Lucy's mother, Janelle Hadler. She'd told Frank about it one afternoon out by the mailbox. The night Lawrence Hadler hit the road, she said, he prepared a lavish dinner—prime rib, mashed potatoes, roasted asparagus—and wrapped it all in aluminum foil to be reheated when Janelle and Lucy returned from Lucy's dance recital. In addition to this meal, he left a long, handwritten letter on the kitchen table explaining that he just couldn't do it anymore, this lie he was living here in New Hampshire, and he hoped Janelle and Lucy would come to understand.

"I've come to understand I married a coldhearted, goddamn asshole," Janelle had told Frank.

Frank wished he had something good to say to Lucy now, some scrap of fatherly wisdom to bestow upon the lonely little girl in the backseat. But all he could muster was, "It's a great song."

Back home, he parked the truck and told Ethan to bring inside the left-over pizzas and the chocolate cake he'd picked up at Hannaford on the drive home. "Be right back, bud," he said, and he walked Lucy next door. It was a cool September afternoon, and Janelle Hadler was raking leaves. Foliage season had started early this year: five cold nights in a row and now the whole neighborhood was a postcard limbo of red and orange and bright green. Janelle leaned against the rake as Frank and Lucy approached. She was still in her work clothes: black pants, tucked-in white blouse, hair pulled back in a simple bun. She sold real-estate—"I used to sell real-estate," she'd once joked with Frank, expounding on the downturn in the economy, the piss-poor interest rates—and it made Frank a little depressed to see her out here working like this in her house-selling outfit.

"How was it?" she asked.

"The turnout wasn't stellar," Frank said.

Janelle sighed. "Sorry to hear that. I wish I could've come, but I had to catch up on a few things around the house."

"Lucy was great," Frank said. "Told me I'm going to be reincarnated as a dolphin."

"Is that so?" Janelle said. "Better than a silverback gorilla. That's my destiny, right, love?"

"Dolphins and gorillas are highly intelligent," Lucy said.

"Intelligence," Janelle said. "That'll be a refreshing change."

"Bye, Mr. Rudman!" Lucy shrieked, and she ran into the house, banging the screen door shut behind her. Frank and Janelle were alone in the yard. Frank holstered his hands in his pockets and let his eyes wander over the colorful leaf piles punctuating the lawn. Since Bonnie's death, he'd found small talk like this almost excruciating, not because he was inherently anti-social—he wasn't, he hoped—but because lately he felt as though people possessed some secret knowledge he himself did not; as though every citizen in Outlook Springs had X-ray vision when it came to Frank Rudman, an ability to spot tumors in his bones or dementia rooting in the soft pulp of his brain, and yet they could not reveal this information to Frank, lest the concealed calamities befall themselves instead.

Of course this was ridiculous. There was no secret knowledge. You didn't need X-ray vision to know about Bonnie's car accident. It was in the local papers, and discussed like all tragedies are discussed in a small town.

Still, in the months following Bonnie's death, Frank had had a difficult time shaking the feeling that there was another highly combustible disaster looming on the margins of his life, some finishing blow that could be ignited by the simple spark of a lie—*I'm doing fine, just fine, thanks for asking*—and for a time he'd sequestered himself in his bedroom, performing, he realized later, the cliché hermitage of grief. Rarely had he emerged from that room: to heat up a frozen pizza for Ethan, or to sit with him on the couch and stare at an episode of *Star Trek*, or to gather in cardboard boxes those belongings of Bonnie's he could no longer bear to have around—a hair-clotted brush, a pair of Scrabble-tile earrings, a jar of sea glass she'd gathered during their honeymoon in Morocco. He'd brought these boxes to the basement, and stacked them on top of one another like a shrine devoted to the life she should have had.

But the rest of the world had their misfortunes, too. Little focused apocalypses from which lives barely escaped. Like Janelle Hadler, for instance. Like Lucy.

Like Ethan.

Frank said, "I should head home."

Janelle nodded. She pulled a maple leaf from one of the rake's tines and broke it apart, letting it sift through her fingers like confetti.

She smiled. "I had something to tell you, Frank, but I've forgotten what it was."

"It'll come back," Frank said.

"I hope so," Janelle said.

Ethan was penciling the names of countries onto a map of Europe when Frank returned from the Hadler's. Frank removed the plastic-domed lid from the chocolate cake and stuck his finger into the buttercream frosting.

"Much better than coffee cake," he said.

"I liked the coffee cake," Ethan said.

"Don't let me off the hook, bud. I bungled it."

"It's not your fault I don't have friends."

Frank took two plates and two forks from the cupboard. He slid a wedge of cake toward Ethan. "Eat," he said. Ethan stuck the back of his pencil into the cake and licked the frosting from the eraser.

"You have friends," Frank said, as if simply stating this out loud made it true.

"I have three Spock posters in my room, Dad."

"You could take 'em down," Frank said.

"I'm not that desperate," Ethan said.

Frank let a breath of silence pass, then said, "I didn't plan the thing well enough. That's the problem. I just sort of, well, thought it would turn out all right."

"Bloody Mary was kinda cool," Ethan said.

"I'm the King of Kinda Cool," Frank said.

Ethan filled in Germany, Poland, Belarus.

"Did you see something in that mirror, Dad?" he asked.

"See something?" Frank said. "Bloody Mary, you mean?"

"I don't know. You looked—*weird*."

Frank took a bite of cake. "I was thinking about an old crush, if you want to know the truth. Trisha Malamoff. This was way before Mom."

Before Mom. That magical epoch for a child, in which the world is all rumor and myth.

"How come you were thinking about her?" Ethan asked.

"Bloody Mary. I used to play it with Trisha and her brother, Seth. Seth was my best friend."

Slovakia, Austria, Hungary.

"Have I met them?"

"Seth and Trisha? Nope."

It occurred to Frank that he didn't know much about Seth and Trisha anymore. The last time he saw either of them was at Seth's wedding at Peninsula Park in Portland, Oregon, on a blue-sky afternoon in June. At that point he'd only been dating Bonnie four months, but she came along to Portland, too.

During the reception, Frank marveled at the fact that Seth Malamoff had solidified into a man with a mortgage and a soon-to-be-baby-girl on the horizon. Seeing him up there with the roses and the new wife and the priest, Frank had realized that their friendship was over, though the two of them might go on for years and years pretending otherwise. Through a miraculous transformation spelled out on this side of their shared childhood, Frank and Seth had left an entire world behind: fishing down at Livermore River; late-night talks after middle school dances about girls gifted in breaking your heart three-hundred-and-eleven times in an afternoon; summers between the end of one school year and the start of another in which the only thing they had to do was sit in front of a fan and think about the heat.

Frank hadn't known how much he'd loved Seth until he no longer knew him. The only thing he could do now, he had told himself as teary-eyed Seth said, "I do," was hold the hand of the pretty girl sitting beside him in the rose garden and trust that this new world might make moments half as good as the old.

Back at the Marriott after the post-reception party, Bonnie had come out of the bathroom brushing her long black hair and said, "Did you used to date that girl? Seth's sister, I mean."

Frank laughed. He'd talked to Trisha for just a minute or two—she had a plump, drooling baby balanced on each knee and a Marine husband keen on taking full advantage of the open bar—and so he couldn't imagine how Bonnie had reached that conclusion. She wasn't jealous, just curious, and Frank confessed he'd had a crush on Trisha from fifth to tenth grade, though of course it hadn't been anything serious.

"Funny," Bonnie had said. "She kept glancing over like you two almost had a life together."

"She did?" Frank said.

Bonnie nodded. "Like you missed it by an inch or two."

Listening to Bonnie sleep later that night, Frank had thought about the lives he'd almost had. It was impossible to know these almost-lives, but sometimes he made them up in his head—entire lineages and histories unspooling into nowhere. Even if these unhatched realities weren't any good, it seemed unfair and cruel that they never got a chance to exist.

"Dad?"

Frank looked up to see Ethan balancing a lump of cake on the tip of his pencil.

"Yeah, bud?"

"Do you still talk to Trisha and Seth?"

"Nope."

"How come?"

"I guess we've all sort of moved on."

"Do you miss them?"

Frank considered his answer. Yes or no? He didn't know which was sadder.

"I have presents for you," he said. "Let's open those, okay?"

Ethan slid his geography textbook across the table. "Help me with some capitals first."

Frank leaned back in his chair and stared at the colorful pages.

"France," he said.

"Easy," Ethan said. He sucked cake from the tip of his pencil. "Paris."

"*Spock*tacular," Frank said.

Ethan groaned.

The phone rang at quarter till nine. The Caller I.D. said it was Janelle Hadler. It was not like her to call this late.

Then Frank remembered: The big boob lady! Ms. Taft. He'd forgotten all about the incident.

"Hi, Frank," she said.

"Hi there, Janelle. How's it going?"

From the couch, Ethan mouthed, *What does she want?* Frank had the portable phone cradled between his ear and shoulder, and he put his hands in front of his chest as though he were balancing a couple of huge cantaloupes. Ethan threw back his head with silent laughter.

"Look, Frank, I'm sorry to bother you," Janelle said.

"No, no, it's fine. Ethan's just going through his presents."

"Oh, good," Janelle said. She breathed heavily into the phone. "It's about Lucy. She's really upset and—"

"I'm so sorry, Janelle," Frank said. He paced from the living room to the kitchen. "I had no idea that woman would be out there without a shirt on. It was Ms. Taft. Do you know her? Chester's mom?" He tried to defuse the tension with a laugh. "To be honest," he continued, "her, umm, ample bosom"—Jesus, ample bosom?—"upset me quite a bit, too. I meant to explain all this before."

For a moment, Janelle was silent. Then she started laughing.

"I had no idea about that," she said. "Don't worry about it, though. I'm sure Lucy's seen worse, whatever the hell it was."

Frank sat on the arm of the couch. Ethan looked up from his lapful of presents—two Xbox games, a chessboard with pieces modeled after Lord of the Rings characters, a Dustin Pedroia jersey—and mouthed, *Is she mad?* Frank shook his head.

"I'm actually calling about Bloody Mary," Janelle said.

"Bloody Mary?"

"Lucy's all worked up about it. She said she saw the woman in the bathroom mirror. Now she can't sleep."

"Jesus," Frank said. "That's my fault. I thought I kept the whole thing pretty PG. Lucy's so smart for her age. Sometimes I forget she's just a little girl."

"She did some research on the internet when she got home," Janelle said. "She's officially a Bloody Mary expert now."

"Is there anything I can do?"

"I was hoping you could talk to her."

The humor drained out of her voice, leaving it brittle, the voice of a mother doing everything on her own. "She looks up to you," she said. "Do you know what she told me the other night? She told me you sleep on the moon."

"I don't get it," Frank said.

"I don't either," Janelle said. "But she made it sound like it's the greatest compliment in the world."

For some reason, Frank imagined Janelle talking to him from her dark bathroom, sitting on the edge of the tub, perhaps, waiting for Bloody Mary to reveal herself.

"I'm more than happy to talk to her," Frank said.

"Can I put her on the phone?"

Frank nodded, as though Janelle could somehow sense this movement through the phone's connection. Ethan was now watching an episode of *Dr. Who*. It was raining again. Fat drops the size of grapes thumped the roof and rushed down the windows like melting pewter, sloshing in the gutter, hissing on Emerson Street.

Frank said, "How about I come over?"

"Oh, you don't need to go through all that trouble," Janelle said, though Frank could hear in her voice that she'd been considering this option, too. "It's late."

"No trouble," Frank said. "Please? Let me repent for my sins in person."

"Okay, well, *sure*, if you don't mind. That'd be nice, Frank."

There was a measure of silence between them. Then Frank said, "Don't let Bloody Mary out of the mirror until I get there."

Janelle sighed. "Deal."

"Oh, and Janelle?"

"Yes, Frank?"

"It might take me a minute or two to get over there. I'm coming all the way from the moon, you know."

Ethan zipped up his Nike sweatshirt and stepped into a pair of Frank's much-too-large sandals, duck-walking around the living room, laughing. Frank rummaged in the closet for an umbrella—*portable ceilings*, Bonnie used to call them—and found one under a heap of coats. Mildew from last summer's storms clung to the fabric, and Frank thought of Bonnie standing right here in the space beneath the umbrella's cover. Beneath this portable ceiling.

"I can't believe Lucy's so freaked out," Ethan said.

"She's only nine," Frank said. "I don't know what I was thinking."

"The King of Kinda Cool strikes again!" Ethan said.

Janelle held the screen door open with her shoulder as Frank and Ethan tromped up the steps. She was no longer dressed in her real-estate outfit, Frank was glad to see. Instead, she wore a long-sleeved shirt that read CAPE COD, I MISS YOU! and flannel pajama pants. In the light of the overhead bulb, her hair was almost blue, as if each strand were a filament charged with starry voltage. Frank closed the umbrella, slapped off the accumulated rain.

"Let me take that," Janelle said, and Frank handed it to her.

It had been a long time since he'd visited this house. Years. The place was totally revamped: new couches, new kitchen cupboards, the prints of Monet and Renoir replaced by framed photographs of Lucy. The alterations surprised Frank, though why should they? Houses changed.

Back in the old days—Before Mom!—Frank and Bonnie had come here on several occasions to play cards with Janelle and Lawrence, the four of them sipping Manhattans around this same granite-island table-top, scratchy music spilling from an old record player—Mississippi John Hurt, Van Morrison, Stravinsky—and reveling in that particular cama-raderie reserved for young marrieds, still without children, living in a world that seemed custom-built for their lives. Looking around the bright kitchen now, Frank remembered Bonnie sitting beside Janelle on that table, both women open-mouthed as Frank and Lawrence flung pista-chios from across the room, counting aloud the ones their wives caught, all of them laughing and half-drunk as a November blizzard whirled madly outside.

"Mr. Rudman!" Lucy shrieked. She was sitting at the table with a glass of milk. "Ethan!"

"Hi, Lucy," Ethan said.

Janelle held up a bottle of Merlot like a trophy. "Can I interest y'all in something to drink?" she said.

"Milk, please," Ethan said. "Dad'll have the wine."

"I will?" Frank said.

"Yes," Ethan said. "You will."

Frank sat beside Lucy at the table. He thrummed his fingers on the table. There was a bowl of green grapes, and Frank took one, peeling the tart skin back with his teeth. He cleared his throat. But before he could speak, Lucy said, "I know why you're here, Mr. Rudman. But I saw her. I know I did."

"Look," Frank said. "I shouldn't have shown you that game. It was a joke. Bloody Mary doesn't exist."

"She was in the mirror," Lucy said. She shifted in her seat, then added, "Her hands were pressed against the other side of the glass, Mr. Rudman. I'm telling the truth. Her fingers got all white from the pressure. She wasn't scary looking—not like you said she'd be. She just looked really, really scared. Like I was the ghost or something."

"Scared?" Frank said, realizing even as he spoke that he was feeding into her delusion.

"She was crying."

Frank touched Lucy's hand. She'd drawn little smiling hearts on each knuckle. "It's just a game," he told her. "Like hide-and-seek or tag. It doesn't mean anything."

Frank looked at Janelle. She just shrugged and sipped her wine. He should have come over and said something after Lawrence walked out, he suddenly thought. After Bonnie died, Janelle had brought a tray of manicotti to the house. Couldn't Frank have done that much, at least? Some small gesture to let her know he was there if she needed help?

"I'm not scared," Lucy said.

"That's good," Frank said. "There's nothing to be scared of, right?"

"I'm *sad*." Her big green eyes flooded.

"I don't understand," Janelle said patiently. "Tell us what's wrong, love. Please." "She's stuck behind that mirror," Lucy said. "Forever and ever. She has a pretty red dress on, and she can't go anywhere. It's not fair."

She began to cry. Janelle came around the table and put her arm around the girl's quaking shoulders. Frank took a sip of wine. He didn't know what to do. How could he convince Lucy that Bloody Mary wasn't real? That there was no woman trapped behind the glass? That it was all in her head. Like the Brain Drain Man, Frank thought, the monster who crawled out of the bathtub drain each night and traipsed around Frank's childhood home, sniffing for brains to slurp out of Frank's ear like warm Jell-O. How long had Frank believed in the Brain Drain Man? How many rituals had he invented to prevent that creature from entering his bedroom? The aluminum-covered doorknob. The length of fishing line rigged with little bells.

He could perform the Bloody Mary routine with Lucy, he thought, and show her the woman she'd seen—the red gown, the white fingertips—was nothing more than a trick of candlelight. The same way a coat draped over a chair might assume the likeness of the Grim Reaper. The way crumpled blankets on a bed might look like the curled body of a sleeping woman, though in the end it's nothing.

"Dad," Ethan whispered, placing his hands palms-up on the table, running the point of a grape stem along the intersecting lines. Frank looked at his own hands and understood.

"Lucy," he said. "Look at me one moment, okay?"

Lucy peeked through a mask of her own splayed fingers.

"I want you to read my fortune," Frank said. "Can you do that for me?"

"I already did," Lucy said warily.

"But there's got to be more," Frank said. "I win the lottery. I'm reincarnated as a dolphin. I know all that. It's old news! But what about the other stuff? I mean, I have lots of lines on these old palms." He showed his hands to Lucy for proof. "Look at this one," he said, tracing a long diagonal line with his thumb. "This is, what, a '67 Corvette? How about this one? Loads of grandkids?" He glanced at Ethan and smiled. *Grandkids?* Ethan mouthed, as though it were some terrible diagnosis. "Please, Lucy," Frank said. "I'm begging you."

"I want another reading, too," Ethan said. "It's my birthday, after all."

Lucy beamed. She swiped tears and snot from her face with the sleeve of her T-shirt and took Frank's right hand in her own, pulling it close. She had such small, delicate fingers. Little fingernails with half-moons. Hearts on each knuckle.

"Okay," she said, "but first you need to take a deep, deep breath."

Frank did as he was told.

"Deeper than that, Dad," Ethan teased.

Frank made a production of sucking in more air, and when he exhaled Janelle pretended to wobble on her feet, as though the gust were too much for her.

"Good," Lucy said, giggling. Frank smelled the sweet milk on her breath.

"How does it look?" Frank said. "Be straight with me."

Lucy made a clicking sound with her tongue as she examined the lines. "This is interesting," she said, tapping a spot in the middle of Frank's palm. "I can't believe I didn't see *this* before."

"Tell us what you see," Janelle said.

305

"It's incredible," Lucy said, and gasped.

Frank squeezed Ethan's knee with his free hand. Twelve years old! It didn't seem possible. Outside, the rain made the same delicate hissing sound ten thousand different ways. Inside, the lights above the kitchen table flickered but did not go out.

"I'm ready," Frank said, and he waited for the little girl holding his hand to tell him all the wonderful things that would happen in the course of his long, long life, if only he were patient, if only he believed as much as she did.

Nominated by Southern Indiana Review,
Thomas Paine

THE CLEARING

by ALLISON ADAIR

from THE SOUTHEAST REVIEW

THE CLEARING

What if this time instead of crumbs the girl drops
teeth, her own, what else does she have, and the prince

or woodcutter or brother or man musty with beard and
thick in the pants collects the teeth with a wide rustic hand

holds their gray roots to a nostril to smell the fresh
feminine rot, fingers the bony stems of her

fear, born of watered-down broths, of motherlessness,
of an owl's sharp beak crooking back around into itself?

The wolf licks his parts with a sandpaper tongue
and just like that we've got ourselves a familiar victim.

It is written: the world's fluids shall rush into a single birch
tree and there's the girl, lying in a clearing we've never seen

but know is ours. Undergrowth rattles like the shank
of a loose pen. We'll write this story again and again,

how her mouth blooms to its raw venous throat—that tunnel
of marbled wetness, beefy, muted, new, pillow for our star

sapphire, our sluggish prospecting—and how dark birds come
after, to dress the wounds, no, to peck her sockets clean.

Nominated by The Southeast Review

GUERRILLA MARKETING

fiction by SANJAY AGNIHOTRI

from ONE STORY

Vikram dropped onto his knees and prayed to the goddess Lakshmi for a cash windfall. In less than six months, his only daughter, Heena, was getting married in Baroda, India, and he didn't have money for the plane ticket home, let alone the wedding spread. If anyone should understand his desperation, it was the goddess of prosperity, and so—in the Balaji temple in Parsippany, New Jersey—Vikram bent down and prayed like he used to when he was a boy, when he believed the gods could deliver anything.

Vikram hadn't come to the Balaji temple alone. He'd brought along one of his roommates, the ex-con and cook Sethi. Sethi, a lapsed Sikh, waited outside, claiming the eyeless statues of gods and goddesses spooked him. He leaned against a lamppost, smoking cigarettes and ogling the Hindu girls as they made their way across the parking lot to the temple for the free Prasad dinner.

For a couple of weeks now, Vikram had been investing in prayer, but tonight, when dollars didn't fall from the temple ceiling, he grabbed the old Brahmin priest and pronounced the goddess Lakshmi a whore. The priest, who was accompanying a youth group, passed off his heavy load of Sanskrit texts, adjusted his cotton dhoti, and pushed Vikram out the temple doors. The usually reserved teenagers laughed, and so did Sethi—until he realized he might not eat that night. Some skinny-ankled Brahmin wasn't going to stop him from getting his Prasad dinner. He had scraped together enough to buy a bottle of Cutty Sark and didn't intend to drink on an empty stomach.

Sethi went seething into the temple, ready for a confrontation; he walked away carrying two plates of steaming food to go.

"They couldn't have been more kind," he said, with a tone of disappointment.

In the parking lot, the two roommates clawed at the hot food and split the bottle of Cutty Sark. The whiskey went straight to Vikram's head, even with his belly full of greasy samosas. On the bus ride back to the boarding house, he bemoaned the depth of his debts, raged against the bastards around the world who had screwed him over, and confessed the growing stack of American dollars he owed their boss, Mr. Raj, the restaurant proprietor, for picking up Vikram's H1 visa fees and relocation expenses from Los Angeles to New Jersey. He worried about his daughter's marriage. She was his only child, and if he didn't find the money—shit, she was thirty-six, and this was her last shot. Sethi listened carefully, patiently. The ex-con concluded that their only option was to rob the Indian grocer on Route 46. "After all," he said, "by the end of the day, he must have five hundred sitting in the register."

"I don't have the stomach for it," Vikram said. The idea of thieving frightened him more than it excited him. He wasn't some street criminal. He was a fifty-seven-year-old accountant with a degree in finance from Baroda University. Since his family's apothecary business in Baroda had gone bust seven years ago, he'd travelled around—mostly in the Middle East—trying to start import/export and other businesses. He'd worked a bootleg tape shop in Yanbu, Saudi Arabia; sold rugs in Ethiopia; paved roads in Dubai; and peddled remote-control toy cars in the alleyways of Kuwait City. Los Angeles was to have been his breakthrough. He'd exaggerated to his family about steady revenue as a hotelier and promised to relocate them from India to California within one year.

His wife and daughter in Baroda would have drowned themselves in the Mahi River if they'd discovered the truth: months ago he'd been run out of Los Angeles, where he'd been working as the night manager at a pay-by-the-hour motel in Ventura, and he was now living in Parsippany with fifteen wayward Indian men in an overcrowded clapboard trap, making lousy tips as a waiter at Mr. Raj's Spice Grill.

The next morning, Vikram ducked into the Spice Grill bathroom to change into his waiter uniform: a poorly fitted polyester jacket, tight-in-the-crotch pants, and pinching leatherette shoes from Target. Through the bathroom wall came the clanking of pans and iron cookware from the kitchen—Sethi and the kitchen staff prepping for the lunch buffet—and Mr. Raj's wife's bullying, caustic voice. Every morning it was the same routine: Raj's wife scolding the kitchen staff and threatening to confiscate their work papers, turn the illegals over to Homeland Security, withdraw green card applications, or sic the police on them for doing drugs.

Vikram buttoned his jacket with shaky fingers and stepped outside the restaurant into the frozen air. He walked a few stores down to the Dunkin' Donuts. Showkat, the Bangladeshi kid behind the counter, recognized the familiar signs of a hangover in Vikram's suffering face and poured him a large coffee, one sugar, no cream.

Outside Vikram braced himself against the guardrail. He took a sip of coffee, swished it around, and spat. He felt clammy, dizzy. He could feel his ass sweating through his underwear.

Despite the mess he'd left behind in California, he missed Los Angeles. He longed for the heat, the palm trees, the empty streets of Ventura after midnight. If he could have just one palm tree—delivered express via the monkey god Hanuman, faster than FedEx. And the beaches. *A beach to go, Hanuman, while you're at it. And a beautiful woman to lounge with in the sun.* Where were all the pretty Indian girls in New Jersey? These dashi girls—skinny-boned Gujaratis—didn't compare to the lush blondes in L.A.

He tossed the unfinished coffee into the trash. As he was on his way back to Spice Grill, a Mercedes pulled quickly alongside him, making a wide, sweeping turn into one of Mr. Raj's private parking spots. The Mercedes came to a short stop, and Boss Bhatti, a Spice Grill regular and Raj's business partner, stepped out in a suit and tie. Boss Bhatti called Vikram over to the car. He needed help carrying crates of mangoes into the restaurant. Vikram reached inside the Mercedes and grabbed a stack.

"My son gets them from a contact in Edison," Boss Bhatti said. "Best mangoes around, even out of season."

Inside Spice Grill, Vikram placed the stack on the serving tables alongside the steaming buffet trays. Boss Bhatti took off his jacket and slipped his iPad from his briefcase, settling in for business. "I get lousy Wi-Fi in here. Is Raj around?"

Vikram had seen only Raj's wife.

"She doesn't know Wi-Fi," Bhatti said. From his suit pocket, he took a long distance phone card and slipped it into Vikram's chest pocket.

"And that's not a shitty thirty-minute one. That's two hours international. Call your family. Tell them how much you miss them," Boss Bhatti turned back to his iPad and continued to poke at the screen, checking his various bank accounts. "Bank of America," he said. "Did you know an Indian is the CEO?"

"Sure," Vikram said, encouraged by Bhatti's unexpected desire to talk to him. "Deshpande."

Boss Bhatti did not look up. He poked at the screen. "Yes, Deshpande. He's an asshole. He snubbed me at a charity event in Manhattan. Then he found out about my businesses, that I'm not some day laborer. You follow the financials?"

"At the library on the Internet."

"You have to walk all the way to the library? Raj should at least spring for a computer at that shit hole. What's your mattress like?"

"I sleep on the floor."

"That bad?"

"I got used to it when I worked in Kuwait. It was the only way to sleep in the heat."

"Last year, before you arrived, all the waiters had head lice. Raj shaved their heads. It looked like a bunch of Buddhist monks worked here."

Vikram glanced at the iPad and saw a balance of $157,000 in a personal account.

"Look at all this clutter on the screen," Boss Bhatti said, referring to the Bank of America website. "I can't tell tit from tat. Deshpande should be less concerned with Manhattan charity events and more with cleaning up the site."

Vikram agreed that it didn't seem right.

"You're from Anand, right?" Boss Bhatti said.

"Baroda."

"Raj told me Anand. And you're an engineer—electrical?"

"I'm an accountant."

"Really?" Boss Bhatti lifted his head and looked Vikram full in the face for the first time ever. "My son has his CPA. He's starting an accounting firm. I staked him. We should talk. He got his degree from Rutgers."

"Very good, Rutgers. Ivy League," Vikram said.

At that moment, Raj's wife came through the swinging kitchen doors into the dining room. Vikram knew he was caught. Her crazed eyes spun Vikram around and back into the kitchen faster than a hot shell. He should not have been speaking with Boss Bhatti.

Bhatti shot her a look. "Use some of that hostile energy to get your Wi-Fi running right," he said, rising out of his seat. "What's the point of my doing business here otherwise?"

After the lunch crowd rush, Vikram and Sethi shared a smoke out back. They stood in the cold sun, the wind blowing through the empty trees, scattering ashes into the creases of the ex-con's saffron turban. Sethi held his hand-rolled cigarette between his teeth and examined the phone card Boss Bhatti had placed in Vikram's pocket.

"He knows I'm an accountant," Vikram said.

"You're a waiter."

"You know what I mean. His son's new business—maybe he needs another accountant. I think he's going to offer me a job."

"Forget it," Sethi said.

The back door of Dunkin' Donuts swung open, and Showkat stepped out, hauling a bag of garbage.

Sethi shouted, "Box o' joe!"

Showkat heaved the garbage bag into the dumpster, nearly falling in with the trash. He brushed himself off and disappeared back into the Dunkin' Donuts.

"How does Bhatti change the phone cards from thirty minutes to two hours? You should ask him," Sethi said.

"I need a new sponsor."

"Raj isn't going to be happy."

"I'll never be out of debt to him."

"We should start a franchise," Sethi said.

"Franchise is old hat. That's year 2000 thinking. I'm too old. My feet hurt."

A few minutes later, the Dunkin' Donuts' back door opened again, and Showkat walked toward them carrying a box of coffee. "How much longer do I have to get you free stuff? My father is going to catch on."

Sethi smirked. "You want me to tell him you're stealing *Hustler* magazines from Dilip's shop and jerking off behind the dumpsters?"

Showkat grabbed his crotch and told the ex-con to bite it.

"Okay," Sethi said. "Can you get me some pot?"

"Of course. My cousin Ramesh, he's a DJ, works the clubs. He can get it for you. Oxycontin too."

"Just pot to help me sleep."

"Sure."

"Get me a *Hustler* too. Vikram has the goddess Lakshmi praying for you."

Showkat, a Hindu, made the sign of the cross, turned on his heels, and left.

Spice Grill's back door opened, and Mr. Raj walked out, gut first, breathing hard in the cold air like a broken mule. Steam rose from his nostrils, the top of his toupee, his hairy ears. He bummed one of the hand-rolled cigarettes from Sethi.

"What, twenty-minute breaks now? I've got a party in the banquet hall tonight. Chop, chop. Pharmaceutical dinner. This sales rep, she's hot and she gives me free samples of Cialis. I think it's a come-on," he said, winking at Sethi.

"Tell her you accidentally overdosed and need four-hour mouth-to-cock," Sethi said.

Sethi and Vikram kicked their cigarettes under the dumpster. Mr. Raj followed them inside. As Vikram headed toward the bathroom to clean up, Mr. Raj took hold of his arm and turned him around.

"I need you at my gas station," Mr. Raj said.

"So I'm not here anymore?"

"No, you're still workings days here. And the graveyard at my Shell station."

"The graveyard?" Vikram said. "Really?"

"Before you leave, walk by the banquet hall. You got to see the tits on this rep."

Vikram understood the graveyard gas station detail was punishment for commiserating with Boss Bhatti. Raj's wife had ratted him out. She deployed a kind of crude and antiquated caste system hierarchy at the restaurant, and Vikram was at the bottom.

Sethi was probably right: Bhatti wasn't going to offer him any job in his start-up. When Vikram got home, he used the calling card Bhatti had given him to phone his family in Baroda. His daughter, Heena, answered. Vikram kept up the story about the motels. His life in California. Told her he was being groomed for the role of CFO for the thriving motel franchise. There would be money soon. His daughter cut in, reminding him there hadn't been money in months. Did he have any idea how much the most basic wedding cost, she asked, her voice shaking on the line. They didn't have money for invitations, for the mandap, for new saris. And what about the catering costs? Vikram demanded to speak with his wife. There was a brief silence on the line, and Vikram could hear his daughter smothering her tears. Finally, she replied, "She's at uncle's house. He's going to pay for the wedding."

There was a moment of relief—until Vikram realized he did not even have enough money for the plane ticket home. But he did not tell Heena this. He spoke to her about Los Angeles—the palm trees, the Pacific Ocean, the breakfast burritos—as he looked out the filthy windows of the boarding house at the dead trees and pitted winter roads of New Jersey.

That night he started working at the gas station, returning to the boarding house after 8 a.m. He had to be back at Spice Grill by 11 a.m. Mr. Raj shut off the boarding house's heat during the day, so it was too cold for Vikram to sleep on the floor, but he couldn't sleep comfortably on the bed. After two weeks of working double shifts, he got sick. He blamed Sethi for taking him to a chicken wings dhaba—Cluck-U— where he'd eaten veggie wings and convinced himself the rancid cooking oil had given him bronchitis. He missed a day of work, placing him at the top of Mr. Raj's shit list. All day he had fever dreams about stealing money from the Shell station's till and walking back to California.

He woke in the dark, sweating and disoriented. Sethi sat beside him on the edge of the bed, turbanless, his black hair falling long and loose over his shoulders. He'd found Vikram passed out on the bathroom floor, he said. "I thought you'd broken your neck, the way you were all twisted up, like a hanged man."

The young Muslim, Naseer, stood in the doorway, his Bluetooth earpiece blinking. Vikram wondered if Naseer was receiving secret codes to detonate a bomb. Naseer passed Sethi a cup of chai. "I put some Cutty Sark in it, to break up the junk in his chest."

Sethi held the cup as Vikram took little sips like an invalid.

"I'm going to cover your shift at the station, uncle," Naseer said, tapping his Bluetooth.

"It was the chicken," Vikram insisted.

"Superstition," Sethi said, maintaining a gentle, patient tone. "Cluck-U doesn't cause the flu. And anyway, you had the veggie wings."

For five days Vikram was bedridden, so for five days he didn't get paid. On the sixth night, it was back to the graveyard shift for the still sick

315

Vikram. Around 1 a.m., a car full of drunk teenagers pulled into the gas station. A girl went into the bathroom and vomited, missing the toilet. Vikram spent an hour splashing down the walls with disinfectant and cold water—so cold the floors iced over. He left the shit box coughing and dumped the bucket of slosh behind the dumpster.

Out front there was a car waiting at the pumps—Boss Bhatti's black Mercedes S-something, windows tinted. Vikram wiped his hands and adjusted his Shell cap to hide his watering, bloodshot eyes. Boss Bhatti rolled down the window and with his ring-studded hand beckoned Vikram inside.

Vikram fell into the leather seat as if he'd fallen into a pit. The bones in his back pressed against the leather, and he knew he'd lost too much weight. A Lakshmi murti was perched on the dashboard, the goddess of prosperity idolized in eighteen-karat rose gold.

Boss Bhatti wore a Fila track suit, wrinkled in the crotch, he boasted, from a dozen lap dances that night. Once he started talking, alcohol fumes filled the cabin, though he didn't appear drunk. He explained his absence from Spice Grill—he'd been helping his son, Ginger, with the new business venture, Liberty Tax Company. He needed men for the team, competent men. *Start-up. Good money.* Boss Bhatti spoke urgently and with more animation than usual. He was on something—cocaine, Vikram guessed. *Lots of work to be done. Tax season. Busy time. We need your accounting background. You need a new sponsor. I heard you were sick. You might have walking pneumonia. I know a good Ayurvedic doctor. He'll give you a turmeric paste to apply to your throat and chest.*

Bhatti talked at a fast clip, alternating between Gujarati and Hindi, waxing lyrical on acupuncture and Ayurvedic medicine. He called out Raj for his lousy business practices and the terrible conditions at the boarding house. "You probably saw better conditions in the gulf states." He went on about how Raj would be nothing without him, how he had sponsored Raj and his wife to come to America. He told Vikram he should quit Raj, quit working as a waiter.

And he knew all about Vikram's "scandalous" period in L.A. He knew about the teenage girl who had overdosed on heroin at the motel on Vikram's watch. He knew about the married woman from the Mexican food truck he was screwing at the time when he should have been at the front desk. Vikram waved off the accusations, saying in Gujarati, "That is false." Boss Bhatti placed a hand on his shoulder. "You think it matters to me?" he said. "You don't think I know about Naseer and the others blowing through dollars at the strip clubs and on whores every chance they get? You know how many Indian doctors I know supporting stripper girlfriends on the side?"

Vikram closed his burning eyes. When he opened them, a strange thing happened: the gold Lakshmi murti on the dashboard had vanished, and now the goddess herself appeared, cross-legged, hovering above the hood of the Mercedes. Boss Bhatti didn't seem to notice; he was going on about how Indian doctors were just greedy businessmen at heart. Vikram squeezed his eyes shut, afraid he might be losing his mind. But when he reopened them, there she was, the beautiful goddess Lakshmi of his adolescent fantasies—enormous breasts, lustful green eyes, smooth feet clad in gold sandals.

Though she spoke Sanskrit, he understood her every word. "Vikram, you fool," she said, floating in the moonlight. She unfolded her legs and rose fifteen feet tall. "Did you think I'd allow you to remain in debt and spend your days serving buffet lunches to ugly Americans? All this time you believed I abandoned you, that I wouldn't find a way for your daughter's wedding to be a success. Did your despair turn so black? Did you really think I wouldn't help you to repay Raj and the other dozen men you owe? Don't you know one day you will return to India a triumphant hero?"

Vikram muttered—"Yes, yes, yes, I knew it"—and the goddess pressed her lips against the windshield. "Boss Bhatti is going to take care of you," she whispered as she floated toward the stars. "He is going to give you a job. You are going to be part of his son's enterprise. You are going to sit in an office and work with other professional men. You are going to wear a suit. You are going to have clean fingernails . . ."

The goddess's words faded, and Boss Bhatti's rough, arrogant voice broke through the magic. "You're going to be the accountant. I'll pick you up here Friday at 3 p.m. Take you to the office. Get started. Paperwork. Once the business gets rolling, I'm going to have a party at my house in Short Hills, and there you'll make useful contacts, and I'll pick up the cost of the flight back to India for your daughter's wedding, and . . ."

Vikram closed his eyes and said a silent prayer of gratitude to the goddess for not steering him wrong.

Vikram didn't tell anybody, not even Sethi, about Boss Bhatti's job proposition. He didn't tell anybody that Bhatti had given him a cash advance of $150. And he certainly didn't mention his vision of the goddess. He woke in the morning in good spirits, despite Mr. Raj having scheduled him for a double shift at the gas station. He felt strong and did five push-ups. On the way to the bathroom, however, a coughing fit brought him to his knees on the stairs. He crawled back to his room and sat on the edge of the bed, sipping a glass of cloudy tap water Sethi had poured for him the day before.

In the afternoon, Mr. Raj's wife pulled into the gas station. She pressed on the horn, forcing Vikram out of the office. She scolded him for not standing sentinel at the pumps.

Vikram blew his nose into the filthy gasoline rag he kept in his pocket. "I can't stop sweating," he said, "and I can't get warm."

Raj's wife called him a lazy dashi freeloader. She said he could count on more of the graveyard shift. But first Raj wanted Vikram for a Friday night sweet sixteen party for a doctor's daughter. "You break one fucking glass," she said, "and Raj will take you by the ear to Immigration."

Vikram coughed a wad of mucus into the rag and tossed it into the car, onto the lap of Mr. Raj's wife. "My resignation letter to Raj," he said. He wanted to say more, but when he opened his mouth, he could not stop coughing. Raj's wife said nothing. Her eyes seemed to smile as though she had stolen something from right under his nose. She left the filthy rag in her lap, closed the window, and drove away at a snail's pace.

Vikram did not return to the boarding house. He had nothing there to retrieve. He walked through the cold to the nearest strip mall and purchased a dress shirt, a pair of slacks, new shoes, and, most importantly, Drakkar Noir cologne. He went into the restroom and changed out of his Shell uniform and into his new clothes. With profound satisfaction, he threw his Shell uniform into the dumpster behind the mall. He had about fifty dollars remaining from Bhatti's advance and spent it all on a room at the Route 46 motel managed by his friend Sharma, who gave him a good rate for one night and complimented Vikram on his "new IT professional look."

The next day Vikram walked with his hands in his pockets two long miles from the hotel to the Shell station and waited in the back, out of sight of the old man, Ashok, who had assumed Vikram's shift. The bitter cold gnawed at his ears. At 3 p.m., Boss Bhatti's Mercedes pulled into the station. The driver—Vikram couldn't see a face behind the tinted windows—unlocked the passenger door, and Vikram got in. At the wheel sat a young white man in a black suit, smoking a cigarette. Vikram assumed he was Bhatti's private driver. A pack of red Dunhills lay on the dash, and Vikram noticed that the Lakshmi murti had been removed.

The young man reached out a freckled hand and introduced himself as Ginger, Boss Bhatti's son and owner of the new business. Ginger noticed Vikram's surprise and smiled. He took a short drag on his cigarette and said, "My mother is white, Danish."

Vikram coughed into his fist and apologized.

"Don't feel bad," Ginger said, resting the cigarette on the dash. "My dad should have told you."

Vikram couldn't find anything in the young man's face or gestures to identify him as Bhatti's son. His hair was blond and his eyes bright blue. There was not a trace of Indian. And this he liked. No more dashi runarounds. Ginger reminded Vikram of the Berlin businessmen he'd seen walking the lobbies of the hotels in Dubai. Sometimes Vikram would sit in the lobby and read the European newspapers, snapping the pages, hoping to be noticed, longing to enter into a fruitful conversation—until he realized he was the only one reading a paper. All the foreign businessmen gleaned the news from handhelds.

Ginger was impressed with Vikram's "cosmopolitan" background, his education, his tenure as an accountant, his robust "international" travel. Vikram couldn't deny the rekindled entrepreneurial energy flowing through him. The cold symptoms vanished: he could talk without coughing; his head was clear.

"Everybody is pitching in," Ginger said. "Even I make the coffee. No job is beneath anybody in this new venture."

Vikram liked everything he heard. He said he'd do anything to be part of it.

Ginger told him he was pleased to hear this—he had no doubts about Vikram's work ethic and his commitment to the start-up. Ginger reached inside his suit pocket, withdrew a postcard, and handed it to Vikram. The postcard pictured the Statue of Liberty, and across the top were the words "LIBERTY LIVES."

"You know it?" Ginger asked.

"Of course," Vikram said. "Although I have not had the pleasure of visiting yet."

Ginger leaned into Vikram. "That, my friend, is the heart of our marketing campaign. The image of the Statue of Liberty is undeniable in its power to draw people in, to make them trust us, to convince them that we at Liberty Tax Company will do everything in our power to provide our clients with the greatest refund."

Vikram found himself nodding along. Ginger's enthusiasm and confidence were contagious.

Ginger reached into the backseat and pulled a Whole Foods shopping bag onto his lap. He plunged his hand into the bag as if he were performing a magic trick, but instead of pulling out a rabbit, he produced a green foam crown. "Vikram, director of marketing, I would like for you to be our Statue of Liberty." He passed the crown to Vikram.

Vikram looked at the crown, the shopping bag, and Ginger, trying to connect the dots.

"I am an accountant, Mr. Ginger." Vikram placed the crown on the dashboard.

"You're too humble." Ginger lifted the crown off the dash and placed it on Vikram's head. "King Vikram, chief marketing officer of Liberty Tax!"

The foam costume crown felt weightless on his head, much lighter than the Shell baseball cap he was so used to wearing. Ginger nodded as if charged with a solemn initiation. Vikram did his best to model the crown for his new employer, turning his head left and right, raising his chin, as Ginger requested. The heat of humiliation flushed Vikram's cheeks.

"The rest of the uniform is in this bag. Why don't you go into the restroom and try it on? It should fit comfortably over your coat."

Vikram took off the crown and carried the bag with him into the bathroom that once again smelled of vomit, trying not to be seen by Ashok, who was watching DVDs in the office. Ginger was correct—the costume fit perfectly, as if tailored for him.

Ginger pulled at Vikram's sleeves and adjusted the crown. "So on your business card it shall read, 'Vikram, manager of marketing operations.'"

"Not chief marketing officer?" Vikram said, recalling one of Ginger's earlier pronouncements.

"Any title you like!" Ginger smiled, put the car into gear, and drove Vikram to a parking lot at the busy intersection of Route 46 and Beverwyck Road. Across the street was a strip mall, drab as peeling cardboard, featuring the usual stores: a dry cleaner, bagel shop, Chang Liquor, Khan Markets, community bank. An Applebee's stood like an island in the middle of the parking lot. Ginger took a pole sign out of the trunk. The big block letters read: "LIBERTY TAX COMPANY—FAST REFUNDS—LOCAL 973-555-0147."

"Think of it as your scepter," Ginger said, passing the sign to Vikram. "Take no prisoners. Display it proudly, CMO." He pointed to the corner across the street and instructed Vikram to "get noticed." Ginger called it "guerrilla marketing." "Two hours," he said, placing his hand on Vikram's shoulder like a valued colleague. "That's all I ask."

Vikram planted his feet on the corner and for the first hour or so held the sign high, waving and spinning the pole to catch the eyes of drivers and bus commuters. He performed like a man inspired. Hope superseded self-consciousness. He smiled like he imagined Lady Liberty herself might smile if she could.

After a while, the pole splintered and chewed into his hands. His cough started up. He got thirsty and reached for his wallet. Inside only two crumpled dollar bills remained. "No matter," he said aloud for reassurance, though his voice sounded hollow. "Soon the company car will return for me." A car full of teenagers honked at him and swerved close, one of the kids taunting, "Nice costume, tranny!"

The streetlights turned on but did little to cut the darkness. Vikram did not know what time it was. He could not remember what time Ginger was supposed to pick him up. The cold air around him went dead still and found a way deeper into his bones. His feet throbbed hot and cold. He could not stop coughing. He was really thirsty now—sick thirsty. He looked across the road to the parking lot for the Mercedes. What time was it, anyway? Had fifteen minutes passed, or an hour? The wind picked up, and the crown atop his head flapped about like a clipped bird. Purple clouds scudded across the lowering sky, and then the wind started. Vikram got scared. The atmosphere twisted him inside out, so he couldn't catch his breath. It began to snow, and the snow blew sideways into his face, bruising his eyes. He wanted to hide. He wanted to dig a hole in the ground. When he lived in Dubai, that's what you did when you were caught in the open during a sandstorm. You dug a hole and hid. That was not an option here, on a frozen street corner in Parsippany, New Jersey.

Vikram unglued his shoes from the frozen pavement. He limped across Route 46 and crashed through the entrance of the Applebee's, dragging the destroyed sign toward the bar. The small happy hour crowd stared. Vikram felt too sick to care. He found the bathroom and chipped his feet out of his frozen shoes. He lifted them, one at a time, into a sink full of warm water. The bathroom door opened and a skinny young man—a kid, really—walked in.

"I'm the manager," the kid said. "You can't be doing that in here."

"Please, sir," Vikram said, "give me a moment or two. Please, my friend."

The baby-manager looked unconvinced.

Vikram asked him for a phone. He explained that he was an important executive with Liberty Tax Company. He must call the company now, he demanded, shivering, bracing himself between a stall and a sink. The company car must be summoned. The manager placed an orange safety cone in front of the bathroom.

The manager didn't want Vikram touching his phone, so he dialed and put the phone on speaker.

The phone rang three times. A gruff, impatient voice answered, all business: "Yeah, Liberty Tax."

"Sir Bhatti?" Vikram asked in English.

"Who is this? This is Liberty Tax."

"This is Vikram K.," he replied, now in Gujarati. "I'm working with Boss Bhatti and his son for the organization. I am—"

"Who?"

"I need my driver to pick me up."

"Bhatti's not here—who, Ginger?"

"Yes."

"Ginger's gone."

The line went dead.

The manager said he was going to call the cops if Vikram didn't get his shoes out of the sink and vacate the premises. Vikram didn't want trouble. He had no ID, no work papers, nothing. He put his frozen shoes back on. He could hear low whispers and muffled laughter as he made his way past the bar to the front door.

Vikram stepped outside into the storm. He pointed his feet in the direction of Spice Grill and "dashi row." The bones in his feet crunched like broken glass inside his shoes. The Liberty Tax sign was destroyed, but he used what was left of the pole as a sort of walking stick. Few cars passed, and the traffic lights wobbled on the wires and blinked red. He could hear the faraway beeps of trucks and snowplows. He took what he thought might be a shortcut across a corporate parking lot and followed a path alongside a wooded area with picnic tables.

From deep within the woods came the sound of fast-moving water, the sound of the Whippany River. When he was a child, he'd watched a group of village women pull a girl, a classmate of his, out of the village river. Each of the old women grabbed a limb of the bloated, blackening body and dragged it to high ground. Only years later did he learn that the girl had been drowned, a victim of a dowry dispute.

Vikram could not think about that girl, his onetime classmate, her body pulled from the river, without thinking of the girl who had died on his watch at the motel in Ventura. For the rest of his life, the two would be forever wedded. At the motel, Vikram, in a moment of panic, had told the police she had tried to drown herself in the bathtub. The police found a needle sticking out of her arm and dismissed Vikram as an immigrant fool. She had snuck into the motel and stolen a room key. She was seventeen.

The motel owners—devout Jains, or so they claimed—fired Vikram on the spot. They called him a deviant and accused him of getting oral sex from one of the prostitutes when he should have been manning the desk. But there was no blowjob. Vikram had made the ill-fated decision to leave his post for a side deal with a Mexican kid he'd met at Krispy Kreme. He'd been bargaining for bootlegged DVDs to sell on the street, to pay for his daughter's wedding.

Vikram walked along the path, which led to an industrial complex alongside a shuttered strip mall. After an hour or so, he closed in on "dashi row" and Spice Grill. In the parking lot, four tall, bearded men—sanitation workers—stood beside their idling garbage trucks fitted with plows. They were smoking and laughing, excited for the storm and overtime cash. Vikram watched as the snow gathered in their beards and hair.

Except for the Dunkin' Donuts and Spice Grill's banquet hall, the shops had all closed. Vikram limped across the parking lot. The men got into their trucks and drove off. He could hear music coming from the banquet hall as the strobe lights pulsed against the window. It was the sweet sixteen party for Dr. Malhotra's daughter. Vikram had almost forgotten. Had he not quit, he would have worked the event, perhaps been paid overtime.

Vikram crouched beside the window, careful to stay out of sight. With the back of his hand, he cleared away the condensation and pressed his face against the glass. The music changed to classical sitar and tabla, and the Indian girls showed the American girls how to dance. The lights softened; all the girls, even the Americans, wore saris. He had never seen American girls in saris—and how well they danced! It was a glamorous

affair, full of wealthy Indians. The men—mostly doctors, no doubt—
wore suits, and everybody was drinking. Even the Hindu women smiled,
holding what looked like glasses of pink champagne. The gang was in-
side: Raj's wife was dancing; Sethi manned the bar, pouring Johnnie
Walker Blue. Raj had found Showkat a spot at the DJ table. The party
was in full swing, and nobody seemed to be aware of the storm outside.
Watching the scene, Vikram felt the distance between himself and his
family in India, the many years away from home, and he knew it would
never be possible to close that gap.

Vikram turned from the window and made his way down the slip-
pery sidewalk of empty and darkened storefronts to the Dunkin' Do-
nuts. He left his sign outside. There were no customers inside, but the
place was charged with activity: the entire Parikh clan seemed to be
working that night, preparing for the waves of sanitation workers and
contractors who would arrive after midnight and not stop coming until
dawn. Showkat's father carried trays of doughnuts from the kitchen,
cursing his wayward son for his marijuana smoking, his rock star day-
dreams, and for abandoning the family for the con artist Raj. Showkat's
sisters, still in high school, counted change; their mother labored over
the coffee urns, switching out filters, swapping out pots; the frail grand-
mother mopped the floor behind the counter. Other cousins, nephews,
and nieces performed menial tasks such as stocking and sweeping. Not
one of them gave Vikram a second glance when he walked in: he didn't
approach the counter, so he wasn't a customer.

An old man at a table in the back waved Vikram over to join him. It
took a moment for Vikram to get his broken body into the chair. The old
man pushed a tin cup of water toward him, but Vikram could not grip it
with his hands. He let it sit. Vikram now recognized the old man: it was
Showkat's grandfather, working like everybody else. He wore the Dunkin'
Donuts uniform and a name tag that read "Peter," although Vikram
knew his name to be Vishwamatra. All the Parikhs wore name tags, each
with an Anglicized modification: Pratiiti became Penny, Shoktu became
Steven.

The old man was on his break, eating okra and potato shak with his
hands. He pushed his tin plate toward Vikram and said in Gujarati,
"Take off your hat. Rest a while. You don't look so good." Vikram had
forgotten about his crown. It had frozen to his head, and he could not
feel it. The old man smiled, nodded for no apparent reason, and clicked
his tongue, slightly demented. Vikram's presence seemed a welcome

324

distraction for him. Though his family showered him with sentimental respect, they often ignored him, and he almost always ate alone.

After a while of sitting and thawing out, Vikram was able to pick up the tin cup and take a drink of water and a bite of chappati bread and potato shak. Old Vishwamatra rose slowly from the table, his knees cracking. It was time to get back to work. The old man shuffled toward a mop and pail outside the bathroom. Somehow Vikram found the strength to get up from the table and reached the mop before he did. Vikram plunged the mop into the slop and splashed down the bathroom floor. He needed the work. Old Vishwamatra didn't seem to mind, and neither did his son, the owner. They needed all the help they could get.

Nominated by One Story

THE WONDER OF THE LOOK ON HER FACE

by BRIAN DOYLE

from CREATIVE NONFICTION

I was in an old wooden church recently, way up in the north country, and by chance I got to talking to a girl who told me she was almost nine years old. The way she said it, you could hear the opening capital letters on the words *Almost* and *Nine*. She had many questions for me. Did I know the end of my stories before I wrote them? Did my stories come to me in dreams? *Her* stories came to her in dreams. Did the talking crow in one of my books go to crow school? *Where* did crows have their schools? Did the crow's friends talk, too? Did they have jokes that only crows know? Did I write with a typewriter like her grandfather? Did I use a computer? If you write on a computer, do the words have electricity in them? Is it *too* easy to write on a computer? Do you write better if you write slower? *She* wrote with a pencil. *She* was about to start writing her third book. Her first book was about bears, and her second book was about her grandfather's fishing boat. Her grandfather still owned the boat even though he was too old to go fishing. He would go sit in the boat sometimes when it was at the dock, though. It took him a long time to get into and out of the boat, but he wouldn't let anyone help him in and out of the boat because he was a Mule-Headed Man. He let a young man go fishing in the boat, though. The young man wanted to buy the boat, but her grandfather wouldn't sell it no matter what. So the young man paid her grandfather in money and fish he caught when he used the boat. Her family ate an *awful lot of fish* sometimes. She thought her *third* book was going to be about a mink. She wasn't sure yet. Could you write a book if you didn't know what would happen in it? I said yes, you could. I said that, in fact, it seemed to me that the writing was a lot more fun if you were regularly surprised and startled and even stunned by what happened. I said that maybe one way to write a good book was to just show up ready to listen to the people and animals and trees in the book, and write down what they said and did. I said that I supposed you *could* know everything that was going to happen, and even draw yourself a map of what should happen, and then try hard to make that happen, but that didn't seem as much fun as having a rough idea what *might* happen and then being startled quite often by what *did* happen. I said that I rather enjoyed that the people and animals in my books didn't listen too much to what I thought should happen, hard as it was sometimes for me to watch. I said that I wasn't saying one way was *better* than another way, and that probably you could write good books in all *sorts* of ways, certainly I was not particularly wise about how to write good books, because I only wrote one book at a time, and very slowly, too, and whatever *I* learned while writing one book seemed to be utterly lost the next time I wrote a book, because the books were as different as people or animals or trees are, and whatever you think you know about a person or an animal or a tree because it is a certain species or color or nativity is probably egregiously wrong, because assumptions are foolish, as far as I could tell. She said that one of her ambitions was to someday write a book with a *really good pen*, and I said that, by happy chance, I had a *terrific* pen on my person, in the shirt pocket where I always carry pens with which to start books if book-starting seems necessary, and that one thing authors should be with each other is generous with good pens. So I gave her my pen, observing that it might have a very good book in it, especially if the book was about minks, or otters, which are fascinating animals, as everyone knows. She accepted the pen gingerly, with great care, with a look on her face that I wish I could express in words. But even excellent words like *astonishment* and *joy* and *gravity* and *awe* and *reverence* do not quite catch the wonder of the look on her face.

Nominated by Creative Nonfiction,
Krista Bremer

UDFJ-39546284

by RICK BAROT

from ARROYO LITERARY REVIEW

In *bunraku*, when you are watching *bunraku*,
there is that sweet moment in your mind

when you stop noticing the three puppeteers hovering
around each puppet like earnest ghosts

and begin to follow the story being told
by the puppets, the chanter sitting off to the side

voicing the love, connivance, outrage,
and eventual reconciliation at the heart of each play,

though often what reconciliation actually meant
was everyone banished, broken, or dead.

The seeing and non-seeing that makes humans
humans: I'm thinking now of the placid

English estates where the servants had to face the wall
whenever anyone of importance was near,

where workers had to cut the lawns with scissors
in candlelight, to save the master the trouble

of seeing and hearing all that effort.
What the mind does with this kind of information

is probably the knot within the *post-*
in what we call *post-modernism*, knowing all we know

now about the cruelty that made modernism
modernism. In the Philippines, growing up among

servants, I loved the servants the same way
I loved my parents, with helplessness and tyranny.

Walking in the exhibit of the black artist's paintings
of young black men in brocaded tableaus,

I am absorbed by their beauty as much
as I am by finding out that the intricate backgrounds

were outsourced to painters in Beijing, taking part
in the functional ambiguity between

one kind of labor and another. I guess all this matters
only as much as you want it to matter,

the mind making its focal adjustments
between foreground and context, present and past,

as well as it can. For example, this morning
my sister sent me a photograph of my grandmother's

hands. Sitting outside in her wheelchair, taking in
the gold sunshine, my grandmother

had her hands folded in her lap, and I looked at them
until I had to stop. This is foreground.

For context, today I learned that the farthest galaxy
we know of, located by scientists in 2011,

is 100,000,000,000,000,000,000,000 miles away.
It goes by the name of UDFj-39546284,

for reasons that I haven't yet looked up.
In the photograph you can see online, the galaxy looks

like the dusty stuff in the corner of a windowpane,
something you could look at sometimes,

something that is nothing, and has nothing
to do with what you know about distance and time.

Nominated by Arroyo Literary Review,
Fleda Brown

TACO NIGHT

fiction by JULIE HECHT

from CATAPULT

There was a man who owned a tree farm in our town. That's the way I knew him—I used to go to the farm to look at all the trees. But then there was a falling out between him and his brother, and he went to South America for a while. When he came back, his mother gave him a smaller nursery where they sold shrubs and perennials and annuals, but not on as big a scale as the first tree farm.

When he worked at the first place, I bought some clethra. The clever common name was bottlebrush. And then I realized I had no room for it, because I have hardly any land to plant things on. But I keep trying to buy every beautiful plant I see.

The man agreed to pick up the two giant clethra after he saw that I had no room. And when I mentioned this to the woman salesperson who worked at the tree farm, she said, "*He* picked something up? I can't believe that—how did you get him to pick it up?"

"Well, I just told him there was no room and then he looked and agreed."

After that happened I saw this man on and off for a few years, here and there. Once he drove me around the big tree farm in a little cart, a scary little cart, and he drove very fast.

I begged him to let me out. He obviously was some kind of madman. He told me what kind of madman he was. He said he was deranged by his former life of drugs and alcohol and wildness of every kind.

At the time, when we were at the nursery in the cart, he told me that he was in love with a woman he'd met in South America, but she couldn't move here and he couldn't move there. One of those stories. But then she eventually did move here and at some point the two star-crossed lovers got married. But he still wasn't happy. He was still unhappy because his brother had the big farm and he had the small nursery. And whenever I asked him about any plant, he wasn't interested because he wanted to sell only trees and massive quantities of plant material in order to compete with his brother. He did have good plants, and every year there were bigger and better plants and trees.

Any time I asked him whether he knew a pruner for our overgrown trees, he would come to look and say, "I'll do it. I'll chop them down. What do you need these trees for?" So I figured he wasn't the right person for us. Because what kind of tree pruner hates trees?

We used to have a tree pruner who could spend two days in a big old cherry tree. He knew exactly what to prune off. And then there was always one more twig he wanted to prune. He volunteered that he had obsessive-compulsive disorder. Once when I was bidding him farewell as he sat in his truck, I saw about ten bottles of prescription drugs, thrown about on the passenger seat. He told me he had to take all of them to maintain his sanity.

But he wasn't sane. He would tell clients he was going to take over their whole property, and the reason for the takeover—he had really good reasons—and what he was going to do. It turns out he didn't hire anyone to do any of it. It was a one-man band. He'd spend a week putting mulch down, when most landscapers have some Hispanic slaves— I say this in the most sympathetic way—to do that for them. It became apparent that the trees weren't getting pruned, and neither was the huge old privet. Then it got to be the season when it was too late to cut privet and we couldn't find another pruner. So every year I would ask the nursery owner, "Could you please find us a pruner?" And he'd say, "No, they're all the same. None of them are good."

Then it was That Night in November, and I was still begging him for a pruner. He said, "Oh, look, call this one—it says in the phone book he's been in business twenty years." He gave me a phone number.

I called and made an appointment, but no one ever showed up. There's an ad in the Yellow Pages here titled "We Show Up." I once called that guy, and he didn't show up either.

* * *

That Night in November, it was around five o'clock, and the nursery man said over the phone, "I have to go home and make tacos."

"Why?" I asked.

"Because it's Taco Night."

"What's Taco Night?"

"Oh, I hand-make the tacos and I invite over our kids who have moved out. And their girlfriends and a neighbor or two," he said. His wife was away for a time, on a buying trip. Buying waterfalls and garden furniture for their wealthy clients.

"Well, you're not going to watch the thing, are you?" I said.

"God, no. I'm just going to make tacos and get blind drunk and then serve Eskimo pies."

"Why serve Eskimo pies, when you can get Rice Dreams?" I asked.

One thing this guy and I had in common was that we were vegans, and we went to the same health food store or we'd meet in the organic aisle of the regular supermarket. So I figured he knew what Rice Dream pies were. He said he didn't eat the ice cream pies anyway. They were just for the guests and the guests all ate junk food.

"What am I going to do?" I said. "You know my husband's going to some thing in New York, where they're going to watch it. I can't watch, no matter what. I can feel the bad vibrations. But it's too creepy to be alone here, knowing what's going on. Even if the worst didn't happen, I couldn't bear the tension and the pressure."

Then he said, "I guess you could come to Taco Night. You might not like it."

I asked who was going to be there, and he repeated the guest list.

I went to his house—or I tried to go to his house—but I couldn't see which house it was in the dark. I had to call him from my cell phone, and he never answers his house phone or his cell phone. But he somehow managed to call me back, and said, "Oh, no, you have to turn left. It's not on the street. You have to turn."

So I did that. And then there were no lights on his lawn, if you could call it his lawn—a little tiny piece of grass that led to his door—and there was no way to see which door to get in. So I just knocked on a door. He came and opened the door and rushed back to his taco-making. There he was, making the tacos, on a special taco machine. He seemed to be under some pressure. Even then, I felt a pall hanging over the evening. The people assembled there seemed worried.

The table was set—there were dark red candles. And he had all kinds of little dishes of things to go with the tacos, like mashed avocados without anything else in them, mashed sweet potatoes. He didn't have anything that wasn't vegan. He had fake vegan sausages, which he bought for those kids, who were in their twenties.

First, we had to sit down and talk in the living room. I noticed that each person who came into the living room had a dog. It appeared that there were more dogs than people, or there was one dog for every person, or the dogs were really big. They weren't the fluffy kind. They were the flat, skinny kind. One of these kids was lying on the couch with the dog stretched out next to him, and they were the same length. Even the dog knew something bad was going on. I could tell.

Then another dog came in, and it was spotted with different colors. It was like a jigsaw puzzle. That dog went and sat somewhere else. And soon every person was sitting with a dog. I tried not to panic, but it looked unreal. Some of these dogs weren't too attractive.

I tried talking to another guest who was invited to Taco Night. But I immediately saw that we weren't going to be able to communicate. Either she wasn't listening or she just didn't have the capacity. She didn't have the wavelength—she was just out there somewhere.

It eventually was time to have the taco dinner. Then I saw that the host was drunk; he was bleary-eyed. His eyes were bloodshot and glassy. Maybe he'd smoked some marijuana earlier on. And then these kids started looking at their cell phones and they began talking about which states were which color.

I said, "Oh, no, I thought there wasn't going to be any of this. I thought we were going to pretend this wasn't happening."

The host said, "They don't know anything—they're just kids, you know how they're always on their phones. They don't know what's going on."

"Yes, but we do," I said. "And we don't like to hear about it."

Next he showed me how to put together a taco—how you put this on, then you put that on, then you roll it up. I tasted the taco, and it really was the best taco I'd ever tasted, and I'm not even a taco fan; I don't know the difference between a taco, a burrito, and the other ones. I told him how good it was, and then I said, "Oh, you cooked brown rice."

"Yes, of course," he said. "I soaked the beans myself. I cooked the beans myself. I did everything myself."

I forgot to say that this man is six-foot-four and he's a big athlete and rides a dirt bike every morning at six, in the woods and on the sand, even though he's in his sixties.

These kids kept looking at their phones and saying, "Now it's blue," and "Now it's red."

"It doesn't mean anything unless you turn on the TV and watch some-one interpret it," I said. "You can't just do it this way."

But they didn't care. One of them said he didn't even vote. He gave some reason he hadn't registered. But who cares. Anyway, I was too sickened to care.

Then I said to the host, "What is that thing that looks like a sausage?"

And he said, "Oh, it's an awful vegan thing. It's for them. I don't like it. But here, you should taste it." He cut off four inches.

I said, "No, no. Just cut off half an inch."

He said, "No, just . . . here. Take this."

He cut off half, and I attempted to taste it. "This is so terrible," I said. "It's not like food."

He said, "Right." I put the rest back on his plate. He was more and more intoxicated, so he didn't really care.

As the phone commentary went on, I said, "I'm going to the TV room. I just want to see what they say." I think it was only 7:30 then. Maybe it was eight o'clock.

I turned on MSNBC. How could I have been so stupid. I saw Chris Matthews's face. And on his face was a ghastly expression. I never saw him look like that, ever. And on the face of that woman whom I don't like to hear talk about anything, there was also a grim, horrified, desperate look. I turned it off right that instant. I thought, Oh, that's it. It happened.

I quickly found Turner Classics. I heard the host putting things away. I heard him whistling and singing and then he came in and sat down on the couch.

I said, "Don't you know any smarter people?"

He laughed and said, "Well, I tried to dumb it down, just to amuse you."

I said, "Well, you dumbed it down, but it wasn't amusing. There wasn't even a conversation I could follow."

He kept laughing.

"People just look at their phones and call out what they see? That's not a conversation."

"He's going to win," the tired host said.

"Oh no, don't say that! Let's not talk about it. Let's watch TCM."

"What's the difference? Just don't watch anything."

"But I have to be distracted," I said.

Then he yawned a few times. I asked, "Isn't it your bedtime? Don't you go to sleep early because you get up so early?"

"Yeah, I do," he said. "I don't know how I'm going to be able to talk to my mother tomorrow if he wins. She'll be out of her mind."

"I can't think about that. It's too much. I'll go home so you can go to sleep."

And that's what I did. He let me take the Pellegrino that I had brought for everybody but which nobody wanted. I said, "Can I take one of these bananas?" There were many bananas. I don't even like bananas, but they looked like a still life.

"Take whatever you want," he said.

Then he walked me to the car.

"Thank you. That's the best taco I ever tasted."

"Oh yeah, you're welcome," he said. He didn't care one way or the other. That's alcohol.

And then I went home. I turned on TCM, and luckily found that guy Mankiewicz was talking about Alfred Hitchcock and what a great film they were going to show. They were going to show *Saboteur*, which isn't even one of my favorites, but I was so happy that I would have it to watch. I've seen it maybe fifty times.

After a while, my husband called from New York. He said, "I went home. I couldn't take it. But all the people in the know said, It's still going to turn out all right."

"No, it's not!" I said. "Don't call me unless something good happens."

I watched all of *Saboteur*. And it was so suspenseful that I figured they'd chosen it for that reason. It was about those people who had wished to destroy our country. Some clever person must have chosen it for the suspense and the plot. There's the part where Norman Lloyd's character, named Frank Fry, is on the torch of the Statue of Liberty with Robert Cummings, one of the first health nuts in Hollywood—I had read something about his drinking carrot juice in the 1960s, when this was unheard of, except maybe in California. The other well-known carrot-juice drinker was Cary Grant's former roommate Randolph Scott. Bob Cummings is holding onto the saboteur's sleeve to keep him from falling, and the stitching in the saboteur's jacket starts to rip at the shoulder seam, and it keeps ripping, a stitch a second. And it's so unbearably suspenseful and so like what I assumed was on the other channels, and I was completely distracted since this is the part of the movie I usually can't stand to watch. It still was hard to watch, but I was grateful to be seeing that instead of the other.

As a special bonus, they were going to show an interview with the villain, Frank Fry, the actor Norman Lloyd, filmed last year when he was 101 years old, in perfect physical and mental condition—someone who acts sixty-five or seventy at the most, someone who told funny stories about his long, great career in Hollywood, how he worked with and was friends with Alfred Hitchcock and Orson Welles. This went on for so long and was so fascinating that I actually forgot what was happening on the other channels and in the world.

Next, they said *Limelight* would be on, and although I don't like *Limelight*, I decided I was going to watch.

I remember I'd seen it some years before and I didn't like it then, either. I guess it's Charlie Chaplin's worst film. At some point I fell asleep. I left the TV on TCM without the sound, and I woke up every hour, but I would not turn the news on.

Then in the morning I didn't take in the paper. The phone didn't ring. It was a gray day, completely quiet and still. It was as if the world had ended and I was the only one left.

✻ ✻ ✻

My husband called in the afternoon, and the first thing I said was, "Don't tell me anything. I'm not watching the news. I'm not reading the paper—I think I'm just going to lie down. I'm so tired."

Then I fell asleep for two hours. Not a peaceful sleep. A half sleep—it was like the sleep of the damned. Knowing the badness while asleep—that's not sleeping.

There was nothing I could think of doing. I still hadn't learned how to meditate. Without David Letterman, I had only *Downton Abbey* to look forward to at night. I wasn't yet as tired of the Crawleys' problems as I became after watching three whole seasons in the next week—I planned to think about the maroon velvet dresses and peach-colored upholstery and the green outdoors and trees of their land and trees everyplace around there.

At four or five, I went to a plant nursery—not the plant nursery owned by the man who was the host of Taco Night, but an even smaller one that has greenhouses with all kinds of plants and flowers. The guy who runs this one is someone I'd also gotten to be friendly with through discussing horticultural topics about which he's an expert, having gone to what he calls the Cornell Ag school and liking to talk at length about horticulture and other interesting, odd things.

When I saw this horticultural man, the Subject came up somehow, and he said that he'd voted for that person. I was quickly able to forget it, and see him the way he was before I knew. Since his midsection is so large, it gets in the way of thoughts, and he wears a large plaid overshirt, the same one every day. I resolved to get him a new one as a Christmas

337

present, more for my sake than his, because he doesn't care. I just have to look at something else—maybe a solid color, like navy blue. It would make that area look less big.

Then I remembered our conversation of the day before: He had told me this, when I'd asked him where he went to vote, and we'd discussed the hideousness of the voting places, schools built in the '70s, '60s, and '50s. He'd said, "I don't even know who I'm voting for." And I said, "How could you not know?" That was a mistake because I thought of this man as a sort of friend. He said, "I'll make up my mind when I get there."

"But how can you not know?" I couldn't help asking.

"Because she's a liar," he said.

"Most politicians are liars," I said. "But let's not talk about it." I'd said that sentence every day for many weeks and months.

Then I'd said to this man who was almost a friend, "Why don't you just write in the one from Vermont?"

"Well, I'd like to," he said. "I'd like to vote for him."

"But if you'd like to vote for him, how can you consider the other?" Then I said, "Oh, never mind." "Because she's a liar," he said again, and he started naming the lies. I hate when they start the naming—then you know it's hopeless. You're beyond the let's-not-talk-about-it stage. I finally left without any flowers or even a plant.

That night I watched the first *Downton Abbey* they were showing on TV that season. Or maybe it was the second; maybe I missed one. So I went back and took out my own set of *Downton Abbey* DVDs and tried to figure out which one came next. And then I thought, I don't care. I'm going to fast-forward through all the bad parts anyway—war, illness, fatal accidents, all the prison scenes. I just want to see the beautiful things, petty squabbles among the servants, the family—their little problems, not their big problems.

It was going downhill with all the silly parts with the boyfriends of Lady Mary, the final boyfriend with hair that appeared to be part of a partial toupee. It was clear that the talented Fellowes was above writing this kind of drivel plot. The episode with the Duke of Windsor might have been the worst. The actor bore no resemblance to the handsome and weird Duke.

Worse than that, the boyfriend-turned-husband was smoking. Before his appearance on the program, only the villains, the downstairs servant-villains, smoked: the handsome footman and Lady Grantham's evil maid.

I must have stayed up until four. That was when I got tired of the Crawleys' problems, even the little ones, as I'd already seen every epi-

sode about five or ten times when the show was on the first time. I fig-
ured I could just keep looking at the clothes and furniture without the
sound. If only I'd had a bigger TV, I could have seen all of that in bet-
ter detail. Big TVs are so unsightly. I'd made this choice.

I wondered what my life was going to be, just watching BBC programs
like this and *Doc Martin*.

Since I don't work in an office, I couldn't imagine how people could
go to work that day. So I decided to call an office of anyone I knew. The
young woman assistant who answered the phone sounded as if she had a
cold and/or was crying. And I said, "Do you still have a cold from last
week?"

And she said, "Yes, I still have it."

"I thought maybe you were crying," I said.

"I was," she said, "but I'm not right now."

I said, "Aren't there any groups like sympathy, grieving, mourning,
or communal comfort groups?"

I'd heard from a friend that in Nantucket two churches were open.
The Unitarian church and one other. I had asked my friend—a half-
friend, a Democrat seamstress—"Well, what's it like there?"

She'd told me about the churches and that people were in the most
terrible condition, worse than after the Kerry thing, those years ago.
That was when I'd received a present from the owner from Nantucket
Bookworks. The present consisted of some tiny notecards I'd had put
aside but never picked up. Each one had a beautiful basket of hand-
painted watercolor flowers. And they were in a small brown paper bag
on which she'd written, "A little present on this dark November day." I
should have framed it right away.

I knew I'd spend a few hours looking for it in order to frame it. It was
a real piece of history. I remember people telling me what that day was
like on Nantucket, and so I just couldn't imagine what it could be like
this time. I guess it's not good to sit alone, imagining things.

* * *

The next day when I was out, I went to a place to take out a cup of in-
ferior green tea. Three people were sitting down in a booth—a man
and two teenage children. I heard the man say, with a lot of feeling,
"Why is it so hard to talk to people!"

And I just looked at him, and I wanted to say, "May I ask what you mean
by that? Do you mean why is it so hard to make things clear? Or why is
it so hard to say what you need to say? Or why is it so hard to be social?"

But I refrained from asking him, and then was sorry because all I could think of was, What did he mean? They didn't look like deep thinkers. They looked like regular town people. But that would have made it more interesting. And if I go back to the place, in search of the man and his teenager children, I may never see them again. I guess I could go and wait there, every evening, at the same hour. They were sitting at a booth—who knows what terrible dinner they were going to order.

I smiled at the man when he asked his rhetorical question, and he smiled back. So I guess I could have said, "Excuse me, do you mind if I inquire?" These questions are often answered in a disappointing way.

✻ ✻ ✻

But back to the seamstress. She usually has some false, crazy hope. She said, "You know what I think is going to happen? He's not going to be able to deal with what it means to be president, and he's going to have a massive coronary within the first year."

"But they would both need to have massive coronaries," I said, "and all their henchmen would have to, in order for it to have any effect."

"Oh," she said. She sounded disappointed.

"Anyway he's able to deny to himself what it is to be president. He even said, after meeting the real president, that he didn't realize what a big job it was."

"What an idiot! I can't think of one person on earth who doesn't realize what a big responsibility it is to be president," she said.

"I guess he has some special thing in his brain that allows him to not know things that are obvious."

I'd always heard that it was all lit up in Nantucket in the most beautiful way. And I'd never seen that. I said, "Oh, I've never been there Christmastime. What will it be like this Christmas?" I asked. "Will it be different because of the thing that happened?"

"I guess it will," she said. She sounded sad.

Then she started trying to talk about it again, and I begged her not to. All she said was "he" and I said, "Please. We can't talk about it."

"But my mother voted for him and my father passed away," she said.

✻ ✻ ✻

Whatever happened to the taco man? I think I called him every day. Not about the thing that had happened, but to ask about the tree pruner he'd recommended. He never called back.

340

I finally had to give up. I hoped I wouldn't meet him at the grocery store, where he buys Bob's Red Mill Dried Soup Mix. A macho man who's a good cook—that's unusual.

I remembered how we'd gotten to be almost friends. It was something that had to do with his mother, because his mother ran the smaller nursery before he did. She was always enraged about some political situation going on. This was during the George W. B. era. And then she got to be in her eighties and she wasn't there that much. She wanted to have more fun.

The other thing about her was she was always planning something like a rib roast dinner. When she knew I was a vegan, she said, "Oh, my son and his wife are that. I don't know what to cook for them when they come over." I said, "Just give them the side dishes. Give them the vegetables."

"I don't like to do that. I like to cook a main course—a roast."

She started naming all the kinds of roasts she liked to cook: rib roast, roast beef, roasted this animal, roasted that animal. It was hard for me to listen. I don't have Paul McCartney by my side for vegan support, although he has a house near hers. Then she said, "You know, they wouldn't even deviate from it for one night."

I said, "No, it's not the health food thing, it's the animal thing."

Once, when I was talking to her son, I said, "You know, I just had a conversation with your mother. I'm all worn out."

He laughed and said, "Oh, god, I know what you mean." He just kept laughing. "How do you think I feel? I've had a lifetime of those conversations."

I guess we had a bond over the difficulties of talking to his mother about being vegans. One day, a few years ago, he was outside his landscape office, out where the plants were. There was a big, long wooden box, the kind people keep outdoor cushions in, and he was sitting on the box. "How's your mother?" I said. "I haven't seen her."

Then he lay down on the box, and he started talking about his mother and other people in his family. He said, "You don't know what's going on in my family—my mother, my brothers, my cousins. You don't know how dysfunctional it is."

"You know, this is like analysis," I said. It had just struck me how it looked. "You're lying down and I'm listening to the problems." I remembered that psychotherapists don't usually listen, but still I said, "Why don't you go to some kind of family therapy? I have similar problems, but I don't know how to help."

341

"They don't know how to help either," he said. Then he did a lot of sighing and moaning, saying, "Oh, god."

It sure looked crazy, the way he was lying on that big box. He was wearing long shorts—it was spring or fall—and he was such a big, macho man, suffering from his family problems. I guess that was the psychoanalytic bond we made because I never saw a big athletic guy like that talk about his problems that way. And this was before I knew he knew how to cook.

✻　✻　✻

I haven't seen him since Taco Night. We had to order tacos from a taco place, and they weren't half as good as his. But that's the way it goes. Worse things are happening.

I wonder what his mother thinks. I don't want to hear it. But the thing I wonder about most is how did it happen, the thing that happened on Taco Night.

One good thing to come about was the absence of many "Happy New Year" greetings this year. I noticed that people seemed to have to force themselves to say the words, and when they said the phrase it was without any hope of happiness to come.

Right on New Year's Eve afternoon, a sad teenaged clerk in a health food store said the words. I had asked him the ingredients of a number of things they sold. One of the questions was, "Are the chickpeas canned or dried?" and he didn't seem to mind.

When I left and he said the Happy-New-Year thing, I looked at his sad eyes and said, "How?"

"We're all down," he said.

I thought of that great Beatles song Paul McCartney wrote, "I'm Down," with the line: "How can you laugh when you know I'm down?" I read that Paul McCartney said he wrote the song after performing "a lot of Little Richard's stuff" and wanted to write something of his own. He wrote the song in 1965. I read somewhere that it was "the most frantic rocker in the Beatles' whole catalogue." Paul McCartney—great musician and fellow vegan.

That stayed on my mind: "How can you laugh when you know I'm down?"

But I didn't hear any laughter. I kept trying to remember what it would sound like.

Nominated by Catapult

I FIGURE

fiction by KIM CHINQUEE

from NOON

After he gets up to use the bathroom, I lie on my back, still naked, balancing my wineglass on my stomach, flexing my muscles to try to keep the glass upright. I put my hands in close proximity to the glass, and when it looks like it might tip, I flex some more, picking up the glass when I have to. The wine is white. I figure it's harmless.

I met him online, and after a couple phone calls, we had drinks at a low-lit bistro down the road. He's a surgeon. A recent transplant. He lives across the street from where I used to live until last year, when I moved into my new place.

I used to walk past this building all the time. It was my neighborhood. Every morning and night I'd take my dog out, first with one boyfriend, then another, then another. I lived there for five years, the longest I've lived anywhere.

After this guy elevatored me up to his apartment and I looked out, I saw only the brick of a building I used to see the other side of all the time. His kitchen is smaller than his bathroom.

It's kind of disappointing.

I wonder what he's doing now other than taking off the condom.

When we met, he said he was famous for heart surgery. He showed me his hands. He has pretty fingers. Dark skin and darker circles under his even darker eyes. Thick black hair. Not tall but certainly not short. Muscular. A runner.

I'm a chemist, I had to remind him. I'm decent with equations.

We fucked. I figured it was harmless.

I focus on my abs, on balancing the glass. I flex.

When he comes back, I point to the glass and I say, See?

He says, You're very balanced.

He's naked, his things hanging. He gets in bed again. I watch the glass. I work on balancing. He laughs and says, You're very balanced. He laughs so hard he makes the bed move. I don't think it's funny.

Shut the fuck up, I say. The glass almost tips.

I figure I am harmless.

Nominated by Noon,
Jean Thompson

FAITH FOR MY FATHER CIRCA 1980

by ERIK CAMPBELL

from NIMROD

When I think about it, usually at his grave,
where I try to think funny things, faith

for my father was pragmatic in deed,
evidenced best by the night he bought

the microwave oven and made popcorn
in a bag for the first time, which was

so modern, NASA-like for my brother
and me, we were suddenly science fiction,

one of the *Space Giants* or crewmembers
of Ark II. Our father squinted and jabbed

the start button, flinched slightly, retreated,
made us stand as far away from the machine

as the kitchen and Cold War would allow,
stood with arms outstretched in front of us,

Bruce Banner-style, against newly nefarious air.
And we were proud of him, would have thought

How intrepid he is, if we'd known the adjectives
to fit our impossible, periodic father. Soon,

we knew, we would push past the moon; it was
what we three so wanted and tacitly wooed,

a world of unbound horizons that smelled of popcorn,
aluminum, and prescience fulfilled. "If you can

smell it," he breathed over his plaid shoulder,
"particles are escaping. So, stay behind me, for

Christ's sake." Then he lit a cigarette, inhaled and
held it, and we waited, breath bated, for the future.

Nominated by Bill Trowbridge

THE WHITEST GIRL

fiction by BRENDA PEYNADO

from ECOTONE

From day one, Terry Pruitt was too good and too white, the whitest girl we'd ever seen. Most of us at Yuma Catholic Girls High School were some version of Hispanic, but Terry was whiter even than those whose families were high-class from whatever island we came from and so were blessed with Spaniard instead of Indo or plantation genes and shot out of our mothers' bellies as pale as little Europeans. There were other Anglo girls of course, but they lay in tanning beds, wore too-dark makeup shades that made them glow orange, studied Spanish, and flashed gold hoops to blend in. But Terry Pruitt didn't even make an effort. Her skin was so pale it was transparent, and we could see the web of veins underneath, including one throbbing blue line that split her forehead in half. Her teeth were jagged and yellow, the front teeth pocked with metal fillings. She had pale gray eyes the color of dirty dishwater, and her hair was a dull mouse-brown, not like our locks of black or chestnut hair we gelled up into ponytails. Her first day of school, all we could do was stare at the audacity of her whiteness.

A group of us followed her home after that first week of school and discovered that she lived in a trailer park with a herd of brothers and sisters, all as translucent and bad-teethed as Terry. Their parents had died and so their grandmother was raising them. She was too old to drive, so they had to walk everywhere. We were horrified. How did she get admitted to our school? When people that white yelled at us in the grocery store, or assumed we couldn't speak English, or that we were somehow unintelligent, their anger mystified us. When others wanted to dismiss us, we were lumped together with Terry's kind of trailer white, these creatures we didn't understand. We watched her run after a chicken that wandered underneath the trailer, watched her pluck its eggs out from their hiding places to feed her gang of siblings. When the siblings screamed and ran around her and she looked about to break, we saw her put a pillowcase over her head. Then her breathing seemed to slow. She looked peaceful, faceless, that blob of white sagging over her shoulders. We were fascinated.

After that first time we followed her home, we wanted more from the whitest girl we'd ever seen. We were like circus-goers who gasped at the bearded lady and then wanted desperately to know if, underneath all that hair, she was beautiful. We wanted to know Terry's secrets, we wanted to know who she loved, who she hated, what she dreamed of in the bed she shared with her sisters. This is not what we admitted to each other, of course. We said that we hated her, we wanted to ruin her life, or at least get her kicked out of school, and *haz mel favor*, how dare she? So we became her dark shadows, assigning one of us for every moment she might have been alone. Some of us protested at our cruelty, but the rest of us framed it as a game. Then it all seemed harmless.

One of us reported back that she had joined the choir, but she sang like a cat in heat. Another said she tried to play the clarinet, but couldn't muster enough breath for anyone to hear the notes. She spoke with a lazy Southern drawl that made us wonder if she was, in general, slow, except we heard she had a scholarship. We discovered she was religious in a Puritan, sanctimoniously abstinent way, and not in the ostentatious kissing-crosses-and-crying-Jesus way, which was the one we understood. When she passed through a room, you thought at first she was a ghost or a saint, except that when she smiled with those teeth, you knew she wasn't a thing from the heavens.

She seemed not to be bothered by glimpsing so many familiar faces where before there were none: in the next aisle at the grocery store, behind her when she walked home from school, crowding by her locker. She seemed not to notice. We *could* have just befriended her. We could have invited her to everything we did, pried her open with questions with all the bluntness of an oyster knife. But we didn't want to. We imagined it would look like she was running the show, a white girl, nearly glowing, surrounded by a sea of brown and tan and orange. So instead, we trailed behind her in the grocery line as she cashed her grandmother's Social Security check. She did none of the normal things, like hang out at the movies, socialize with the guys from the all-boys across the street, or anything that wasn't school or taking care of her siblings.

Once, she hesitated for just a moment, turning toward the parking lot where the boyfriends from other schools waited to pick their girlfriends up. Then she continued down the street. We thought this meant that she wanted to be a part of our lives, that she regretted never inviting us over to her squalid trailer piled high with children and her grandmother's doll collections and trash, that she wanted to be invited to our quinceañeras as elaborate as balls. We thought this meant she wanted to be us.

One day after the closing bell rang, we caught her in the broom closet, hand around a fluorescent bulb, her eyes cast down, the young janitor explaining to her how to connect the wiring to a light switch. We'd barely noticed him before, except to know his name was Joseph. We'd heard he was a dropout from the all-boys, but he couldn't have been more than college age. His hair hung past his ears. He was tall and muscled, arms as hairy as forests—a man, unlike our own boyish boyfriends, those of us who had them. This is what made us discount him, that he was old and dropped-out and scrubbing our toilets. But at the moment he extended his hands to show Terry Pruitt something in his palm, his long sandy hair framing his face, we thought he looked like Jesus. We wanted his chocolate eyes full of mercy to glance toward us instead. Then he and Terry bent their heads over his hands as he twisted two ends of stripped wire together, and their pale backs in their white uniform shirts looked like the outline of a white elephant.

After that, we caught her in places she'd never been before. She went furtively into the makeup section of the grocery store, but then counted her change and put down the glistening tubes. The youngest of the Pruitt herd played on a swing set at a playground near their school, and Terry drifted two streets down, head in the clouds. She walked into a bar during a local band's ska set. Having assumed she was at home and asleep for the night, we stared from our seats with surprise. She was dressed in a turtleneck with sleeves down to her wrists, despite the heat. Always that throbbing blue vein in the middle of her forehead. We thought she was alone, and then we saw Joseph bring her a Coke, unsheath the straw from its paper for her pale, thin lips. Then we saw her terrible smile.

We were horrified. Didn't he see what we saw? What magic did she have that none of us did? His eyes slid past us. We were the color of smooth pecans, our eyes dark and full of mysteries, our plump lips deep purple and moistened. Some of us were even white with blue eyes. Some, willing to do things with him that Terry could only have dreamed of.

Some just as virginal as she, though we didn't look it. Some in the running for valedictorian. Some of us would end up scattered to colleges across the states, dragging our boyfriends with us to more exciting lives. We could entertain anyone with stories about how our families had crossed this ocean or that desert or were pursued by an evil dictator. Some of our dads were even janitors, though we were embarrassed by them. But none of us were as poor as white trash. We wouldn't glow in the moonlight as Joseph walked us back to our cars.

The next week at school, we analyzed her in desperation. The way her mouth opened to screech out a note, her fingers soft around rosary beads at weekly mass, the frail hunch of her shoulders, the throb of her forehead. Joseph, who was watching her through the classroom windows as intently as we were, was on to us. Although Terry was not able to imagine that her running into us held anything but good wishes, Joseph had been cleaning up after our messes for years, had found our crumpled notes. He knew the cutting things we said to each other. The first time his car passed by one of ours as we trailed Terry from school, his eyes catching the hunger in our own, he was not confused for very long. After that, she waited after school for him to drive her home, and he drove fast, shaking us every time. Our constant eye on her dwindled into only what we could observe from school hours. Other than making messes to take up Joseph's time on the other side of the campus from her, blocking hallways, taking up bathroom stalls when she needed them, rolling our eyes at her answers, and commenting on her bad singing as much as we dared, she had slipped from our grasp.

Quinceañera after quinceañera rolled by, each of us despairing that despite our elaborate ball gowns on the night we turned fifteen, the relatives and people we'd invited, the boys who were our dates, none of it was enough. The clinking of our bangles sounded like chains, the gel in our hair too much like grease and dirt, our clothing tight and suffocating when we peeled off our uniforms. We started wearing less jewelry, discarding the bangles, leaving our name plates at home, as if we had forgotten who we were. We wanted to be good so badly—to do the right thing, to have everyone love us—even though we knew that good and love didn't always mix. What did it mean to be as angelic as Terry? But we saw glimpses of her at school that disturbed us. Terry hiding from the nuns, Terry refraining from Eucharist during the weekly mass, Terry forgetting to mouth the words to the rosary after school, beads hanging limp in her hands.

Finally, we spoke to her. Did you have sex, we asked her, as if we were her friends. She turned bright red, the only color we'd ever seen her except white, but she said no. We didn't think she was capable of lying.

In the month of Yasmín's quince, we had an idea. Have your party, we told Yasmín. Invite Terry. Then she will again be in our grasp, and so will Joseph. We would be dressed as elaborately as princesses, but we suspected Terry would sew her own dress. So Yasmín sent her one of the invitations tied in a mint-green ribbon, which began, Dear Terry, Special Guest.

The days leading up to her quince, we planned. The one of us who wanted to be a movie star said, We have to set the stage. The one of us most chonga, gesticulating wildly, said, Let me get my fingernails on her if she even touches my man. The one whose uncle was an ousted president of a South American country said, Please, no need to get obviously ugly. One white girl, honorary member of the group, who had refused to discard her name plate and gold hoops, said we could throw spray tan on her to ruin her paleness. Someone proposed only talking in Spanish, but only half of us knew Spanish. All of it seemed too much. All of it seemed not enough. What had she done to us? She was just one shimmering, pearlescent drop in an endless sea of what we hated. And wasn't hate as useful as love?

Terry arrived at the quince on Joseph's arm, her shoulders sloped bare in a silver dress, hunching in a way we'd never noticed before. She wore no makeup, and the lights that had been arranged all over the ballroom floor drowned out her features, so she looked like a ghostly blob. We'd planned the lights, of course. There were other white girls there, people from other schools, and dates that Yasmín's cousins had brought. Yasmín's parents were old-school Mexican, which meant her quince was the biggest and fanciest we would ever go to. Everyone she knew was there, dresses as full with lace as icing on cupcakes, everyone graceful and immaculate, as much as high school girls could be. We looked both wild and regal, like Lady Godiva and her horse. This was what we wanted. Her quince happened during many colleges' spring breaks, so everyone who had fled for the year, cousins and older friends and boyfriends, strolled about looking fresh from a war. Some of us were overwhelmed and kept going to the bathroom to escape. Some of us took to the lights like we'd been born in them, flashing our smiles and our bare shoulders. Some offered Terry and Joseph cups of spiked punch. The room where Yasmín and her court danced the opening dances in their poofy gowns and tuxedos and we waited to join in, was hot and made for thirst. We watched the ruby liquid pour down their throats.

Of course Joseph knew that the punch had alcohol. But this made him no less eager for refills, for himself or Terry. We tried to talk to them in passing. She was quiet and kept ducking her head behind her hair, which sprouted from her forehead frazzled and stiff. She was sweetly shy. We were drinking too, and though we would never have admitted it, the fuzziness of the evening, the unreality, was bringing us out of our hatred for her. Her eyes were wide. She was drowning in the grandness of everything she didn't have, and we were sorry for her. Joseph kept his grip tight on her arm. With his other hand, he tossed back his long hair. Everything in his manner said that he was above it all.

Who is that guy? said some of the cousins from out of state, eyes passing over the white and gray blur that was Terry.

We started to explain that he was our janitor and he was dating Terry, keeping the horribleness of our motivations behind tight smiles, but the dates and cousins back from college interrupted us. He's your janitor? they said, incredulous. They shook their heads. At an all-girls?

What's the matter? we said. Can only women serve women?

Haven't you heard why he got kicked out? they said. Why he never finished school?

The story they told us was that, some years ago, he had raped a girl at a party, a white girl from one of the public schools no one had been friends with, who showed up because someone was related to her and their parents made them bring her. She'd gotten drunk to deal with the awkwardness. Someone found him just as he was finishing, in the master bedroom, the masters being absent. Most of the guys there were his friends, so everyone stayed quiet, although the party ended soon after. But the guy whose cousin he had raped, he wanted to ruin Joseph. The girl refused to press charges because she didn't want her name on the public record. But her cousin's parents had donated a lot of money to the school, and got him kicked out almost at the end of the year when no other school would take him. He never went back. A few years after that is when he must have shown up at our school, rag, mop, bucket soon in hand.

We shook our heads, for the first time feeling dumb, in all our months watching them. It could have been one of us, we told each other.

Then the court's dances were over and people streamed to the dance floor. We looked over at Terry. Her ghostly figure swayed with drink. The hem of her dress swished up, and we saw she wore tattered, dirty

352

sneakers. She looked up at Joseph with those drowning eyes that meant she was in love. We saw through his facade then. He no longer looked like Jesus, more like a rat with pinched features and uncut hair. The music rocked us against our dates. Some of us joined the dancing, sliding our bodies in the air like snakes. In some of us, pity sank like a stone.

We all wanted to tell her. No matter what our motives, each girl would be fulfilled. Some felt that telling her would be the last revenge, the last betrayal of this girl who in our heads was no longer a girl. She was a Frankenstein cobbled together, made of what we hated, what hated us, the disinterest and disregard that bunched us together with these disgusting people, with their potatoes and bad music, bad manners, their self-satisfied boredom, their blinders that meant they could only see their own bare patch of ground. Some of us felt that telling her would be a kindness. Others felt that we could take with one hand what the other gave. Our whispers hid underneath the reggaetón and merengue and bachata. At some point a real mariachi band walked in, costumes flashing wildly beneath their instruments. Some of us kept dancing with straight faces.

We tried to pry her away from him. We said, Terry, come dance, but he followed. She shifted her feet from side to side, beaming at the fact that we'd asked her to do anything. We said, Terry, come sit, and he pulled a chair out for her. We had our dates glare at him and make him feel unwelcome, but it seemed like he enjoyed this. Finally, Terry had to use the restroom, the one place he could not follow.

We recognized her sneakers poking out under the stall, white strips of leather flayed off and dangling. She was a captive audience. Terry, we called.

Yes, she said.

Terry, we just heard something we have to tell you. It would be the only kind thing to do.

I'm so grateful Yasmín invited me, she said.

Oh, we said. The music stopped for a moment.

Quick, she said, tell me before the music starts again.

So we told her. We heard the toilet flush. That's impossible, she said. He's been more kind than anyone. Then the toilet flushed again and there was silence.

We waited. You shouldn't be alone with him anymore, we said. We're so sorry you had to hear this way.

The music began again, muffled by the bathroom walls and the bass notes trembling the mirrors. When she finally came out, her eyes were puffy, but dry, and her fingers twitched like they were fingering rosary beads for novenas, but of course she hadn't brought them with her. The vein in the middle of her forehead throbbed and tapped. She seemed full of a strength we hadn't seen in her before. As she washed her hands, she said, Have you never heard of forgiveness?

For that? we called after her, as she walked out. For that?

Then, finally, we were divided. We saw the differences between even ourselves. Some of us wanted to leave her alone. Those of us who felt the hate that had been poured into us chilling and condensing, wanted to prove it to her, what he had done. Some felt we should still try to convince her for other reasons, because who knew what kind of danger her naiveté would drag her into? A few, who had never believed anything and were becoming the outcast atheists, said, How do we know it's true? How do we ever know it's true, what we believe? Many felt he was the one we should break. Watching the mariachi band with their gentle guitars and brazen trumpets capture us in an amber wash of music so we were all waves in a sea, some of us wondered if that was what forgiveness felt like. It was a moment those few of us would treasure until we died.

We dispersed on the ballroom floor. Joseph put his arm around Terry. We could see her stiffen, then flash that horrible smile. She seemed determined to stay until the end. Some of us felt sick and asked our dates to take us home. Those of us thrilled by the dark caught Joseph's eyes, full of all the danger we wanted to tempt, and gyrated for him, our hips carving up the smoky air. Some lied through perfect teeth and said, Terry, you look so beautiful, you could have any guy here. Some of us questioned the ones who had told us the story. Some gave the couple more punch. Then Joseph had to use the bathroom. We noticed, when he walked out of the room, that he stumbled. Then one of us, when he came out, told him Terry was outside.

The smokers saw him trip and peer out the door like a blind mouse into the dark. Terry, he called. Crickets and our voices met his call. Some of us blocked his entrance back inside.

What do you want from Terry? we asked. Why did you do it? we wanted to know. We didn't ask, Why not us, when he could have picked the noblest of us to ruin, the most beautiful of us, the darkest of us, the palest of us, the one from Argentina who spoke four languages, the one who looked like she'd crawled out of the Garden of Eden, dark hair down to her knees. We didn't ask, Why that one girl? What did she do to you? We knew full well that hate did not require an initial offense. Only original sin, only being born.

Little girls, he said. It was the first time he'd spoken directly to us, done something other than pick up our trash. He said, Would you believe that none of you know what you're talking about? None of this is your business.

Is it true? we asked. About why you got kicked out? Does our principal know?

He clenched his hands, but we knew there was strength in numbers, an entire group, easy to misunderstand but impossible to ignore.

Meanwhile, Terry had ventured out onto the dance floor with the rest of us. She did her strange swaying, and then a few of us ditched our dates and grabbed her hands and pushed her hips around like ours. She even mouthed the words to one of the punk songs, but thankfully the music drowned out her screeching voice. She seemed both rattled and happy, but holding no grudges about what we had told her. For a moment, we thought she could have been one of us. For a moment, we were just a mass of dancing bodies in the strobing smoke, and we were celebrating our fifteen years on earth.

Then she asked, Where's Joseph? and one of us said, I saw him go out.

We had pushed him toward the parking lot. We held hands like a game of Red Rover, and we tried to pin him out by the dumpster where he belonged. We were girls. How could he have been so threatened? But the fear in his eyes was what we wanted. It was the permanent paradox, that you longed for and wanted to destroy what you feared.

He must have thought he could take us all. He ran toward the smallest girl with the highest stilettos. The girl went toppling, head over heels, and Joseph tripped and fell on top of her.

This was when Terry walked outside. When she saw Joseph on top of a girl on the ground, struggling to get up, all of us yelling and crowding behind him, finally, she was not an idiot. Her face, all of its whiteness, seemed to fold into itself like dough. She turned softly on her ratty sneakers. She started walking home. None of us in our high heels or our bare feet could keep up with her, the ones who wanted to explain. Joseph called after her on the sidewalk.

That night, Terry disappeared into the forest. We saw what we loved, what we hated, what we had destroyed but could not live without. Some of us were still tripping to catch up, propelled forward on tottering heels. Our exclusion of her trembled in our guts, on our skin. We felt the very edges of us shred apart. We were only each girl, one and one and one, alone. For just a moment, she turned toward us on the sidewalk. She glittered translucent and unsmiling, beautiful because she was the moonlight, formless and ungraspable. Then she stepped into the woods in the direction of her trailer and was gone.

She would never come back to school, but we'd see glimpses of her in town, her hair cut short and ragged like she'd allowed each sibling to cut a lock, that blue vein throbbing electric like a river of knowledge. Years later, when we would hear she'd joined the nuns, our guilt would drive us to visit her, but she was cloistered away in a secluded part of the convent. She would never marry, never bear children, never pass on those terrible genes. Then our pride settled on our heads like thorns. After that, the only time we'd remember her was driving by her old trailer, where a few of her sisters still lived, the moon-blue glow of an old television flickering, us uninvited.

Later that night, after running to her trailer and back, coming up empty-handed, Joseph did sleep with one of us. Loss engraved on his face, he sat in his car. We sent out the one of us best at martyrdom, also the best at being a mirror for what boys wanted to hear. She said, Joseph, I've left you notes among the trash. Later, we saw him hunched over her, then over the steering wheel as the rest of us leaving the party passed by the car, satisfied and terrified.

Nominated by Ecotone,
David Gessner,
Sujata Shekar

THE HUNTER

by GABRIEL DANIEL SOLIS

from OXFORD AMERICAN

Hunting season swept through my hometown with the crisp northern winds that sent leaves and trash dancing down King Street, near the Old Spanish Trail. In late fall, the town's annual hunters' gathering—Buck Fever—packed the county fairgrounds with guns and taxidermy and families wearing matching camouflage outfits, scents of damp hay and manure and hot funnel cakes swirling together in the cool dry air. It seemed like everyone in Seguin went to Buck Fever, and even though we weren't real hunters, my family went, too.

I was never comfortable at Buck Fever like I was at the Diez y Seis dance during the same season, a night of commemoration that packed the placita with gritos and laughter and kids running through the old oaks, with aunts and uncles and familiar faces from Our Lady of Guadalupe dancing together in a perfect rhythmic trance to the conjunto beat. With scents of roasted corn and barbecue and the band's synthetic fog. With drunk, sweaty men fighting on the courthouse lawn, their wet obsidian bodies twisting into each other and my dad's rock-calloused hand reaching through the crowd to pull me away.

One of my closest childhood friends was from an old Anglo hunting family. Their home looked like a Spanish castle and sat on a perfect green lawn surveying hundreds of acres of land. Above the stone fireplace, among the family portraits, hung several deer heads with antlers that looked like small bare trees in the winter. The pictures of long-dead relatives and the deer heads were arranged in a way that always brought my eyes to the similarities in the faces: living and dead animals with the same fake expression of the energy of life. At my friend's house, I'd

357

sometimes hear hunters shooting in the distance. I was never comfortable there either.

Our house didn't have dead deer on the walls or a manicured lawn. Our house sat on a small plot of dirt, the only one made of brick in a row of crooked wooden houses. Our neighborhood was wedged between the county salvage yard and Interstate 10, separated from town by railroad tracks that went toward San Antonio in one direction, the ports of Houston in the other.

On Harper Street, we had no expansive views of family lands, only family—and family extended beyond the walls of our little house. An electrician down the street became my godfather, his wife a second mother. On Harper Street, neighbors helped each other as they could, looking after babies while young parents worked long hours, keeping watchful eyes on kids playing in the dim-lit streets, yelling from the porch when cars screeched around the corner. On Harper Street, kids ate dirt because they had nothing else to eat. They'd press their round faces against our window at night, watching us with hungry eyes as we shoveled cheap pink beef and fideo, soaking up the brown juice with tortillas, waves of gratitude rippling across our plates. On Harper Street, gunshots broke the silence of the night, and we'd lie on the floor still as toppled statues, our faces pressed against the cold tile. But there were no hunters outside.

I was at my friend's house late one night when his dad returned from a weekend hunt. In the back of his truck were multiple dead deer stacked high, their bodies covered with a tarp, their round black eyes, wide open, peeking beneath the edges of their blue plastic shroud. I stood quietly and watched as his dad unloaded the deer from the truck, tossing them into the yard one by one, their limp bodies contorting as they slid across the dewy grass. I twisted my hands together and sweat ran through the prophetic creases of my palms like swelling creeks.

My friend's dad kneeled down and held up a deer's head by its antlers; its cracked dry tongue hung down, licking the grass. My friend retrieved a camera, and his dad smiled proudly. The flash illuminated the night like lightning in the distance, like a storm coming. His dad grabbed the deer by its hind legs, dragged it to a nearby tree and hoisted it up with a large hook, wounds pulled open by the subtle grip of gravity. He slashed the deer into an unrecognizable mess, leaving the leftovers there to swing in the breeze. This was an impressive buck, I was told, a twelve-pointer. He would escape the trash-pile cremation, and his hide—crumpled in the yard like a deflated balloon after a summer birthday party—would be taken to the local taxidermist.

Looking back, I think of Frida Kahlo's painting of the wounded deer, her expressionless face on the animal's bloody body. Every arrow that strikes her body is like a century of violence plunged deep into her being. Blood drips out, tracing delicately the contour of her form. She moves nowhere, toward nothingness, while electrical storms move toward her. Perhaps she considers diving into the deep blue ocean, into pure madness. Her strength of life is fading fast, but her face remains calm even as her body dies: only the animal in her cares. I often feel like the stag follows me, creaking the floorboards in my shadow's wake. When I turn around to catch her eyes her face disappears and becomes a mirror . . .

In junior high, my friend wore his camouflage pants and jacket and boots to school, marching through the halls like a willing boy soldier. He beamed when he talked about killing hogs and bucks, and especially when he talked about the place he called "the lease"—such a bland name for a place he seemed to revere as almost mystical. Never before had I heard of anything like it: designated land to kill animals, a beautiful arena of death. *Your family pays money to hunt there? But what about all the land your family already owns?* My friend could not have answered my sincere questions even if he tried. They didn't teach us that history.

My friend always had stories about his weekend hunting trips to the lease, stories born from cold nights when fathers and sons crammed together in camouflaged boxes among the trees, stories anchored in whiskey and lust, in tests of masculinity, as they waited for a fine buck to come upon their corn feed. I'll never forget the story about "the Mexican," one my friend frequently told, about a morning he and his dad were hunting in the Río Grande Valley. They saw an object in the distance hovering parallel to the horizon. It grew into the form of an animal, some kind of desert beast. They soon realized that it wasn't a beast but a man, his dark chest exposed against a white bandana draped around his neck like a levitating triangle, upside-down.

"It was a Mexican!" my friend would yell, his voice hoarse with excitement and fear. Mexicans were dangerous, he would explain. Mexicans broke into their hunting cabin and stole food and clothes. In his young mind, molded like clay by the ideologies around him, Mexicans

359

were like bloodthirsty animals roaming the land with calloused hides immune to barbed wire.

He and his father watched the Mexican as he walked across the land, their eyes following his every step—right into the crosshairs of his dad's rifle.

His dad pulled the trigger.

The man collapsed to the ground, still and silent. Suddenly, in an explosion of movement, he jumped to his feet and ran away, fast, zigzagging, home. "Fucking Mexicans," the father said to his son. "Fucking Mexicans," the son repeated to us.

My friend told the story around me without hesitation. And why wouldn't he? He couldn't see the Mexican in me. He could not have known that the Mexican and I were the same, connected and separated by the histories of violence that haunt the borderlands. Or maybe he did know but denied it because denial made him feel better—safer—around me. The Mexican is sometimes hard to recognize in seventh-generation Tejanos like me, who in many ways are more American than Mexican, immensely proud of our heritage and culture even as we struggle to speak its language, to embody its distinct ways of knowing the world around us. Like descendants of other colonized peoples, twenty-first century Tejanos and Tejanas are contradictory, volatile, stunning mosaics of psychocultural tensions.

Still, some will point and laugh and call us quintessential pochos, Mexico's lost children, permanent tourists, coconuts. The ones-with-soft-hands who dive headfirst into the violent superficiality of American dreams despite feeling the danger in our mere existence on this land. Still, we embrace the empire with our eyes shut tight, relegating its violence to darkness, its hatred to the shadows of the stars and stripes whipping in the wind.

Juan Nepomuceno Seguín, a Tejano who served in the Army of the Republic during the Texas War of Independence, once believed that Tejanos living in Texas could at the same time be proud mexicanos and loyal Texans. Then he witnessed the increasing brutality waged against Tejanos with every new wave of Anglo settlers. Even the Tejanos who fought alongside Anglos against Santa Anna's army weren't immune to the constant threat of the noose. By 1838, Anglos "were already beginning to work their dark intrigues against the native families," Seguín wrote in his personal memoirs. "Could I leave them defenseless, exposed to the assaults of foreigners, who, on the pretext that they were Mexican, treated them worse than brutes?"

That same year Seguín realized he had no choice but to leave Texas, and he fled with his family to Mexico. Although many Texans have labeled Seguín a traitor, his bones were returned to Texas nearly a century after his death and buried on a hill in the town that bears his name—the town where I grew up. The inscription on Seguín's tomb says nothing of the "dark intrigues" that forced him to Mexico; neither does the plaque on his bronze statue that keeps watch over the placita. Like the acento in his Spanish name, those histories have disappeared, replaced by something cleaner, more ideologically symmetrical, whitewashed.

My friend could not have known that history had forced me away, too. Carried me away from the Mexican like driftwood swept out to sea by a rogue tide that never returned to shore. Perhaps it was that distance that led me to believe that I needed to be more like my white friends. That I needed to be a hunter like them.

My dad had gone hunting only a few times with friends from church. I usually declined his invitations to join, but one day, to his surprise, I said yes. I wanted hunting stories of my own. If my friends and their families saw me as a hunter like them, then maybe my inclusion in the group would be unquestioned. Maybe I'd finally be included in the gifted and talented classes at school. Maybe I'd finally make the all-star baseball team.

When dove-hunting season came around, my dad arranged for us to tag along on a morning hunt on a ranch outside of town. The night before the hunt, we raided Walmart and he bought me everything a new hunter could ever need: jacket, hat, gloves, pants, boots—all camouflage. He gave me his old shotgun and watched proudly as I practiced over and over how to pump and reload it.

A neon blue horizon sat on a blood-orange ridge in the distance. It was quiet, only the sound of rustling leaves pierced by an occasional bird-call. We huddled together for a group photograph. The sun struck the brims of our caps, sending shadows over our faces. We all bowed our heads and said a prayer for our safety, for clear skies, for a good hunt. We said nothing for the birds.

The group walked in a straight line, slowly, a search party looking to kill. A solitary tree in the distance held my attention for most of the morning. It was like el Árbol de Teneré, once the most isolated tree in the world. Unlike el Árbol, an acacia twisted sideways by the Sirocco winds, this tree found its beauty in its symmetry. If el Árbol's roots reached the aquifers deep beneath the Sahara, this tree's roots might have reached the Gulf of Mexico. A dark cloud passed overhead, a gray chill covered us, and the tree took the form of Seguin's Whipping Oak, where runaway slaves were lashed and which still sits among the placita's walkways, or the old hanging tree that used to weep and sway in the shadow of the Plaza Hotel.

On the land where the Lipan Apache once tracked buffalo migrations across the blackland prairies, the rain from the night before had erased the topsoil like an archaeologist's careful brush. While the hunters scanned the sky, my eyes scanned the ground for flint sculpted by dead hands—relics from their battles with the Tonkawa—for evidence of peace when the Caddo and Coahuiltecan people camped together near the springs, waiting for the buffalo to come kiss the water.

When I was young, my dad taught me how to study the ground with focused patience, how not to fall for the mind's trick of imposing sharp crafted angles where there are only the accidents of nature. Together, walking like hunchbacks, we found many arrowheads on the land now owned by the river authority. I ran my fingers across the rocky surface and imagined the tribes huddled in the dusty red light of dusk, only the glimmer of sweat illuminating tattooed lines crawling like black vines around their bodies. It was like they were trying to tell me something, something about origins, but I couldn't understand what they were saying.

Suddenly a flock of doves flew over us, mobilizing the hunters into position. Gun blasts shocked the natural quiet. A hunter yelled in my direction, his voice drowned out by gunfire. *Shoot!* It was an order, and I followed it. I raised my gun and let the long barrel follow the birds across the sky. I had never noticed the perfection of their collective movement, a pointillist-mass throbbing in telepathic harmony. I froze.

Shoot!

I pulled the trigger.

A single bird fell from the sky and bounced with a dull thud out in front of me. I kneeled down beside it. Small burgundy dots expanded in perfect circles across its smooth gray chest. A man I didn't know walked over and congratulated me with a hard slap on the back. He walked over to the dove, now fluttering in a circle, and pressed his boot firmly onto its head. He wrapped his hand around its body and pulled it apart with a quick jerk of his arm. He placed the body into my pouch and the head into my hand. It looked like a little moon with two craters. Was it chance or some deeper cruelty that put pellets through her eyes?

Nearly twenty years later, I still think about that morning hunt. The city is a mirror of nostalgia for the placita, for the land. Black smoke billows, imposing dark shadows over my window, erasing the sun. Broken birds on the sidewalk are symbols of the memory's haunting. And while I know that to be human is to be haunted by memory, I can't help but yearn to understand the meaning of the guilt, the deep shame I feel twist into me like a screw jagged with truth every time I recall myself in the image of a hunter. It arises slowly at first, as if coming to a boil, then grows rapid, furious, consuming my body with heat and weakness. Sweat runs down my face like plastic tears melting down the mannequin of Buñuel's Lavinia, thrown into the fire by the jealous Archibaldo.

That morning hunt has come to represent everything I'm ashamed to have been and fear to become again, the wound of mimicry that Octavio Paz describes as a "wound that is also a grotesque, capricious, barbaric adornment. A wound that laughs at itself and decks itself out for the hunt." This wound neither bleeds nor festers but scabs into a deep scar. Even as I try to scratch it off. Even as the ones who came before tell us to heed the wisdom in wounds, the knowledge in scabs, and the axioms in scars.

It wasn't until I encountered the writings of queer Chicana philosopher Gloria Anzaldúa that I began to truly understand the guilt. In her poem "Cervicide," Anzaldúa tells of a young girl, Prieta, and her pet fawn, Venadita. Prieta finds the fawn when it is just a few hours old, after a hunter has killed its mother. Prieta nurses Venadita back to life, cares for the fawn as if it were her own. But even this is not to be tolerated. La guardia, the town's Anglo game warden, is on his way with his hounds. Prieta fears he will put her father in jail if he finds Venadita.

> In the shed behind the corral, where they'd hidden the fawn,
> Prieta found the hammer. She had to grasp it with both hands.
> She swung it up. The weight folded her body backwards. A
> thud reverberated on Venadita's skull, a wave undulated down
> her back. Again, a blow behind the ear. Though Venadita's long
> lashes quivered, her eyes never left Prieta's face. Another thud,
> another tremor. *La guardia* and his hounds were driving up

the front yard. The *venadita* looked up at her, the hammer rose and fell. Neither made a sound. The tawny, spotted fur was the most beautiful thing Prieta had ever seen.

La guardia drives away, and Prieta's family stays together another day. The young girl is not possessed by the land's evil spirits or seduced by the Devil's calling light. Prieta understands that Venadita felt every single blow. She knows what would have happened if la guardia had imprisoned her father: the land's memory is in her. As Prieta swings up the hammer, one sees in the shadow of annihilation an act of love, an act of resistance.

Anzaldúa has compelled me to look deeper, beyond the kill, to the archeology of the act itself. Hunting is no longer a sacred dance of silence and secrets, of life. The hunter kills not for the sustenance of human bodies but as a sacrifice to the human god he has manufactured out of his own skin. Caressing the gun's trigger, a strange euphoria consumes him. He feels supreme over nature. Believes he embodies the power to kill without guilt. Adorns himself with the sovereignty of the colonizer.

Becoming a hunter was much more than a transgression against my history and culture: it was an act of violence against history and future, bodies now and coming.

On that land, not far from the fields of Geronimo where my grandmother picked cotton as a girl, I was like an actor on a stage; the mesquite trees, dry brush, wild rabbits, and snakes, its props. In a picture from that morning that still sits on my father's desk, I am kneeling in the brush, looking toward the sky. My shotgun rests against me, safety off, trigger ready. I was decked out for the hunt. I was posing for the camera. I was guilty of betrayal.

Nominated by Oxford American,
Ben Stroud

ONE DEFINITION OF TIME

by ALBERT GOLDBARTH

from GETTYSBURG REVIEW

She was photogenically pretty—so important
if media coverage is intended to last—and young; and
so her death (her crimson Volvo skeetered over ice
and into the river) became the point
from which her life was retroengineered to fit
the needs of either 1) the "scandalous" (with that,
you'd think her days were spent entirely
at the strip club Baby-O's: its infamous
"VIP Room" promised the hungry media gossips
endless opportunities for seedy speculation) or 2) a brand
of secular saintliness (the volunteering at Rest Care Manor,
the Children's Urban Literacy Foundation Drive: again,
the sense was these entirely represented her energy
and hours) . . . but of course when we step back in Time

(as any science-fiction story demonstrates, or
there isn't a plot), we superimpose; it might be
with the innocence of chrono-tourists casually
lollygagging about the nineteenth century ("Look!
A butter churn!") or might instead be with the conscious
agenda of altering the "flow of events" ("With luck,
we'll downtime in Washington on April 14, 1865,
just moments before he exits the carriage
with Mrs. Lincoln . . . ."); either way, Time,
in its travel from the Big Bang

to the farthest eventual fadeout rim of Expansion, is
an ever-forward impulse, and refuses backward
tampering. An entire subgenre of science fiction
posits unflagging Time Patrol detectives, alert

for the glitter of pop tops in the muck of the Paleozoic,
for a button-size spy camera in the grand salons
of gold rush San Francisco . . . then they try to smooth
that fourth dimension wound. Of course our minds
don't have such vigilant constabulary;
offer us the chance to reinvent ourselves "back then"
as heroes, or (sometimes the rewards are as great for this)
as victims, and the past . . . ah, but there isn't any "the past"
as a singular construct . . . no, there's really
as many pasts as there's us. One example here
would be the downy cloud of her breath
in the alley, laughing with Thick and Dazzle the way
that people do at 3:00 a.m. with one last Jack-and-Coke,
and then the snow-on-brickwork crunching as she teeters

to the Volvo, and the small clicks of her three attempts
(the last a success) to slip the fucking key in the ignition.
The moon in the clouds is where the sun's light goes
to draw up the sheets and sleep for a while. The road
is smooth—or "slick" perhaps, but "smooth" is how
she feels it, smooth and accommodating, and
friendly, and so the sudden uncontrollable skid
at the river bend isn't only unexpected, but a betrayal
by the elements of the night. Her eyes
try to fly from her face like terrified birds, and
if there's a nest, if there's a tree in this metaphor
I'm inventing, it's the long and languorous floating
of her blond hair in the water, for the three days
that it takes before her sunken car

is discovered and reclaimed. All this,
however, is only a story I've forced
against the grain of whatever "actuality" is (or maybe
the verb is "was"). Time doesn't care about the beauty
of my language, or our noble-most intentions,

or about the reshaped history we use
as validation of our grabs for power here and now.
I'm sorry, do-gooder, generous-hearted casters
of Broadway hits and flops, but there were never
sheriffs in the Old West, never any Roman senators,
who were black. There *were*, however, "Negro cowboys"
(some think 10 percent): their absence from the TV Western
   dramas
of my childhood is a milder—but still regrettable—
version of Stalin's well-known "unexisting"

of his political foes: murdering them, well sure, but
then also erasing their ever having been. Anachronism,
then, is not only a positive—those pop tops—but often
a negative space as well. I think I'm trying to suggest
one definition of Time is "integrity."
Thirty-four seconds after the title credits
of John Ford's *Cheyenne Autumn*, a Western
set in 1878, we can see—
and it's shocking, it's a wrongness—streaks
of jet contrails crossing the heavens. They're
lovely, though, the way that things grow lovely
even as they disappear.
I think I'm going to name them
after her dancer name, Skye Bleu.

Nominated by Fleda Brown,
Christopher Kempf

THE WALL

fiction by ROBERT COOVER

from CONJUNCTIONS

Once, there were two lovers, separated by a wall that divided their city, a wall they had helped to build, recruited by the warring city fathers, who declared that only a wall would ensure their freedom. It was across the wall, trowels in their hands, that they first saw each other, lovestruck as soon as seeing. Such amorous gazes between separated wall builders were not rare, but soon were outlawed, stolen glances being treated like common theft and punished with solitary confinement or, when those found guilty were deemed incorrigible, blinding. Looking away became a way of looking, a trowel's clicks a code, the placing of a brick a form of erotic suggestion. Every day there were reports of frustrated lovers being shot while attempting to cross over, whether by burrowing under the wall or by clambering over it. Most of the wall was impenetrably thick, and there were stretches of two separate walls with a no-man's space between, but in a few places it thinned to the depth of a single brick. The lovers sought out these places by knocking on the wall with their wooden bricklaying mallets, their ears pressed to it, and when they found a thin place, they whispered into it, expressing their desires and their frustrations. These whispers stirred a hot wind that authorities said eroded the wall, so that too was soon forbidden and severely punished. Posters appeared that reminded them that freedom was not a given, but was a privilege that required discipline and sacrifice, but such admonitions only further distanced them from the city fathers and confirmed their desires. Once, in a dark crannied crack in the wall, created perhaps by someone attempting to break through, the two lovers were able to touch, which only intensified the fever of their desire. It was dangerous, they could die at any moment, they didn't care; what they could not have, they could imagine, and for a precious moment, in urgent whispers, they spoke to each other of their imaginings. Curfew interrupted them, the terrible sirens. When they returned, the crack had been filled with cement, the wall thickened, and afterward the two lovers had only their memories of what had been until then the most beautiful moment in their lives, memories that brought tears to their eyes.

Slowly, as frustrations mounted, resistance emerged. Trowels were dropped. Graffiti appeared. People were seen carrying emblematic slivers of bricks chipped from the wall and wearing inflammatory "Knock It Down!" pins. Many of these early protesters were martyred, but the numbers steadily grew, each new protester emboldened by the sacrifices of others. Demonstrations sprang up on both sides, demanding the wall's demolition, and the two lovers joined them. There was no time now for stolen glances, passionate whispers into the wall; the fall of the wall became their life's project, their existence all but defined by it. Their hearts told them the wall must come down, and so did their reason, but it was not easy. Many were imprisoned, lives were lost, but yet the resistance spread, up and down the length of the wall, until at last it was broken through. Shots were fired, many of the bravest fell, but the power of the authorities was waning. They could no longer repair the wall as fast as it was being dismantled, and suddenly one night those in power simply vanished, the wall crumbling as if made of sand.

An explosion of happiness! The end of tyranny! Parties broke out across the city. Fireworks, free beer, dancing in the streets! The two lovers ran, stumbling over the rubble, through the crowds of ecstatic strangers into each other's arms, and over the hours and days that followed, celebrated their love in as many ways as possible, and over and over, almost unable to believe what was happening. How could they have surrendered so abjectly to such a bitter fate engineered by others? they asked themselves. The past now seemed as unimaginable as this present had seemed so recently.

What was left of the wall, an insult to humanity itself, was destroyed. Some kept small fragments as souvenirs, but most wanted nothing more to do with such a cruel obscenity. Streets were laid, linking the divided city, and lined by beautiful new buildings, none made of brick. The no-man's-land became a public park with children's playgrounds, and trees were planted, memorializing the fallen. The day the wall fell was declared an official holiday, celebrated with parades and circuses. The "Knock It Down!" pins became collectors' items. The nightmare passed into history, read about in school by the new generation, for whom it was something that happened a long time ago. An excuse for an annual party and a day out of school or off work.

Then, as time passed, the two lovers, along with many others who had lived through the construction and fall of the wall, found that they missed it. They studied old maps, took walks along its buried contours. Sections of the wall were said to exist still; they searched for them, getting lost from one another as they did. They accepted that, discovering that the wall had been a barrier to their desires, and a stimulus to them, but freedom had deprived them of their intensity, provided other options. It was a time of separations, divorces, reconciliations, new loves to be found and lost again. He took a position in a distant neighborhood, she raised the children with a new husband, then later by herself.

And meanwhile, slowly, though none knew how, the myth of the "city fathers" having crumbled with the wall, the wall itself, as if seeded by the chips of bricks that had been left behind, did indeed return, or seemed to, seen by some, if not by all. A kind of personal choice as with all perceptions of reality, though it did not feel like choice. Perhaps its reappearance, to those who witnessed and acknowledged it, was provoked by that longing for a significant life the estranged lovers felt, for there they were, gazing at each other across the wall, real or imaginary. They nodded curtly to each other, looked away. They could have stepped over this young wall, but did not, for their separation had seemed permanent and desirable.

But the rising wall drew them back again and again and, over time, feeling that they had something to share, even if only their disappointment, they allowed a cautious friendship to grow between them. They did not try to breach the wall or recover what they had lost, but conversed quietly over it, recalling dispassionately the tyranny of the old wall, their impassioned resistance to it. Though monstrous, the old wall gave so much meaning to our lives, one said, and the other: Well, meaning, that old delusion. Which, when sought, is just another form of nostalgia. Sort of like love, you mean. No, love, whatever it is, is real in its stupefying way. But it's not enough. No, and there's not much else. That's very sad. It is. Sometimes I cry. We had some good parties, though, which wouldn't have happened without a wall in the way. There's probably a moral, but I don't want to know it. Do you still believe in the city fathers? Sure, they shot people. Well, somebody did. Do you remember those people who were blinded for gazing at one another? Yes, it was horrible. I saw one of them the other day. He's a prophet now, or

claims to be. Wouldn't you know, another blind seer. What is he proph-
esying, the end of the world like everyone else? No, its damnable con-
tinuance. He's a pessimist.

That made them smile, but they didn't know why. Or did know, but
wished not to acknowledge it, even to themselves. Because: if bitterness
overtakes you, what choice remains? They talked about their children
and their children's children, the passing of the elders, what, if anything,
they still believed in (well, the good, the true, the beautiful, they joked),
and whether the return of the wall signaled the return of tyranny. The
tyranny of time maybe, one of them said. Sounds like a popular song title,
said the other: "The Tyranny of Time." Everything's a song title when
meaning's just another tune to play. Like "Knock It Down," that violent
sex song the children are dancing to. I have to confess I still have my old
"Knock It Down" pin, but I never wear it, not even on the national holi-
day. The children, in their terrible innocence, just point at me and
laugh. I know, my old mallet and trowel are still hidden away some-
where like secret sex toys. It's a strange feeling when the story moves
on without you. Yes, at the time, I thought it was about us, but it was
only about itself.

Later, they would wonder why they had remained on opposite sides
of the wall, as if their conversation depended on it, as perhaps it did,
the wall shielding them from anything more disquieting than banter,
while serving at the same time as a kind of playing surface for it. That
surface rose until their wistful sallies were more like lobs. They could
no longer see each other, nor were they hearing each other as clearly as
before, their voices lost in other voices behind the thickening wall. It
might be our ears' fault, one shouted. Our years? the other called back.
No . . . well, maybe. . . . The distance was too great. They turned away,
aware that the loneliness they felt was in effect that freedom they'd been
promised when citizen bricklayers still, and sadly they wished it so.

Nominated by Conjunctions,
Mark Irwin

IRAQ GOOD

by HUGH MARTIN

from CINCINNATI REVIEW

The small boy smiles, kicks roundhouses across
the potholed road, says, *Van Damme good?* & I say, *Yes,*

Van Damme good. The boy punches the warm air while we,
on the street for hours, outside the Sadiyah police compound

walled with Hescos higher than our gunners' heads,
pace circles around the trucks. Two other boys,

maybe nine or ten, chop each other gently with knife-hands,
& one turns, says, *No good Saddam, Saddam very no,*

& he points to his sandal's heel, *Saddam no.* & so it went:
Bruce Lee good, Zamzam good, falafel good, even

Michael Jackson good, even *Bush good*, even *America very
good.* We stood, speaking on ground where written words

were first made, where Enheduanna, Sargon's daughter,
wrote her poems, blunt reed on wet clay, the clay

that made the walls those children slept behind at night,
that filled the Hescos behind our backs to protect

from blasts & bullets. We leaned, a few feet from the boys,
against Humvees—two hundred grand apiece—made

in Indiana. Insurgents were paid—we knew—
to blow one apart: five hundred US cash. Sometimes,

as the boys spoke to each other, their Arabic muffled
by passing traffic & muezzin calls, we'd talk, too,

among ourselves, asking, just steps from the boys,
which one might, in five or ten years or less, fight us. Still,

these silences, brief, would break when one of the boys
might point to our rifles hanging over our vests, muzzles

aimed at the road, the black red-dot scopes clipped
to the carrying handles, & say, *Laser . . . good,*

then point to our dark ballistic sunglasses, say,
X-ray yes, good, &, although we'd agree, there was really no

laser, no *X-ray,* but if we kept those boys there, talking,
on that street as evening came, we'd be, for the moment,

okay if only we kept it going: *Ali Baba no good,*
chicken good, Sadiyah good, Iraq good, & good, & good.

Nominated by Cincinnati Review

ACCEPTANCE SPEECH

fiction by DAVID NAIMON

from BOULEVARD

It is fitting, I suppose, standing here before you, a room of fellow gardeners, that I confess to a dirty little secret. For what is dirt if not a repository of such things? Non-gardeners the world over stomp across its surface without a thought. They imagine it as a flat and homogenous thing, merely a stage for their lives, if they imagine it at all. Never do they break the skin; never do they willingly, solely for the pleasure of it, or with great purpose and design, stick their hands deep down in the stuff. Someone wise once said we know more about the stars at the outer edge of our galaxy than we know about the goings-on of bacteria at the root nodes of plants, more about the farthest sun than the dark dirt beneath our very own feet. Seems to me a matter of attention. Of skull orientation. Of orientation period. We gardeners are always unearthing secrets, the subterranean love affair between taproots and earthworms, the unconquerable underground of morning glory networks, the white softness of larvae in the fetal position, so little and helpless in the darkness, yes. But also human things, turn-of-the-century pharmacy bottles woefully absent their drugs, green mesh from a long-gone sheet of sod, maybe even a tin penny. We peddle in these dirty things. And, I've been told, the dirtiest of them all, bacteria, are our true ancestors. Older than us, older than everything alive, these germs germinated us all. The wisest, if comparatively quite young (laughably so, really), human scientists say these bacteria are quite remarkable. They cooperate across species, share survival tips, trade adaptation strategies, leave messages of what they've learned or encountered for the benefit of the whole bacterial family tree. These same sweetly confident scientists also say we

374

are more bacteria than human, more other than self, ten bacterial cells for every one of ours in each and every human form. But, I must confess, my husband and I, while we too leave messages and presumably are merely, like you, just two human-shaped bacterial colonies ourselves, we fight about the smallest of things. Take my nighttime gardening for instance. He thinks it is barbaric, that *I'm* barbaric, due to the apparent joy I display, the insecticidal gleam in my eye from the scissoring of slugs by flashlight, their fat tiger-striped bodies snipped cleanly in two, draped doubly across my escarole beneath a springtime moon. He prefers the "humanity" of beer traps to methods he considers not only unnecessarily but unbearably cruel. But, I ask you, isn't the whole gardening enterprise full of cruelty, a task best suited for sociopaths and tyrants? If not them, what mentality best suits a pastime where we alone choose what deserves to live and what deserves to die, that demands we constantly kill things to groom and nourish the others we prefer? Does it really matter that my husband wants to lure them, that he wants it to happen passively, when he isn't looking? He still engineers it to happen, he still lays the trap even as he pretends otherwise. And honestly, isn't that worse, the dishonesty of it? My husband eats meat; we both do. He makes an admittedly transcendent osso bucco, fills the house with its aroma while ants in the sunroom gather at his trap of poisoned sugar gel. Bit by bit they bring it back to their queen, slowly, quietly, and unwittingly poisoning her and her community while he sips wine and sings his best Caruso. I just squish them with my thumb. Drone, drone operator, and hellfire missile all rolled in one, I get it done. I crumble their bodies between my fingers and sprinkle them down the drain with no more or less thought than my husband. But without all the moral sleight of hand. Yet somehow I'm the barbarian. We can argue the effectiveness of a given strategy but certainly not moral superiority of one over the other, I complain. These are our fights, existential ones of the garden variety. We don't fight over ordinary things. Or rather, we too, like you, fight about the ordinary things, but for us they are only a thin film across an extraordinary abyss. I suffer a misery of vertigo every time we skim off that layer. Take recycling. We recycle as I imagine all you gardeners do. And like you, I'm sure, my husband sees it as a virtue, as a nod toward nature, toward coexistence, toward the merits of human economy. But we fight about it because it seems like a terrible lie to me. Even if we put aside that so many of our recyclables just end up as trash in landfills in Asia, or that the recycling process is a ridiculous Band-Aid on the open sore that is consumer capitalism, even if we imagined that recycling worked, doesn't it just keep the human farce going? Wouldn't it be more honest to realize the world has a fever for a reason, that it is trying, like all good fevers, to kill something off, the question being not whether it will kill us but when and how quickly? I say, let's look to our ancestors and to their ancestral wisdom for the answer. When we place bacteria in a petri dish with an abundant food supply, what happens? They reproduce rapidly, exponentially. They are unstoppable. That is, until they choke to death on their own waste, an ending to their story that is beautifully scatological and eschatological, both. That patrimonial urge is so clear in us. I say let's embrace it, embrace our humanity instead of half-assing it, hedging against it with recycled toilet paper. Let's be fully, *naturally* human, live and die as we are, until we are taken care of. I'm serious here. My husband knows it and says I'm a misanthrope. But it isn't that simple. I hate anything that is elevated without proper cause. We all know humans aren't humane. That humans are, in fact, inhuman. I don't need to tell you that. So let's take for example the universally loved otter, those adorably furry mustachioed animals that float on their backs holding hands with their mates, who drift asleep together tethered to strands of seaweed as if in a fairy tale. What could be more cute than that? I don't disagree. But they rape baby seals. They herd them off the beach into the water, bite and claw at their faces, lacerate their eyes and noses, hold them below the surface and mount them. They rape baby seals and often continue raping them for hours or days after they've raped them to death. But when I tell people this, they get mad at me, not the otters. Seems strange. My husband still loves them and still gets mad at me when I grumble about recycling. But to be fair to him, if it wasn't for my husband, I wouldn't be here accepting this Happy Valley Horticultural Society Green Thumb Award from you tonight. One day, the fateful day in fact, he rescued yet another recycle-approved plastic yogurt container from our trash and waved it in my face, pointing at the recycle symbol, a Bermuda triangle of self-referential arrows embossed on its bottom, in grave accusation. "Why won't you have babies then?" he yelled in a weird and random flourish. "If, as you say, we should accept the purpose of the fever, if we should stop recycling to advance it to its inevitable conclusion, then why on earth won't you have kids with me? *That* would be the ultimate act toward filling the petri dish, wouldn't it? Both the most *natural* of human things to do *and* the most effective embodiment of your warped world view?" Needless to say, I was furious. So furious that I stormed out of the house and drove straight to the nursery. And I came home with the absolute ugliest plant I could find, the lumbering purple-leaved Sambucus Black Tower. I brought it home and, flummoxed where to put it, saw the azalea my husband loved so much and decided to put it right there, uprooting the azalea and recycling it in the bin for yard debris. It seemed like poetry. But unbelievably he didn't even notice. Or if he did he didn't say a thing about it. Which only made me return to the nursery yet again. Absent any grand plan, other than the floral expression of my rage, I was torn between the reptilian creepiness of Brunette Snakeroot and the terribly unremarkable purple of the castor bean plant. When the employee told me the seeds of the latter looked like engorged ticks, explaining that its Latin name, *ricinus*, comes from the same root as that of the bloodsucker (a wonderful marriage of etymology and entymology), that the plant was so poisonous that it was never planted near playgrounds, that the consumption of a mere twelve seeds would kill an adult human male, I was sold. So much so I took, in my giddiness, the Snakeroot home as well. Again, to be clear, I recycled. I did. This time the honeysuckle and one of our prettier rose bushes to make space, to make room for the new. Of course, I expected my husband to be furious. He always rolled his eyes when I referred to weeding as a way to get in touch with my inner serial killer, but certainly now he would cry bloody murder as I uprooted, not a weed, but the very architecture of our yard. Or so I thought. So far I had just received some queer sidelong glances but was left by him, suspiciously, to my own devices. It made me feel a little randy, to be honest, a little dirty, even more keen to recycle. And almost as if by magic, my destructive rage turned into constructive delight as the unexpected synergy of the dark corner I had created, of unnaturally black, poisonously purple, and uncannily lizard-like plants suggested a plan to move forward from, a blueprint for an alternate garden in my mind. A garden with the complete absence of greenery. Many of you have asked me tonight if I took my cues from Joris Karl Huysmans's 1884 novel *Against Nature*, if I was inspired by Des Esseintes's desire for a collection of the most artificial looking plants possible to accompany his jewel-encrusted pet turtle. It's true, I won't deny it, I do envy his collection. Who wouldn't drool at his vegetal ghouls, shaped like rolled-back tongues, sporting glandular hairs, turgid stalks, voracious trumpets, or shiny pouches that ooze a viscous glue? But I had not yet read his book, no. Instead, my own dark corner began to suggest the next step to me. And with each new plant added, the next revealed itself as the inevitable new member of the family. I listened to my gut. I used my gut instinct. And what better

377

thing to use? For far more neural tissue resides there than in our skulls, and interestingly, so do pounds of bacteria. What are they, our neurons and these bugs, this dirt, saying to each other? No one knows, for the conversation between them is no less mysterious than the one at the root nodes of trees. But we *can* think with our guts. And we *do* think with them. That is, if we are indeed the ones thinking down there at all. Perhaps instead we are being thought, thought through our guts by our invisible ancestors. But regardless of who is deciding, I or we, me or other, I continued with texture and color, to plant plants the hue of skin and rust, that shined like metal or plastic, recycling a weeping Japanese maple, an unruly quince, a row of redolent sweet box in the process. And slowly but surely the garden began to take shape, to swallow light as the dark bruise of a corner became a full black and blue yard. I'd be lying if all this time there wasn't a hiccup from my husband. No, we did not fight, not with words or thrown objects, when I excavated our fig, the same one we had planted when we first moved into the house, a traditional gesture toward good luck and fertility at the time. But something stirred as I did, sunken and subterranean, behind my husband's silent eyes. A secret swam there, not his but mine, a secret that I was hiding in and hiding from, that my dead-wrong husband was right about one thing all along. Faced with my first day with nothing left to plant, no trips to the nursery yet to make, the very day the first tree we planted became the last green thing removed from our garden, the day I completed my mission, my vision, through its death, the day my brain-child, so carefully conceived, had been delivered, like a miracle, complete, I knew, from my husband's wounded puss that the garden, however glorious, was no reply to his infant questions unanswered, but a terrible lie. That it was I performing a moral sleight of hand. That it was my garden, the one you have so kindly bestowed this award upon today, that was ill-conceived, a misconception, a noisy masquerade, a hide-and-seek from the fact that nothing did fulfill my philosophy more fully than hominid propagation, even if somehow it also, disturbingly, satisfied my husband's hackneyed hope for humanity's future as well. But I must admit that while I have now conformed my life to the shape of its own logic, I still sometimes fear that my husband has lured me here. In the end it doesn't matter. For now when I go out with my scissors amidst my award-winning garden at twilight, one absent the song of birds or the scurry of squirrels, who have both forsaken it, I can almost hear the bacteria hum. I've heard that some reproduce so quickly, five hundred thousand times faster than us humans, that there is a new generation every twenty minutes. Perhaps it is this I am hearing, the binary fission of bacterial cell division. Or perhaps it is that much slower divide happening within me now. That bundle of implanted cells, half-me, half-other, sequestering my blood supply for its own purposes, an engorged tick, a swallowed castor bean seed, that I hear as it splits and grows, splits and grows some more. I place my hand below my navel as the sky continues to darken, blacker, bluer, and the yard releases its musk. I fake a drag off an imaginary cigarette and watch a fat tiger-striped slug slide in the moonlight. I decide not to scissor it. Not yet. I decide to leave it whole, as my husband would prefer, leave it unsplit, undivided for yet another moment. But the hum, it is unmistakable. I like to think it is both that I hear, the bacteria and me, the hum of our division, as together we feed the fever and add to the dish. The garden and I, we are so full, so full of life. Thank you for this great honor.

Nominated by Boulevard

I KEPT GETTING

BOOKS ABOUT BIRDS

by CATHERINE PIERCE

from GETTYSBURG REVIEW

as if recognizing the yellow-winged one
at the feeder, the shiny black one hopping
through the grass might somehow
become enough. As if knowing *grackle* or *thrush*
or *prothonotary warbler* might give me a handle
of sorts—something to hold as all around me
the books piled up and the hours too,
time unrolling like a lush carpet
that caught me again and again,
foot sinking into the plush, and there went
three hours, six days, half a year.
I kept getting books about birds as if
in the Great Ledger of What I Had Accomplished
I could simply fill in some Latin names
and notes on skeletal pneumaticity
and be done. I kept getting books about birds
because those days I had no reason
to go to bed, and so the night stretched
and yawned and stayed awake,
because my corn fritters from scratch
didn't pan out, because the garden had all
the hot peppers the neighborhood could eat,
but the tomatoes stayed hard and green
no matter how I coaxed them, because
I wanted to write a novel but never made it

past a protagonist, because I wanted
to understand how some people galloped
through their lives as if they were astride
tall white horses, and here I was
spending my drawn-out days researching
ailments and likelihoods. I kept getting
books about birds, and they were beautiful,
the books, glossy and thin, and I looked
at them, and I stroked their smooth covers,
but I'd be lying if I said I ever read one.
They were so dull, with their migration
pattern charts and seed particulars,
and I knew as I looked at the congregating
backyard starlings or whatever they were
that the only real solution was to walk outside
and startle them so that they rose in one
of their gorgeous rivers, one of their gorgeous
bed sheets, one of their gorgeous
choreographies of shadow, and to see, at last,
in that one bright, cacophonous moment
something I had made.

Nominated by John Allman,
Gary Fincke,
Mark Irwin

LET THE DEVIL SING

by ALLEGRA HYDE

from THE THREEPENNY REVIEW

The road to hell is narrow, bordered by a serpentine river and sheer mountain cliffs that swagger upwards and out of sight. Road signs warn of tumbling rocks, landslides, car crashes at the blind corners. The weather is fair and crisp. My husband drives our rented Peugeot. He does this calmly, effortlessly, while I sit in the passenger seat and stare at the road unblinking, as if I might intuit the speeding approach of a brakeless eighteen-wheeler or the meteoric plummet of falling rocks. But what would I do if I could? A car bound for hell will get there one way or another.

Dyavolsko Garlo, the locals call it. The Devil's Throat. A cavern plumbing Bulgaria's Rhodope Mountains. The site where, according to legend, Orpheus descended into the underworld to seek his beloved Eurydice, who had died of a snakebite soon after they wed.

My husband is six feet tall—just a touch taller than me—and sturdily built, with thick brown hair and facial scruff that arrives in an inexplicable rust-colored red. Driving has put him in a quiet mood. His fingers strum the steering wheel, tapping along with the pop-folk flowing from the radio: accordion strains overlaid with brassy vocals praising easy money, women.

"The Devil's Throat," reads a sign, "44 km."

My husband and I love one another, but our marriage feels like a sham. This is one of our problems. The other is living in Bulgaria.

Eurydice had died too soon, so Orpheus traveled to hell to bring her back. Orpheus—that famous Thracian, the musically blessed son of Apollo and Calliope—had strummed his famous lyre at the feet of Hades and Persephone, pronouncing his heartbreak in melodies so sweet the cold-souled King of the Dead was moved. So moved, the story says, the king shed iron tears. Plunk. Plunk. Plunk. The noise echoed through the underworld.

My husband and I have lived in Bulgaria for six months, lived in this country often confused for other places. "You'll have to brush up on your French," said a friend before I left the U.S., believing me bound for Algeria. "Enjoy the northern lights," said another. Bulgaria is one of the forgotten nations once tucked behind the Iron Curtain, its cities now stocked with crumbling Soviet tenements and silent factories and stray dogs too hungry to bark. In the winter, in Haskovo—the city where I teach English to three hundred hardened teenagers—the air thickens to a gray haze as residents burn brush and scraps of trash to heat their homes. The smoke makes me cough, makes my eyes sting, makes my thoughts turn dark.

Today, though, we have left Haskovo. We have left winter as well. The first spring blossoms are starting to show, forsythia yellowing the countryside. As the road to the Devil's Throat continues its manic winding route through the Rhodopes, we pass the occasional village of squat red-roofed dwellings, laundry lines strung with colorful underwear like prayer flags. Chickens bustle after bugs. Kids kick soccer balls on smears of new grass.

"21 km," says a sign.

Even in the presence of spring, I feel nervous. I can't help imagining the ways we might die on this mountain road, squeezed between cliffs and a squalling river. It's a bad habit of mine: envisioning worst-case scenarios. I picture our car tumbling end to end over a ledge, the windshield shattered, our bodies flecked with glass. I do this despite also worrying that if I envision such things I might make them come true.

My husband gives no sign of noticing my nervousness. He's absorbed by the purely physical task of driving. Or perhaps by thoughts of what's to come: this purported entrance to hell. A myth made real. A myth, in many ways, still in the making. Odd things are said to happen inside the Devil's Throat. Having rushed down from peaks of the Rhodopes, the Trigrad River enters the cavern in a spectacular waterfall—the highest in the Balkans—then disappears into an underground siphon. No one knows where the river goes, what it does, as it courses through the earth. If a person were to send a log into this siphon, or a marked flotation device, it would never come out. There have been two diving expeditions, back in the Seventies. Both divers disappeared; their bodies were never recovered. Since then, no one has tried.

"5 km," says a sign. The landscape begins to change. Cliffs lean over the road, as if to engulf our car, swallow us. As we gain elevation, the air turns chilled, icicles spearing down from the rockface like a thousand sharpened teeth. The river changes too. The water becomes wilder, more tangled as it scrambles past the skinny leafless trees lining the river banks, their branches decked with pale shreds of shopping bags. They have a wraith-like quality, these shreds. They look like the torn edges of ghosts.

I imagine our car flipping sideways, the cold spill of water over my limbs.

My husband taps his fingers to the music, turns the radio up.

Samo mi pokashi chmi obichash, croons a young man. Just show me that you love me.

"She died too soon," Orpheus sang to Hades, strumming his lyre all those miles underground, his words echoing through the fleshless spirit world, the legions of the dead. "We had so little time together."

Bulgaria has its share of gifts. There are the savory delights of homemade *lyutenitsa*, the noisy neighborhood gatherings on warm afternoons, the layered history that places Thracian ruins next to Byzantine churches next to Ottoman mosques. But the country is also stymied by poverty, youth-drain, and the worst corruption in the E.U. Recently, Bulgaria experienced a wave of self-immolations. Citizens burned themselves on the capitol's steps because there seemed no other way to protest. The gulf between Communistic orderliness and the promise of Capitalist salvation has stretched wide and grim and endless. My role, as an English teacher, is to help bridge that gulf—to distribute language like a currency—but my job often feels like thinly veiled imperialism. Really, I'm a cultural missionary, sponsored by the U.S. government, stationed abroad in a not-so-

384

subtle bid to win the allegiance of young Bulgarians. "The West," they should learn to say, without rolling their R's or pronouncing their I's like E's, "has our best interests at heart."

Regardless, my teaching hasn't been especially successful. My students receive my lessons with jaded apathy, view me with suspicion. Some speculate that I'm an FBI agent. Maybe they aren't so far off. I tell them to call me "Mrs. McElroy," using my husband's surname. It feels like an alias. I don't use the name anywhere else. After school, I return to our apartment, take off my wedding ring. My husband does the same. Our rings don't feel natural. These cheap gold zeros we purchased at a pawnshop: we got them for our slapdash wedding, planned a day in advance, so that my husband—then boyfriend—could get his visa paperwork.

"You must be the first people in history," a friend said, "to get married for a visa to Bulgaria."

I look at my husband, driving the car with quiet concentration, his eyes fixed forward, his jawline scruffy with an encroaching beard. I wouldn't have gone abroad if he hadn't come with me. And if I hadn't gone abroad, we might not have signed those binding papers. The two things feel inextricable now—Bulgaria and our marriage—which in turn feels problematic. My husband has become part of the great gray weight of this country, the crush of its despair. He doesn't have the pressure of a government job, or even legal working privileges. Because of this, I often get resentful—even angry—especially as my inner film reel of calamities spins ever faster. But these emotions also make me feel ashamed. Perhaps Bulgaria, if anything, has kept us together: rendered us co-dependent in a city with no other native English speakers except a pair of skittish Mormons. Perhaps beyond Bulgaria we will disintegrate, dissolve.

Perhaps he has his own resentments.

My husband continues to drive, his lips sealed, his mind distant. I wonder if this is how marriages begin to end. Not so much in shouting as in silence.

"Please," sang Orpheus. "Give us another chance."

My husband pulls our car into a parking lot, empty. On one side a sheer cliff rises, a tiny doorway at its base like a mouse hole in a Tom & Jerry cartoon. A man knocks on our car's windshield and tells us that tickets to enter cost five *leva* each. The tour starts in ten minutes.

We get out, stretch our legs. My husband produces a notebook and begins to scribble observations, glancing around at the jagged peaks, the arrow-straight pine trees, sniffing the sharp mountain air. Feeling the pang of exclusion, I take out my own notebook and make my own scribblings. We stay in physical proximity, but barricade our thoughts. This is a far cry from when we first started dating, both transplants to a new city, both unable to resist the contents of the other's mind. My future husband would invite himself over to my apartment to swim in an old over-chlorined pool, and there we would bob in circles, talking and talking until our fingers pruned, doling out our lives to one another—so much at the beginning of something that every word felt like a new invention.

Now, though, it seems more like an incursion to share the thoughts inside me, to unravel my knotted anxiety, to expose the hot coals lining my mind.

"Another chance."

We pay for our tickets and walk into the mountain. Behind us comes the tour guide speaking with sardonic familiarity to several young Bulgarian couples who had arrived at the last minute. The men have a toughened demeanor, their heads shaven, their bodies lumpy and neckless beneath their tracksuits. The women wear shiny leather jackets and tight jeans, cigarettes balanced on their fingers, lips plumped, eyebrows plucked, hair pulled back tight enough to stretch skin.

We hurry on ahead of them. As we descend, the air turns stale. The tunnel walls press closer. I sink into subterranean unease, imagining earthquakes, the suffocating trap of a collapsed ceiling, a mountain river rising too fast to escape. My breath quickens. The tunnel worms deeper, well beyond the reach of natural light. Piss-colored lamps line the path, their glow throwing more shadows than illumination, dim phantasms cast here and there disguising the tunnel's turns until, finally, they reveal a huge cavern thundering with the muscular plunge of the river.

The Devil's Throat is ballroom big. Ceilings swell upward as if inflated by sound. On the floor, puddles gather and glint from the waterfall's spray. Dark patches of bat colonies fleck the walls. There is a musty smell. I feel disoriented, both by the river's roar and the heady hugeness of the space. My husband disappears into a dim corner, scribbling in his notebook. The ache of exclusion becomes unbearable. I call to him but he does not hear me. I call again. I call and call and call.

At last he comes, putting his arm around me. We lean over a railing, marveling at the sheer force of the river. It feels good to look closely at the same thing. It feels important. I suggest that we should each send something into the river. We should send something to be taken into the earth and never returned. A feeling maybe. Or a fear. My husband likes this idea. With exaggerated decorum, we both make silent vows of absolution, then spit them into the river.

Resentment, I think. *Anger. Be gone.*

Then I hug my husband, fiercely, as if to rediscover the strength in my own body, my own solidity, my own living form.

Hades shed iron tears and they dropped to the ground with a plunk, plunk, plunk, his sympathy sounding through the underworld. "Go," he said to Orpheus, to Eurydice—called up from the depths—"go live long full lives and return when you are ready."

The tour guide and the Bulgarian couples are coming up into the cavern behind us. Their presence seems to push us forward, out, as if the men's wide-legged swagger, the women's eyerolling, might poison our moment of intimacy. We move through the cavern, across the slick ground, past a stone altar where pilgrims have placed glittering piles of copper *stotinki,* red and white bracelets called *martenitsi,* and little portraits of saints. Then we come to three hundred steps. "Do not attempt to climb," reads a large sign, "if you have a fear of heights, claustrophobia, high or low blood pressure, diabetes . . ."

The list continues on, naming what seems like every conceivable ailment. My spirits falter. What if, I wonder, one's mind inevitably spins through deadly scenarios? What if one often loses hold of her real world?

"There's just one condition," said Hades to Orpheus, about to climb out of hell, to take Eurydice with him. "Listen closely . . ."

We begin climbing. My husband first and then me. The steps are narrow, puddled with mud and slippery with river spray, steep. If a person leans backwards, even slightly, she will plummet. She has to grip the railings tightly. She has to grip them even though they are made from iron rebar and are shockingly cold, almost too cold to touch. Even though she feels dizzy with the foreboding workings of her imagination.

". . . Until you have reached the living world, do not look at your wife. Do not look back."

Too cold to touch, and yet they must to be touched. Must be squeezed and clung to. I long for gloves. I long to put my hands in my pockets or to warm them with my breath, and yet to do such a thing would mean giving in to gravity, grasping at air until I'm dashed on the rocks, flung into the churning river that would suck me into the earth and make me disappear.

Hades' instruction: at once simple and impossible, arbitrary and inevitable. Orpheus traveled up and out of the underworld, Eurydice close behind, when—and here different versions of the story provide different explanations, though the action remains the same—Orpheus could not resist glancing at his resurrected bride. He looked back. And when he did, death reclaimed Eurydice, drew her down into the underworld forever.

Ahead, on the stairs, my husband climbs steadily towards a crevice of light.

Orpheus was heartbroken, the stories tell us, bound for suffering and hardship and death by disembowelment, but I have always wondered about Eurydice. Was she also heartbroken? Or was the look, in a way, a thing of comfort? Orpheus had lost her, but she had gained him.

"What, then, could she complain of," writes Ovid, "except that she had been loved?"

My husband pauses climbing, turns to look back at me briefly. Then he continues. He has made sure that I'm okay, that I'm still going. Perhaps this is marriage, I think. It's not the paperwork, signed for one reason or another; it's two pairs of feet making the same steady climb, the same bid for light. Two souls seeking the same fate, doomed or otherwise.

I let my scared self fall backward, peel away, that ghost of me, bottled up and angry. I grip the railings tighter. I scramble upward after my husband, back into Bulgaria, our daily struggles, our yearnings, the grayness and the poverty, and I hear the waterfall roaring in the cavern behind me, the Devil's Throat loud with its heady music, made from a river tonguing deep into a mountain, carrying things in and bringing nothing out, like a lover's heart, a promise, a tale told for the dead as much as for the bereaved.

Nominated by The Threepenny Review,
Angela Woodward

WONDER DAYS

by NOMI STONE

from NEW ENGLAND REVIEW

What I meant is that when the child shook the branch,
the beetles, quiet, somnolent, darkly, fell and again fell
like plums. Once woken, they bzzzed towards
the street lamps, loving each light well, thwacking
against them until they landed face down or face
up, trying to find their feet, reminding me of Eve's face
as a baby when she tried to lift her head on her stem
of a neck before yet she could. Upon the child's shoulders,
beetles landed, kinging him. The dusk's gray mute
unfolded its scrolls, while his mother made toast
with boysenberry jam, his father played solitaire,
and think of his sister doing her biology homework.
But they are under the tree, he is, the bright ones falling
upon him like stars, and as they fall, he names them:
some doctors, some cooks, depending on the size
of their antennae. His face was a diary of leaves: dark,
lit, risen with laughter, then suddenly at rest. This
was one way to be inside the world rather than outside
looking into a bright window.

Nominated by Chloe Honum

THE WHITE ROAD

by DANIEL TOBIN

from PLUME

I am walking along the dazzling ruin of a road I knew
When I was fourteen, summer, and the days stretch out
Like the road itself, or like that song about a road heading
Somewhere far off into the unseen and the one walking,
Caminante no hay camino, knows he's come upon his life
Rising up to him in white quartz macadam and heat-haze.
Along the slapdash shoulder a few almost teenage boys
Are shaving down stalks of goldenrod in afternoon sun,
The better to whip the heads off weeds, or whip each other
Before nothing much calls them to loiter off elsewhere
To Grossi's junkyard or the Shale Pit or, today, saunter
The dirt lane down to the Lower Lake where in three years
Dante Tedeschi will fashion a ramp out of cast-off
Plywood and scrap, aiming to accomplish something
No one has dared before—to tear down Heart Attack Hill
Past Hendershot's house, in full view of the ball courts,
The beach where Patty Curiale, all glistening skin and breasts
In her string bikini, suns her blonde self, her feet dangling
From the wooden dock; or she's out on the raft readying
To dive with a lithe grace into the unseeable-into-murk
Of the middle of that dammed up pond we called a lake—
Which is, approximately, the medium into which Dante aims
To take flight, hauling from the hill top at top speed
Toward the ramp he's sturdied beside the bridge, as if
He were on his father's Harley and not some souped-up

Almighty Schwinn, its raised handles, its roll bar,
The flared banana seat, as though this were a road bike
And he some mythical Easy Rider twisting the hand grips
To gun it beyond sound or sense into a catalytic future.

We called him Boone, even our fathers called him Boone,
Our mothers, arrayed in neon polyester like kitsch
Statuary outside their jerry-built summer houses—
Coolers of beer and whisky sours all evening long
Under citronella torches, weekend parties that made
The rounds from porch to patio while their children
Wandered off. Here he comes now, Dante aka Boone,
With his incongruous swagger and coke-bottle glasses,
Twirling a cut-down stick in his left hand that he now
Pretends is a Louisville Slugger he summons to swing,
A dead pull hitter blithely turning on the invisible,
The fastball deposited somewhere deep in the vetch
Across the sweltering pitch and glitter of the White Road.
His laugh was a kind of rapid-fire staccato, shuttling
Between a case of hiccups and a howitzer, unfettered,
Pure enjoyment admixed to a purer derision.
Like when, playing chess on Garrity's lawn, he'd stare
Expressionless at his opponent's spread of forces, pawns
Advancing, bishops slicing slantwise over the squares,
And in no time their Queen taken, King checkmated,
So it shot up uncontrollable, infiltrating the canopy,
The shade trees sheltering the picnic table, echoing
Off the rusted shed: that impishly jocular spattering
Of genius immodestly, no surprise to us, surprising
Itself once again with its own manic and rarified life.
Always he attained whatever he desired, slaughter
On the game board, sliding catches in left-center
On Power's Field, even the soft-limbed Patty of dreams.
He'd take her nightly to Schuman's porch, the house
disused, or abandoned, the rest of us pent and waiting
With the unkempt fevers of our bodies that longed
To trespass beyond their churning borders. Like a spoon
Slipping into honey, he'd say, letting his simile float
In the air awhile among us like a fraying wing of smoke,
The blazon of his carnal knowing.

He was first to go,
The buzz coming by phone one winter evening
After those summers had disbanded to intimations
Of more necessary longings, for jobs, for departures,
The bullet passing clean through his skull at a sister's
Wedding, the trigger pulled by the groom's hand.
What he had done or said, none of us would come
To know, though all of us could hear inside
That rapid fire laugh, haughty, untamable, and saw
His shambling, self-assured walk as in a heatwave
Off the White Road, Dante alias Boone, in saddle
On his Schwinn wheeling breakneck from on high
Down Heart Attack in the mind's would-be perpetual
Now, hair flying, pot-holes loose gravel be damned,
Down to where the rigged ramp rose upward above
The waiting lake, our crowd of bored numb-nuts cheering
As bike and rider flew treacherously up into the air
And out beyond the shore, and disappeared—circlets
Of waves radiating out like visible ticks from a clock face,
Slowly softening into nothing one by one by one
As we waited for the quick-eyed, impudent head to rise.

Nominated by Plume,
Bruce Beasley,
William Wenthe

A SUBURBAN WEEKEND

fiction by LISA TADDEO

from GRANTA

On a scorching Sunday in late August, Fern and Liv lay out in the sun at Liv's parents' country club. At twenty-seven, they were old to be coming in from the city for the weekend, swimming in the pool and eating chicken salad lunches on the patio, signing the bill to Liv's fat father's account.

But last night was weird—broken rubbers, lukewarm digestifs—and to stay in Manhattan after that kind of night, during a heat wave, would have been too much.

They chose two lounge chairs next to the pool. Little girls splashed and squealed and twiggy boys walked underwater, their palms periscoping like shark fins. Even the children with very long hair didn't need swimming caps at the club. Caps were for the town pool, where the members shed and had split ends.

Club employees in cream polos and khaki shorts jotted drink orders and then took forty minutes to retrieve Diet Cokes with sturdy lemon wedges. The girls looked at their feet, and past their feet to the annoying kids in the water. They looked up and felt the sun on their necks. The suburban sky was a Windex blue, whereas in Manhattan the blue was washed-out, blue like you had just slept with some guy in the same small room in which your best friend had slept with some other guy.

Fern and Liv were always trying to decide who was prettier, hotter, who could bypass the line to get into Le Bain, who looked more elegant drinking cortados at a cafe with crossed legs. The answer flickered, depending on whether they were assessing themselves from far away or up close, and what each was wearing, how her hair looked, how much rest she'd gotten and, of course, who had recently been hit on hardest by tall guys with MBAs.

The facts. Fern was skinnier than Liv, but Liv was blonde and tall and her breasts were enormous and thrillingly spaced. Liv could have been called chubby in certain circumstances, in jeans or leggings for example, or at power yoga. Fern's face could look misshapen, in weird lighting, with no makeup. Liv had a better chance of being called beautiful, especially by black guys and Danes. Fern was more often sexy, mysterious. Small, Jewish men liked her. Also, men from any of the Latin countries, and Italians from Jersey or Delaware. Cleft-lipped financiers and Bushwick bloggers. Irish guys went for both girls. Bartenders liked neither.

Fern was reading *The Executioner's Song*; she welcomed the way the heavy book felt against the tops of her thighs. She wanted to be ground down. Liv had one of her graphic novels; she was the funny one, the one who stayed at the bar the latest with the people who were either waiting around to hook up, or the alcoholics who never thought it was time to go home. Liv was more the latter. She didn't want to hook up as much as she wanted to *be out*. She made others feel lame for going home before two in the morning.

Fern was thinking about her empty childhood house. Though it was less than three miles away, her family hadn't belonged to this club. They'd summered at the township pool. They would spread their brown-horse towel and the light-yellow irregular Nautica towel on the hot cement; her parents smoked while she swam. First her father, and then her mother, drew cancer from the wheel of how you will die. Fern imagined this wheel was in a shitty part of London, spun by a man with brown teeth and coke fingernails. Her mother was incinerated just a few months ago.

Now the family home was for sale, plus all of its contents: the Capodimonte statuettes of old Italian men playing bocce, eating speck, licking their dark fingers; the Encyclopedia Britannica; her father's marble pen holder; the aluminum bowls belonging to Puppy, who lived for four years before getting hit by an Escalade on South Orange Avenue.

Not for sale: the yellowed stacks of TV Guides Fern's mother collected, especially the Fall Previews; and a bowl of handmade Venetian candies called *lacrime d'amore*. Tears of love. They were little pellets about twice the size of a peppercorn, fine pastel shells filled with a drop of *rosolio*, an Italian liqueur made from rose petals. They evaporated in your mouth like racy air. When they'd arrived in the mail, all the way from Marghera, Fern's mother cast her leather neck back and cried with joy. Some cousin recently told Fern you could find them out near Newark now, an Italian importer. But by then Fern's mom had already turned gray. *It's the lack of oxygen,* a hipster resident at St Barnabas Medical said with confidence. *See how our faces are pink? That's oxygenated blood. Your mother's is quickly dwindling. It's like her blood can't breathe.*

As though reading aloud from her graphic novel, Liv hummed.

'Uh, uh, uh, uh, oh, oh, ohmygod, ohmygod, ohmygod, OHMYFUCK-INGGOD!'

Fern laughed. She kicked Liv's considerable calf with her little foot.

'Your sex noises,' Liv continued, not joining in the laughter, 'are ultra-soft-core. HBO circa 1996.'

'Ew. Fuck you.'

'They're like. Husband-pleasing.'

'Dude your kissing noises are pretty homo. *Ooom-wah, ooom-wah.* It sounded like an annoying washing machine.'

'What does that even mean?'

'In fucking Sears.'

'Can you pass me the Pirate's Booty?'

Fern tossed Liv the bag of butter-colored food product that Liv's mom kept in their pantry of bright, fat-people items. Fern, who had no parents, loved the pantry. She loved Liv's mom.

'Liv, Liv,' Fern said with a Latin accent. 'You are so glamorous, Liv, when you eat the Booty.'

Fern knew that whenever Liv was upset, it was best to poke fun harmlessly and, in doing so, incidentally worship her.

Now Liv laughed. 'How about those Argentineans?' she said.

'Jesus Christ,' said Fern. 'My thighs are still quivering.'

Last night had begun at the Arthur Ashe Stadium. Round one of the Men's US Open. Liv's father worked in marketing for Mercedes, a platinum sponsor, and had got the girls two good seats to one of the matches. A Swede who was hot versus a Brit who was not. It was luminous and Waspy in the stadium. Ruddy women in hats and men in crisp Bonobos. Cologne, lemon dresses, the occasional Chinatown fan. Some Staten Island dads with clapping hats. The place was mostly packed, but for two empty seats beside the girls. They drank light beers from plastic cups and raised their tanned arms in the air whenever the Swede got a point.

'Fifteen Love,' they would preempt the announcer.

Fern wore a red skater dress with a pair of navy espadrille wedges. Liv wore a floral romper and leather flats and made fun of Fern for wearing heels.

'They're not heels, they're wedges.'

'Whatever, hooker.'

'You're just jealous because I'm not an Amazon and I can wear heels without freaking people out.'

'Hey, Fur, why don't you go hook yourself in the boxes? Lots of Deutsche douches looking for a GFE.'

'Yum, prime rib under carving lights. Fuck. Should we crash a box?'

'I don't know. I keep looking at these two empty seats, imagining the loves of our lives coming in and sitting down.'

Fern rolled her eyes; she used to feel the same, but now she was a person who didn't care who sat down beside her. The courthouse, the subway. Maybe if she took the Effexor that she'd been prescribed, she would give a flying fuck.

Two men were suddenly standing above them. The girls looked up, shielding their eyes from the sun. The men were dads, golfers, bald, buzzed.

'These seats taken?' said the one wearing a Masters polo from the previous year.

'I don't understand,' Fern said. 'Are they yours?'

'No,' said the other, holding curly fries.

'Then yes,' Fern said, 'they're taken by the people who paid for them.'

But she did the full body version of batting her eyelashes. The only thing that had lately survived in Fern was a desire to make men want to fuck her. All men. Every single man she saw. Hot dog vendors. UPS drivers across the street. Liv called her a slut. It made Liv angry. A lot of things about Fern made Liv angry. But then, Liv did nice things. She spoke to Fern in Fern's mother's Italian accent, for example.

The guy with the curly fries looked past Fern to Liv.

'Hello, excuse me, are you one of the players?' Liv did look like one of the Slavic stars with her white teeth and voracious forearms.

'Yes,' she said. 'But I'm like ninth seed, so.'

'Oh, wow! What is it like, at a women's match? Are there a lot less spectators?'

'Yeah, about 95 per cent less.'

'That many, wow.'

'Yeah. But this year we're giving out Thinx. That's the period underwear. So we're hopeful.'

The guy in the polo brought out a newly purchased visor and a black Sharpie and Liv signed the name Paulina Pornikova to the lid.

The girls watched some more tennis, yawned, texted, and got up to get another pair of beers, and a jumbo soft pretzel to share.

When they returned, two nice-looking young men were sitting in the spare seats beside them.

'Are you fucking kidding me right now?' Liv whispered to Fern.

The boys seemed as pleased as the girls. The dark-haired one was Sebastián and the blond was Axel. They were Argentinean derivatives traders, working in Latin American markets in the city. Sebastián, whose father was an ambassador, wore a Rolex, while Axel was more sporty, with goofy teeth and horny blue eyes. They were both well-dressed and vaguely soulless.

They watched the rest of the match together. At some point it seemed both young men wanted Liv, and at another point it seemed they both wanted Fern. Sebastián told them to call him Seb. He was quiet while Axel was hyper. In many ways their relationship to one another mirrored Fern and Liv's. When the match was over they all rode the 7 train back into the city.

'Let's get off here,' Sebastián said, as they neared Gramercy. 'We will have a drink at Pete's Tavern.'

They were slightly warmer than American boys, and they paid for all the cocktails without question. Fern knew, for as little or as long as she lived, that she would never fall in love; she thought it was so childish that Liv believed in fairy-tale romance like an idiot. That was why she liked Seb better. He was the colder of the two boys, and he seemed like he could take the girls or leave them, while Axel seemed bent on getting laid.

'It's getting late,' Seb said, around eleven. 'I have a squash game in the morning.'

'You are right,' Axel said. 'Let's go up to your place for a nightcap.'

'Are you sleeping over?'

'Yes, brother,' Axel said. 'Come on girls, you can see what a bomb site my friend lives in.'

Seb's place was right across the street from the bar. The girls were shocked to see it was a studio. Granted, it was a doorman building in a prime location, but the idea of an ambassador's son living in a studio with all his dry cleaning hanging from the rusty rod of his shower dulled the thrill of the hunt.

Seb brought out four mismatched glasses and poured Fernet Branca. 'Ok,' he said, it is time for me to collect on my win.' Earlier, at the game, they'd bet on the point spread of the game, and the stakes had been that the winner could make a rule, any rule he wanted.

'Do you know what you want?' Liv said, rubbing her pink lips around the rim of her glass.

'I think I do,' Seb said. He walked into the bedroom section of his studio and came back with a paisley tie. He proposed blindfolding Axel and suggested that both girls should kiss him, and Axel would try to figure out which was which, and who was better. Seb would go after.

Fern went second, both times. She used a different technique with each boy. With Seb she didn't even touch his body; she just matched her lips to his and kissed lightly and seductively. With Axel, she moved one hand along his waist and brought her other around his neck. Then she sucked on his tongue like a porn star.

Liv kissed both boys the way Liv kissed. Fern knew something about that because she'd once woken in the middle of the night with Liv's mouth on hers. Liv had been holding Fern's hands, like teenagers on a park bench. Liv took a lot of Adderall which acted like cocaine at high dosages, so she would pass out hard and then do weird shit in her sleep. In the morning Liv, bleary-eyed, said, *Yo man did you try to make out with me last night?* Anyway, Fern knew Liv's kiss style was *true love.*

Axel was more diplomatic but basically both boys said the second girl was the better kisser.

Liv, of course, was pissed. Fern excelled at most things. It was because Fern wanted to win. It was all she had.

They talked and laughed some more and drank as though the kissing never happened. But the smell of blood was in the air, a slutty rivalry radiating between the girls. Fern assumed it was for Seb, since that was the Argentinean she wanted. When Liv got up to go to the bathroom, Fern turned her face to his and flashed a spiritual fuck-me gaze.

Eventually it ended up with Fern and Seb in Seb's bed, and Liv and Axel on the banana-leaf futon by the door. There was rustling and then there was nothing and then there was the sound of heavy sliding, like repo men in the middle of the night.

'Fur, are you doing it?' Liv asked from across the room.

Fern giggled. Seb said, *Shhh,* and they fucked dementedly. She felt more at peace with this boy she barely knew than with Liv, who always needed to know what she was doing, and how she was feeling.

＊　＊　＊

The country club pool looked like a giant Blue Hawaiian. That was the cocktail, Fern knew, that caused Liv to fail her bartender exam. It was made with curaçao, rum, pineapple juice and cream of coconut. Instead of cream of coconut, Liv used sour mix. But that was a Blue Hawaii. Fern would never had made that mistake. She was a more precise person.

'I can't believe you had sex,' Liv said.

'What the fuck do you mean? I thought you were doing it, too. What does it matter?'

'It just does. It's just weird. Like, I'm right there. I thought we were just making out with them.'

'I don't get why it matters.'

'I just think it's kind of, I don't know, low-class.'

That was the shit Fern couldn't abide. Liv calling *her* low-class? Liv regularly got wasted and smeared her lipstick, making coral bridges to her nose, and she embarrassed herself with superiors and told doormen they were handsome young men. Did she want Seb? Who knew? All Fern knew was that she had always been scared of disease, and now she wasn't. She didn't care that the Durex broke last night and the ambassador's son fell asleep inside of her, dribbling. Contracting HIV would be a godsend.

Her therapist said she was clinically depressed, making it sound like the flu. His name was Sanford; he was wet granola, from Bend, Oregon, with sandy hair and long sideburns. He wore knit ties on top of flannel shirts, like an executive who lived in a tree. *My parents died,* Fern screamed at him, the third session. *Both of them, and we were close. And there is literally nothing left. I'm not depressed. I'm just done. You don't seem to get it, fucking no one does.*

And Sanford replied, soulfully, *I, too, have lost many people.* And proceeded to tell her, for twenty-one minutes on her dime, that he had a meth addict father who left when he was five and a mom that drank tons of boxed white wine and laughed very loudly when any kind of man was around. She smoked Winstons and went out a fair amount, so young Sanford ate a lot of Kraft Cheese and macaroni; she would make a family-size package on Sunday, which was the only night she was definitely home, and Sanford would eat it congealed on Mondays, Tuesdays and Wednesdays, cool and pale orange and flavorless. Towards the week-ends it was frozen dinners. Salisbury steak and Creamed Chipped Beef. The latter was his favorite, but he burned himself once opening the steaming plastic and thereafter it was just another thing he loved but was afraid to get close to.

That's not the same thing, Fern had said quietly. To which Sanford countered, *How are your bowel movements?* She fucking hated it when he asked about bowel movements. Once, he gave her a jar of Friendly Fiber. Yoga and fiber were the keys to a healthy soul.

To Liv she said, 'Fine, I'm low-class, whatever man.'

'I'm sorry. I didn't mean that. I just think. You're like. Acting out.'

'I need to pee.'

Liv nudged her chin in the direction of the water and winked.

At half past noon the girls pulled on their cover-ups—a turquoise and magenta Roberta Roller Rabbit tunic for Liv, a black velour onesie for Fern—and were seated at the patio for a poolside lunch.

Liv always ordered stupid things. Veal tonnato or duck confit over fri-sée. This day she had the sourdough rabbit sandwich. It smelled like earth and vitamins. Fern ordered the lemon Caesar salad with shards of Parmesan and shimmering anchovy filets.

A conga line of suntanned, blonde women with tight, tight faces ap-proached their table in succession. Liv's mom's friends. They wanted to talk about what their daughters were doing versus what Liv was doing. Liv was doing stand-up and Upright Citizens Brigade. She had a day job as the executive assistant to the guy who founded Beardz, the app linking gay men with the girls who wanted to go to Barneys and eat lunch with them.

One of the women, Sheila, lingered for nearly five minutes. She had red hair and old-lady freckles and her neck looked two decades older than her face. Her daughter, Jess, had married an 'entrepreneur' and they lived all the way out in Vail. Jess was seven months pregnant, but still hiking. 'Your mom is so lucky,' Sheila said, after confirming Liv was single, 'to have you close to home.' Fern marveled at how many dead people were still alive.

While Sheila droned, Fern looked through her phone. No messages, nothing from Seb, or any of the other men she had lately provided with off-the-cuff orgasms. She was still getting used to not having to call her mother in the morning.

When Sheila walked away, Liv hissed, 'You can't have your phone out at the club!'

Fern placed her phone down and stared at her.

'My dad could get written up.'

'What a stupid rule.'

'You don't have to be here.'

'Fine,' Fern said, pushing out her rattan chair, scraping the slate floor.

'I'm sorry,' Liv said. 'I think I'm getting my period. Can you sit down?'

'Is this about last night?'

'What? No.'

'Did you like the other one?'

'No. I didn't like either of them, I don't care okay. Look can you just please try my fucking rabbit sandwich? You'll love it.' Pause, smile. 'It's what the courtesans used to eat.'

Fern smiled, too. 'I can't.' Fern was worried about gaining weight. She was thin like a snake, and it meant a lot to her. It felt like she took up less room and so when she went, it would be like a thread of angel hair slipping through the hole of a colander.

'Just try it,' Liv said, holding out a taupe forkful, 'you can puke it up after.'

Fern ate it; Liv watched her with a big smile. And Fern remembered how it used to be, in the honeymoon of their friendship, after Fern's father died but before her mother was diagnosed. They'd attended nearby high schools but hadn't met until a Thanksgiving Eve party hosted by a mutual friend. They clicked that night, Fern liked how Liv was pounding shots while knitting a blanket. They quickly became close, texting constantly throughout the workday and going out at night, leaving notes for bearded maître d's, sharing tea cakes with Japanese businessmen.

Liv suggested a trip to Capri that summer, where the girls wore linen sundresses and white bikinis and paid thirty euros for muslin sacks and laid out on the black rocks over the Tyrrhenian, shoulder to shoulder. Fern showed Liv the restaurant under the lemon grove where her parents had their first date. Liv insisted on ordering the same dishes they did. The crust on the white pizza gave like the flesh of a child's arm. Liv had never seen fried zucchini flowers. They drank limoncello from cordial glasses and squeezed the sweet-smelling lemons on everything, their fish, their wrists, and a waiter made them garlands of bougainvillea and thyme to wear around their heads.

But their love was cemented the following spring, after the second funeral, when Fern texted Liv, *come get me?* And Liv showed up within the hour, in her father's cherry red Aston Martin convertible, blasting LCD Soundsystem, and they drove out to the Colorado Cafe where they drank everything they could think of and rode the mechanical bull and pulsed onstage with the Kenny Rogers cover band and wound up in some New Jersey cowboy's apartment, taking turns puking in the bathroom while the cowboy tried to finger whoever was waiting her turn on the couch.

In the morning, when they drove home and Fern said at least nobody was worried about her, Liv brought her back to her house, where Liv's mom raged at them both.

So Fern knew it was important to let Liv know the plan.

'Did I ever tell you how I was obsessed with Jeremy Mullen when I was twelve, you know, from that stupid movie at the aquarium?'

'The child actor who hung himself.'

'When I found out he killed himself, I was like fuck. I thought, if only he knew how I loved him. I would have taken care of him. You know? I would have done his laundry or told the maid what was dry-clean only.'

'Yeah,' said Liv, sounding exhausted.

'Now I'm like, fuck no. Whatever ridiculous child actor nonsense. I would have just stolen his pills.'

'Probably he had a small dick. That's why he killed himself.'

'My point is, it doesn't matter. He killed himself because it was time. Every night is the same, going to clubs, whatever, it doesn't fix anything.'

'I think if we were celebrities going to the Chateau every night, we'd make it work, you and me. Anyway I totally disagree with you. I think people can be saved by people who love them. You just have to be dedicated. You have to like, be there, every day.'

'I couldn't save my mom.'

'Your parents died of fucking *can*cer, man.'

'My mom's was basically suicide. Suicide by cancer.'

Liv snorted. But covered Fern's hand with her own. Liv's nails were bitten but she had pretty, feminine fingers. Fern's hands were small, boyish. They looked silly giving hand jobs.

'What did your mom call your dad again?' Liv said.

Liv was obsessed with Fern's dead parents. Because the girls had only become very close in the last several years, Liv hadn't known Fern's parents very well, but she'd made it a mission to understand who they were, how they would answer a certain question. She often made Fern tell her the romantic story of how they met in the Conad, next to the piadina display. And in general would say things like, I bet your mom would tell you that you look like a slut right now.

'Pip,' Fern said, removing her hand from under Liv's.

Liv smiled and nodded. 'Pip,' she repeated. Then she sat up straight in her chair. 'Oh my god, see that guy?'

'Which?'

'Hot dad, twelve o'clock, curly salt-and-pepper hair. And the wife, that polar blonde, and their two little girls, oh my god I'm obsessed. Look at those curly ringlets! They are the perfect family. He's the CFO of the USGA. They live on Flat Pond Road, that sick house with the fucking turrets.'

'Awesome.'

'That's what I want. He's in the city all week, killing it, she's lounging at the pool with her kids, he comes home on the weekend, they have hot sex and then whatever, she goes to the movies, makes cashew milk. That could be you and me. With powerful husbands, I mean.'

'Dude he probably cheats on her all week.' Where Liv liked to imagine perfect marriages because they made her feel she would someday have one, too, Fern liked to expose the rot at the bottom of the bowl of organic vegetables. She looked at the man, tall and patrician in Vilebrequin shorts and fine leather sandals. The wife, with a former model look, in a white linen shirt over a black bikini.

'No way,' Liv said. 'Look at her.'

'She looks like a cleaner, less-bloated version of you. Who cares? All women get cheated on.'

'You're full of poisonous energy. I'm gonna need to do a juice cleanse when I get home.'

'Yeah vodka's a great base for a cleanse. Listen. Do you want to come back to my house with me? I have to pick up the surrogate certificate for the lawyer.' Fern didn't like showing up to the house alone unless she was blasted. And she knew Liv never wanted the day to end.

'Of course. Let's just say hi.'

Liv introduced Fern to the man. His name was Chip. He didn't look like a Chip. He looked like a Luther. His lips were fleshy and his skin was moist. The wife looked bored but she asked after Liv's mom. Chip said he wanted to play with Liv's dad in the Labor Day scramble. But the whole time Chip was looking at Fern and Fern was looking back. Even when another tan man in tennis whites walked past and clapped Chip on the shoulder, saying, *Drink later?* Chip nodded, said, *Always*, but kept his shark eyes on Fern.

❀ ❀ ❀

Fern's house was a museum of mid-century nothing special. Things that were semi-expensive but mismatched, and dowry items from Fiesole. Persian rugs and parquet floors. Silver tea sets on baroque tables. Her parents had kept two entire rooms in the house unused. The couches had just barely escaped those giant plastic condoms. Like her mother before her, Fern never opened the windows or drew the shades. Skeins of sunlight slithered through moth holes in the curtains, and died inside the cracks of the parquet.

Liv was reverential in the house, gliding around like Fern's parents were merely asleep.

Fern couldn't wait to get rid of everything, all the knickknacks. She was going to sell the junk at one of those estate sales usually reserved for the dusty passing of grandparents. A lady named Tabitha would come and man a cash register. Women with skeletal noses would haggle over the price of costume jewelry and oven mitts.

'Your mom had such regal taste,' Liv said, her hand resting on a yellow silk scarf with a fringe of tinkling gold leaves.

'You want that? You can have it.'

'No, don't be silly.'

'Seriously, take it. Or somebody's grandmother will be wearing it to chemo next week.'

'Okay, thanks.' Liv wrapped it around her neck. She disappeared upstairs, where she spritzed herself with Fern's mom's L'Air du Temps and returned with her nose scrunched up.

'It smells kinda bad in the upstairs bathroom.'

'Why'd you go in there? I said don't go in there.'

'Sorry, I forgot. Are these them?' Liv's hand hovered by the bowl of candies on the kitchen table.

'Yeah.'

'Wow. They're pretty cool-looking. Where do you get them?'

'Some cousin sent those from Italy, but I heard some store in Cranford sells them now. My mom would have been psyched. Or maybe she wouldn't have been. Nothing made that bitch happy.'

Liv was about to have one. Fern looked at her.

'What?'

405

'Nothing. I was just kind of doing a thing.'

'What kind of a thing, weirdo?'

'I don't know. When they're all gone, I was thinking of killing my-self.' For the past few months, every time Fern did something gross, she would eat a candy. The bowl had been dwindling slowly but surely.

'You fucking idiot. That's retarded.'

'Pancreatic, metastatic,' Fern whisper-sang, like a rap.

'Will you please come to dinner with us. Don't make me do it alone.'

Liv had dinner plans with her former prom-queen sister in the city that night. They would eat somewhere that served peppery Pinot Noir in ball jars and Liv's sister would talk about her latest private equity douche-bag and tell Liv she might land a boyfriend if she lost fifteen pounds.

'Nah,' Fern said.

'Dude, you can't stay in your dead mom and dead dad's house. Come back to the city with me. Or I can stay? I'll cancel on the hyena.'

'No.'

'Ew, you have a suburban dick appointment. A fucking dentist with a wet bar.'

'No, man. I just want to like, sit in the house, go through stuff before the house sale. I'm fine. Just leave me alone.' Often, Fern made the pain of her parent's loss bigger to get out of doing things she didn't want to do. Other times, she felt it more acutely than it was possible to explain.

'It's weird you have no soul, when your parents had all this love for each other, and for you.' Liv scratched at Fern's chest like a chipmunk. 'Where's your thump thump, Baby Jane?'

Fern pushed her away.

'Dude. Stop.'

* * *

After Liv left and just before sunset, Fern put on her mother's snake dress. It was a short-sleeved beige shift with a cream-and-gray viper that twisted around the body. She selected the fawn Trussardi bag from her mother's good bag shelf and slipped in her license and sixty dollars in cash.

She drove her father's aquamarine Chevy Cavalier to Martini. She played no music. The sky was peach, hot orange and lilac. She passed sated lawns, cobblestone drives, Maremma sheepdogs. Fast walkers with bony butts in a rainbow of lululemon black.

Martini was the town bar and it was full of big-bellied insurance lawyers, divorcees in open-toed boots.

Fern sat down and ordered a Blue Hawaii.

Across the bar she saw the man from the country club. His greasy tendrils of black-and-silver hair looked alive. He wore a shirt with a contrast collar and was surrounded by middle-aged men with shiny lips and no wives.

Fern sipped her drink. She could be mostly normal in the day and then the second it got dark, her skin and scalp would itch and she'd grow dizzy and exhausted. Next, a sting behind her heart, where the pancreas was, and her lungs would feel heavy and soft with water, like her mother's. (*It's like your mother's lungs are drowning*, the hipster resident had said, that final week.) *Hypochondria*, Fern's therapist said a month later, nodding, jotting it down with his Yellowstone Park twig pencil.

She'd gotten her period that afternoon, so at least she wouldn't be pregnant with the ambassador's son's baby. That would suck, being pregnant. Would she get the abortion and *then* exterminate herself? Or just kill two birds with one bottle of Ambien. Bam.

She'd met a guy here a few years back, just after her dad died and before she met Liv. His name was Teddy. He had a new beagle puppy at home and asked if Fern wanted to meet him. He was one of those rich kids with no focus. A few lame producer credits, several gaudy friends in the fashion world. His fingers became a butterfly inside of her, nice, but otherwise she drove home at four a.m., feeling like garbage. Her mother was waiting in the foyer—smoking, gaunt, medieval. *How dare you?* she said. *How dare you to make me worry?*

This night Fern didn't feel pretty; she'd used up all her pretty the previous night. But it didn't matter in New Jersey. In New Jersey you just had to be under forty, under 130 pounds, and your hair shoulder-length or longer. Preferably straight and dark. That was really it.

Chip sauntered over. Frank Sinatra was pining from the speakers.

'You're Bob Long's daughter's friend, we met today.'

'Oh, right.'

'Is—uh—hmm here?'

'Liv? No. She went back to the city.'

'Must be nice to be young and living in the city.'

'The time of our lives.'

'You here by yourself?'

'Yup.'

'Can I buy you a drink? You wanna come hang with a couple of old fogeys?'

He sniffed. Clearly he had cocaine.

Fern sniffed, winked. He smiled. He got close and moved a tiny vial into her palms. He pressed it down with the pork of his thumb. 'When you're done,' he said, 'meet us on the patio for a Cuban.'

In the faux-elegant bathroom, Fern saw the makeup on her face was like a mask. It looked like it could be peeled off to reveal a dead person.

She snorted two lines off the tank of the toilet with a one-dollar bill. She rubbed some on her gums. She wondered if her parents were watching.

The patio was full of white wizard smoke blown from the mouths of the horniest men she had ever seen. Chip was hitting on one of the waitresses who drove in every day from Linden. Fern pretended she hadn't seen him and began to walk back inside. She felt a hand on her shoulder, and smelled his clean laundry.

'You almost missed us,' he said.

She ordered a Glenfiddich on his tab. She asked the waitress for honey and poured some into her glass, saying this is what they did in Scotland.

'Is that a fact?' said the fattest man.

'Yeah. Plus it takes the sting off the liquor, for the baby.'

'Say what? You're pregnant?'

'Yup,' Fern said, rubbing her belly. 'I'm drinking for two.'

'She's joking,' said Chip, smiling.

'She's funny. Hey, you're funny.'

'Beautiful babies,' said another man. 'You know that? You're beautiful babies.' He was looking from Fern to the waitress and back, as though they knew each other. The waitress had chunky highlights and a pierced eyebrow.

One of the other guys, who looked like he'd had a face lift, bought a whole bottle of Patron. Fern did shots with them. Chip held the lime wedge as she sucked it.

Face Lift said, 'Snapper these days, drink like men.'

Chip asked her what her father did. Actually, he said, 'Who's your father?' But it was the same question.

'Nobody,' Fern said. She thought how her father had never gone to a bar with the guys in all the years she'd known him.

She heard the fattest man say, 'Daddy issues,' under his breath. She swayed and Chip caught her. She whispered something into his ear.

'You wanna go where?' he said.

She said it again.

He raised his eyebrows and smiled. 'I know just the place.'

They passed the florist with the mirrored door and she checked her body in the mirror. Her mother's best dress, her tan legs. They got into Chip's olive Jaguar. He was drunk, too. Fern was impressed that certain men always knew how to drive, to move through toll booths without scraping the sides, even when they were three martinis deep. At home the Ambien was in the medicine closet with the cancer accoutrements— steroids, laxatives, vibrant head scarves. Fern felt like she was in a sensory deprivation tank. She thought of Liv's sunny face and wished she was with her now, her warm, solid arms around Fern.

They pulled up to a cement building, seemingly windowless. A pink scripted sign said, Cheeques.

Had she suggested this? She didn't remember. Probably she did.

Inside a guy wearing a Method Man shirt gave them a spot in the front row. Red velvet banquettes, glass tables, purple lighting. Chip ordered kamikaze shots and scotch and beer.

Most of the dancers were younger than Fern. One dark-skinned girl was absolutely beautiful, she could have been working in Abercrombie and dating someone with a good family.

There weren't many people in there, so the stripper concentrated on them, specifically on Fern; she whooshed her long mane in Fern's face. Fern inhaled. Salon Selectives conditioner, she was positive, probably from a dollar store, left over from 1994. It was her mother's brand. Crème rinse, the old lady called it.

Not to be outdone, Fern stood and did a dance for Chip. She ripped the seams of her mother's dress, straddling his lap. She licked the outlines of his giant lips with her tongue. The look on his face was not shock, or even happy surprise. It was almost judgmental. She just wanted to feel sexier than the stripper.

He drove her back to her car, parked in the unlit lot outside of Maximilian Furs and the out-of-business toy store. It was past three in suburbia and there was no one on the streets. He turned to look at her, then they were kissing again; his tongue was cold and his mouth tasted like iceberg lettuce. Eventually he got his manicured hands up her mother's dress. She remembered her tampon, yanked it out, opened the door and tossed it in the street. What they did after that didn't register. All Fern could think was that she would be eating two candies when she got home.

Last month over Sazeracs at Buvette, Liv said: *When I get married I'm going to have to watch my husband around you. You, and your shifty labia.* Liv said that because she'd just met Teddy—of the beagle and the butterfly fingers—through her parents, and told Fern about him, and Fern said, *Oh, I effed that loser.* Liv ended up going on two dates with Teddy. She didn't like him, but she slept with him. *Did you enjoy my sloppy seconds?* Fern said. *Why are you a dick*, Liv said. *What does it do for you?* Later that night, they really got into it. They'd moved onto a dim Mexican speakeasy on the Lower East Side. Liv was blasted on tequila. The fight erupted at the bar, quiet and nasty, their eyes locked on one another. Fern threw down a fifty-dollar bill—she was flush with cash these days—and walked fast down Ludlow. Liv threw open the door of the place and came after her, plastering Fern's little body against a parked SUV. She held Fern's neck against a cool window with her big hands. *What are you so proud of?* Liv said, nearly spitting in Fern's face. *You're jealous of me*, Fern said, smirking. *You're a cunt*, Liv said. *A fucking loveless whore.* They wrestled in each other's arms, pushing, pinching skin between gel nails, pulling hair. In the end, Fern had a split lip and in the morning Liv touched her middle finger to her mouth, then inspected her finger for blood, mimicking Fern the night before.

Now Fern drove home from Martini, falling asleep several times at the wheel and waking only when her car slid into the dirt off the shoulder. When she saw the bricks of her dark house, she was shocked she'd made it back alive.

She crept in as though her parents would hear her if she made noise. In the upstairs bathroom she vomited in the sink and not the toilet, because the toilet contained some precious urine—her mother's final home pee, lime-colored now and smelling like science. She laid in her parents' bed, a king made out of two twin mattresses. But vomiting had diluted forty percent of the drunk, while the coke was still blooming, and now she couldn't sleep.

She thought of the bowl of candies, and said out loud, *Three.* This night deserved three.

Quietly she slunk down the stairs. She passed the antique mirror on the wall, which as a child she thought could reflect the demons in her soul. Now it said $25 or best offer.

It was bizarre, to be in the house without the snores of the dog and the fear of the parents. So weird how a whole house of people could disappear over the course of three Fall Previews.

She wasn't exactly shocked, but her jaw did kind of drop when she saw the bowl of candies utterly replenished. She imagined Liv, driving out to the importer in Cranford, coming back and letting herself in the screen door at the back, a burglar in a beach cover-up. Filling the bowl, *lacrime d'amore* tinkling the glass.

Fern admired them. Pale shells, delicate as the eyelids of newborns. Here were hundreds more shitty things she could do to herself. On South Orange Avenue an ambulance awayoed, followed by the silence of the upper-middle dead.

She sat down and started popping the candies in her mouth, one after another. *Beautiful babies*, she thought, laughing, *all of us.*

Nominated by Granta

AUTISM SCREENING QUESTIONNAIRE—SPEECH AND LANGUAGE DELAY

by OLIVER DE LA PAZ

from POETRY

1. DID YOUR CHILD LOSE ACQUIRED SPEECH?

A fount and then silence. A none. An ellipse
between—his breath through
the seams of our windows. Whistle
of days. Impossible bowl of a mouth—
the open cupboard, vowels
rounded up and swept under the rug.

2. DOES YOUR CHILD PRODUCE UNUSUAL NOISES OR INFANTILE SQUEALS?

He'd coo and we'd coo back. The sound
passed back and forth between us like a ball.
Or later, an astral voice. Some vibrato
under the surface of us. The burst upon—
burn of strings rubbed
in a flourish. His exhausted face.

3. IS YOUR CHILD'S VOICE LOUDER THAN REQUIRED?

In an enclosure or a cave it is difficult to gauge
one's volume. The proscenium of the world.
All the rooms we speak of are dark places. Because
he cannot see his mouth, he cannot imagine
the sound that comes out.

4. DOES YOUR CHILD SPEAK FREQUENT GIBBERISH OR JARGON?

To my ears it is a language. Every sound
a system: the sound for dog or boy. The moan
in his throat for water—that of a man with thirst.
the dilapidated ladder that makes a sentence
a sentence. This plosive is a verb. This liquid
a want. We make symbols of his noise.

5. DOES YOUR CHILD HAVE DIFFICULTY UNDERSTANDING BASIC THINGS
   ("JUST CAN'T GET IT")?

Against the backdrop of the tree he looks so small.

6. DOES YOUR CHILD PULL YOU AROUND WHEN HE WANTS SOMETHING?

By the sleeve. By the shirttail. His light touch
hopscotching against my skin like sparrows.
An insistence muscled and muscled again.

7. DOES YOUR CHILD HAVE DIFFICULTY EXPRESSING HIS NEEDS OR
   DESIRES USING GESTURES?

Red-faced in the kitchen and in the bedroom
and the yellow light touches his eyes
which are open but not there. His eyes
rest in their narrow boat dream and the canals
are wide dividing this side from this side.

8. IS THERE NO SPONTANEOUS INITIATION OF SPEECH OR
   COMMUNICATION FROM YOUR CHILD?

When called he eases out of his body.
His god is not our words nor is it
the words from his lips. It is entirely body.
So when he comes to us and looks we know
there are beyond us impossible cylinders
where meaning lives.

9. DOES YOUR CHILD REPEAT HEARD WORDS, PARTS OF WORDS, OR
   TV COMMERCIALS?

The mind circles the mind in the arena, far in—far in
where the consonants touch and where the round
chorus flaunts its lambs in a metronomic trot. Humming
to himself in warm and jugular songs.

10. DOES YOUR CHILD USE REPETITIVE LANGUAGE (SAME WORD OR
    PHRASE OVER AND OVER)?

A pocket in his brain worries its ball of lint.
A word clicks into its groove and stammers
along its track, Dopplering like a car with its windows
rolled down and the one top hit of the summer
angles its way into his brain.

11. DOES YOUR CHILD HAVE DIFFICULTY SUSTAINING A CONVERSATION?

We could be anywhere, then the navel of the red moon
drops its fruit. His world. This stained world drips its honey
into our mouths. Our words stolen from his malingering afternoon.

12. DOES YOUR CHILD USE MONOTONOUS SPEECH OR WRONG PAUSING?

When the air is true and simple, we can watch him tremble
for an hour, plucking his meaning from a handful of utterances
and then ascend into the terrible partition of speech.

13. DOES YOUR CHILD SPEAK THE SAME TO KIDS, ADULTS, OR OBJECTS
    (CAN'T DIFFERENTIATE)?

Because a reference needs a frame: we are mother and father
and child with a world of time to be understood. The car radio
plays its one song. The song, therefore, is important.
It must be intoned at a rigorous time. Because rigor
is important and because the self insists on constant vigils.

14. DOES YOUR CHILD USE LANGUAGE INAPPROPRIATELY (WRONG WORDS
    OR PHRASES)?

Always, and he insists on the incorrect forms.
The wrong word takes every form for love—
the good tree leans into the pond,
the gray dog's ribs show, the memory
bound to the window, and the promise of the radio
playing its song on the hour. Every wrong form
is a form which represents us in our losses,
if it takes us another world to understand.

Nominated by Ayse Papatya Bucak,
Maxine Skates,
Shelley Wong

DO I LOOK SICK TO YOU? (NOTES ON HOW TO MAKE LOVE TO A CANCER PATIENT)

fiction by C. J. HRIBAL

from BELLEVUE LITERARY REVIEW

At first you don't. You hold back, stroking the small of her back. You kiss her ear. You nestle in behind her. Finally she says, "What, you're afraid I'll break? You're afraid it's contagious? Trust me, the cancer will not stick to your dick. It's not gonna rush up your urethra, pummeling your little spermies on the way, and explode like an IED in your insides. It's only trying to do that to *me*."

This is how it's going to be—she is going to kick cancer in the ass. Everyone says this, "She is going to kick cancer in the ass," until it becomes a mantra. Everything is going to be as it was before, only now you are "living with cancer."

"'Living with cancer?'" she says when her oncologist uses this phrase. "What, I've lent out rooms? I'm just supposed to think it's a particularly sloppy roommate? It leaves its clothes everywhere, its dishes mound up in the sink, it leaves its towels on the bathroom floor and clots of hair in the drain, and when I say, 'This is not working out,' my cancer roommate gets to say, 'Screw you, I'm staying'? That is *so* not right." Her oncologist and her nurses love her. So do you. She is going to kick cancer in the ass.

Later, when her hair falls out in clumps, she plays games with her kids, "Look, Mommy's shedding!" and the kids take turns plucking out her hair, creepily fascinated, until she says brightly, "That's enough!" and

416

you make love that night with her hair spider-webbing against the pillow and she's crying, and she says, "I'm going to be fucking bald." Note to self: this is NOT the time to say "That's okay. I'll pretend I'm Captain Kirk making it with a hot alien," as you do, which goes over a lot less well than you'd think. She's crying and laughing simultaneously, and then she says, "Honey, about this? Only one of us gets to be a comedian, and it's not you."

Better when she makes the jokes, such as when you are at the Courage Clinic for the first time, and she says, "Are you fucking kidding me? The Courage Clinic? Really? Who does their marketing? The same people who came up with Peacekeeper Missiles? Why don't they name it for what it really is? They should call it The Despair Clinic. The Terror Clinic. The Give Up All Hope All Ye Who Enter Here Clinic."

At the wig shop they also sell scarves and hats and books on healing and small stones with similar treacle faux-carved in them—*Hope, Health, A Journey of a Thousand Miles*, etc. Again she explodes. "They should have 'Help Me' stamped in them, and 'Unfucking Believable' and 'Go fuck yourself, Cancer.'" You make love that night after that first trip to the Courage Clinic, and it still bothers her. "What the hell were they thinking?" she says, and then she lowers her breasts to your face while she's riding you and she says, "So tell me, do I look sick to you?"

The next day she calls a friend who owns a salon. After hours, so there are no other clients, the friend supervises the shaving of both your heads because you are going sympathetically bald, too, and she takes particular glee when, to get her in the mood before her own head is shaved, the friend hands her the clippers and says, "Here, you do him," and she takes your hair down to its nubbins saying, "So how does it feel to have collaborated with the Germans, hmm?" And to her friend she says, "You know what's kind of cool about this? I'm essentially getting a chemo-Brazilian," because even though her own gorgeous, thick, chemically auburn hair is about to be shaved off, she is going to kick cancer in the ass.

* * *

How to make love to a cancer patient? For a long time you don't. You say, "If I'd have known we'd be having this little sex, I'd have asked you to marry me." Which is when you do.

And she says, "Okay, but I'm going to want a big fucking ring to remember you by when this doesn't work out."

And later, when she is missing her eyebrows, and she does indeed have a chemo Brazilian, and there is something like a Captain Kirk—alien monkey—love thing going on here because you're newly engaged and you tell her she's beautiful, she says, "Bullshit, but thank you for trying."

When you make love to a cancer patient in a chemo ward, you close the door and arrange yourselves carefully around the tubes going into her chest, and you cradle her head and you whisper in her ear, "I love you." There are creases in her now-papery forehead from the green polyester Green Bay Packers skull cap she's been wearing, and she's missing her eyelashes, and there are tears leaking out the sides of her eyes, or falling on your chest when she is on top of you, and she is beautiful, beautiful in the most elemental way one can be, and you say, "I love you," and she says, "Thank you."

When you make love to a cancer patient, they want to be loved for themselves, they want not to be pitied—the worst thing you could do is pity them—and they are afraid they are no longer themselves, that the cancer has taken over, and they worry that it's the cancer husk you are making love with. They worry you're making love to them not because you want to, but because you're afraid they need you to. They are no longer sure they are themselves, they are only their disease, and you are making love to them out of obligation, or memory. They are afraid you cannot look at them, and so they look away, or close their eyes. They do not want to come, they do not want to give themselves up, to feel something larger than themselves taking hold of them because something larger than themselves has already taken hold of them, and won't let go. So letting go is not to be trusted. Their bodies have let them down. The notion of pleasure suddenly seems strange to them. And so they are wary. Can they trust your wanting to be inside them, desiring them, commingling with them—and cancer makes three? Cancer always, always makes three. It washes away the feeling that they could possibly be desired,

418

which is why the most common words you hear after you make love with a cancer patient are "Thank you." And you feel awful when they say that.

How do you make love to a cancer patient? Much of the time you don't. There are times you want to run away screaming, and she knows this. "It must be hard," she says, "wanting to break up with me so you don't have to be here for this, but then you'd be the guy who broke up with the cancer patient, and that must suck. Gingrich, Edwards, and you. Yep, yep," she says, "it must suck to be you." You know what she is doing, picking fights and throwing this in your face—*Can you take it? Can you take it? Can you?*—because she only wants people around who'll be there through all of it, and also, she is trying to give you an out, being a bitch, because then she'll feel justified, dying alone, and she can curse you as well as God, though she doesn't say any of this. What she's really saying is, "It's going to be tough, babe, don't leave me. Please, don't leave me." You are scorched by her being right—you do, at various times, want to run away screaming. But what you say is, "I love you," and she says, "So, are we gonna fuck or are we gonna fight? I'd rather not fight." And it bothers you a little that it's stated as a negative—not that she'd like to make love, but rather that she'd rather not fight. So you say, "I'd rather not fight either." And she says, "Well, I'm too angry to fuck right now, so give me a minute." Then she pushes you backwards onto the bed and arranges herself on top of you and says, "There, better."

And later, when a work colleague who's been out of the loop asks, "Is this a new look?" and wonders why you are looking like the guy from *Breaking Bad*—you have a starter goatee to compensate for your shaved head—you say, "Charlotte has cancer," and watch his face try to recover. That you take a perverse pleasure in this—you have never liked this colleague, and saying "Charlotte has cancer" feels exactly like saying, "Fuck you!"—forces you to realize that this is deep shit territory you are in now, and you, too, are sinking.

And later, when you go to Jamaica—her Make-a-Wish trip only with booze and jerk chicken—after the chemo and before the radiation, when she is wearing sunglasses and a big straw hat at customs, and the officer says, "You don't look like your passport picture, miss, I'm going to have to ask you to lose the hat and the glasses," and she takes them off and stands there in her sun dress, proud and fierce, and the officer says, "Oh," and "I'm sorry"—that night you want to make love tenderly, but she is angry, and what she wants is to pound you and herself into oblivion, but you both know that's not what she wants pounded into oblivion.

More and more she makes love with a kind of ferocity. It is as if she is trying to fuck cancer to death, or maybe to outfuck death itself. But she is mistaken. You cannot fuck cancer to death. That is the conundrum— the thing is in her, it feeds on her, and it's so happy to be alive inside her it's going to keep growing until it kills her. Death comes on little cat feet—like fog—and it sits at the end of the bed, licking its paws and cleaning its whiskers, patiently waiting for you to finish.

And always she says, in the midst of riding you, her breasts, beautiful, lowered to your face, brushing against your cheek—"Do I *look* sick to you? Do I look *sick* to you? Do *I* look *sick* to *you?*"

Note to self: Later, when her hair comes back, and it's like peach fuzz, call it that when she asks you to touch it, and resist the urge to say, "It's like petting a dog's groin," unless you want to be swiftly kneed in yours. Remember, there is only one comedian when making love with a cancer patient, and it is not you.

It's only later, after the chemo and radiation have failed, and her oncologist stops talking in specifics—*It's shrunk 9 millimeters, its overall mass is down 17 millimeters*—and he starts talking in generalities—*There's been some growth. We think it's spread to your omentum membrane, but we think we might be able to contain it with more chemo*—that the love-making turns tender again.

But even then misunderstandings abound: You are extra careful because you really are worried that you're going to hurt her. You worry she will feel sore later, and whether she gets anything out of it at all. You worry that this thing has taken her over now, and isn't a cock in-

420

side her just one more invasive species, like those mussels crowding out everything else living in Lake Michigan? Soreness, dryness, discomfort—those are the physical worries. She names the other one. "How can you possibly find me attractive right now?" she asks. You understand—she's bald, there are tubes in her, ports for putting drugs in and draining things away. She's bloated here, skinny there. She asks, "Isn't it like making love to that malnourished kid in those 'you can donate now or you can turn the page' ads that used to make you feel guilty when you did turn the page?" You say, "No, I love you," and she says, "Babe," and then she's softly singing, a little off-key, *If you feel like giving me a lifetime of devotion*, but she breaks it off there.

It only works with her on top now, and you no longer sleep together. It's too painful for her to have you in her bed. Still, she says, "Make love to me, baby," and you do. You notice, though, that she has given up wanting foreplay, that time you spent happily at the juncture of her thighs. She really is doing this now for you as a gift, just to get you to come. She is making a nod to memory, to what you used to be, and are still, or at least are trying to be. It's not much, but it's something.

You do not sleep much, and neither does she, but you no longer are sleepless together. You're in the spare room and you get one of those baby monitors, and the sound of her glucose pump goes all night. It's like an asthmatic old man wheezing, the suck of the air in and letting it out. Soon enough it will be her making that sound, and you wonder, with each pause at the end of the intake suck, and then the release, if it's the machine doing that or if it's her.

And later, after her brain surgery because it's spread there, too, and the radiation that follows that, and the ascites that causes her belly to swell like a late term pregnancy, which gets catheterized so it can be drained daily—three liters, four liters, where is all this goddamn fluid coming from? you wonder as you empty the bags into the toilet—when she asks, "Wanna make love?" you say, "Can we just cuddle?" And she says in a tiny voice, her grin exhausted, "Why, do I look sick to you?"
    Then she sees the look in your face.

"You're really afraid you're going to hurt me, aren't you?" she says, and you say, 'Yes." And when the tears start to your eyes, she says, "Good, I was waiting for that."

"I won't break," she says, but instead of climbing on top of you, she lays next to you, her thumb rubbing the spot between your thumb and your forefinger. And that's when it hits you that you will never make love with her again and that this is only the smallest of your losses.

Her tenderness tears you in two.

This is how you make love to a cancer patient:

You pull her towards you as closely as you can and your thumb plays over each of her knuckles and you say, "I love you."

You say, "I love you."

You say, "I love you."

She says, "I know."

Nominated by Bellevue Literary Review

FIELD THEORIES

by SAMIYA BASHIR

from BETTERING AMERICAN POETRY

sold for poker chips
left cold left thawed left

bent into the yawp
ass up

let be
let air

bones
unknowns

ash
everywhere

curved space
dark—breath

dark—breath
dark—what?

sold for bluff on blind
left choked

left down
left bent

left passed
catch

How a body grabs a body.
Hungry. Even Jesus let

his bakers dozen fend
for themselves once

they got to snipping and
sipping too comfortably.

According to the literature.
Jesus. That first bite.

Its sharp. Its ache.
Its nectar. We'll

build a fort and fill it
with maple trees gone gaudy

with cobalt wishing stones.
We'll crawl inside and imagine

how maybe we used to laugh.
Fuck Orpheus and fuck them

for loving him harder for not
loving who we love when

we're the ones down here
rotting in hell. Huh? Music?

Anyone ever really heard us sing?
Let's move this: anyone ever asked?

Even so we sing all day. Even so we pass
our days whatever ways we can—

We know some folk don't listen.
Just look. And trace. Look:

What is a thing of beauty
if not us?

Bear where a clothespin clips a nose
and breath is held until—

Bear it then keep walking
toward light. Right? Wait—

We'll ask them to name something
blue and maybe they'll say:

popsicle tongue
broken finger

black eye. Easy enough
to say You. Don't.

What does anyone out here know
of us? How

our tar-stained wings hide what
ergot saddles we ride. How

between our teeth we mash
the fur of maritime beasts. Still

some folk never thanks us
to manifest their pleas. Yet

what is a thing of beauty
if not us? Repeat:

dark—breath
dark—breath

dark—things we do as
we turn slowly blue:

lead laser dots through another
chalk outline; pick up today's

halloween dress; cry
at commercials; obey; pay

defense department rates
for a sandwich; unremember

memorable jingles; jaw
sandwiches that taste just like

sandwiches; figure we can't
expect much more than that; don't.

Some slaves only get free enough
to crouch in Kentucky foxholes

with Cincinnati just over
one last swift river.

Our own acrid smell finally
wakes us. Eras. Halfwoke

slowroll through the wet spot.
Panic. Floor. Hard. Years.

The worst kiddie-porn
we'll never say we see.

Bottles. Cans. Pizza box
hotels. Crusty burrito

bits. Razor blades.
Mirror shards. Cat puke.

Half a joint. Shuffled match.
Broken brick. Bloody steps.

Lit joint. Burnt fingers. Better.
Wash the hair/don't wash the hair.

Wash the hair/don't wash the hair.
Wash the hair/don't wash the hair.

Own no time. Late as fuck. Strip
the bed. Consider the stain. Don't.

The murk we blow to cool.
The slop and bang we curse.

The hum of incandescence.
The lip burns we nurse.

The best skin of our lives.
The best skins of our lives.

What is a thing of beauty
if not us?

Repeat

Nominated by Bettering American Poetry,
D.A. Powell

HOW DO YOU
RAISE A BLACK CHILD?

by CORTNEY LAMAR CHARLESTON

from TELEPATHOLOGIES (SATURNALIA BOOKS)

From the dead. With pallbearers who are half as young
as their faces suggest and twice the oxen they should be.
Without a daddy at all, or with a daddy in prison, or at home,
or in a different home. With a mama. With a grandmama
if mama ain't around, maybe even if she is. In a house, or not.
In the hood. In the suburbs if you're smart or not afraid of white
fear or even if you are. Taking risks. Scratching lottery tickets.
Making big bets. On a basketball court. Inside a courtroom.
Poorly in the ever-pathological court of opinion. On faith. Like
a prayer from the belly of a whale. In church on Sunday morning,
on Monday, Tuesday and every other. Before school and after.
In a school you hope doesn't fail. In a school of thought named
for Frederick Douglass. Old school or not at all. With hip-hop or
without. At least with a little Curtis Mayfield, some Motown,
sounds by Sam Cooke. Eating that good down-home cooking.
Putting some wood to their behind. With a switch. With a belt
to keep their pants high. Not high all the time. On all-time highs
at all times until they learn not to feel and think so lowly of
their aims. To be six feet tall and not under. With a little elbow
grease and some duct tape. Sweating bullets. On a short leash.
Away from the big boys on the block. Away from the boys in blue.
Without the frill of innocence. From the dead, again. Like a flag.

Nominated by Saturnalia Books

PATHETIC FALLACY

by EMILIA PHILLIPS

from POEM-A-DAY

the sap that I am springtime
        makes me want to reread Virgil's

Georgics while eating *cacio*
        e pepe with fresh-shelled

peas this morning over coffee I
        watched a video of spinach

leaves washed of their cellular
        information and bathed in stem

cells until they became miniature
        hearts vascular hopes capable

of want to roll down a hill
        of clover to cold-spoon chrysanthemum

gelato or to stop whenever
        their phones autocorrect *gps*

to *god* the sublime is a suspension
        of disbelief the earth has gotten

sentimental this late in the game
        with its smells of gasoline

rosemary and woodsmoke the Rorschach
        of vitiligo on my eyes mouth

and throat the ongoing
        argument between self

and selfhood the recognition
        of the storm the howling

wind I wish I could scream
        into someone else's rain

Nominated by Poem-A-Day,
Diane Seuss,
Lee Upton,
David Wojahn

QUARRY

by MELISSA STEIN

from KNOW ME HERE (WORDTEMPLE PRESS)

A girl is swimming naked
in dark water. She doesn't see herself
as graceful but the water tells otherwise,
the way it loosens and strikes
and burnishes. Exposed
ledges, rock's crumble on surfaces
and the surface of the water broken
by her body, marine and white.
There is also a freckled boy
contained in his body's wish
to outstrip but for now
mere stripling, too slight
for the shoulders and limbs
that pummel and thrash
to make himself bigger.
The girl and boy
pinwheel in the water
and do not touch
but are connected
by invisible currents
their bodies manufacture.
Her eyes are closed
but she knows where he is,
diving from the turtle rock
a little clumsily, the muscles

like lozenges
in his thin legs twitching
as they push off.
Days of this. Weeks.
Then, detaching itself from
sun, water, blasted rock
another body comes,
a grown man, all smiles
and cigarettes
and offering. I still dream
that the red-haired boy held my head
under water
to spare me what the man did.

Nominated by WordTemple Press,

Idris Anderson,

Robert Thomas

PEDAL, PEDAL, PEDAL

by HEATHER SELLERS

from THE SUN

On a bike I have wings and a kingdom. On a bike I'm a taller, stronger, wiser version of myself—the person I wish to be on land. It's always been this way.

When I was three or four years old, and the neighbors' big dog, Smackey, came waddling across the street to try to lick me, I was safe if I was on my trike: I could ride circles around her. If Smackey came over and I wasn't on my trike, I had to go back inside, where my strange, bone-thin mother did not let anyone come near her, or make noise, or turn on the lights. Sometimes she was lying on top of her bedspread, looking like a wax figure. Other times I found her hiding in her closet.

On my trike I had no mother. I was above the dog, above the earth, above myself.

At the age of five I received a red bike with bright-white training wheels and red and white plastic streamers on the handlebar grips. I rode in figure eights on our shiny black driveway: a girl in a blue cotton dress, a girl with skinned elbows, a girl who traveled through life above the dog, above the earth, above herself. No one told her to keep pedaling, but every day she did.

When I turned ten, I was given a purple bike with a white banana seat. It was a fine ride for a couple of years, until it was stolen. By then my mother had gotten worse. She didn't want me to leave the house or talk to anyone—it was too dangerous.

My mother had a dusty, old green bicycle that she never rode. It seemed impossibly uncool and matronly to me, and I didn't think to touch it, much less ride it, until one bikeless day I was out in the garage and saw her bike as if for the first time. Suddenly it seemed like a fabulous *tank* of a bike. It had a wire-basket, a bell, and a cursive S— for Schwinn—on the green-and-white vinyl seat. I pretended the S was for Sellers, and I named her Greenie and rode her as much as possible.

By the time I was fourteen, I was pedaling Greenie all over downtown Orlando, Florida—to baby-sitting and lawn-mowing jobs, to the grocery store, to the pool—often in a sundress with a towel and my bathing suit and a bike lock in the basket. I caught myself smiling as I rode.

I stood on the pedals, strong and tan and thin, surveying my kingdom, the most all-seeing girl in town. What harm could come to me? My long ponytail flew behind me like a windsock. I could ride sidesaddle. I even worked out a way to ride on my stomach, one hand cranking the pedal, the other on the handlebars.

For a lonely girl in an American city, a bike is a horse longing to be ridden. My relationship with Greenie was the deepest and happiest of my life to that point.

You're taller on a bike, and faster, and the air is cooler, because riding creates a breeze—a blessing in Florida summers. On a bike the world seems made just for you. The tires carry on a conversation with the road, and you are both a part of it and listening to it all at once.

In high school I was still riding that old green bike everywhere—I had no car—when my mother told me I couldn't borrow it without permission. She said primly, *Please ask first if you want to use my bicycle.*

On principle I refused to ask her permission to borrow anything— her cashmere sweater, her perfume, her jeweled evening bag. So I definitely would not ask to borrow that bike, *my* bike. I felt angry and humiliated that she had even suggested it.

One evening I brought Greenie right into the foyer of our house. I did this to irritate my mother, and it worked. She said, *I don't appre-*

ciate this funny business. I said whatever I usually said to her, and she replied, *You can't talk to me that way.* She was wrong. Straddling Greenie in the small foyer, my hands on the handlebars, I *could* talk to her that way. I might as well have had a fighter jet between my legs.

My mother's fear of people contributed to my shyness. I could not figure out how to interact socially in a light, carefree way: not at school, not at the restaurant where I hostessed, and not at Disney World, where I ran a cash register. I was often mute, unable to get my words to move out of me and into the world.

Whenever I went for a ride, though, I breathed easy, because of the way a bike moves through space: fast, quiet, smooth, each moment unfurling into the next. I could sing and often did: songs from *The Sound of Music, Man of La Mancha, West Side Story.* When I was on my bike, I could not only envision a happy, outgoing future self; I *was* her. The true me was the girl I was on the bike, and the other me was like a girl under the spell of a horrid witch in a fairy tale.

In the fall after my high-school graduation, against my mother's strict orders and with the help of a guidance counselor's letter and my savings, I managed to go to Florida State University in Tallahassee, a five-hour drive from Orlando. I'd wanted desperately to get into a better school, preferably one farther away from my mother, but I felt lucky to be leaving town at all. At college I'd been expecting to find wise professors, studious young people, and a new intellectual life waiting for me to step into it. Instead the campus was inhabited by heavily made-up girls with jewelry and sandals, and smug-faced boys in chinos and polo shirts—perfectly groomed, confident, and involved in one long conversation that I couldn't join. I walked around the campus in a daze, unable to fit a single syllable into their flow of words.

I got a black Schwinn road bike that I kept next to my bed in my dorm—because I did not want it to get rained on—and instead of going to parties on Friday and Saturday nights, I went riding up and down hills. Orlando is completely flat, so the gently rolling terrain of Tallahassee was like the Alps to me. Somehow it was the landscape and not the beautiful campus or the textbooks or even the library that made me feel smarter than I had been in Orlando. On my bike I could fly through the clusters of other students. I was free.

When I told my mother over winter break that I was returning to the university for the spring semester, she said she had to end our relationship; I caused her too much concern. She stopped taking my calls.

I biked along country roads all over Leon County: Wakulla Highway, Old Miccosukee, Thomasville Road. I never saw another cyclist—not one—but there was a lot to swerve around: snakes, potholes, glass, sand, sticks, rocks, car parts, and dead possums, squirrels, raccoons, armadillos, birds, and frogs. On Crawfordville Highway a man in a pickup truck yelled, *I shore wish my face was your bicycle seat!* I never cycled on that road again. Other guys threw cans, bottles, or bags of fast-food trash at me. Teenagers hung from car windows and screamed. Women honked, swerved, and yelled, *Get on the sidewalk, girl!* But sidewalks were for baby strollers and pedestrians. I put my head down and kept pedaling.

On the bike was the only time I thought I was beautiful: sleek black helmet, long black hair, dark sunglasses, red lipstick, tight shorts, white tank top, black sneakers. I was strong and fast, and I could ride for hours. I felt like a bird. But in the rest of my life I continued to feel awkward and out of place. I went on a date to a restaurant and couldn't think of a single thing to say. I went out to a bar with a construction worker who was helping build the university's new business building. I had no idea how to act.

I preferred to ride bikes on dates: no talking. I once kissed a boy while we sped along, and it was so much fun, we did it again and again. We held hands on our bikes. We tied a rope around my waist and his and rode single file—do not ask me why. We rode in the rain and in the dark. We rode to swimming holes. I raced a college-basketball star, turning my head back to watch him watch me. That boy would come by my dorm and ride slow circles outside my window until I'd carry my bike outside, get on, and go.

And then there was Derry at the bike shop: gray apron and blue eyes and straw-colored hair pulled back in a ponytail. Derry rode for the Alfa Romeo cycling team. And now here he was holding my bike in one hand and grinning at me.

Hi.

Hi.

In the bike shop I was not my mother's daughter. I found my words. I was talking, almost chatting, with a boy. He asked if I wanted to ride with him sometime, and I said sure.

When would be good for you? he asked.

How about now? I said, shocked and thrilled and more than a little nervous that I could be so bold.

I can't say I learned how to love because of bicycles, but I learned something about the geometry of love. The feeling of being in his arms, of making dinner together or going dancing, was similar to what I felt on my bike: a kind of light but forceful movement into the future. Being *with* made me better than I was alone.

In 1995 I finished my PhD in English, got my hair cut into a bob, bought pumps and pantyhose, and moved to San Antonio, Texas. I left Derry and the black bike behind in Tallahassee, along with my long hair and flip-flops and other markers of my youth.

I never saw a cyclist in Texas, where I lived for three years. When my teaching career took me to Michigan, my first purchase was a hybrid Giant bike that I named Blackie, because I thought the paint was black, though it turned out to be dark blue.

The college where I taught was downhill from my house, and I coasted to work, feeling young and effective. I wore teacherly dresses and perfected a rolling dismount. I kept Blackie in my office, and at the end of the day I would pump my way home uphill.

I married a strong, lean sweetheart of a man who ran every night after work. In college he'd run two miles in under nine minutes, and he could still run fast and far.

My husband refused to get on a bike because he feared he might hurt his knees or hips and adversely affect his running. So I took up running, too. He taught me to lean forward and stop bouncing up and down. He taught me where to position my hands, elbows, stomach, and shoulders, and how to approach a corner. We spent a lot of our time running, or talking about running, or getting ready to run, or recovering from running, or nursing running injuries. (That last part was mostly me.)

The week after the divorce was final, I showed up at the bike shop on Main Street, and there they were: the same sort of boys I remembered from Tallahassee, but far too young for me now. The tall, tattooed one stepped over an aging golden retriever—the shop in Tallahassee had had a golden retriever, too—while the others listened to edgy music on a radio beside the workbenches. An elfin chatterbox, blond bangs hanging over his blue eyes, set me up with a shining, new Bianchi and asked if I wanted to join the shop's riding group. Yes. Definitely.

I rode that night and discovered that, even in the raw grief after the divorce, I could still find happiness on my bike.

That winter I trained indoors at the bike shop, and when May came around, I began riding during the week with a group of women. My depression lifted, and I spoke freely again: *You're getting so strong. You're a good rider. Let's do the Blueberry Fest ride together.* We wore matching jerseys and shouted and laughed and waited at stop signs for the older women in the group—Doris was in her seventies; Alice, eighty—to catch up. Those were some of the happiest hours of my life, tearing down the long, straight country roads in western Michigan; past corn fields, orchards, farms, and lakes; six or seven or eight women talking in one glorious sentence about nothing. We didn't discuss illness, debt, or work. I didn't even know what most of the women did during the day. Like children, we were free from the tyranny of the house, the job, the burden of being. You're always a kid on a bike.

I still often rode with the bike-shop boys on Monday nights and Saturday mornings, trying to stand on the pedals at stoplights like they did, never putting a foot down to touch the pavement. We were above the pavement, lords of the air. We took turns being at the front of the pack. When the lead cyclist hit his hip with his hand and slid out of the line, the person behind him took his place. The idea was for the pack to constantly rotate leaders; when you got to the front, you pedaled for a while, then dropped off the side and let the pack pass you until you were in the rear again. So the line was really a loop, always moving counterclockwise in a circle. It felt like we were doing ballet on a roadway.

In my turn at the front I worked hard to keep my speed at exactly twenty-two miles per hour. Whenever we saw a green county road sign, the boys would challenge each other to impromptu races to the next sign. Sometimes I'd start to speed up when there was no sign, just to watch all of them leap forward like grasshoppers.

The lead cyclist warned the rest about approaching hazards, which we couldn't see because the pack was so tight. He yelled, *Hole up.*

Branches up. Wood up. Water up. Sand up. Rocks up. Walker up. Debris up. And once, *Mattress up.* And we yelled to the riders behind us. The last in line yelled, *Car back, car back, car back.*

At each intersection, when it was safe to cross, the person in front would shout, *Clear.* And, as in a game of telephone, the *clears* traveled back.

Cars sometimes came so close to me I could smell the passengers' cigarettes and hamburgers.

I rode fifty miles, seventy miles, a hundred miles. I tried to keep exact count, but I always lost track. There were those in the group who insisted on reaching a precise number and would pedal in a circle in the bike-store parking lot at the end of the ride to do it. "Mile whores," they were called. I didn't care exactly how many miles I went.

Viva Italia! the boys shouted when I pedaled hard to pass them or when I peeled off toward home at dusk, my dark hair flying behind me—everything behind me.

Viva! I shouted into the night. *Viva!*

Riding in a pack, you have to stay together and move as one. This group movement activated some deep cellular sense of belonging in me. I became a fish with a dozen other fish forming one big, safe school. You can cycle faster and farther with others than on your own. The talking and energy and laughter carry you along. You're fueled by joy itself.

Before joining the group rides, I'd hated and avoided groups. Even departmental meetings at work were hard for me. I never felt I was going with the flow, working toward a common purpose. After cycling with the friendly women and the bike-shop boys—learning the exquisite timing required to keep a steady distance from the riders in front, in back, and next to me—I became more at ease with people on land. Once, at a Tuesday department meeting, having ridden forty miles with a group the night before, I cracked a joke, and every one of my colleagues laughed. I was as surprised as they were.

One evening in late summer three friends and I rode down to Saugatuck and back. Afterward we chatted for a bit in my driveway, straddling our bikes. The sky was a dusky blue-gray, the trees a darkening green. As I was chattering away, I wondered how long it had been since I'd struggled to find my words. Seated on my aluminum horse, with my fellow riders on their steeds, I felt as though I'd traveled across the world to reach this point. And, in a way, I had.

When I moved back to Florida a few years ago, it was to St. Petersburg, a city with bike lanes and bike trails and bike shops and the largest cycling organization in the state. We have a coffee shop called The Bikery, where you can take your bike inside with you and see famous bicycles mounted on the walls, including one ridden by U.S. Olympian John Sinibaldi in the 1930s. Like me, he would only ride Italian.

I ride the Pink Streets neighborhood (just what it sounds like) along the glittering bay. The great Olympian's daughter-in-law, Lenore, shows me the way. I ride under the palms and live oaks and the blistering sun, and I wonder whatever happened to Greenie, my mother's old Schwinn. I look for a similar bike on eBay and find just the saddle, with its white cursive *S*, selling for eighty-five dollars.

In this new life I once again have wings and a kingdom. I know how to make friends now. It's still not easy, but is it for anyone? I plan to see at least two friends a week; a walk with Jennifer, drinks with Debbie, a ride with Lenore or Katherine or Bob or Jim or Ezra. "Heather," my friend Helen says one day, "you could make friends with a doorknob."

On Saturday mornings I ride in a group. My old Bianchi is still fast. We form a tight pack, like geese in formation. It takes concentration to override your desire for safety and space. *Close the gap!* Wendy keeps yelling at me. *Get up on her wheel.* I don't know these riders well. I can't read their micro movements. The wind gusts coming off the bay are fearsome.

When someone in the pack isn't pedaling but coasting, you hear a clicking, a *chicka-chicka-chicka* sound that makes the experienced riders anxious. *Pedal, pedal, pedal!* someone will always shout. You can't coast in the pocket. You want to—it's so cozy and easy to be carried along—but it's dangerous: if one person slows down, even by a hair, the pack begins to break apart. You have to keep pedaling fast, just inches from all that metal and flesh and bone.

Pedal, pedal, pedal.

On land I have fallen so many times. On my bike I have not fallen—not ever, not once.

Nominated by The Sun,
Krista Bremer

KRA-DIN

by EMMANUEL OPPONG-YEBOAH

from KWELI JOURNAL

i. okra (soul)

I pray my dead speak to me / / and my dead stay silent
I pray my dead speak to me / / and my dead say "no"
I pray my dead speak to me / / and my dead say _____

which I don't hear / / in a foreign language
which is to say / / my own

I pray my dead speak to me / / and my dead grapple at my throat
drag me to the river / / lay me as a boat

I pray my dead to speak to me / / and my dead clap back
my dead speak / / and all my language ruins me

my dead speak / / and I become a hole
my dead speak / / what parts of you
have you lost / / that you now seek our forgiveness

what anchorage / / have you found
that breaks your back towards home?

my dead / / show me a man / / holding his head in his hands / / say
after a man has his head cut off he no longer fears anything

my dead / / show me / /a man / / hanging by his neck / / say
all different forms of death / / are death

my dead / / speak / / and all their bubbles froth my mouth
call me towards / / my one true name

my dead / / show me a tortoise / / holding a baby tortoise in its
    mouth
my dead / / show me a bird / / with head turned looking backwards

I show my dead a canoe / / I beat me as a drum
I am learning let me succeed / / I am learning let me succeed

ii. sunsum (spirit)

like when you are going, like a night, shadow, it's sunsum. but also
spirit, back home, when we say sunsum bono. we mean a bad spirit,
when we say sunsum papa we mean all that glimmers in the night
when the moon looks into the face of a brackish pool.

iii. mogya (blood)

my brother, my mother, her mother before then. bone to my bone.
an endless array of ashes. who comes back from billows to stacks of
black smoke? my grandfather, a cathedral humbled to the ground
and named holy. this much I know. someone once knew this name
and knew this blood, clinging. eager to the skin. a betrothal. for lambs
that did not know slaughter. or did. and let sheers through their skin
in the name of survival. akata fuo. the name for all our taken. my
mother's hands before my eyes. kata wo nei—

> son, you come from a place called love
> all our people are held in your name

> a king once split himself from his blood mirror
> loved his people more than his throne

> it's said, an entire sea of peoples pulled before a full moon
> it's said, the waves puddled and now each one carries their
>   names

442

son, you come from what remains of them
our people braved water and discovered flame

a dog ran through our village carrying a torch in its mouth
we took the torch's flame and named it—motive.

Nominated by Kweli Journal

BLUE COMING

by THYLIAS MOSS

from ABSTRACT MAGAZINE TV

Poetry is connected to the body,

part of my fingertips, just as blue as anything
that ever was or will be blue—

—blue that dye aspires to, *true blue*
denied to any sapphire, Logan sapphire included, even

if she wears some
on those blue fingers, blue spreads, consumes her

as if she hatched from *an Araucana egg:*

SHE IS BLUE, fingers, bluest hands ever, Tunisian blue. Djerban
blue hands, shoulders, breasts, every
nook and cranny blue, big bad wolf says: *how blue you are*!
The better to blue you. . . .

She, so blue today, visits
Offices of the *National Enquirer* to report
on this surging of blue epidemic, Blue
bottle fly bluer than any sound buzzing, fly buzzing
as blue as it can, making the Blues, making

The Blues mean something very different—such music from
beating of wings, some of what has spread blue
throughout her bluing body,

444

blue buzz

even layers of atmosphere: *blue buzz*: name
of a new Crayola crayon and marker, manufactured
from her fingertips
Blue Buzz Blood group
She bleeds an orgasmic paint set. She bleeds
a blue layer
her lover's face becoming
blue she's dreaming of again, blue as his face
That defines blue for
her blue orgasm, so much blue everywhere
world become
blue for her—story of this massive bluing
—true story on the cover
of papers—turning blue once in her atmosphere

Blue static
Blue stuttering

Blue hands

Blue—*Code Blue*—
coming together, what a mighty tincture,
—not exactly at the same time, but coming, connected
to coming
Her fingertips writing a

Blue coming.

Nominated by Abstract Magazine TV

CODESWITCH DECOMPOSING INTO LIL WAYNE LYRIC

by JULIAN RANDALL

from NINTH LETTER

After Danez Smith

<u>Lord Please Forgive Me for My Brash Delivery</u>
A face is for other people's benefit, a brochure gospel
undone by a mouth, I am the most marketable sin since 2004.
A smile that yields only bones, a mouth slick with restraint.
I am a good filament, a bright obedient electric. I speak,
and sometimes am found.

<u>Lord Please Forgive Me for My Brash</u>
body and especially my mouth, for-
give me my scholarships, for-
give me my name brand ambition, for-
give me my tattered skin on my G-Unit sneakers
how easy I drenched all the photographs

<u>Lord Please Forgive Me</u>
my jagged epiphanies

                                        my tarnished
jaw gleaming w/excess & all
                                        my un-flayed dark

<u>Lord Please</u>
y'all knew I was a storm when you Found me
once a white boy asked me for a Skin-Colored Marker

I say Whose skin? and stare until he buss out cryin'
Imma flood   waiting to happen   been like this since '99

<u>Lord</u>

You know

      I'mma make it rain

I'm da hurricane son

Nominated by Ninth Letter,
Aimee Nezhukumatathil

TRANSITION: THE RENAMING OF HOPE

by MOLLY COONEY

from THE GEORGIA REVIEW

I will miss *Anne,* with the well-placed *e* and easy shape. Steep climb, perfect point, and the slide into the runout of three short, round letters. The way the letters smooth across the page in a tiny creek of repeat, *nn,* and slip into silence. *Anne.* I will miss the way her name sighs. *Anne.* It's quite ordinary, really, the taper into nothing and the beauty of that sweep.

I will miss the way Anne fits with Molly and Ellis. *I'm Molly, and this is my partner Anne and my kid Ellis.* Anne doesn't say her name, unless she's standing in front of an extended hand, forced to own something. But I say it, like a mantra sometimes, a reminder of where my feet stand. *Molly, Anne, and Ellis.* A reminder of where her toes are headed. She doesn't even know her own name yet.

I will miss the voice of a decade of whispers, of vocal cords still short and lithe. The voice that hides behind compression shirts and silence and my willingness to speak, that presses down and adjusts its register, wishing for longer, thicker cords pushing sounds to a depth her small voice can only imagine now.

I hope she lets me record *I love you* before I have to let her voice go.

Anne and I have been discussing transition for years: her genderqueer childhood, boy clothes and bullying, harassment and fear, bras and binding and decades of depression. Forty years she's been dreaming of this, creeping infinitesimally closer to himself. Finally Anne is shedding the *she* and the trappings of that pronoun and walking away from her name

448

toward the open empty of trans, whatever that shift will mean for her. For me. For our family. She to He, maybe T. No matter. I will miss Anne—parts of her anyway.

Anne wants big biceps and broad shoulders, her hips shaved straight. She wants a new voice, and a new name that fits the way she feels. She wants confidence and safety. She wants height she cannot have.

"I'll be a short guy," Anne said one winter day, a half-smile deepening her dimple. "It'll give me away."

We were flipping through pants hangers in the men's section at Savers thrift store in Midtown Minneapolis because Anne needed dress clothes for a work conference. Lots of decade-old khakis, pleated, with 34″ inseam. She's 5′ 5″ and will walk on those hems. Anne fiddled with her hair, cut boy-short in back and rumpled on top, her blue eyes scanning hopefully for the right hanger.

"Let's cruise over and check out the boys' section," I said, pulling her in for a hug.

"I'm a shrimp," she whispered to my chest.

Turns out, one of the best places for Anne to buy clothes is The Children's Place. But it's hard to stand with authority and present a paper at the American Association of Museums conference on developing a standardized lexicon of culturally sensitive ethnographic collections when you're wearing the same pinstriped pants as the teenager checking badges at the door.

Testosterone can't grow a femur, can't lengthen the tibia and fibula like a drawbridge rising. Even weekly injections have a limit. But T will rearrange her face, redistribute fat to thicken her forehead and broaden her jaw line. I imagine tiny globs tumbling over each other, connecting, combining, and redividing on the slow migration to their new home. Fat slips from hips and thighs. Voice drops. Skin toughens. Body hair grows thicker on every surface, face becomes coarse with the slow emergence of stubble. Many of these changes are permanent, but some last only as long as the hormone remains in the blood. Most of them happen so slowly—wisps of whiskers can take years to show up—but the voice plunge happens in the first few months, and once it deepens, can't be reversed.

Not all transpeople take hormones or have surgery. Many linger somewhere in the middle between male and female, in just the place Anne has stood her whole life, facing the world in a genderqueer body. Living this ambiguity is sometimes by choice and sometimes by circumstance because it's expensive to go to the doctor and fill prescriptions, and it costs thousands to go under the knife. Anne doesn't (yet) take testosterone and hasn't made any medical transitions. Likely she will. Or maybe not. We're saving money, just in case. But those choices don't determine whether or not Anne is trans, they just let other people recognize her intentions when she walks down the street. A beard helps.

Testosterone regulates hair growth patterns and the maternal line decides who goes bald, so, will Anne's sandy brown tousle slowly recede off her newly prominent forehead? Maybe. Anne's dad and brother are bald. Her maternal grandfather, too. No one's sure what happens when T visits and stays a good long while in a body already sculpted by estrogen. No one can say exactly which hereditary patterns and family traits translate when someone so deep into life moves from female to male. FTM. No one really knows just yet. Ellis will grow up knowing.

Anne first started telling people she was trans during the summer I was pregnant with Ellis, but only her parents and closest friends. I was proud of her and hoped she'd tell others, get it out of the way before our lives grew infinitely more complicated by a newborn. But that's not Anne's way. She takes quiet, measured steps. It took her nearly two years after Ellis's birth to come out to a few more people, to hedge closer to a new name and even consider testosterone.

Ellis was born on 9 September 2012 in the barely morning hours, covered in meconium and shouting from his very first breaths. With his fair skin and light hair, his giant cheeks and blue eyes, his deep right-cheek dimple, he looked like Anne from the second he came out.

The OB glanced at Anne: "If I didn't just deliver this guy, I'd guess he came from you."

In his first couple years of life, Ellis grew to look more and more like Anne. Yes, he had my eyes and chin, but mostly he looked like Anne. Not just his features and skin; the resemblance was more nuanced than that. Small gestures and expressions: something in the pucker of his lips, and the way he tucked his thumb between his ring finger and middle finger; the way his thick feet flexed and wiggled, his toes actually able to grasp things; the way he smiled so big his eyes disappeared in folds of joy.

"Seriously, Anne," the pediatrician said at one of Ellis's check-ups. "He looks like you. I mean, just like you."

"It's just because I look more like a baby," Anne said, scrunching her nose.

And she did a little bit, or youthful anyway, with sweet soft cheeks, gentle blue eyes, and a dimple that wouldn't quit. Her plaid button-ups and Levi's 285 jeans. Broad shoulders, strong legs, and sturdy feet. She stood grounded in her brown hikers and walked with solid steps, even if she didn't always feel that confidence. When I walked next to Anne, my body shaped from years of wilderness travel and softened by pregnancy, dark hair clipped short in back and angled past my cheekbones, wearing my black hoodie and striped scarf . . . well, we looked as though we belong together.

I can't remember the very first time Anne told me she wanted a new voice. It was before we had Ellis, but I can't place the moment specifically in the timeline of our decade together. I imagine a dramatic conversation in the canoe while we paddled the Canadian Quetico lakes for two weeks; I know we discussed it one darkening day on Agnes Lake while the thunderheads marched in on whitecaps and wind. But maybe those canoe conversations were more theoretical and not so personal. I can picture a conversation on the jungle trail in the Osa Peninsula after a twelve-hour hike to the river crossing where crocodiles lingered, but maybe that was when we talked about a friend's transition and his emerging voice. There was the conversation in our tent at the base of Mount Lemon and another in the kayak off Orcas Island. I can almost hear her voice.

I do remember the moment when Anne's desire for a new voice indelibly wrote itself into the pages of our story. It was deep winter in 2014 when Ellis was about sixteen months old and we were living in our century-old house in South Minneapolis. One night we were lying with the soft moon shining on our mattress, blankets tight, Anne nestled in the spoon of my hips.

"When I talk, everyone knows I'm a girl," she whispered. "I really need a lower voice."

My breath caught, my feet tingled. "Oh, boy."

"Exactly," she said. "I really want it to be deeper."

Ellis woke us the next day, clutching a book as big as he was. "Want to read with me?"

I squeezed Anne's sleepy hand, then scooped Ellis into bed. Sitting between us in his Darth Vader T-shirt and pink whale pants, a toilet paper roll for a bracelet, Ellis narrated the story, flipping pages as if he were reading.

Listening to that tiny voice, I couldn't fathom that someday it would drop and deepen, that he'd become a cracking-voiced teenager and then a deep-voiced man. Anne leaned over and whispered to me, "What will we do with a man-child?" I just couldn't imagine. But it wasn't hard for Anne to imagine, to anticipate the day her son's voice will drop lower than her own ever will, testosterone or not. She told me as much a couple weeks later.

We were eating pancakes at the breakfast table, Ellis poking strawberries onto his fingers, and Anne said, "When Ellis was born, I mean, that first night in the hospital, I stayed up all night watching him breathe."

I imagined Anne staring at the rise and fall of his tiny rib cage, "I didn't know"

"Staring at him, I kept thinking, *He's my kid. I get to watch him grow. My little boy.*" Anne paused. "Then it occurred to me. *I have a son? Really?*" I pictured Anne shaking her head a little as she reached out to touch his sleepy cheek.

Anne spoke softly, head bowed and eyes glancing at Ellis chattering away to his strawberry finger puppets. I wasn't exactly sure what she meant and I didn't ask, but I heard the nostalgia in her voice and realized that she was going to watch her son have the childhood she wished she'd had, or the childhood body anyway, and that to witness him grow up would be beautiful and painful and, perhaps, draped with moments of jealousy.

Ellis talked constantly from the moment he was born. Shouted, really. His newborn grunts became animated shrieks punctuated by flailing limbs and, at a freakishly young age, before he could even stand on his own, he started to speak—literally.

Anne and I would listen to his nonstop baby babbling all day and sometimes even at night when he cooed and giggled in his sleep. We'd look at each other across the dinner table, in the grocery store, on stroller walks, while Ellis was holding forth in a garble of sounds, and we'd laugh. I'd say, *What's going to happen when he can talk? When he has actual words?* Anne would smile and shake her head.

One July day when Ellis was ten months old we were hanging out in the backyard. I was sitting in the grass, stretching to get ready for a jog, and Ellis was lying in the hammock with Anne. Quiet breeze. Gentle sun. Suddenly Ellis pointed his chubby finger straight up into the branches of the giant maple and said, "Tree."

Anne looked at me, eyes wide, and silently mouthed, *Are you kidding me?*

"What did you say?" I whispered to Ellis, "Say it again, bubba."

There it was—*Tree.* He said it on an evening walk past a row of ash trees, reading a bedtime book, and looking out our bedroom window at the birch raising its peeling white trunk into the deep morning sky. *Tree. Tree. Tree.* And so we learned exactly what would happen when Ellis had more words: he would say them all the time, over and over again. His voice clear and bold, just the opposite of Anne's childhood experience.

As a kid, Anne could go days without talking. Silence at school was easy because the teachers knew her whip-smart brain and straight As, knew how her shy eyes trailed the ground, and how without much pressure at all Anne would cry. They let her be quiet. She helped the librarian reshelve books at lunch and left immediately after school. She didn't play sports or go to pep rallies or dances. In fact, any day she could find an excuse, Anne didn't go to school at all.

When she did go, she was harassed and bullied relentlessly. She didn't know how to get help because there was none—no support groups or safe spaces for gender nonconforming kids, or even the language to describe them. The school counselor told Anne not to cry because that made the bullies tease her more; that counselor essentially told twelve-year-old Anne the ridicule was her own fault.

At home she didn't have much room for her voice, either. The airspace was filled with two other voices: Anne's mother narrating everything she did and talking about her students or friends or the book she was reading about immigration while she served pizza and garlic bread; and Anne's brother, all-star on the football field, state champ on the wrestling mat, and student body president, telling story after story about high school as his pepperoni cooled. While Anne's mom and brother talked over one another, her dad shook too much salt on his food, winked at Anne, and turned to watch the birds at the feeder outside the dining room window. Anne picked at her food, rolling quiet on the curve of her tongue.

"Five days," she said. "Once I didn't say anything all week and no one noticed."

"What made them realize?"

"They didn't. I got too sad and asked my dad to pass the salt," she said. "He didn't hear me."

Anne's parents may not have acknowledged the silence at their dinner table, but maybe they always heard it and just didn't know what to say, because there were no words. No household term for *trans,* no

453

language to even imagine what their daughter was going through. And so their support was offered in muted gestures and quiet allowances. They let Anne buy clothes from the boys' section and have her hair cut boy-short starting in preschool. They bought her a dirt bike and a BB gun. Didn't push dolls or ruffles or Easy-Bake Ovens.

Her parents' quiet support was a kindness deeper than Anne could understand as a kid, but one she has grown to see with time and distance. And maybe it wasn't enough, hard to say, but Anne did know she was loved by them, even if they didn't know what words to offer.

Shyness was not all that silenced Anne throughout her childhood. She also didn't talk because her careful gender ambiguity crumbled with every syllable she spoke: the slight lift at the end of a sentence, the reach of her range, and the softness of the vowels betrayed her every time—her voice and her name forced her to be a girl. I can imagine the awkward interactions with a reluctant grade-school Anne.

What's your name? a grocery clerk or receptionist would ask.

Anne would whisper, if she spoke at all.

Can you say it again? I didn't quite hear you, a new neighbor might say.

Anne would stare at the ground, clutching her thumbs and shuffling her feet.

Did you say Ian? Silence. *Sam?*

Or sometimes it was Dan, or Ethan, or Evan. No one ever heard *Anne* in the swallowed syllables she spoke to her toes. No one could imagine that a girl named Anne lived in the short-haired, high-top-wearing, baggy-shirted body before them—not even Anne.

Even now, when she's an adult, it's hard for people to imagine that someone named Anne lives in her still genderqueer body—until she speaks. She can't sneak past her high voice. The apologies come after Anne has been sir'ed by someone: a store clerk, a flight attendant, a waiter. *I'm so sorry. Excuse me* They flutter their hands. *I mean, of course you're a woman. It was just a quick glance. I don't have my glasses on.* Often people bend in too close to her face: *I'm so, so sorry.* What they don't know is that the apology should really come after they refer to Anne as *she* or *ma'am.* What they don't notice is that when they say *he* or *sir,* Anne flushes with pride, even in the face of frantic hands. Someday Anne will leave that high pitch behind, exchange it for a coarser sound, and avoid the frazzled apologies.

Even if she takes hormones, Anne's voice will likely not register quite like a man's. When a testosterone-taking trans guy speaks, the voice is often a giveaway to the people who know to notice. Not my mom, though, or the bank teller or the barista. It's difficult to identify exactly what is different, but there is usually a quality to a voice forced lower with hormones, a certain roughness to the sounds as they elbow their way through newly thickened vocal cords, that is distinctly trans.

Anne and I know transfolks who never lost the scratch and croak of their transition voice, and some whose voices deepened and passed as male but were never smooth or pleasing to listen to. Anne worries those problems will happen to her, and they could. There's no way to prevent her voice from cracking or to anticipate what it will sound like in the end.

Anne brought this up one still-frozen March day, not long after the night she admitted wanting a deeper voice. We were walking from the grocery store to the car with eighteen-month-old Ellis humming and draped over Anne's back like a cape and my arms loaded with paper bags.

"Sweetie," she said, "I'll probably sound like a teenager at first. Sort of squashed and crackly."

I took a deep breath. "Then I'll be your sugar mama."

"Or it might be smooth as butter," she said, a coy smile. "You never know." The checkout guy had been trans. He'd smiled shyly while he fumbled our apples and yogurt into a bag. Seeing Anne, he knew he was both visible and safe, not a usual combo for a transperson to experience.

"But seriously," she sighed, scraping the icy windshield. "I'm worried it'll sound weird."

"It might," I said, shrugging. "No biggie." Then I shoved the groceries in the trunk and slipped behind the wheel, thinking, *Who cares? Either way, you'd be happier.*

Anne and Ellis tumbled into the backseat singing "The Bear Went over the Mountain." I sat quietly waiting for the car to heat up, considering my own question: *Who does care?*

Anne kept singing, "Grrr went the bear and roar went the cub," while she buckled Ellis into his car seat and tightened the shoulder straps. I thought again. *Maybe I do.* Anne's voice is the one that I'll hear every day for the rest of my life, the one that will whisper *I love you* late at night and *I'm here* when a fever spikes, that will shout, *Go, go, go!* at Ellis's soccer games and embarrassingly cheer *Bravo! Encore!* at his cello recitals. Hers is the voice that will grow old and raspy next to mine.

Sitting there in the warming car, I realized that it was *me* who cared. A lot. I wanted to scream, *No, I don't want your new voice. I don't want any of it.* But I glanced at Anne in the rearview mirror—her deep eyes holding the years of pain and silence, her fragile smile holding a thin line of hope, her hand holding Ellis's—and I stayed quiet.

"Ready?" I said. Then I put the car into gear and slipped into the icy flow of Lake Street traffic.

After that night, I began to wonder how scratchy Anne's voice might be, if it will still seem like hers, if it will still sound sexy to me. But if taking T means Anne will talk, will order pizza or call Ellis's doctor, will speak to the neighbor about the weather or to the coffee guy about the weekend, will tell Ellis stories or wake up excited to say even just one word, then the change will be worthwhile. If she's speaking she's growing, even if there is gravel in her voice.

Anne tiptoes toward hope on the rise and fall of every letter lilting off her tongue, because her transition depends not on hormones but on the words she shares with the world and those she swallows again.

One September evening, just after Ellis turns two, Anne and I are on a date, the kind that starts with therapy and ends with wine because that's the kind of time we get together these days. We are sitting on a restaurant patio eating curry, a twinkle of lights strung above us, a tall wooden fence separating us from rush of cars and busses on University Avenue. We are discussing parenting and groceries, top surgery and hormones, a new name.

"I want to have it figured out by my birthday," Anne says.

"Sounds realistic," I say, my mouth full. "What does 'figured out' mean?"

"Done. Cured," she smiles. "Gender puzzle solved."

I hold up nine fingers. September to June. A perfect gestation.

We drift to Ellis stories and weekend plans, but names simmer on the table between us, *Evan, Lewis, Maxwell?*

I pack the leftovers while Anne heads to the bathroom. She doesn't usually go to public restrooms alone. We go together, my clearly gendered body announcing us, because most women don't like genderqueer folks in the stall next to them or sharing sink space and paper towels. But we know this bathroom is single-stall and no one will harass Anne. That's how she survives each day—one safe pee at a time.

The tap of breeze on crisp sunset leaves. My purple striped scarf loose and long. The slant of sun on my plate. Anne emerges from the patio door, and as she walks toward me with strong steps on the cobblestones, I see him—really *see* the emerging him wearing Anne's blue gingham button-up. There he is in her jeans and hikers, stealing her stride with each footfall.

As she moves past tiny hanging lanterns and tables of laughter, I can feel her gentle face slide into a strong-jawed smile. Blink. I can touch her once-soft forearms through muscles and hair. Blink. I can smell his sharp sweat. My breath catches the sweet sigh of her name, *Anne,* and I watch him walk toward me, still tracing the shift of those shoulders I fell in love with a decade ago.

"What?" she whispers.

I smile, take his hand, and wonder at the tightness of the grip.

Most transmen on T have hands disproportionately small for their new bodies. They can grow muscle and shift fat with hormones and workouts, but the structure of the hands, the basic foundation of how the palm meets the fingers, stays constant. Their hands can muscle up, but they'll only be so long.

"I like my hands," Anne says, turning them over and back again, fingers stretched wide, veins wrapping tendons.

She doesn't like much about her body, but she believes in her tough hands—strong bone structure, square palm, fingers just the right density and agility to be equally skilled at labor and art. She can chop wood and lay brick with the same precision and grace that steady her hand to examine a thousand-year-old pot. When I watch Anne teach Ellis to trace with a crayon, tighten a screw, or hold a cricket, the quiet curve of her fingers cradling his, I hold my breath and hope that Anne's hands can carry her through transition, that they will still feel tough at the end of her someday-hairy arms. I hope they will still feel like hers when they belong to him. I hope they will still feel like mine.

There are layers and layers of learning how to re-gender yourself. It's not just new clothes and a new name. Not just wide stance and strong shoulders, nor just taking up space and talking loudly. For many transmen it's about how a guy props the door with his foot, that imperceptible difference in the kick of leg and tilt of hip. The tight nod hello. How a guy holds his toddler, no hip, arm crooked high. To teach yourself gender is to walk through the world as an artist, noticing details not meant to be noticed, watching each shift and sway and breath to find out how we codify and signify gender, and then to try on that skin day after day after day.

But re-gendering is also about a shifting wardrobe and a new configuration of letters to make a name. The clothes seem to be much easier to change, one shirt at a time, a new way of tucking or rolling, or not. Yes, it's heading to the men's or boys' section, but it's also about figuring out which stores carry extra-small button-up shirts and men's size 8 shoes. Not many, as it turns out. And it's also about discerning which styles accentuate shoulders and de-accentuate hips, a much trickier task. There is no manual, no checklist, no comprehensive website; the process is mostly about so many details that are learned along the way, observing people and listening to stories shared by other genderqueer and transpeople, and it's about so much patience.

When we met ten years ago, Anne still wore women's clothes. Not particularly girlie ones, but still. She had earrings, 16-gauge stretched, but earrings just the same. She wore Hanes-Her-Way and fumbled with clips on an underwire. The accumulation of women's clothes were lead on her shoulders and she walked slightly hunched over, offering only flashes of eye contact and a beautiful smile touched with sadness. But that's who I fell in love with, that complex and gentle person, bursting with compassion and patience, shy and open, solid, and living what felt to me a tender ambiguity. I fell in love with her as she was, chest and all.

Slowly Anne has shed this life, a decade of subtle shifts. Shirts to the thrift store. Ears stripped naked. Sideburns cut straight. Her shoulders lifted ever so slightly. Boxers and boy jeans. Tight sports bras to try to flatten her chest.

So many quiet changes.

Then, one spring a couple years before Ellis was born, Anne visited a friend in St. Louis and returned with a suitcase of thrift-store clothes and a whole new style. Her friend is a professor of masculinity studies and a dapper queer—a perfect companion for someone teetering on the edge of trans identity. She led Anne through the basics of Dressing Male 101.

A front pocket distracts people's eyes. One pocket. Not two.

Patterns, like plaid and gingham, mask bumps and bulges.

Shoulder detail—buttons, flaps, visible seams—draws attention and makes them look broader

Men roll sleeves three times and tuck their shirts.

When I went to pick up Anne at the airport, warm breeze drifting off the tarmac, I looked right past her, thinking she was a teenage boy. I actually drove the loop again before I spotted her. There, on the sunspeckled sidewalk, Anne began to shed her name and crawl away from the pronoun *she*. A painfully slow transition, but I could see it starting to happen, even if she couldn't say so yet. She had left for the trip in a baggy T-shirt and shorts, then returned in a plaid green button-up tucked into dark jeans and standing straighter than I'd ever seen, shoulders relaxed and hands quiet, looking at people walking by. Our eyes met, and I blushed.

"Oo-la-la," I said, slapping her butt as she loaded the suitcase.

She teased my hand away. "Too many people."

I pulled her in for a kiss, held her there a while, then whispered, "They're just jealous."

We got in the car, windows down as we merged onto the highway.

"What do you think?" Anne said.

"It's good," I said. "I like it."

And I meant it. Despite how it caves me to remember that significant shift, that emerging of the more masculine Anne, I thought she looked hot in her new boy clothes.

"Me too," she said, settling in to the blow of the wind, eyes closed.

Anne wore her new confidence as well as she wore her new style, and for a few months that carried her. But button-ups and rolled cuffs have their limitations, and the clothes still bulged slightly over her chest. She wanted to hide more. Stifling sports bras weren't enough, and Ace bandages would bruise her ribs and damage her lungs, so Anne turned to tight nylon compression shirts to flatten her chest. Years of binding have broken down her breast tissue, essentially pressing it back into the body, and for a while that has hidden enough. Someday surgery will likely take the tiny bit of breast tissue that remains.

When Anne first started to wear compression shirts, we didn't talk about it. I got some old ones from a trans friend and tossed them in the laundry. Anne put the clean clothes in the dresser and the compression shirts disappeared from my drawers. She wore the old, stretched-out shirts for months, and when I rubbed her back, I felt the seamless slip of my hand over nylon. Still, we were silent. Eventually Anne ordered new ones, longer and tighter. Shirts so tight she got stomachaches; shirts so tight she stood and faced the world in a whole new way. Back tall and feet steady, even if she couldn't feel it at first.

For a while, even through these changes, I could sometimes still touch her chest, if I asked. It was always quick and short, and never during sex. Then not at all. Now I can't imagine touching her chest, reminding Anne that she has breasts, has curves, underneath the binding. I don't even know the slide of her back without the weave of a compression shirt. I don't know how it feels to wrap my arms around her nakedness and hold the softness of her belly, the boldness of her bare back. It's been five and a half years and I don't know if I will ever know that skin again.

Naming a human being is hard. I have no idea how to do it, and neither does Anne. It felt nearly impossible for us to name our baby, just a tiny being whose spirit we barely knew, yet even with just those first flutterings of personality our child had a name. We had to find it, shape it, and give it to him to carry in his still-tight fists. Anne and I needed a week, and a changed birth certificate, to hand Ellis his name. To really feel it and know it and share it.

Because we didn't know the sex of the baby before the birth, Anne and I went to the hospital with a list of possible names and the hope that one would work. We knew the middle name was Ellis regardless of the baby's sex. Ellis, inspired by Melissa, a late aunt Anne adored. We left the hospital with a name on the birth certificate, but did so reluctantly. We told our families and closest friends, but made no larger announcement, no Facebook post or group email. We spent the first days of our baby's life calling him nicknames—*bubba, love bug, tiny E*—but never his actual given name. It just wasn't his. I wrote an email to our families: "Hold the monogramming, we're changing the name." And so we renamed our one-week-old the name we'd grown to love but had relegated to the middle, the name that finally chose our kid—Ellis.

So, if it's that hard to name a newborn, how do you name a person with forty years of history, decades of connections, and a lifetime of expectations? How do you find a name that tells those stories and the ones still growing? How do you find a name you want to call yourself? How do you plant your feet *here*?

"I don't want a trans name," Anne said while we were jogging along the Mississippi one Sunday, Ellis asleep in the stroller. "You know, the obvious ones, like Aiden, Myles, Rae."

I glanced at Anne, eyebrows raised, "But you are trans."

"I don't need the world to know that up front," she replied.

That's exactly what I need, I thought, *People to know up front*.

"Makes sense," I said with a shrug. We were silent for a few paces, then as the path narrowed and we headed downhill single file, I whispered to myself, *You shouldn't have chosen me*.

Anne knows I don't hide things, especially emotional things, very well. She knows I don't want to. When something joyful happens, I tell my family and friends, and sometimes the guy on the bus. When I'm grieving or stewing or fuming, I tell people just the same. Anne knows that conversations with people untangle my feelings and give me breathing room. She also knows that sometimes her silence suffocates me. And *I* know that sometimes that same silence saves her.

Anne's been researching names for years. She has lists in notebooks, on the computer, in her journals, and even on a giant poster on the bedroom wall, which hung next to another giant poster with potential baby names on it before Ellis was born. There was some crossover, including the name our kid ended up getting. A few months after Ellis was born, I said to Anne, "You could go with Ellis II. Baby first and parent follows."

She laughed. "Another way to queer our family."

Exactly.

Anne could change her name a million ways. She could, like so many transmen we know, use a male version of her given name or a similar-sounding name. Anne would become Andrew or Andy, maybe Dan or Stan or Graham, all of which she rejected immediately. She could reclaim her mom's maiden name of Wells, or adopt Whidbey, the island where she was born. Some trans-people ask their parents to rename them, but that's risky and definitely not Anne's style.

Her favorite research technique is movie credits. We slouch in our seats until the very last words scroll away, whispering every possibility, and every absurdity. Names of catering companies are fair game, but mostly we look for real options.

Steven. George. Mike. Jack—too much our dads' generation.

Milo. Byron. Linus—too hip.

Maxfield—possible. Calloway—thumbs up. Lucas—on the short list.

Anne and I discuss the growing and shrinking lists. Some names persist—Charlie. Sam. Obie. We try names at home, but that mostly makes us giggle, or cry, and so far nothing has stuck.

It's not quite right, she says about each name, even the favorites. *Doesn't feel like me.*

Of course, I think. *Because it's not you yet. But it would be.*

Makes sense, I say in my most patient moments. *You'll figure it out.*

If you don't try something, you'll never know, I say in my less patient moments.

In my darkest moments, I say nothing at all and stare at the list penciled in the spiral notebook—Nolan, Elliot, Lewis, Theodore, Ethan—and imagine meeting new people. "This is my kid, Ellis, and my partner, _____," I would say. I watch the fictitious neighbors filing away

461

their assumptions and expectations about me and my straight family, and I start to cry.

Anne and I discuss names, but ultimately I don't get to decide. Anne is naming herself. It's her identity and she isn't really asking my opinion. It's not that I think she should, but I feel so powerless, as though I'm supposed to accept the lists and be open to whatever she chooses, supposed to play it cool. But I hate Lewis and cringe to think of saying it every day. Nolan reminds me of a high school bully I knew, and Ted is an ex-boyfriend I don't want to think about during sex. But I'm not invited to be that honest. I have no eraser to wield. Just silence and sadness. And brewing anger. And shame for feeling those things.

When we meet someone and fall in love, the name is there, being worn. If we don't like it, we simply deal with it. If it's awkward, we get over it. But we enter the relationship knowing. I committed my life to Anne knowing her name, her body, and suddenly I didn't. And still don't.

There is no word for a genderqueer person raising a kid. There isn't a standard name for a child to call a "mom/dad." I mean, yes, there is the word *parent*, but who wants to wake up to, *Good morning, parent*, or hear, *Parent! Parent!* shouted across the swings and sand? Maybe if we drank afternoon tea while wearing elbow patches or spoke French at the dinner table. But we're more the rolling-in-the-grass kind of crowd. *Anne, Ellis, and I.*

Anne researched options and found ways that other queer families have made do with the gaps in our language. There weren't many prospects—Maddy, Mapa, Baba, Moppy—and none of them appealed to Anne.

Most of the queer parents we know went with Mom and Momma, regardless of gender identity. But Anne couldn't do it, couldn't compromise—with her parent name, her style, or her behavior. Not now, not in high school, not when she was a toddler. Anne has a photo album from her childhood and in it there is a picture of her wearing a pink dress with lace cuffs and matching bloomers, her wispy blond hair curled around her chubby cheeks. It's the last one of her in a dress; she was two years old.

As Anne grew up and suffered through puberty, she couldn't grow her hair or wear make-up to stop the world from staring. She couldn't walk lightly then, and she wasn't going to enter parenthood with quiet steps. For all her shyness and shame, Anne always knew where she couldn't compromise. There were some things she couldn't change no matter who pressured her. There was a clear line Anne couldn't step over no matter how lonely she became, because if she did, she knew she would shatter from the inside out.

When Ellis was born Anne decided, tentatively at first, on Poppy. She liked it, but was nervous to tell people, curious how the name would be received. I imagined her practicing introducing herself: "Poppy." "Yup, I go by Poppy." "He calls me Poppy." "Yes, P-o-p-p-y, like the flower."

I watched her during those brave moments when she first told people her parent name, and I could almost feel the flush rise in her, despite the solid way she stood, feet wide and shoulders set, her hope hanging on to the steep round of the capital letter P. *Poppy.*

Anne didn't tell her parents she was to be called Poppy until a month after Ellis was born. They lived far away and didn't ask questions during phone calls; they simply waited. Perhaps her mom and dad knew the name would be something different, something difficult to hear. Or perhaps they didn't think about it, assumed she'd be Mom because that fit what they thought of their little girl grown parent.

Poppy. Her dad integrated it seamlessly into his very next sentence and didn't look back. He spoke to Ellis about his Poppy, spoke for Ellis and addressed his Poppy. Anne's mom managed to call her nothing for a couple months. For her, the situation went deeper than a name. She had imagined her little girl would birth a baby, adding a branch to the Iverson family tree and a girl to the Daughters of the American Revolution. She loves genealogy, finding connections and bloodlines of ancestors as far back as possible. What to do with a non-bio baby? Then, a Poppy to boot. She just couldn't say it.

I don't remember how long Anne's mom took to start calling her Poppy, or what made her change. Maybe it was watching Ellis's baby cheeks scrunch with joy when Anne held him close and said, *Hey Peanut, I'm your Poppy.* Or maybe it was seeing the flush of joy on Anne's cheeks when everyone else called her Poppy. Or maybe it just took time for her mom to unravel the dream she had for her daughter, and to rewrite how she fit into Poppy's new story. And maybe her mom wishes she'd done something more or something quicker, or maybe not. But in the end, she started saying *Poppy* with apparent joy on her own face.

Anne's mom wasn't alone in avoiding the word. People we know well—coworkers, neighbors, even Ellis's babysitter—still refer to Anne as Mom. It seems like sometimes they just forget, but I think most of the time people are uncomfortable using an offbeat name. When Anne is alone with Ellis and people say, *Go find your Mom,* or *Sit on your Mama's lap,* Ellis looks right through Anne, leans to peek around her, turns in circles looking for me and says, "Where is Mama? She's not here." Anne is Poppy; for Ellis, that is enough. He knows that some kids have a Daddy, and some don't, but no one else gets to have a Poppy.

We've taught Ellis to call toddlers *babies* or *kids* and to refer to adults as *grown-ups* or *parents*. He hugs Anne and me close and says, *You're my parents. We're a whole family.* Ellis doesn't have to say *she* and *he* when *they* works just fine. There is no need to make binary distinctions with a toddler, or any of us, really. When a pronoun is unavoidable, two-year-old Ellis moves gracefully between *he* and *she* when he talks about Poppy, intuitively shifting pronouns depending on context and conversation, taking cues from me or the people around him. When Ellis transposes *he* and *she* or substitutes *they*, he isn't making a mistake; he's living linguistic fluidity and accepting difference unconditionally. He's not gender bound. If we listen, he's teaching us how language doesn't have to define identity, that we are bigger than the pronouns people use to describe us, that we don't have to be one thing or the other because we can simply be both, or many.

Not long after the date night, Ellis and I were crossing the Lake Street bridge, his wispy toddler hair blowing in the fall breeze, when I heard the term *trans-trender* for the first time. We were walking behind a pierced, cis-gendered teenager wearing an off-shoulder sweater and skinny jeans who said to her iPhone friend, "He's totally trans-trender. You know, for attention." This comment slipped casually from her mouth, as if being trans is as cool and easy as getting a tattoo. But there is truly nothing trendy about being trans. There is mostly fear and danger, and plenty of shame. And trying not to be noticed.

It's not hip. It's not a fad. It's scary.

As a teenager, Anne stayed home as much as possible, and she still does so as an adult—avoiding public places, opting out of concerts and dinner parties, skipping hikes with friends. I go, taking Ellis's hand and heading to the park or the restaurant. Yes, Anne stays home because she's introverted, but also because, no matter what one's age, it's hard to be genderqueer and stared at. Anne still freezes around teenagers, haunted by high school bullies. She melts when she witnesses kids mocking each other, sinks into her small-framed heart that took the blows of the cruelty that defined her childhood. She won't hold hands in public or walk by a group of men at night because no matter how much the queer community and academia discuss gender spectrum, the average

American wants the binary boxes on forms to make sense and be absolute reality. Anne doesn't want to face that animosity while eating ice cream on a summer night with her family.

For her, the worst part about being out in public is not having anywhere to pee, or at least anywhere safe. Not the men's bathroom, and not the women's. She has learned to hold her pee for up to ten hours to avoid a public restroom, especially a multiple-stall one. But occasionally it's unavoidable and Anne has to walk past the sign with the stick figure in a skirt and deal with whoever is in there. Sometimes it's fine, and sometimes it's terrifying. But peeing in public is always intense and totally exhausting. Anne has lived this dynamic her entire life, and it never gets easier to stand there on her own two feet when the meanness gets right in her face:

"What are you?" said a woman to the Wrangler-wearing ten-year-old Anne in a roadside Texaco bathroom. Grabbing her own daughter's hand, the woman then said, "Jesus, where's your mother?"

"Prove it," said the pack of sixth graders to second-grader Anne in the school bathroom one fall day.

What the hell are you doing? says one woman after another. *You're in the wrong place.*

Anne lives an echo of *You're in the wrong bathroom* and *You're not supposed to be here,* which, over a lifetime, sounds a lot like *You're wrong* and *You're not supposed to be.* Shame wraps Anne, binding her breath to her ribs and forcing her to fold instead of stand tall. There she is, standing with dripping hands in bathrooms across the country while the air grows tight around her.

I've watched women enter the bathroom, see Anne at the sink, and step back to check the sign on the door. Most come in again and ignore her, some glare, a few wait outside until she leaves. Sometimes women report that there is a man in the women's restroom. I stare at the mean faces, my feet planted, and say to Anne, "Take up all the space you need."

I imagine the day Anne changes her name, starts testosterone, and begins to pass as a guy. I imagine she will shed her shame and walk lighter, more open to people and engaged in the world. The difficulty won't recede; it will just be renamed and redistributed. Our lives will likely get easier, or at least less scary—but still hard, a new kind of hard. For me anyway.

Sometimes on long runs by the river or in the silent moonlight on our mattress, I say to the imagined vial of testosterone and still-wrapped syringe, *I know you are, but what am I?*

It's not that I worry about how my identity will change once Anne transitions more physically, more publicly. I'll know my face and how my clothes fit. I'll know his eyes and how he sees the world. What makes me panic is how the world will see *me*. I imagine my queer identity fading into Anne's facial hair, and my ability to own my queerness drowned by her deepening voice. To out myself will be to out Anne. I don't see how I won't become invisible.

I fought hard for my queer identity. Growing up in a military Catholic family, I had some work to do in my twenties. Nose ring. Big boots. Dykey glasses. Buttons and bumper stickers about the binary gender system. Pride parades and drag shows—too late and too raunchy, but I showed up. My body didn't necessarily read as queer, so I could choose when to come out and when to fade into the safe, straight walls. I could put on my privilege like a cape of good intentions. Most of the time I stood with conviction laced into my Dr. Martens and tucked into my big belt, fighting to be seen.

Holding Anne's hand queered me. Standing next to her gender-nonconforming cuteness outed me to the world. What a relief. Anne fought all her life to blend in and I clamored to be noticed. As Anne transitions, she'll shift from being seen as a queer dyke to being a straight white guy—suddenly tossed up from years of isolation to the place of privilege in our narrow mainstream world. And me? What will become of me? I'll be seen as a straight girl living in the Longfellow neighborhood of South Minneapolis with her husband, toddler, two cats, and a dog in our two-story house with a porch in front, raspberries in the garden, and a giant maple out back. I try to imagine the assumptions people will make about my family and my life, about who I am and what I stand for. You can see us now, standing side by side. Hand in hand. Ellis tight on my hip. Anne's feet facing forward and my toes outturned, the way they always are.

This is not what I signed on for.

Nominated by The Georgia Review,
Nancy Geyer,
Joan Murray

JUST THE ONE EPISODE

by JOHN ASHBERY

from LITMAG

My thanks for these various emails,
and regrets for not responding sooner.
I was weighing myself on the old-fashioned scale
in front of the druggist. It delivers your fortune
along with your weight—"you wate and fate."
Mine was, to say the least, distressing,
but, like all prophecies, contained
in the narrow groove of its delivery.
The French doors of truth are closed
against the tragically hemispheric
wall of our deliverance, and my eyes are open.
Otherwise there's not much to say.
The apples gave it (me) away.
Of such painted rags are our days woven.
The horoscope wasn't wrong, only a little late,
while I have stuff to do, and crates to open.

Nominated by Litmag

MONOMOY

by CARL PHILLIPS

from POETRY

Somewhere, people must still do things like fetch
water from wells in buckets, then pour it out
for those animals that, long domesticated, would
likely perish before figuring out how to get
for themselves. That dog, for example, whose
refusal to leave my side I mistook, as a child,
for loyalty—when all along it was just blind . . . What
is it about vulnerability that can make the hand
draw back, sometimes, and can sometimes seem
the catalyst for rendering the hand into sheer force,
destructive? *Don't you see how you've burnt almost
all of it, all the tenderness, away,* someone screams
to someone else, in public—and looking elsewhere,
we walk quickly past, as if even to have heard
that much might have put us at risk of whatever fate
questions like that

                    spring from. Estrangement—
like sacrifice—begins as a word at first, soon it's
the stuff of drama, cue the follow-up tears that
attend drama, then it's pretty much the difference
between waking up to a storm and waking up
inside one. Who can say how she got there—
in the ocean, I mean—but I once watched a horse
make her way back to land mid-hurricane: having

468

ridden, surfer-like, the very waves that at any moment
could have overwhelmed her in their crash to shore, she
shook herself, looked back once on the water's restlessness—
history's always restless—and the horse stepped free.

Nominated by David Baker,
Michael Collier,
Martha Collins,
Andrea Hollander,
Lloyd Schwartz,
Maxine Scates

HE

by JANE MEAD

from AMERICAN POETRY REVIEW

•

Out of quarry-dust
he comes running.
Running as a crab runs

he comes out of the hills
the hills that own him—
as a lie comes to own

its person, like that.
And the hackles of the land
rise up behind him.

•

On the sub-zero
range-land the deer
bed down. He—

harrowed, and holds
rivers of snow
and forgetting—he

beds down.

•

In the morning, he—

stooped and stretches—
signs a song of praise
from long-ago, while

a little sun strikes
a little frost
on the skin of the earth:

Some say the gate out is the river
some say the gate out is rain—
but I agree with those who say
that every gate is a gate of praise . . .

then the sagebrush rattles
then out limps a tattered
sheepdog, thin and just like

that.

•

He had a father
and a mother!
His dreams were

cathedral homes
for beetles, of which
there are 450,000

different species so far
identified. Or, Could you
take down the heaviest

book from the top
shelf please? Read
to me more about

A is for Aviary?

he would inquire.
Now sleep is all
the cathedral he desires

please.

•

He lives on the steps
of the cathedral now.
Cardboard, wind-tug

and rattle. And sometimes
the trash does a dull
little dance. Rash

stiff and throb
inhabit. He is
insect rat and rust

hampered. Danger
is his host—
and all forgetting

or maybe dreaming—
or maybe just all

dreaming.

•

His hands

are bitten and grease—
one thumb
no longer performing.

At the way top
of the cathedral
the Angel Gabriel looks

out over the city
and blows his little horn—
say some, though he

thinks it could just
as well be a Native
American with a peace pipe,

who could possibly know
from here he argues.

And it is a strong
argument.

•

In the little park
behind the cathedral
he gives the stray cats

water in an old
anchovy tin when
the heat shoots up

and everybody who can
leaves town, including
the cat volunteers.

Good thing he is there
to rinse out the tin
in the drinking fountain

and fill it again.
The cats do not
let him touch them

and when he hums
they pretend not
to listen. Sometimes

the cats eat beetles
sometimes ants, though
for eating they prefer

the warm blooded creatures.
Either way they have
made up their minds

about certain things:
like people,
no exceptions.

•

He says he has seen
the sky and the steps
of the cathedral

and the little apple
branches that reach
over the wall

enough. He says
the thoughts
in his mind have

been in his mind
a long time now.
He doesn't have

a star, he doesn't
have a certificate
for a star. Maybe just

his mind now.

Plus a green wool hat.

Plus a crumble of cheese

for the mad dog who runs
through his memory

blinded.

•

Sometimes a deep
humming warms him
as if his heart

were a tuning fork
the world set going—
It is not God.

It is not whisky.
It is not even
the mad dog snoring.

It is just everything
humming the same note
at the same time—

and he is invited,

thank you.

•

Well, he whose
singing was a matter
of grave opinion

is now otherwise
employed. He is harness
and wind now, wind

and harness.

•

Sometimes a child
wanders through
the cathedral park—

looking for a lost
mitten or hat, her sitter
trailing. The stray cats

retreat and crouch
under the tangled
bushes, but they never

stop watching.

—*For John*

Nominated by American Poetry Review,
James Harms

FROM "INTERRUPTIVE"

by PHILLIP WILLIAMS

from POETRY

What can I do but make of the eyes of others
my own eyes, but make of the world a ghazal
whose radif is a haunting of *me, me, me?*

Somewhere there are fingers still whole
to tell the story of the empire that devours fingers.
Somewhere there is a city where even larvae

cannot clean the wounds of the living
and cannot eat on the countless dead
who are made to die tomorrow and tomorrow.

Carrion beetles and boot bottoms grind corpses
powder-soft to feed the small-mouthed gods
of gardens and wind. Roses made to toss their silk

to earth like immolated gowns, hills
spewing ribbons of charred air from cities
occupied by artillery and pilfered grain, limbs

blown from their bodies and made into an alphabet
that builds this fool song, even now, presented
before you as false curative, as vacant kiss—even

what is lost in the fabrication of strangers needs naught
from strangers. Even *somewhere* stings with stillness,
stings with a home not surrendered but a given.

•

But I have not been with my feet on the earth
there where bullets make use of skin like flags
make use of the land. My thinking is as skeletal

as the bombed-out schools and houses
untelevised. What do I know of occupation
but my own colonized thinking to shake

free from. While my days themselves tremble
from time and shake off place to feel falsely
placeless, a hollow empathy as if its soft chisel

could make of this wall—my ignorance mighty
before me upon which drawn figures alight
against the stone—my own; what is mine is

the wall my votes and non-votes, my purchases
wrapped in unthought have built and stretched,
undead gray. There are no secrets in debris.

I have a home I hate, its steel and lights
red and blue upon me. Home itself a mist
through which I pass and barely notice.

Home, to assume you are home is to assume
I am welcome in you—to what degree let the wounds
say so—and can come and go as I please.

The television tells me *Over there*, and one must point
with a fully extended arm to show how far from,
how unlike here *there* really is. *Over there*

where they blow each other up over land and God.
And it feels good to stretch as if from waking—
this silence could be called a kind of sleep—and think

beyond, where I am not and where those who are
are not—wall upon which drawings of fists
strike skyward and faces of activists stare into me

from my Google search. Turnstiles separate
home from home. Barbed wire catches clouds
in its coil saws. What do I know of injustice

but having a home throughout which bullets,
ballots, and brutality trifecta against
people who were here before here was here

and people were brought here to change
the landscape of *humanity?* That word has rolling hills
and towering walls. To hammer against it not to get

to the other side—believe nothing is there—
but to make obsolete *side*—know there is nothing.
I know this: my metaphors have small arms,

my wallet has made monstrous my reflection,
I have done terrible things by being alive.
I have built a wonder of terror with my life.

•

[Image of an eight-meter-tall wall, constructed by connected prefabrications. Interspersed among them are surveillances (I'll make them pay). What is closed opens then settles. Spill: a scream, what makes it. On the wall a body leans, which is a caption: "This is not prayer." (Which side are you on?) Here where there is no here, endurance measured by a field's disruption and around it what makes possible a furthering (to settle this in court or to settle in this courtyard). Argument: this thinking is real because it has been made touchable if touch is the mutual rejection of objects from entering into the other (let's settle this once and for all) who's going to pay for what reaches toward and fails at heaven? To settle the debt, settle in silence. If it is not silent (this roaring (is it fire / stone / a pen lifting (ban no ban no b—) or falling?) is it home?) make it so.]

Between his war with self and the war
in a sand-sealed country neither of us could spell,
juvie took from R what little childhood

Chicago hadn't taken. Between bloody showers
and rushed meals, him forced by bigger boys
until pain became expectation and expectation

pleasure. A shortened sentence meant fighting
for a country against people for whom R held
no hatred while hating the ones he fought for.

There is venom in coercion misnamed loyalty.
Boys and bloody water in his head when he left
to fight in heat and camo. Then in the barracks

shower, three soldiers raped R. Sand is the Plaza
of Pardon. Wind draws its name across the grains
and leaves the grains with the name it gave.

Who would I be after so many tried to live
in me forcibly? R in the desert, our Skype
lost connection when an explosion blew out

what little service he had. *Oh shit,*
we been hit. Then blackout silence
and my pulse explicit. Let us rejoice in this:

war is a love song that makes your body dangerous
to others, that makes you unlivable. You become more
private. You are always early to yourself.

When I saw him again, marijuana discharged him
dishonorably and the men inside him shooting guns
and shooting cum went with him. This is one veteran's

legacy, one man I know and have lost to distance,
my own pulling me from everything I'm meant to

hold close. What do I know of exile but self-imposed

self-removal. When R kissed my forehead goodbye
the first time I felt citizenly, patriotic, my white
handkerchief au revoir-ing a friend from my mind

who returned with sand hissing down his pant legs.
A hero is an hourglass. For what
does his countdown drop its grains, skull to heel?

•

One night, words came, swift
as if prayed for, showing
myself to me to correct myself:

> Grief unhides beneath bombed mosques
>   while the sky blows into pale blue absence
>   dust and vaporized skin.
>
> Grief and sky, unrequited lovers. Whose hurt
>   could hold the other's? Grief knows the passage
>   of the worm and the temperatures of dirt.
>
> Sky knows the neon of kite sail and tail.
>   Fifteen thousand names written in the air
>   by ribbon, rhombi billowed into shields,
>
> glide into the Guinness Book of Records, memories
>   passed page to page across oceans and treaties
>   in ink out-blacking smoke. Waves leave soft creases
>
> on the Gaza Strip and know airborne diamonds
>   by the shadows of their measured shapes
>   tethered like falcons to a child's quick hands . . .

How to mistake American arrogance for love,
to think kites could humanize the already-human
and hide the anti-human from its history.

Why cloak our custom of cloaking? To make

palatable the blade we turn on ourselves we turn it
on others. In good light the metal will give

us back to ourselves. Does the wolf know
it has a reflection? Ask the water if it shows
to us its beast self or has one given to it.

•

[Image of an eight-meter-tall wall, over which is painted "Is you coming or
going or is I?" A ray of light ballistic through the form is both answer and re-
jection of an answer's possibility.]

•

Tragedy disturbs tragedy.
There can never be just one
way to see the end to ourselves.

The Mediterranean has endless room
where capsized boats of hundreds bloomed
once with refugees. Water can't be trusted.

The wind with its countless hands hasting
water into waves can't be seen so can't be
trusted even though we feel it, even when we

know along its unseen force bobs curt hymns
from the dead to the living. We don't hear them
rising from the salt like fins. We hear bombs

and think *Each storm carries the broken cries
of a broken nation in its contortion.* Alibi
for the living is the land: it's the earth

itself that refuses the dead a home in burr
or field, in the stone plateaus or tableaux
of scree from a city of wild boars and roads

that lead to a burning garden, a gutted church,
a school uniform hemmed by soldiers, a birch
limned with blood and pointing dually

west to a row of houses roofless but for crows and east
to a rifle hung above a threshold like a saint.
Something's always watching, well-aimed

and unkind, empty and on fire or just-
finished burning. And the water will rust
the skin, will extinguish the fire and the flesh.

Baptism is what the living do. The rest
are left to idols of fish and worm, are left
with the living's pens and books bereft

and intricate as mausolea woven from husks
of stories the dead cannot tell. They brux
in our renditions as we cull their truth for our song.

•

The wilderness within us creeps closer
to the surface of thought and burial.
We drag ourselves from the selves

that laid bear traps that trapped us into our own
dragging, one leg limp behind like a memory
pain brings forward. Low grass collects

pockets of our blood as if any gloss
could reduce droughts in the smallest needs.
If we make eye contact with the most beleaguered

of us, we pray the remains of god would shower
spears to smite clean such embarrassment. We are not
neighbors, just near. We are failures of nature

and the stars burn down through trees no light
we can trust. Because we were shrewd with conviction
the pads of our right hands' digits have singed

483

into them one letter each to spell *faith*. What we touch
with that hand will fell our enemies
who are ourselves. We draw a maze with our blood,

follow paths drawn from the cruelties sculpted
into another's body. I am losted by a child's missing eye,
dead-ended by a family encrusted with shrapnel.

If I follow my own disaster more closely,
if I allow buzzards spiraling above prophecy
enough to reveal time as caught in the loop

of their pinions, if I remove my shirt
from my bloodied torso and twist
from it my own oil, if in my pocket

I find the final ballot before the mine
was tripped in god's patience, if I see my vote
had predicted the immolation of seasons

and the beheading of goats sacrificed to rain
that washed away no blood and emulsified
sickness into the oceans and seas, if pain rises

from the mouths of the dead in the shape
the dead took when alive, if all this time
we've been building tombs and calling them home—

•

[Image of an eight-meter-tall wall bearing a hole in its center, or a
1.7272-meter-tall wall, which is me, bearing a hole in my center. I am the wall
and the hole is what makes me better. I want to be better.]

•

Hajjar, does a body on its back act as the body's own
grief? Is a body downed the mind's shadow? If we must love
our souls, does that mean we must love what leaves?

Nominated by Ye Chun,
Chloe Honum

BRACE YOURSELF

fiction by LESLIE JILL PATTERSON

from PRIME NUMBER

SHORT FICTION

Note from David Jauss, judge: In my forty-four years of teaching and editing, I've read countless stories about abused women but never one like this. Without a single scene of abuse (and the sensationalism such scenes almost inevitably create), the story parses its soul-shattering effects. At one point, the narrator says, "It's odd, even savage, how lies are sometimes tender while truth can surprise you, like a backhand across the cheek." This story surprises us with just such a truth. Reader, brace yourself.

BRACE YOURSELF

You like to claim you landed at Eagle Hill by mistake. A misunderstanding of some kind. Truth is, Billy Scales and his ranch hands found you in a bar named True Grit, and they knew, from minute one, who you were.

They knew you stuffed your suitcase in a hurry and surely didn't come to Colorado for camping in the mountains—because it was fifty degrees outside and dropping, and, even so, you wore a sleeveless dress and city-girl sandals with leather daisies arching over your foot. You avoided eye contact, propping a book around your plate and pretending to read when they took the bar stools next to yours. You ordered off the kid's menu and packed half of it out in a to-go box, so you were clearly guarding every dime. They probably even knew you tucked your wedding ring inside your purse before you walked through The Grit's door. And

485

when Billy invited you to his equine program—where women caught in hazardous marriages learned to tug a rein resolutely, steering their lives away from vows they should have never spoken—your story was so obvious, he pitched his invitation in the same pragmatic vein that he mentioned where you could find a low-rent apartment and which local bank offered free checking.

Three days later—though you told Billy, *Thanks, but no*, you didn't have any reason to saddle a horse, *really, no*—you drive out to Eagle Hill. And who knows if you do so because you're ready to conquer fear or because you're attracted to it. No question: Billy and his cowboys ought to frighten you. They're the hardscrabble types who own only the necessities: toilet paper, milk, wire-cutters to mend barbed fences, hatchets to shatter winter ice, and guns loaded and well-sighted and always within reach.

When you arrive at the barn, a pack of wild dogs surrounds your car. They bark and lunge at the rear tires, then the driver's door. You slam on the brakes. One of them, a blue heeler that looks like a coyote, rises on his hind legs and scrapes his front paws on your window and growls. Your car inches forward, herded into a parking space by the dogs. Snarling, they stand at a distance, their feet planted, refusing to let you out of your automobile.

When the commotion draws Billy from his office, your addiction to apologies surfaces. You're sorry for rousing the dogs. You're sorry to interrupt the routine of riding and breaking colts, to soak up daylight when the afternoon is already draining into evening. You're sorry for the very fact that you know nothing about horses.

Billy whistles at his dogs, and they heel, and then he smiles at you. He looks exactly like Wilford Brimley: a handlebar mustache; full-moon cheeks that eclipse his eyes when he laughs; a bowling-pin belly lapping over the waistband of his Wranglers; and a copper bracelet, neckerchief, and Stetson. The hat is cocked at an upward angle this afternoon, and Billy wraps an arm around your shoulders and leads you into the barn. "I've taught handicapped kids before," he says. "If you can spell *horse*, you can ride one."

He halters and ties Juan, a chestnut quarter horse whose shoulders are a good head taller than you, to a post in the barn's alley. Then he heaves a sixty-pound saddle onto Juan's back, cinching it so fast it looks like a magic trick. "Tomorrow," Billy warns, "you'll do this yourself."

Let's be clear here: what's ticker-taping through your head right at this moment isn't the fear that you're too stupid to manage a saddle

486

without a chaperone. No, what you're calculating is how easily you can sucker Billy into respecting your husband's third-rate opinion of you, because if there's one lesson you've learned the hard, punishing way, it's that it's safer for a man to believe you're hopeless from the get-go than for you to fail at one of his assigned tasks. If he expects nothing, he won't argue later that you intentionally botched the job to provoke him.

Holding the bridle and reins, Billy's right hand rests on Juan's forehead, ready to slip the tack over the horse's ears. His other hand grips Juan's chin, ready to pry open his mouth. Billy tells you a horse can bite hard enough to break bone, and suspiciously, his right thumb is missing a knuckle. His left, you guess, might be next. Too, you hear the smack of slobber, and it doesn't sound pretty. When Billy pinches Juan's jaw, it drops, and the metal bit glides into place. Juan jerks his head, rears, then settles. Now that he has the bit in his mouth and suspects you'll soon be holding the reins, he angles his head to keep an eye on you, his ears spun and flat. Cautious, too, you cut a wide arc around his backend, and Billy notices and laughs.

It's not funny how women are taught to fear trouble. Your granddad was a rancher who never let you sit a horse unless he himself held the reins. And you've heard the family stories—how a colt planted an angry hoof against your granddad's forehead one summer, furrowing a scar on his brow that never vanished. Always, he warned you that a hoof stomping a little girl's foot shod in steel-toed boots would slice off her toes. You haven't worn your city-girl sandals to Eagle Hill—when Billy invited you out, he advised you to buy decent shoes, and you obeyed— but your Payless bargain boots aren't much better. Juan shifts nervously in the alley; his hooves clomp against the rubber mats. His hips are as solid as old tree trunks. His hind legs alone outweigh you by two hundred pounds. At point-blank range, a kick from Juan can kill.

Of course, it's possible you're imagining Juan's hostility. Back home, when you broached the subject of your husband's anger, he swore he loved you. The first therapist encouraged you to point out the early signs of rage—his eyes, like gunnery scopes, locked on yours; his lungs, his chest, swollen with air and holding; his chin edged forward; his jaw cinched—so your husband, who adored you, could recognize himself then temper his stance. But when a man of fury swears he's Mr. Charming, offering evidence to the contrary won't mollify him. It's not "communicating better." What it is, is dangerous. The therapist's suggestion only taught your husband a new trick: in the middle of an argument, his body language enflamed, his mood on the ledge between sanity and the E.R., but his voice rational and calm, he said, *You be sure and tell me when I'm mad.* What he meant was, *I dare you.*

"Horses can't see directly behind them without turning their heads, and we've hitched Juan's to a post." Billy swipes his palm across Juan's rump as he walks around his back end, showing you how to stay in a horse's radar. "He'll only kick if he can't figure where you are."

"Right." You shrug. "So you say. But it looks like we're just showing him where to aim, when to fire."

Out on the trail, you riding Juan and Billy riding Scout, this cowboy's smart enough not to remark upon certain subjects—like, *Why are you alone in Colorado?* and *Does anyone back home know you're missing?* Instead, he rattles on about his family's ranch in Whitewater, his sister's fight with Lupus. He says he sleeps in the barn so he can hear his horses breathe easy at night, and when he cranks open the doors every morning and sees the view outside, he's grateful for a life in Colorado though it means eliminating luxuries like indoor plumbing, electricity, maybe a wife. His laughter carries across the valley floor. You can see how his world—the mountains snow-fluffed in winter and sunbaked in summer, aspen with leaves the color of apples, a pack of dogs loyal and quick-witted—could make a poor man, or even a broke woman, feel rich.

Billy studies how you sit in the saddle. After a while, he lifts the brim of his hat, swipes a hand across his brow. "Don't arch your back, Dolly. Juan knows you're nervous."

You ponder Billy's posture. His denim jacket curves around the slump of his shoulders; his hands, one of them missing that half-thumb, coil loosely around the reins. You try to slouch, too, and ease your grip.

The two of you scoot along in silence now, Billy having run out of things to gab about. Occasionally, he whistles at his dogs to keep them close. And just when you relax, aren't simply faking the posture of an experienced rider, Billy says, "So my manners were rusty at The Grit, and I didn't ask what you do for a living."

Billy's trying to convince you, or maybe himself, that ferreting for information is polite and not inquiring rude, but he can't look you in the face when he says this, and because he can't, and because you've seen coworkers and your parents, and that furniture salesman one year the day before Christmas, glance away right before bulldozing in with the real interrogation, you brace yourself for the questions Billy wants to ask most, the pointed ones, which are surely coming next. Should he rev up the chitchat, you'll lie to him because learning the truth makes some people demand a reckoning of your husband's crimes, but others, an apology for yours.

It seems harmless to admit that you were, are, a professor; you teach English. But even as the words fall from your mouth, you worry that you've given too many particulars. Details are the map that will lead your husband to you.

"I like Cormac McCarthy," Billy offers.

You stare at him, studying his expression for motive—because he's yanking your chain shamelessly; he's conjured that name from some high school memory, probably hasn't held a book, open or closed, in decades. Then you realize, with a twinge in your gut, that you don't care if he's lying. You're grateful he's found a subject that puts you at ease. But just as you open your mouth, ready to share what you know about McCarthy—a man who answers questions about his writing but, like you, clamps silent when asked about his life—you think how silly that conversation will sound. "Okay," you admit, "I'm a nerd. Bullies have always known where to find me. In junior high, the kids shut me in a bass drum, then a tuba case. It wasn't pretty." You laugh at your own joke in hopes that the conversation will stay light-hearted.

Billy's head pitches backward, and he laughs so hard he nearly chokes. "By God, that's damn ugly." Then he steals a look at you to make sure you're still smiling.

When you are, he clucks his tongue, asking Scout to bypass the trail and descend a steep slope. Juan follows, lurching downhill. The angle is so sharp you'd swear you're standing upright in the stirrups while also reclining in the saddle, your head nearly resting on Juan's rump. His hooves slip. Gravel skitters underfoot. Your weight pitches forward, and it feels like you and Juan will tumble head over hoof, your hands and feet hogtied by the reins and stirrups. Billy has told you that horses spook easily. On the trail, even a mature horse can buck and flail if it's surprised by the scent of fresh bear scat or the scuffle of wind in the trees. There isn't room in the mountains, on paths skinny as needles, for emotional outbursts. And as you and Juan reel downhill, you wait for him to panic—because fear is a habit that's hard to break.

But Juan is more experienced than you. When you yank the reins nervously, his head shakes off the tug the same way it tosses to swat away flies. He steps, skids, steps then skids—level ground a goal he knows how to reach.

At the bottom, when the world rights itself again, Billy says, "I had similar troubles growing up. Bullies and such."

Now he's outright lying. The way folks at The Grit gathered around and offered to buy his supper and beer the night you met, you can tell Billy has always been popular. He's faking common ground because he suspects you need some company. It's odd, even savage, how lies are sometimes tender while truth can surprise you, like a backhand across the cheek.

Scout winds through the brush; Juan trails behind him. The sun begins heading home for the night, and already, the moon hovers above Owl Creek Pass like a blue china dish. Billy points out two bucks hiding in the chaparral. In the fading light, you can barely discern them.

Then Billy asks if you hunt and stares you in the eye. "I can teach you to fire a gun," he says, "if you need it."

When the two of you return to the barn, it's twilight. Having finished their day jobs in town, Jim Merritt and Egan Anderson, Billy's two volunteer ranch hands, arrive, looking to ride colts or help power down for the night. Unlike Billy, Jim is slender as a rope, and though black strands linger in his hair, his Vandyke is ice-white. Egan is so young, by a decade or more, that he still misses college—hence, the Cornhusker's T-shirt and ball cap. All three of them head out in Billy's truck to feed and water the horses stashed in the pasture, and they tell you to water the barn while they're gone. You stare at the industrialsized hose, nearly as thick as your arm, and then consider the buckets inside each of the stalls, where the horses, all enormous and snorting and knocking their hooves against the walls, wait for you to enter.

Maybe you should just get in your car and drive away.

This is how you arrived in Colorado in the first place. Your husband called home from work one afternoon and asked you to cook your rosemary chicken for a group of his friends, and you knew: you'd bake it too long, or not long enough; you'd serve it on a platter that wasn't presentable; you'd unwittingly give another man a chicken breast plumper than the one you spatulaed onto your husband's plate. After dinner, there'd be the stack of dishes leaning precariously in the sink, the steam rising from hot water, and your husband locking the door behind the last of the guests—the kind of setting details that foreshadow what's to come. That final afternoon, you stood in the kitchen, the phone in your hand, him waiting on the line, the both of you pretending he wasn't telling you but was instead asking a genuine question—Were you inclined to cook or no? Did you have the time and ingredients?—and you weren't pondering what dessert paired well with chicken. No, you were remembering how the women at the last shelter gave you what they called a safety plan: Never again, they warned, let an argument start

490

in the kitchen. That's where the knives are. And imagining the disquiet in the house after the guests would be gone, you said, Yes, I can do that, but then hung up the phone, grabbed a duffle, stuffed it, and ran.

But running means you can't come back.

You stare at the hose, heavy and tangled on the ground. One of the horses whinnies and bangs his water bucket against the wall. You take a step forward, then another, and another; then suddenly, you're cranking on the water and filling all the pails in Billy's barn. Sure, you can't control the industrial hose while wrestling open the stall doors. It bucks in your hand, jetting water so icy your breath catches when it splashes in your face. You douse the horses, their shavings, the alley. And you worry there'll be trouble when the men return and find everything soaked and you covered in mud.

Not that the three of them look any better. Dust cakes Billy's eyes; his shirt is wrinkled and untucked; and dirt, or maybe manure, is wedged under his fingernails. His Justin ropers have rusted spurs. Jim's jeans may be starched and pressed, the crease down each pant leg sharp as a blade, but hay clings to his jacket, and his hair, damp with sweat and flattened by his hat, is filthy. Egan's hand is bleeding.

To your surprise, they don't gripe one word about the mess you've made but instead invite you to join them near the round pen for a makeshift happy hour. Outside, the stars glisten like coins tossed into the sky's well, and Billy and his ranch hands pull vests and woolly jackets over their sweaty shirts to keep warm. They offer you one to wear, too. Then they're drinking beer and teasing you about your Payless boots.

Jim points his bottle of Sierra Nevada at them. "I hope you didn't pay good money for that bullshit Western wear."

Egan nods. "Salesmen around here can smell a Texan coming."

So your boots aren't Tony Lamas or Justin ropers, but they are two tall, fleece-lined bargains, warm for winter when she arrives and with the appropriate heels for stirrups. "The pair of them cost only $12," you say, holding your feet out in front of you so everyone can admire your purchase. Really, they look like big black galoshes.

Billy's laughter spills free. "Where the hell did you get those motorcycle boots, Dolly? Do we have to take you shopping?"

"Are you buying?" you ask. The question, a bona fide joke some men might mistake for impertinence, flies from your mouth before you think about consequences.

Billy only laughs harder, his face turning red. Jim warns him that if you get the right shoes on your feet, you just might kick his ass. And this, Jim's punch line with a little zest, makes you want to laugh out loud for the first time in years. You almost don't recognize the feeling.

For certain, you don't recognize where you are.

By now, eleven beer bottles line up on the ground, and Egan and Billy are using two other empties as spittoons. Billy hasn't even asked your name yet but is simply calling you *Dolly*. These men are nothing like your husband, an English professor like you, who carries a briefcase and wears Perry Ellis slacks, button-down tailored shirts, and matching silk ties. They're nothing like anyone you've ever been attracted to, all the old boyfriends whose manners were clean and sober. So they shouldn't cause any trouble. At least, not the way your husband defines *trouble*.

Here's the truth though: what you're doing is reckless. You're sitting around a campfire with three strangers, all of them drinking, and they might not know your name, but, rest assured, they know who you are and what you've given your husband permission to do. And for some men, that's an invitation.

When the three men quit laughing, the silence catches you off-guard. In the backcountry, far from city traffic, you can hear every noise: wind, a clock ticking, even the sound of your own breathing. Jim shuffles his feet and fidgets with the buttons on his jean jacket. Egan takes another swig of beer and wipes his sleeve across his mouth. Billy stares off into the distance, scanning the horizon, maybe watching for coyotes or mountain lions.

Back home, quietude usually meant a man seething, a man jonesing to take a swing. But today, for now, you hope it's not the ratchet of danger you hear in the emptiness. You pray it's the sound of life when it's finally safe. Far away, a truck mumbles down the road, and the Uncompahgre River purls downstream, flush with snowmelt. Biscuit and Dweeb, Billy's two heelers, patter around the campfire, panting and happy. And one of the three cowboys starts humming, soft as a fiddle.

Nominated by Prime Number
Ayse Papatya Bucak,
David Jauss

POWDER HOUSE

BY MOLLY GALLENTINE

FROM FOURTH GENRE

Outside 77 St. Mark's Place in Manhattan, an old man walks a minia-
ture dog, and a skateboarder sweeps past them on the street. Inside, I
blink and slowly dig my spoon into a half-crystallized, fishy gelatin, slunk
out of a plastic bowl. The apartment belongs to a friend of mine from
grad school named Brandon. A tenement built in 1845, it is a typical nar-
row railroad layout with the rare prize of a balcony on either side.

When my mother first walked down St. Mark's, with its line of smoke
shops, open mic venues, and its tattoo parlor doubling as a coffee shop,
she called it "a circus." I was drawn to the neighborhood as I was drawn
to Brandon's character—to his inquisitiveness and loud laugh. Brandon
embraced eccentricities. He was always working on quirky projects,
constructing things: a coffee table, a costume for Burning Man, a black-
and-white film on his Super 8 camera.

Brandon and I make the movie together. In the film, my hand picks
up a small antler and places it into a pot of boiling water on his stove.
It's the first step in our gelatin recipe: sterilizing cartilage.

*　*　*

Peter Cooper, New Yorker and inventor of instant gelatin, made much
of his fortune manufacturing glue. He stated, "I determined to make
the best glue, and found out every method and ingredient looking to
that end, and so it has always been in demand." In order to make the
stuff, Peter collected glue stock, lime, sulfuric acid, scrap zinc, coal, and
water. From the tanner, he gathered the roundings, skivings, and

493

trimmings from hides of deer, goat, sheep, and cattle. From the butchers, Peter received calves feet and pates—all materials needed to create his ten uniform grades of product (the lowest being Jell-O). He took out several patents for the manufacture. The most successful was signed by President Andrew Jackson in 1830. It was for "making glue from the foot-water or liquor from the boiling of bone of all kinds of animals in double-floored evaporating pans."

*　*　*

A recipe for molded orange jelly hangs on foam board at the Jell-O Museum in LeRoy, New York; this is the recipe we choose to follow. It was written by a woman named Hannah Glasse and published in *Art of Cookery Made Plain and Easy*, a cookbook staple during the Revolutionary War. When questioned about the quality of the recipe, the woman at the museum's front desk says, "I've never made that old stuff. It probably doesn't taste very good." Instructions include vague measurements and unfamiliar ingredients: hand-ground hartshorn, and isinglass, a collagen made from the dried swim bladders of fish.

Brandon receives two deliveries from eBay; he uses house keys to cut the tape on the boxes. The cloudy isinglass arrives in what looks like transparent ketchup packets. If you squish one with your index finger, it springs back. There is still dried blood and dirt on the hartshorn.

Hartshorn no longer requires the dry distillation of horns, but is produced by heating a mixture of ammonium chloride, or ammonium sulfate and chalk. Neither sounds appetizing. Using ammonia while baking can result in the creation of acrylamide (a carcinogen). Knowledge of this potential carcinogen led to a health study on the dangers of gingerbread in the *Journal of Agriculture and Food Chemistry* (scientists concluded it was safe enough).

Hartshorn is now foreign to most home cooks, but it wasn't always so. While used to treat fevers, sunstroke, and snakebites, salt of hartshorn, or "baker's ammonia," served as a precursor to baking powder in the seventeenth and eighteenth centuries. It acts as a leavening agent in bread and cookies. Today, 2.7 ounces sells for about nine dollars. But Brandon insists we go straight to the source—we go "old school" and make it ourselves.

We do not own proper utensils for the job and instead utilize a cheese grater. Brandon and I take turns scraping antlers, rotating them, searching for soft spots. We want to fill a small bowl with bone. It takes forever.

Brandon points his camera at me.

✿　✿　✿

In the film, bone floats down like snow. Little flecks litter the hardwood floor of his living room.

✿　✿　✿

The blog for the Greenwich Village Society for Historical Preservation displays a photograph of Brandon's apartment, telling readers that Marxist revolutionary Leon Trotsky "wrote in this building for the Moscow publication *Novy Mir* (The New World)." After him, poet W. H. Auden would live in the building for nearly twenty years. Auden's friend Hannah Arendt recalled, "When his slum apartment was so cold that the water no longer functioned . . . he had to use the toilet in the liquor store at the corner." Brandon lives in less squalor than Auden, although his home seems more like an evolving workshop than a spread in *Better Homes and Gardens.* He has running water, and even a toilet seat cover picturing a crouching leopard. In fact, a lot of Brandon's decor is animal-themed or taxidermied. A giant buffalo head hangs next to his couch. I often stroke its mangled fur as if it were a living pet. It is impressive, despite the nose, which is a little too dry and on the verge of cracking.

Brandon named the buffalo head Cornelius, proudly claiming it was something he'd stolen from an ex-boyfriend of his sister who had "knocked her up" when she was too young. I see the animal as a relic, a symbol of his childhood growing up in a small town of teenaged mothers, a place where people shoot guns without irony. Most people I meet in New York are intensely curious about Brandon's land of cowboys and my own home of Iowa, which holds a certain Midwestern mystique. Theirs is a blind admiration. Where Brandon and I come from, people wear flannel shirts because it is winter. East Village men grow beards and wear flannel shirts as a kind of throwback to a time when we crafted things with our hands. The resulting impression is more lumberjack dandy. In our New York, everyone seemingly lives in a glorified renaissance of their own imaginations, filled with costumes that can be put on or taken off at will.

✿　✿　✿

In retrospect, it was clear we were living at the end of something—the big city dream we'd held on to in adolescent desperation was now home to trust fund kids and tall, modern buildings built with international money. Even St. Mark's Place was turning into something different, housing more and more frozen yogurt shops. In a year or two, St. Mark's Bookshop wouldn't be able to make rent. The Chelsea Hotel, where Dylan Thomas died and Sid Vicious killed Nancy, where poor tenants paid their occupancy through gifting artwork, and where I had once stayed before permanently moving to New York, was bought—the art removed from the walls, supposedly for the works' "own protection." I flagged these happenings as quintessential of our time, the casualties of economic disparity, a cleansing during a time America battled its own fear and a rhetorical War on Terror.

My first year in New York, the boiler room under my apartment caught fire. I startled from my book, my street full of swirling red lights and a knock at the door. The firemen had put out the fire. One of them scratched his number onto a piece of paper. He asked me to accompany him to a 9/11 memorial banquet. It was difficult for me to understand what was worse: asking a girl out on a first date that would surely center around an attack that resulted in nearly 3,000 deaths, or not being the date to someone who had survived an attack that resulted in nearly 3,000 deaths. The morning of September 11, 2001, I remember taking a difficult anatomy test. I was still a teenager living in Iowa, and my teacher had told the class, "Life goes on, even amidst tragedy." I thought it was a cruel statement and that he must not care much for New Yorkers, but now see that this is probably not the case. I never called the fireman and avoided walking by his station at all costs, feeling that accepting an invitation to rehash a tragedy that I was absent for would be disingenuous. From it had sprung forth a war that I wasn't well-versed in talking about, that was much too complicated for the patriotism that it demanded. I assumed the fireman sought allegiance as well as my love, but I would not give these things to him.

* * *

Brandon is one of a small handful of my friends to have said "I love you" and meant it in a deep, platonic way. In the beginning of our relationship, he told me I was "weird" and "macabre," but I quickly learned to take it as a compliment. These were things about my personality that he could clearly understand and accept. Brandon was the only person who seemed to full-heartedly embrace my strange curiosity about gela-

496

tin, its absurd existence—nourishment from bones. A part of me be-
lieved Jell-O should not exist—a food with hardly any nutritional value,
dunked in chemicals so many times that it was no longer deemed an
animal product. Yet the product thrives via American consumers,
passed around during Thanksgiving and 4th of July picnics, fed to
children and the elderly. It's found in grocery stores all across the
country. If a teenaged Brandon drove south from the town of Broken
Arrow, Oklahoma, where he went to public school, past Gore, stopping
19 miles northwest of the town of Hartshorne, he would have found a
wall of Jell-O at the Super Walmart. Instead, he found it later, while a
patient in the hospital.

✱　✱　✱

After spending a lifetime readying himself to live a *Top Gun* fantasy, to
go to war for his country, Brandon was discharged from the Air Force
for having Crohn's disease. He got very sick and tried to hide his ill-
ness, but someone found him passed out in the bathroom. I only knew
Brandon post-uniform, after he had grown a hippie haircut, walked
from Mexico to Canada, taught scuba diving in the Florida Keys, sailed
from Africa to Antarctica, and tracked wolves in the Rocky Mountains.
Like Jell-O, Brandon embodied creativity and invention; a phoenix
who picked himself up from the ashes of his own childhood and career,
he molded himself into a new person. Brandon was taking film and
audio courses when we met. He hauled his equipment with him across
the country, interviewing friends and comrades who had stayed in the
military and gone to war. These recorded conversations were usually
bleak, but they made Brandon happy to be alive and intact—to have
been plucked from the path of service. He might have a chronic dis-
ease, but at least he hadn't killed anyone.

✱　✱　✱

W. H. Auden's World War II poem, "September 1, 1939," had a surge in
popularity in the aftermath of the 2001 terrorist attack. It's easy to see
why adoration for the poem was reinvigorated with lines like "Waves of
anger and fear / Circulate over the bright / And darkened lands of the
earth." It was broadcast on the radio. During a time of immense mourn-
ing, it did what poems are good for, quietly sinking into the public
consciousness and attempting to heal an entire population. Edward
Mendelson, Auden's hand-selected literary executor, describes how
Auden grew to think of the work as false sentiment. In 1957, while he

497

was living in what would become Brandon's apartment, Auden wrote to the literary critic Laurence Lerner, "Between you and me, I loathe that poem." As a reflection of his growing distaste, Auden edited his own line "We must love one another or die" to "We must love one another *and* die."

Now, when people quote this work they generally use the lines, interchangeably without much notice. But in September 1964, Lyndon B. Johnson quoted Auden's original line in his famous "Daisy" ad, which was run in order to link a hypothetical doomed future to the election of Republican Senator Barry Goldwater. In it, a three-year-old girl counts daisy petals in a field. Over her voice, a more ominous countdown begins, and then the shot suddenly cuts to a mushroom cloud explosion. At the end, Johnson loudly proclaims, "We must love one another or die," but it comes off as more of a threat than encouragement.

I spend time thinking about the subtle distinction in the wording of the poem. Even though the War on Terror is supposedly over, a gray-haired woman in my neighborhood's Episcopal church reads the names of dead soldiers every week off her iPhone, praying for those who, even though they were cared for by doting family members, could not be saved from themselves.

❊ ❊ ❊

The same year Auden wrote about his secret aversion to his poem to Laurence Lerner, Jell-O published an advertisement in verse form. A play on a popular nursery rhyme, a black sheep trades his wool for "deep, dark, delicious treats for deep, dark me." At the bottom of the advertisement is a box of black cherry gelatin, but you get the idea that the text is not talking about hue. It seems to be saying that Jell-O is for people who have complex underbellies, who have complex histories. It was for people like Auden, who obsessed over the difference between "love or die" and "love and die" in his poem. It was for women who donated their aluminum Jell-O molds during World War II so that they might be melted down and forged into airplanes, so that the men they loved could bomb men who were doing atrocious things (but were also loved). Americans killed so that life could return to normal—so that the world would become right again.

❊ ❊ ❊

In Latin, gelatin means "frozen" or "to freeze," which may be one of the many reasons we associate it with a kind of utopian America. What

Jell-O tapped into and sold to its consumers exists both in and out of time. It's a depiction of an America we are nostalgic for, even if our memory of it is a shared delusion. In a Jell-O America, families have a mother and a father, a high—if not superior—moral standard, and everyone dines on roasted bird and treats from the icebox. A woman unveils her molded gelatin creation to her family, garnering squeals of delight. The woman stands proud. It is a food of perfection, a substance that allows her to assert control over otherwise unwieldy fruits and vegetables. Psychologically speaking, it is a food that encapsulates and controls.

❖ ❖ ❖

Six years after 9/11, the satirical newspaper *The Onion* described a fictional attack on the Sears Tower. "Conceptual terrorists" have come to Chicago and have molded a Jell-O salad around the building. The supposed terrorist group leaks a video stating, "[Terrorism] is not your simple bourgeois notion of destructive explosions and weaponized biochemical agents. True terror lies in the futility of human existence." When I read this, the line lingered like a depressive, hovering cloud; as in most comedy, it contains a bit of truth and sadness. The article echoes loss felt in Manhattan—countless deaths, shortened lives, executed human potential, but also the pointlessness of an existence that is meant only to destroy or be destroyed. In addition, the Jell-O imagery makes a farce out of civilian hope: that chaos can be ordered through creativity, that our homes and landmarks are impenetrable. Through the fake journalistic account, satirists illuminated our country's difficult struggle with vulnerability and fear, which, after six years, had not dissipated.

❖ ❖ ❖

In a Brooklyn brownstone, a poet writes DEATH on a piece of paper. He hands the paper to me. "You talk about Jell-O, but you are really talking about this." I believe he is being too dramatic, simplifying a culinary subject of great depth, although he has sniffed out Jell-O's darker meaning. Wendy Wall, author of the article "Shakespearean Jell-O: Mortality and Malleability in the Kitchen," describes jelly as something that "reveals the most abject part of being human. It exposes the potential for decay and ill that is carried through mortality itself." When Shakespeare writes, "Out, vile jelly!" it is a plea to be rid of poisonous humors, those that have the power to change human nature.

The saying that a person "turns to jelly" when afraid? It means invol- untary movement, shifting earth. To many, alterability is unnatural.

It is the last thing eaten by a handful of passengers on the Titanic— peaches in a chartreuse jelly followed by cold waters, sinking bodies, a pitch black night.

❊ ❊ ❊

Instead of experiencing combat firsthand, instead of wearing the title of masculine hero, Auden traveled to Germany only after European hostilities had ended. He was sent with the rank of major in the U.S. Strategic Bombing Survey, where he observed at close hand the effects of area bombing on the defeated German population. What he found was eerie silence and a changed landscape. Essayist and poet Charles Simic writes, "Just in Germany where British planes attacked by night and American planes by day, the Allies dropped nearly two million tons of bombs. . . . There were 31.1 cubic meters of rubble for every person in Cologne and 42.8 cubic meters for every inhabitant of Dres- den." Maybe because of this exposure, Auden became known as a "panoramic" writer, a label given to him by critics and scholars. Or perhaps the fact that he was already a writer made him a perfect sur- veyor. "The pilot's-eye view is . . . desirable for the writer," Auden wrote in a letter to poet John Pudney.

❊ ❊ ❊

Ghosts of factories now dot LeRoy, New York—Salt Company, Can- ning Company, Cotton Company, Plow Company, Paper Company— reminders of a once-booming industrial America. In 1964, the same year the slogan "There's always room for Jell-O" was introduced, the General Foods Company (which merged with the Postum Cereal Co.— later General Foods, now Kraft Foods—which merged with Heinz) decided to end its ties to the town, and shifted all production to Dover, Delaware. Many people were laid off and the Jell-O warehouse was converted into a paintball field.

❊ ❊ ❊

The LeRoy Historical Society prints an article in the local newspaper titled "I Never Knew That," focused on providing facts about the town. It explains that the town is named after a man who never lived in Le- Roy. The proper pronunciation is "luh roy" and not "lee roy." The orig- inal town was named Bellona, for the Greek goddess of war.

500

Instead of salt, canning, cotton, plow, paper, LeRoy now sells explosives.

❂   ❂   ❂

I find it no longer possible to "sing of war" as the great poems and great ballads do. When I think of war, I think of Brandon talking to his now-damaged buddies as they battle their own realities, tired wives whispering into his ear, "I'm so glad you came." I think of hollow pits of death, and Auden circling them from a cold distance. I'm reminded of the valley of dry bones in Ezekiel's vision. As a child, the story terrified me—a sea of dead bodies in a place lacking the water of life. A desert. It had always seemed so mystical, so dreamlike—I'd forgotten or ignored that there was a literal desert with actual Israelites living in it until our War on Terror began. In the Middle East, American soldiers received packages of sunscreen and flavored ice pops from their mothers while they waited for orders and for something to happen in the sandy terrain. Mothers continued to send packages, too. They shipped them because it was one of the only ways they knew how to honor their children's choices, display their own love from across the world. Packaged, preserved, artificial food was mailed in cardboard boxes. Food whose flavors merely mimic flavors of real food.

W. H. Auden tells *The Paris Review* that Chianti does not travel well. "When you drink it here, [it] always tastes like red ink," he says. The interview is supposed to be about the art of poetry, but there is a kind of hiccup in the middle where the interviewer examines the pots and pans hanging from Auden's kitchen wall, and you get the impression that the poet might care for more than the sustenance of words. Auden unashamedly speaks of his fondness for tongue, tripe, brain, and one time when he got a "craze" for turnips. He speaks of these things as if speaking of them might be a matter of importance—as if by scrutinizing his consumption, one might come closer to Auden's poetry, understand his pleasures, his passions.

❂   ❂   ❂

In his poem "In Memory of W.B. Yeats," Auden writes, "For poetry makes nothing happen: it survives. From ranches of isolation and the busy griefs / Raw towns that we believe and die in; it survives, / A way of happening, a mouth." Many critics have come to the conclusion that he is speaking about the performative nature of lyric poetry, but the word "mouth" continues to generate inquiry. "In Memory . . ." is excerpted in a book called *Romanticism after Auschwitz*; the author goes on to ask, "Does it—poetry—survive as a mouth? Does it survive in our mouths? Does it survive because of our mouths or because it gives us mouths?" I believe the answer is "all of the above." I also believe that poetry and food are oftentimes interchangeable.

Who were Brandon and I but people looking for "a way of happening" in the ingredients of a recipe and the mundane, performative nature of its making?

❖ ❖ ❖

At the time, I don't believe Brandon and I thought much of Auden's presence, the fact that he once resided in the same space, cooked in a similar kitchen. We didn't consider his words when we drank mugs of strong coffee, or when we scrubbed a pound of mussels over the sink and cooked them in wine and butter. But now, it all comes flooding back to me: the coffee, the mussels, the day we decided to make gelatin from scratch. We cooked because, as prolific writer M.F.K. Fisher puts it, "three basic needs, for food and security and love, are so mixed and mingled and entwined that we cannot straightly think of one without the others." She wrote these words after her lover shot himself at the beginning of World War II. W. H. Auden said of Fisher, "I do not know of anyone in the United States who writes better prose."

❖ ❖ ❖

The lot on which Peter Cooper's first glue factory was built originally housed ammunition. The space is referred to as "powder house lots" in city records: barrels of gunpowder had to be removed before he could begin production. Peter Cooper and his descendants continued to call their glue and gelatin-making buildings after their original intended purpose—as if they were just borrowing the space. Powder House: a paradoxical name. Powder would make a sorry home. Pitiful protection. It would just take one bad wolf to blow it all down, scatter the structure into the air.

I imagine this scene while I shave antlers. If I breathe, the bone disperses and misses the bowl. I kneel down and touch escaped flecks with the tips of my fingers. They stick to my hands like glitter, and I wonder then if this is what it would have been like inside a rendering factory: everything covered in a thin layer of dust. If so, Peter Cooper must've spread these fragments wherever he traveled, tracking them into his living room, the dining room, the bed in which he slept.

Shavings are all over us. Brandon and I bend down to brush them off.

Bone sticks to our bodies. It does not leave.

* * *

I am riding the PATH train from New Jersey to Manhattan when I hear about the death of Marcy Borders, whom CNN calls the "Dust Lady." The news flashes on a television screen while I travel underneath the Hudson River. The nickname comes from a now-famous photograph of Marcy. In the image, she has just emerged from the damaged North Tower, her hands held out helplessly in front of her, searching the air. She is wearing business attire, pearls, and covered in white powder. The news tells me Marcy has died of stomach cancer, likely as a result of exposure to chemical carcinogens released during the building's collapse.

On the train, passengers lean on railings. Some, like me, read captions on the television screen about Ms. Borders. The car is packed solid, people are going to work, and a woman's purse taps my back like Morse code. When my parents visit, they say about these crowded rides, "It's like animals being taken to slaughter." Their statement catches me off guard—the casual nature in which they can sometimes be so insensitive. I tell my parents this is how I live now. In the city, space is what I adapt to, pass through, and share with others. When a stranger brushes my arm while walking past, I'm reminded of the person's realness. A body outside of my own.

* * *

Powder House: A Film

I am the hand. The pose. I touch each ingredient and each ingredient seems imperfect.

Our water is not spring but tap; our oranges are not Seville but navel. Our recipe is actually quite specific about these items. But we say, *this will work.* We want it to work. I squish and stir. Brandon points his camera at the pot into which I have thrown powdered bone and isinglass. He stops, laughs, holds his nose. In Brandon's kitchen, the air has turned sickeningly strong: metallic, like blood, like ocean. I cut citrus, squeeze the flesh to mask smell and add flavoring. Juice runs down my arm into a small cut and stings.

Brandon and I watch the mixture activate, thicken, and bubble. We pour it into a bowl, place it in the fridge, and wait.

503

The next day, it has not quite solidified, so we stick the bowl in the freezer like sly cheaters. Brandon says *this will work*. He wants it to come out of the bowl as one solid, molded shape. What comes out is part gelatinous, part ice crystal. We place the molded creation on the table beside the leftover antlers and begin to film. You cannot see our failure in the recording. Off-camera, we lift spoons to our mouths and taste what we have done. It is not pleasant, and the gelatin quickly makes a puddle on the countertop.

❋   ❋   ❋

A San Francisco artist constructs the New York City skyline out of gelatin. She has something to say about "the fragility of the familiar city grid." She likes to watch the material glisten and dissolve. She likes to watch her towers lean on each other in support. The artist says, this is what gives Jelly NYC "human quality." It exists somewhere in the act of touching.

❋   ❋   ❋

I meet a young artist named Veronica, whose job is to repair patina and wax on parapets surrounding the memorial pools and the railings inside the 9/11 Memorial Museum. She does this in the middle of the night, like Santa Claus or the tooth fairy. She leaves no corrosive fingerprints behind. Veronica makes it look as though no one has been there. She is a restorationist, a preservationist—one that makes everything appear okay from the outside.

In her personal practice, she paints with rust on paper—paintings that look like forests. I view these works as an act of acknowledging and honoring entropy.

❋   ❋   ❋

There is a model museum in Jersey City hidden inside a now-defunct tobacco factory. If you call to make an appointment, a person will unlock the door. Here, you will find the miniature-sized work of architect Richard Meier and his partners—building complexes, whole cityscapes constructed out of delicate balsa wood—whose structures reach upward like little stalagmites. The models are all done by hand, an impressive sight of dedication and detail. The trees on the models even have leaves.

There are tiny people inside the buildings too, hanging out in park areas, conversing on balconies. I spy on them and notice that they have

504

facial expressions. They gesture: put their hands on their hips or head, point straight ahead with index fingers. The people—even their clothes—are white. On the wall hangs a framed, rejected plan for the 9/11 memorial. On the blueprint someone has written, "an echo of what was lost, an anti-creation." It reminds me of the dust lady. All of a sudden, the room is full of tiny specters. Little white bodies gesturing into space, touching nothing at all.

*   *   *

The 9/11 memorial pools look like deep, never-ending pits. Like Niagara Falls, I get wet when I stand too close to one of them. Wind carries the water and sprays me in a fine mist. I see the pool for the first time on my way to a freelance job. A food magazine has asked me to be a hand model for a film shoot. Their offices and test kitchen have moved into the new World Trade Center—now called the Freedom Tower— and I am to go to the 35th floor. I think it is a bold move for a bunch of foodies to work within a building charged with past tragedy, but Auden once wrote, "It is only through [art] that we are able to break bread with the dead, and without communion with the dead a fully human life is impossible." So I commune, and a woman gives me brandied cherries: one to eat and one to place into a cocktail I make in front of the cameras. "Aren't these the best?" The woman is a food stylist and she gingerly arranges whole spices in a tiny bowl. The film crew has placed me right in front of a wall of windows, and when I look up, I am floating above Manhattan. "Look," says the woman. For a moment I think she is talking about the view or something outside, but she wants to instruct me on how to hold a bottle of bitters. "Like this," she motions. "Beautiful."

Nominated by Fourth Genre

SPECIAL MENTION

(The editors also wish to mention the following important works published by small presses last year. Listings are in no particular order.)

FICTION

J Bloom — Molly (Notre Dame Review)
MK Malik — Call Ladies (Bellevue Literary Review)
Alexander Weinstein — Fall Line (Pleiades)
Claire Davis — Fix-It Man (Gettysburg Review)
Bryan Washington — Bayou (One Story)
Iheoma Nwachukwu — Urban Gorilla (Southern Review)
T. Coraghessan Boyle — Warrior Jesus (Narrative)
Lily King — A Man At The Door (Harvard Review)
Noelle O'Reilly — Glacier (Conjunctions)
Joan Silber — Secrets of Happiness (Southern Review)
April Vazquez — Rebirth (Ruminate)
Joyce Carol Oates — Fractal (Conjunctions)
Michael Pritchett — A Sort of Woman (New Letters)
Christie Hodgen — The War of The Worlds (American Short Fiction)
Kevin Wilson — Door to Door (Kenyon Review)
Eric Severn — Jocasta (The Pinch)
Helen Elaine Lee — Blood Knot (Ploughshares)
Alexander Maksik — The Old Masters (Sewanee Review)
Amber Caron — Bending the Map (Agni)
Amy Neswald — Bruce, on Ice (Green Mountains Review)

Michael Jaime-Becerra — Dale, Dale, Dale ! (Zyzzyva)

Jill McCorkle — The Lineman (Ecotone)

Mark Jacobs — Other Men's Fields (Hudson Review)

Mike Alberti — Prairie Fire, 1899 (One Story)

Wendy Herlich — Silence Is Golden — (Mississippi Review)

John Chandler — Tourette's (Chicago Quarterly Review)

Sonya Larson — The Kindest (American Short Fiction)

Justin Reed — The Remedy to Every Fear (Consequence)

JP Vallieres — Big Walmart (Santa Monica Review)

Leslie Pietrzyk — People Love A View (Arts & Letters)

Kirby Williams — The Mermaid and the Firefly (Blue Fountain)

Jack Driscoll — At Any Given Time (Georgia Review)

Christine Sneed — In The Park (LitMag)

Kelsey Yoder — Ocean Bound (Five Points)

Rick DeMarinis — Planing Ahead (Antioch Review)

Lee Upton — Visitation (Bennington Review)

Brooke Bullman — The Gray Horse (Southern Review)

Kristina Gorcheva-Newberry — All of Me (Prairie Schooner)

Rolf Yngve — An August Taxi, la Sirena (Five Points)

Viet Dinh — The Food Chain (Copper Nickel)

Jacob M. Appel — Prisoners of the Multiverse (The Liars' Asylum,
    Black Lawrence Press)

Elizabeth Wagner — The Violinist (Mississippi Review)

Kathleen J. Woods — When You Are Thus Changed (Western
    Humanities Review)

Lilly Hunt — Bulletin Board Dragon (One Teen Story)

Alex Taylor — The Gypsy Rib (Southwest Review)

Greg Sarris — Citizen (Zyzzyva)

Jeff Albers — My Appearance (Notre Dame Review)

Krystal Sanders — Drown (Black Warrior Review)

Kimberly King Parsons — Nothing Before Something (Indiana Review)

Rebecca McClanahan — The New Couple in 5A (Literal Latte)

Celia Laskey — Snow Angel (Minnesota Review)

A.A. Weiss — Opyata (Zone 3)

Jennifer Maritza McCauley — Torsion (Vassar Review)

Tim Griffith — The Boathouse (Tin House)

CC Humphreys — The Ankle Bracelet (Pulp Literature)

Matthew Young — Coping Mechanisms (Consequence Magazine)

Ngwah-Mbo Nana Nkweti — It Takes A Village Some Say
    (The Baffler)

Phong Nguyen — We're So Blessed, We're So Lucky (River Styx)

Molly Quinn — A Danger To Ourselves (Iowa Review)

Scott L. Sanders — House For Sale By Owner (Zone 3)

Stephen Dixon — The Kiss (Agni)

Sigrid Nunez — The Blind (Paris Review)

Zeynep Özakat — Aviculture (Black Warrior Review)

Andría Nacina Cole — Men Be Either Or, But Never Enough (New Letters)

Anya Ventura — Vanishing Point (The Common)

Lindsey Drager — The Two-Body Problem (Cincinnati Review)

Idra Novey — The Last Summer of Our Patriarch (Ploughshares)

Janice Obuchowski — Mountain Shade (Grist)

Gwen E. Kirby — First Woman Hanged For Witchcraft in Wales, 1594 (New Delta Review)

E.C. Osondu — Alien Mark (Threepenny Review)

Rita Bullwinkel — Decor (Tin House)

Andrew Porter — Rhinebeck (Epoch)

Wendell Berry — The Art of Loading Brush (Threepenny Review)

Meg Wolitzer — Deep Lie The Woods (Southampton Review)

Kendra Fortmeyer — Monomyth (Cincinnati Review)

Marian Crotty — What Counts As Love (Potomac Review)

NONFICTION

Andrew Blevins — The Egg Man (Crazyhorse)

Art Hanlon — The Brilliant Present (Narrative)

Andrew Kay — Pilgrim At Tinder Creek (The Point)

Benjamin Hertwig — Home From The War (The Sun)

Barbara Hurd — Letter To America (Terrain.org)

Naa Baako Ako-Adjei — Why It's Time Schools Stopped Teaching To "Kill A Mockingbird" (Transition)

David Klein — Einhorn's Kosher Palace (Hudson Review)

Alyssa Knickerbocker — X-Men (Tin House)

Sinead Gleeson — Second Mother (Granta)

Richard Russo — Getting Good (Sewanee Review)

Bruce Ballenger — Return To The Typewriter (Fourth Genre)

A. Lyn Carol — I Plead The Blood (Redivider)

Elizabeth Benedict — Do You Come Here Often? (Kitchen Work)

Steven Koteff — Saint Bart (The Point)

Jacqueline Jones LaMon — Bergamot (Crab Orchard Review)

John Kimmey — Fear and Trembling (Ruminate)

Jenn Shapland — Illness Is Metaphor (Tin House)

Jes Loy Nichols — To The Hedgerows About Trump (Caught on The River)

Robert Wrigley — Nemerov's Door (Missouri Review)

Karl Taro Greenfeld — We Not Die (Kenyon Review)

Jennifer Hope Choi — My Mongolian Spot (American Scholar)

Askold Melnyczuk — And The Living Are Silent (Ploughshares)

Ye Chun — To Say (Denver Quarterly)

Colleen Mayo — Knockers Up (The Sun)

William Pierce — In Uniform (Consequence)

Christopher Ketcham — The Fallacy of Endless Economic Growth (PSMAG.Com)

Phil Christman — On Being Midwestern (Hedgehog Review)

Julie Marie Wade — 503A (Iowa Review)

Philip Metres — Singing The Darkness (Image)

Maureen McCoy — Bats: Teen Worker (Antioch Review)

Brian Castner — Bethlehem Revisited (River Teeth)

Erin Slaughter — On Grief (Another Chicago Magazine)

Clint McCown — A Lesson From My Father's Suitcase (Colorado Review)

Eric Puchner — Expression (Hopkins Review)

Christina Olson — The Lion of Ladysmith (Third Coast)

Kerry Muir — Blur (River Teeth)

LaTanya McQueen — Points of Interest (Passages North)

Thomas Larson — What It Was My Father Came Here To Get Away From (River Teeth)

Kim McLarin — Eshu Finds Work (New England Review)

Ben Fountain — One Hundred Million Years of Solitude (Sewanee Review)

John Barth — Out of The Cradle (Granta)

Rosellen Brown — Offstage (New Letters)

Jo Scott-Coe — This American Monster (Tahoma Literary Review)

Jesse Chehak — The Soldier And The Soil (Orion)

Toni Jensen — Women In The Fracklands (Catapult)

Kristopher Jansma — The Corps of Discovery (Zyzzyva)

Brian Turner — Ashes, Ashes (Georgia Review)

Lia Purpura — Walk With Snowy Things (Agni)

Idrissa Simmonds — Satiate (Room)

Erika Krouse — Comfort Woman (Granta)

Leath Tonino — The Doe's Song (Orion)

POETRY

Julia B. Levine — Ordinary Psalm After Failing Another Child (Zone 3)

Melissa Hunter Gurney — Eating Shadows (Great Weather For Media)

Martha Collins — In Time (Salamander)

Joel Oppenheimer — Houses (Selected Poems, White Pine Press)

Zeina Hashem Beck — Broken Ghazal: Speak Arabic (Louder Than Hearts, Bauhan Publishing)

Layli Long Soldier — from Whereas (Poetry)

Carolyn Forché — Tapestry (World Literature Today)

Tommy Pico — from Junk (Poetry)

Betsy Sholl — Philomela (Field)

Eleanor Wilner — To Bear Them Up (Birmingham Poetry Review)

Chase Twichell — What's Wrong With Me (Georgia Review)

Kathy Fagan — Cooper's Hawk (Blackbird)

David Wojahn — Still Life: Stevens's Wallet On a Key West Hotel Dresser (Agni)

Bob Hicok — Say Uncle (Southern Review)

Laura Kasischke — The Breath (Arroyo)

Erika Meitner — The Practice of Depicting Matter as it Passes from Radiance to Decomposition (New England Review)

Patricia Smith — Mammy Two-Shoes, Rightful Owner of Tom, Addresses the Lady of the House (Hunger Mountain)

Susan Cohen — Report on the State of the World's Children, (Tar River Poetry)

Corey Van Landingham — On the Theory of Descent, (The Adroit Journal)

Emily Tuszynska — Firstborn (Salamander)

Jennie Malboeuf — Hubris (New South Journal)

Ilya Kaminsky — We Lived Happily During the War (American Poetry Review)

Jehanne Dubrow — Self-Portrait with Cable News Graffiti, Weather (Copper Nickel)

Joseph J. Capista — Notes for the Next God, (Cutbank)

Grant Clauser — The Tattooist's Lament (Poetry South)

Caitlin Doyle — The Dress Code, (The Yale Review)

Mihaela Moscaliuc — The Wandering Womb Borrows Language from Aretaeus, 2nd Century (Poet Lore)

Rachel Marie Patterson — Connemara (Gulf Stream)

Donald Platt — 'Iluminación (Crazyhorse)

Kevin Prufer — The Art of Fiction (Copper Nickel)

Taije Silverman — Who the Letters Were From (The Southern Review)

Elizabeth Vignalí — 'Mortgage, (The Cincinnati Review)

Kathryn Smith — Rehearsal for the Apocalypse (Book of Exodus, Scablands Books)

PRESSES FEATURED IN THE PUSHCART PRIZE EDITIONS SINCE 1976

A-Minor
About Place Journal
Abstract Magazine TV
The Account
Adroit Journal
Agni
Ahsahta Press
Ailanthus Press
Alaska Quarterly Review
Alcheringa/Ethnopoetics
Alice James Books
Ambergris
Amelia
American Circus
American Journal of Poetry
American Letters and Commentary
American Literature
American PEN
American Poetry Review
American Scholar
American Short Fiction
The American Voice
Amicus Journal
Amnesty International
Anaesthesia Review
Anhinga Press
Another Chicago Magazine

Antaeus
Antietam Review
Antioch Review
Apalachee Quarterly
Aphra
Aralia Press
The Ark
Arroyo
Art and Understanding
Arts and Letters
Artword Quarterly
Ascensius Press
Ascent
Aspen Leaves
Aspen Poetry Anthology
Assaracus
Assembling
Atlanta Review
Autonomedia
Avocet Press
The Awl
The Baffler
Bakunin
Bat City Review
Bamboo Ridge
Barlenmir House
Barnwood Press

Barrow Street

Bellevue Literary Review

The Bellingham Review

Bellowing Ark

Beloit Poetry Journal

Bennington Review

Bettering America Poetry

Bilingual Review

Black American Literature Forum

Blackbird

Black Renaissance Noire

Black Rooster

Black Scholar

Black Sparrow

Black Warrior Review

Blackwells Press

The Believer

Bloom

Bloomsbury Review

Blue Cloud Quarterly

Blueline

Blue Unicorn

Blue Wind Press

Bluefish

BOA Editions

Bomb

Bookslinger Editions

Boston Review

Boulevard

Boxspring

Briar Cliff Review

Brick

Bridge

Bridges

Brown Journal of Arts

Burning Deck Press

Butcher's Dog

Cafe Review

Caliban

California Quarterly

Callaloo

Calliope

Calliopea Press

Calyx

The Canary

Canto

Capra Press

Carcanet Editions

Caribbean Writer

Carolina Quarterly

Catapult

Cave Wall

Cedar Rock

Center

Chariton Review

Charnel House

Chattahoochee Review

Chautauqua Literary Journal

Chelsea

Chicago Quarterly Review

Chouteau Review

Chowder Review

Cimarron Review

Cincinnati Review

Cincinnati Poetry Review

City Lights Books

Cleveland State Univ. Poetry Ctr.

Clown War

Codex Journal

CoEvolution Quarterly

Cold Mountain Press

The Collagist

Colorado Review

Columbia: A Magazine of Poetry and Prose

Conduit

Confluence Press

Confrontation

Conjunctions

Connecticut Review

Constellations

Copper Canyon Press

Copper Nickel

Cosmic Information Agency

Countermeasures

Counterpoint

Court Green

Crab Orchard Review
Crawl Out Your Window
Crazyhorse
Creative Nonfiction
Crescent Review
Cross Cultural Communications
Cross Currents
Crosstown Books
Crowd
Cue
Cumberland Poetry Review
Curbstone Press
Cutbank
Cypher Books
Dacotah Territory
Daedalus
Dalkey Archive Press
Decatur House
December
Denver Quarterly
Desperation Press
Dogwood
Domestic Crude
Doubletake
Dragon Gate Inc.
Dreamworks
Dryad Press
Duck Down Press
Dunes Review
Durak
East River Anthology
Eastern Washington University Press
Ecotone
El Malpensante
Electric Literature
Eleven Eleven
Ellis Press
Empty Bowl
Ep;phany
Epoch
Ergol
Evansville Review
Exquisite Corpse

Faultline
Fence
Fiction
Fiction Collective
Fiction International
Field
Fifth Wednesday Journal
Fine Madness
Firebrand Books
Firelands Art Review
First Intensity
5 A.M.
Five Fingers Review
Five Points Press
Florida Review
Forklift
The Formalist
Foundry
Four Way Books
Fourth Genre
Fourth River
Frontiers: A Journal of Women Studies
Fugue
Gallimaufry
Genre
The Georgia Review
Gettysburg Review
Ghost Dance
Gibbs-Smith
Glimmer Train
Goddard Journal
David Godine, Publisher
Graham House Press
Grand Street
Granta
Graywolf Press
Great River Review
Green Mountains Review
Greenfield Review
Greensboro Review
Guardian Press
Gulf Coast
Hanging Loose

Harbour Publishing
Hard Pressed
Harvard Review
Hawaii Pacific Review
Hayden's Ferry Review
Hermitage Press
Heyday
Hills
Hollyridge Press
Holmgangers Press
Holy Cow!
Home Planet News
Hopkins Review
Hudson Review
Hunger Mountain
Hungry Mind Review
Ibbetson Street Press
Icarus
Icon
Idaho Review
Iguana Press
Image
In Character
Indiana Review
Indiana Writes
Intermedia
Intro
Invisible City
Inwood Press
Iowa Review
Ironwood
I-70 Review
Jam To-day
J Journal
The Journal
Jubilat
The Kanchenjunga Press
Kansas Quarterly
Kayak
Kelsey Street Press
Kenyon Review
Kestrel
Kweli Journal

Lake Effect
Lana Turner
Latitudes Press
Laughing Waters Press
Laurel Poetry Collective
Laurel Review
L'Epervier Press
Liberation
Linquis
Literal Latté
Literary Imagination
The Literary Review
The Little Magazine
Little Patuxent Review
Little Star
Living Hand Press
Living Poets Press
Logbridge-Rhodes
Louisville Review
Lowlands Review
LSU Press
Lucille
Lynx House Press
Lyric
The MacGuffin
Magic Circle Press
Malahat Review
Manoa
Manroot
Many Mountains Moving
Marlboro Review
Massachusetts Review
McSweeney's
Meridian
Mho & Mho Works
Micah Publications
Michigan Quarterly
Mid-American Review
Milkweed Editions
Milkweed Quarterly
The Minnesota Review
Mississippi Review
Mississippi Valley Review

Missouri Review
Montana Gothic
Montana Review
Montemora
Moon Pie Press
Moon Pony Press
Mount Voices
Mr. Cogito Press
MSS
Mudfish
Mulch Press
Muzzle Magazine
n+1
Nada Press
Narrative
National Poetry Review
Nebraska Poets Calendar
Nebraska Review
Nepantla
Nerve Cowboy
New America
New American Review
New American Writing
The New Criterion
New Delta Review
New Directions
New England Review
New England Review and Bread Loaf
   Quarterly
New Issues
New Letters
New Madrid
New Ohio Review
New Orleans Review
New South Books
New Verse News
New Virginia Review
New York Quarterly
New York University Press
Nimrod
9×9 Industries
Ninth Letter
Noon

North American Review
North Atlantic Books
North Dakota Quarterly
North Point Press
Northeastern University Press
Northern Lights
Northwest Review
Notre Dame Review
O. ARS
O. Bl k
Obsidian
Obsidian II
Ocho
Oconee Review
October
Ohio Review
Old Crow Review
Ontario Review
Open City
Open Places
Orca Press
Orchises Press
Oregon Humanities
Orion
Other Voices
Oxford American
Oxford Press
Oyez Press
Oyster Boy Review
Painted Bride Quarterly
Painted Hills Review
Palo Alto Review
Paris Press
Paris Review
Parkett
Parnassus: Poetry in Review
Partisan Review
Passages North
Paterson Literary Review
Pebble Lake Review
Penca Books
Pentagram
Penumbra Press

Pequod

Persea: An International Review

Perugia Press

Per Contra

Pilot Light

The Pinch

Pipedream Press

Pitcairn Press

Pitt Magazine

Pleasure Boat Studio

Pleiades

Ploughshares

Plume

Poem-A-Day

Poems & Plays

Poet and Critic

Poet Lore

Poetry

Poetry Atlanta Press

Poetry East

Poetry International

Poetry Ireland Review

Poetry Northwest

Poetry Now

The Point

Post Road

Prairie Schooner

Prelude

Prescott Street Press

Press

Prime Number

Prism

Promise of Learnings

Provincetown Arts

A Public Space

Puerto Del Sol

Purple Passion Press

Quaderni Di Yip

Quarry West

The Quarterly

Quarterly West

Quiddity

Radio Silence

Rainbow Press

Raritan: A Quarterly Review

Rattle

Red Cedar Review

Red Clay Books

Red Dust Press

Red Earth Press

Red Hen Press

Release Press

Republic of Letters

Review of Contemporary Fiction

Revista Chicano-Riqueña

Rhetoric Review

Rhino

Rivendell

River Styx

River Teeth

Rowan Tree Press

Ruminate

Runes

Russian *Samizdat*

Salamander

Salmagundi

San Marcos Press

Santa Monica Review

Sarabande Books

Saturnalia

Sea Pen Press and Paper Mill

Seal Press

Seamark Press

Seattle Review

Second Coming Press

Semiotext(e)

Seneca Review

Seven Days

The Seventies Press

Sewanee Review

The Shade Journal

Shankpainter

Shantih

Shearsman

Sheep Meadow Press

Shenandoah

A Shout In the Street
Sibyl-Child Press
Side Show
Sixth Finch
Small Moon
Smartish Pace
The Smith
Snake Nation Review
Solo
Solo 2
Some
The Sonora Review
Southeast Review
Southern Indiana Review
Southern Poetry Review
Southern Review
Southampton Review
Southwest Review
Speakeasy
Spectrum
Spillway
Spork
The Spirit That Moves Us
St. Andrews Press
Stillhouse Press
Storm Cellar
Story
Story Quarterly
Streetfare Journal
Stuart Wright, Publisher
Subtropics
Sugar House Review
Sulfur
Summerset Review
The Sun
Sun & Moon Press
Sun Press
Sunstone
Sweet
Sycamore Review
Tab
Tamagawa
Tar River Poetry

Teal Press
Telephone Books
Telescope
Temblor
The Temple
Tendril
Texas Slough
Think
Third Coast
13th Moon
THIS
Thorp Springs Press
Three Rivers Press
Threepenny Review
Thrush
Thunder City Press
Thunder's Mouth Press
Tia Chucha Press
Tiger Bark Press
Tikkun
Tin House
Tipton Review
Tombouctou Books
Toothpaste Press
Transatlantic Review
Treelight
Triplopia
TriQuarterly
Truck Press
Tule Review
Tupelo Review
Turnrow
Tusculum Review
Undine
Unicorn Press
University of Chicago Press
University of Georgia Press
University of Illinois Press
University of Iowa Press
University of Massachusetts Press
University of North Texas Press
University of Pittsburgh Press
University of Wisconsin Press

University Press of New England
Unmuzzled Ox
Unspeakable Visions of the Individual
Vagabond
Vallum
Verse
Verse Wisconsin
Vignette
Virginia Quarterly Review
Volt
The Volta
Wampeter Press
War, Literature & The Arts
Washington Writer's Workshop
Water-Stone
Water Table
Wave Books
West Branch
Western Humanities Review
Westigan Review
White Pine Press

Wickwire Press
Wigleaf
Willow Springs
Wilmore City
Witness
Word Beat Press
Wordsmith
World Literature Today
WorldTemple Press
Wormwood Review
Writers' Forum
Xanadu
Yale Review
Yardbird Reader
Yarrow
Y-Bird
Yes Yes Books
Zeitgeist Press
Zoetrope: All-Story
Zone 3
ZYZZYVA

THE PUSHCART PRIZE FELLOWSHIPS

The Pushcart Prize Fellowships Inc., a 501 (c) (3) nonprofit corporation, is the endowment for The Pushcart Prize. "Members" donated up to $249 each. "Sponsors" gave between $250 and $999. "Benefactors" donated from $1000 to $4,999. "Patrons" donated $5,000 and more. We are very grateful for these donations. Gifts of any amount are welcome. For information write to the Fellowships at PO Box 380, Wainscott, NY 11975.

FOUNDING PATRONS

The Katherine Anne Porter Literary Trust
Michael and Elizabeth R. Rea

PATRONS

Anonymous
Margaret Ajemian Ahnert
Daniel L. Dolgin & Loraine F. Gardner
James Patterson Foundation
Neltje
Charline Spektor
Ellen M. Violett

BENEFACTORS

Anonymous
Russell Allen
Hilaria & Alec Baldwin
David Caldwell
Ted Conklin
Bernard F. Conners
Catherine and C. Bryan Daniels
Maureen Mahon Egen
Dallas Ernst
Cedering Fox
H.E. Francis

Mary Ann Goodman & Bruno Quinson Foundation
Bill & Genie Henderson
Bob Henderson
Marina & Stephen E. Kaufman
Wally & Christine Lamb
Dorothy Lichtenstein
Joyce Carol Oates
Warren & Barbara Phillips
Stacey Richter
Glyn Vincent
Margaret V. B. Wurtele

SUSTAINING MEMBERS

Agni
Margaret A. Ahnert
Dick Allen
Hilaria & Alec Baldwin
Jim Barnes
Ellen Bass
Ann Beattie
Wendell Berry
Rosellen Brown
David Caldwell
Bonnie Jo Campbell
Mary Casey
Dan Chaon
Luchinda Clark
Suzanne Cleary
Martha Collins
Linda Coleman
Ted Colm
Stephen Corey
Lisa Couturier
Ed David
Josephine David
Dan Dolgin & Loraine Gardner
Jack Driscoll
Wendy Druce
Penny Dunning
Wendy Durden
Maureen Mahon Egen
Elizabeth Ellen
Alan Furst
Alice Friman
Carol & Laurene Frith
Ben & Sharon Fountain
Robert Giron
Myrna Goodman
Helen Hardley
Jeffrey Harrison
Alex Henderson
Bob Henderson
Lee Hinton
Jane Hirsfield
Helen Houghton
Mark Irwin
Diane Johnson
Don Kaplan

Peter Krass
Edmund Keeley
Wally & Christine Lamb
Linda Lancione
Sydney Lea
Stephen O. Lesser
William Lychack
Maria Matthiessen
Alice Mattison
Robert McBrearty
Rebecca McClanahan
John Mullen
Joan Murray
Neltje
Joyce Carol Oates
Daniel Orozco
Barbara & Warren Phillips
Horatio Potter
C.E. Poverman
Elizabeth R. Rea
Stacey Richter
Valerie Sayers
Schaffner Family Fdn.
Alice Schell
Dennis Schmitz
Sharasheff-Johnson Fund
Sybil Steinberg
Jody Stewart
Sun Publishing
Summerset Review
Elaine Terranova
Susan Terris
Upstreet
Elizabeth Veach
Glyn Vincent
Rosanna Warren
Michael Waters
BJ Ward
Susan Wheeler
Diane Williams
Kirby E. Williams
Henny Wenkart
Eleanor Wilner
Sandra Wisenberg
Margaret Wurtele

SPONSORS

Altman / Kazickas Fdn.
Jacob Appel
Jean M. Auel
Jim Barnes
Charles Baxter

Joe David Bellamy
Laura & Pinckney Benedict
Wendell Berry
Laure-Anne Bosselaar
Kate Braverman

Barbara Bristol
Kurt Brown
Richard Burgin
Alan Catlin
Mary Casey
Siv Cedering
Dan Chaon
James Charlton
Andrei Codrescu
Linda Coleman
Ted Colm
Stephen Corey
Tracy Crow
Dana Literary Society
Carol de Gramont
Nelson DeMille
E. L. Doctorow
Karl Elder
Donald Finkel
Ben and Sharon Fountain
Alan and Karen Furst
John Gill
Robert Giron
Beth Gutcheon
Doris Grumbach & Sybil Pike
Gwen Head
The Healing Muse
Robin Hemley
Bob Hicok
Jane Hirshfield

Helen & Frank Houghton
Joseph Hurka
Diane Johnson
Janklow & Nesbit Asso.
Edmund Keeley
Thomas E. Kennedy
Sydney Lea
Stephen Lesser
Gerald Locklin
Thomas Lux
Markowitz, Fenelon and Bank
Elizabeth McKenzie
McSweeney's
John Mullen
Joan Murray
Barbara and Warren Phillips
Hilda Raz
Stacey Richter
Schaffner Family Foundation
Sharasheff—Johnson Fund
Cindy Sherman
Joyce Carol Smith
May Carlton Swope
Glyn Vincent
Julia Wendell
Philip White
Kirby E. Williams
Eleanor Wilner
David Wittman
Richard Wyatt & Irene Eilers

MEMBERS

Anonymous (3)
Stephen Adams
Betty Adcock
Agni
Carolyn Alessio
Dick Allen
Henry H. Allen
John Allman
Lisa Alvarez
Jan Lee Ande
Dr. Russell Anderson
Ralph Angel
Antietam Review
Susan Antolin
Ruth Appelhof
Philip and Marjorie Appleman
Linda Aschbrenner
Renee Ashley
Ausable Press
David Baker
Catherine Barnett
Dorothy Barresi

Barlow Street Press
Jill Bart
Ellen Bass
Judith Baumel
Ann Beattie
Madison Smartt Bell
Beloit Poetry Journal
Pinckney Benedict
Karen Bender
Andre Bernard
Christopher Bernard
Wendell Berry
Linda Bierds
Stacy Bierlein
Big Fiction
Bitter Oleander Press
Mark Blaeuer
John Blondel
Blue Light Press
Carol Bly
BOA Editions
Deborah Bogen

Bomb
Susan Bono
Brain Child
Anthony Brandt
James Breeden
Rosellen Brown
Jane Brox
Andrea Hollander Budy
E. S. Bumas
Richard Burgin
Skylar H. Burris
David Caligiuri
Kathy Callaway
Bonnie Jo Campbell
Janine Canan
Henry Carlile
Carrick Publishing
Fran Castan
Mary Casey
Chelsea Associates
Marianne Cherry
Phillis M. Choyke
Lucinda Clark
Suzanne Cleary
Linda Coleman
Martha Collins
Ted Conklin
Joan Connor
J. Cooper
John Copenhaver
Dan Corrie
Pam Cotney
Lisa Couturier
Tricia Currans-Sheehan
Jim Daniels
Daniel & Daniel
Jerry Danielson
Ed David
Josephine David
Thadious Davis
Michael Denison
Maija Devine
Sharon Dilworth
Edward DiMaio
Kent Dixon
A.C. Dorset
Jack Driscoll
Wendy Druce
Penny Dunning
John Duncklee
Elaine Edelman
Renee Edison & Don Kaplan
Nancy Edwards
Ekphrasis Press
M.D. Elevitch

Elizabeth Ellen
Entrekin Foundation
Failbetter.com
Irvin Faust
Elliot Figman
Tom Filer
Carol and Lauerne Firth
Finishing Line Press
Susan Firer
Nick Flynn
Starkey Flythe Jr.
Peter Fogo
Linda Foster
Fourth Genre
John Fulton
Fugue
Alice Fulton
Alan Furst
Eugene Garber
Frank X. Gaspar
A Gathering of the Tribes
Reginald Gibbons
Emily Fox Gordon
Philip Graham
Eamon Grennan
Myrna Goodman
Ginko Tree Press
Jessica Graustain
Lee Meitzen Grue
Habit of Rainy Nights
Rachel Hadas
Susan Hahn
Meredith Hall
Harp Strings
Jeffrey Harrison
Clarinda Harriss
Lois Marie Harrod
Healing Muse
Tim Hedges
Michele Helm
Alex Henderson
Lily Henderson
Daniel Henry
Neva Herington
Lou Hertz
Stephen Herz
William Heyen
Bob Hicok
R. C. Hildebrandt
Kathleen Hill
Lee Hinton
Jane Hirshfield
Edward Hoagland
Daniel Hoffman
Doug Holder

Richard Holinger
Rochelle L. Holt
Richard M. Huber
Brigid Hughes
Lynne Hugo
Karla Huston
Illya's Honey
Susan Indigo
Mark Irwin
Beverly A. Jackson
Richard Jackson
Christian Jara
David Jauss
Marilyn Johnston
Alice Jones
Journal of New Jersey Poets
Robert Kalich
Sophia Kartsonis
Julia Kasdorf
Miriam Polli Katsikis
Meg Kearney
Celine Keating
Brigit Kelly
John Kistner
Judith Kitchen
Stephen Kopel
Peter Krass
David Kresh
Maxine Kumin
Valerie Laken
Babs Lakey
Linda Lancione
Maxine Landis
Lane Larson
Dorianne Laux & Joseph Millar
Sydney Lea
Donald Lev
Dana Levin
Gerald Locklin
Rachel Loden
Radomir Luza, Jr.
William Lychack
Annette Lynch
Elzabeth MacKiernan
Elizabeth Macklin
Leah Maines
Mark Manalang
Norma Marder
Jack Marshall
Michael Martone
Tara L. Masih
Dan Masterson
Peter Matthiessen
Maria Matthiessen
Alice Mattison

Tracy Mayor
Robert McBrearty
Jane McCafferty
Rebecca McClanahan
Bob McCrane
Jo McDougall
Sandy McIntosh
James McKean
Roberta Mendel
Didi Menendez
Barbara Milton
Alexander Mindt
Mississippi Review
Martin Mitchell
Roger Mitchell
Jewell Mogan
Patricia Monaghan
Jim Moore
James Morse
William Mulvihill
Nami Mun
Joan Murray
Carol Muske-Dukes
Edward Mycue
Deirdre Neilen
W. Dale Nelson
New Michigan Press
Jean Nordhaus
Celeste Ng
Christiana Norcross
Ontario Review Foundation
Daniel Orozco
Other Voices
Paris Review
Alan Michael Parker
Ellen Parker
Veronica Patterson
David Pearce, M.D.
Robert Phillips
Donald Platt
Plain View Press
Valerie Polichar
Pool
Horatio Potter
Jeffrey & Priscilla Potter
C.E. Poverman
Marcia Preston
Eric Puchner
Osiris
Tony Quagliano
Quill & Parchment
Barbara Quinn
Randy Rader
Juliana Rew
Belle Randall

Lily Henderson
Paul Bresnick
Philip Schultz

Daniel Dolgin
Kirby E. Williams

ADVISORY COUNCIL

Rick Bass
Charles Baxter
Madison Smartt Bell
Marvin Bell
Sven Birkerts
T. C. Boyle
Ron Carlson
Andrei Codrescu
Billy Collins
Stephen Dunn
Daniel Halpern
Edward Hoagland

John Irving
Ha Jin
Mary Karr
Joan Murray
Wally Lamb
Rick Moody
Joyce Carol Oates
Sherod Santos
Grace Schulman
Charles Simic
Gerald Stern
Charles Wright

CONTRIBUTING SMALL PRESSES FOR PUSHCART PRIZE XLIII

(These presses made or received nominations for this edition.)

A&U: America's AIDS Magazine, 25 Monroe St., #205, Albany, NY 12210

aaduna, 144 Genesee St., Ste. 102-259, Auburn, NY 13021

A3 Review, PO Box 65016, London N5 9BD, UK

About Place Journal, 4520 Blue Mounds Trail, Black Earth, WI 53515

Abstract MagazineTV, 1305 E. Boyd St., Norman, OK 73071

Abyss & Apex Magazine, 116 Tennyson Dr., Lexington, SC 29073

The Account, 2501 W. Zia Rd., #8204, Santa Fe, NM 87505

Across the Margin, 299 6th Ave., Unit 4, Brooklyn, NY 11215

Adirondack Review, 11 Smith Terrace, Highland, NY 12528

Adoree, 13309 Lake George PL, Tampa, FL 33618

The Adroit Journal, 1223 Westover Rd., Stamford, CT 06902

After Happy Hour, 1120 N. Euclid Ave., #2, Pittsburgh, PA 15206

Agni Magazine, Boston Univ., 236 Bay State Rd., Boston, MA 02215

Airlie Press, P.O. Box 82653, Portland, OR 97282

Alaska Quarterly Review, ESH 208, 3211 Providence Dr., Anchorage, AK 99508-4614

Alice James Books, 114 Prescott St., Farmington, ME 04938

Altadena Poetry Review, 468 East Marigold St., Altadena, CA 91001

Alternating Current Press, PO Box 270921, Louisville, CO 80027

Alternative Press 45, 261 Derosa Dr., Hampton, VA 23666

Always Crashing, 407 W. Green St., #6, Urbana, II 61801

Amberjack Publishing, P.O. Box 4668, #89611, New York, NY 10163

American Chordata, 589 Flatbush Ave., #2, Brooklyn, NY 11225

American Journal of Poetry, 14969 Chateau Village Dr., Chesterfield, MO 63017

American Literary Review, 1155 Union Cir, #311307, Denton, TX 76203

American Poetry Journal, 43 Nathan Pierce Court, Pawling, NY 12564

American Poetry Review, 3205, Broad St., Philadelphia, PA 19102

The American Scholar, 1606 New Hampshire Ave. NW, Washington, DC 20009

American Short Fiction, PO Box 4152, Austin, TX 78765

Amsterdam Quarterly, Choisyweg 2-B, 3701 TA Zeist, The Netherlands

Anapest, Paragon Press, 325 N. Union St., #1, Middletown, PA 17057

Anaphora Literary Press, 1898 Athens St., Brownsville, TX 78520

Animal, 264 Fallen Palm Dr., Casselberry, FL 32707

Annorlunda Books, 3077-B Clairemont Dr., #310, San Diego, CA 92117

Anomaly, 2031 Arch St., #105, Philadelphia, PA 19103

Another Chicago Magazine, 1301 W. Byron St., Chicago, IL 60613-2818

Anthropology and Humanism, 1986 Paquita Dr., Carpinteria, CA 93013

The Antioch Review, PO Box 148, Yellow Springs, OH 45387-0148

Antrim House Books, 21 Goodrich Rd., Simsbury, CT 06070

Apogee Journal, 418 Suydam St., Apt. 1L, Brooklyn, NY 11237

Appalachia Journal, 41 Bridge St., Deep River, CT 06417

Appalachian Heritage, Berea College, CPO 2166, Berea, KY 40404

Apple Valley Review, 88 South 3rd St., #336, San José, CA 95113

apt, 81 Lexington St., #1, Boston, MA 02128

Aquifer, UCF, English, PO Box 161346, Orlando, FL 32816-1346

Arctos Press, 16 Cloud View Rd., Sausalito, CA 94965

Arcturus Magazine, 1 W. Superior St., #3412, Chicago, IL 60654

The Ardent Writer Press, PO Box 25, Brownsboro, AL 35741

Argot, 253 10th St. NE, Washington, DC 20016

Arkana, Thompson Hall, 2019 Bruce St., Rm. 324, Conway, AR 72034

The Arkansas International, Univ. of Arkansas, Fayetteville, AR 72701

Arroyo Literary Review, CSU, English, MB 2579, Hayward, CA 94542

Arts, Im Breien 11, D-44894 Bochum, GERMANY

Arts & Letters Journal, Campus Box 89, Georgia College, Milledgeville, GA 31061

Ascent, Concordia, English, 901 8th St. S., Moorhead, MN 56562

Ashland Poetry Press, 401 College Ave., Ashland, OH 44805

Asia Literary Review, 145 Copse Hill, London SW20 054, UK

Asian American Literary Review, 9903 Traverse Way, Fort Washington, MD 20744

Asian American Writers' Workshop, 112 W. 27th St., 6th FL, New York, NY 10001

Aster(ix), Univ. of Pittsburgh, 4200 Fifth Ave., Pittsburgh, PA 15260

Atticus Review, 22 Hickory Rd., West Orange, NJ 07052

Autonomous Press, 420 Brockway Pl., Albion, MI 49224

Autumn House Press, 5530 Penn Ave., Pittsburgh, PA 15206

Autumn Sky Poetry Daily, 5263 Arctic Circle, Emmaus, PA 18049

Awst, P.O. box 49163, Austin, TX 78765-9163

Bacopa Literary Review, 4000 NW 51st St., G-121, Gainesville, FL 32606

The Baltimore Review, 6514 Maplewood Rd., Baltimore, MD 21212

Bamboo Ridge Press, PO Box 61781, Honolulu, HI 96839-1781

Bards and Sage Publishing, 201 Leed Ave, Bellmawr, NJ 08031

Barrelhouse, 793 Westerly Parkway, State College, PA 16801

Bath Flash Fiction, 6 Old Tarnwell, Stanton Drew, Bristol, BS39 4EA, UK

Bauhan Publishing, PO Box 117, Peterborough, NH 03458

Bayou, UNO, English, 2000 Lake Shore Dr., New Orleans, LA 70148

Bear Star Press, 185 Hollow Oak Drive, Cohasset, CA 95973

Bedazzled Ink, 2137 Pennsylvania Ave., Fairfield, CA 94533

Beecher's, 1445 Jayhawk Blvd., Lawrence, KS 66045

Belletrist Magazine, 3000 Landerholm Circle SE, Bellevue, WA 98007

Bellingham Review, MS-9053, WWU, 516 High St., Bellingham, WA 98225

Beloit Poetry Journal, PO Box 1450, Windham, ME 04062

Beltway Poetry Quarterly, 626 Quebec Pl. NW, Washington, DC 20010

Ben Yehuda Press, 122 Ayers Court, Ste. 1-B, Teaneck, NJ 07666

Bennington Review, 1 College Dr., Bennington, VT 05201

Better Than Starbucks, 7711 Ashwood Lane, Lake Worth, FL 33467

Bettering America Poetry, PO B 101, Shandaken, NY, 12480

Bhashalipi Publishers, 24 Raga Lane, Kolkata - 700009, West Bengal, India

Big Muddy, SMSU Press, 1 University Plaza, MS 2650, Cape Girardeau, MO
   63701

Big Table, 383 Langley Rd., #2, Newton Centre, MA 02459

Big Windows Review, Washtenaw Community College, 4800 E. Huron Dr.,
   Ann Arbor, MI 48105-4800

The Binnacle, 19 Kimball Hall, Univ. of Maine, 116 O'Brien Ave., Machias,
   ME 04654

bioStories, 175 Mission View Dr., Lakeside, MT 59922

Bird's Thumb, 701 S. Wells St., #2903, Chicago, IL 60601

Birmingham Poetry Review, HB 215, UAB, Birmingham, AL 35294-1260

BkMk Press, UMKC, 5100 Rockhill Rd., Kansas City, MO 64110-2499

Black Fox, 336 Grove Ave., Ste. B, Winter Park, FL 32789

Black Heart, PO Box 1799, Alpine, CA 91903

Black Lawrence Press, 279 Claremont Ave., Mount Vernon, NY 10552

Black Warrior, Univ. of Alabama, Box 870170, Tuscaloosa, AL 35487

Blackbird, English Dept., PO Box 843082, Richmond, VA 23284-3082

Blank Spaces, 282906 Normanby/Bentinck Townline, Durham ON NOG 1R0,
   Canada

Blink Ink, P.O. Box 5, North Branford, CT 06471

Blue Fifth Review, 267 Lark Meadow Circle, Bluff City, TN 37618

Blue Heron, N66W38350 Deer Creek Ct., Oconomowoc, WI 53066

Blue Light Press, 1563 45th Ave., San Francisco, CA 94122

Blue Mesa, UNM English, 1 University of New Mexico, Albuquerque, NM 87131-0001

Blue Unicorn, 13 Jefferson Ave., San Rafael, CA 94903

Blueshift Journal, PO Box 16009, 531 Lasuen Mall, Stanford, CA 94309

bluestem, English Dept., EIU, Charleston, IL 61920-3011

BOA Editions, 250 North Goodman St., Ste. 306, Rochester, NY 14607

Bodega Magazine, 451 Court St., #3R, Brooklyn, NY 11231

The Boiler, 311 Jagoe St., #7, Denton, TX 76201

Bombus Press, 3 Geddes Heights Dr., Ann Arbor, MI 48104

Book Ex Machina, P.O. Box 23595, Nicosia 1685, CYPRUS

Booth, Butler Univ., English, 4600 Sunset Ave., Indianapolis, IN 46208

Border Crossing, 650 W. Easterday Ave., Sault Ste. Marie, MI 49783

Bottom Dog Press, Firelands College, P.O. Box 425, Huron, OH 44839

Boulevard, 4125 Juniata St., #B, St. Louis, MO 63116

Braddock Avenue Books, PO Box 502, Braddock, PA 15104

Brain Mill Press, 1051 Kellogg St., Green Bay, WI 54303

Breakwater Review, U. Mass., 100 Morrissey Blvd., Boston, MA 02125

Brevity, 265 E State, Athens, OH 45701

The Briar Cliff Review, 3303 Rebecca St., Sioux City, IA 51104-2100

Brick, P.O. Box 609, Stn. P, Toronto, Ontario, M5S 2Y4, Canada

Brick Road Poetry Press, 513 Broadway, Columbus, GA 31901

Bridge Eight, 11 E. Forsyth St., #701, Jacksonville, FL 32202

Broad River, PO Box 7224, Gardner-Webb, Boiling Springs, NC 28017

Broadstone Books, 418 Ann St., Frankfort, KY 40601-1929

This Broken Shore, 15 Sandspring Dr., Eatontown, NJ 07724

Buffalo Arts Publishing, 179 Greenfield Dr., Tonawanda, NY 14150

Burnt Pine Magazine, 642 Stumer Rd., Rapid City, SD 57701

C&R Press, 1869 Meadowbrook Dr., Winston-Salem, NC 27104

Caffeinated Press, 3167 Kalamazoo Ave. SE, #203, Grand Rapids, MI 49508-1475

cahoodaloodaling, 2100 College Dr., #65, Baton Rouge, LA 70808

Calamus Journal, 17002 Point Pleasant Ln, Dumfries, VA 22026

California Quarterly, PO Box 2672, Del Mar, CA 92014

Calliope, 2506 SE Bitterbrush Dr., Madras, OR 97741-9452

Calypso Edition, 2540 Goldsmith, Houston, TX 77030

Cantabrigian Magazine, 72 Dimick St., Somerville, MA 02143

The Cape Rock, SMSU Press, 1 University Plaza, MS 2650, Cape Girardeau, MO 63701

Carve Magazine, PO Box 701510, Dallas, TX 75370

Catamaran, 1050 River St., #118, Santa Cruz, CA 95060

Catapult, 1140 Broadway, Ste. 704, New York, NY 10001

Central Square Press, 450B Paradise Rd., #442, Swampscott, MA 01907

Chaffey Review, 5885 Haven Ave., Rancho Cucamonga, CA 91737-3002

Chattahoochee Review, Georgia State University, 555 North Indian Creek Dr., Clarkston, GA 30021

Chatter House, 7915 S. Emerson Ave., B-303, Indianapolis, IN 46237

Chautauqua, Creative Writing Dept., 601 South College Rd., Wilmington, NC 28403-5938

Cheap Pop, 8102 E. Jefferson Ave., B-210, Detroit, MI 48214

Cherry Tree, Washington College, 300 Washington Ave., Chestertown, MD 21620

Chicago Quarterly Review, 517 Sherman Ave., Evanston, IL 60202

Chiron Review, 522 E. South Ave., St. John, KS 67576-2212

ChiZine, 1410 Hetherington Dr., Peterborough, ON K9L 1Z5, Canada

Choice 575 Main St., #300, Middletown, CT 06457

Cholla Needles, 6732 Conejo Ave., Joshua Tree, CA 92252

Chrome Baby, 445 S. Western Ave., #303, Los Angeles, CA 90020

Cimarron Review, OSU, 205 Morrill Hall, Stillwater, OK 74078

Cincinnati Review, PO Box 210069, Cincinnati, OH 45221-0069

Circling Rivers, P.O. Box 8291, Richmond, VA 23226

Cirque, 3978 Defiance St., Anchorage, AK 99504

Clare Songbirds Publishing, 140 Cottage St., Auburn, NY 13021

Cleaver, 8250 Shawnee St., Philadelphia, PA 19118

Cleveland State University Poetry Center, 2121 Euclid Ave., Cleveland, OH 44115-2214

Clockhouse, 51 Park Ave., Brockport, NY 14420

Cloudbank, PO Box 610, Corvallis, OR 97339-0610

Cold Creek Review, 122 Arabian Dr., Madison, AL 35758

Cold Mountain Review, English Dept., Appalachian State Univ., Boone, NC 28608

The Collagist, G. Blackwell, 2905 E. Jackson St., Pensacola, FL 32503

The Collapsar, 1628 Fairview St., #1, Berkeley, CA 94703

Colorado Review, Colorado State Univ., Fort Collins, CO 80523-9105

Columbia Poetry Review, 600 So. Michigan Ave., Chicago, IL 60605

Comment, 185 Young St., Hamilton, ON L8N 1V9, Canada

The Common, Amherst College, Amherst, MA 01002-5000

Compose, 544 Fishermens' Point Rd., Shuniah, ON, P7A 0J4, Canada

Concho River Review, ASU Station #10894, San Angelo, TX 76909

concis, PO Box 82826, Fairbanks, AK 99708

Conclave, 12600 W. Glen Ct., Choctaw, Ok 73020

Concrete Wolf, PO Box 445, Tillamook, OR 97141

Confrontation, English Dept., LIU/Post, Brookville, NY 11548-1300

Conjunctions, Bard College, Annandale-on-Hudson, NY 12504-5000

Connecticut River Review, 3 Edmund PL, West Hartford, CT 06119

Consequence Magazine, P.O. Box 323, Cohasset, MA 02025-0323

Constellations, 127 Lake View Ave., Cambridge, MA 02138

Conversations, 105 McCornell Circle, Brandon, MS 39042

Copper Canyon Press, PO Box 271, Port Townsend, WA 98368

Copper Nickel, UCD, Campus Box 175, Denver, CO 80217-3364

Corporeal Writing, 5111 SE Tolman St., Portland, OR 97206

Cosmonauts Avenue, 252 West St., #18, Amherst, MA 01002

Court Green, 600 South Michigan Ave., Chicago, IL 60605-1996

The Courtship of Winds, 55 Cortland Lane, Boxborough, MA 01719

Cowboy Jamboree, 10695 Old Hwy 51 N, Cobden, IL 62920

Crab Creek, P.O. Box 1682, Kingston, WA 98346

Crab Fat Magazine, 900 W. South Blvd., Petersburg, VA 23805

Crab Orchard Review, Mail Code 4503, SIUC, 1000 Faner Dr., Carbondale. IL 62901

Crack the Spine, 6449 Sea Isle, Galveston, TX 77554

Craft, 818 SW 3rd Ave., #221-5911, Portland, OR 97204

Crazyhorse, Charleston College, 66 George St., Charleston, SC 29424

Creative Nonfiction, 5119 Coral St., Pittsburgh, PA 15224

Creative Talents Unleashed, PO Box 605, Helendale, CA 92342

Crisis Chronicles, 3431 George Ave., Parma, OH 44134

Cross-Cultural Communications, 239 Wynsum Ave., Merrick, NY 11566-4725

Crystal Lake Publishing, Eads, 42 Haig Ave., Bristol, CT 06010

Cultural Weekly, 3330 S. Peck Ave., #14, San Pedro, CA 90731

Cutthroat, A Journal of the Arts, PO Box 2414, Durango, CO 81302

D. M. Kreg Publishing, 3985 Wonderland Hill Ave., #201, Boulder, CO 80304

Dalhousie Review, Dalhousie University, Halifax NS B3H 4R2, Canada

Daniel & Daniel, Publishers, PO Box 2790, McKinleyville, CA 95519

Dark Matter, 1028 Laurier E., Montreal, QC H2J 1G6, Canada

Darkhouse Books, 160 J St., #2223, Niles, CA 94536

David R. Godine, Publisher, 15 Court Square, #320, Boston, MA 02108

Dead Housekeeping, 1014 Loxford Terrace, Silver Spring, MD 20901

Deaf Poets Society, 4405 Fair Stone Dr., #301, Fairfax, VA 22033

december, P.O. Box 16130, St. Louis, MO 63105

decomP, 3002 Grey Wolf Cove, New Albany, IN 47150

Deerbrook Editions, P.O. Box 542, Cumberland, ME 04021-0542

Delmarva Review, PO Box 544, St. Michaels, MD 21663

Denver Quarterly, English Dept., 2000 E. Ashbury, Denver, CO 80208

Diagram, New Michigan Press, 8058 E. 7th St., Tucson, AZ 85710

Dialogist, Loruss, 1 Stone Cottages, Osmaston, Ashbourne, Derbyshire, DE6 1LW, UK

Diaphanous Press, 44 Poplar Dr., Windsor, CT 06095

Dime Show Review, PO Box 760, Folsom, CA 95763-0760

Diode Editions, PO Box 5586, Richmond, VA 23220

The DMQ Review, 16393 Bonnie Lane, Los Gatos, CA 95032

Dos Gatos Press, 6452 Kola Court NW, Albuquerque, NM 87120-4285

Dos Madres Press, PO Box 294, Loveland, OH 45140

drDoctor, 4266 Cheval Circle, Stow, OH 44224

Dream Pop Press, 825 Upper Ranchitos Rd., Taos, NM 87571

Dreams and Nightmares, 1300 Kicker Rd., Tuscaloosa, AL 35404

Drunk Monkeys, 252 N. Cordova St., Burbank, CA 91505

Dunes Review, PO Box 2355, Traverse City, MI 49685

East Bay Review, Posell, 876 32nd St., Oakland, CA 94608

Eastern Iowa Review, 6332 33rd Avenue Dr., Shellsburg, IA 52332

Eclectia, 6030 N. Sheridan Rd., #805, Chicago, IL 60660

ecotone, UNCW, 601 S. College Rd., Wilmington, NC 28403-3201

Edify Fiction, 212 Tocoa Circle, Helena, AL 35080

Edizioni Esordienti E Book, Strada Vivero 15, 10024 Moncalieri (Torinio) Italy

805 Lit+Art, 1301 Barcarrota Blvd W, Brandenton, FL 34205

Ekphrasis/Frith Press, PO Box 161236, Sacramento, CA 95816-1236

El Zarape Press, D. Ordaz, 1413 Jay Ave., McAllen, TX 78504

Electric Lit, 147 Prince St., Brooklyn, NY 11201

Ellipsis Zine, 3 Murdoch Mews, Cotteridge Rd., Birmingham B30 3AZ, UK

Elm Leaves, English Dept., 1300 Elmwood Ave., Buffalo, NY 14222

Empty Sink, 2330 Boxer Palm, San Antonio, TX 78213

Emrys Journal, PO Box 8813, Greenville, SC 29604

Encircle Publications, P.O. Box 187, Farmington, ME 04938

Entre Rios Books, 733 25th Avenue So., Seattle, WA 98144

EOAGH, 677 Classon Ave., Apt., 3LF, Brooklyn, NY 11238

Epic Rites Press, PO Box 80002 Woodbridge, Sherwood Park, Alberta, T8A 5T4, Canada

Epigram Books, 1008 Toa Payon North, #03-08, 318996 Singapore

Epiphany Literary Journal, 71 Bedford St., New York, NY 10014

Epoch, 251 Goldwin Smith Hall, Cornell University, Ithaca NY 14853

Escape Into Life, Kirk, 108 Gladys Dr., Normal, IL 61761

eSkylark, 10 Hillcross Ave., Morden Surrey, SM4 4EA, UK

The Evansville Review, 1800 Lincoln Ave., Evansville, IN 47722

Event, PO Box 2503, New Westminster, BC, V3L 5B2, Canada

Exit 7, WKCTC, 4810 Alben Barkley Dr., Paducah, KY 42001

Exit 13, PO Box 423, Fanwood, NJ 07023

Exposition Review, 2611 4th St., Santa Monica, CA 90405

Eye Flash Poetry, 7 Trevor Rd., I.O.W. PO30 SD2, UK

Fabula Press, 752 A/2, Block P, New Alipore, Kolkata, West Bengal, India 700053

failbetter, 2022 Grove Ave., Richmond, VA 23220

Fantastic Floridas, PO Box 533709, Orlando, FL 32853

Fantasy and Science Fiction, PO Box 8420, Surprise, AZ 85374

Fem Rag Lit Mag, 3409 N. Pulaski Rd., #1, Chicago, IL 60641

Fiction International, English Dept., SDSU, San Diego, CA 92182-6020

Fiction River, WMG Publishing, PO Box 269, Lincoln City, OR 97367

Fiction Week Literary Review, 887 S. Rice Rd., Ojai, CA 93023

Fictive Dream, 79 Court Lane, Dulwich, London SE21 7EF, UK

Fiddlehead, Box 4400, Univ. New Brunswick, NB E3B 5A3, Canada

Field, 50 North Professor St., Oberlin, OH 44074-1091

Fields Magazine, 3702 Tower View Court, Austin, TX 78723

Fifth Wednesday, P.O. Box 4033, Lisle, IL 60532-9033

Fighting Cock Press, 45 Middlethorpe Dr., York, YO24 1NA, UK

Finishing Line Press, P.O. Box 1626, Georgetown, KY 40324

First, UMKC, 5101 Rockhill Rd., Kansas City, MO 64110-2499

Five Oaks Press, 6 Five Oaks Dr., Newburgh, NY 12550

Five Points, Georgia State University, Box 3999, Atlanta, GA 30302

Fjords Review, 1869 Meadowbrook Dr., Winston Salem, NC 27104

Flash, Univ. of Chester, English, Parkgate Rd., Chester, CH1 4BJ, UK

Flash Fiction Online, 110 Canter Lane, Pinehurst, NC 28374

Flash Frontier, 267 Lark Meadow Cr., Bluff City, TN 37618

Fledging Rag, 1716 Swarr Run Rd., J-108, Lancaster, PA 17601

Fleur-de-Lis Press, 901 So. 4th St., Louisville, KY 40203-3205

The Flexible Persona, 1070-1 Tunnel Rd., #10-244, Asheville, NC 28805

Flock, PO Box 7944, Roanoke, VA 24019

Florida Review, UCF, PO Box 161346, Orlando, FL 32816-1346

Flying Horse Press, 311 Shingle Hill Rd., West Haven, CT 06516

Flying Island, 1125 E. Brookside Ave., Indianapolis, IN 46201

Flying South 2017, 546 Birch Creek Rd., McLeansville, NC 27301

Flyway, English Dept., 206 Ross Hall, Iowa State Univ., Ames, IA 50011

Foglifter, 214 Grand Ave., #90, Oakland, CA 94610

Folded Word, 79 Tracy Way, Meredith, NH 03253-5409

Foothill, Arts & Humanities, 150 E. 10th St., Claremont, CA 91711

Forge, 4018 Bayview Ave., San Mateo, CA 94403

Foundlings Magazine, 128 Wellington Rd., Buffalo, NY 14216

Foundry, 10 Halley St., Yonkers, NY 10704

Fourteen Hills, Creative Writing, SFSU, 1600 Holloway Ave., San Francisco, CA 94132

Fourth Genre, 434 Farm Ln, 235 Bessey, MSU, East Lansing, MI 48824

The Fourth River, Chatham U., 1 Woodland Rd., Pittsburgh, PA 15232

Free State Review, 3222 Rocking Horse Lane, Aiken, SC 29801

Front Porch Journal, TSU, 601 University Dr., San Marcos, TX 78666

Frontier Poetry, 818 SW 3rd Ave., #221-5911, Portland, OR 97204

Full Grown People, 106 Tripper Ct., Charlottesville, VA 22903

Gamut, PO Box 964, Mundelein, IL 60060-0964

Garden Oak Press, 1953 Huffstatler St., #A, Rainbow, CA 92028

Gemini Magazine, PO Box 1485, Onset, MA 02558

The Georgia Review, University of Georgia, Athens, GA 30602-9009

The Gettysburg Review, Gettysburg Coll., #2446, Gettysburg, PA 17325

Ghost Parachute, 909 Pinegrove Ave., Orlando, FL 32803

Gigantic Sequins, 209 Avon St., Breaux Bridge, LA 70517

Gingerbread House, 378 Howell Ave., Cincinnati, OH 45220

Gival Press, PO Box 3812, Arlington, VA 22203

Glass Lyre Press, PO Box 2693, Glenview, IL 60025

Glass Poetry Press, 1667 Crestwood, Toledo, OH 43612

Glassworks, Rowan Univ., 201 Mullica Hill Rd., Glassboro, NJ 08028

Gnarled Oak, 9412 Billingham Trail, Austin, TX 78717

Gold Man Review, 4626 Nantucket Dr., Redding, CA 96001

Golden Dragonfly Press, 87 Colonial Village, Amherst, MA 01002

Golden Rock Books, 825-C Merrimon Ave., #243, Asheville, NC 28804

Golden Walkman Magazine, 11 Holbrook St, Palmer, MA 01069

Good Men Project, 823 Drummond Ave., Asbury Park, NJ 07712

Goose River Press, 3400 Friendship Rd., Waldoboro, ME 04572

Granta, 12 Addison Ave., Holland Park, London W11 4QR, UK

Graphic Arts Books, PO Box 3225, Durango, CO 81302

Grayson Books, PO Box 270549, West Hartford, T 06127

great weather for MEDIA, 515 Broadway, #2B, New York, NY 10012

Green Hills Literary Lantern, Truman State Univ., English, Kirksville, MO 63501

Green Linden Press, 208 Broad Street South, Grinnell, IA 50112

Green Silk Journal, 228 N. Main St., Woodstock, VA 22664

Green Writers Press, 139 Main St., #501, Brattleboro, VT 05301

Grist, 301 McClung Tower, Univ. of Tennessee, Knoxville, TN 37996

Guernica Magazine, 81 Prospect St., Brooklyn, NY 11201

Gulf Coast, University of Houston, Houston, TX 77204-3013

Gulf Stream, 3000 NE 151st St., ACI-338, North Miami, FL 33181

Gunpowder Press, PO Box 60035, Santa Barbara, CA 93160

Gutwrench, 240 N. Highland Ave. NE, #3520, Atlanta, GA 30307
Gyroscope Review, 1891 Merrill St., Roseville, MN 55113

Half Mystic Journal, 67 Rosewood Dr., #05-33, Singapore, SG 737876
Halophyte, 450 East 100 South, #17, Salt Lake City, UT 84102
Hand Type Press, P.O. Box 3941, Minneapolis, MN 55403-0941
Harbour Publishing, Box 219, Madeira Park, BC V0N 2H0, Canada
Harvard Review, Lamont Lib., Harvard Univ., Cambridge, MA 02138
Hay House, 665 Broadway, Ste. 1200, New York, NY 10012
Hayden's Ferry Review, P.O. Box 870302, Tempe, AZ 85287-0302
Hawai'i Pacific Review, Hawai'i Pacific University, 1060 Bishop St., LB507,
    Honolulu, HI 96813
Headmistress Press, P.O. Box 275, Eagle Rock, MO 65641
Heartland Review Press, 600 College St. Rd., Elizabethtown, KY 42701
Hedgehog Review, P.O. Box 400816, Charlottesville, VA 22904-4816
Hedgerow Review, 71 South Pleasant St., Amherst, MA 01002
Hematopoiesis Press, 175 S. Lexington Ave., #306, Asheville, NC 28801
Heyday, P.O. Box 9145, Berkeley, CA 94709
HiConcept Magazine, 46 Ocean Ave., Bayport, NY 11705-1819
Highland Park Poetry, 376 Park Ave., Highland Park, IL 60035
Hip Pocket Press, 5 Del Mar Court, Orinda, CA 94563
Hippocampus Magazine, 222 E. Walnut St., #2, Lancaster, PA 17602
Hobart, PO Box 1658, Ann Arbor, MI 48106
The Hollins Critic, P.O. Box 9538, Roanoke, VA 24020-1538
The Hopkins Review, Johns Hopkins Univ., 3400 N. Charles St., Baltimore,
    MD 21218
Hotel, 126 Winston Rd., London N16 9LJ, UK
Hub City Press, 186 West Main St., Spartanburg, SC 29306
The Hudson Review, 33 West 67th St., New York, NY 10023
Hunger Mountain, Vermont Coll., 36 College St., Montpelier, VT 05602
Hypertext Review, 1821 W. Melrose St., Chicago, IL 60657-2001
Hypertrophic Press, P.O. Box 423, New Market, AL 35761
Hyphen Magazine, 7002 Blvd. E. 12D, Guttenberg, NJ 07093

I-70 Review, 5021 S. Tierney Dr., Independence, MO 64055
I Write Press, Dibyajyoti Sarma, 187/I Patparganj, Mayur, Vihar I, New Delhi,
    India 110091
Ibbetson Street Press, Endicott, 376 Hale St., Beverly, MA 01915
Illuminations, Coll. of Charleston, 66 George St., Charleston, SC 29424
Illya's Honey, 1621 Brighton Dr., Carrolton, TX 75007
Image, 3307 Third Avenue West, Seattle, WA 98119
Inanna Publications, 210 Founders College, York University, 4700 Keele St.,
    Toronto, ON M3J 1P3, Canada

Indiana Review, 1020 E. Kirkwood Ave., Bloomington, IN 47405-7103

Indianapolis Review, 5906 W. 25th St., #13, Speedway, IN 46224

Indigent Press, 16 Seymour St., #3, Montclair, NJ 07042

Indigo Dreams, 24, Forest Houses, Halwill, Beaworthy, Devon EX21 5UU, UK

Inflectionist Review, 11322 SE 45th Ave., Milwaukie, OR 97222

Ink & Letters, 1120 N. Louisa Ave., Shawnee, OK 74801

Interim, UNLV, English, 4505 S. Maryland Pkwy, Las Vegas, NV 89154

Into the Void, 112 Claremont St., Toronto, ON M6J 2M5, Canada

The Iowa Review, 308 EPB, University of Iowa, Iowa City, IA 52242

Irrupciones, Bemabe Rivera 1506, 11200 Montevido, Uruguay

J Journal, English Dept., 524 West 59th St., 7th Fl, New York, NY 10019

Jabberwock Review, MSU., P.O. Box E, Mississippi State, MS 39762

Jacar Press, 6617 Deerview Trail, Durham, NC 27712

Jelly Bucket, 521 Lancaster Ave., Mattox 101, Richmond, KY 40475

Jerry Jazz Musician, 2207 NE Broadway, Portland, OR 97232

Jersey Devil Press, 3722 Keagy Rd. SW, Roanoke, VA 24018

Jet Fuel Review, English, Box 1214, De La Salle, 1 University Pkwy, Rome-
    oville, IL 60446-2200

JMF Publications, 92 Parkview Loop, Staten Island, NY 10314

jmww, 2105 E. Lamley St., Baltimore, MD 21231

Josephine Quarterly, 625 Piedmont Ave. NE, #1013, Atlanta, GA 30308

The Journal, English Dept., Ohio State Univ., 164 West 17th Ave., Columbus,
    OH 43210

Joyland Magazine, 302 Nassau Ave., #3R, Brooklyn, NY 11222

Juked, 3941 Newdale Rd., #26, Chevy Chase, MD 20815

Kelsay Books, 1185 N 850 E., Pleasant Grove, UT 84062

Kelsey Review, MCCC, 1200 Old Trenton Rd., West Windsor, NJ 08550

Kenyon Review, Finn House, 102 W. Wiggin St., Gambier, OH 43022

Kerf, College of Redwoods, 883 W. Washington Blvd., Crescent City, CA 95531

Kestrel, Fairmont State Univ., 1201 Locust Ave., Fairmont, WV 26554

kitchen work, Heirloom Café, 2500 Folsom St., S. F., CA 94110

Kore Press, PO Box 42315, Tucson AZ 85733-2315

Kweli Journal, P.O. Box 693, New York, NY 10021

KYSO Flash, Gibbons, 4805 106th St. NE, Marysville, WA 98270

L'Éphémère Review, 11376 236A St., Maple Ridge, BC V2W 2A3, Canada

La Presa, 39 Charles St., Livingston, NJ 07039

La Vague, 7809 Estancia St., Carlsbad, CA 92009

Lagoons Editions, 11600 2nd St., Huntley, IL 60142

Lake Effect, Humanities, 4951 College Drive, Erie, PA 16563-1501

Lao American Review, 503 Irving Ave. N, #100-A, Minneapolis, MN 55405

Lavender Review, P.O. Box 275, Eagle Rock, MO 65641

Left Hooks, 11414 Xavis St. NW, Coon Rapids, MN 55433

Library Partners Press, 1834 Wake Forest Rd., Winston-Salem, NC 27106

Light, 1515 Highland Ave., Rochester, NY 14618

Likely Red Magazine, 206 Nob Hill Ln., #2, Louisville, KY 40206

Lindenwood Review, 400 N. Kingshighway, St. Charles, MO 63366

Lips, P.O. Box 616, Florham Park, NJ 07932

Liquid Imagination, 7800 Loma Del Norte Rd. NE, Albuquerque, NM 87109

Litbreak Magazine, 9459 Springfield Blvd., Queens Village, NY 11428

LitMag, Greeley Square Station, PO Box 20091, New York, NY 10001

Literal Latté, 41 Fifth Ave., #413, New York, NY 10003

Literary Alchemy, 955 N. Duesenberg Dr., #6314, Ontario, CA 91764

Literary Matters, English Dept., Catholic University of America, Washington, DC 20064

Little Balkans Press, 315 South Hugh St., Frontenac, KS 66763

Little Fiction/Big Truths, 1608-1910 Lake Shore Blvd. W., Toronto, ON M6S 1A2, Canada

Little Patuxent Review, 11243A Skilift Ct., Columbia, MD 21004

Little Red Tree Publishing, 509 W. 3rd St., North Platte, NE 69101

The Lonely Crowd, 62 Kings Rd., Pontcanna, Cardiff, CF11 9DD, UK

Longreads, 275 Fair St., #11, Kingston, NY 12401

Longshot Press, 1455 Larkspur Ave., Eugene, OR 97401

Loose Moose Publishing, 303 E. Gurley St., #449, Prescott, AZ 86301

Lost Balloon, 1402 Highland Ave., Berwyn, IL 60402

Lost Horse, 105 Lost Horse Lane, Sandpoint, ID 83864

Louisville Review, Spalding U., 901 South 4th St., Louisville, KY 40203

Loving Healing Press, 5145 Pontiac Trail., Ann Arbor, MI 48105-9238

Lowestoft Chronicle Press, 1925 Massachusetts Ave., #8, Cambridge, MA 02140

Lumina, Sarah Lawrence College, 1 Mead Way, Bronxville, NY 10708

Lummox Press, PO Box 5301, San Pedro, CA 90733

Lunch Ticket, MFA Dept., Antioch University Los Angeles, 400 Corporate Pointe, Culver City, CA 90230

The MacGuffin, 18600 Haggerty Rd., Livonia, MI 48152-2696

Madcap Review, 245 Wallace Rd., Goffstown, NH 03045

Make Literary Productions, 2712 W. Medill Ave., Chicago, IL 60647

Malahat Review, University of Victoria, Box 1700, Stn CSC, Victoria BC V8W 2Y2, Canada

Mambo Academy of Kitty Wang, PO Box 5, No. Branford, CT 06471

Manhattan Review, 440 Riverside Dr., #38, New York, NY 10027

The Mantle, 974 Delaware Ave., Columbus, OH 43201

Massachusetts Review, Photo Lab 309, 211 Hicks Way, Amherst, MA 01003

Masters Review, 818 SW 3rd Ave., #221-5911, Portland, OR 97204

Matador Review, 1019 S. Oakley Ave., #2, Chicago, IL 60612

matchbook, 9 Dana St., Apt. 1, Cambridge, MA 02138

McSweeney's, 849 Valencia St. San Francisco, CA 94110

The Meadow, VISTA B300, 7000 Dandini Blvd., Reno, NV 89512

Meadowlark Books, PO Box 333, Emporia, KS 66801

Méasure, English Dept., Univ. of Evansville, 1800 Lincoln Ave., Evansville, IN 47722

Meerkat Press, 200 River Vista Dr., Ste. 522, Atlanta, GA 30339

Memorious, 28 N. Wright St., Naperville, IL 60540

Mercer University Press, 1400 Coleman Ave., Macon, GA 31207-0001

Mid-American Review, Bowling Green State University, Bowling Green, OH 43403

Midway Journal, 216 Banks St., #2, Cambridge, MA 02138

Midwest Review, UW-M, 21 N. Park St., #7101, Madison, WI 53715

Midwest Villages & Voices, PO Box 4024, Saint Paul, MN 55104

Midwestern Gothic, PO Box 4341, Des Plaines, IL 60016

the minnesota review, Virginia Tech, ASPECT, Blacksburg, VA 24061

Misfit Magazine, 143 Furman St., Schenectady, NY 12304

Mississippi Review, USM, English, #5037, Hattiesburg, MS 39406

Missouri Review, 357 McReynolds Hall, University of Missouri, Columbia, MO 65211

Mobius, Journal of Social Change, 149 Talmadge, Madison, WI 53703

Modern Creative Life, 813 Eagle Run Dr., Centerville, OH 45458

Modern Language Studies, Univ. of North Dakota, English, Grand Forks, ND 58202-7209

Mojave River, 12277 Apple Valley Rd., #449, Apple Valley, CA 92308

Molotov Cocktail, 1218 NE 24th Ave., Portland, OR 97232

Mom Egg Review, PO Box 9037, Bardonia, NY 10954

Monkeybicycle, 611-B Courtland St., Greensboro, NC 27401

Moon City, English, MSU, 901 South National Ave., Springfield, MO 65897

MoonPark Review, PO Box 87, Dundee, NY 14837

Moon Pie Press, 16 Walton St., Westbrook, ME 04092

Moss, 30 Columbia PL, #AF, Brooklyn, NY 11201

The Moth, Ardan Grange, Milltown, Belturbet, Co. Cavan, Ireland

Mount Hope, Roger Williams U., One Old Ferry Rd., Bristol, RI 02809

Mud Season Review, 110 Main St., #3C, Burlington, VT 05401

Muddy River Poetry Review, 15 Eliot St., Chestnut Hill, MA 02467

Muse-Pie Press, 73 Pennington Ave., Passaic, NJ 07055

Museum of Americana, Waarala, 2676 Bluewater, Ypsilanti, MI 48198

Muzzle, S. Edwards, 2218 North Lake Trail, Denton, TX 76201

Nabillera: Contemporary Korean Literature, 12 Dearborn Rd., Somerville, MA 02144

Narrative, 2443 Fillmore St., #214, San Francisco, CA 94115

Narratively, 30 John St., Brooklyn, NY 11201

Nasty Women Poets, Kane, 200 Pine St., Natchitoches, LA 71457

Nat. Brut, 5995 Summerside Dr., Unit 796032, Dallas, TX 75379

Natural Bridge, English, UMSL, 1 University Blvd, St. Louis, MO 63121

Naugatuck River Review, 45 Highland Ave. #2, Westfield, MA 01085

Nazim Hikmet Poetry, ATA-NC, 303 E. Durham Rd., #F, Cary, NC 27513

Neologism Poetry, 34 Glenbrook Dr., #2C, Greenfield, MA 01301

Neon, 5 Court Close, Bitterne, Southampton, Hampshire S018 5EJ, UK

Nerve Cowboy, PO Box 4973, Austin, TX 78765

New Academia Publishing, 4401-A Connecticut Ave., #236, Washington, DC 20008

New Delta Review, LSU, Allen Hall 9, Baton Rouge, LA 70803

The New Engagement, 664 West 163rd St., #56, New York, NY 10032

New England Review, Middlebury College, Middlebury, VT 05753

New Millennium Writings, 402 Garden Dr., Knoxville, TN 37918

The New Guard, Writer's Hotel, PO Box 472, Brunswick, ME 04011

New Issues Poetry & Prose, 1903 W. Michigan Ave., Kalamazoo, MI 49008-5463

New Letters, UMKC, 5101 Rockhill Rd., Kansas City, MO 64110-2499

New Limestone Review, U. of Kentucky, English, Lexington, KY 40506

New Madrid, FH - 7C, Murray State Univ., Murray, KY 42071-3341

New Ohio Review, Ohio University, 360 Ellis Hall, Athens, OH 45701

New Orleans Review, Loyola Univ., Box 195, New Orleans, LA 70118

New Poetry in Translation, 616 Storrs Rd., Mansfield Center, CT 06250

New Pop Lit, 2074 17th St., Wyandotte, MI 48192

The New Quarterly, 290 Westmount Rd. N, Waterloo, ON N2L 3G3, Canada

New Rivers Press, 1104 7th Ave. S., Moorhead, MN 56563

new south, Campus Box 1894, Georgia State Univ., Atlanta, GA 30303

New Verse News, Les Belles Maisons H-11, Jl. Serpong Raya, Serpong Utara, Tangerang-Baten 15310, Indonesia

New World Writing, 85 Hardwood Rd., Glenwood, NY 14069

New York Quarterly, PO Box 2015, Old Chelsea Stn., N. Y., NY 10113

New York Tyrant, 5114 Iroquois St., College Park, MD 20740

Newfound, 4505 Duval St., #156, Austin, TX 78751

Newtown Literary, 61-15 97th St. #11C, Rego Park, NY 11374

NewTown Writers, 320 S. Ridgeland Ave., Oak Park, IL 60302

Nightboat Books, PO Box 10, Callicoon, NY 12723

Nightjar Review, 1880 Wolf River Blvd., Collierville, TN 38017

Nightwood Editions, Harbour Publishing, PO Box 219, Madeira Park, BC V0N 2H0 Canada

Nimrod, Univ. of Tulsa, 800 South Tucker Dr., Tulsa, OK 74104

1932 Quarterly, 5783 Oakland Terrace, #4, Indianapolis, IN 46220

Ninth Letter, Univ. of Illinois, 608 S. Wright St., Urbana, IL 61801

Nirala Publications, 4637/20 Ground Floor, #127, Munish Plaza, Ansari Road, Daryaganj, New Delhi 110002, India

Nixes Mate Review, PO Box 1179, Allston, MA 02134

No Tokens, 300 Mercer St., #26E, New York, NY 10003

Noble/Gas Quarterly, Fissenden, 627 Whitehaven Crescent, London ON N6G 4V4, Canada

Nodin Press, 5114 Cedar Lake Rd., Minneapolis, MN 55416

Nomadic Press, 2926 Foothill Blvd., #1, Oakland, CA 94601

Noon, 1324 Lexington Ave., PMB 298, New York, NY 10128

The Normal School, 5245 N. Backer Ave., PB 98, CSU, Fresno, CA 93740-8001

North American Review, 1222 W. 27th St., Cedar Falls, IA 50614-0516

North Carolina Literary Review, ECU Mailstop 555, Greenville, NC 27858-4353

North Country Books, 220 Lafayette St., Utica, NY 13502

Northern New England Review, 35 Walnut St, Northampton, MA 01060

Northern Virginia Review, 6901 Sudley Rd., Manassas, VA 20109

Nostrovia! Press, 2041 Miramonte Ave., #37, San Leandro, CA 94578

Notre Dame Review, B009C McKenna, UND, Notre Dame, IN 46556

O-Dark-Thirty, 5812 Morland Dr. N., Adamstown, MD 21710

Oakwood, South Dakota State University, English Dept., Scobey 014, Box 504, Brookings, SD 57007

Obsidian, Illinois State U., Campus Box 4241, Normal, IL 61790-4241

Ocean State Review, U.R.I., 60 Upper College Rd., Kingston, RI 02881

Ocotillo Review, 1801 E. 51st St., Ste. 365-246, Austin, TX 78723

Offing Magazine, PO Box 22730, Seattle, WA 98122

Old Cove Press, 501 W. 6th St., Ste. 250, Lexington, KY 40508

Old Mountain Press, P.O. Box 66, Webster, NC 28788

Olive Press, UMO, 634 Henderson Dr., Mt. Olive, NC 28365

One Story, 232 3rd St., #A108, Brooklyn, NY 11215

One Teen Story, 232 3rd St., #A108, Brooklyn, NY 11215

Ooligan Press, Portland State Univ,, PO Box 751, Portland, OR 97202

Open, 3150 Dunlop Lane, Clarksville, TN 37043

The Opiate Magazine, 344 Starr St., #F, Brooklyn, NY 11237

Orange Quarterly, Peters, 210 E. Pine St., Cadillac, MI 49601

Orchards Poetry Journal, 24600 Mountain Ave. 35, Hemet, CA 92544

Orion Magazine, 187 Main St., Great Barrington, MA 01230

Osiris, 106 Meadow Lane, Greenfield, MA 01301

Out of Stock, Walsh, 1556 S. Grant Ave., Boise, ID 83706

Outrider Press, Inc., 2036 North Winds Drive, Dyer, IN 46311

Ovunque Siamo, 17 Douglas St., Ambler, PA 19002

Owl Canyon Press, 621 Pleasant St., Boulder, CO 80302

Oyster River Pages, PO Box 991, Groton, MA 01450

Pacific Literary Review, 2317 E. Lynn St., #2, Seattle, WA 98112

Pacific Standard, 801 Garden St., #101, Santa Barbara, CA 93101

Paddock Review, 452 Gen. John Payne Blvd., Georgetown, KY 40324

Palewell Press, 384 Upper Richmond Rd West, London SW14 7JU, UK

[PANK], 1869 Meadowbrook Dr., Winston Salem, NC 27104

Panorama, Clark, 442 Willoughby Ave., #1, Brooklyn, NY 11205

Paraclete Press, P.O. Box 1568, Orleans, MA 02653

Paragon Journal, 325 N. Union St., #1, Middletown, PA 17057

The Paris Review, 544 West 27th St., New York, NY 10001

Parthian Books, 22 Keir Hardie, Swansea University, Singleton Park, Swansea, SA2 8PP, Wales

Passages North, English Dept., N.M.U., Marquette, MI 49855-5363

Peach, 124 Highland Ave., Buffalo, NY 14222

Peacock Journal, 12702 Eldrid Pl, Silver Spring, MD 20904

The Penn Review, 3805 Locust Walk, Philadelphia, PA 19104

Pebblebook Press, PO Box 1254, Sheboygan, WI 53082-1254

Pembroke Magazine, P.O. Box 1510, Pembroke, NC 28372-1510

Pen & Anvil Press, PO Box 15274, Boston, MA 02215

Penny, 1825 Buccaneer Dr., Sarasota, FL 34231

Permafrost, P.O. Box 755720, Fairbanks, AK 99775

Perugia Press, PO Box 60364, Florence, MA 01062

Petigru Review, 4711 Forest Dr., Ste. 3, PMB 189, Columbia, SC 29206

Petite Hound Press, 8119 Defiance Ave., Las Vegas, NV 89129

Phantom Drift, P.O. Box 3235, La Grande, OR 97850

Phoebe, GMU, MSN 2C5, 4400 University Place, Fairfax, VA 22030

Phoenicia Publishing, 207-5425 de Bordeaux, Montreal QC H2H 2P9, Canada

Pigeon Pages, 443 Park Ave. S., #1004, New York, NY 10016

The Pinch, English Dept., 467 Patterson Hall, Memphis, TN 38152

Pinesong, 131 Bon Aire Rd., Elkin, NC 28621

Pittsburgh Poetry Review, 1216 Middletown Rd, Greensburg, PA 15601

Places, 2875 21st St., #15, San Francisco, CA 94110

Platypus Press, 67 Cordwell Park, Shropshire SY4 5BE, UK

Pleiades, UCM, PO Box 800, MAR 336, Warrensburg, MO 64093-5069

Ploughshares, Emerson Col., 120 Boylston St., Boston, MA 02116-4624

Plume, 740 17th Ave N., St. Petersburg, FL 33704

Poet Lore, 4508 Walsh St., Bethesda, MD 20815

Poetry Box, 2228 NW 159th Pl., Beaverton, OR 97006

Poetry Magazine, 61 West Superior St., Chicago, IL 60654

Poetry Northwest, 2000 Tower St., Everett, WA 98201-1390

Poetry Pacific, 1550 68th Ave. W., Vancouver, BC V6P 2V5 Canada

Poetry Salzburg Review, University of Salzburg, English & American Studies, Unipark Nonntal, Erzabt-Klotz-Str.1, 5020 Salzburg, Austria

Poetry South, MUW-1634, 1100 College St., Columbus, MS 39701

The Poet's Billow, 6135 Avon St., Portage, MI 49008

The Poet's Haven, PO Box 1501, Massillon, OH 44648

Poets Wear Prada, 533 Bloomfield St., #2, Hoboken, NJ 07030-4960

The Point, 2 N. LaSalle St., Ste. 2300, Chicago, IL 60602

Point Petre Publishing, 1515 County Rd., #24, RR#1, Milford, ON K0K, 1P0, Canada

Ponder Review, MUW-1634, 1100 College St., Columbus, MS 39701

Porkbelly Press, 5046 Relleum Ave., Cincinnati, OH 45238

Portland Review, Portland State U., PO Box 751, Portland, OR 97207

Posit, 245 Sullivan St., #8A, New York, NY 10012

Post Road, Boston College, 140 Commonwealth Ave., Chestnut Hill, MA 02467

Potomac Review, 51 Mannakee St., MT/212, Rockville, MD 20850

Prairie Journal, 28 Crowfoot Terrace NW, PO Box 68073, Calgary, AB, T3G 3N8, Canada

Prelude, 589 Flushing Ave., #3E, Brooklyn, NY 11206

Presence, English Dept., Caldwell Univ., 120 Bloomfield Ave, Caldwell, NJ 07006

Press 53, 560 No. Trade St., #103, Winston-Salem, NC 27101

Pretty Owl Poetry, 648 Montclair St., Pittsburgh, PA 15217

Priestess & Hierophant Press, 4432 Myrtlewood Dr. NW, #D, Huntsville, AL 35816

Prime Number Magazine, 560 North Trade St., #103, Winston-Salem, NC 27101

Prism International, UBC, Buch E462 – 1866 Main Mall, Vancouver BC V6T 1Z1, Canada

Prism Review, Univ. of La Verne, 1950 Third St., La Verne, CA 91750

Promethean, CCNY, 160 Convent Ave., New York, NY 10031

Provincetown Arts, 650 Commercial St., Provincetown, MA 02657

Psaltery & Lyre, 4917 E. Oregon St., Bellingham, WA 98226

Psychopomp, 17574 Gillette Way, Lakeville, MN 55044

Puerto del Sol, NMSU., PO Box 30001, Las Cruces, NM 88003-8001

Pulp Literature Press, 8540 Elsmore Rd., Richmond, BC V7C 2A1, Canada

Punctuate, Columbia College Chicago, 600 South Michigan Ave., Chicago, IL 60605-1996

Puritan Magazine, 50 Lowther Ave., Toronto, ON M5R 1C6, Canada

Quarterly West, Univ. of Utah, English/LNCO 3500, 255 S. Central Campus Dr., Salt Lake City, UT 84112-9109

Quatrain.Fish, 115 Ramoa Ave., El Cerrito, CA 94530

Quiddity, PO Box 1046, Murphysboro, IL 62966

Quiet Lightning, 734 Balboa St., SF, CA 94118

Quiet Lunch, 234 5th Ave., New York, NY 10001

Quill and Parchment, 2357 Merrywood Dr., Los Angeles, CA 90046

r.kv.r.y literary journal, 72 Woodbury Dr., Lockport, NY 14094

Rabbit Catastrophe Press, 147 N. Limestone, Lexington, KY 40507

Rabid Oak, 8916 Duncanson Dr., Bakersfield, CA 93311

Radar Poetry, 19 Coniston Ct., Princeton, NJ 08540

Radius, 65 Paine St., #2, Worcester, MA 01605

Raleigh Review, Box 6725, Raleigh, NC 27628

Raritan, Rutgers, 31 Mine St., New Brunswick, NJ 08901

Rascal, 45 Pinehurst Ave., #43, New York, NY 10033

Raven Chronicles, 15528 12th Avenue NE, Shoreline, WA 98155

Read Furiously, 15 Civic Center Dr., #1, East Brunswick, NJ 08816

Red Bone Press, PO Box 15571, Washington, DC 20003

Red Dashboard, 4408 Sayre Drive, Princeton, NJ 08540

Red Fez, 3811 NE 3rd Ct., Apt. G208, Renton, WA 98056

Red Hen Press, 1335 N. Lake Ave., #200, Pasadena, CA 91104

Red Hook Editions, 33 Flatbush Ave., 4th fl., Brooklyn, NY 11217

Red River Review, 4669 Mountain Oak St., Fort Worth, TX 76244

Red Rock Review, English Dept. J2A, College of Southern Nevada, 3200 East Cheyenne, North Las Vegas, NV 89030

Redactions, 604 N. 31st Ave., Apt. D-2, Hattiesburg, MS 39401

redbat books, 2901 Gekeler Ln, La Grande, OR 97850

Redivider, Emerson College, 120 Boylston St., Boston, MA 02116

Reginetta Press, P.O. Box 7042, Aurora, IL 60507

Relief Journal, Taylor Univ., 236 W. Reade Ave., Upland, IN 47348

Remembered Arts, 2776 S. Arlington Mill Dr., #142, Ste. 805, Arlington, VA 22206

Rescue Press, 526 Reno St., Iowa City, IA 52245

Reservoir Journal, 511 1st St. North, #302, Charlottesville, VA 22902

Resolute Bear Press, PO Box 14, Robbinston, ME 04671

Rhino, The Poetry Forum, PO Box 591, Evanston, IL 60204

Riddled with Arrows, 117 McCann Rd., Newark, DE 19711

Riggwelter Press, 58 John St., Heyrod, Stalybridge, Cheshire, SK15 3BS, UK

Rising Phoenix, 500 W. Rosedale Ave., #C7 Trinity, West Chester, PA 19382

Ristau, 1935 Gardiner Lane, #A-8, Louisville, KY 40205

River Styx, 3139A South Grand, Ste. 203, St. Louis, MO 63118-1021

River Teeth, Ashland University, 401 College Ave., Ashland, OH 44805

Roanoke Review, English Dept., 221 College Ln, Salem, VA 24153-3794

Rock & Sling, 300 W. Hawthorne Rd., Spokane, WA 99251

Rockhurst Review, 1100 Rockhurst Rd., Kansas City, MO 64110

Rogue Agent Journal, 5541 Beacon St., Pittsburgh, PA 15217

Room Magazine, P.O. Box 46160, Stn. D, Vancouver, BC V6J 5G5, Canada

Rumble Fish Quarterly, 2020 Park Ave., Richmond, VA 23220

Ruminate, 1041 N. Taft Hill Rd., Ft. Collins, CO 80521

The Rumpus, 742 Halstead Ave., Mamaroneck, NY 10543

Rust + Moth, 2409 Eastridge Court, Fort Collins, CO 80524

The Rusty Toque, 2-680 Shaw St., Toronto, ON M6G 3L7, Canada

Sagging Meniscus Press, 115 Claremont Ave., Montclair, NJ 07042

Salamander, Suffolk Univ., English, 8 Ashburton Pl, Boston, MA 02108

Salmagundi, 815 N. Broadway, Saratoga Springs, NY 12866-1632

the Same, 12911 Peach View Dr., Knoxville, TN 37922

San Francisco Peace and Hope, PO Box 8057, Berkeley, CA 94707

San Pedro River Review, Blue Horse Press, 318 Avenue I, #760, Redondo Beach, CA 90277

Sand Journal, L. Pfister, Prinz-Georg-Str. 7, 10827 Berlin, Germany

Santa Monica Review, Santa Monica College, 1900 Pico Blvd., Santa Monica, CA 90405

Saranac Review, SUNY, English, 101 Broad St., Plattsburgh, NY 12901

Saturnalia Books, 105 Woodside Rd., Ardmore, PA 19003

Saw Palm: Florida Literature & Art, English Dept., University of South Florida, 4202 E. Fowler Ave., Tampa, FL 33620

Scablands Books, 1312 E. 41st Ave., Spokane, WA 99203

Scarlet Leaf, 26-1225 York Mills Rd., Toronto ON M3A 1Y4, Canada

The Schuylkill Valley Journal, 334 Crawford Ave., #5, Morgantown, WV 26505

The Scores, 1/7 Livingstone PL, Edinburgh EH9 1PB, Scotland

Scoundrel Time, 5425 Wisconsin Ave., 6th Fl., Chevy Chase, MD 20815

Scrutiny Journal, Meckes, 18 Lanark Rd., Chapel Hill, NC 27517

Seems, Lakeland Univ., W3718 South Drive, Plymouth, WI 53073-4878

The Sewanee Review, 735 University Ave., Sewanee, TN 37383

The Shade Journal, WUSL, English, Campus Box1122, 1 Brookings Dr., St. Louis, MO 63130-4899

Shade Mountain Press, PO Box 11393, Albany NY 12211

Sheila-Na-Gig, 203 Meadowlark Rd., Russell, KY 41169

Sibling Rivalry Press, P.O. Box 26147, Little Rock, AR 72221

Side Street Press, 3400 West 111th St., #412, Chicago, IL 60655

Silver Birch Press, P.O. Box 29458, Los Angeles, CA 90029

Silver Pen, 9041 Hickory Lane, Saint John, IN 46373

Silverfish Review Press, PO Box 3541, Eugene, OR 97403

Sinister Wisdom, 2333 McIntosh Rd., Dover, FL 33527

sitio *tiempo* press, PO Box 10064, Berkeley, CA 94709

Six Ft. Swells Press, 732 Burgundy St., Apt. A, New Orleans, LA 70116

Sixfold, 10 Concord Ridge Rd., Newtown, CT 06470

Sixteen Rivers Press, PO Box 640663, San Francisco, CA 94164-0663

Sixth Finch, 95 Carolina Ave., #2, Jamaica Plain, MA 02130

Skylark Publications, 10 Hillcross Ave., Morden Surrey, SM4 4EA, UK

Slag Glass City, English Dept., 2315 No. Kenmore Ave., Chicago, IL 60614-3210

Slag Review, Whaley, 457 Zaicek Rd., Ashford, CT 06278

Sleet Magazine, 1846 Bohland Ave., St. Paul, MN 55116

Slice, PO Box 659, Village Station, New York, NY 10014

The Sligo Journal, Montgomery College, 7600 Takoma Ave., Takoma Park, MD 20912

Slippery Elm, Univ. of Findlay, 1000 N. Main, Findlay, OH 45840-3653

Slipstream, Box 2071, Niagara Falls, NY 14301

Smartish Pace, 2221 Lake Ave., Baltimore, MD 21213

SmokeLong Quarterly, 5229 Sidebum Rd., Fairfax, VA 22032

Sojourners, 408 C St. NE, Washington, DC 20002

Solstice, PO Box 920653, Needham, MA 02492

Sonora Review, University of Arizona, English, Tucson, AZ 85721

The Southampton Review, 239 Montauk Hwy., Southampton, NY 11968

The Southeast Review, English, FSU, Tallahassee, FL 32306

Southern Humanities Review, 9088 Haley Center, Auburn Univ., Auburn, AL 36849

Southern Indiana Review, USI, 8600 Univ. Blvd., Evansville, IN 47712

Southern Review, LSU, 338 Johnston Hall, Baton Rouge, LA 70803

Southwest Review, PO Box 750374, Dallas, TX 75275-0374

Spadina Literary Review, 101-639 Dupont St., Toronto, ON M6G 1Z4, Canada

Spillway, 11 Jordan Ave., San Francisco, CA 94118

Spiritus, Burrows, Im Breien 11, D-44894 Bochum, Germany

Split Lip, 10906 Braewick Dr., Carmel, IN 46033

Split This Rock, 1301 Connecticut Ave. NW, Washington, DC 20036

Spoon River Poetry Review, ISU, Box 4241, Normal, IL 61790-4241

Squares & Rebels, PO Box 3941, Minneapolis, MN 55403-0941

St. Katherine Review, 2639 W. Homer St., Chicago, IL 60647

Stairwell, 161 Lowther St., York, YO31 7LZ, UK

Star 82 Review, PO Box 8106, Berkeley, CA 94707

Stellar Day, 900 S. Lamar Blvd., #307, Austin, TX 78704

Still, 89 W. Chestnut St., Williamsburg, KY 40769

Still Point Arts Quarterly, 193 Hillside Rd., Brunswick, ME 04011

Stillwater Review, Poetry Ctr., Sussex County Coll., Newton, NJ 07860

Stoneboat, P.O. Box 1254, Sheboygan, WI 53082-1254

Story Quarterly, Rutgers, English, 311 N. Fifth St., Camden, NJ 08102

Straylight, U. of Wisconsin, English, 900 Wood Rd, Kenosha, WI 53141

Streetlight, 56 Pine Hill Lane, Norwood, VA 24581

subTerrain, P.O. Box 3008 MPO, Vancouver, BC V6B 3X5, Canada

Sugar House Review, PO Box 13, Cedar City, UT 84721

The Summerset Review, 25 Summerset Dr., Smithtown, NY 11787

The Sun, 107 North Roberson St., Chapel Hill, NC 27516

Sundog Lit., 429 Woodward Ave., Kalamazoo, MI 49007

Sun Star Review, 3013 SE Hawthorne Blvd., #308, Portland, OR 97214

SurVision, 36 Glasthule Bldg. S, Glasthule Rd., Dun Laoghaire, County Dublin, Ireland

Sweet, 10144 Arbor Run Dr., Unit 157, Tampa, FL 33647

Sweet Tree Review, 121 NW 85th St., #311, Seattle, WA 98117

SWWIM, 9301 NE 9th Place, Miami Shores, FL 33138

Sycamore Review, English, Purdue Univ,, West Lafayette, IN 47907

TAB: The Journal of Poetry & Poetics, Chapman University, One University Drive, Orange, CA 92866

Tahoma Literary Review, 3727 80th Ave. SE, Mercer Island, WA 98040

Tailwinds Press, 401 Commons Park S., #673, Stamford, CT 06902

Tar River Poetry, East Carolina Univ., #159, Greenville, NC 27858-4353

Terrain.org, P.O. Box 19161, Tucson, AZ 85731-9161

Terrapin Books, 4 Midvale Ave., West Caldwell, NJ 07006

Tethered By Letters, 3494 S. Dexter St., Denver, CO 80222

The Texas Observer, 54 Chicon St., Austin, TX 78702

Texas Review Press, SHSU, Box 2146, Huntsville, TX 77341-2146

TEXTure Magazine, 3412 Newport Ave., Annapolis, MD 21043

Third Coast, Western Michigan University, Kalamazoo, MI 49008-5331

Third Flatiron, 4101 S. Hampton Circle, Boulder, CO 80301

Thirty West, 2622 Swede Rd. (C-8), Norristown, PA 19401

32 Poems, Valparaiso Univ., 1320 Chapel Hill Dr., Valparaiso, IN 46383

Thomas-Jacob Publishing, P.O. Box 390524, Deltona, FL 32739

3: A Taos Press, P.O. Box 370627, Denver, CO 80237

3 Elements Review, 198 Valley View Rd., Manchester, CT 06040

Three Mile Harbor Press, PO Box 1, Stuyvesant, NY 12173

Three Rooms Press, 561 Hudson St., #33, New York, NY 10014

Threepenny Review, PO Box 9131, Berkeley, CA 94709

Thrush Poetry Journal, 889 Lower Mountain Dr., Effort, PA 18330

Tiferet, 211 Dryden Rd., Bernardsville, NJ 07924

Tiger Bark Press, 202 Mildorf St., Rochester, NY 14609

Tinderbox, 6932 Kayser Mill Rd. NW, Albuquerque, NM 87114

the tiny, 1350 Caroline Ave., Clinton, IA 52732

Tipton Poetry Journal, 642 Jackson St., Brownsburg, IN 46112

The Tishman Review, PO Box 605, Perry, MI 48872

Transition Magazine, 104 Mt. Auburn St., #3R, Cambridge, MA 02138

Trestle Creek Review, North Idaho College, 1000 W. Garden Ave., Coeur d'Alene, ID 83814

TriQuarterly, 339 E. Chicago Ave., 6th Fl., Chicago, IL 60611

True Story, 5119 Coral St., Pittsburgh, PA 15224

Truman State Univ. Press, 100 E. Normal Ave., Kirksville, MO 63501

The Trumpeter, St. Joseph's College, Univ. of Alberta, Edmonton, Alberta T6G 2J5 Canada

Tupelo Press, P.O. Box 1767, North Adams, MA 01247

Turnip Truck(s), 305 Cleveland St., Lafayette, LA 70501

Turtle Point Press, 208 Java St., 5th Fl., Brooklyn. NY 11222

The Tusk, 1477 Bedford, #4, Brooklyn, NY 11216

Twitteriztion, Schaufler, 3161 N. 82nd St., Milwaukee, WI 53074

Two Cities Review, 1 Hanson Place, Apt. PHA, Brooklyn, NY 11243

Two Lines Press, 582 Market St., Ste. 700, San Francisco, CA 94104

Two Sylvias Press, PO Box 1524, Kinston, WA 98346

Typehouse Magazine, PO Box 68721, Portland, OR 97268

U.S. 1 Poets' Cooperative, PO Box 127, Kingston, NJ 08528-0127

Ugly Duckling Presse, 232 Third St., #E-303, Brooklyn, NY 11215

Umbrella Factory, Ilacqua, 838 Lincoln St., Longmont, CO 80501

unbound CONTENT, 160 Summit St., Englewood, NJ 07631

Unbroken Journal, Adams, 109 So. Gallaher View Rd., #108, Knoxville, TN 37919

Under the Gum Tree, Studio J, 1812 J St., #21, Sacramento, CA 95811

Under the Sun, 1622 Edgefield Ct., Cookeville, TN 38506

University of Arizona Press, PO Box 210055, Tucson, AZ 85721-0055

University of Iowa Press, 119 West Park Rd., Iowa City, IA 52242-1000

University of New Mexico Press, MSC05 3185, 1 University of New Mexico, Albuquerque, NM 87131-0001

University of North Texas Press, 1155 Union Circle #311336, Denton, TX 76203-5017

The Unpublishables, Unit C – 18F, Wan Shun Gardens, 898 King's Rd., Hong Kong

Up the Staircase Quarterly, 716 4th St., SW, Apt. A, Minot, ND 58701

Upper Hand Press, PO Box 91179, Bexley, OH 43209

upstreet, P.O. Box 105, Richmond, MA 01254-0105

Vagabond City, 727 Country Club Rd, Columbus, OH 43213.

Vagabondage Press, PO Box3563, Apollo Beach, FL 33572

Valley Voices, MVSU 7242, 14000 Hwy 82 W., Itta Bena, MS 38941

Valley Press, Woodend, The Crescent, Scarborough, YO11 2PW, UK

Vallum, 5038 Sherbrooke West, PO Box 20377 CP Vendome, Montreal, QC H4A 1T0, Canada

Varnish, 3720 Clarington Ave., #105, Los Angeles, CA 90034

Vassar Review, 124 Raymond Ave., Box 464, Poughkeepsie, NY 12604

Veliz Books, PO Box 920243, El Paso, TX 79912

Vestal Review, 127 Kilsyth Rd., #3, Brighton, MA 02135

Vida Review, Heath, 1724 N. Sumner St., Potland, OR 97217

Vinyl Poetry, 1 College Dr., Bennington, VT 05201

Voices, 120 Connecticut Ave. NW, Ste. 710, Washington, DC 20036

Volt Books, 354 Nichols Hall, SSU, 1801 E. Cotati Ave, Rohnert Park, CA 94928

vox poetica, 160 Summit St., Englewood, NJ, 07631

Waccamaw, Coastal Carolina Univ., PO Box 261954, Conway, SC 29528

The War Horse, PO Box 399, Richlands, NC 28574

War, Literature & the Arts, 2354 Fairchild Dr., Ste. 6D-149, USAF Academy, CO 80840-6242

Ward Street Press, 620 Ward St., #502, Seattle, WA 98109

Washington Square Review, 58 W. 10th St., New York, NY 10011

Watershed Review, CSU, Chico, 400 West First St., Chico, CA 95929

The Wax Paper, 837 N. Wolcott Ave., Chicago, IL 60622

Waxwing Magazine, 3336 N. Schevene Blvd., Flagstaff, AZ 86004

Wayne State University Press, 4809 Woodward Ave., Detroit, MI 48201

Waywiser Press, PO Box 6205, Baltimore, MD 21206

West Branch, Bucknell Hall, Bucknell Univ., Lewisburg, PA 17837

West Marin Review, P.O. Box 1302, Point Reyes Station, CA 94956

West Texas Literary Review, PO Box 65851, Lubbock, TX 79464

Western Humanities Review, English Dept., 255 S. Central Campus Dr., Salt Lake City, UT 84112-0494

Whale Road Review, 3900 Lomaland Dr., San Diego, CA 92106

Whiskey Island, CSU, 2121 Euclid Ave., Cleveland, OH 44115

White Pine Press, PO Box 236, Buffalo, NY 14201

Whitefish Review, 708 Lupfer Ave., Whitefish, MT 59937

Wigleaf, UM - English, 114 State Hall, Columbia, MO 65211-1500

Wild Goose Poetry Review, 838 4th Avenue Dr. NW, Hickory, NC 28601

Willow Springs, 668 N. Riverpoint Blvd., #259, Spokane, WA 99202

Wings Press, 627 E. Guenther, San Antonio, TX 78210

Wink, 14051 Oakview Lane N., Dayton, MN 55327

Wipf & Stock Publishers, 199 W. 8th Ave., #3, Eugene, OR 97401-2960

The Wire's Dream, Lydia, 180 N. 1st St., #115, El Cajon, CA 92021

Witness, UNLV, Box 455085, Las Vegas, NV 89154

WMG Publishing, PO Box 269, Lincoln City, OR 97367

The Worcester Review, PO Box 804, Worcester, MA 01613

Word Fountain, 71 S. Franklin St., Wilkes-Barre, PA 18701

The Word Works, PO Box 42164, Washington, D.C. 20015

Words Without Borders, 147 Prince St., Brooklyn, NY 11231

Wordspace, 66 Lindley St., York, YO24 4Jf, UK

WordTech, PO Box 541106, Cincinnati, OH 45254-1106

World Literature Today, 630 Parrington Oval, Ste. 110, Norman, OK 73019-4033

World Poetry Books, 365 Fairfield Way, #1057, Oak Hall East SSHB, Room 224, Storrs, CT 06269

World Stage Press, 4321 Degnan Blvd., Los Angeles, CA 90008

World Weaver Press, PO Box 21924, Albuquerque, NM 87154

Woven Tale Press, PO Box 2533, Setauket, NY 11733

Write Bloody Publishing, 1800 N. New Hampshire Ave., #302, Los Angeles, CA 90027

The Write Launch, 943 West Walnut St., Lancaster, PA 17603

Writing Disorder, P.O. Box 93613, Los Angeles, CA 90093-0613

Writing Knights Press, PO Box 9364, Canton, OH 44711

Xenox Books, PO Box 16433, Las Cruces, NM 88004

Yemassee Journal, English, USC, Columbia, SC 29208

Yes Yes Books, 1614 NE Alberta St., Portland, OR 97211

Zephyr Press, 50 Kenwood St., Brookline, MA 02446

zimZalla, 30 Lynwood Grove, Sale, Cheshire, M33 2AN, UK

Zoetic Press, PO Box 1354, Santa Cruz, CA 95061

Zoetrope: All Story, 916 Kearny St., San Francisco, CA 94133

Zone 3 Press, APSU, P.O. Box 4565, Clarksville, TN 37044

ZYZZYVA, 57 Post St., Ste. 604, San Francisco, CA 94104

CONTRIBUTORS' NOTES

ALLISON ADAIR lives in Boston and teaches at Boston College and Grub Street. His work has been published in *American Poetry Review*, *Field*, and *Subtropics* among other journals.

SANJAY AGNIHOTRI is the publisher of *Local Knowledge*, a literary and arts journal. He lives in Morristown, New Jersey

JOHN ASHBERY (1927–2017) won the Yale Younger Poets Prize in 1955, and published more then two dozen volumes of poetry, most recently *Commotion of The Birds*, 2016.

POE BALLANTINE's novel, *Whirlaway*, is just out from Hawthorne Books. He lives in Chadron, Nebraska.

MARY JO BANG is the author of eight poetry books including *Elegy*, which received the National Book Critics Award. She teaches at Washington University.

RICK BAROT has published three volumes of poetry, all from Sarabande Books. He is poetry editor for *New England Review*.

ELI BARRETT is a librarian at an elementary school for the creative arts. This is his first published story.

SAMIYA BASHIR is associate professor of creative writing at Reed College. Her books include *Field Theories*, *Gospel* and *Where The Apple Falls*.

GABRIEL BROWNSTEIN teaches at St. John's University. His novel, *The Curious Case of Benjamin Button*, won the PEN / Hemingway award.

JESSICA BURSTEIN is an associate professor in the English Department at the University of Washington, Seattle.

ERIK CAMPELL is the author of the poetry collections *Arguments for Stillness* (Curb-stone) and *The Corpse Pose* (Red Hen).

JUNG HAE CHAE's work has appeared in *Calyx*, *Third Coast*, and *Crab Orchard Review*.

KRISTIN CHANG's debut chapbook, *Past Lives, Future Bodies*, is just out from Black Lawrence Press. She lives in Cupertino, California.

VICTORIA CHANG's poetry collections are *The Boss*, *Salvinia Molesta* and *Circle*. Her children's book is *Mommy?*

CORTNEY LAMAR CHARLESTON is the author of *Telepathologies* (Saturnalia Books). He has received awards from The Poetry Foundation, Cave Canem, and The New Jersey State Council on the Arts.

KIM CHINQUEE's collections include *Oh Baby*, *Pretty*, *Pistol*, *Veer* and *Shot Girls*. She is senior editor of *New World Writing*.

TIANA CLARK teaches at Southern Illinois University. Her debut collection of poetry is *I Can't Talk About The Trees Without The Blood* (University of Pittsburgh Press, 2018).

MICHAEL COLLIER is the author of seven books of poetry and is the Director of the Creative Writing Program at the University of Maryland.

MOLLY COONEY is a queer writer, mother and teacher. She lives with her partner and two kids in Minneapolis.

ROBERT COOVER authored twenty books of fiction and plays, most recently *Going For A Beer : Selected Short Fiction* (W.W. Norton).

HAL CROWTHER is the author of *Gather At The River*, a finalist for the National Book Critics Circle Award, and other books. He previously appeared in the 2014 Pushcart Prize.

OLABAJO DADA teaches English at Central Piedmont Community College. He was born and raised in Nigeria and now lives in Fairfax, Virginia.

BRIAN DOYLE (1947–2017) was editor of *Portland Magazine* and was the author of many books of essays and fiction. This is his fourth selection for The Pushcart Prize.

MOLLY GALLENTINE holds an MFA from The New School. She lives in New Jersey and has been published in *The Rumpus*, *Brooklyn Rail* and elsewhere.

ALBERT GOLDBARTH lives entirely offline in Wichita, Kansas. He has twice received the National Book Critics Circle Award.

JULIE HECHT is the author of *Do The Windows Open?* and other books. She is at work on her next novel, *Every Single* Thing.

ROBERT HASS was United States Poet Laureate from 1995 to 1997, He has been awarded a National Book Award and The Pulitzer Prize.

TONY HOAGLAND's most recent poetry collection is published by Graywolf Press. His craft book, *The Art of Voice*, will be published by W.W. Norton next year.

J. M. HOLMES lives in North Hills, California. His novel, *How Are You Going to Save Yourself?*, is just out from Little, Brown.

ANTHONY MARRA is author of *A Constellation of Vital Phenomena*, winner of the John Leonard Prize From The National Book Critics Circle. He lives in Oakland, California.

HUGH MARTIN is a veteran of the Iraq War and the author of *The Stick Soldiers* and *In Country*, both from BOA Editions.

JANE MEAD is the author of five poetry collections, most recently *Made and Unmade* (Alice James). She lives in Napa, California.

ANDREW MITCHELL received the Barthelme Prize for Short Fiction. He lives in Dover, New Hampshire.

RICK MOODY is the author of five novels, including *Garden State*, *Purple America*, and *The Ice Storm*. He won Pushcart's Editors Book Award and a Guggenheim Fellowship.

THYLIAS MOSS is Professor Emerita at the University of Michigan, the author of thirteen books, and the recipient of MacArthur and Guggenheim recognitions.

PAM HOUSTON is the author of six books of fiction and nonfiction, all published by W.W. Norton. She lives in Colorado at 9,000 feet above sea level.

C. J. HRIBAL is the author of the novels *The Company Car* and *American Beauty*, and two short fiction collections. He teaches at Marquette University.

ALLEGRA HYDE's short story collection is *Of This New World*. She lives in Houston, Texas.

JOHN LANDRETTI's work appears frequently in *Orion*. He lives in Minnesota and teaches at a state prison.

VICTOR LAVALLE teaches at Columbia University. He is the author of a short story collection, four novels and two novellas.

SU-YEE LIN has written for *Day One*, *The Offing*, and *NANO fiction*. She was a 2012 Fulbright Fellow to China.

DAVID LONG's stories have won O. Henry and Pushcart Prize awards. His novels include *Falling Boy* and *Inhabited World*.

DAVID NAIMON is a host of the radio and podcast program "Between The Covers." He lives in Portland, Oregon.

D. NURKSE teaches at Sarah Lawrence College and has published eleven poetry collections.

OLUFUNKE OGUNDIMU was born in Lagos, Nigeria. She holds an MFA from the University of Nevada and is at work on a short story collection and a novel.

EMMANYEL OPPONG-YEBOAH is a Ghanaian-American poet living in Boston. He is associate editor for Pizza Pi Press.

LESLIE JILL PATTERSON edits *Iron Horse Literary Review*, teaches at Texas Tech University and won the 2014 Soros Justice Fellowship, among other awards.

OLIVER DE LA PAZ's most recent poetry collection is *Post Subject: A Fable*. He teaches at The College of The Holy Cross.

BRENDA PEYNADO teaches at The University of Central Florida and is at work on a novel.

CARL PHILLIPS teaches at Washington University. His most recent book of poems is *Wild Is The Wind* (FSG, 2018).

EMILIA PHILLIPS is the author of two books from The University of Akron Press. She teaches at Centenary College.

CATHERINE PIERCE's books are published by Saturnalia Books. She co-directs the writing program at Mississippi State University.

SARAH RESNICK lives in New York. Her writing has appeared in *Bookforum*, *Art in America*, *Triple Canopy* and *Best American Essays* 2017.

DANA ROESER's fourth book, *All Transparent Things Need Thunder Shirts*, is due in 2019 from Two Sylvias Press. She lives in West Lafayette, Indiana.

DAVID J. ROTHMAN lives in Crested Butte, Colorado. He is director of the Graduate Creative Writing Program at Western State Colorado University.

MARY RUEFLE's most recent book is *My Private Property* (Wave Books). She lives in Vermont.

KAREN RUSSELL is the author of the novel *Swamplandia!* and two story collections. She lives in Portland, Oregon.

JULIAN RANDALL's first book, *Refuse*, is winner of the Cave Cavern Poetry Prize and is just out from The University of Pittsburgh Press. He was winner of the 2015 National College Slam.

HEATHER SELLERS lives in St. Petersburg, Florida. She is the author of several books, and her work has appeared in *Tin House*, *Five Points*, *The New York Times* and *Best American Essays 2017*.

TOM SLEIGH's books include *Station Zed*, *Army Cats* and *Space Walk*. His recognitions include the John Updike and Kingsley Tufts awards.

MAGGIE SMITH is author most recently of *Good Bones* (Tupelo Press, 2017), named one of the five best poetry books of the year by *The Washington Post*. She lives in Bexley, Ohio.

GABRIEL DANIEL SOLIS is director of the Texas After Violence Project, a restorative justice organization that documents the impacts of violence on families and communities.

MELISSA STEIN's poetry collections are *Terrible Blooms* and *Rough Honey*. She lives in San Francisco.

STEVE STERN's *The Wedding Jester* won the National Jewish Book Award. He teaches at Skidmore College.

JUSTIN ST. GERMAIN is the author of the memoir *Son of A Gun*. He teaches at Oregon State University.

NOMI STONE's second poetry collection, *Kill Class*, is forthcoming from Tupelo Press. She lives in Bethesda, Maryland.

LISA TADDEO received an MFA in fiction from Boston University. Her debut nonfiction will appear soon from Simon and Schuster.

MYRON TAUBE was professor emeritus at the University of Pittsburgh where he specialized in Victorian era literature. He died in August, 2017.

DANIEL TOBIN is the author of nine books of poems. He has received many awards for his writing and lives in Dorchester, Massachusetts.

CLAIRE VAYE WATKINS is one of *Granta's* "Best Young American Novelists" and is founder of The Mojave School, a creative writing workshop in the Mojave Desert.

PHILLIP B. WILLIAMS won the Tufts Discovery Award and a Whiting Award. He teaches at Bennington College.

INDEX

The following is a listing in alphabetical order by author's last name of works reprinted in the *Pushcart Prize* editions since 1976.

564

565

577

578

585

592